PRAISE FOR

THE NEW SPACE OPERA

Edited by GARDNER DOZOIS
and JONATHAN STRAHAN

"Inside the science fiction I love the best there's a rip-roaring space opera just waiting to take me for a ride. This anthology is a reminder of why science fiction captured the hearts and minds of generations of readers."

Orson Scott Card

"Grand adventures across space and time . . . Modern themes approached with modern sensibilities . . . Twenty-first century seers show that science fiction has not lost its power to evoke the sense of wonder."

Joe Haldeman

"In sheer breathtaking, mind-expanding scope, this collection of some of the finest tale-spinning the subgenre has to offer delivers hours of exhilarating reading."

Booklist

"THE NEW SPACE OPERA carries us deep into the young, vital core of science fiction: adventure, wonder, far places, strange beings—friends. Two pseudopods up! Highly recommended!"

Greg Bear

"Editors Dozois and Strahan bring together some of the finest writers in the field—to take us once more to the stars."

Vernor Vinge

Edited by
Gardner Dozois & Jonathan Strahan

THE NEW SPACE OPERA 2
THE NEW SPACE OPERA

THE NEW SPACE OPERA 2

EDITED BY
GARDNER DOZOIS AND
JONATHAN STRAHAN

An Imprint of HarperCollinsPublishers

A continuation of the copyright page appears on page 625–626.

EOS
An Imprint of HarperCollins*Publishers*
10 East 53rd Street
New York, New York 10022-5299

Copyright © 2009 by Gardner Dozois and Jonathan Strahan;
individual stories copyrighted by the authors
ISBN 978-0-06-156236-5
www.eosbooks.com

First Eos paperback printing: April 2010
First Eos trade paperback printing: July 2009

HarperCollins® and Eos® are registered trademarks of HarperCollins Publishers.

Printed in the U.S.A.

10 9 8 7 6 5 4 3 2 1

For Jessica and Sophie,
who are far more likely to see the stars than me

CONTENTS

THE NEW
SPACE
OPERA
2

INTRODUCTION

The true heart of science fiction has always been the space-opera story; the thrilling adventure tale of powerful rocket ships, dashing heroes, and far frontiers—stories of immense scope and scale, color and action, taking us to the ultimate limits of both time and space. Two years ago, when compiling the book that became *The New Space Opera*, we looked to present a snapshot of how the space-opera story had evolved from what Bob Tucker had in 1941 contemptuously defined as "the hacky, grinding, stinking, outworn space-ship yarn" to one of the most popular forms of science fiction of the eighties, the nineties, and the oughts, and one where much of the cutting-edge work in today's genre is being done.

As we noted in the introduction to that book, starting in the early 1970s, writers on both sides of the Atlantic (Iain M. Banks, M. John Harrison, Barrington Bayley, Samuel R. Delany, Bruce Sterling, Vernor Vinge), building on the work of earlier eras, from the twenties to the sixties, by such great pioneers as Edmond Hamilton, Leigh Brackett, A. E. van Vogt, Poul Anderson, Jack Vance, and many others, started experimenting with what had in some ways by then become an old and threadbare form, investing it with a much more rigorous approach to science, a greater depth of characterization, better writing, and an increased sensitivity to political realities. While "old space opera" continued—and continues—to be written, part of the established spectrum of science fiction, this "new space opera" caught the imagination of the reading public, and to this day many writers identified with the form are among the best-selling authors in the field.

Our intention with compiling *The New Space Opera* was not to assemble a movement-defining book—a task that still remains to be done, in our opinion—but to map at least some of the territory covered by this sprawling (and sometimes contradictory: the line between New Space Opera and Old Space Opera, and just plain science fiction, for that matter, is often subjective and hard to draw, and no two people draw it in the same place) new form, providing a broad range of stories by some of the best writers working in the field at the time. And, of course, to provide as entertaining an anthology as possible in the process, one that would make the readers think that their money had not been ill-spent. Much ink was spilled over the result, with some critics drawing lines in the sand and declaring that some of the stories in the book were not really New Space Opera by their definition, while other critics drew other lines in the sand and came to exactly opposite conclusions about what was canonical and what was not.

No doubt the book you hold in your hand will provoke a similar range of arguments.

The subgenre of New Space Opera has become broad enough that we were able to provide a completely fresh slate of contributors for this anthology, not needing to reuse anyone from the first book—and coming along behind *them* is yet another entirely new rank of New Space Opera creators who may yet someday also get a shot of their own.

We're proud to say that the book at hand compiles new work from eighteen of the best current practitioners of the New Space Opera, from relatively new writers to experienced veterans of the field: Robert Charles Wilson, Peter Watts, John Kessel, Cory Doctorow, John Barnes, Kristine Kathryn Rusch, Neal Asher, Garth Nix, Sean Williams, Bruce

Sterling, Bill Willingham, John Meaney, Elizabeth Moon, Jay Lake, Tad Williams, Justina Robson, John Scalzi, Mike Resnick, and John C. Wright—as good a list of authors, we think, as you're likely to find in any other science-fiction anthology this year.

We think there's something here for everyone, with the stories ranging from cool, cutting extrapolation on the extreme edge of cosmology to baroque romanticism to the swashbuckling adventures of space pirates. There's variety and breadth, color and life, scale and scope, drama and conflict, romance and glory—and not a little humor. While it's a completely different book than its predecessor, we think that it's nonetheless a worthy successor to *The New Space Opera*. We can only hope you'll agree.

—Gardner Dozois/Jonathan Strahan

UTRIUSQUE COSMI

ROBERT CHARLES WILSON

Robert Charles Wilson made his first sale in 1974, to *Analog*, but little more was heard from him until the late eighties, when he began to publish a string of ingenious and well-crafted novels and stories that have since established him among the top ranks of the writers who came to prominence in the last two decades of the twentieth century. His first novel, *A Hidden Place*, appeared in 1986. He won the John W. Campbell Memorial Award for his novel *The Chronoliths*, the Philip K. Dick Award for his novel *Mysterium*, and the Aurora Award for his story "The Perseids." In 2006, he won the Hugo Award for his acclaimed novel *Spin*. His other books include the novels *Memory Wire*, *Gypsies*, *The Divide*, *The Harvest*, *A Bridge of Years*, *Darwinia*, *Blind Lake*, *Bios*, and *Axis*, and a collection of his short work, *The Perseids and Other Stories*. His most recent book is a new novel, *Julian*. He lives in Toronto, Canada.

Here he tells the compelling story of a young woman faced with the most significant choice she will ever make in her life—after which, *nothing* will ever be the same.

Diving back into the universe (now that the universe is a finished object, boxed and ribboned from bang to bounce),

Carlotta calculates ever-finer loci on the frozen ordinates of spacetime until at last she reaches a trailer park outside the town of Commanche Drop, Arizona. Bodiless, no more than a breath of imprecision in the Feynman geography of certain virtual particles, thus powerless to affect the material world, she passes unimpeded through a sheet-aluminum wall and hovers over a mattress on which a young woman sleeps uneasily.

The young woman is her own ancient self, the primordial Carlotta Boudaine, dewed with sweat in the hot night air, her legs caught up in a spindled cotton sheet. The bedroom's small window is cranked open, and in the breezeless distance a coyote wails.

Well, look at me, Carlotta marvels: skinny girl in panties and a halter, sixteen years old—no older than a gnat's breath—taking shallow little sleep-breaths in the moonlit dark. Poor child can't even see her own ghost. Ah, but she will, Carlotta thinks—*she must*.

The familiar words echo in her mind as she inspects her dreaming body, buried in its tomb of years, eons, kalpas. *When it's time to leave, leave. Don't be afraid. Don't wait. Don't get caught. Just go. Go fast.*

Her ancient beloved poem. Her perennial mantra. The words, in fact, that saved her life.

She needs to share those words with herself, to make the circle complete. Everything she knows about nature of the physical universe suggests that the task is impossible. Maybe so . . . but it won't be for lack of trying.

Patiently, slowly, soundlessly, Carlotta begins to speak.

Here's the story of the Fleet, girl, and how I got raptured up into it. It's all about the future—a bigger one than you believe in—so brace yourself.

It has a thousand names and more, but we'll just call it the Fleet. When I first encountered it, the Fleet was scattered from the core of the galaxy all through its spiraled tentacles of suns, and it had been there for millions of years, going about its business, though nobody on this planet knew anything about it. I guess every now and then a Fleet ship must have fallen to Earth, but it would have been indistinguishable from any common meteorite by the time it passed through the atmosphere: a chunk of carbonaceous chondrite smaller than a human fist, from which all evidence of ordered matter had been erased by fire—and such losses, which happened everywhere and often, made no discernible difference to the Fleet as a whole. All Fleet data (that is to say, all *mind*) was shared, distributed, fractal. Vessels were born and vessels were destroyed, but the Fleet persisted down countless eons, confident of its own immortality.

Oh, I know you don't understand the big words, child! It's not important for you to hear them—not *these* words— it's only important for me to *say* them. Why? Because a few billion years ago tomorrow, I carried your ignorance out of this very trailer, carried it down to the Interstate, and hitched west with nothing in my backpack but a bottle of water, a half-dozen Tootsie Rolls, and a wad of twenty-dollar bills stolen out of Dan-O's old ditty bag. That night (tomorrow night: mark it) I slept under an overpass all by myself, woke up cold and hungry long before dawn, and looked up past a concrete arch crusted with bird shit into a sky so thick with falling stars it made me think of a dark skin bee-stung with fire. Some of the Fleet vectored too close to the atmosphere that night, no doubt, but I didn't understand that (any more than *you* do, girl)—I just thought it was a big flock of shooting stars, pretty but meaningless. And, after a while, I slept some more. And come sunrise, I waited for the morning traffic so I could catch another ride . . . but the only cars that came by were all weaving or speeding, as if the whole world was driving home from a drunken party.

"They won't stop," a voice behind me said. "Those folks already made their decisions, Carlotta. Whether they want to live or die, I mean. Same decision you have to make."

I whirled around, sick-startled, and that was when I first laid eyes on dear Erasmus.

Let me tell you right off that Erasmus wasn't a human being. Erasmus just then was a knot of shiny metal angles about the size of a microwave oven, hovering in midair, with a pair of eyes like the polished tourmaline they sell at those roadside souvenir shops. He didn't *have* to look that way—it was some old avatar he used because he figured that it would impress me. But I didn't know that then. I was only surprised, if that's not too mild a word, and too shocked to be truly frightened.

"The world won't last much longer," Erasmus said in a low and mournful voice. "You can stay here, or you can come with me. But choose quick, Carlotta, because the mantle's come unstable and the continents are starting to slip."

I half-believed that I was still asleep and dreaming. I didn't know what that meant, about the mantle, though I guessed he was talking about the end of the world. Some quality of his voice (which reminded me of that actor Morgan Freeman) made me trust him despite how weird and impossible the whole conversation was. Plus, I had a confirming sense that *something* was going bad *somewhere*, partly because of the scant traffic (a Toyota zoomed past, clocking speeds it had never been built for, the driver a hunched blur behind the wheel), partly because of the ugly green cloud that just then billowed up over a row of rat-toothed mountains on the horizon. Also the sudden hot breeze. And the smell of distant burning. And the sound of what might have been thunder, or something worse.

"Go with you where?"

"To the stars, Carlotta! But you'll have to leave your body behind."

I didn't like the part about leaving my body behind. But what choice did I have, except the one he'd offered me? Stay or go. Simple as that.

It was a ride—just not the kind I'd been expecting.

There was a tremor in the Earth, like the devil knocking at the soles of my shoes. "Okay," I said, "whatever," as white dust bloomed up from the desert and was taken by the frantic wind.

Don't be afraid. Don't wait. Don't get caught. Just go. Go fast.

Without those words in my head, I swear, girl, I would have died that day. Billions did.

* * *

She slows down the passage of time so she can fit this odd but somehow necessary monologue into the space between one or two of the younger Carlotta's breaths. Of course, she has no real voice in which to speak. The past is static, imperturbable in its endless sleep; molecules of air on their fixed trajectories can't be manipulated from the shadowy place where she now exists. Wake up with the dawn, girl, she says, steal the money you'll never spend—it doesn't matter; the important thing is to *leave*. It's time.

When it's time to leave, leave. Of all the memories she carried out of her earthly life, this is the most vivid: waking to discover a ghostly presence in her darkened room, a white-robed woman giving her the advice she needs at the moment she needs it. Suddenly Carlotta wants to scream the words: *When it's time to leave—*

But she can't vibrate even a single mote of the ancient air, and the younger Carlotta sleeps on.

Next to the bed is a thrift-shop night table scarred with cigarette burns. On the table is a child's night-light, faded cutouts of SpongeBob SquarePants pasted on the paper shade. Next to that, hidden under a splayed copy of *People* magazine, is the bottle of barbiturates Carlotta stole from Dan-O's ditty bag this afternoon, the same khaki bag in which (she couldn't help but notice) Dan-O keeps his cash, a change of clothes, a fake driver's license, and a blue steel automatic pistol.

Young Carlotta detects no ghostly presence . . . nor is her sleep disturbed by the sound of Dan-O's angry voice and her mother's sudden gasp, two rooms away. Apparently, Dan-O is awake and sober. Apparently, Dan-O has discovered the theft. That's a complication.

But Carlotta won't allow herself to be hurried.

The hardest thing about joining the Fleet was giving up the idea that I had a body, that my body had a real place to be.

But that's what everybody believed at first, that we were still whole and normal—everybody rescued from Earth, I mean. Everybody who said yes to Erasmus—and Erasmus, in one form or another, had appeared to every human being on the planet in the moments before the end of the world. Two and a half billion of us accepted the offer of rescue. The rest chose to stay put and died when the Earth's continents dissolved into molten magma.

Of course, that created problems for the survivors. Children without parents, parents without children, lovers separated for eternity. It was as sad and tragic as any other incomplete rescue, except on a planetary scale. When we left the Earth, we all just sort of reappeared on a grassy plain as flat as Kansas and wider than the horizon, under a blue faux sky, each of us with an Erasmus at his shoulder and all of us wailing or sobbing or demanding explanations.

The plain wasn't "real," of course, not the way I was accustomed to things being real. It was a virtual place, and all of us were wearing virtual bodies, though we didn't understand that fact immediately. We kept on being what we expected ourselves to be—we even wore the clothes we'd worn when we were raptured up. I remember looking down at the pair of greasy secondhand Reeboks I'd found at the Commanche Drop Goodwill store, thinking: in heaven? *Really*?

"Is there any place you'd rather be?" Erasmus asked with a maddening and clearly inhuman patience. "Anyone you need to find?"

"Yeah, I'd rather be in New Zealand," I said, which was really just a hysterical joke. All I knew about New Zealand was that I'd seen a show about it on PBS, the only channel we got since the cable company cut us off.

"Any particular part of New Zealand?"

"What? Well—okay, a beach, I guess."

I had never been to a real beach, a beach on the ocean.

"Alone, or in the company of others?"

"Seriously?" All around me people were sobbing or gibbering in (mostly) foreign languages. Pretty soon, fights would start to break out. You can't put a couple of billion human beings so close together under circumstances like that and expect any other result. But the crowd was already thinning, as people accepted similar offers from their own Fleet avatars.

"Alone," I said. "Except for *you*."

And quick as that, there I was: Eve without Adam, standing on a lonesome stretch of white beach.

After a while, the astonishment faded to a tolerable dazzle. I took off my shoes and tested the sand. The sand was pleasantly sun-warm. Salt water swirled up between my toes as a wave washed in from the coral-blue sea.

Then I felt dizzy and had to sit down.

"Would you like to sleep?" Erasmus asked, hovering over me like a gem-studded party balloon. "I can help you sleep, Carlotta, if you'd like. It might make the transition easier if you get some rest, to begin with."

"You can answer some fucking *questions*, is what you can *do*!" I said.

He settled down on the sand beside me, the mutant offspring of a dragonfly and a beach ball. "Okay, shoot," he said.

It's a read-only universe, Carlotta thinks. The Old Ones have said as much, so it must be true. And yet, she knows, she *remembers*, that the younger Carlotta will surely wake and find her here: a ghostly presence, speaking wisdom.

But how can she make herself perceptible to this sleeping child? The senses are so stubbornly material, electrochemical data cascading into vastly complex neural networks . . . is it possible she could intervene in some way at the borderland of quanta and perception? For a moment, Carlotta chooses to look at her younger self with different eyes, sampling the fine gradients of molecular magnetic fields. The child's skin and skull grow faint and then transparent as Carlotta shrinks her point of view and wanders briefly through the carnival of her own animal mind, the buzzing innerscape where skeins of dream merge and separate like fractal soap bubbles. If she could manipulate even a single boson—influence the charge at some critical synaptic junction, say—

But she can't. The past simply doesn't have a handle on it. There's no uncertainty here anymore, no alternate outcomes. To influence the past would be to *change* the past, and, by definition, that's impossible.

The shouting from the next room grows suddenly louder and more vicious, and Carlotta senses her younger self moving from sleep toward an awakening, too soon.

Of course, I figured it out eventually, with Erasmus's help. Oh, girl, I won't bore you with the story of those first few years—they bored *me*, heaven knows.

Of course "heaven" is exactly where we weren't. Lots of folks were inclined to see it that way—assumed they must have died and been delivered to whatever afterlife they happened to believe in. Which was actually not *too* far off the mark, but, of course, God had nothing to do with it. The Fleet was a real-world business, and ours wasn't the first sentient species it had raptured up. Lots of planets got destroyed, Erasmus said, and the Fleet didn't always get to them in time to salvage the population, hard as they tried—we were *lucky*, sort of.

So I asked him what it was that caused all these planets to blow up.

"We don't know, Carlotta. We call it the Invisible Enemy. It doesn't leave a signature, whatever it is. But it systematically seeks out worlds with flourishing civilizations and marks them for destruction." He added, "It doesn't like the Fleet much, either. There are parts of the galaxy where we don't go—because if we *do* go there, we don't come back."

At the time, I wasn't even sure what a "galaxy" was, so I dropped the subject, except to ask him if I could see what it looked like—the destruction of the Earth, I meant. At first, Erasmus didn't want to show me; but after a lot of coaxing, he turned himself into a sort of floating TV screen and displayed a view "looking back from above the plane of the solar ecliptic," words that meant nothing to me.

What I saw was . . . well, no more little blue planet, basically.

More like a ball of boiling red snot.

"What about my mother? What about Dan-O?"

I didn't have to explain who these people were. The Fleet had sucked up all kinds of data about human civilization,

I don't know how. Erasmus paused as if he was consulting some invisible Rolodex. Then he said, "They aren't with us."

"You mean they're dead?"

"Yes. Abby and Dan-O are dead."

But the news didn't surprise me. It was almost as if I'd known it all along, as if I had had a vision of their deaths, a dark vision to go along with that ghostly visit the night before, the woman in a white dress telling me *go fast*.

Abby Boudaine and Dan-O, dead. And me raptured up to robot heaven. Well, well.

"Are you sure you wouldn't like to sleep now?"

"Maybe for a while," I told him.

Dan-O's a big man, and he's working himself up to a major tantrum. Even now, Carlotta feels repugnance at the sound of his voice, that gnarl of angry consonants. Next, Dan-O throws something solid, maybe a clock, against the wall. The clock goes to pieces, noisily. Carlotta's mother cries out in response, and the sound of her wailing seems to last weeks.

"It's not good," Erasmus told me much later, "to be so much alone."

Well, I told him, I *wasn't* alone—he was with me, wasn't he? And he was pretty good company, for an alien machine. But that was a dodge. What he *meant* was that I ought to hook up with somebody human.

I told him I didn't care if I ever set eyes on another human being ever again. What had the human race ever done for *me*?

He frowned—that is, he performed a particular contortion of his exposed surfaces that I had learned to interpret as disapproval. "That's entropic talk, Carlotta. Honestly, I'm worried about you."

"What could happen to me?" Here on this beach, where nothing ever *really* happens, I did not add.

"You could go crazy. You could sink into despair. Worse, you could die."

"I could *die*? I thought I was immortal now."

"Who told you that? True, you're no longer *living*, in the strictly material sense. You're a metastable nested loop embedded in the Fleet's collective mentation. But everything's mortal, Carlotta. Anything can die."

I couldn't die of disease or falling off a cliff, he explained, but my "nested loop" was subject to a kind of slow erosion, and stewing in my own lonely juices for too long was liable to bring on the decay that much faster.

And, admittedly, after a month on this beach, swimming and sleeping too much and eating the food Erasmus conjured up whenever I was hungry (though I didn't really need to eat), watching recovered soap operas on his bellyvision screen or reading celebrity magazines (also embedded in the Fleet's collective memory) that would never get any fresher or produce another issue, and just being basically miserable as all hell, I thought maybe he was right.

"You cry out in your sleep," Erasmus said. "You have bad dreams."

"The world ended. Maybe I'm depressed. You think meeting people would help with that?"

"Actually," he said, "you have a remarkable talent for being alone. You're sturdier than most. But that won't save you, in the long run."

So I tried to take his advice. I scouted out some other survivors. Turned out, it was interesting what some people had done in their new incarnations as Fleet-data. The Erasmuses had made it easy for like-minded folks to find one another and to create environments to suit them. The most successful of these cliques, as they were sometimes called, were the least passive ones: the ones with a purpose. Purpose kept people lively. Passive cliques tended to fade into indifference pretty quickly, and the purely hedonistic ones soon collapsed into dense orgasmic singularities; but if you were curious about the world, and hung out with similarly curious friends, there was a lot to keep you thinking.

None of those cliques suited me in the long run, though. Oh, I made some friends, and I learned a few things. I learned how to access the Fleet's archival data, for instance—a trick you had to be careful with. If you did it right, you could think about a subject as if you were doing a Google search, all the relevant information popping up in your mind's eye just as if it had been there all along. Do it too often or too enthusiastically, though, and you ran the risk of getting lost in the overload—you might develop a "memory" so big and all-inclusive that it absorbed you into its own endless flow.

(It was an eerie thing to watch when it happened. For a while, I hung out with a clique that was exploring the history of the nonhuman civilizations that had been raptured up by the Fleet in eons past . . . until the leader of the group, a Jordanian college kid by the name of Nuri, dived down too far and literally fogged out. He got this look of intense concentration on his face, and, moments later, his body turned to wisps and eddies of fluid air and faded like fog in the sunlight. Made me shiver. And I had liked Nuri—I missed him when he was gone.)

But by sharing the effort, we managed to safely learn some interesting things. (Things the Erasmuses could have just *told* us, I suppose; but we didn't know the right questions to ask.) Here's a big for-instance: although every species was mortal after it was raptured up—every species eventually fogged out much the way poor Nuri had—there were actually few very long-term survivors. By that, I mean individuals who had outlived their peers, who had found a way to preserve a sense of identity in the face of the Fleet's hypercomplex data torrent.

We asked our Erasmuses if we could meet one of these long-term survivors.

Erasmus said no, that was impossible. The Elders, as he called them, didn't live on our timescale. The way they had preserved themselves was by dropping out of realtime.

Apparently, it wasn't necessary to "exist" continuously from one moment to the next. You could ask the Fleet to turn you off for a day or a week, then turn you on again. Any moment of active perception was called a *saccade*, and you could space your saccades as far apart as you liked. Want to live a thousand years? Do it by living one second out of every million that passes. Of course, it wouldn't *feel* like a thousand years, subjectively; but a thousand years would flow by before you aged much. That's basically what the Elders were doing.

We could do the same, Erasmus said, if we wanted. But there was a price tag attached to it. "Timesliding" would carry us incomprehensibly far into a future nobody could predict. We were under continual attack by the Invisible Enemy, and it was possible that the Fleet might lose so much cohesion that we could no longer be sustained as stable virtualities. We wouldn't get a long life out of it, and we might well be committing a kind of unwitting suicide.

"You don't really go anywhere," Erasmus summed up. "In effect, you just go fast. I can't honestly recommend it."

"Did I ask for your advice? I mean, what *are* you, after all? Just some little fragment of the Fleet mind charged with looking after Carlotta Boudaine. A cybernetic babysitter."

I swear to you, he looked *hurt*. And I heard the injury in his voice.

"I'm the part of the Fleet that cares about you, Carlotta."

Most of my clique backed down at that point. Most people aren't cut out to be timesliders. But I was more tempted than ever. "You can't tell me what to do, Erasmus."

"I'll come with you, then," he said. "If you don't mind."

It hadn't occurred to me that he might *not* come along. It was a scary idea. But I didn't let that anxiety show.

"Sure, I guess that'd be all right," I said.

Enemies out there too, the elder Carlotta observes. A whole skyful of them. As above, so below. Just like in that old drawing—what was it called? *Utriusque cosmi.* Funny what a person remembers. Girl, do you hear your mother crying?

The young Carlotta stirs uneasily in her tangled sheet.

Both Carlottas know their mother's history. Only the elder Carlotta can think about it without embarrassment and rage. Oh, it's an old story. Her mother's name is Abby. Abby Boudaine dropped out of high school pregnant, left some dreary home in South Carolina to go west with a twenty-year-old boyfriend who abandoned her outside Albuquerque. She gave birth in a California emergency ward and nursed Carlotta in a basement room in the home of a retired couple, who sheltered her in exchange for housework until Carlotta's constant wailing got on their nerves. After that, Abby hooked up with a guy who worked for a utility company and grew weed in his attic for pin money. The hookup lasted a few years, and might have lasted longer, except that Abby had a weakness for what the law called "substances," and couldn't restrain herself in an environment where coke and methamphetamine circulated more or less freely. A couple of times, Carlotta was bounced around between foster homes while Abby Boudaine did court-mandated dry-outs or simply binged. Eventually, Abby picked up ten-year-old Carlotta from one of these periodic suburban exiles and drove her over the state border into Arizona, jumping bail. "We'll never be apart again," her mother told her, in the strained voice that meant she was a little bit high or hoping to be. "Never again!" Blessing or curse? Carlotta wasn't sure which. "You'll never leave me, baby. You're my one and only."

Not such an unusual story, the elder Carlotta thinks, though her younger self, she knows, feels uniquely singled out for persecution.

Well, child, Carlotta thinks, try living as a distributed entity on a Fleet that's being eaten by invisible monsters, *then* see what it feels like.

But she knows the answer to that. It feels much the same.

"Now you *steal* from me?" Dan-O's voice drills through the wall like a rusty auger. Young Carlotta stirs and whimpers. Any moment now, she'll open her eyes, and then what? Although this is the fixed past, it feels suddenly unpredictable, unfamiliar, dangerous.

Erasmus came with me when I went timesliding, and I appreciated that, even before I understood what a sacrifice it was for him.

Early on, I asked him about the Fleet and how it came to exist. The answer to that question was lost to entropy, he said. He had never known a time without a Fleet—he couldn't have, because Erasmus *was* the Fleet, or at least a sovereign fraction of it.

"As we understand it," he told me, "the Fleet evolved from networks of self-replicating data-collecting machine intelligences, no doubt originally created by some organic species, for the purpose of exploring interstellar space. Evidence suggests that we're only a little younger than the universe itself."

The Fleet had outlived its creators. "Biological intelligence is unstable over the long term," Erasmus said, a little smugly. "But out of that original compulsion to acquire and share data, we evolved and refined our own collective purpose."

"That's why you hoover up doomed civilizations? So you can catalog and study them?"

"So they won't be *forgotten*, Carlotta. That's the greatest evil in the universe—the entropic decay of organized information. Forgetfulness. We despise it."

"Worse than the Invisible Enemy?"

"The Enemy is evil to the degree to which it abets entropic decay."

"Why does it want to do that?"

"We don't know. We don't even understand what the Enemy *is*, in physical terms. It seems to operate outside of the material universe. If it consists of matter, that matter is nonbaryonic and impossible to detect. It pervades parts of the galaxy—though not *all* parts—like an insubstantial gas. When the Fleet passes through volumes of space heavily infested by the Enemy, our loss-rate soars. And as these infested volumes of space expand, they encompass and destroy life-bearing worlds."

"The Enemy's growing, though. And the Fleet isn't."

I had learned to recognize Erasmus's distress, not just because he was slowly adopting somewhat more human features. "The Fleet is my home, Carlotta. More than that. It's my body, my heart . . ."

What he didn't say was that by joining me in the act of surfing time, he would be isolating himself from the realtime network that had birthed and sustained him. In realtime, Erasmus was a fraction of something reassuringly immense. But in slidetime, he'd be as alone as an Erasmus could get.

And yet, he came with me, when I made my decision. He

was *my* Erasmus as much as he was the Fleet's, and he came with me. What would you call that, girl? Friendship? At least. I came to call it love.

The younger Carlotta has stolen those pills (the ones hidden under her smudged copy of *People*) for a reason. To help her sleep, was what she told herself. But she didn't really have trouble sleeping. No: if she was honest, she'd have to say the pills were an escape hatch. Swallow enough of them, and it's, hey, fuck you, world! Less work than the highway, an alternative she was also considering.

More shouting erupts in the next room. A real roust-up, bruises to come. Then, worse, Dan-O's voice goes all small and jagged. That's a truly bad omen, Carlotta knows. Like the smell of ozone that floods the air in advance of a lightning strike, just before the voltage ramps up and the current starts to flow.

Erasmus built a special virtuality for him and me to time-trip in. Basically, it was a big comfy room with a wall-sized window overlooking the Milky Way.

The billions of tiny dense components that made up the Fleet swarmed at velocities slower than the speed of light, but timesliding made it all seem faster—scarily so. Like running the whole universe in fast-forward, knowing you can't go back. During the first few months of our expanded Now, we soared a long way out of the spiral arm that contained the abandoned Sun. The particular sub-swarm of the Fleet that hosted my sense of self was on a long elliptical orbit around the super-massive black hole at the galaxy's core, and from this end of the ellipse, over the passing days, we watched the Milky Way drop out from under us like a cloud of luminous pearls.

When I wasn't in that room, I went off to visit other timesliders, and some of them visited me there. We were a self-selected group of radical roamers with a thing for risk, and we got to know one another pretty well. Oh, girl, I wish I could tell you all the friends I made among that tribe of self-selected exiles! Many of them human, not all: I met a few of the so-called Elders of other species and managed to communicate with them on a friendly basis. Does that sound strange to you? I guess it is. Surpassing strange. I thought so too, at first. But these were people (mostly people) and things (but things can be people too) that I mostly liked and often loved, and they loved me back. Yes, they did. Whatever quirk of personality made us timesliders drew us together against all the speedy dark outside our virtual walls. Plus—well, we were survivors. It took not much more than a month to outlive all the surviving remnant of humanity. Even our ghosts were gone, in other words, unless you counted *us* as ghosts.

Erasmus was a little bit jealous of the friends I made. He had given up a lot for me, and maybe I ought to have appreciated him more for it. Unlike us formerly biological persons, though, Erasmus maintained a tentative link with realtime. He had crafted protocols to keep himself current on changes in the Fleet's symbol-sets and core mentation. That way, he could update us on what the Fleet was doing—new species raptured up from dying worlds and so forth. None of these newcomers lasted long, though, from our lofty perspective, and I once asked Erasmus why the Fleet even bothered with such ephemeral creatures as (for instance) human beings. He said that every species was doomed in the long run, but that didn't make it okay to kill people—or to abandon them when they might be rescued. That instinct was what made the Fleet a moral entity, something more than just a collection of self-replicating machines.

And it made *him* more than a nested loop of complex calculations. In the end, Carlotta, I came to love Erasmus best of all.

Meanwhile the years and stars scattered in our wake like dust—a thousand years, a hundred thousand, a million, more, and the galaxy turned like a great white wheel. We all made peace with the notion that we were the last of our kind, whatever "kind" we represented.

If you could hear me, girl, I guess you might ask what I found in that deep well of strangeness that made the water worth drinking. Well, I found friends, as I said—isn't that enough? And I found lovers. Even Erasmus began to adopt a human avatar, so we could touch each other in the human way.

I found, in plain words, a *home*, Carlotta, however peculiar in its nature—a *real* home, for the first time in my life.

Which is why I was so scared when it started to fall apart.

In the next room, Abby isn't taking Dan-O's anger lying down. It's nearly the perfect storm tonight—Dan-O's temper and Abby's sense of violated dignity both rising at the same ferocious pitch, toward some unthinkable crescendo.

But her mother's outrage is fragile, and Dan-O is frankly dangerous. The young Carlotta had known that about him from the get-go, from the first time her mother came home with this man on her arm; knew it from his indifferent eyes and his mechanical smile; knew it from the prison tattoos he didn't bother to disguise and the boastfulness with which he papered over some hole in his essential self. Knew it from the meth-lab stink that burned off him like a chemical perfume. Knew it from the company he kept, from the shitty little deals with furtive men arranged in Carlotta's mother's home because his own rental bungalow was littered with incriminating cans of industrial solvent. Knew it most of all by the way he fed Abby Boudaine crystal meth in measured doses, to keep her wanting it, and by the way Abby began to sign over her weekly Wal-Mart paycheck to him, like a dutiful servant, back when she was working checkout.

Dan-O is tall, wiry, and strong despite his vices. The elder Carlotta can hear enough to understand that Dan-O is blaming Abby for the theft of the barbiturates—an intolerable sin, in Dan-O's book. Followed by Abby's heated denials and the sound of Dan-O's fists striking flesh. All this discovered, not remembered: the young Carlotta sleeps on, though she's obviously about to wake; the critical moment is coming fast. And Carlotta thinks of what she saw when she raided Dan-O's ditty bag, the blue metal barrel with a black gnurled grip, a thing she had stared at, hefted, but ultimately disdained.

We dropped back down the curve of that elliptic, girl, and suddenly the Fleet began to vanish like drops of water on a hot griddle. Erasmus saw it first, because of what he was, and he set up a display so I could see it too: Fleet-swarms set as ghostly dots against a schema of the galaxy, the ghost-dots dimming perilously and some of them blinking out altogether. It was a graph of a massacre. "Can't anyone stop it?" I asked.

"They would if they could," he said, putting an arm (now that he had grown a pair of arms) around me. "They will if they can, Carlotta."

"Can *we* help?"

"We are helping, in a way. Existing the way we do means they don't have to use much mentation to sustain us. To the Fleet, we're code that runs a calculation for a few seconds out of every year. Not a heavy burden to carry."

Which was important, because the Fleet could only sustain so much computation, the upper limit being set by the finite number of linked nodes. And that number was diminishing as Fleet vessels were devoured wholesale.

"Last I checked," Erasmus said (which would have been about a thousand years ago, realtime), "the Fleet theorized that the Enemy is made of dark matter." (Strange stuff that hovers around galaxies, invisibly—it doesn't matter, girl, take my word for it; you'll understand it one day.) "They're not material objects so much as *processes*—parasitical protocols played out in dark matter clouds. Apparently, they can manipulate quantum events we don't even see."

"So we can't defend ourselves against them?"

"Not yet. No. And you and I might have more company soon, Carlotta. As long-timers, I mean."

That was because the Fleet continued to rapture up dying civilizations, nearly more than their shrinking numbers could contain. One solution was to shunt survivors into the Long Now along with us, in order to free up computation for battlefield maneuvers and such.

"Could get crowded," he warned.

"If a lot of strangers need to go Long . . ." I said . . .

He gave me a carefully neutral look. "Finish the thought."

"Well . . . can't we just . . . go Longer?"

* * *

Fire a pistol in a tin box like this ratty trailer and the sound is ridiculously loud. Like being spanked on the ear with a two-by-four. It's the pistol shot that finally wakes the young Carlotta. Her eyelids fly open like window shades on a haunted house.

This isn't how the elder Carlotta remembers it. *Gunshot?* No, there was no *gunshot*; she just came awake and saw the ghost—

And no ghost, either. Carlotta tries desperately to speak to her younger self, wills herself to succeed, and fails yet again. So who fired that shot, and where did the bullet go, and why can't she *remember* any of this?

The shouting in the next room has yielded up a silence. The silence becomes an eternity. Then Carlotta hears the sound of footsteps—she can't tell whose—approaching her bedroom door.

In the end, almost every conscious function of the Fleet went Long, just to survive the attrition of the war with the dark-matter beings. The next loop through the galactic core pared us down to a fraction of what we used to be. When I got raptured up, the Fleet was a distributed cloud of baseball-sized objects running quantum computations on the state of their own dense constituent atoms—*millions and millions* of such objects, all linked together in a nested hierarchy. By the time we orbited back up our ellipsis, you could have counted us in the thousands, and our remaining links were carefully narrowbanded to give us maximum stealth.

So us wild timesliders chose to go Longer.

Just like last time, Erasmus warned me that it might be a suicidal act. If the Fleet was lost, we would be lost along with it . . . our subjective lives could end within days or hours. If, on the other hand, the Fleet survived and got back to repro-ducing itself, well, we might live on indefinitely—even drop back into realtime if we chose to do so. "Can you accept the risk?" he asked.

"Can *you*?"

He had grown a face by then. I suppose he knew me well enough to calculate what features I'd find pleasing. But it wasn't his ridiculous fake humanity I loved. What I loved was what went on behind those still-gemlike, tourmaline eyes—the person he had become by sharing my mortality. "I accepted that risk a long time ago," he said.

"You and me both, Erasmus."

So we held on to each other and just—*went fast.*

Hard to explain what made that time-dive so vertiginous, but imagine centuries flying past like so much dust in a windstorm! It messed up our sense of *place*, first of all. Used to be we had a point of view light-years wide and deep . . . now all those loops merged into one continuous cycle; we grew as large as the Milky Way itself, with Andromeda bearing down on us like a silver armada. I held Erasmus in my arms, watching wide-eyed while he updated himself on the progress of the war and whispered new discoveries into my ear.

The Fleet had worked up new defenses, he said, and the carnage had slowed; but our numbers were still dwindling.

I asked him if we were dying.

He said he didn't know. Then he looked alarmed and held me tighter. "Oh, Carlotta . . ."

"What?" I stared into his eyes, which had gone faraway and strange. "*What is it?* Erasmus, tell me!"

"The Enemy," he said in numbed amazement.

"What about them?"

"I know what they are."

The bedroom door opens.

The elder Carlotta doesn't remember the bedroom door opening. None of this is as she remembers it should be. The young Carlotta cringes against the backboard of the bed, so terrified she can barely draw breath. *Bless you, girl, I'd hold your hand if I could!*

What comes through the door is just Abby Boudaine. Abby in a cheap white nightgown. But Abby's eyes are yellow-rimmed and feral, and her nightgown is spattered with blood.

See, the thing is this. All communication is limited by the speed of light. But if you spread your saccades over time, that speed limit kind of expands. Slow as we were, light seemed to cross galactic space in a matter of moments. Single thoughts consumed centuries. We felt the super-massive black hole at the center of the galaxy beating like a ponderous heart. We heard whispers from nearby galaxies, incomprehensibly faint but undeniably manufactured. Yes, girl, we were *that* slow.

But the Enemy was even slower.

"Long ago," Erasmus told me, channeling this informa-tion from the Fleet's own dying collectivity, "long ago, the Enemy learned to parasitize dark matter . . . to use it as a computational substrate . . . to evolve *within* it . . ."

"*How* long ago?"

His voice was full of awe. "Longer than you have words for, Carlotta. They're older than the universe itself."

Make any sense to you? I doubt it would. But here's the thing about our universe: it oscillates. It *breathes*, I mean, like a big old lung, expanding and shrinking and expanding again. When it shrinks, it wants to turn into a singularity, but it can't do that, because there's a limit to how much mass a quantum of volume can hold without busting. So it all bangs up again, until it can't accommodate any more emptiness. Back and forth, over and over. Perhaps ad infinitum.

Trouble is, no information can get past those hot chaotic contractions. Every bang makes a fresh universe, blank as a chalkboard in an empty schoolhouse . . .

Or so we thought.

But dark matter has a peculiar relationship with gravity and mass, Erasmus said; so when the Enemy learned to colo-nize it, they found ways to propagate themselves from one universe to the next. They could survive *the end of all things material*, in other words, and they had already done so— many times!

The Enemy was genuinely immortal, if that word has any meaning. The Enemy conducted its affairs not just across galactic space but across the voids that separate galaxies, clusters of galaxies, superclusters . . . slow as molasses, they were, but vast as all things, and as pervasive as gravity, and very powerful.

"So what have they got against the Fleet, if they're so big and almighty? Why are they killing us?"

Erasmus smiled then, and the smile was full of pain and melancholy and an awful understanding. "But they're not *killing* us, Carlotta. They're rapturing us up."

One time in school, when she was trying unsuccessfully to come to grips with *The Merchant of Venice*, Carlotta had opened a book about Elizabethan drama to a copy of an old drawing called *Utriusque Cosmi*. It was supposed to represent the whole cosmos, the way people thought of it back in Shakespeare's time, all layered and orderly: stars and angels on top, hell beneath, and a naked guy stretched foursquare between divinity and damnation. Made no sense to her at all. Some antique craziness. She thinks of that drawing now, for no accountable reason. *But it doesn't stop at the angels, girl. I learned that lesson. Even angels have angels, and devils dance on the backs of lesser devils.*

Her mother in her bloodstained nightgown hovers in the doorway of Carlotta's bedroom. Her unblinking gaze strafes the room until it fixes at last on her daughter. Abby Boudaine might be standing right here, Carlotta thinks, but those eyes are looking out from someplace deeper and more distant and far more frightening.

The blood fairly drenches her. But it isn't Abby's blood.

"Oh, Carlotta," Abby says. Then she clears her throat, the way she does when she has to make an important phone call or speak to someone she fears. "Carlotta . . ."

And Carlotta (the invisible Carlotta, the Carlotta who dropped down from that place where the angels dice with eternity) understands what Abby is about to say, recognizes at last the awesome circularity, not a paradox at all. She pronounces the words silently as Abby makes them real: "Carlotta. Listen to me, girl. I don't guess you understand any of this. I'm so sorry. I'm sorry for many things. But listen now. When it's time to leave, you leave. Don't be afraid, and don't get caught. Just go. Go *fast*."

Then she turns and leaves her daughter cowering in the darkened room.

Beyond the bedroom window, the coyotes are still complaining to the moon. The sound of their hooting fills up the young Carlotta's awareness until it seems to speak directly to the heart of her.

Then comes the second and final gunshot.

I have only seen the Enemy briefly, and by that time, I had stopped thinking of them as the Enemy.

Can't describe them too well. Words really do fail me. And by that time, might as well admit it, I was not myself a thing I would once have recognized as human. Just say that Erasmus and I and the remaining timesliders were taken up into the Enemy's embrace along with all the rest of the Fleet—all the memories we had deemed lost to entropy or warfare were preserved there. The virtualities the Enemies had developed across whole kalpas of time were labyrinthine, welcoming, strange beyond belief. Did I roam in those mysterious glades? Yes I did, girl, and Erasmus by my side, for many long (subjective) years, and we became—well, larger than I can say.

And the galaxies aged and flew away from one another until they were swallowed up in manifolds of cosmic emptiness, connected solely by the gentle and inexorable thread of gravity. Stars winked out, girl; galaxies merged and filled with dead and dying stars; atoms decayed to their last stable forms. But the fabric of space can tolerate just so much emptiness. It isn't infinitely elastic. Even vacuum ages. After some trillions and trillions of years, therefore, the expansion became a contraction.

During that time, I occasionally sensed or saw the Enemy—but I have to call them something else; say, *the Great Old Ones*, pardon my pomposity—who had constructed the dark-matter virtualities in which I now lived. They weren't people at all. Never were. They passed through our adopted worlds like storm clouds, black and majestic and full of subtle and inscrutable lightnings. I couldn't speak to them, even then; as large and old as I had become, I was only a fraction of what they were.

I wanted to ask them why they had destroyed the Earth, why so many people had to be wiped out of existence or salvaged by the evolved benevolence of the Fleet. But Erasmus, who delved into these questions more deeply than I was able to, said the Great Old Ones couldn't perceive anything as tiny or ephemeral as a rocky planet like the Earth. The Earth and all the many planets like her had been destroyed, not by any willful calculation but by autonomic impulses evolved over the course of many cosmic conflations—impulses as imperceptible and involuntary to the Old Ones as the functioning of your liver is to *you*, girl.

The logic of it is this: life-bearing worlds generate civilizations that eventually begin playing with dark matter, posing a potential threat to the continuity of the Old Ones. Some number of these intrusions can be tolerated and contained—like the Fleet, they were often an enriching presence—but too many of them would endanger the stability of the system. It's as if we were germs, girl, wiped out by a giant's immune system. They couldn't *see* us, except as a somatic threat. Simple as that.

But they could see the *Fleet*. The Fleet was just big enough and durable enough to register on the senses of the Old Ones. And the Old Ones weren't malevolent: they perceived the Fleet much the way the Fleet had once perceived *us*, as something primitive but alive and thinking and worth the trouble of salvation.

So they raptured up the Fleet (and similar Fleet-like entities in countless other galaxies), thus preserving us against the blind oscillations of cosmic entropy.

(Nice of them, I suppose. But if I ever grow large enough or live long enough to confront an Old One face to face, I mean to lodge a complaint. Hell *yes* we were small—people are some of the smallest thought-bearing creatures in the cosmos, and I think we all kind of knew that even before the end of the world . . . *you* did, surely. But pain is pain and grief is grief. It might be inevitable, it might even be built into the nature of things, but it isn't *good*, and it ought not to be tolerated, if there's a choice.)

Which I guess is why I'm here watching you squinch your eyes shut while the sound of that second gunshot fades into the air.

Watching you process a nightmare into a vision.

Watching you build a pearl around a grain of bloody truth.

Watching you *go fast*.

The bodiless Carlotta hovers a while longer in the fixed and changeless corridors of the past.

Eventually, the long night ends. Raw red sunlight finds the window.

Last dawn this small world will ever see, as it happens; but the young Carlotta doesn't know that yet.

Now that the universe has finished its current iteration, all its history is stored in transdimensional metaspace like a book on a shelf—it can't be changed. Truly so. I guess I know that now, girl. Memory plays tricks that history corrects.

And I guess that's why the Old Ones let me have access to these events, as we hover on the brink of a new creation.

I know some of the questions you'd ask me if you could. You might say, *Where are you really?* And I'd say, *I'm at the end of all things, which is really just another beginning.* I'm walking in a great garden of dark matter, while all things known and baryonic spiral up the ladder of unification energies to a fiery new dawn. I have grown so large, girl, that I can fly down history like a bird over a prairie field. But I cannot remake what has already been made. That is one power I do not possess.

I watch you get out of bed. I watch you dress. Blue jeans with tattered hems, a man's lumberjack shirt, those thrift-shop Reeboks. I watch you go to the kitchen and fill your vinyl Bratz backpack with bottled water and Tootsie Rolls, which is all the cuisine your meth-addled mother has left in the cupboards.

Then I watch you tiptoe into Abby's bedroom. I confess I don't remember this part, girl. I suppose it didn't fit my fantasy about a benevolent ghost. But here you are, your face fixed in a willed indifference, stepping over Dan-O's corpse. Dan-O bled a lot after Abby Boudaine blew a hole in his chest, and the carpet is a sticky rust-colored pond.

I watch you pull Dan-O's ditty bag from where it lies half under the bed. On the bed, Abby appears to sleep. The pistol is still in her hand. The hand with the pistol in it rests beside her head. Her head is damaged in ways the young Carlotta can't stand to look at. Eyes down, girl. That's it.

I watch you pull a roll of bills from the bag and stuff it into your pack. Won't need that money where you're going! But it's a wise move, taking it. Commendable forethought.

Now go.

I have to go too. I feel Erasmus waiting for me, feel the tug of his love and loyalty, gentle and inevitable as gravity. He used to be a machine older than the dirt under your feet, Car- lotta Boudaine, but he became a man—*my* man, I'm proud to say. He needs me, because it's no easy thing crossing over from one universe to the next. There's always work to do, isn't that the truth?

But right now, you go. You leave those murderous pills on the nightstand, find that highway. Don't be afraid. Don't wait. Don't get caught. Just go. Go fast. And excuse me while I take my own advice.

THE ISLAND

PETER WATTS

Self-described as "a reformed marine biologist," Peter Watts is quickly establishing himself as one of the most respected hard-science writers of the twenty-first century. His short work has appeared in *Tesseracts*, *The Solaris Book of Science Fiction*, *On Spec*, *Divine Realms*, *Prairie Fire*, and elsewhere. He is the author of the well-received Rifters series, including the novels *Starfish*, *Maelstrom*, *Behemoth: B-Max*, and *Behemoth: Seppuku*. His short work has been collected in *Ten Monkeys, Ten Minutes*. His most recent book is the novel *Blindsight*, which has been widely hailed as one of the best hard SF books of the decade. He lives in Toronto, Canada.

In the powerful and innovative story that follows, he paints a picture of a work crew compelled to labor on through all eternity, even though they're no longer sure whom they're working for or why, and who come smack up against an obstacle unlike any even they have ever seen.

You sent us out here. We do this for *you*: spin your webs and build your magic gateways, thread the needle's eye at sixty thousand kilometers a second. We never stop, never even dare to slow down, lest the light of your coming turn us to plasma. All so you can step from star to star without dirtying your feet in these endless, empty wastes *between*.

Is it really too much to ask, that you might talk to us now and then?

I know about evolution and engineering. I know how much you've changed. I've seen these portals give birth to gods and demons and things we can't begin to comprehend, things I can't believe were ever human; alien hitchhikers, perhaps, riding the rails we've left behind. Alien conquerors.

Exterminators, perhaps.

But I've also seen those gates stay dark and empty until they faded from view. We've inferred diebacks and dark ages, civilizations burned to the ground and others rising from their ashes—and sometimes, afterward, the things that come out look a little like the ships *we* might have built, back in the day. They speak to one another—radio, laser, carrier neutrinos—and sometimes their voices sound something like ours. There was a time we dared to hope that they really were like us, that the circle had come around again and closed on beings we could talk to. I've lost count of the times we tried to break the ice.

I've lost count of the eons since we gave up.

All these iterations fading behind us. All these hybrids and posthumans and immortals, gods and catatonic cavemen trapped in magical chariots they can't begin to understand, and not one of them ever pointed a comm laser in our direction to say *Hey, how's it going?* or *Guess what? We cured Damascus Disease!* or even *Thanks, guys, keep up the good work!*

We're not some fucking cargo cult. We're the backbone of your goddamn empire. You wouldn't even be *out* here if it weren't for us.

And—and you're *our* children. Whatever you've become, you were once like this, like me. I believed in you once. There was a time, long ago, when I believed in this mission with all my heart.

Why have you forsaken us?

* * *

And so another build begins.

This time, I open my eyes to a familiar face I've never seen before: only a boy, early twenties perhaps, physiologically. His face is a little lopsided, the cheekbone flatter on the left than the right. His ears are too big. He looks almost *natural*.

I haven't spoken for millennia. My voice comes out a whisper: "Who are you?" Not what I'm supposed to ask, I know. Not the first question *anyone* on *Eriophora* asks, after coming back.

"I'm yours," he says, and just like that, I'm a mother.

I want to let it sink in, but he doesn't give me the chance: "You weren't scheduled, but Chimp wants extra hands on deck. Next build's got a situation."

So the chimp is still in control. The chimp is always in control. The mission goes on.

"Situation?" I ask.

"Contact scenario, maybe."

I wonder when he was born. I wonder if he ever wondered about me, before now.

He doesn't tell me. He only says, "Sun up ahead. Half light-year. Chimp thinks, maybe it's talking to us. Anyhow . . ." My—son shrugs. "No rush. Lotsa time."

I nod, but he hesitates. He's waiting for The Question, but I already see a kind of answer in his face. Our reinforcements were supposed to be *pristine*, built from perfect genes buried deep within *Eri*'s iron-basalt mantle, safe from the sleeting blueshift. And yet this boy has flaws. I see the damage in his face, I see those tiny flipped base-pairs resonating up from the microscopic and *bending* him just a little off-kilter. He looks like he grew up on a planet. He looks borne of parents who spent their whole lives hammered by raw sunlight.

How far out must we be by now, if even our own perfect building blocks have decayed so? How long has it taken us? How long have I been dead?

How long? It's the first thing everyone asks.

After all this time, I don't want to know.

* * *

He's alone at the tac Tank when I arrive on the bridge, his eyes full of icons and trajectories. Perhaps I see a little of me in there, too.

"I didn't get your name," I say, although I've looked it up on the manifest. We've barely been introduced and already I'm lying to him.

"Dix." He keeps his eyes on the Tank.

He's over ten thousand years old. Alive for maybe twenty of them. I wonder how much he knows, whom he's met during those sparse decades: does he know Ishmael or Connie? Does he know if Sanchez got over his brush with immortality?

I wonder, but I don't ask. There are rules.

I look around. "We're it?"

Dix nods. "For now. Bring back more if we need them. But . . ." His voice trails off.

"Yes?"

"Nothing."

I join him at the Tank. Diaphanous veils hang within like frozen, color-coded smoke. We're on the edge of a molecular dust cloud. Warm, semiorganic, lots of raw materials. Formaldehyde, ethylene glycol, the usual prebiotics. A good spot for a quick build. A red dwarf glowers dimly at the center of the Tank: the chimp has named it DHF428, for reasons I've long since forgotten to care about.

"So fill me in," I say.

His glance is impatient, even irritated. "You too?"

"What do you mean?"

"Like the others. On the other builds. Chimp can just squirt the specs, but they want to *talk* all the time."

Shit, his link's still active. He's *online*.

I force a smile. "Just a—a cultural tradition, I guess. We talk about a lot of things, it helps us—reconnect. After being down for so long."

"But it's *slow*," Dix complains.

He doesn't know. Why doesn't he know?

"We've got half a light-year," I point out. "There's some rush?"

The corner of his mouth twitches. "Vons went out on schedule." On cue, a cluster of violet pinpricks sparkle in the Tank, five trillion klicks ahead of us. "Still sucking dust mostly, but got lucky with a couple of big asteroids, and the refineries came online early. First components already extruded. Then Chimp sees these fluctuations in solar output— mainly infra, but extends into visible." The Tank blinks at us: the dwarf goes into time-lapse.

Sure enough, it's *flickering*.

"Non-random, I take it."

Dix inclines his head a little to the side, not quite nodding.

"Plot the time-series." I've never been able to break the habit of raising my voice, just a bit, when addressing the chimp. Obediently (*obediently*—now *there's* a laugh and a half), the AI wipes the spacescape and replaces it with

..... • • • • • • • • • • • • • •   •   •   •   •   •

"Repeating sequence," Dix tells me. "Blips don't change, but spacing's a log-linear increase cycling every 92.5 corsecs. Each cycle starts at 13.2 clicks/corsec, degrades over time."

"No chance this could be natural? A little black hole wob-bling around in the center of the star, something like that?"

Dix shakes his head, or something like that: a diagonal dip of the chin that somehow conveys the negative. "But way too simple to contain much info. Not like an actual conversation. More—well, a shout."

He's partly right. There may not be much information, but there's enough. *We're here. We're smart. We're powerful enough to hook a whole damn star up to a dimmer switch.*

Maybe not such a good spot for a build after all.

I purse my lips. "The sun's hailing us. That's what you're saying."

"Maybe. Hailing *someone*. But too simple for a rosetta signal. It's not an archive, can't self-extract. Not a bonfer-roni or fibonacci seq, not pi. Not even a multiplication table. Nothing to base a pidgin on."

Still. An intelligent signal.

"Need more info," Dix says, proving himself master of the blindingly obvious.

I nod. "The vons."

"Uh, what about them?"

"We set up an array. Use a bunch of bad eyes to fake a good one. It'd be faster than high-geeing an observatory from this end or retooling one of the on-site factories."

His eyes go wide. For a moment, he almost looks frightened for some reason. But the moment passes and he does that weird head-shake thing again. "Bleed too many resources away from the build, wouldn't it?"

"It would," the chimp agrees.

I suppress a snort. "If you're so worried about meeting our construction benchmarks, Chimp, factor in the potential risk posed by an intelligence powerful enough to control the energy output of an entire sun."

"I can't," it admits. "I don't have enough information."

"You don't have *any* information. About something that could probably stop this mission dead in its tracks if it wanted to. So maybe we should get some."

"Okay. Vons reassigned."

Confirmation glows from a convenient bulkhead, a complex sequence of dance instructions that *Eri*'s just fired into the void. Six months from now, a hundred self-replicating robots will waltz into a makeshift surveillance grid; four months after that, we might have something more than vacuum to debate in.

Dix eyes me as though I've just cast some kind of magic spell.

"It may run the ship," I tell him, "but it's pretty fucking stupid. Sometimes you've just got to spell things out."

He looks vaguely affronted, but there's no mistaking the surprise beneath. He didn't know that. He *didn't know.*

Who the hell's been raising him all this time? Whose problem is this?

Not mine.

"Call me in ten months," I say. "I'm going back to bed."

It's as though he never left. I climb back into the bridge and there he is, staring into tac. DHF428 fills the Tank, a swollen red orb that turns my son's face into a devil mask.

He spares me the briefest glance, eyes wide, fingers twitching as if electrified. "Vons don't see it."

I'm still a bit groggy from the thaw. "See wh—"

"The *sequence*!" His voice borders on panic. He sways back and forth, shifting his weight from foot to foot.

"Show me."

Tac splits down the middle. Cloned dwarves burn before me now, each perhaps twice the size of my fist. On the left, an *Eri*'s-eye view: DHF428 stutters as it did before, as it presumably has these past ten months. On the right, a compound-eye composite: an interferometry grid built by a myriad precisely spaced vons, their rudimentary eyes layered and parallaxed into something approaching high resolution. Contrast on both sides has been conveniently cranked up to highlight the dwarf's endless winking for merely human eyes.

Except that it's only winking from the left side of the display. On the right, 428 glowers steady as a standard candle.

"Chimp: any chance the grid just isn't sensitive enough to see the fluctuations?"

"No."

"Huh." I try to think of some reason it would lie about this.

"Doesn't make *sense*," my son complains.

"It does," I murmur, "if it's not the sun that's flickering."

"But *is* flickering—" He sucks his teeth. "You *see* it—wait, you mean something *behind* the vons? Between, between them and us?"

"Mmmm."

"Some kind of *filter*." Dix relaxes a bit. "Wouldn't we've seen it, though? Wouldn't the vons've hit it going down?"

I put my voice back into ChimpComm mode. "What's the current field-of-view for *Eri*'s forward scope?"

"Eighteen mikes," the chimp reports. "At 428's range, the cone is 3.34 lightsecs across."

"Increase to a hundred lightsecs."

The *Eri*'s-eye partition swells, obliterating the dissenting viewpoint. For a moment, the sun fills the Tank again, paints the whole bridge crimson. Then it dwindles as if devoured from within.

I notice some fuzz in the display. "Can you clear that noise?"

"It's not noise," the chimp reports. "It's dust and molecular gas."

I blink. "What's the density?"

"Estimated hundred thousand atoms per cubic meter."

Two orders of magnitude too high, even for a nebula. "Why so heavy?" Surely we'd have detected any gravity well strong enough to keep *that* much material in the neighborhood.

"I don't know," the chimp says.

I get the queasy feeling that I might. "Set field-of-view to five hundred lightsecs. Peak false-color at near-infrared."

Space grows ominously murky in the Tank. The tiny sun at its center, thumbnail-size now, glows with increased brilliance: an incandescent pearl in muddy water.

"A thousand lightsecs," I command.

"There," Dix whispers: real space reclaims the edges of the Tank, dark, clear, pristine. DHF428 nestles at the heart of a dim spherical shroud. You find those sometimes, discarded castoffs from companion stars whose convulsions spew gas and rads across lightyears. But 428 is no nova remnant. It's a *red dwarf*, placid, middle-aged. Unremarkable.

Except for the fact that it sits dead center of a tenuous gas bubble 1.4 AU's across. And for the fact that that bubble does not *attenuate* or *diffuse* or *fade* gradually into that good night. No, unless there is something seriously wrong with the display, this small, spherical nebula extends about three hundred and fifty lightsecs from its primary and then just *stops*, its boundary far more knife-edged than nature has any right to be.

For the first time in millennia, I miss my cortical pipe. It takes forever to saccade search terms onto the keyboard in my head, to get the answers I already know.

Numbers come back. "Chimp. I want false-color peaks at three hundred thirty-five, five hundred, and eight hundred nanometers."

The shroud around 428 lights up like a dragonfly's wing, like an iridescent soap bubble.

"It's *beautiful*," whispers my awestruck son.

"It's photosynthetic," I tell him.

Phaeophytin and eumelanin, according to spectro. There are even hints of some kind of lead-based Keipper pigment, soaking up X-rays in the picometer range. Chimp hypothesizes something called a *chromatophore*: branching cells with little aliquots of pigment inside, like particles of charcoal dust. Keep those particles clumped together and the cell's effectively transparent; spread them out through the cytoplasm and the whole structure *darkens*, dims whatever EM passes through from behind. Apparently there were animals back on Earth with cells like that. They could change color, pattern-match to their background, all sorts of things.

"So there's a membrane of—of *living tissue* around that star," I say, trying to wrap my head around the concept. "A, a meat balloon. Around the whole damn *star.*"

"Yes," the chimp says.

"But that's—Jesus, how thick would it be?"

"No more than two millimeters. Probably less."

"How so?"

"If it was much thicker, it would be more obvious in the visible spectrum. It would have had a detectable effect on the von Neumanns when they hit it."

"That's assuming that its—cells, I guess—are like ours."

"The pigments are familiar; the rest might be too."

It can't be *too* familiar. Nothing like a conventional gene would last two seconds in that environment. Not to mention whatever miracle solvent that thing must use as antifreeze . . .

"Okay, let's be conservative, then. Say, mean thickness of a millimeter. Assume a density of water at STP. How much mass in the whole thing?"

"1.4 yottagrams," Dix and the chimp reply, almost in unison.

"That's, uh . . ."

"Half the mass of Mercury," the chimp adds helpfully.

I whistle through my teeth. "And that's *one* organism?"

"I don't know yet."

"It's got organic pigments. Fuck, it's *talking*. It's intelligent."

"Most cyclic emanations from living sources are simple biorhythms," the chimp points out. "Not intelligent signals."

I ignore it and turn to Dix. "Assume it's a signal."

He frowns. "Chimp says—"

"*Assume*. Use your imagination."

I'm not getting through to him. He looks nervous.

He looks like that a lot, I realize.

"*If* someone were signaling you," I say, "*then* what would you do?"

"Signal . . ." Confusion on that face, and a fuzzy circuit closing somewhere ". . . back?"

My son is an idiot.

"And if the incoming signal takes the form of systematic changes in light intensity, how—"

"Use the BI lasers, alternated to pulse between seven hundred and three thousand nanometers. Can boost an interlaced signal into the exawatt range without compromising our fenders; gives over a thousand watts per square meter after diffraction. Way past detection threshold for anything that can sense thermal output from a red dwarf. And content doesn't matter if it's just a shout. Shout back. Test for echo."

Okay, so my son is an idiot *savant*.

And he still looks unhappy—"But Chimp, he says no real *information* there, right?"—and that whole other set of misgivings edges to the fore again: *he*.

Dix takes my silence for amnesia. "Too simple, remember? Simple click train."

I shake my head. There's more information in that signal than the chimp can imagine. There are so many things the chimp doesn't know. And the last thing I need is for this, this *child* to start deferring to it, to start looking to it as an equal, or, God forbid, a *mentor*.

Oh, it's smart enough to steer us between the stars. Smart enough to calculate sixty-digit primes in the blink of an eye. Even smart enough for a little crude improvisation should the crew go too far off-mission.

Not smart enough to know a distress call when it sees one. "It's a deceleration curve," I tell them both. "It keeps *slowing down*. Over and over again. *That's* the message."

Stop. Stop. Stop. Stop.

And I think it's meant for no one but us.

We shout back. No reason not to. And now we die again, because what's the point of staying up late? Whether or not this vast entity harbors real intelligence, our echo won't reach it for ten million corsecs. Another seven million, at the earliest, before we receive any reply it might send.

Might as well hit the crypt in the meantime. Shut down all desires and misgivings, conserve whatever life I have left for moments that matter. Remove myself from this sparse tactical intelligence, from this wet-eyed pup watching me as though I'm some kind of sorcerer about to vanish in a puff of smoke. He opens his mouth to speak, and I turn away and hurry down to oblivion.

But I set my alarm to wake up alone.

I linger in the coffin for a while, grateful for small and ancient victories. The chimp's dead, blackened eye gazes down from the ceiling; in all these millions of years, nobody's scrubbed off the carbon scoring. It's a trophy of sorts, a memento from the early incendiary days of our Great Struggle.

There's still something—comforting, I guess—about that blind, endless stare. I'm reluctant to venture out where the chimp's nerves have not been so thoroughly cauterized. Childish, I know. The damn thing already knows I'm up; it may be blind, deaf, and impotent in here, but there's no way to mask the power the crypt sucks in during a thaw. And it's not as though a bunch of club-wielding teleops are waiting to pounce on me the moment I step outside. These are the days of détente, after all. The struggle continues but the war has gone cold; we just go through the motions now, rattling our chains like an old married multiplet resigned to hating each other to the end of time.

After all the moves and countermoves, the truth is we need each other.

So I wash the rotten-egg stench from my hair and step

into *Eri*'s silent cathedral hallways. Sure enough, the enemy
waits in the darkness, turns the lights on as I approach, shuts
them off behind me—but it does not break the silence.

Dix.

A strange one, that. Not that you'd expect anyone born and
raised on *Eriophora* to be an archetype of mental health,
but Dix doesn't even know what side he's on. He doesn't
even seem to know he has to *choose* a side. It's almost as
though he read the original mission statements and took
them *seriously*, believed in the literal truth of the ancient
scrolls: Mammals and Machinery, working together across
the ages to explore the Universe! United! Strong! Forward
the Frontier!

Rah.

Whoever raised him didn't do a great job. Not that I blame
them; it can't have been much fun having a child underfoot
during a build, and none of us were selected for our parent-
ing skills. Even if bots changed the diapers and VR handled
the infodumps, socializing a toddler couldn't have been anyone's idea of a good time. I'd have probably just chucked the
little bastard out an airlock.

But even I would've brought him up to speed.

Something changed while I was away. Maybe the war's
heated up again, entered some new phase. That twitchy kid
is out of the loop for a reason. I wonder what it is.

I wonder if I care.

I arrive at my suite, treat myself to a gratuitous meal, jill
off. Three hours after coming back to life, I'm relaxing in
the starbow commons. "Chimp."

"You're up early," it says at last.

I am. Our answering shout hasn't even arrived at its destination yet. No real chance of new data for another two
months, at least.

"Show me the forward feeds," I command.

DHF428 blinks at me from the center of the lounge: *Stop.
Stop. Stop.*

Maybe. Or maybe the chimp's right, maybe it's pure physiology. Maybe this endless cycle carries no more intelligence
than the beating of a heart.

But there's a pattern inside the pattern, some kind of *flicker* in the blink. It makes my brain itch.

"Slow the time-series," I command. "By a hundred."

It *is* a blink. DHF428's disk isn't darkening uniformly, it's *eclipsing*. As though a great eyelid were being drawn across the surface of the sun, from right to left.

"By a thousand."

Chromatophores, the chimp called them. But they're not all opening and closing at once. The darkness moves across the membrane in *waves*.

A word pops into my head: *latency*.

"Chimp. Those waves of pigment. How fast are they moving?"

"About fifty-nine thousand kilometers per second."

The speed of a passing thought.

And if this thing *does* think, it'll have logic gates, synapses—it's going to be a *net* of some kind. And if the net's big enough, there's an *I* in the middle of it. Just like me, just like Dix. Just like the chimp. (Which is why I educated myself on the subject, back in the early tumultuous days of our relationship. Know your enemy and all that.)

The thing about *I* is, it only exists within a tenth-of-a-second of all its parts. When we get spread too thin—when someone splits your brain down the middle, say, chops the fat pipe so the halves have to talk the long way around; when the neural architecture *diffuses* past some critical point and signals take just that much longer to pass from A to B—the system, well, *decoheres*. The two sides of your brain become different people with different tastes, different agendas, different senses of themselves.

I shatters into *we*.

It's not just a human rule, or a mammal rule, or even an Earthly one. It's a rule for any circuit that processes information, and it applies as much to the things we've yet to meet as it did to those we left behind.

Fifty-nine thousand kilometers per second, the chimp says. How far can the signal move through that membrane in a tenth of a corsec? How thinly does *I* spread itself across the heavens?

The flesh is huge, the flesh is inconceivable. But the spirit, the spirit is—

Shit.

"Chimp. Assuming the mean neuron density of a human brain, what's the synapse count on a circular sheet of neurons one millimeter thick with a diameter of five thousand eight hundred ninety-two kilometers?"

"Two times ten to the twenty-seventh."

I saccade the database for some perspective on a mind stretched across thirty million square kilometers: the equivalent of two quadrillion human brains.

Of course, whatever this thing uses for neurons have to be packed a lot less tightly than ours; we can see right through them, after all. Let's be superconservative, say it's only got a thousandth the computational density of a human brain. That's—

Okay, let's say it's only got a *ten*-thousandth the synaptic density, that's still—

A *hundred* thousandth. The merest mist of thinking meat. Any more conservative and I'd hypothesize it right out of existence.

Still twenty billion human brains.

Twenty *billion*.

I don't know how to feel about that. This is no mere alien.

But I'm not quite ready to believe in gods.

I round the corner and run smack into Dix, standing like a golem in the middle of my living room. I jump about a meter straight up.

"What the hell are you doing here?"

He seems surprised by my reaction. "Wanted to—talk," he says after a moment.

"You *never* come into someone's home uninvited!"

He retreats a step, stammers: "Wanted, wanted—"

"To talk. And you do that in *public*. On the bridge, or in the commons, or—for that matter, you could just *comm* me."

He hesitates. "Said you—*wanted* face to face. You said, *cultural tradition*."

I did, at that. But not *here*. This is *my* place, these are my *private quarters*. The lack of locks on these doors is a safety protocol, not an invitation to walk into my home and *lie in wait*, and stand there like part of the fucking *furniture* . . .

"Why are you even *up*?" I snarl. "We're not even supposed to come online for another two months."

"Asked Chimp to get me up when you did."

That fucking machine.

"Why are *you* up?" he asks, not leaving.

I sigh, defeated, and fall into a convenient pseudopod. "I just wanted to go over the preliminary data." The implicit *alone* should be obvious.

"Anything?"

Evidently it isn't. I decide to play along for a while. "Looks like we're talking to an, an island. Almost six thousand klicks across. That's the thinking part, anyway. The surrounding membrane's pretty much empty. I mean, it's all *alive*. It all photosynthesizes, or something like that. It eats, I guess. Not sure what."

"Molecular cloud," Dix says. "Organic compounds everywhere. Plus it's concentrating stuff inside the envelope."

I shrug. "Point is, there's a size limit for the brain, but it's *huge*, it's . . ."

"Unlikely," he murmurs, almost to himself.

I turn to look at him; the pseudopod reshapes itself around me. "What do you mean?"

"Island's twenty-eight million square kilometers? Whole sphere's seven quintillion. Island just happens to be between us and 428, that's—one in fifty billion odds."

"Go on."

He can't. "Uh, just . . . just *unlikely*."

I close my eyes. "How can you be smart enough to run those numbers in your head without missing a beat and stupid enough to miss the obvious conclusion?"

That panicked, slaughterhouse look again. "Don't—I'm not—"

"It *is* unlikely. It's *astronomically* unlikely that we just happen to be aiming at the one intelligent spot on a sphere one and a half AU's across. Which means . . ."

He says nothing. The perplexity in his face mocks me. I want to punch it.

But finally, the lights flicker on: "There's, uh, more than one island? Oh! A *lot* of islands!"

This creature is part of the crew. My life will almost certainly depend on him some day.

That is a very scary thought.

I try to set it aside for the moment. "There's probably a whole population of the things, sprinkled through the membrane like, like cysts I guess. The chimp doesn't know how many, but we're only picking up this one so far, so they might be pretty sparse."

There's a different kind of frown on his face now. "Why *Chimp*?"

"What do you mean?"

"Why call him Chimp?"

"We call it *the* chimp." Because the first step to humanizing something is to give it a name.

"Looked it up. Short for *chimpanzee*. Stupid animal."

"Actually, I think chimps were supposed to be pretty smart," I remember.

"Not like us. Couldn't even *talk*. Chimp can talk. *Way* smarter than those things. That name—it's an insult."

"What do you care?"

He just looks at me.

I spread my hands. "Okay, it's not a chimp. We just call it that because it's got roughly the same synapse count."

"So gave him a small brain, then complain that he's stupid all the time."

My patience is just about drained. "Do you have a point or are you just blowing CO_2 in—"

"Why not make him smarter?"

"Because you can never predict the behavior of a system more complex than you. And if you want a project to stay on track after you're gone, you don't hand the reins to anything that's guaranteed to develop its own agenda." Sweet smoking Jesus, you'd think *someone* would have told him about Ashby's Law.

"So they lobotomized him," Dix says after a moment.

"No. They didn't *turn* it stupid, they *built* it stupid."

"Maybe smarter than you think. You're so much smarter, got *your* agenda, how come *he's* still in control?"

"Don't flatter yourself," I say.

"What?"

I let a grim smile peek through. "You're only following orders from a bunch of other systems *way* more complex than you are." You've got to hand it to them, too; dead for stellar lifetimes and those damn project admins are *still* pulling the strings.

"I don't—*I'm* following?—"

"I'm sorry, dear." I smile sweetly at my idiot offspring. "I wasn't talking to you. I was talking to the thing that's making all those sounds come out of your mouth."

Dix turns whiter than my panties.

I drop all pretense. "What were you thinking, chimp? That you could send this sock-puppet to invade my home and I wouldn't notice?"

"Not—I'm not—it's *me*," Dix stammers. "*Me* talking."

"It's *coaching* you. Do you even know what 'lobotomized' *means*?" I shake my head, disgusted. "You think I've forgotten how the interface works just because we all burned ours out?" A caricature of surprise begins to form on his face. "Oh, don't even fucking *try*. You've been up for other builds, there's no way you couldn't have known. And you know we shut down our domestic links too, or you wouldn't even be sneaking in here. And there's nothing your lord and master can do about that because it *needs* us, and so we have reached what you might call an *accommodation*."

I am not shouting. My tone is icy, but my voice is dead level. And yet Dix almost *cringes* before me.

There is an opportunity here, I realize.

I thaw my voice a little. I speak gently: "You can do that too, you know. Burn out your link. I'll even let you come back here afterward, if you still want to. Just to—talk. But not with that thing in your head."

There is panic in his face, and, against all expectation, it almost breaks my heart. *"Can't,"* he pleads. "How I *learn* things, how I *train*. The *mission* . . ."

I honestly don't know which of them is speaking, so I answer them both: "There is more than one way to carry out the mission. We have more than enough time to try them all. Dix is welcome to come back when he's alone."

They take a step toward me. Another. One hand, twitching, rises from their side as if to reach out, and there's something on that lopsided face that I can't quite recognize.

"But I'm your *son*," they say.

I don't even dignify it with a denial.

"Get out of my home."

A human periscope. The Trojan Dix. That's a new one.

The chimp's never tried such overt infiltration while we were up and about before. Usually, it waits until we're all undead before invading our territories. I imagine custom-made drones never seen by human eyes, cobbled together during the long dark eons between builds; I see them sniffing through drawers and peeking behind mirrors, strafing the bulkheads with X-rays and ultrasound, patiently searching *Eriophora*'s catacombs millimeter by endless millimeter for whatever secret messages we might be sending one another down through time.

There's no proof to speak of. We've left trip wires and telltales to alert us to intrusion after the fact, but there's never been any evidence they've been disturbed. Means nothing, of course. The chimp may be stupid, but it's also cunning, and a million years is more than enough time to iterate through every possibility using simpleminded brute force. Document every dust mote; commit your unspeakable acts; put everything back the way it was, afterward.

We're too smart to risk talking across the eons. No encrypted strategies, no long-distance love letters, no chatty postcards showing ancient vistas long lost in the redshift. We keep all that in our heads, where the enemy will never find it. The unspoken rule is that we do not speak, unless it is face to face.

Endless idiotic games. Sometimes I almost forget what we're squabbling over. It seems so trivial now, with an immortal in my sights.

Maybe that means nothing to you. Immortality must be
ancient news to you. But I can't even imagine it, although
I've outlived worlds. All I have are moments: two or three
hundred years, to ration across the life span of a universe.
I could bear witness to any point in time, or any hundred-
thousand, if I slice my life thinly enough—but I will never
see *everything*. I will never see even a fraction.

My life will end. I have to *choose*.

When you come to fully appreciate the deal you've
made—ten or fifteen builds out, when the trade-off leaves
the realm of mere *knowledge* and sinks deep as cancer into
your bones—you become a miser. You can't help it. You
ration out your waking moments to the barest minimum: just
enough to manage the build, to plan your latest countermove
against the chimp, just enough (if you haven't yet moved
beyond the need for human contact) for sex and snuggles and
a bit of warm mammalian comfort against the endless dark.
And then you hurry back to the crypt, to hoard the remains
of a human life span against the unwinding of the cosmos.

There's been time for education. Time for a hundred post-
graduate degrees, thanks to the best caveman learning tech.
I've never bothered. Why burn down my tiny candle for a
litany of mere fact, fritter away my precious, endless, finite
life? Only a fool would trade book-learning for a ringside
view of the Cassiopeia Remnant, even if you *do* need false-
color enhancement to see the fucking thing.

Now, though. Now, I want to *know*. This creature crying
out across the gulf, massive as a moon, wide as a solar
system, tenuous and fragile as an insect's wing: I'd gladly
cash in some of my life to learn its secrets. How does it
work? How can it even *live* here at the edge of absolute zero,
much less think? What vast, unfathomable intellect must it
possess, to see us coming from over half a lightyear away, to
deduce the nature of our eyes and our instruments, to send a
signal we can even *detect*, much less understand?

And what happens when we punch through it at a fifth the
speed of light?

I call up the latest findings on my way to bed, and the
answer hasn't changed: not much. The damn thing's already

full of holes. Comets, asteroids, the usual protoplanetary junk careens through this system as it does through every other. Infra picks up diffuse pockets of slow outgassing here and there around the perimeter, where the soft vaporous vacuum of the interior bleeds into the harder stuff outside. Even if we were going to tear through the dead center of the thinking part, I can't imagine this vast creature feeling so much as a pinprick. At the speed we're going we'd be through and gone far too fast to overcome even the feeble inertia of a millimeter membrane.

And yet. *Stop. Stop. Stop.*

It's not us, of course. It's what we're building. The birth of a gate is a violent, painful thing, a spacetime rape that puts out almost as much gamma and X as a microquasar. Any meat within the white zone turns to ash in an instant, shielded or not. It's why *we* never slow down to take pictures.

One of the reasons, anyway.

We can't stop, of course. Even changing course isn't an option except by the barest increments. *Eri* soars like an eagle among the stars, but she steers like a pig on the short haul; tweak our heading by even a tenth of a degree, and you've got some serious damage at 20 percent light-speed. Half a degree would tear us apart: the ship might torque onto the new heading, but the collapsed mass in her belly would keep right on going, rip through all this surrounding super-structure without even feeling it.

Even tame singularities get set in their ways. They do not take well to change.

We resurrect again, and the Island has changed its tune.

It gave up asking us to *stop stop stop* the moment our laser hit its leading edge. Now it's saying something else entirely: dark hyphens flow across its skin, arrows of pigment converging toward some offstage focus like spokes pointing toward the hub of a wheel. The bull's-eye itself is offstage and implicit, far removed from 428's bright backdrop, but it's easy enough to extrapolate to the point of convergence six light-secs to starboard. There's something else, too: a shadow, roughly circular, moving along one of the spokes like a bead running along a string. It too migrates to starboard, falls off the edge of the Island's makeshift display, is endlessly reborn at the same initial coordinates to repeat its journey.

Those coordinates: exactly where our current trajectory will punch through the membrane in another four months. A squinting God would be able to see the gnats and girders of ongoing construction on the other side, the great piecemeal torus of the Hawking Hoop already taking shape.

The message is so obvious that even Dix sees it. "Wants us to move the gate . . ." and there is something like confusion in his voice. "But how's it know we're *building* one?"

"The vons punctured it en route," the chimp points out. "It could have sensed that. It has photopigments. It can probably see."

"Probably sees better than we do," I say. Even something as simple as a pinhole camera gets hi-res fast if you stipple a bunch of them across thirty million square kilometers.

But Dix scrunches his face, unconvinced. "So sees a bunch of vons bumping around. Loose parts—not that much even *assembled* yet. How's it know we're building something *hot*?"

Because it is very, very smart, you stupid child. Is it so hard to believe that this, this—*organism* seems far too limiting a word—can just *imagine* how those half-built pieces fit together, glance at our sticks and stones and see exactly where this is going?

"Maybe's not the first gate it's seen," Dix suggests. "Think there's maybe another gate out here?"

I shake my head. "We'd have seen the lensing artifacts by now."

"You ever run into anyone before?"

"No." We have always been alone, through all these epochs. We have only ever run *away*.

And then always from our own children.

I crunch some numbers. "Hundred eighty-two days to insemination. If we move now, we've only got to tweak our bearing by a few mikes to redirect to the new coordinates. Well within the green. Angles get dicey the longer we wait, of course."

"We can't do that," the chimp says. "We would miss the gate by two million kilometers."

"Move the gate. Move the whole damn site. Move the refineries, move the factories, move the damn rocks. A couple hundred meters a second would be more than fast enough if we send the order now. We don't even have to suspend construction, we can keep building on the fly."

"Every one of those vectors widens the nested confidence limits of the build. It would increase the risk of error beyond allowable margins, for no payoff."

"And what about the fact that there's an intelligent being in our path?"

"I'm already allowing for the potential presence of intelligent alien life."

"Okay, first off, there's nothing *potential* about it. It's *right fucking there.* And on our current heading, we run the damn thing over."

"We're staying clear of all planetary bodies in Goldilocks orbits. We've seen no local evidence of spacefaring technology. The current location of the build meets all conservation criteria."

"That's because the people who drew up your criteria *never anticipated a live Dyson sphere*!" But I'm wasting my breath, and I know it. The chimp can run its equations a million times, but if there's nowhere to put the variable, what can it do?

There was a time, back before things turned ugly, when we had clearance to reprogram those parameters. Before we discovered that one of the things the admins *had* anticipated was mutiny.

I try another tack. "Consider the threat potential."

"There's no evidence of any."

"Look at the synapse estimate! That thing's got order of mag more processing power than the whole civilization that sent us out here. You think something can be that smart, live that long, without learning how to defend itself? We're assuming it's *asking* us to move the gate. What if that's not a *request*? What if it's just giving us the chance to back off before it takes matters into its own hands?"

"Doesn't *have* hands," Dix says from the other side of the Tank, and he's not even being flippant. He's just being so stupid I want to bash his face in.

I try to keep my voice level. "Maybe it doesn't *need* any."

"What could it do, *blink* us to death? No weapons. Doesn't even control the whole membrane. Signal propagation's too slow."

"We *don't know*. That's my *point*. We haven't even tried to find out. We're a goddamn road crew; our onsite presence is a bunch of construction vons press-ganged into scientific research. We can figure out some basic physical parameters, but we don't know how this thing thinks, what kind of natural defenses it might have—"

"What do you need to find out?" the chimp asks, the very voice of calm reason.

We can't find out! I want to scream. *We're stuck with what we've got! By the time the onsite vons could build what we need, we're already past the point of no return! You stupid fucking machine, we're on track to kill a being smarter than all of human history and you can't even be bothered to move our highway to the vacant lot next door?*

But of course if I say that, the Island's chances of survival go from low to zero. So I grasp at the only straw that remains: maybe the data we've got in hand is enough. If acquisition is off the table, maybe analysis will do.

"I need time," I say.

"Of course," the chimp tells me. "Take all the time you need."

The chimp is not content to kill this creature. The chimp has to spit on it as well.

Under the pretense of assisting in my research, it tries to *deconstruct* the Island, break it apart and force it to conform to grubby earthbound precedents. It tells me about earthly bacteria that thrived at 1.5 million rads and laughed at hard vacuum. It shows me pictures of unkillable little tardigrades that could curl up and snooze on the edge of absolute zero, felt equally at home in deep ocean trenches and deeper space. Given time, opportunity, a boot off the planet, who

knows how far those cute little invertebrates might have
gone? Might they have survived the very death of the homeworld, clung together, grown somehow colonial?

What utter bullshit.

I learn what I can. I study the alchemy by which photo-
synthesis transforms light and gas and electrons into living
tissue. I learn the physics of the solar wind that blows the
bubble taut, calculate lower metabolic limits for a life form
that filters organics from the ether. I marvel at the speed of
this creature's thoughts: almost as fast as *Eri* flies, orders of
mag faster than any mammalian nerve impulse. Some kind
of organic superconductor perhaps, something that passes
chilled electrons almost resistance-free out here in the freezing void.

I acquaint myself with phenotypic plasticity and sloppy
fitness, that fortuitous evolutionary soft-focus that lets species exist in alien environments and express novel traits they
never needed at home. Perhaps this is how a life form with
no natural enemies could acquire teeth and claws and the
willingness to use them. The Island's life hinges on its ability to kill us; I have to find *something* that makes it a threat.

But all I uncover is a growing suspicion that I am doomed
to fail—for violence, I begin to see, is a *planetary* phenomenon.

Planets are the abusive parents of evolution. Their very
surfaces promote warfare, concentrate resources into dense
defensible patches that can be fought over. Gravity forces you
to squander energy on vascular systems and skeletal support,
stand endless watch against its endless sadistic campaign to
squash you flat. Take one wrong step, off a perch too high,
and all your pricey architecture shatters in an instant. And
even if you beat those odds, cobble together some lumbering
armored chassis to withstand the slow crawl onto land—how
long before the world draws in some asteroid or comet to
crash down from the heavens and reset your clock to zero? Is
it any wonder we grew up believing life was a struggle, that
zero-sum was God's own law and that the future belonged to
those who crushed the competition?

The rules are so different out here. Most of space is *tran-*

quil: no diel or seasonal cycles, no ice ages or global tropics,
no wild pendulum swings between hot and cold, calm and
tempestuous. Life's precursors abound: on comets, clinging
to asteroids, suffusing nebulae a hundred lightyears across.
Molecular clouds glow with organic chemistry and life-
giving radiation. Their vast, dusty wings grow warm with
infrared, filter out the hard stuff, give rise to stellar nurseries
that only some stunted refugee from the bottom of a gravity
well could ever call *lethal*.

Darwin's an abstraction here, an irrelevant curiosity. This
Island puts the lie to everything we were ever told about the
machinery of life. Sun-powered, perfectly adapted, immortal, it won no struggle for survival: where are the predators,
the competitors, the parasites? All of life around 428 is one
vast continuum, one grand act of symbiosis. Nature here is
not red in tooth and claw. Nature, out here, is the helping
hand.

Lacking the capacity for violence, the Island has outlasted
worlds. Unencumbered by technology, it has outthought civilizations. It is intelligent beyond our measure, and—

—and it is *benign*. It must be. I grow more certain of that
with each passing hour. How can it even *conceive* of an
enemy?

I think of the things I called it, before I knew better. *Meat
balloon*. *Cyst*. Looking back, those words verge on blas-
phemy. I will not use them again.

Besides, there's another word that would fit better, if the
chimp has its way: roadkill. And the longer I look, the more
I fear that that hateful machine is right.

If the Island can defend itself, I sure as shit can't see how.

"*Eriophora*'s impossible, you know. Violates the laws of
physics."

We're in one of the social alcoves off the ventral noto-
chord, taking a break from the library. I have decided to start
again from first principles. Dix eyes me with an understandable mix of confusion and mistrust; my claim is almost too
stupid to deny.

"It's true," I assure him. "Takes way too much energy to

accelerate a ship with *Eri*'s mass, especially at relativistic speeds. You'd need the energy output of a whole sun. People figured if we made it to the stars at all, we'd have to do it in ships maybe the size of your thumb. Crew them with virtual personalities downloaded onto chips."

That's too nonsensical even for Dix. "*Wrong*. Don't have mass, can't fall toward anything. *Eri* wouldn't even *work* if it was that small."

"But suppose you can't displace any of that mass. No wormholes, no Higgs conduits, nothing to throw your gravitational field in the direction of travel. Your center of mass just *sits* there in, well, the center of your mass."

A spastic Dixian head-shake. "*Do* have those things!"

"Sure we do. But for the longest time, we didn't *know* it."

His foot taps an agitated tattoo on the deck.

"It's the history of the species," I explain. "We think we've worked everything out, we think we've solved all the mysteries, and then someone finds some niggling little data point that doesn't fit the paradigm. Every time we try to paper over the crack, it gets bigger, and before you know it, our whole worldview unravels. It's happened time and again. One day, mass is a constraint; the next, it's a requirement. The things we think we know—they *change*, Dix. And we have to change with them."

"But—"

"The chimp can't change. The rules it's following are ten billion years old and it's got no fucking imagination—and really that's not anyone's fault, that's just people who didn't know how else to keep the mission stable across deep time. They wanted to keep the mission on track, so they built something that couldn't go off it; but they also knew that things *change*, and that's why *we're* out here, Dix. To deal with things the chimp can't."

"The alien," Dix says.

"The alien."

"Chimp deals with it just fine."

"How? By killing it?"

"Not our fault it's in the way. It's no threat—"

"I don't care whether it's a *threat* or not! It's alive, and it's intelligent, and killing it just to expand some alien empire—"

"*Human* empire. *Our* empire." Suddenly, Dix's hands have stopped twitching. Suddenly, he stands still as stone.

I snort. "What do *you* know about humans?"

"*Am* one."

"You're a fucking trilobite. You ever see what comes *out* of those gates once they're online?"

"Mostly nothing." He pauses, thinking back. "Couple of—ships once, maybe."

"Well, I've seen a lot more than that, and believe me, if those things were *ever* human, it was a passing phase."

"But—"

"Dix—" I take a deep breath, try to get back on message. "Look, it's not your fault. You've been getting all your info from a moron stuck on a rail. But we're not doing this for humanity, we're not doing it for Earth. Earth is *gone*, don't you understand that? The sun scorched it black a billion years after we left. Whatever we're working for, it—it won't even *talk* to us."

"Yeah? Then why do this? Why not just, just *quit*?"

He really doesn't know.

"We tried," I say.

"And?"

"And your *chimp* shut off our life support."

For once, he has nothing to say.

"It's a *machine*, Dix. Why can't you get that? It's *programmed*. It can't change."

"*We're* machines. Just built from different things. We're programmed. *We* change."

"Yeah? Last time I checked, you were sucking so hard on that thing's tit you couldn't even kill your cortical link."

"How I *learn*. No *reason* to change."

"How about acting like a damn *human* once in a while? How about developing a little rapport with the folks who might have to save your miserable life next time you go EVA? That enough of a *reason* for you? Because, I don't mind telling you, right now I don't trust you as far as I could throw the tac tank. I don't even know for sure who I'm talking to right now."

"Not my fault." For the first time, I see something outside the usual gamut of fear, confusion, and simpleminded computation playing across his face. "That's *you*, that's *all* of you. You talk *sideways. Think* sideways. You all do, and it *hurts.*" Something hardens in his face. "Didn't even need you online for this," he growls. "Didn't *want* you. Could have managed the whole build myself, *told* Chimp I could do it—"

"But the chimp thought you should wake me up anyway, and you always roll over for the chimp, don't you? Because the chimp always knows best, the chimp's your *boss*, the chimp's your fucking *god.* Which is why I have to get out of bed to nursemaid some idiot savant who can't even answer a hail without being led by the nose." Something clicks in the back of my mind, but I'm on a roll. "You want a *real* role model? You want something to look up to? Forget the chimp. Forget the mission. Look out the forward scope, why don't you? Look at what your precious chimp wants to run over because it happens to be in the way! That thing is better than any of us. It's smarter, it's peaceful, it doesn't wish us any harm at—"

"How can you know that? Can't know that!"

"No, *you* can't know that, because you're fucking *stunted*! Any normal caveman would see it in a second, but *you*—"

"That's crazy," Dix hisses at me. *"You're* crazy. You're *bad."*

"I'm bad!" Some distant part of me hears the giddy squeak in my voice, the borderline hysteria.

"For the mission." Dix turns his back and stalks away.

My hands are hurting. I look down, surprised: my fists are clenched so tightly that my nails cut into the flesh of my palms. It takes a real effort to open them again.

I almost remember how this feels. I used to feel this way all the time. Way back when everything *mattered*; before passion faded to ritual, before rage cooled to disdain. Before Sunday Ahzmundin, eternity's warrior, settled for heaping insults on stunted children.

We were incandescent back then. Parts of this ship are still scorched and uninhabitable, even now. I remember this feeling.

This is how it feels to be awake.

I am awake, and I am alone, and I am sick of being outnumbered by morons. There are rules and there are risks, and you don't wake the dead on a whim, but fuck it. I'm calling reinforcements.

Dix has got to have other parents, a father at least, he didn't get that Y chromo from me. I swallow my own disquiet and check the manifest; bring up the gene sequences; cross-reference.

Huh. Only one other parent: Kai. I wonder if that's just coincidence, or if the chimp drew too many conclusions from our torrid little fuckfest back in the Cyg Rift. Doesn't matter. He's as much yours as mine, Kai, time to step up to the plate, time to—

Oh shit. Oh no. Please no.

(There are rules. And there are risks.)

Three builds back, it says. Kai and Connie. Both of them. One airlock jammed, the next too far away along *Eri*'s hull, a hail-Mary emergency crawl between. They made it back inside but not before the blueshifted background cooked them in their suits. They kept breathing for hours afterward, talked and moved and cried as if they were still alive, while their insides broke down and bled out.

There were two others awake that shift, two others left to clean up the mess. Ishmael and—

"Um, you said—"

"You fucker!" I leap up and hit my son hard in the face, ten seconds' heartbreak with ten million years' denial raging behind it. I feel teeth give way behind his lips. He goes over backward, eyes wide as telescopes, the blood already blooming on his mouth.

"*Said* I could come back—!" he squeals, scrambling backward along the deck.

"He was your fucking *father*! You *knew*, you were *there*! He died right in *front* of you and you didn't even *tell* me!"

"I— I—"

"Why didn't you tell me, you asshole? The chimp told you to lie, is that it? Did you—"

"Thought you knew!" he cries. "Why *wouldn't* you know?"

My rage vanishes like air through a breach. I sag back into the 'pod, face in hands.

"Right there in the log," he whimpers. "All along. Nobody hid it. How could you not know?"

"I did," I admit dully. "Or I— I mean . . ."

I mean I *didn't* know, but it's not a surprise, not really, not down deep. You just—stop looking, after a while.

There are *rules*.

"Never even *asked*," my son says softly. "How they were doing."

I raise my eyes. Dix regards me wide-eyed from across the room, backed up against the wall, too scared to risk bolting past me to the door. "What are you doing here?" I ask tiredly.

His voice catches. He has to try twice: "You said I could come back. If I burned out my link . . ."

"You burned out your link."

He gulps and nods. He wipes blood with the back of his hand.

"What did the chimp say about that?"

"He said—*it* said that it was okay," Dix says, in such a transparent attempt to suck up that I actually believe, in that instant, that he might really be on his own.

"So you asked its permission." He begins to nod, but I can see the tell in his face. "Don't bullshit me, Dix."

"He—actually suggested it."

"I see."

"So we could talk," Dix adds.

"What do you want to talk about?"

He looks at the floor and shrugs.

I stand and walk toward him. He tenses but I shake my head, spread my hands. "It's okay. It's okay." I lean back against the wall and slide down until I'm beside him on the deck.

We just sit there for a while.

"It's been so long," I say at last.

He looks at me, uncomprehending. What does *long* even mean, out here?

I try again. "They say there's no such thing as altruism, you know?"

His eyes blank for an instant, and grow panicky, and I know that he's just tried to ping his link for a definition and come up blank. So we *are* alone. "Altruism," I explain. "Un-selfishness. Doing something that costs *you* but helps some-one else." He seems to get it. "They say every selfless act ultimately comes down to manipulation or kin-selection or reciprocity or something, but they're wrong. I could—"

I close my eyes. This is harder than I expected.

"I could have been happy just *knowing* that Kai was okay, that Connie was happy. Even if it didn't benefit me one whit, even if it *cost* me, even if there was no chance I'd ever see either of them again. Almost any price would be worth it, just to know they were okay.

"Just to *believe* they were . . ."

So you haven't seen her for the past five builds. So he hasn't drawn your shift since Sagittarius. They're just sleep-ing. Maybe next time.

"So you don't check," Dix says slowly. Blood bubbles on his lower lip; he doesn't seem to notice.

"We don't check." Only I did, and now they're gone. They're both gone. Except for those little cannibalized nucleotides the chimp recycled into this defective and mal-adapted son of mine.

We're the only warm-blooded creatures for a thousand lightyears, and I am so very lonely.

"I'm sorry," I whisper, and lean forward, and lick the blood from his bruised and bloody lips.

Back on Earth—back when there *was* an Earth—there were these little animals called cats. I had one for a while. Some-times I'd watch him sleep for hours: paws and whiskers and ears all twitching madly as he chased imaginary prey across whatever landscapes his sleeping brain conjured up.

My son looks like that when the chimp worms its way into his dreams.

It's almost too literal for metaphor: the cable runs into his head like some kind of parasite, feeding through old-fashioned fiberop now that the wireless option's been burned away. Or *force*-feeding, I suppose; the poison flows *into* Dix's head, not out of it.

I shouldn't be here. Didn't I just throw a tantrum over the violation of my own privacy? (Just. Twelve lightdays ago. Everything's relative.) And yet, I can see no privacy here for Dix to lose: no decorations on the walls, no artwork or hobbies, no wraparound console. The sex toys ubiquitous in every suite sit unused on their shelves; I'd have assumed he was on antilibinals if recent experience hadn't proven otherwise.

What am I doing? Is this some kind of perverted mothering instinct, some vestigial expression of a Pleistocene maternal subroutine? Am I that much of a robot, has my brain stem sent me here to guard my child?

To guard my *mate*?

Lover or larva, it hardly matters: his quarters are an empty shell, there's nothing of Dix in here. That's just his abandoned body lying there in the pseudopod, fingers twitching, eyes flickering beneath closed lids in vicarious response to wherever his mind has gone.

They don't know I'm here. The chimp doesn't know because we burned out its prying eyes a billion years ago, and my son doesn't know I'm here because—well, because for him, right now, there *is* no here.

What am I supposed to make of you, Dix? None of this makes sense. Even your body language looks like you grew it in a vat—but I'm far from the first human being you've seen. You grew up in good company, with people I *know*, people I trust. Trusted. How did you end up on the other side? How did they let you slip away?

And why didn't they warn me about you?

Yes, there are rules. There is the threat of enemy surveillance during long, dead nights, the threat of—other losses. But this is unprecedented. Surely someone could have left something, some clue buried in a metaphor too subtle for the simpleminded to decode . . .

I'd give a lot to tap into that pipe, to see what you're seeing now. Can't risk it, of course; I'd give myself away the moment I tried to sample anything except the basic baud, and—

—wait a second—

That baud rate's way too low. That's not even enough for hi-res graphics, let alone tactile and olfac. You're embedded in a wireframe world at best.

And yet, look at you go. The fingers, the eyes—like a cat, dreaming of mice and apple pies. Like *me*, replaying the long-lost oceans and mountaintops of Earth before I learned that living in the past was just another way of dying in the present. The bit rate says this is barely even a test pattern; the body says you're immersed in a whole other world. How has that machine tricked you into treating such thin gruel as a feast?

Why would it even want to? Data are better grasped when they *can* be grasped, and tasted, and heard; our brains are built for far richer nuance than splines and scatterplots. The driest technical briefings are more sensual than this. Why settle for stick figures when you can paint in oils and holograms?

Why does anyone simplify anything? To reduce the variable set. To manage the unmanageable.

Kai and Connie. Now *there* were a couple of tangled, unmanageable datasets. Before the accident. Before the scenario *simplified*.

Someone should have warned me about you, Dix.

Maybe someone tried.

And so it comes to pass that my son leaves the nest, encases himself in a beetle carapace, and goes walkabout. He is not alone; one of the chimp's teleops accompanies him out on *Eri*'s hull, lest he lose his footing and fall back into the starry past.

Maybe this will never be more than a drill, maybe this scenario—catastrophic control-systems failure, the chimp and its backups offline, all maintenance tasks suddenly thrown onto shoulders of flesh and blood—is a dress rehearsal for a crisis that never happens. But even the unlikeliest scenario approaches certainty over the life of a universe; so we go through the motions. We practice. We hold our breath and dip outside. We're on a tight deadline: even armored, moving at this speed, the blueshifted background rad would cook us in hours.

Worlds have lived and died since I last used the pickup in my suite. "Chimp."

"Here as always, Sunday." Smooth, and glib, and friendly. The easy rhythm of the practiced psychopath.

"I know what you're doing."

"I don't understand."

"You think I don't see what's going on? You're building the next release. You're getting too much grief from the old guard so you're starting from scratch with people who don't remember the old days. People you've, you've *simplified*."

The chimp says nothing. The drone's feed shows Dix clambering across a jumbled terrain of basalt and metal matrix composites.

"But you can't raise a human child, not on your own." I know it tried: there's no record of Dix anywhere on the crew manifest until his mid-teens, when he just *showed up* one day and nobody asked about it because nobody *ever* . . .

"Look what you've made of him. He's great at conditional if/thens. Can't be beat on number-crunching and do loops. But he can't *think*. Can't make the simplest intuitive jumps. You're like one of those—" I remember an earthly myth, from the days when *reading* did not seem like such an obscene waste of life span—"one of those wolves, trying to raise a human child. You can teach him how to move around on hands and knees, you can teach him about pack dynamics, but you can't teach him how to walk on his hind legs or talk or be *human* because you're *too fucking stupid*, Chimp, and you finally realized it. And that's why you threw him at me. You think I can fix him for you."

I take a breath, and a gambit.

"But he's nothing to me. You understand? He's *worse* than nothing, he's a liability. He's a spy, he's a spastic waste of O_2.

Give me one reason why I shouldn't just lock him out there until he cooks."

"You're his mother," the chimp says, because the chimp has read all about kin selection and is too stupid for nuance.

"You're an idiot."

"You love him."

"No." An icy lump forms in my chest. My mouth makes words; they come out measured and inflectionless. "I can't love anyone, you brain-dead machine. That's why I'm out here. Do you really think they'd gamble your precious never-ending mission on little glass dolls that needed to bond?"

"You love him."

"I can kill him any time I want. And that's exactly what I'll do if you don't move the gate."

"I'd stop you," the chimp says mildly.

"That's easy enough. Just move the gate and we both get what we want. Or you can dig in your heels and try to reconcile your need for a mother's touch with my sworn intention of breaking the little fucker's neck. We've got a long trip ahead of us, Chimp. And you might find I'm not quite as easy to cut out of the equation as Kai and Connie."

"You cannot end the mission," it says, almost gently. "You tried that already."

"This isn't about ending the mission. This is only about slowing it down a little. Your optimal scenario's off the table. The only way that gate's going to get finished now is by saving the Island, or killing your prototype. Your call."

The cost-benefit's pretty simple. The chimp could solve it in an instant. But still it says nothing. The silence stretches. It's looking for some other option, I bet. It's trying to find a workaround. It's questioning the very premises of the scenario, trying to decide if I mean what I'm saying, if all its book-learning about mother love could really be so far off-base. Maybe it's plumbing historical intrafamilial murder rates, looking for a loophole. And there may be one, for all I know. But the chimp isn't me, it's a simpler system trying to figure out a smarter one, and that gives me the edge.

"You would owe me," it says at last.

I almost burst out laughing. *"What?"*

"Or I will tell Dixon that you threatened to kill him."

"Go ahead."

"You don't want him to know."

"I don't care whether he knows or not. What, you think he'll try and kill me back? You think I'll lose his *love*?" I linger on the last word, stretch it out to show how ludicrous it is.

"You'll lose his trust. You need to trust each other out here."

"Oh, right. *Trust*. The very fucking foundation of this mission!"

The chimp says nothing.

"For the sake of argument," I say, after a while, "suppose I go along with it. What would I *owe* you, exactly?"

"A favor," the chimp replies. "To be repaid in future."

My son floats innocently against the stars, his life in balance.

We sleep. The chimp makes grudging corrections to a myriad small trajectories. I set the alarm to wake me every couple of weeks, burn a little more of my candle in case the enemy tries to pull another fast one; but for now it seems to be behaving itself. DHF428 jumps toward us in the stop-motion increments of a life's moments, strung like beads along an infinite string. The factory floor slews to starboard in our sights: refineries, reservoirs, and nanofab plants, swarms of von Neumanns breeding and cannibalizing and recycling one another into shielding and circuitry, tugboats and spare parts. The very finest Cro Magnon technology mutates and metastasizes across the universe like armor-plated cancer.

And hanging like a curtain between *it* and *us* shimmers an iridescent life form, fragile and immortal and unthinkably alien, that reduces everything my species ever accomplished to mud and shit by the simple transcendent fact of its existence. I have never believed in gods, in universal good or absolute evil. I have only ever believed that there is what works and what doesn't. All the rest is smoke and mirrors, trickery to manipulate grunts like me.

But I believe in the Island, because I don't *have* to. It does not need to be taken on faith: it looms ahead of us, its existence an empirical fact. I will never know its mind, I will never know the details of its origin and evolution. But I can *see* it: massive, mind-boggling, so utterly inhuman that it can't *help* but be better than us, better than anything we could ever become.

I believe in the Island. I've gambled my own son to save its life. I would kill him to avenge its death.

I may yet.

In all these millions of wasted years, I have finally done something worthwhile.

Final approach.

Reticles within reticles line up before me, a mesmerizing infinite regress of bull's-eyes centering on target. Even now, mere minutes from ignition, distance reduces the unborn gate to invisibility. There will be no moment when the naked eye can trap our destination. We thread the needle far too quickly: it will be behind us before we know it.

Or, if our course corrections are off by even a hair—if our trillion-kilometer curve drifts by as much as a thousand meters—we will be dead. Before we know it.

Our instruments report that we are precisely on target. The chimp tells me that we are precisely on target. *Eriophora* falls forward, pulled endlessly through the void by her own magically displaced mass.

I turn to the drone's-eye view relayed from up ahead. It's a window into history—even now, there's a time-lag of several minutes—but past and present race closer to convergence with every corsec. The newly minted gate looms dark and ominous against the stars, a great gaping mouth built to devour reality itself. The vons, the refineries, the assembly lines: parked to the side in vertical columns, their jobs done, their usefulness outlived, their collateral annihilation imminent. I pity them, for some reason. I always do. I wish we could scoop them up and take them with us, reenlist them for the next build—but the rules of economics reach everywhere, and they say it's cheaper to use our tools once and throw them away.

A rule that the chimp seems to be taking more to heart than anyone expected.

At least we've spared the Island. I wish we could have stayed awhile. First contact with a truly alien intelligence, and what do we exchange? Traffic signals. What does the Island dwell upon, when not pleading for its life?

I thought of asking. I thought of waking myself when the time-lag dropped from prohibitive to merely inconvenient, of working out some pidgin that could encompass the truths and philosophies of a mind vaster than all humanity. What a childish fantasy. The Island exists too far beyond the grotesque Darwinian processes that shaped my own flesh. There can be no communion here, no meeting of minds.

Angels do not speak to ants.

Less than three minutes to ignition. I see light at the end of the tunnel. *Eri*'s incidental time machine barely looks into the past anymore; I could almost hold my breath across the whole span of seconds that *then* needs to overtake *now*. Still on target, according to all sources.

Tactical beeps at us.

"Getting a signal," Dix reports, and yes: in the heart of the Tank, the sun is flickering again. My heart leaps: does the angel speak to us after all? A thank-you, perhaps? A cure for heat death?

But—

"It's *ahead* of us," Dix murmurs, as sudden realization catches in my throat.

Two minutes.

"Miscalculated somehow," Dix whispers. "Didn't move the gate far enough."

"We did," I say. We moved it exactly as far as the Island told us to.

"*Still in front of us!* Look at the *sun*!"

"Look at the *signal*," I tell him.

Because it's nothing like the painstaking traffic signs we've followed over the past three trillion kilometers. It's almost—random, somehow. It's spur-of-the-moment, it's *panicky*. It's the sudden, startled cry of something caught utterly by surprise with mere seconds left to act. And even though I

have never seen this pattern of dots and swirls before, I know
exactly what it must be saying.

Stop. Stop. Stop. Stop.

We do not stop. There is no force in the universe that
can even slow us down. Past equals present; *Eriophora*
dives through the center of the gate in a nanosecond. The
unimaginable mass of her cold black heart snags some distant dimension, drags it screaming to the here and now. The
booted portal erupts behind us, blossoms into a great blinding corona, every wavelength lethal to every living thing.
Our aft filters clamp down tight.

The scorching wavefront chases us into the darkness as
it has a thousand times before. In time, as always, the birth
pangs will subside. The wormhole will settle in its collar.
And just maybe, we will still be close enough to glimpse
some new transcendent monstrosity emerging from that
magic doorway.

I wonder if you'll notice the corpse we left behind.

"Maybe we're missing something," Dix says.

"We miss almost everything," I tell him.

DHF428 shifts red behind us. Lensing artifacts wink in
our rearview; the gate has stabilized and the wormhole's
online, blowing light and space and time in an iridescent
bubble from its great metal mouth. We'll keep looking over
our shoulders right up until we pass the Rayleigh Limit, far
past the point it'll do any good.

So far, though, nothing's come out.

"Maybe our numbers were wrong," he says. "Maybe we
made a mistake."

Our numbers were right. An hour doesn't pass when I
don't check them again. The Island just had—enemies, I
guess. Victims, anyway.

I was right about one thing, though. That fucker was *smart*.
To see us coming, to figure out how to talk to us; to use us as
a *weapon*, to turn a threat to its very existence into a, a . . .

I guess *flyswatter* is as good a word as any.

"Maybe there was a war," I mumble. "Maybe it wanted the
real estate. Or maybe it was just some—family squabble."

"Maybe didn't *know*," Dix suggests. "Maybe thought those coordinates were empty."

Why would you think that? I wonder. *Why would you even care?* And then it dawns on me: he doesn't, not about the Island, anyway. No more than he ever did. He's not inventing these rosy alternatives for himself.

My son is trying to comfort me.

I don't need to be coddled, though. I was a fool: I let myself believe in life without conflict, in sentience without sin. For a little while, I dwelt in a dream world where life was unselfish and unmanipulative, where every living thing did not struggle to exist at the expense of other life. I deified that which I could not understand, when in the end it was all too easily understood.

But I'm better now.

It's over: another build, another benchmark, another irreplaceable slice of life that brings our task no closer to completion. It doesn't matter how successful we are. It doesn't matter how well we do our job. *Mission accomplished* is a meaningless phrase on *Eriophora*, an ironic oxymoron at best. There may one day be failure, but there is no finish line. We go on forever, crawling across the universe like ants, dragging your goddamned superhighway behind us.

I still have so much to learn.

At least my son is here to teach me.

EVENTS PRECEDING THE HELVETICAN RENAISSANCE

JOHN KESSEL

Born in Buffalo, New York, John Kessel now lives with his family in Raleigh, North Carolina, where he is a professor of American Literature and the director of the Creative Writing program at North Carolina State University. Kessel made his first sale in 1975. His first solo novel, *Good News from Outer Space*, was released in 1988 to wide critical acclaim, but before that he had made his mark on the genre primarily as a writer of highly imaginative, finely crafted short stories, many of which have been assembled in collections such as *Meeting in Infinity* and *The Pure Product*. He won a Nebula Award in 1983 for his novella *Another Orphan*, which was also a Hugo finalist that year, and has been released as an individual book. His story "Buffalo" won the Theodore Sturgeon Award in 1991, and his novella *Stories for Men* won the prestigious James Tiptree Jr. Memorial Award in 2003. His other books include the novels *Corrupting Dr. Nice*, *Freedom Beach* (written in collaboration with James Patrick Kelly), *Ninety Percent of Everything* (written in collaboration with James Patrick Kelly and Jonathan Lethem), and an anthology of stories from the famous Sycamore Hill Writers Workshop (which he also helps to run), called *Intersections*, coedited by Mark L. Van Name and Richard Butner. His most recent books are two anthologies coedited with James Patrick Kelly, *Feeling Very Strange: The Slipstream Anthology* and *Rewired: The Post-Cyberpunk Anthology*, and a new collection, *The Baum Plan For Financial Independence and Other Stories*.

◖ When my mind cleared, I found myself in the street. A god spoke to me then: *The boulevard to the spaceport runs straight up the mountain. And you must run straight up the boulevard.*

The air was full of wily spirits, and moving fast in the Imperial City was a crime. But what is man to disobey the voice of a god? So I ran. The pavement vibrated with the thunder of the great engines of the Caslonian Empire. Behind me the curators of the Imperial Archives must by now have discovered the mare's nest I had made of their defenses, and perhaps had already realized that something was missing.

Above the plateau the sky was streaked with clouds, through which shot violet gravity beams carrying ships down from and up to planetary orbit. Just outside the gate to the spaceport a family in rags—husband, wife, two children—used a net of knotted cords to catch fish from the sewers. Ignoring them, prosperous citizens in embroidered robes passed among the shops of the port bazaar, purchasing duty-free wares, recharging their concubines, seeking a meal before departure. *Slower, now.*

I slowed my pace. I became indistinguishable from them, moving smoothly among the travelers.

To the Caslonian eye, I was calm, self-possessed; within me, rage and joy contended. I had in my possession the means to redeem my people. I tried not to think, only to act, but now that my mind was rekindled, it raced. Certainly it would go better for me if I left the planet before anyone understood what I had stolen. Yet I was very hungry, and the aroma of food from the restaurants along the way enticed me. It would be foolishness itself to stop here.

Enter the restaurant, I was told. So I stepped into the most elegant of the establishments.

The maître d' greeted me. "Would the master like a table, or would he prefer to dine at the bar?"

"The bar," I said.

"Step this way." There was no hint of the illicit about his manner, though something about it implied indulgence. He was proud to offer me this experience that few could afford.

He seated me at the circular bar of polished rosewood. Before me, and the few others seated there, the chef grilled meats on a heated metal slab. Waving his arms in the air like a dancer, he tossed flanks of meat between two force knives, letting them drop to the griddle, flipping them dexterously upward again in what was as much performance as preparation. The energy blades of the knives sliced through the meat without resistance, the sides of these same blades batting them like paddles. An aroma of burning hydrocarbons wafted on the air.

An attractive young man displayed for me a list of virtualities that represented the "cuts" offered by the establishment, including subliminal tastes. The "cuts" referred to the portions of the animal's musculature from which the slabs of meat had been sliced. My mouth watered.

He took my order, and I sipped a cocktail of bitters and Belanova.

While I waited, I scanned the restaurant. The fundamental goal of our order is to vindicate divine justice in allowing evil to exist. At a small nearby table, a young woman leaned beside a child, probably her daughter, and encouraged her to eat. The child's beautiful face was the picture of innocence as she tentatively tasted a scrap of pink flesh. The mother was very beautiful. I wondered if this was her first youth.

The chef finished his performance, to the mild applause of the other patrons. The young man placed my steak before me. The chef turned off the blades and laid them aside, then ducked down a trap door to the oubliette where the slaves were kept. As soon as he was out of sight, a god told me, *Steal a knife*.

While the diners were distracted by their meals, I reached

over the counter, took one of the force blades, and slid it into my boot. Then I ate. The taste was extraordinary. Every cell of my body vibrated with excitement and shame. My senses reeling, it took me a long time to finish.

A slender man in a dark robe sat next to me. "That smells good," he said. "Is that genuine animal flesh?"

"Does it matter to you?"

"Ah, brother, calm yourself. I'm not challenging your taste."

"I'm pleased to hear it."

"But I am challenging your identity." He parted the robe—his tunic bore the sigil of Port Security "Your passport, please."

I exposed the inside of my wrist for him. A scanlid slid over his left eye and he examined the marks beneath my skin. "Very good," he said. He drew a blaster from the folds of his cassock. "We seldom see such excellent forgeries. Stand up, and come with me."

I stood. He took my elbow in a firm grip, the bell of the blaster against my side. No one in the restaurant noticed. He walked me outside, down the crowded bazaar. "You see, brother, that there is no escape from consciousness. The minute it returns, you are vulnerable. All your prayer is to no avail."

This is the arrogance of the Caslonian. They treat us as non-sentients, and they believe in nothing. Yet as I prayed, I heard no word.

I turned to him. "You may wish the absence of the gods, but you are mistaken. The gods are everywhere present." As I spoke the plosive "p" of "present," I popped the cap from my upper right molar and blew the moondust it contained into his face.

The agent fell writhing to the pavement. I ran off through the people, dodging collisions. My ship was on the private field at the end of the bazaar. Before I had gotten halfway there, an alarm began sounding. People looked up in bewilderment, stopping in their tracks. The walls of buildings and stalls blinked into multiple images of me. Voices spoke from the air: "This man is a fugitive from the state. Apprehend him."

I would not make it to the ship unaided, so I turned on my perceptual overdrive. Instantly, everything slowed. The voices of the people and the sounds of the port dropped an octave. They moved as if in slow motion. I moved, to myself, as if in slow motion as well—my body could in no way keep pace with my racing nervous system—but to the people moving at normal speed, my reflexes were lighting fast. Up to the limit of my physiology—and my joints had been reinforced to take the additional stress; my muscles could handle the additional lactic acid for a time—I could move at twice the speed of a normal human. I could function perhaps for ten minutes in this state before I collapsed.

The first person to accost me—a sturdy middle-aged man—I seized by the arm. I twisted it behind his back and shoved him into the second, who took up the command. As I dodged through the crowd up the concourse, it began to drizzle. I felt as if I could slip between the raindrops. I pulled the force blade from my boot and sliced the ear from the next man who tried to stop me. His comic expression of dismay still lingers in my mind. Glancing behind, I saw the agent in black, face swollen with pustules from the moondust, running toward me.

I was near the field. In the boarding shed, attendants were folding the low-status passengers and sliding them into dispatch pouches, to be carried onto a ship and stowed in drawers for their passage. Directly before me, I saw the woman and child I had noticed in the restaurant. The mother had out a parasol and was holding it over the girl to keep the rain off her. Not slowing, I snatched the little girl and carried her off. The child yelped, the mother screamed. I held the blade to the girl's neck. "Make way!" I shouted to the security men at the field's entrance. They fell back.

"Halt!" came the call from behind me. The booth beside the gate was seared with a blaster bolt. I swerved, turned, and, my back to the gate, held the girl before me.

The agent in black, followed by two security women, jerked to a stop. "You mustn't hurt her," the agent said.

"Oh? And why is that?"

"It's against everything your order believes."

Master Darius had steeled me for this dilemma before sending me on my mission. He told me, "You will encounter such situations, Adlan. When they arise, you must resolve the complications."

"You are right!" I called to my pursuers, and threw the child at them.

The agent caught her, while the other two aimed and fired. One of the beams grazed my shoulder. But by then I was already through the gate and onto the tarmac.

A Port Security robot hurled a flame grenade. I rolled through the flames. My ship rested in the maintenance pit, cradled in the violet anti-grav beam. I slid down the ramp into the open airlock, hit the emergency close, and climbed to the controls. Klaxons wailed outside. I bypassed all the launch protocols and released the beam. The ship shot upward like an apple seed flicked by a fingernail; as soon as it had hit the stratosphere, I fired the engines and blasted through the scraps of the upper atmosphere into space.

The orbital security forces were too slow, and I made my escape.

I awoke battered, bruised, and exhausted in the pilot's chair. The smell of my burned shoulder reminded me of the steak I had eaten in the port bazaar. The stress of accelerating nerve impulses had left every joint in my body aching. My arms were blue with contusions, and I was as enfeebled as an old man.

The screens showed me to be in an untraveled quarter of the system's cometary cloud; my ship had cloaked itself in ice so that on any detector I would simply be another bit of debris among billions. I dragged myself from the chair and down to the galley, where I warmed some broth and gave myself an injection of cellular repair mites. Then I fell into my bunk and slept.

My second waking was relatively free of pain. I recharged my tooth and ate again. I knelt before the shrine and bowed my head in prayer, letting peace flow down my spine and relax all the muscles of my back. I listened for the voices of the gods.

I was reared by my mother on Bembo. My mother was an extraordinarily beautiful girl. One day, Akvan, looking down on her, was so moved by lust that he took the form of a vagabond and raped her by the side of the road. Nine months later, I was born.

The goddess Peri became so jealous that she laid a curse on my mother, who turned into a lawyer. And so we moved to Helvetica. There, in the shabby city of Urushana, in the waterfront district along the river, she took up her practice, defending criminals and earning a little *baksheesh* greasing the relations between the Imperial Caslonian government and the corrupt local officials. Mother's ambition for me was to go to an off-planet university, but for me the work of a student was like pushing a very large rock up a very steep hill. I got into fights; I pursued women of questionable virtue. Having exhausted my prospects in the city, I entered the native constabulary, where I was reengineered for accelerated combat. But my propensity for violence saw me cashiered out of the service within six months. Hoping to get a grip on my passions, I made the pilgrimage to the monastery of the Pujmanian Order. There I petitioned for admission as a novice, and, to my great surprise, was accepted.

It was no doubt the work of Master Darius, who took an interest in me from my first days on the plateau. Perhaps it was my divine heritage that had placed those voices in my head. Perhaps it was my checkered career to that date. The Master taught me to distinguish between those impulses that were the work of my savage nature and those that were the voices of the gods. It is not an easy path. I fasted, I worked in the gardens, I practiced the martial arts, I cleaned the cesspool, I sewed new clothes and mended old, I tended the orchards. I became an expert tailor and sewed many of the finest kosodes worn by the masters on feast days. In addition, Master Darius held special sessions with me, putting me into a trance during which, I was later told by my fellow novices, I continued to act normally for days, only to awake with no memories of my actions.

And so I was sent on my mission. Because I had learned

how not to think, I could not be detected by the spirits who guarded the Imperial Archives.

Five plays, immensely old, collectively titled *The Abandonment*, are all that document the rebirth of humanity after its long extinction. The foundational cycle consists of *The Archer's Fall*, *Stochik's Revenge*, *The Burning Tree*, *Close the Senses*, *Shut the Doors*, and the mystical fifth, *The Magic Tortoise*. No one knows who wrote them. It is believed they were composed within the first thirty years after the human race was re-created by the gods. Besides being the most revered cultural artifacts of humanity, these plays are also the sacred texts of the universal religion and claimed as the fundamental political documents by all planetary governments. They are preserved only in a single copy. No recording has ever been made of their performance. The actors chosen to present the plays in the foundational festivals on all the worlds do not study and learn them; through a process similar to the one Master Darius taught me to confuse the spirits, the actors *become* the characters. Once the performance is done, it passes from their minds.

These Foundational Plays, of inestimable value, existed now only in my mind. I had destroyed the crystal containing them in the archives. Without these plays, the heart of Caslon had been ripped away. If the populace knew of their loss, there would be despair and riot.

And once Master Darius announced that the Order held the only copy in our possession, it would only be a matter of time before the Empire would be obliged to free our world.

Three days after my escape from Caslon, I set course for Helvetica. Using an evanescent wormhole, I would emerge within the planet's inner ring. The ship, still encased in ice, would look like one of the fragments that formed the ring. From there I would reconnoiter, find my opportunity to leave orbit, and land. But because the ring stood far down in the gravitation well of the planet, it was a tricky maneuver.

Too tricky. Upon emergence in the Helvetican ring, my ship collided with one of the few nickel-iron meteoroids in the belt, disabling my engines. Within twenty minutes, Caslonian hunter-killers grappled with the hull. My one advantage was that by now they knew that I possessed the plays, and therefore they could not afford to blast me out of the sky. I could kill them, but they could not harm me. But I had no doubt that once they caught me, they would rip my mind to shreds seeking the plays.

I had only minutes—the hull door would not hold long. I abandoned the control room and retreated to the engine compartment. The place was a mess, barely holding pressure after the meteoroid collision, oxygen cylinders scattered about and the air acrid with the scent of burned wiring. I opened the cat's closet, three meters tall and two wide. From a locker I yanked two piezofiber suits. I turned them on, checked their readouts—they were fully charged—and threw them into the closet. It was cramped in there with tools and boxes of supplies. Sitting on one of the crates, I pulled up my shirt, exposing my bruised ribs. The aluminum light of the closet turned my skin sickly white. Using a microtome, I cut an incision in my belly below my lowest rib. There was little blood. I reached into the cut, found the nine-dimensional pouch, and drew it out between my index and middle fingers. I sprayed false skin over the wound. As I did, the artificial gravity cut off, and the lights went out.

I slipped on my night vision eyelids, read the directions on the pouch, ripped it open, removed the soldier, and unfolded it. The body expanded, became fully three dimensional, and, in a minute, was floating naked before me. My first surprise: it was a woman. Dark skinned, slender, her body was very beautiful. I leaned over her, covered her mouth with mine, and blew air into her lungs. She jerked convulsively and drew a shuddering breath, then stopped. Her eyelids fluttered, then opened.

"Wake up!" I said, drawing on my piezosuit. I slipped the force blade into the boot, strapped on the belt with blaster and supplies, shrugged into the backpack. "Put on this suit! No time to waste."

She took in my face, the surroundings. From beyond the locker door I heard the sounds of the commandos entering the engine room.

"I am Brother Adlan," I whispered urgently. "You are a

soldier of the Republican Guard?" As I spoke I helped her into the skinsuit.

"Lieutenant Nahid Esfandiar. What's happening?"

"We are in orbit over Helvetica, under attack by Caslonian commandos. We need to break out of here."

"What weapons have we?"

I handed her a blaster. "They will have accelerated perceptions. Can you speed yours?"

Her glance passed over me, measuring me for a fool. "Done already." She sealed her suit and flipped down the faceplate on her helmet.

I did not pay attention to her, because as she spoke, a god spoke to me. *Three men beyond this door.* In my mind I saw the engine room and the three soldiers who were preparing to rip open the closet.

I touched my helmet to hers and whispered to Nahid, "There are three of them outside. The leader is directly across from the door. He has a common blaster, on stun. To the immediate right, a meter away, one of the commandos has a pulse rifle. The third, about to set the charge, has a pneumatic projector, probably with sleep gas. When they blow the door, I'll go high, you low. Three meters to the cross corridor, down one level and across starboard to the escape pod."

Just then, the door to the closet was ripped open, and through it came a blast of sleep gas. But we were locked into our suits, helmets sealed. Our blaster beams, pink in the darkness, crossed as they emerged from the gloom of the closet. We dove through the doorway in zero-G, bouncing off the bulkheads, blasters flaring. The commandos were just where the gods had told me they would be. I cut down one before we even cleared the doorway. Though they moved as quickly as we did, they were trying not to kill me, and the fact that there were two of us now took them by surprise.

Nahid fired past my ear, taking out another. We ducked through the hatch and up the companionway. Two more commandos came from the control room at the end of the corridor; I was able to slice one of them before he could fire, but the other's stunner numbed my thigh. Nahid torched his head and grabbed me by the arm, hurling me around the corner into the cross passageway.

Two more commandos guarded the hatchway to the escape pod. Nahid fired at them, killing one and wounding the other in a single shot. But instead of heading for the pod she jerked me the other way, toward the umbilical to the Caslonian ship.

"What are you doing?" I protested.

"Shut up," she said. "They can hear us." Halfway across the umbilical, Nahid stopped, braced herself against one wall, raised her blaster, and, without hesitation, blew a hole in the wall opposite. The air rushed out. A klaxon sounded the pressure breach, another commando appeared at the junction of the umbilical and the Caslonian ship—I burned him down—and we slipped through the gap into the space between the two ships. She grabbed my arm and pulled me around the hull of my own vessel.

I realized what she intended. Grabbing chunks of ice, we pulled ourselves over the horizon of my ship until we reached the outside hatch of the escape pod. I punched in the access code. We entered the pod and while Nahid sealed the hatch, I powered up and blasted us free of the ship before we had even buckled in.

The pod shot toward the upper atmosphere. The commandos guarding the inner hatch were ejected into the vacuum behind us. Retro fire slammed us into our seats. I caught a glimpse of bodies floating in the chaos we'd left behind before proton beams lanced out from the Caslonian raider, clipping the pod and sending us into a spin.

"You couldn't manage this without me?" Nahid asked.

"No sarcasm, please." I fought to steady the pod so the heat shields were oriented for atmosphere entry.

We hit the upper atmosphere. For twenty minutes we were buffeted by the jet stream, and it got hot in the tiny capsule. I became very aware of Nahid's scent—sweat and a trace of rosewater; she must have put on perfume before she was folded into the packet that had been implanted in me. Her eyes moved slowly over the interior of the pod.

"What is the date?" she asked.

"The nineteenth of Cunegonda," I told her. The pod bounced violently and drops of sweat flew from my forehead. Three red lights flared on the board, but I could do nothing about them.

"What year?"

I saw that it would not be possible to keep many truths from her. "You have been suspended in nine-space for sixty years."

The pod lurched again, a piece of the ablative shield tearing away. She sat motionless, taking in the loss of her entire life.

A snatch of verse came to my lips, unbidden:

Our life is but a trifle
A child's toy abandoned by the road
When we are called home.

"Very poetic," she said. "Are we going to ride this pod all the way down? They probably have us on locator from orbit and will vaporize it the minute it hits. I'd rather not be called home just now."

"We'll eject at ten kilometers. Here's your chute."

When the heat of the reentry had abated and we hit the troposphere, we blew the explosive bolts and shot free of the tumbling pod. Despite the thin air of the upper atmosphere, I was buffeted almost insensible, spinning like a prayer wheel. I lost sight of Nahid.

I fell for a long time, but eventually managed to stabilize myself spread-eagled, dizzy, my stomach lurching. Below, the Jacobin Range stretched north to southwest under the rising sun, the snow-covered rock on the upper reaches folded like a discarded robe, and below the thick forest climbing up to the tree line.

Some minutes later, I witnessed the impressive flare of the pod striking just below the summit of one of the peaks, tearing a gash in the ice cover and sending up a plume of black smoke that was torn away by the wind. I tongued the trigger in my helmet, and with a nasty jerk, the airfoil chute deployed from my backpack. I could see Nahid's red chute some five hundred meters below me; I steered toward her, hoping we could land near each other. The forested mountainside came up fast. I spotted a clearing on a ledge two thirds of the way up the slope and made for it, but my burned shoulder wasn't working right, and I was coming in too fast. I caught a glimpse of Nahid's foil in the mountain scar ahead, but I wasn't going to reach her.

At the last minute, I pulled up and skimmed the treetops, caught a boot against a top limb, flipped head over heels, and crashed into the foliage, coming to rest hanging upside down from the tree canopy. The suit's rigidity kept me from breaking any bones, but it took me ten minutes to release the shrouds. I turned down the suit's inflex and took off my helmet to better see what I was doing. When I did, the limb supporting me broke, and I fell the last ten meters through the trees, hitting another limb on the way down, knocking myself out.

I was woken by Nahid rubbing snow into my face. My piezo-suit had been turned off, and the fabric was flexible again. Nahid leaned over me, supporting my head. "Can you move your feet?" she asked.

My thigh still was numb from the stunner. I tried moving my right foot. Though I could not feel any response, I saw the boot twitch. "So it would seem."

Done with me, she let my head drop. "So, do you have some plan?"

I pulled up my knees and sat up. My head ached. We were surrounded by the boles of the tall firs; above our heads the wind swayed the trees, but down here the air was calm, and sunlight filtered down in patches, moving over the packed fine brown needles of the forest floor. Nahid had pulled down my chute to keep it from advertising our position. She crouched on one knee and examined the charge indicator on her blaster.

I got up and inventoried the few supplies we had—my suit's water reservoir, holding maybe a liter, three packs of *gichy* crackers in the belt. Hers would have no more than that. "We should get moving; the Caslonians will send a landing party, or notify the colonial government in Guliston to send a security squad."

"And why should I care?"

"You fought for the republic against the Caslonians. When the war was lost and the protectorate established, you had yourself folded. Didn't you expect to take up arms again when called back to life?"

"You tell me that was sixty years ago. What happened to the rest of the Republican Guard?"

"The Guard was wiped out in the final Caslonian assaults."

"And our folded battalion?"

The blistering roar of a flyer tore through the clear air above the trees. Nahid squinted up, eyes following the glittering ship. "They're heading for where the pod hit." She pulled me to my feet, taking us downhill, perhaps in the hope of finding better cover in the denser forest near one of the mountain freshets.

"No," I said. "Up the slope."

"That's where they'll be."

"It can't be helped. We need to get to the monastery. We're on the wrong side of the mountains." I turned up the incline. After a moment, she followed.

We stayed beneath the trees for as long as possible. The slope was not too steep at this altitude; the air was chilly, with dying patches of old snow in the shadows. Out in the direct sunlight, it would be hot until evening came. I had climbed these mountains fifteen years before, an adolescent trying to find a way to live away from the world. As we moved, following the path of a small stream, the aches in my joints eased.

We did not talk. I had not thought about what it would mean to wake this soldier, other than how she would help me in a time of extremity. There are no women in our order, and though we take no vow of celibacy and some commerce takes place between brothers in their cells late at night, there is little opportunity for contact with the opposite sex. Nahid, despite her forbidding nature, was beautiful: dark skin, black eyes, lustrous black hair cut short, the three parallel scars of her rank marking her left cheek. As a boy in Urushana, I had tormented my sleepless nights with visions of women as beautiful as she; in my short career as a constable I had avidly pursued women far less so. One of them had provoked the fight that had gotten me cashiered.

The forest thinned as we climbed higher. Large folds of granite lay exposed to the open air, creased with fractures and holding pockets of earth where trees sprouted in groups. We had to circle around to avoid coming into the open, and even that would be impossible when the forest ended completely. I pointed us south, where Dundrahad Pass, dipping below three thousand meters, cut through the mountains. We were without snowshoes or trekking gear, but I hoped that, given the summer temperatures, the pass would be clear enough to traverse in the night without getting ourselves killed. The skinsuits we wore would be proof against the nighttime cold.

We saw no sign of the Caslonians, but when we reached the tree line, we stopped to wait for darkness anyway. The air had turned colder, and a sharp wind blew down the pass from the other side of the mountains. We settled in a hollow beneath a patch of twisted scrub trees and waited out the declining sun. At the zenith, the first moon Mahsheed rode, waning gibbous. In the notch of the pass above and ahead of us, the second moon Roshanak rose. Small, glowing green, it moved perceptibly as it raced around the planet. I nibbled at some *gichy*, sipping water from my suit's reservoir. Nahid's eyes were shadowed; she scanned the slope.

"We'll have to wait until Mahsheed sets before we move," Nahid said. "I don't want to be caught in the pass in its light."

"It will be hard for us to see where we're going."

She didn't reply. The air grew colder. After a while, without looking at me, she spoke. "So what happened to my compatriots?"

I saw no point in keeping anything from her. "As the Caslonians consolidated their conquest, an underground of Republicans pursued a guerrilla war. Two years later, they mounted an assault on the provincial capital in Kofarnihon. They unfolded your battalion to aid them, and managed to seize the armory. But the Caslonians sent reinforcements and set up a siege. When the rebels refused to surrender, the Caslonians vaporized the entire city—hostages, citizens, and rebels alike. That was the end of the Republican Guard." Nahid's dark eyes watched me as I told her all this. The tightness of her lips held grim skepticism.

"Yet here I am," she said.

"I don't know how you came to be the possession of the Order. Some refugee, perhaps. The masters, sixty years ago, debated what to do with you. Given the temperament of the typical guardsman, it was assumed that, had you been restored to life, you would immediately get yourself killed in assaulting the Caslonians, putting the Order at risk. It was decided to keep you in reserve, in the expectation that, at some future date, your services would be useful."

"You monks were always fair-weather democrats. Ever your Order over the welfare of the people, or even their freedom. So you betrayed the republic."

"You do us an injustice."

"It was probably Javeed who brought me—the lying monk attached to our unit."

I recognized the name. Brother Javeed, a bent, bald man of great age, had run the monastery kitchen. I had never thought twice about him. He had died a year after I joined the Order.

"Why do you think I was sent on this mission?" I told her. "We mean to set Helvetica free. And we shall do so, if we reach Sharishabz."

"How do you propose to accomplish that? Do you want to see your monastery vaporized?"

"They will not dare. I have something of theirs that they will give up the planet for. That's why they tried to board my ship rather than destroy it; that's why they didn't bother to disintegrate the escape pod when they might easily have shot us out of the sky."

"And this inestimably valuable item that you carry? It must be very small."

"It's in my head. I have stolen the only copies of the Foundational Dramas."

She looked at me. "So?"

Her skepticism was predictable, but it still angered me. "So—they will gladly trade Helvetica's freedom for the return of the plays."

She lowered her head, rubbed her brow with her hand. I could not read her. She made a sound, an intake of breath. For a moment, I thought she wept. Then she raised her head and laughed in my face.

I fought an impulse to strike her. "Quiet!"

She laughed louder. Her shoulders shook, and tears came to her eyes. I felt my face turn red. "You should have let me die with the others, in battle. You crazy priest!"

"Why do you laugh?" I asked her. "Do you think they would send ships to embargo Helvetican orbital space, dispatch squads of soldiers and police, if what I carry were not valuable to them?"

"I don't believe in your fool's religion."

"Have you ever seen the plays performed?"

"Once, when I was a girl. I saw *The Archer's Fall* during the year-end festival in Tienkash. I fell asleep."

"They are the axis of human culture. The sacred stories of our race. We are *human* because of them. Through them the gods speak to us."

"I thought you monks heard the gods talking to you directly. Didn't they tell you to run us directly into the face of the guards securing the escape pod? It's lucky you had me along to cut our way out of that umbilical, or we'd be dead up there now."

"*You* might be dead. I would be in a sleep tank having my brain taken apart—to retrieve these dramas."

"There are no gods! Just voices in your head. They tell you to do what you already want to do."

"If you think the commands of the gods are easy, then just try to follow them for a single day."

We settled into an uncomfortable silence. The sun set, and the rings became visible in the sky, turned pink by the sunset in the west, rising silvery toward the zenith, where they were eclipsed by the planet's shadow. The light of the big moon still illuminated the open rock face before us. We would have a steep three-hundred-meter climb above the tree line to the pass, then another couple of kilometers between the peaks in the darkness.

"It's cold," I said after a while.

Without saying anything, she reached out and tugged my arm. It took me a moment to realize that she wanted me to move next to her. I slid over, and we ducked our heads to keep below the wind. I could feel the taut muscles of her body beneath the skinsuit. The paradox of our alienation hit me. We were both the products of the gods. She did not believe this truth, but truth does not need to be believed to prevail.

Still, she was right that we had not escaped the orbiting commandos in the way I had expected.

The great clockwork of the universe turned. Green Roshanak sped past Mahsheed, for a moment in transit looking like the pupil of a god's observing eye, then set, and an hour later, Mahsheed followed her below the western horizon. The stars shone in all their glory, but it was as dark as it would get before Roshanak rose for the second time that night. It was time for us to take our chance and go.

We came out of our hiding place and moved to the edge of the scrub. The broken granite of the peak rose before us, faint gray in starlight. We set out across the rock, climbing in places, striding across rubble fields, circling areas of ice and melting snow. In a couple of places, we had to boost each other up, scrambling over boulders, finding hand- and footholds in the vertical face where we were blocked. It was farther than I had estimated before the ground leveled and we were in the pass.

We were just cresting the last ridge when glaring white light shone down on us, and an amplified voice called from above. "Do not move! Drop your weapons and lie flat on the ground!"

I tongued my body into acceleration. In slow motion, Nahid crouched, raised her blaster, arm extended, sighted on the flyer, and fired. I hurled my body into hers and threw her aside just as the return fire of projectile weapons splattered the rock where she had been into fragments. In my head, the voices of the gods screamed: *Back. We will show you the way.*

"This way!" I dragged Nahid over the edge of the rock face we had just climbed. It was a three-meter drop to the granite below; I landed hard, and she fell on my chest, knocking the wind out of me. Around us burst a hail of sleep-gas pellets. In trying to catch my breath, I caught a whiff of the gas, and my head whirled. Nahid slid her helmet down over her face and did the same for me.

From above us came the sound of the flyer touching down. Nahid started for the tree line, limping. She must have been hit or injured in our fall. I pulled her to our left, along the face of the rock. "Where—" she began.

"Shut up!" I grunted.

The commandos hit the ledge behind us, but the flyer had its searchlight aimed at the trees, and the soldiers followed the light. The fog of sleep gas gave us some cover.

We scuttled along the granite shelf until we were beyond the entrance to the pass. By this time, I had used whatever reserves of energy my body could muster and passed into normal speed. I was exhausted.

"Over the mountain?" Nahid asked. "We can't."

"Under it," I said. I forced my body into motion, searching in the darkness for the cleft in the rock that, in the moment of the flyer attack, the gods had shown me. And there it was, two dark pits above a vertical fissure in the granite, like an impassive face. We climbed up the few meters to the brink of the cleft. Nahid followed, slower now, dragging her right leg. "Are you badly hurt?" I asked her.

"Keep going."

I levered my shoulder under her arm and helped her along the ledge. Down in the forest, the lights of the commandos flickered, while a flyer hovered above, beaming bright white radiance down between the trees.

Once inside the cleft, I let her lean against the wall. Beyond the narrow entrance the way widened. I used my suit flash and, moving forward, found an oval chamber of three meters with a sandy floor. Some small bones give proof that a predator had once used this cave for a lair. But at the back, a small passage gaped. I crouched and followed it deeper.

"Where are you going?" Nahid asked.

"Come with me."

The passage descended for a space, then rose. I emerged into a larger space. My flash showed not a natural cave, but a chamber of dressed rock, and opposite us, a metal door. It was just as my vision had said.

"What is this?" Nahid asked in wonder.

"A tunnel under the mountain." I took off my helmet and spoke the words that would open the door. The ancient mechanism began to hum. With a fall of dust, a gap appeared at the side of the door, and it slid open.

The door closed behind us with a disturbing finality, wrapping us in the silence of a tomb. We found ourselves in a corridor at least twice our height and three times that in width. Our lights showed walls smooth as plaster, but when I laid my hand on one, it proved to be cut from the living rock. Our boots echoed on the polished but dusty floor. The air was stale, unbreathed by human beings for unnumbered years.

I made Nahid sit. "Rest," I said. "Let me look at that leg."

Though she complied, she kept her blaster out, and her eyes scanned our surroundings warily. "Did you know of this?"

"No. The gods told me, just as we were caught in the pass."

"Praise be to the Pujmanian Order." I could not tell if there was any sarcasm in her voice.

A trickle of blood ran down her boot from the wound of a projectile gun. I opened the seam of her suit, cleaned the wound with antiseptic from my suit's first aid kit, and bandaged her leg. "Can you walk?" I asked.

She gave me a tight smile. "Lead on, Brother Adlan."

We moved along the hall. Several smaller corridors branched off, but we kept to the main way. Periodically, we came across doors, most of them closed. One gaped open upon a room where my light fell on a garage of wheeled vehicles, sitting patiently in long rows, their windows thick with dust. In the corner of the room, a fracture in the ceiling had let in a steady drip of water that had corroded the vehicle beneath it into a mass of rust.

Along the main corridor our lights revealed hieroglyphics carved above doorways, dead oval spaces on the wall that might once have been screens or windows. We must have gone a kilometer or more when the corridor ended suddenly in a vast cavernous opening.

Our lights were lost in the gloom above. A ramp led down to an underground city. Buildings of gracious curves, apartments like heaps of grapes stacked upon a table, halls whose walls were so configured that they resembled a huge garment discarded in a bedroom. We descended into the streets.

The walls of the buildings were figured in abstract designs of immense intricacy, fractal patterns from immense to microscopic, picked out by the beams of our flashlights. Colored tiles, bits of glass and mica. Many of the buildings were no more than sets of walls demarcating space, with horizontal trellises that must once have held plants above them rather than roofs. Here and there, outside what might have been cafés, tables and benches rose out of the polished floor. We arrived in a broad square with low buildings around it, centered on a dry fountain. The immense figures of a man, a woman, and a child dominated the center of the dusty reservoir. Their eyes were made of crystal, and stared blindly across their abandoned city.

Weary beyond words, hungry, bruised, we settled against the rim of the fountain and made to sleep. The drawn skin about her eyes told me of Nahid's pain. I tried to comfort her, made her rest her legs, elevated, on my own. We slept.

When I woke, Nahid was already up, changing the dressing on her bloody leg. The ceiling of the cave had lit, and a pale light shone down, making an early arctic dawn over the dead city.

"How is your leg?" I asked.

"Better. Do you have any more anodynes?"

I gave her what I had. She took them, and sighed. After a while, she asked, "Where did the people go?"

"They left the universe. They grew beyond the need of matter, and space. They became gods. You know the story."

"The ones who made this place were people like you and me."

"You and I are the descendants of the re-creation of a second human race three million years after the first ended in apotheosis. Or of the ones left behind, or banished back into the material world by the gods for some great crime."

Nahid rubbed her boot above the bandaged leg. "Which is it? Which child's tale do you expect me to believe?"

"How do you think I found the place? The gods told me, and here it is. Our mission is important to them, and they are seeing that we succeed. Justice is to be done."

"Justice? Tell the starving child about justice. The misborn and the dying. I would rather be the random creation of colliding atoms than subject to the whim of some transhumans no more godlike than I am."

"You speak out of bitterness."

"If they are gods, they are responsible for the horror that occurs in the world. So they are evil. Why otherwise would they allow things to be as they are?"

"To say that is to speak out of the limitations of our vision. We can't see the outcome of events. We're too close. But the gods see how all things will eventuate. Time is a landscape to them. All at once they see the acorn, the seedling, the ancient oak, the woodsman who cuts it, the fire that burns the wood, and the smoke that rises from the fire. And so they led us to this place."

"Did they lead the bullet to find my leg? Did they lead your Order to place me on a shelf for a lifetime, separate me from every person I loved?" Nahid's voice rose. "Please save me your theodical prattle!"

"'Theodical.' Impressive vocabulary for a soldier. But you—"

A scraping noise came from behind us. I turned to find that the giant male figure in the center of the fountain had moved. As I watched, its hand jerked another few centimeters. Its foot pulled free of its setting, and it stepped down from the pedestal into the empty basin.

We fell back from the fountain. The statue's eyes glowed a dull orange. Its lips moved, and it spoke in a voice like the scraping together of two files: "Do not flee, little ones."

Nahid let fly a shot from her blaster, which ricocheted

off the shoulder of the metal man and scarred the ceiling of the cave. I pulled her away and we crouched behind a table before an open-sided building at the edge of the square.

The statue raised its arms in appeal. "Your shoes are untied," it said in its ghostly rasp. "We know why you are here. It seems to you that your lives hang in the balance, and of course you value your lives. As you should, dear ones. But I, who have no soul and therefore no ability to care, can tell you that the appetites that move you are entirely transitory. The world you live in is a game. You do not have a ticket."

"Quite mad," Nahid said. "Our shoes have no laces."

"But it's also true—they are therefore untied," I said. "And we have no tickets." I called out to the metal man, "Are you a god?"

"I am no god," the metal man said. "The gods left behind the better part of themselves when they abandoned matter. The flyer lies on its side in the woods. Press the silver pentagon. You must eat, but you must not eat too much. Here is food."

The shop behind us lit up, and in a moment the smell of food wafted from within.

I slid over to the entrance. On a table inside, under warm light, were two plates of rice and vegetables.

"He's right," I told Nahid.

"I'm not going to eat that food. Where did it come from? It's been thousands of years without a human being here."

"Come," I said. I drew her inside and made her join me at the table. I tasted. The food was good. Nahid sat warily, facing out to the square, blaster a centimeter from her plate. The metal man sat on the plaza stones, cross-legged, ducking its massive head in order to watch us. After a few moments, it began to croon.

Its voice was a completely mechanical sound, but the tune it sang was sweet, like a peasant song. I cannot convey to you the strangeness of sitting in that ancient restaurant, eating food conjured fresh out of nothing by ancient machines, listening to the music of creatures who might have been a different species from us.

When its song was ended, the metal man spoke: "If you wish to know someone, you need only observe that on which he bestows his care, and what sides of his own nature he cultivates." It lifted its arm and pointed at Nahid. Its finger stretched almost to the door. I could see the patina of corrosion on that metal digit. "If left to the gods, you will soon die."

The arm moved, and it pointed at me. "You must live, but you must not live too much. Take this."

The metal man opened the curled fingers of its hand, and in its huge palm was a small, round metallic device the size of an apple. I took it. Black and dense, it filled my hand completely. "Thank you," I said.

The man stood and returned to the empty fountain, climbed onto the central pedestal, and resumed its position. There it froze. Had we not been witness to it, I could never have believed it had moved.

Nahid came out of her musing over the man's sentence of her death. She lifted her head. "What is that thing?"

I examined the sphere, surface covered in pentagonal facets of dull metal. "I don't know."

In one of the buildings, we found some old furniture, cushions of metallic fabric that we piled together as bedding. We huddled together and slept.

SELENE:
Hear that vessel that docks above?
It marks the end of our lives
And the beginning of our torment.

STOCHIK:
Death comes
And then it's gone. Who knows
What lies beyond that event horizon?
Our life is but a trifle,
A child's toy abandoned by the road
When we are called home.

SELENE:
Home? You might well hope it so,
But—
[Alarums off stage. Enter *a god*]

GOD:
The hull is breached!
You must fly.

In the night I woke, chasing away the wisps of a dream.
The building we were in had no ceiling, and faint light from
the cavern roof filtered down upon us. In our sleep, we had
moved closer together, and Nahid's arm lay over my chest,
her head next to mine, her breath brushing my cheek. I turned
my face to her, centimeters away. Her face was placid, her
eyelashes dark and long.

As I watched her, her eyelids fluttered and she awoke. She
did not flinch at my closeness, but simply, soberly looked
into my own eyes for what seemed like a very long time. I
leaned forward and kissed her.

She did not pull away, but kissed me back strongly. She
made a little moan in her throat, and I pulled her tightly to
me.

We made love in the empty, ancient city. Her fingers entwined with mine, arms taut. Shadow of my torso across her
breast. Hard, shuddering breath. Her lips on my chest. Smell
of her sweat and mine. My palm brushing her abdomen. The
feeling of her dark skin against mine. Her quiet laugh.

"Your leg," I said, as we lay in the darkness, spent.

"What about it?"

"Did I hurt you?"

She laughed again, lightly. "Now you ask. You are indeed
all man."

In the morning, we took another meal from the ancient
restaurant, food that had been manufactured from raw molecules while we waited, or perhaps stored somewhere for
millennia.

We left by the corridor opposite the one by which we had

entered, heading for the other side of the mountain range.
Nahid limped but made no complaint. The passage ended in
another door, beyond which a cave twisted upward. In one
place, the ceiling of the cave had collapsed, and we had to
crawl on our bellies over rubble through the narrow gap it
had left. The exit was onto a horizontal shelf overgrown with
trees, well below the pass. It was mid-morning. A misting
rain fell across the Sharishabz Valley. In the distance, hazed
by clouds of mist, I caught a small gleam of the white buildings of the monastery on the Penitent's Ridge. I pointed it out
to Nahid. We scanned the mountainside below us, searching
for the forest road.

Nahid found the thread of the road before I. "No sign of
the Caslonians," she said.

"They're guarding the pass on the other side of the mountain, searching the woods there for us."

We descended the slope, picking our way through the
trees toward the road. The mist left drops of water on our
skinsuits but did not in any way slow us. My spirits rose. I
could see the end of this adventure in sight, and wondered
what would happen to Nahid then.

"What will you do when we get to the monastery?" I
asked her.

"I think I'll leave as soon as I can. I don't want to be there
when the Caslonians find out you've reached your Order
with the plays."

"They won't do anything. The gods hold the monastery in
their hands."

"Let us hope they don't drop it."

She would die soon, the statue had said—if left to the
gods. But what person was not at the mercy of the gods?
Still, she would be much more at risk alone, away from the
Order. "What about your leg?" I asked.

"Do you have a clinic there?"

"Yes."

"I'll take an exoskeleton and some painkillers and be on
my way."

"Where will you go?"

"Wherever I can."

"But you don't even know what's happened in the last sixty years. What can you do?"

"Maybe my people are still alive. That's where I'll go—the town where I grew up. Perhaps I'll find someone who remembers me. Maybe I'll find my own grave."

"Don't go."

She strode along more aggressively. I could see her wince with each step. "Look, I don't care about your monastery. I don't care about these plays. Mostly, I don't care about *you*. Give me some painkillers and an exo, and I'll be gone."

That ended our conversation. We walked on in silence through the woods, me brooding, she limping along, grimacing.

We found the forest road. Here the land fell away sharply, and the road, hardly more than a gravel track, switchbacked severely as we made our way down the mountainside. We met no signs of pursuit. Though the rain continued, the air warmed as we moved lower, and beads of sweat trickled down my back under the skinsuit. The boots I wore were not meant for hiking, and by now my feet were sore, my back hurt. I could only imagine how bad it was for Nahid.

I had worked for years to manage my appetites, and yet I could not escape images of our night together. With a combination of shame and desire, I wanted her still. I did not think I could go back to being just another monk. The Order had existed long before the Caslonian conquest, and would long outlast it. I was merely a cell passing through the body of this immortal creation. What did the gods want from me? What was to come of all this?

At the base of the trail, the road straightened, following the course of the River Sharishabz up the valley. Ahead rose the plateau, the gleaming white buildings of the monastery clearly visible now. The ornamental gardens, the terraced fields tended by the Order for millennia. I could almost taste the sweet oranges and pomegranates. It would be good to be back home, a place where I could hide away from the world and figure out exactly what was in store for me. I wouldn't mind being hailed as a hero, the liberator of our people, like Stochik himself, who took the plays from the hands of the gods.

The valley sycamores and aspens rustled with the breeze. The afternoon passed. We stopped by the stream and drank. Rested, then continued.

We came to a rise in the road, where it twisted to climb the plateau. Signs here of travel, ruts of iron wheels where people from the villages drove supplies to the monastery. Pilgrims passed this way—though there was no sign of anyone today.

We made a turn in the road, and I heard a yelp behind me. I turned to find Nahid struggling in the middle of the road. At first, I thought she was suffering a seizure. Her body writhed and jerked. Then I realized, from the slick of rain deflected from his form, that she was being assaulted by a person in an invisibility cloak.

This understanding had only flashed through my mind when I was thrown to the ground by an unseen hand. I kicked out wildly, and my boot made contact. Gravel sprayed beside me where my attacker fell. I slipped into accelerated mode, kicked him again, rolled away, and dashed into the woods. Above me I heard the whine of an approaching flyer. *Run!* the voice of a god told me.

I ran. The commandos did not know these woods the way I did. I had spent ten years exploring them, playing games of hide and hunt in the night with my fellow novices; I knew I could find my way to the monastery without them capturing me.

And Nahid? Clearly this was her spoken-of death. No doubt it had already taken place. Or perhaps they wouldn't kill her immediately, but would torture her, assuming she knew something, or even if they knew she didn't, taking some measure of revenge on her body. It was the lot of a Republican Guard to receive such treatment. She would even expect it. *The Order comes first.*

Every second took me farther from the road, away from the Caslonians. But after a minute of hurrying silently through the trees, I felt something heavy in my hand. I stopped.

Without realizing it, I had taken the object the metal man
had given me out of my belt pouch. *She would not want you
to return. The freedom of her people comes before her personal safety.*

I circled back, and found them in the road.

The flyer had come down athwart the road. The soldiers
had turned off their cloaks, three men garbed head to toe
in the matte gray of light deflection suits. Two soldiers had
Nahid on her knees in the drizzle, her hands tied behind her
back. One jerked her head back by her hair, holding a knife
to her throat while an officer asked her questions. The officer
slapped her, whipping the back of his gloved hand across
her face.

I moved past them through the woods, sound of rain on
the foliage, still holding the metal sphere in my hand. The
flyer sat only a few meters into the road. I crouched there,
staring at the uncouth object. I rotated it in my palm until
I found the surface pentagon that was silvered. I depressed
this pentagon until it clicked.

Then I flipped it out into the road, under the landing pads
of the flyer, and fell back.

It was not so much an explosion as a vortex, warping the
flyer into an impossible shape, throwing it off the road. As
it spun, the pilot was tossed from the cockpit, his uniform
flaring in electric blue flame. The three men with Nahid were
sucked off their feet by the dimensional warp. They
jerked their heads toward the screaming pilot. The officer
staggered to his feet, took two steps toward him, and one
of the men followed. By that time, I had launched myself
into the road and slammed my bad shoulder into the small
of the back of the man holding Nahid. I seized his rifle and
fired, killing the officer and the other soldier, then the one
I had just laid flat. The pilot was rolling in the gravel to
extinguish the flames. I stepped forward calmly and shot
him in the head.

Acrid black smoke rose from the crushed flyer, which lay
on its side in the woods.

Nahid was bleeding from a cut on her neck. She held her
palm against the wound, but the blood seeped steadily from

between her fingers. I gathered her up and dragged her into the woods before reinforcements could arrive.

"Thank you," Nahid gasped, her eyes large, and fixed on me. We limped off into the trees.

Nahid was badly hurt, but I knew where we were, and I managed, through that difficult night, to get us up the pilgrim's trail to the monastery. By the time we reached the iron door we called the Mud Gate, she had lost consciousness and I was carrying her. Her blood was all over us, and I could not tell if she yet breathed.

We novices had used this gate many times to sneak out of the monastery to play martial games in the darkness, explore the woods, and pretend we were ordinary men. Men who, when they desired something, had only to take it. Men who were under no vow of nonviolence. Here I had earned a week's fast by bloodying the nose, in a fit of temper, of Brother Taher. Now I returned, unrepentant over the number of men I had killed in the last days, a man who had disobeyed the voice of a god, hoping to save Nahid before she bled out.

Brother Pramha was the first to greet me. He looked at me with shock. "Who is this?" he asked.

"This is a friend, a soldier, Nahid. Quickly. She needs care."

Together we took her to the clinic. Pramha ran off to inform the Master. Our physician, Brother Nastricht, sealed her throat wound, and gave her new blood. I held her hand. She did not regain consciousness.

Soon, one of the novices arrived to summon me to Master Darius's chambers. Although I was exhausted, I hurried after him through the warren of corridors, up the tower steps. I unbelted my blaster and handed it to the novice—he seemed distressed to hold the destructive device—and entered the room.

Beyond the broad window that formed the far wall of the chamber, dawn stained the sky pink. Master Darius held out his arms. I approached him, humbly bowed my head, and he embraced me. The warmth of his large body enfolding me was an inexpressible comfort. He smelled of cinnamon. He let me go, held me at arm's length, and smiled. The kosode he wore I recognized as one I had sewn myself. "I cannot tell you how good it is to see you, Adlan."

"I have the plays," I announced.

"The behavior of our Caslonian masters has been proof enough of that," he replied. His broad, plain face was somber as he told me of the massacre in Radnapuja, where the colonial government had held six thousand citizens hostage, demanding the bodily presentation, alive, of the foul villain, the man without honor or soul, the sacrilegious terrorist who had stolen the Foundational Plays.

"Six thousand dead?"

"They won't be the last," the Master said. "The plays have been used as a weapon, as a means of controlling us. The beliefs which they embody work within the minds and souls of every person on this planet. They work even on those who are unbelievers."

"Nahid is an unbeliever."

"Nahid? She is this soldier whom you brought here?"

"The Republican Guard you sent with me. She doesn't believe, but she has played her role in bringing me here."

Master Darius poured me a glass of fortifying spirits and handed it to me as if he were a novice and I the master. He sat in his great chair, had me sit in the chair opposite, and bade me recount every detail of the mission. I did so.

"It is indeed miraculous that you have come back alive," Master Darius mused. "Had you died, the plays would have been lost forever."

"The gods would not allow such a sacrilege."

"Perhaps. You carry the only copies in your mind?"

"Indeed. I have even quoted them to Nahid."

"Not at any length, I hope."

I laughed at his jest. "But now we can free Helvetica," I said. "Before any further innocents are killed, you must contact the Caslonian colonial government and tell them we have the plays. Tell them they must stop or we will destroy them."

Master Darius held up his hand and looked at me piercingly—I had seen this gesture many times in his tutoring of me. "First, let me ask you some questions about your tale. This is what my mentor, the great Master Malrubius, called a 'teaching moment.' You tell me that, when you first came to consciousness after stealing the plays in the Imperial City, a god told you to run. Yet to run in the Caslonian capital is only to attract unwelcome attention."

"Yes. The god must have wanted to hurry my escape."

"But when you reached the port bazaar, the god told you to stop and enter the restaurant. You run to attract attention, and dawdle long enough to allow time for you to be caught. Does this make sense?"

My fatigue made it difficult for me to think. What point was the Master trying to make? "Perhaps I was not supposed to stop," I replied. "It was my own weakness. I was hungry."

"Then, later, you tell me that when the commandos boarded your ship, you escaped by following Nahid's lead, not the word of the gods."

"The gods led us out of the engine room. I think this is a matter of my misinterpreting—"

"And this metal man you encountered in the ancient city. Did he in fact say that the gods would have seen Nahid dead?"

"The statue said many mad things."

"Yet the device he gave you was the agent of her salvation?"

"I used it for that." Out of shame, I had not told Master Darius that I had disobeyed the command of the god who told me to flee.

"Many paradoxes." The Master took a sip from his own glass. "So, if we give the plays back, what will happen then?"

"Then Helvetica will be free."

"And after that?"

"After that, we can do as we wish. The Caslonians would not dare to violate a holy vow. The gods would punish them. They know that. They are believers, as are we."

"Yes, they are believers. They would obey any compact

they made, for fear of the wrath of the gods. They believe what you hold contained in your mind, Adlan, is true. So, as you say, you must give them to me now, and I will see to their disposition."

"Their disposition? How will you see to their disposition?"

"That is not something for you to worry about, my son. You have done well, and you deserve all our thanks. Brother Ishmael will see to unburdening you of the great weight you carry."

A silence ensued. I knew it was a sign of my dismissal. I must go to Brother Ishmael. But I did not rise. "What will you do with them?"

Master Darius's brown eyes lay steady on me, and quiet. "You have always been my favorite. I think perhaps you know what I intend."

I pondered our conversation. "You—you're going to destroy them."

"Perhaps I was wrong not to have you destroy them the minute you gained access to the archives. But at that time I had not come to these conclusions."

"But the wrath of the Caslonians will know no limit! We will be exterminated!"

"We may be exterminated, and Helvetica remain in chains, but once these plays are destroyed, never to be recovered, then *humanity* will begin to be truly free. This metal man, you say, told you the gods left the better part of themselves behind. That is profoundly true. Yet there is no moment when they cease to gaze over our shoulders. Indeed, if we are ever to be free human beings, and not puppets jerked about by unseen forces—which may or may not exist—the gods must go. And the beginning of that process is the destruction of the Foundational Plays."

I did not know how to react. In my naiveté I said, "This does not seem right."

"I assure you, my son, that it is."

"If we destroy the plays, it will be the last thing we ever do."

"Of course not. Time will not stop."

"Time may not stop," I said, "but it might as well. Any things that happen after the loss of the gods will have no meaning."

Master Darius rose from his chair and moved toward his desk. "You are tired, and very young," he said, his back to me. "I have lived in the shadow of the gods far longer than you have." He reached over his desk, opened a drawer, took something out, and straightened.

He is lying. I stood. I felt surpassing weariness, but I moved silently. In my boot, I still carried the force knife I had stolen from the restaurant on Caslon. I drew out the hilt, switched on the blade, and approached the Master just as he began to turn.

When he faced me, he had a blaster in his hands. He was surprised to find me so close to him. His eyes went wide as I slipped the blade into his belly below his lowest rib.

STOCHIK:
Here ends our story.
Let no more be said of our fall.
Mark the planting of this seed.
The tree that grows in this place
Will bear witness to our deeds;
No other witness shall we have.

SELENE:
I would not depart with any other
My love. Keep alive whatever word
May permit us to move forward.
Leaving all else behind we must
Allow the world to come to us.

The Caslonian government capitulated within a week after we contacted them. Once they began to withdraw their forces from the planet and a provisional government for the Helvetican Republic was reestablished in Astara, I underwent the delicate process of downloading the foundational dramas from my mind. *The Abandonment* was once again embodied in a crystal, which was presented to the Caslonian legate in a formal ceremony on the anniversary of the rebirth of man.

The ceremony took place on a bright day in midsummer in that city of a thousand spires. Sunlight flooded the streets, where citizens in vibrantly colored robes danced and sang to the music of bagpipes. Pennants in purple and green flew from those spires; children hung out of second-story school windows, shaking snowstorms of confetti on the parades. The smell of incense wafted down from the great temple, and across the sky flyers drew intricate patterns with lines of colored smoke.

Nahid and I were there on that day, though I did not take a leading role in the ceremony, preferring to withdraw to my proper station. In truth, I am not a significant individual. I have only served the gods.

I left the Order as soon as the negotiations were completed. At first the brothers were appalled by my murder of Master Darius. I explained to them that he had gone mad and intended to kill me in order to destroy the plays. There was considerable doubt. But when I insisted that we follow through with the plan as the Master had presented it to the brothers before sending me on my mission, they seemed to take my word about his actions. The success of our thieving enterprise overshadowed the loss of the great leader, and indeed has contributed to his legend, making of him a tragic figure. A drama has been written of his life and death, and the liberation of Helvetica.

Last night, Nahid and I, with our children and grandchildren, watched it performed in the square of the town where we set up the tailor's shop that has been the center of our lives for the last forty years. Seeing the events of my youth played out on the platform, in their comedy and tragedy, hazard and fortune, calls again to my mind the question of whether I have deserved the blessings that have fallen to me ever since that day. I have not heard the voices of the gods since I slipped the knife into the belly of the man who taught me all that I knew of grace.

The rapid decline of the Caslonian Empire, and the Helvetican renaissance that has led to our current prosperity, all date from that moment in his chambers when I ended his plan to free men from belief and duty. The people, joyous on their knees in the temples of twelve planets, give praise to the gods for their deliverance, listen, hear, and obey.

Soon I will rest beneath the earth, like the metal man who traduced the gods, though less likely than he ever to walk again. If I have done wrong, it is not for me to judge. I rest, my lover's hand in mine, in the expectation of no final word.

TO GO BOLDLY

CORY DOCTOROW

Here's a sly tale of the collision of the Old and the New—*one* of which is going to have to give way to the other . . .

Cory Doctorow is the coeditor of the popular *Boing Boing* website (boingboing.net), a cofounder of the Internet search-engine company OpenCola.com, and until recently was the outreach coordinator for the Electronic Frontier Foundation (www.eff.org). In 2001, he won the John W. Campbell Award as the year's Best New Writer. His stories have appeared in *Asimov's Science Fiction, Science Fiction Age, The Infinite Matrix, On Spec, Salon,* and elsewhere, and were collected in *A Place So Foreign and Eight More.* His well-received first novel, *Down and Out in the Magic Kingdom,* won the Locus Award as Best First Novel, and was followed shortly by a second novel, *Eastern Standard Tribe,* then by *Some-one Comes Town, Someone Leaves Town.* Doctorow's other books include *The Complete Idiot's Guide to Publishing Science Fiction,* written with Karl Schroeder, a guide to *Essential Blogging,* written with Shelley Powers, and, most recently, *Content: Selected Essays of Technology, Creativity, Copyright, and the Future of the Future.* His most recent books are a new collection of his short work, *Overclocked,* and a new novel, *Little Brother*, which debuted at #9 on the *New York Times* bestseller list. He has a website at www.craphound.com.

Captain Reynold J. Tsubishi of the APP ship *Colossus II* was the youngest commander in the fleet. He knew he owed his meteoric rise through the ranks to the good study habits he'd acquired in the Academy: specifically, the habit of studying what people cared about and *embodying those things* for them. Thus he was an expert in twentieth-century culture (the mark of distinguished taste in the Academy for two hundred years); a sudden-death bare-knuckles martial artist; a rakish flirt; and a skilled three-harp player. He led nearly every away-team, didn't screw the junior officers, and—

And he didn't have the faintest idea what to do about The Ball.

The Ball had been detected in the middle of the second shift, when the B-string had the conn and the bridge. No one called them the B-string, but they were. Some ships had tried evenly spreading the top people across all three shifts, but no one who was any good wanted to work ship's night and anyone with clout filed for transfers to ships that let the As congregate in A spaces during "daylight" hours. So now it was the A-string from ship's 9 to ship's 17, the B-string from 17 to 1, and the miserable Cs on the truly nocturnal 1 to 9.

Tsubishi was in the middle of his first REM when his headband brought him swiftly to the surface of his mind, dialing up the lights and the smell of wintergreen and eucalyptus as the holo of First Lieutenant !Mota, framed by the high back of the command chair, filled the room.

"Sir," !Mota said, ripping off a precise salute (his exoskeleton made all routine movement precise, but the salute was a work of art, right down to the tiny "ping" as the tip of zer metal-sheathed tentacle grazed zer forelobe), "my apologies for rousing you. The forward sensor array detected a yufo, and, on closer inspection, we believe it may be evidence of a potentially hostile garrison." The B-string commander was actually pretty good at zer job, and would have likely had zer own command by now but for the fact that the admiralty was heavily tilted to stock humans and loathe to promote non- and trans-humans to the higher eschelon. As a Wobblie (not a flattering name for an entire advanced starfaring race, but an accurate one, and no one with humanoid mouth-parts could pronounce the word in Wobbliese), !Mota was forever doomed to second-banana.

"On bridge in three," Tsubishi said, with a slightly sleepy salute of his own. His fresher had already cleaned and hung his uniform—a limitless supply of hard vac gave new meaning to the phrase "dry cleaning," and the single-piece garment was as crisp as the ones he'd assiduously ironed as a kay-det on old Mars. He backed into the fresher and held his arms up while it wrapped him in the fabric. All on-ship toilets had an automated system for dressing and undressing uniformed personnel, while the away-teams made do with sloppier (but easier to shuck) baggies, or, in the rare event that a green ensign forgot to change before beaming down, relying on teammates to help with the humiliating ritual of dressing and undressing.

The duty officer barked "Captain on deck" before he'd even managed to set his foot down, and the whole B-squad was on its feet and saluting before his back leg came up to join it. !Mota made a formal gesture of handing over the conn, and Tsubishi slid into his chair just as it finished its hurried reconfiguration to suit his compact, tightly wound frame. The ship beamed a double cappuccino—ship's crest stamped into the foam—into the armrest's cup-holder, and he sipped it pensively before nodding to !Mota to make his report.

!Mota—the model of second-banana efficiency—had whomped up an entire slideshow (with music and animated transitions, Tsubishi noted, with an inward roll of his eyes) in the time it had taken him to reach the bridge. The entire command crew watched him closely as !Mota stepped through it.

"We were proceeding as normal in our survey of the Tesla Z-65 system," !Mota said, the bridge holo going into orrery mode, showing the system and its 11 planets and 329 planetesimals, the fourth planet out glittering with a safety-orange highlight. "We'd deployed the forward sensor arrays here, to Tesla Z-65-4, for initial detailed surveys. Z-65-4 is just over one AU from the star, and pulls 1.8 gees, putting it in the upper bound of high-value/high-interest survey targets." The holo swept forward in dizzying jumps as the sensor packages beamed each other closer and closer to the planet in a series of hops, leaving them strung out in a lifeline from the ship's safe position among Z-65's outer rim to Z-65-4, ninety AU's away. The final stage established a long, elliptical orbit, and beamed its tiny progeny into tighter geostationary orbits around the planet's waistline.

"The yufo was detected almost immediately. It had been on the dark side of the planet, in geostationary, and it came into the lateral sensor-range of two of our packages when they beamed in." In a volumetric display, four different views of the yufo: a radar-derived mesh, a set of charts displaying its likely composition, an optical photo of the item in shaky high-mag, and a cartoon derived from the former, showing the yufo as a sphere a mere 1.5 meters in diameter, skinned in something black that the radar-analysis suggested was a damned efficient one-way sheath that likely disguised a Panopticon's worth of sensors, spy-eyes, radar.

The holo transitioned—a genie-back-into-the-bottle effect—and was replaced with a bulleted time line of the encounter, including notations as to when radar incursions on the sensor package emanating from the yufo were detected. !Mota let the chart stand for itself, then clicked to the final slide, the extrapolated cartoon of the yufo again.

!Mota ripped off another artful salute. "Orders, sir?"

"Have you brought one of our packages forward to get a closer look?"

"No sir. I anticipated that contingency and made plans for it, but have not given the order."

"Do it," Tsubishi said, giving one of those ironical little head-tilts that the female kay-dets on Mars had swooned for—and noted the B-shift tactical officer's appreciative wriggle with satisfaction—and watched the holotank as the packet changed its attitude with conservative little thruster-bursts, moving slowly relative to the yufo while the continents below whirled past as it came out of geostationary position. The cartoon yufo resolved itself with ever-more minute details as the packet got closer, closer.

"Packet reports radio chatter, three sigmas off random. Eighty-three percent confidence that it is communication." The comms officer had an unfortunate speech impediment that she'd all but corrected in the Academy, but it was still enough to keep her on the B-squad. Probably wouldn't accept neurocorrection. "Eighty-five. Ninety-five. Signal identified as ultra-wide-band sequence key. Switching to UWB reception now. Playing back 900 MHz to 90 GHz spectrum for ten minutes, using key. Repeating pattern found. Decoding."

It was the standard first contact drill. Any species plying the spaces between the stars was bound to converge on one of a few Rosetta strategies. The holotank showed realtime visualizations of the ship's symbology AI subsystem picking a million digits of Pi out of the chatter, deriving the counting system, then finding calculus, bootstrapping higher symbols out of *that*, moving on to physics and then to the physics of hyperspace. A progress bar tracked the system's confidence that it could decode arbitrary messages from the yufo's originating species, and as it approached completion, Tsubishi took another sip of his cappuccino and tipped his head toward the comms officer.

"Hail the yufo, Ms. De Fuca-Williamson."

The comms officer's hands moved over her panels, then she nodded back at Tsubishi.

"This is Captain Reynold J. Tsubishi of the Alliance of Peaceful Planets ship *Colossus II*. In the name of the Alliance and its forty-two member-species, I offer you greetings in the spirit of galactic cooperation and peace." It was canned, that line, but he'd practiced it in the holo in his quarters so that he could sell it fresh every time.

The silence stretched. A soft chime marked an incoming message. A succession of progress bars filled the holotank as it was decoded, demuxed and remuxed. Another, more emphatic chime.

"Do it," Tsubishi said to the comms officer, and First Contact was made anew.

The form that filled the tank was recognizably a head. It was wreathed in writhing tentacles, each tipped with organs that the computer identified with high confidence as sensory—visual, olfactory, temperature.

The tentacles whipped around as the bladder at the thing's throat inflated, then blatted out something in its own language, which made Wobbliese seem mellifluous. The computer translated: "Oh, for god's sake—*role-players*? You've *got* to be kidding me."

Then the message disappeared. A klaxon sounded and the bridge dimmed; flashing red lights filled the bridge.

"Status?" Tsubishi took another calm sip of his cappuccino though his heart was racing. Captains never broke a sweat. It went with the territory.

"The package has gone nonresponsive. Nearby telemetry suggests with high confidence that it has been destroyed. Another has gone offline. Two more. All packages nonresponsive and presumed under attack."

"Bring us to defcon four," Tsubishi said. "Do it."

The A-team assembled on the bridge in a matter of minutes, freshly wrapped in their uniforms, unceremoniously pushing the unprotesting B-team out of their seats just as the ship's computer beamed their preset high-alert snacks and beverages to their workstations. As a courtesy, !Mota was allowed to remain on the bridge, but the rest of the second shift slunk away, looking hurt and demoralized. Tsubishi pursed his lips at their departing backs and felt the burden of command.

"Bring us to within five AU, Lieutenant," he said, nodding at Deng-Gorinski in the navigator's chair. "I want to get a little closer."

At five AU's, they could beam photon torpedoes to within fifteen minutes of the yufo. If it was anything like their own packages, they could outmaneuver it with the torpedo's thrusters at that range.

The lieutenant showed her teeth as she brought the ship

up to speed, battle-ready and champing to blow the intruder out of the sky.

The ping of another incoming message brought the crew's attention back to the comms post. The progress bars went much faster now, the symbology AI now much more confident of its guesses about the intruder's language.

"Now what are you doing? Can't you see I'm already here? Get lost. This is my patch."

"In the name of the APP, I order you to stand down and power down your offensive systems. Anything less will be construed as a declaration of war. You have thirty seconds to comply. This—is one second."

He crumpled his cappuccino cup and tossed it over his shoulder; the ship obliterated it by beaming it into nullspace before it touched the ground. The holotank was counting down, giving the numbers in the preassigned ultimatum voice: female, calm, cold, with an accent that a twentieth-century Briton would have recognized as Thatcher-posh.

"Oh. Really. Now. You want to shoot at each other? I've got a better idea. Let's meet on the surface and duke it out, being to being, for control of the planet. Capture the flag. First one to get a defensible position on the highest peak of this mountain range gets to claim the whole thing for zer respective empire." Tsubishi noted the neuter pronoun with some interest: neuter species were more common than highly dimorphic ones in the galaxy, and they had a reputation for being meaner than the poor he-she species like h. sap saps. Something about having your primary genetic loyalty to your identical clones as opposed to your family group—it created a certain . . . ruthlessness.

"Why should I bargain at all? I could just blow you out of orbit, right here."

The tentacles writhed in a gesture that the computer badged with the caption "smirk, confidence 86%," and Tsubishi pointed a single finger at the ship's gunner, who flexed in her chiton and clicked delicately at the control interface, priming and aiming it. The computer quietly turned a patch of Tsubishi's armrest into a display and flashed a discreet notification about the spike in hormonal aggression volatiles being detected on the bridge. He waved it away. He didn't need a computer to tell him about the battle-stink. He could smell it himself. It smelled good. First contact was good—but *war . . . war* was what the Alliance of Peaceful Planets lived for.

"You can try," the alien said.

"A warning shot, Lieutenant," he said, tipping his head to Deng-Gorinski. "Miss the yufo by, say, half a million klicks."

The click of Deng-Gorinski's talon was the only sound on the bridge, as every crewmember held zer breath, and then the barely detectable haptic *whoom* as a torpedo left its bay and streaked off in glorious 3-D on the holotank, trailed by a psychedelic glitter of labels indicating its approach, operational status, detected countermeasures, and all the glorious, pointless instrumentation data that was merely icing on the cake.

The torpedo closed on the yufo, drawing closer, closer . . . closer. Then—

Blink

"It's gone, sir." Deng-Gorinski's talons clicked, clicked. "Transporter beam. Picked it right out of the sky."

That's impossible. He didn't bother to say it. Of course it was possible: they'd just seen it happen. But transporting a photon torpedo that was underway and emitting its punishing halo of quantum chaff should have required enough energy to melt a star and enough compute-power to calculate the universe. It was the space-naval equivalent of catching a sword-blade between your palms as it was arcing toward your chest.

"Take us back to seventy AU's," he said, admiring the calmness in his own voice. He had a bad feeling, but it didn't pay to let it show. The armrest gave him another discreet notifier, this one about the changing composition of the pheromones on the bridge. Fear stink. "*Now.*"

The ship's klaxon sounded again, louder than he'd ever heard it outside of the Academy war-games. He silenced it with a flick of a finger and peered into the holotank.

"Incoming yufo, sir."

The tank showed it to them. It was sickeningly familiar.

"That's our torpedo," he said.

"Closing fast," Deng-Gorinski said. "Shields up. Estimated impact in twenty-eight seconds."

"Evasive action," Tsubishi said uselessly. They were already in an evasive pattern, the ship automatically responding to the threat, faster than any human reflexes. "Antimissile battery," he snapped. The smaller missiles streaked toward the torpedo.

"Can we make contact with the control interface on the torpedo?"

The comms officer jabbed furiously at the air around his helmet, making hand-jives known only to the most highly trained communications specialists, each one executing a flurry of commands to the comms computer. "No sir," he muttered around the helmet's visor. "I can establish a three-way handshake with it, but it doesn't respond to my authorization tokens. Fallback tokens no good either."

In the holotank, the antimissiles with their labels went streaking toward the missile. It dodged them, shot at them, dodged them. Then, one of them found its mark and the missile detonated, a silent fireball that collapsed in on itself, lensing the gravity around it and bending space.

"All right then," Tsubishi said. "Hail the yufo, Lieutenant."

"That wasn't very friendly," he said. "I get the feeling we got off to a bad start. Shall we start over again?"

"I've already issued you my challenge, Captain. Personal combat, on-world, first one to the top of the highest peak claims the planet, the loser surrenders it. I'll give you the whole system if you want."

"I see. And if I refuse?"

The klaxon's sound was louder than before. In the tank, dozens of photon torpedoes had just blinked into existence, relentlessly plowing through the depths of space, aimed directly at the ship.

Helpfully, the tank tagged them with countdown labels. The ship was not going to make it.

Tsubishi allowed himself three seconds——————and then he cleared his throat.

"We accept your challenge."

The torpedoes vanished, leaving behind their labels. An instant later, the tank helpfully removed the labels, too.

"Sir, with all due respect, you can't beam down to the surface." !Mota was visibly agitated, and writhed uncomfortably under Tsubishi's calm stare.

"I don't recall asking for your opinion, Commander." He plucked at his baggies and wished for the comforting tautness of his ship-wrapped uniform. Such was the price of leadership. "The alien was very clear on this in any event. It's calling the shots."

"Captain, you are being driven by the alien. You need to get inside its decision-loop and start setting the agenda. It's suicide otherwise. You saw how much power—"

"I saw, Commander. It's well and good to talk about getting inside decision-loops, but sometimes you're outgunned and all you've got is your own bravery and instincts. It's not like we can outrun that thing."

"We could back off—"

"We don't know what its transporter beam range is, but it's clearly far in excess of anything we've ever seen. I'm betting that I have a better chance of getting to some kind of resolution on the surface than I do of being able to pull back to warping distance ahead of its ability to turn us into shrapnel."

"Some kind of resolution, sir?"

"Well, yes. We're intelligent species. We can talk. There's probably something we have that they want. And we're pretty sure that there's something they have that we want— their transporter technology, for starters. That decision-loop stuff is applicable to fighting. We already know we can't do that. We need negotiation."

The Wobbly relaxed visibly. "I see, sir."

"What, did you think I was going on a suicide mission?"

"Sir, of course not, but—"

"Besides, I'm curious to see this thing face to face. That yufo's barely big enough to hold my breakfast. Those ugly bastards must be about three millimeters tall—how do they

accomplish the neuronal density to pack a functional intelligence into something that small?"

"Good question, sir," !Mota said. Tsubishi could tell that
he'd won the argument.

"Commander, I'm de-tasking you from the bridge for
now."

"Me, sir? Who will have the conn?"

"Oh, leave it to Varma," he said. The C-string commander
was always complaining that she never got to run the bridge
when important things were happening.

"Varma." The hurt was palpable, even through the thick
Wobbly accent.

"Of course Varma." He gave forth with one of his ironic
head-tilts. "You can't possibly be in charge." He waited for
one beat, leaving !Mota trembling on zer hook. "You're
coming down to the surface with me."

Emotions chased each other across the Wobbly's face.
Pride. Worry. "Sir? Fleet procedure prohibits having two or
more senior officers in a single landing party—"

"Unless the crewmembers in question possess specific talents or capabilities that are likely to be of necessity during
the on-planet mission. Don't quote regs at me, Commander.
I eat regs for breakfast." Another head-tilt. The Wobbly's
exo gave an all-over shudder that Tsubishi recognized as a
wriggle of pure delight. Tsubishi smiled at zer. Command
wasn't so hard, sometimes.

When he was a kay-det, he'd *hated* the transporter drills.
Yes, they were safe, overengineered to a million nines. But at
the end of the day, Tsubishi just didn't like being annihilated
to a quantum level and reassembled at a great distance by a
flaky, incomprehensible entanglement effect. Deep down in
his cells, annihilation equaled *dread*.

Command meant that you had to like transporters. Love
them. So he'd *gotten over* his dread. He'd found a pliant
transporter technician—an older career woman, the backbone of the fleet—and struck up an *arrangement*. For an
entire month, he'd paged her whenever he needed to go anywhere in the Academy, and she'd beamed him there. A dozen

transports a day. Two dozen. The fresher, quarters, classes, the simulators, the mess-hall. Her room, after hours, where she'd met him wearing a slinky film of machine-wrapped gauze and a smile.

A month of that and he'd changed the equation: annihilation equaled *yawn*.

"Status, Commander !Mota?"

The Wobbly's salute ticked off zer forelobe. "Sir, crew ready for transport."

"Landing coordinates?"

"Here," !Mota said, gesturing at the holotank, which transitioned to a view of the planet below them and quickly zoomed to a prairie at the foot of an impressive mountain range that unevenly split the smaller of the planet's two land-masses.

"And our objective?"

!Mota gestured and the holotank skipped forward, super-imposing a glowing field over one of the mountaintops. Tsub-ishi realized that this was another slide presentation. !Mota really loved slide presentations. It was a Wobbly thing.

"Commander !Mota."

"Yes, sir?"

"If that mountaintop is our objective, why aren't we just beaming down onto it?"

!Mota jumped to the next slide, which zoomed to the mountain range with a bluish bubble superimposed over most of it. "No-go zone, sir. Test transports of enzymatically representative samples proved . . . unreliable."

"Unreliable?"

"The enzymes we retrieved had been denatured sir, as with extensive heat."

"They were barbecued, Cap," said Second Lieutenant !Rena, the mission science officer, a Wobbly who had made a hobby out of twen-cen Earth in a brownnosing effort to ascend through the ranks faster than Wobblies usually man-aged. It was an open secret on the *Colossus II* that the two Wobblies loathed each other. Tsubishi approved of this, and approved even more of !Mota's forbearance in selecting !Rena for the landing party.

"I see."

!Mota flicked to the next slide, a 3-D flythrough of a trail up the mountains. "This appears to be the optimal route to the peak, sir. The seven-leagues have a millimeter-accurate picture of the landscape and they're projecting a 195-minute journey time, assuming no trouble en route." Tsubishi rocked back and forth in his seven-league boots, whose harness ran all the way up to his mid-thigh. Running on these things was *fun*—the kind of thing that made serving on away-teams such a treat.

"I assume we can count on trouble, Commander !Mota. I certainly am."

"Yes, sir," !Mota said, clicking forward one slide. "These are alternate routes through the mountains, and in the worst case, the seven-leagues have a bounce-and-ditch they'll deploy to get us onto the face." That sounded like less fun: the boots would discharge their entire power-packs in one bone-jarring bounce on a near-straight vertical that would launch him like a missile into the mountain face, with only a couple of monosilk drogue chutes to slow him before impact.

"How many more slides, Commander?"

"No more," !Mota said. Tsubishi knew ze was lying, and could tell that ze was disappointed. Make it up later. Time to beam down! His palms were sweating, his heart thudding. Outwardly, he was cool.

"Everyone ready?" All six in the party chorused "Aye, sir," in unison. "Do it," he said to the transporter operator. She smiled at him and engaged the system that would annihilate him and reassemble him millions of klicks away on the surface of a virgin planet. He smiled back in the instant before the machine annihilated him. Horniness was a hazard of his transporter conditioning regime at the Academy, but he could deal with it.

The transporter technician deserved a commendation. Not many of the techs on the bridge were thoughtful enough to land a steaming cappuccino on the planet along with Tsubishi. He liked the attention to detail. He made a mental note and had a sip.

"Report, Commander?"

!Mota had zer comm out and had been busily verifying from the surface all the readings they'd got from orbit, establishing multiple redundant links with the ship, querying the health readouts from the gutbots in the landing parties' bodies. "Nominal, Captain."

"Let's have a little reccy before we kick off, shall we? I was expecting company when we landed. Seems like our friend's style."

"Yes, sir," !Mota said. He unclipped an instrument gun from his exo's thigh and fired it straight into the air. A billion dandelion seeds caught the wind and blew in every direction, settling slowly to the ground or lofting higher and higher. The little sensors on them started to measure things as soon as they were out of the muzzle, while the networking subsystems knit them together into a unified ubiquitous surveillance mesh that spread out for ten kilometers in all directions (though it grew patchier around the edges). "Sir, I have no sign of the alien or its artifacts. Nothing on this planet bigger than a bacterium, and the gutbots have already got their genomes solved and phaged. I recommend beginning the mission."

Tsubishi looked around and finished his cappuccino. The terrain was as depicted in the holotank—sere, rocky, stained in coral colors that swirled together like organic oil-slicks. The temperature was a little chilly, but nothing the baggies couldn't cut, and the wind made an eerie sound as it howled through the rugged mountains that towered all around them.

"All right then, form up, two by two, and then go full auto. Keep your eyes peeled and your guard up." He thought for a moment. "Be on the lookout for very small hostiles—possibly as small as a centimeter." The away-team, six crewmembers with robotic feet, baggies, and looks of grim determination, exchanged glances. "I know. But that is one tiny damned yufo, gang."

They smiled. He finished his cappuccino and set the cup down, then put a rock on top of it to keep it from blowing away. He'd pick it up and return to the ship with it.

"On my mark then. Do it."
And they were off.

The seven-leagues took great pains to establish a regular
rhythm, even though it meant capping the max speed at
about 70 percent of what the body mechanics of the crew
could sustain. But the rhythm was necessary if their brains
were going to converge binocular vision—otherwise the
landscape blurred into a nauseous smear. Tsubishi's command-channel, set deep in his cochlea, counted down the
time to the mountaintop.

It was a marvelous way to travel. Your legs took on a life
of their own, moving with precise, quick, tireless steps that
propelled you like a dream of flying. The most savage terrain
became a rolling pasture, and the steady rhythm lent itself
to musical humming, as though you were waltzing with the
planet itself.

At the halfway mark, Tsubishi called a break and they
broke out hot meals and drinks—he switched to decaf, as
three was his limit in any twenty-four-hour period: more just
made him grumpy. They picnicked on a plateau, their seven-
leagues locked and extended into stools. As they ate, Tsubishi and !Mota circulated among the crewmembers, checking
in with them, keeping morale up, checking the medical diagnostics from their gutbots. The landing party were in fine
form, excited to be off the ship and on an adventure, keen to
meet the foe when and if ze chose to appear.

That was the devil of it, Tsubishi and !Mota agreed, privately, over their subvocal command-channel. Where was
the yufo? The ship confirmed that ze hadn't simply transported to the mountain peak, but neither could it locate zer
anywhere on the planet.

"What sort of game is ze playing?" Tsubishi subvocalized,
keeping his face composed in a practiced expression of easy
confidence.

"Captain, permission to speak freely?"

"Of course."

"The yufo's demonstrated capabilities are unseen in

known space. We have no idea what it might be planning. This may be a suicide mission."

"Commander !Mota, I realize that. But as you say, the yufo has prodigious capabilities and ze made it clear that it was this or be blown out of the sky. When all you have is a least-worst option, there's nothing for it but to make the best of it." This was the kind of can-do thinking that defined command in the fleet, and it was the Wobblies' general incapacity to embrace it that kept them from making the A-squads.

!Mota turned away and pitched in on the clean-up effort.

"You took a *lunch break*?" The voice came from the center of their little circle, and there was something deeply disturbing about it. It took Tsubishi a moment to realize what had made his balls crawl up into his abdomen: it was *his* voice. And there was the yufo, speaking in it: "A *lunch break*? When I made it clear that the stakes were the planet and your lives?" It wasn't two centimeters tall. It was more like three meters, a kind of pyramidal mountain of flesh topped with a head the size of a large pumpkin. The medusa-wreath of tentacles fluttered in the wind, twisting and coiling.

Tsubishi's hand was on his blaster, and he noted with satisfaction that the rest of his crew were ready to draw. Via the command-channel, Varma was whispering that the ship was watching, prepared to give support.

Deliberately, he took his hand off his blaster. "Greetings," he said. "You have an amazing facility for language."

"Flattery? Please." The yufo whacked its tail on the rock. "Not interested. And I distinctly said one-on-one. What are these things doing here?" It waved a flipper derisively at the crew, who stood firm.

"I hoped that we could dispense with challenges and move on to some kind of negotiation. A planet isn't nearly as interesting to the Alliance as a new species. Once again, I bid you greetings in the name of—"

"You don't learn fast, do you?" The flipper twitched again and the crew—*vanished*.

Tsubishi drew his blaster. "What have you done with my crew?" But he knew, he knew from the telltale shimmer as they went. They'd been beamed somewhere—into deep space, to the landing spot, back onto the ship. "You have three seconds. Three—"

The yufo twitched again and the blaster vanished too, tingling in his hands as it went. He looked down at his palm and saw that some of the skin had gone with it. It oozed red blood.

The yufo extended a tentacle in his direction and twitched. "Sorry about that. I'm usually more accurate. As to your crew, I annihilated them. I removed their tokens from the play area. You're a game-player, you should be able to grasp this."

"*Game-player*?" Tsubishi's mind reeled.

"What do you think we're doing here, *Captain*?" The last word dripped with perfectly executed sarcasm. The yufo really did have an impressive language module. With creeping hopelessness, Tsubishi realized that ze couldn't possibly have trained it from their meager conversation to date; ze must have been snaffling up titanic amounts of communication from the *Colossus II*'s internal comms. Ze was thoroughly inside his decision-loop. "Competing. Gaming. You're clearly familiar with the idea, Mr. Role-Player."

"Why do you keep calling me that?"

"You're starting to bore me, *Captain*. Look, it's clear you're outmatched here. You've got a lovely little play area up there in orbit, but I'm afraid you're about to forfeit it."

"No!" Tsubishi's veneer of calm control blistered and burst. "There are hundreds of people on that ship! It would be murder!"

The yufo inflated zer throat-bladder and exhaled it a couple times. "Murder?" ze said. "Come now, Captain, let's be not overly dramatic."

This was the first time that the yufo appeared the least bit off-balance. Tsubishi saw a small initiative and seized it. "Murder! Of course it's murder! We are not at war. It would be an act of sheer murder."

"Act of war? Captain, *I'm not playing your game*. I'm playing—" Its tentacles whipped around its head. Tsubishi got the impression that it was fishing for a word. "I compete to put my flag on a pattern of planets. It is a different game from your little space-marines dramatics."

On that plateau, on that remote world near that unregarded star, Captain Reynold J. Tsubishi experienced satori.

"We are not playing a game. We *are* 'space marines.' Space navy, actually. We are not playing soldiers. We *are* soldiers. Those were real people and you've really, really killed them."

The alien's tentacles went slack and twitched against its upper slopes. It inflated and deflated its bladder several times. The wind howled.

"You mean that you haven't got a recent stored copy of them—"

"Stored copy? Of them?"

The tentacles twitched again. Then they went rigid and stood around zer head like a mane. The bladder expanded and the yufo let out a keening moan the like of which Tsubishi had not heard anywhere in the galaxy.

"You don't make *backups*? What is *wrong* with you?"

The yufo vanished. Instantly, Tsubishi tried to raise the *Colossus II* on the command-channel. Either his comm was dead or—or— He choked down a sob of his own.

The yufo returned to him as he sat on the mountainpeak. He hadn't had anywhere else to go, and the seven-leagues had been programmed for it. From his high vantage, he looked down on wispy clouds, distant, lower mountaintops, the sea. He shivered. The command-channel was dead. He had been there for hours, pacing and doing the occassional calisthenics to stay warm. To take his mind off things.

He was the *Captain*. He was supposed to have *initiative*. He was supposed to be *doing something*. But what could he do?

"You don't have backups?"

The yufo stood before him, a hill of tentacled flesh. It was closer than before, and he could smell it now, a nice smell, a little yeasty. It spoke in !Mota's voice now.

"I don't really understand what you mean." He was cold, shivering. Hungry. He wanted a cappuccino.

"You have the transporter. You scan people to a quantum level. Store the scan. Annihilate them. Reassemble them elsewhere. Are you seriously telling me that *it never occurred to you to store the scans*?"

Captain Reynold J. Tsubishi of the APP ship *Colossus II* was thunderstruck. He really, really wanted a cappuccino now. "I can honestly say that it never had." He fumbled for an excuse. "The ethical conundra. What if there were two of me? Um." He thought. "What if —"

"What is *wrong* with you people? So what if there were two of you?" There were two of the yufo now. Tsubishi was no expert in distinguishing individuals of this race, but he had the distinct impression that they were the same entity. Times two. Times three now. Now there were four. They surrounded him, bladders going in and out.

"Annihilation is no big deal."

"Accepting it is a survival instinct."

"You honestly drag that gigantic lump of metal around the galaxy?"

"What is *wrong* with you people?"

Tsubishi needed some initiative here. This was not a negotiation. He needed to make it one.

"You've murdered five of my crew today. You threatened my ship with torpedoes. We came in peace. You made war. It isn't too late to rescue the relations between our civilizations if you are willing to negotiate as equals in the galactic community of equals."

"Negotiate? Fella—sorry, *Captain*, I don't speak for anyone—" Now there was just one yufo and shimmering space where the others had been. The yufo paused for a second. "Give me a second. Integrating the new memories from those forks takes a little doing. Right. Okay. I'm just here on my own behalf. Yes, I fired on your ship—*after* you fired on me."

"Fired on you? You weren't in that artifact. You wouldn't fit in ten of those things. It was an unmanned sensor package."

"You think I bother to travel around in giant hunks of metal?"

"Why not? You've got impressive transporter technology,

but you can't expect me to believe that you can beam matter over interstellar distances—"

"Of course not. That's what subspace *radio* is for. I upload the latest me to the transporter on the sensor package and then beam as many of myself as I need to the planet's surface. What kind of idiot would actually put zer body in a giant hollow vehicle and ship it around space? The resource requirements are insane. You don't really, *really* do that, do you?"

Tsubishi covered his face with his hands and groaned. "You're telling me that you're just an individual, not representing any government, and that you conquer planets all on your own, using subspace radio and transporter beams?"

"Yes indeed."

"But *why*?"

"I *told* you—I compete to put my flag on a pattern of planets. My friends compete to do the same. The winner is the one who surrounds the largest number of zer opponents' territory. It's fun. Why do you put on costumes and ship your asses around the galaxy?"

The yufo had a remarkable command of Standard. "You've got excellent symbology AI," he said. "Perhaps our civilizations could transfer some technology to one another? Establish trade?" There had to be some way to interest the yufo in keeping Tsubishi around, in letting him back on his ship. The planet was cold and he was hungry. He wanted a cappuccino.

The yufo shrugged elaborately. "It's remarkable what you can accomplish when you don't squander your species resources playing soldier. Sorry, *navy*. Why would we bother with *trade*? What could possibly be worth posting around interstellar distances, as opposed to just beaming submolecular-perfect copies of goods into wherever they're in demand? You people are deeply perverse. And to think that you talked *forty-two* other species into playing along? What a farce!"

Tsubishi tried for words, but they wouldn't come. He found that he was chewing an invisible mouthful of speech, working his jaw silently.

"You've really had a bad day, huh? Right. Okay. Here's what I'll do for you."

There was a cappuccino sitting next to him. He picked it up and sipped reverently at it. It was perfect. It was identical to the one that had been beamed down to him when he arrived on-planet. That meant that the yufo had been sniffing all the transporter beam activity since they arrived. And that meant—

"You can restore the landing party!"

"Oh yes, indeed, I can do that."

"And you don't trade for technology, but you might be persuaded to give me—I mean, the Alliance—access to some of this?"

"Certainly."

"And will you?"

"If you think you want it."

Tsubishi nearly fell over himself thanking the yufo. He was mid-sentence when he found himself back on the transporter deck, along with his entire away-team party.

First things first. Tsubishi headed straight for the fresher, to get out of his baggies and back into uniform. He held his arms over his head and muttered, "Do it," to the computer, received the crackle-starched uniform and lowered his arms, once again suited and booted, every millimeter an officer of the APP Space Navy.

And it felt *wrong*. He didn't feel like he was wearing a uniform at all. He was wearing a *costume*. He knew that now. He had the computer signal his officers to meet him in the executive boardroom, whose long table pulsed with realtime strategic maps of the known galaxy, and as he slid into his seat, he recognized it finally and for the first time for what it really was: a game-board.

"Report, Commander !Mota," he said. Of course !Mota would have a slideshow whipped up by now. He had a whole executive staff dedicated to preparing them on a moment's notice. The slideshow would give him time to gather himself, to recover some of the dignity of his office.

But !Mota just looked at him blankly from within zer exoskeleton, zer big Wobbly eyes unreadable. Tsubishi peered more closely.

"Commander !Mota, are you out of uniform?"

!Mota plucked at zer baggies with a tentacle-tip. "I suppose I am, Reynold."

Tsubishi knew the first signs of mutiny. He'd gotten top marks in Command Psych at the Academy. He looked into the faces of his officers, tried to gauge the support there.

"Commander, you are relieved. Return to your quarters and await my orders."

The Wobbly looked impassively at him. The silence stretched. The other officers looked at him with equal coolness. It wasn't just his command he felt slipping away—it was the *idea* of command itself. The fragility of the traditions, of the discipline, of the great work that bound them all together. It wavered. Panic seized him, tightened his chest, a feeling he hadn't known since those days at the Academy when he was breaking himself of the fear of transporters.

"Please?" he said. It came out in a squeak.

!Mota gave him a lazy salute. "All right, *Captain*. I'll play another round of the game. For now. But it won't do you any good."

Ze moved to the hatch. It irised open. Behind it, a dozen more !Motas. !Mota joined them and turned around and gave him and the rest of the officers another sarcastic salute.

"You all enjoy yourselves now," ze said, and they turned as a body and walked away.

Tsubishi's hand was resting on something. A cappuccino. He lifted it to his lips and had a little sip, but he burned his lip and it spilled down the front of his nice starched uniform.

Costume.

He set it back down and began, very quietly, to cry.

THE LOST PRINCESS MAN

JOHN BARNES

John Barnes is one of the most prolific and popular of all the writers who entered SF in the 1980s. His many books include the novels *A Million Open Doors, The Mother of Storms, Orbital Resonance, Kaleidoscope Century, Candle, Earth Made of Glass, The Merchant of Souls, Sin of Origin, One for the Morning Glory, The Sky So Big and Black, The Duke of Uranium, A Princess of the Aerie, In the Hall of the Martian King, Gaudeamus, Finity, Patton's Spaceship, Washington's Dirigible, Caesar's Bicycle, The Man Who Pulled Down the Sky*, and others, as well as two novels written with astronaut Buzz Aldrin, *The Return* and *Encounter with Tiber*. Long a mainstay of *Analog*, and now a regular at *Jim Baen's Universe*, his short work has been collected in . . . *And Orion* and *Apostrophes and Apocalypses*. His most recent book is the novel *The Armies of Memory*. Barnes lives in Colorado and works in the field of semiotics.

Here he takes us to a grim future dominated by super-powered aristocrats, where death is the penalty for disobedience or even a slip of the tongue, and you'd better walk the tightrope very carefully indeed if you want to stay alive—*especially* if you're a con man working on a job.

What are the people like in the Krevpiceaux country?"
An aristocrat stood over Aurigar's table.

Careful not to spill the carafe of wine or knock the remains of his noodles-and-mussels to the floor, Aurigar staggered up from his chair and bowed. "Lord Leader Sir?"

"You heard the question the first time."

The lord bulged with stimumuscle. His face had been fashionably planed-and-pitched and geneted gun-steel blue; it looked like the entrance to the villain's fortress in a dwell-game.

He will be extremely fast, too, they optimize the nervous system at the same time they grow stimumuscle, and he's legal to carry any weapon and I don't even have resident alien carry permit and Oh! Samwal defend me, I can't run, I can't fight, probably he's even smarter than I am, Aurigar thought.

"I have never been to the Creffenho country, Lord Leader Sir," Aurigar said, "but it is said that—"

"You're telling the truth." Lenses and mirrors flickered in Lord Leader Sir's eye socket, briefly spoiling the illusion of an empty black pit. "But it is disturbing that you are pretending to have misheard the question." The lord extended his hand, palm up, and his fingers flowed forward, splitting into myriad filaments. Through Aurigar's shirt, they stung like jellyfish tentacles and gripped like screws. They moved Aurigar's skin out of the way, then his flesh, flowed around his ribs, and stopped his heart.

Terror restarted his heart; the neural connection from the aristocrat's fingers stopped it again, restarted it, and then made it flutter, before restoring a steady, deep beat.

"When I pull my fingers back out," the blue-faced man asked, eye sockets glittering and whirling silver and glass, "shall I leave you with your heart operating, or not operating?" He raced Aurigar's heart into painful thunder, then slowed it to the low throb of deep meditation. "I will choose *not* operating if you do not make a choice. Operating, or not operating?"

"Operating, if it pleases you, Lord Leader Sir."

"Oh, *whatever* I do will please *me*. Never fear that." The

filaments slid back and out, resolving into fingers just above
Aurigar's chest; the fingers reacquired nails and ridges, and
presently looked like anyone else's. No blood leaked, but
Aurigar's chest tingled where nerves did not quite like how
they had been re-meshed. "Thank you, I *will* have a seat, and
from here on we'll drink on my tab." Gesturing to Aurigar
to resume his seat, the stimumuscled lord sat in the folding chair opposite like a mountain poised upon a dandelion.
"What are the people like in the Krevpiceaux country?"

"Well, Lord Leader Sir, I'd have to say . . . well, stolid.
Quiet, hard-working, eat-what's-in-front-of-you types. You'll
never hear any of them saying that any work is degrading.
Tell'em to shovel shit with a manual shovel, or even their
hands—they do it, and no complaints."

"Stupid, do you think?"

Before Aurigar could answer, the carafes of better wine arrived, and the blue man poured a generous glass and pushed
it across the table to him. "I don't care if you get drunk, but
stay honest. Would you like some appetizers for the table?
I know a man who lives your sort of life often finds great
pleasure in eating until he is ill."

"Yes, Lord Leader Sir." A lifetime of not being sure when
there would be more again had trained Aurigar never to turn
down any good thing, even in a surprisingly pleasant nightmare.

When the lord had tasted his wine and Aurigar had finished a glass—and with the promise of a great heap of food
on the way—the blue-faced man leaned forward and smiled
quite pleasantly. "Now, I already know that you are, by profession, a lost princess man, and that at the moment you
are celebrating a successful season. Your bank account in
Nue Swuisshe is number AFBX-1453-1962-3554-7889. You
booked passage under the name Bifred Prohelo on the *Tam-
bourlaine* tomorrow, stateroom sixteen. I know how Baldor
the Nose met his well-deserved end and why your alibi held
up—excellent job, by the way. You are allergic to asparagus,
the dog you had as a boy was named Magrat, and you are
susceptible to sore feet. Will you accept that it is impossible
to lie to me?"

"Yes, Lord Leader Sir."

"Good answer."

The naneurs in the wine were adjusting Aurigar's taste and smell to appreciate it; it was the wine most exactly to his taste he'd ever had. He tried an experiment—he thought *Rats are bigger than whales*—and instantly the wine tasted like vinegar, his stomach rolled over, and his head hurt. He thought *I will tell my lord anything he wants*; the wine tasted of sunshine on a meadow just after a cool rain.

"Now," the aristocrat said. "Back to the question. Would you say the Krevpiceauxi are stupid?"

"They are pigheadedly proud to be ignorant of anything they find in books, but *not* stupid. They value shrewdness, deception, facing facts, and even verbal quickness, as long as it serves some larger purpose like making a sale or evading police questioning. In fact, they are smart in a way that makes my con easier to work."

"Interesting. Have more wine—oh, and here are the appetizers—and do go on, taking a bit of time between to chew and savor, eh? What you just said interests me very much."

Like anyone whose fortunes have suddenly, inexplicably, improved, Aurigar was becoming more comfortable. For just a moment, after the first delightful fish roll, he thought, *I can tell him that*—and his tongue tasted as if he had been chewing brass. He reminded himself that truth was good and took a sip of excruciatingly delicious wine. "Well, then, Lord Leader Sir, very few people know this about the lost princess business: the girl knows the truth and comes along willingly with the connivance of her family."

"*Really?* I had not heard that."

"Well, you know, Lord Leader Sir, lost princesses are all the rage in dwellgames. Everyone has played a dozen dwellgames in which the smooth talking stranger—that would be me—"

The lord smiled warmly. "You amuse me. My sources say you are very good at it."

"Yes, I suppose I am good at it. I have stayed away from brilliance, which is hazardous."

"And that in itself is brilliant in its own way. So, then,

you—the smooth talker—show up in some remote location where there is an unhappy beautiful girl—"

"Rarely beautiful. Genetion is cheap, and a necessity anyway to put off the insurance-company detectives. The 'lost princess' can be, honestly, plain-faced, with a body that looks like it was piled up at random, and an absolutely lunar complexion. My clients will genete her until she looks better than most real princesses, begging the Lord Leader Sir's pardon if he is related to any."

"Pardon readily granted." The lord knocked back half a glass at a gulp, with a visible shudder. "I am related to thousands of them. So you wander among these stolid farm-folk, and you find some girl to convince that she is a lost princess—usually *the* lost princess?"

"Another myth, Lord Leader Sir. I never tell anyone that she is the Princess Ululara, because she has certainly been warned about strangers who tell her that story. Indeed, I dismiss any such idea; I say, 'Look, sweetie, there's about a billion settled planets under the Imperium, the Emperor's family had *one* baby disappear, so out of maybe four quadrillion humans in the galaxy, *you're* the princess?' Besides, usually their age on their fostindenture papers is wrong for Ululara. I show them that. I say, 'Forget it. If somebody really did snatch Princess Ululara just before the bomb went off, they dropped her down the stairs and killed her, or drowned her in the bathtub, the first day. Then they tossed the little thing into the nearest instant composter and she was potting-soil five minutes later. More likely, it's all just a phantom of the security system and she vaporized with everyone else in the palace. Either way, she's been dead twenty-nine marqs— and you are not she.' Actually, usually I say 'you ain't her,' to fit in better."

"And how do the girls respond to that?"

"They're disappointed—they were harboring the hope, as most unhappy fostindented girls of that generation do. Then I say, 'You seem upset. Perhaps you were hoping that you weren't just another fostindent. You want to know why you don't get along with your family, they don't understand you and worry about ridiculous things—oh, I can see that you're not really one of *them*, it's obvious.' They are, of course, astonished at how well I know them." He flapped a hand to dismiss a lifetime of hard-earned skill. "And so forth, you know. Eventually, I reveal that I am searching for quite a different princess, of a quite minor house, though perfectly verifiable."

"Verifiable?"

"Well, for example, this year I told two girls of sixteen marqs that they might be Princess Pegasa Whon, who would be sixteen, and was kidnapped at about the right date. It's a big galaxy. In four quadrillion people, there are about one hundred million princesses, and, oddly enough, perhaps ten thousand lost ones. At a rough approximation, that's a hundred lost princesses of any particular age, though I don't do much business above forty marqs. One little data search to match age and physical type, and you're in business. Or I am, begging Lord Leader Sir's pardon."

"I do enjoy pardoning you," the lord said. He took a sip and held it in his mouth before swallowing; you were supposed to do that to train the naneurs, Aurigar remembered, and did it himself. The extraordinary wine hastened to surpass itself. The lord asked, "But you say most of them go willingly and knowingly?"

"Well, yes. Only about half the money comes from brothel-owners; the rest is the kickbacks I get in insurance fraud collected by the family. Anyone who buys a fostindent takes out kidnap insurance, and it pays the whole estimated value over the forty-marq indenture and then some. So not only is the girl getting herself a better life, but the family gets a big shot of insurance money, just after one of my false-front companies purchases their outstanding debt at a very deep discount. Then they pay that debt back, to me, at full value. Everyone wins—me, the girl, the family, the family's creditors, the brothel-owners—well, everyone except the insurance companies."

"Given the appeal of the idea, I don't see why these things are not more widely known."

"Honestly, it is in the interests of lost princess men to maintain the horror stories, Lord Leader Sir. It needs to look like a real kidnapping or the insurance company will not pay. Thus, I need to tell the girl a plausible story and make sure she repeats it to several trustworthy blabbermouths—I even coach them to tell it well." He put on a falsetto that he thought was much more girlish than it really was. "'We told her he was a con man and that the lost princess was the oldest con in the book, but she had stars in her eyes, poor thing.' Add a bit of the theatrical to the actual departure— perhaps the girl screaming and her sponsor-parents taking a few wild shots in my direction—and it looks much less like fraud to the detectives."

"And the Krevpiceauxi, who are cunning but not intellectual, are good for this con . . . because?"

"They're blunt, not easily fooled, and hate authority. After listening for a while, the girl says, 'I think you are working the lost princess con, and the minute you have me off planet, you will pump me full of drugs, and I will wake up chained to a bed with a large number of Imperial troops lined up and waiting to have a turn on me.' At which point, I say, 'Well, of course.'"

"You *admit* it?"

"Absolutely, Lord Leader Sir. I then explain that it is better for me if she comes along willingly—fewer clues for the insurance detectives—and that her first stop will be a luxury hospital where she will be geneted into stunning beauty, and tweaked to make her depression-proof, nymphomaniacal, multiorgasmic, and extremely self-confident. Good conversation is highly prized as well, and many men have fetishes for talents like singing or drawing, so the girls also get a year or two developing their most developable talents and receiving a good broad education. The worst is only that during the marq or so it takes to heal into her new form, she will itch a great deal, since her old flesh feels like scar tissue being sloughed off as the new grows in.

"As for Imperial troops, she will encounter them one at a time if at all—and if she's lucky. They are themselves heavily geneted, well educated, highly paid specialists, like herself, and more likely to hire her to come along as a companion on a five-solar-system exotic tour than as fun for a night.

"Besides, under the sumptuary laws, she will be a luxury good. She can't legally be sold to poor or even middle class people unless she is so badly behaved that her owners do so as punishment. As for being owned, we are all theoretically owned by His Supreme Might—"

"His Late Supreme Might," the lord said. "Or had you not heard?"

"I'm a very focused professional; I dwell the crime, investment, and lifestyle instrucks, but not politics, sports, or entertainment." Aurigar hoped that he sounded dignified, but since wayward sauce had spotted his shirt, probably not.

The aristocrat nodded. "Well, then. I am High Supreme Lord Cetuso, which you may know is a junior branch of the Imperial House itself—no, get up, protocol would call for you to get onto the floor entirely facedown, and in this place that would make an utter mess of you, much worse than that little blob on your shirt you keep daubing at. Would you happen to know, since you are concerned with high-ranking lineages, just what the hereditary function of the Cetusos is?"

Aurigar realized. "Samwal defend us!"

"He may have to. Yes. We are the authenticators of the Imperial line. It is well known that the late Emperor was quite mad and could not be geneted into anything that should be allowed to breed, so he died without issue. The Galactic Imperium should now pass to his sister, the lost princess Ululara. If she is alive, we must find her and restore her. If she is dead, there are other, more distant, heirs. But if she is neither proved dead nor found alive . . . well, the fourth Civil War, a thousand years ago, left us with ten thousand vitrified worlds and more than a hundred exploded suns."

"And you think that one of my lost princesses—"

"Seven marqs ago. We have her trail right up to where she talked to you. The insurance-company detectives—a strikingly incompetent lot, by the way—"

"They ought to be incompetent. I pay them enough." Aurigar drained his glass. "Then here's to the new Empress. The only Krevpiceauxi—that's why you asked about that benighted continent on that armpit of a planet, yes?—well, the

Krevpiceauxi of exactly that age would be Miriette Phod-way. I am pleased to inform you, Lord Leader Cetuso Sir, that I can take you straight to her. I think you will get along very well with her."

"Is she—forgive the question—at all mad?"

"Not at all insane, Lord Leader Cetuso Sir. And since she did so well and I did not deceive her in any way, not furious either—in fact she's risen far from that start; nowadays she's one of my best customers, buying a girl or two every marq from me."

"Then you will introduce me. Afterward, I will of course cover the cost of your unused ticket and then put you on a much better liner to wherever you wish to go, with ten lost princesses worth of profit added to your kick—at a mini-mum, more if I need you longer. Is she far off?"

"At Waystonn, and in two days, there's a liner depart-ing—"

"A *liner*? If you can bear to let us pack this food and wine to go, you can resume drinking and dining on my yacht in about twenty minutes, and we can be on our way. Unless you have some matter to settle?"

"I had, but let him live, Lord Leader Sir. Good fortune should be shared."

Aurigar could not think of Miriette as Ululara, though he supposed eventually he would have to. "Right this way," she said, taking his arm, and beckoning Lord Leader Cetuso Sir to follow them. "Where'd you hire the geneted goon?"

"Actually, I work for the Lord Leader," Aurigar said. A glance back told him that Cetuso was mercifully amused at being called a geneted goon—or, considering who had said it, perhaps obsequiously amused.

Waystonn was about the hundredth busiest port in the Galactic Empire—but since there were just over forty-one billion, one hundred nineteen million ports, that was hardly a small distinction. It occupied the entire surface of a con-veniently far-out moon of a conveniently close-in gas giant around a conveniently small star, and the only other occupied orbit of the star, below the gas giant, held a stable Lagrange hex of superheavies. Thus for the port of Waystonn, near the galactic center and with several arm-to-arm trajectories running through it, the total escape velocity was low and the slingshot effect tremendous, so that getting out to jump distance was easy and cheap. Waystonn also had a dense inert-organics atmosphere with a high Reynolds number and a large scale height, and thus aerobraking to the surface was cheap.

Whatever all that meant. Cetuso had assigned him to know it, but had never asked him to repeat it.

Anyway, all that really mattered was that the lost Ululara had progressed from being a hayakawite miner's indentured fosterling to being one of the hundred most important procurers in the Galactic Empire in less than eight marqs.

The Empress-to-be beamed at him like a favorite uncle. "Well, so, you now have an employer, and therefore this must be about his business rather than yours. So . . . ?"

Telling the truth was beginning to come naturally. "Well," he said. "This is Lord Leader Cetuso Sir, keeper of the Imperial bloodline, and it seems I made a mistake when I talked to you."

Cetuso launched into the story. She listened intently through the whole thing and then burst into great, glad, uproarious laughter. "Wow, wow, wow, Aurigar. We have *both* really moved up in the world. So now instead of purported kidnappings of farmers' daughters, you've moved up to capturing successful businesswomen, and you're doing so well that you can afford a geneted actor to make your story plausible. Well, then, let's have a tissue sample from each of you," she said, "and since it will take four hours to run a high-end search, in memory of how much good you did me, Aurigar, and of how much you have both made me laugh, I shall send you up to private rooms where you will each have, so to speak, one on the house."

In Miriette's office, Aurigar sat quietly, occasionally dozing and exhausted, reverently converting the last two hours into perpetual happy memory. Cetuso entered, moving as ever like a dancer half his age and a third of his size, and slipped into the larger chair, appropriating the hassock. A serving robot glided in and set out two glasses for the men. Silently, they toasted and drank.

After a long and equally reverent silence from Cetuso, and a second glass served and begun, Aurigar ventured, "It probably reflects my lack of sophistication, but this was without question the best time I've ever had in a house."

"Whether or not you lack sophistication," the Lord Leader Sir responded, "your experience in no way reflects that, because this was also *my* favorite experience of all time, which is to say, given my resources, appetites, and time devoted to exploration, it might be the finest available anywhere, ever."

Miriette looked into the office. "Well," she said. "That was a very interesting investigation. I trust the accommodations were suitable, Aurigar?"

"Very."

"And Lord Leader Cetuso Sir," she said, dropping a very impressive curtsy. "Also satisfactory?"

"Beyond words," he said, rising to his feet and bowing very low. "Then I take it you have confirmed my identity."

"Oh, yes," she said. "And I am more impressed with Aurigar than ever. To make whatever con he is running plausible, he has actually corrupted a very highly placed public official. I know I want into this deal now, whatever it is, but of course you'll have to tell me what you are actually up to, and cut me in as a partner. Whatever is behind all this must be simply astonishing. I know you'll have to confer with whoever your hidden partners are, but as soon as you can tell me what's really going on, come right back, and we'll see what sort of deal we can do." Her eyes sparkled and she kissed Aurigar on both cheeks. "And Aurigar, even if your partners won't let you tell me, don't be a stranger anyway. You have no idea how much you impress me."

"Really, it's almost to be expected," Lord Leader Cetuso said. "*All* Imperials get extensive genetion. Heirs and near-heirs get even more, beginning right at the embryo stage. Even our late, mad Emperor was a polymathic genius; the madness was due to a botched assassination attempt by his mother, and some unfortunate abuse at the hands of his older brother of equally revered memory. So, naturally, Ululara, or Miriette, is beautiful, competent, cold-blooded, pragmatic, charismatic, all the things she needs to be. She was literally born to rule the galaxy. Climbing up from high-end prostitute to mistress of a hundred brothels in a few short years might have been a challenge for other people, but it was well within her capabilities." He told the robot, "Standard setup for Aurigar."

"I'm not hungry, Lord Leader Sir."

"Have something to eat anyway. It always reduces your worrying and mellows your mood, and that helps you to be the splendid companion you usually are. And it's your clear, calm thought I need now."

The robot brought the platter, and Aurigar munched, forlornly at first, but then resolutely, as if it might be taken away from him, and finally with that certain calm decision that generally preceded his best ideas. He looked up to see Cetuso smiling, and thought he detected a twinkle in one of the mirrors of his eye sockets.

"I do hate being predictable," Aurigar said.

"We all do, but it's part of what makes us useful." Cetuso smiled at him. Aurigar felt cold fear that the Lord Leader Sir might be genuinely fond of him. "Now, if you need to eat all of that and then nap," Cetuso said, "you have plenty of time; considering the distances and numbers involved, we probably have the better part of a marq to get the Empress onto the throne, and loyal client members of my family will make sure no one does anything rash. So rest, eat, and think of what we should do next."

A thought bothered Aurigar, but refused to come to the surface, so he spoke without it. "Just supposing we *do* find a way to persuade her that she is who she actually is, and assuming she wants the job, is there going to be a problem with any of a billion worlds or so realizing that they are being ruled from afar by—pardon the expression, but a former—"

Cetuso laughed. "Oh, there will be a predictable number of uprisings. So long as it's just a planet by itself, the Imperial forces will do the usual—the multiple decimation for which they are famous."

Aurigar shuddered. "I heard stories about that, growing up."

"Notice the durability of the effect. The last time your homeworld rebelled, and had to be set straight, was more than eight thousand marqs ago. There is something about the 'ten tenths' concept that stays in the mind."

Aurigar remembered a vast stone desert stretching out before him, some time before his father left, because he remembered he was holding Magrat's collar and listening to his father explain: "It's simple, Aurie, they 'delete ten tenths,' as they call it. One-tenth of all those of noble blood. One-tenth of all commoners. One-tenth of all slaves. One of the ten largest cities. Ten of the hundred largest cities. One hundred of the thousand largest cities. One-tenth of all livestock. One-tenth of all growing crops. One-tenth of all the forests. All the soil down to rock from one-tenth of the habitable surface. You see, everyone knows the formula, and everyone knows not to rebel, or not to let rebels get control of the planet. And the Emperor is always merciful; overlaps count. By slicing off the piece in front of us, he met not just the soil requirement, but half a dozen of the others as well. Nearly all the cities needed to make up the quota were located there, for example."

Aurigar remembered how much he had hated his father, how sad he had always felt when looking at the decimated parts of worlds from spaceship windows, and how pathetic it seemed to him that he had never once had to coerce or trick a girl into the lost princess routine; every one of them had come willingly, because it was so much better than what she had.

He forced his attention back to the present, but couldn't help asking, "But why does the Emperor care?"

"Empress, as soon as we can make it clear to her that that's what she is."

"I meant in general, Lord Leader Sir," Aurigar said, skirting the edge of the great lord's dislike for lectures not delivered by himself, "but all right, why does the *Empress* care if she has a planet fewer, here and there, out of a billion? She could just seal them off for a while, just a loose blockade to raise prices, and then wait for trade pressure and apathy to bring them back into line."

To Aurigar's surprise, Cetuso sat back, rubbed his bare blue scalp thoughtfully, and said, "Why does anyone do anything, dear fellow? We have the technology to make every one of four quadrillion human beings as rich and comfortable as that person could reasonably consume, and to sustain that forever; between dwell, jump, and nano, there's no reason why anyone would ever need to leave home except for fun, and no reason why there needs to be a charge on anything. So why do you suppose we have people in dreadful and dangerous jobs such as mining, ranching, and prostitution? Why don't we just synthesize materials from lifeless planets, jump it to where the people are, grow perfect food in tanks for everyone, and indulge everyone's sensual whims eternally in dwellspace? We could do that, you know, for everyone, and still have plenty left over for the people who wanted to travel or go camping or whatever."

Aurigar stared at him. "I've never thought of that. I just thought there were a lot of shitty jobs someone had to do. Do you have an answer?"

"Of course, dear fellow. We aristocrats are born with all the answers, you know, it's just a matter of getting them loaded into our heads. And the answer is: there's only one real pleasure; everything else is just satisfactions of urges. And the one real pleasure is getting one's way over and against resistance. The only thing human beings really enjoy is making *other* people do what they don't want to. Simple as that. Why do you think there are waiters, shop clerks, and prostitutes? In this age—and for the past thirty kilomarqs at least—everything they actually do or provide could be done better and cheaper by nano or dwell, and everyone could have as much of that as they want. We *need* poor people, and other gender and biological and spiritual underclasses, so that there will be people who—ideally hating it, or submissively fawning over it—must do what rich people tell them, because otherwise there's no point to being *rich*. That's all. Simple, isn't it, dear fellow—now that you're about to be rich?"

Ninety-four, Aurigar thought, counting the number of times Cetuso called him "dear fellow." He wasn't sure yet why he was counting; he had only started to count them in the last day or so, but now his mind always watched that little register, the "dear fellow" count. *And why am I able to keep it so accurately? For that matter,* he thought, *I knew so much about Waystonn that I would never need to know, and Cetuso prefers my advice to all others, even though I'm just a tenth-rate con man and procurer. And now my father, who was barely there when I was a child, surfaces in a critical memory—*

Aurigar realized. There was no better word—it was the first and only realization of his life.

"Well," he said. "I know how to make this work." He was unsurprised to recall that Geepo owed him a large favor. "I know a man I can get, the best in the Empire in multimapping dwellfaces."

"Why would you know such a person and what would we want with him?"

"Geepo is profoundly useful in salvage operations. Every so often, genetion goes wrong, or a girl decides to balk or try to escape, or for some reason her buyer simply cannot sell her physically, so we put her into dwell, and interface her into a simulation that generates decisions and behavior for some *other* simulation that *is* salable. A girl may dwell the life of a beautiful princess madly in love with a gallant knight, and behave accordingly in dwell, while dozens or hundreds of men assume the role of the traveling salesman— she experiences them as the knight, they experience her as the bored housewife. Not as good as real, but salable in the cheap markets."

"And this Geepo is good at dwellfaces?"

"The very best in the human trades. The three times I've used him, he has been phenomenally expensive, and utterly worth it. He is difficult to work with, like every real artist, but certainly fond of money—"

"Like every real artist. I believe I see your point."

Miriette beamed. "Three of you this time." She smiled particularly at Geepo. "Do you prefer to explain the actual deal yourself, or are you one of those that always wants the lackeys to do the talking?"

"Er, actually," Geepo said, rubbing his upper lip in a way that made Aurigar think of rabbits, "I'm a lackey here myself."

"Oh," she said, fixing him with the "you are fascinating" stare. "We'll *have* to talk. Now, Aurigar, are you going to tell me what all this is about?"

"Well," he said, "I have convinced my principals that you could not be easily tricked into a dwelltank."

"From which I would never emerge?"

"Exactly."

She nodded. "Then let me tell you what I guessed. Your principals, who are probably the owners of a certain very large chain of brothels based in the 11/6 arm of the galaxy—"

"I have not named them," Aurigar said.

"Nor have I. At any rate, these principals of yours estimated that my managerial and business skills were considerably in excess of theirs, true?"

"Actually they believe that left to yourself you would have a galactic monopoly within nineteen marqs."

"I was planning for eleven," she said.

"There is little doubt you know better than they," Cetuso put in.

"There is *no* doubt, Lord Leader Sir. Now, if they could get me to run their enterprise, that monopoly could be theirs, and soon. So you would have taken me to your palace in Jinkhangy, Lord Leader Sir, where all preparation would be under way for my 'coronation.' I would have gone into dwell for an 'extensive briefing' or 'protocol training' or whatever, and never have awakened in reality—but in dwell I would have gone through the coronation, appointed my cabinet, begun the process of ruling the galaxy. Back in reality, I would have been running all the brothels in the galaxy, through a multimapping interface."

"You have discerned the entire thing," Cetuso said gravely. "I hope you are not offended. You must admit it was rather a good scheme."

"It was," she admitted. "And their commitment to it is demonstrated by the sheer enormity of the bribe they must have offered you to take part. Tell me, Aurigar, how many of your other lost princesses are now 'ruling the galaxy' while actually doing accounts receivables for a discount clothing chain?"

Aurigar shrugged, inwardly pleased that he had anticipated the question. "Being able to fake being a great lay is very common," he said. "First-rate administrative talent is much rarer, and most businesses are not large or complex enough to need it. You are rather in the nature of a unique case."

"Of course I am; I should have realized. All right, then, let me propose an alternative. Your principals will hire me to run their entire operation for them, via dwell. For one-fifth of every day, time to be set by me, I will unhook, run my own operation, and do just as I please. My operation will not be absorbed into theirs. I expect generous compensation and a sizable piece of the overall operation. I will take a long list of precautions to make sure that I return from my first dwell, and I will be fully empowered while in dwellspace, so that I can arrange matters such that you will never dare to think of trying to hold me in dwellspace. Does that sound fair?"

"I was carefully instructed," Aurigar said, "not to argue about any issues regarding safeguards, or the definitions of words such as 'generous' or 'sizable.' Our principals are aware of the great need to rebuild the trust that they admittedly squandered. I think you may consider that we have a deal."

"Aurigar, my only remaining question is, why an honest pimp, con man, fraud, and kidnapper like yourself would get involved in something as nasty as large-scale corporate activity?"

"The money was good."

"Oh, but if *that's* your excuse, what will be next? Politics? Well, suit yourself, but I hate to see your talent squandered so squalidly."

"Can you see what she has been doing in there?" Cetuso asked, for the fifth time.

Geepo shrugged, pulled his visor down, and spread his sensegloved fingers into the plextank before him. His fingers danced and wriggled over myriad pseudosurfaces. "Lord Leader Cetuso Sir, she has been through all the business records, penetrated all the locked files, and outcopied everything. She has also set up a remarkably complex and probably unanalyzable system of bombs, traps, alarms, triggers, and poisons so no one can ever hold her in dwellspace against her will."

"Of course," Cetuso said, "you are keeping track of those and can enable us to keep her inside—"

"That is *not* what was agreed to! It would be *extremely* unethical. Even the beginnings of an attempt would make detection certain by a person of ordinary skill, and the princess is building the cleverest protection I've ever seen. We are dealing with no mean or small mind here, Lord Leader Cetuso Sir, and I should be terrified to try to step in contrary to her wishes."

Cetuso's tone was dark and the silver flashes in his eye sockets were ominous. "So there is no way to control her—all we can do is try to stay on her good side?"

Remembering that the lord was three times Geepo's weight in superfast, superstrong muscle—and could not be prosecuted for killing a commoner—Geepo could barely nod.

Cetuso sighed. "Well, Aurigar, from what you know of madams, would *you* want one running the galaxy?"

"Well, yes and no, Lord Leader Sir. No, in that most of them are cruel and petty. Yes, in that they tend to be decisive, knowledgeable about human nature, and focused on the main chance."

"And from what I know of princesses, they have generally been pressured into some semblance of grace and largeness of spirit, but they are obsessed with improving people, prone to vacillating, and disdainful of the most practical and effective way of doing anything. Probably we are about to acquire an Empress with the personal ethics of a pimp and the broad vision of a spoiled aristocrat, about like any other political leadership of the last few kilomarqs. Hard on ordinary people I suppose, but what isn't? And we have no reason to care about them. Time to pursue preferment, eh, dear fellow?"

Four hundred thirty-two, and now it will turn out I already have preferment.

"Already taken care of," Geepo said. "I cast each of us, in the princess's dwellspace, as particularly proficient branch managers, with dwellspace abilities mapped to our real talents on the outside. Your diplomatic ability, Lord Leader Cetuso Sir, for example, maps to a gift for motivating exotic women and attracting discerning customers—"

"You mean I've been cast as a particularly classy pimp for jaded, kinky aristocrats?"

"Exactly, Lord Leader Sir. I would say you are certain to gain a post in the Inner Cabinet. Of course, interacting with you through her interface and yours, she will think you are that pimp, but when she communicates with you, her avatar on the screen will call you by your right name and cabinet rank. After a while, you will barely notice that anything is different."

"This mapping, between pimp and cabinet post—was it easy?"

"Exceedingly so, Lord Leader Sir."

"I guessed as much." The mirrors in his dark eye sockets flashed brightly a few times, and his blue face was still, except for the hint of a satisfied smile.

Aurigar looked around from his command station. There were at least a thousand screenminders within sight, most of them directly over his head, and if it were not for the semicircle of plextanks in which he stood, each showing an aspect of the situation surrounding the six worlds remaining in rebellion, he might have been in any large orbiting office complex around any inhabited planet.

But he was the commander of the Galactic Expeditionary Force, and he could confirm it by looking at the plextank showing six suns, all that remained of the Cleanlist Rebellion against the Empress; she had refused their surrender for the sake of example. At his touch, the plextank display rearranged to show up-close images of each system, no longer to scale, but with all six stars and seventeen inhabited worlds visible as spheres, the systems arranged in a hex around a central data console.

It's not even new, now, but it's still strange, he thought, and idly plucked at the sleeve of the silly getup he had to wear in public.

At his side, Cetuso said, "You've really done well for yourself, dear fellow."

"I suppose so, Lor— er, Cetuso." *Seventeen thousand four hundred twenty-seven.*

The blue man smiled. "Still not used to your peerage?"

"I doubt I ever will be. To judge by the—"

The image in the central tank vanished; Ululara, in full Imperial regalia, appeared. "Supremor Aurigar, are we ready?"

He felt in the plextank once more, for form's sake. "We are."

"Then proceed at once. We have a victory celebration to start."

Aurigar shrugged and spoke the order. More than a thousand screenminders watched for errors or to countermand as thousands of robots, each prepositioned on a sizable asteroid, sprayed the surface with trillions of nanobots. In a matter of a few hundred nanomarqs, well before any remote sensor could hope to detect them, the nanobots had spread their conducting filament-nets of conductors; an instant later, an antimatter fizzle bomb popped up from the main robot and burst, feeding energy into the nanobots' vast antennae, supplying the energy for the transformation.

"Only four not responding, sir," Cetuso said; for this operation he was the Assistant Supremor.

I like "sir" better than "dear fellow." Aurigar nodded. "We expected fifteen to twenty intercepts. This is good." Modern warfare, Aurigar reflected, was now all espionage, remote sensing, and cryptography; with nanobots, quantum computation, and jump tech, you would be hit by every weapon that you didn't detect before it was fired. The four lost weapons had been found and mined by the enemy, killed perhaps three nanomarqs after activation, before they could even deploy their nanobots. Right now, light was spreading out from the antimatter fizzles that powered the conversion, and as the light reached them, a hundred thousand sensors in each of the uninhabited systems would be relaying it through jump transmitters to the enemy. They would know the attack was under way within seventeen micromarqs—but the enemy would not exist within one micromarq.

Still, the enemy backlash must have started by now, their jumpweapons forming and leaping to revenge. Aurigar wondered whether the Imperial forces would take any hits at all; the last time, they had not, but intel estimated a 10 percent chance that the enemy had determined the location of Jinkhangy. To the Empress's image in the plextank before him, he said, "Word on the enemy counterattack?"

Geepo said, "Consider yourself congratulated, sir. Crypto, intel, and search found twenty-six enemy weapon seeds and mined them; they detonated simultaneously with our attack."

"Detonate" was not quite the right word; Aurigar's silent mines had opened wormholes into the cores of blue-white giant stars, and the enemy weapons-to-be had vanished as planet-sized masses of stellar core had burst into existence within the asteroids on which they sat.

"Any jumpspace interceptions?"

"The usual. We sprayed the jumpspace approaches to Jinkhangy with interceptors. Thirteen hits, most of which were probably smugglers or ships that didn't stick to the flight plan, which will certainly teach them a lesson. Our best estimate is that not more than three of them were enemy weapons. All in all, not just a successful operation but a cheap one, and—"

"Silence, please, from everyone," Aurigar said.

They all fell quiet; his peculiar passion for dead silence at the moment of truth was legendary, and the legend was known to be accurate—as were the legends about what happened when he did not get that dread, respectful silence.

Ululara's image ghosted over the hex arrangement of the six Cleanlist systems, arranged to show stars and inhabited planets as spheres and the major stations as points. The countdown in the center of the plextank reached zero.

Thirty-some stations flashed and were gone; an asteroid-mass of vacuum-energy receivers had popped out of jumpspace inside each one, converting instantaneously to relativistic nucleons. *About forty million people*, Aurigar thought, *gone in less time than it takes a signal to cross a synapse.*

The view, with Ululara still ghosted over it, switched to just-activated sleeper satellites over the seventeen planets. Aurigar had just time to think of all the continents and oceans, cities, mountains, deserts, glaciers, temples to a thousand gods, dew-scented mornings and glorious stormy sunsets in progress, kisses never to be finished and hands reaching for each other that would never touch, eighty billion people and a trillion works of art.

The jumpweapons entering the cores of the seventeen worlds opened wormholes to the great black hole at the galaxy's core. Within the space of one breath, planetary surfaces sagged and fell like a deflating balloon. Each place where a planet had been flashed white-hot as the energy just outside the event horizon escaped from the ripping apart and the brutal collisions of the last bits of matter. Then the spy satellites, too, plunged into the black hole.

The view switched briefly to more distant cameras; the black holes swelling from each wormhole were dark spheres, bending starlight weirdly around themselves, swelling for just a moment until the wormholes destabilized and the black ball of the event horizon contracted back to starry void.

There was no point in sending the stars into nova, except as examples. That was all the point the Empress required. The six stars flared brilliantly; over the next few days they would briefly reach far out beyond their former habitable zones, and then gradually recede. Nothing would ever live in those systems again. In a few dekamarqs, the inhabitants of neighboring systems would throw carefully orchestrated festivals to celebrate the brief flarings in their night sky— and be reminded that though she was called "the merciful and mighty," she remained Her Supreme Might.

Aurigar sighed. He wondered how many of the eighty billion had been standing close to someone they loved, so that as that awful fall began, they had been able to clutch a hand or hug close to each other.

Total forever: 17,427. Good enough. Aurigar drew a breath and waited.

Geepo screamed.

Cetuso made a strangled sound.

Aurigar smiled. "That would be Jinkhangy," he said. "Just a start; the provincial capital worlds are going even as we speak, and the galaxy is now swarming with self-replicating robots seeking out and blasting every instrument of Imperial authority into nucleons."

Geepo's and Cetuso's slack expressions were amusing, but Aurigar took no time to relish them. "Oh, the Cleanlists had to go, of course—evil as the Imperium, and ten times madder. Now, for my next act of public service, I eliminate the Imperium. The homeworlds of the high aristocracy are vanishing at this moment, and billions of ships hurrying around on Imperial business are turning to plasma in real space, or unresolvability in jumpspace. The people of each individual planet will work out their own destinies. All the stars are free."

The whole speech rang curiously flat, considering that Aurigar had been mentally rehearsing it since the "dear fellow" count was less than one thousand. *Well, no doubt it is neither the first nor the last line well-composed in advance to be spoiled when it is delivered.*

Cetuso moaned, his jaw hanging open, and the mirrors and lenses in his eye sockets turned slowly and out of coordination; probably he had not yet understood. Aurigar considered taunting him—*your favorite lackey,* my dear fellow! *was not what you thought. You and your adored Empress and the whole aristocracy and system of domination perish* now! *and I shall piss upon your steaming remains.* But whereas the thought was swift as light itself, the words would have been far too slow, so before Cetuso's moan of uncomprehending despair acquired even a hint of comprehension, Aurigar slashed the cutting laser vertically from the blue man's head to his feet, so that he fell into two pieces with steam pouring from his flash-cooked guts in the middle.

Aurigar stepped forward, looked down into the red gap between the blue half-faces, and smelled the roasted reek of the man's entrails. The mirrors and lenses now flashed and turned with the last of their momentum. He holstered his weapon, opened his trousers, and urinated, filling the eye sockets. "For every time you fed me, for every time you said I amused you, and for seventeen thousand four hundred twenty-seven times you called me 'dear fellow.'"

Geepo was sobbing.

Ululara said, "He was my kinsman and you are far too flippant with his body."

I sent four weapons after her physical location on Way-stonn! The plextank displayed nothing.

Aurigar whirled. She stood behind him, rather disarming in pink pajamas, but quite well-armed with a cutting laser pointed at his face. He was acutely aware that he had holstered his own, and then modesty made him reach for his open fly.

"No," she said. "Keep your hands away from your body." She smiled, then, the genuine warm smile she'd had as Miriette, so long ago. "Poor Aurigar, we both had secrets we couldn't tell. I actually knew that I really *was* the Empress after my fourth trip into the multimapped dwellspace you had Geepo build for me. A kidnapper and pimp like you, Aurigar, might not choose to pay attention to politics, but a businessperson with interstellar interests like me has no choice. Once I had confirmed that whatever I did as madam and CEO in my dwellspace had an exact analogy in the actions of the new-crowned Empress, I knew the truth, and shortly I found my way out of the world Geepo built and into the real one. I have been ruling the galaxy directly ever since, just leaving a shell up to fool you, Cetuso, and Geepo."

Geepo moaned, "I am stupid."

"No," Empress Ululara said, "I am competent."

"You cannot stop the robots and replicators already at work," Aurigar said. "You remain alive, and you may kill me, but you can no longer rule your empire; you are an Empress only in name."

"That is exactly right," she said.

And now Aurigar was certain, as he had been for so many marqs, since well before they put her on the throne, and he smiled broadly. "I am tired of this game," he said, "and curious about what I have forgotten and will wake to. You may press that trigger at any time."

"Of course I may," she said. "An Empress does what she likes, always." And she pushed the button down.

For Aurigar, the world ceased. If he had existed to feel it, he would have been startled beyond all words to find that he did not wake into any other existence.

Miriette lifted the dwellcap from her head and shook her damp hair. The clock showed she had been in the simulation for just under two micromarqs. She had a few more micromarqs till old Phodway would come home; the kitchen and the kids were already clean and dinner-ready.

The image of Lord Leader Cetuso Sir appeared at the corner of her screen. "Any luck?"

"Another one who got a bad case of conscience and went radical—very cleverly, too. I've sent you the file. Quite ingenious and well worth study. He assassinated you, by the way, and it seemed rather personal. Generally a bad boy all around. How many more lost princess men do we have left to try?"

"More than a hundred to go, and this was only the twelfth one we've examined, Princess. We'll find you the right one to get you out of the Krevpiceaux country, don't worry. Never fear. At one or two per your day, it won't even take very long."

She felt like pouting, but she did not feel like it nearly enough to do so and spoil her dignity. "I'm getting *very* tired of caring for all Phodway's fostindents, and having to keep him sober, and all that. I really want to start working my way out of hiding."

"Oh, you'll have to hide somewhere till your brother dies,

in any case. I've told you that. And we're working on that too, of course. Just remember that until your memplant woke up and told you to contact me, you had no idea you even *were* in hiding, or that you were anything other than a purchased orphan. Let alone who you actually are." The mirrors in his eye sockets flashed and twinkled. "We *will* find a lost princess man who will stay loyal. And then we *will* get you out of the Krevpiceaux, but not out of hiding. I barely got you out of your mother's palace ahead of the explosion, and your brother's disposition, you may trust me, has not improved in the intervening twenty-nine marqs. *Patience*, Your Supreme Might-to-Be, *patience*."

"I know. I know. It's just I'm facing feeding four kids, sobering up a drunk, cleaning the shack as far as it can be cleaned, and sharing a bed with two of the other fostindents. But I can manage patience. I did have one question to raise— this was the third lost princess man in a row to figure out that he was in a simulation. Like the other ones, he thought it was his and he was the center of it."

"Naturally. What man doesn't think he's the center of the universe?" Cetuso's image on the screen paused for not more than a hundred nanomarqs, then shrugged, the immense blue muscles of his shoulders rising and falling like waves on the sea. "I've scanned his moments of recognition, and I don't think we can change policy; our lost princess man will have to be smart enough to do what we need, simulations cannot be perfect, and many of them will see through it. At least none of them so far has figured out where or how we read and recorded him, or why we're doing it, so there's no danger that one of them will leave behind any warning for the others, and as long as they don't, it doesn't complicate the task, really." He smiled warmly. "And everything really is on course, Princess. Regrettable as it is, just put in another—"

"Miriette!" Henredd was calling from the kitchen. "Miriette, the water is boiling!"

"Drop the noodles in and I'll be there in a moment," she said. Cetuso's image looked disgustingly pitying, so she stuck her tongue out at him before she blanked the screen.

Through the kitchen viewwall, she watched the Krev-piceauxi mistral wail and shriek its way up into a full-blown black-dust storm, the kind that was equally likely to strand them inside for days or blow over before bedtime. Phodway would appreciate a hot meal and a clean bed after making his way home through *that*, anyway. At least he was not unkind and he thanked her often.

Henredd stood beside her, his bony shoulder pressing against her lower ribs, arm around her unself-consciously, and said, "I like being here when you cook." They'd gotten Henredd from an illegal dealer, and the first year they'd had him, he'd barely spoken, mostly just cried; a little kind attention and some efficient care had brought him around, and Miriette had to admit she'd learned how to do that from Phodway's treatment of her when she was young, back before he'd fallen into the bottle. She turned the fish cakes over and rubbed Henredd's head; he snuggled more closely against her.

Once I'm on the throne, I will have Cetuso take care of these people, very, very generously. An empress does not have much need for love, but it is good to know about it, and an empress must show gratitude.

The boy under her arm squirmed and ran off to play; she contemplated her skill in the kitchen with proud dismay. *Patience, patience, patience.*

Cetuso could feel nothing from his extended hand; to get the maximum bandwidth for accessing Aurigar's mind and memories, he'd had to turn every available nerve to the purpose. The lost princess man's facial expression showed that the filaments rushing through Aurigar's body to his heart and brain were painful and distressing; it could and would all be erased at need, if the man lived. The plate of mussels and noodles lay inverted and broken on the floor. Aurigar's boot touched it and slipped slightly, and Cetuso made that foot move to a secure spot on the dry floor behind.

Cetuso had no fear of being disturbed, knowing as he did

that everyone in the place feared to disturb him, or even to look at him to see what he was doing. He relayed the copy of Aurigar to the princess's computer, waited through the micromarqs while she played Aurigar out in simulation, and talked her through the usual disappointment. He might have pointed out that they needed a man of extraordinary abilities to accomplish what was needed, and also one who would not resent how he was used, one who would understand the Imperium as well as the Empress herself and yet feel only deep loyalty. There would be such a man, he was confident, but this was not he.

A few micromarqs later, when he knew she was feeling better, and she had been called off to cook supper for the miner's brats, he turned his attention back to Aurigar. A few people had gotten up and left quietly, not wanting to be witnesses; the rest looked at their drinks, their plates, or the wall.

Cetuso proceeded systematically. First he erased the simulation data from Aurigar's brain, then the memory of their conversation, then all the memories, and finally the instincts, the sensory processing, and the autonomic processes, before his filaments slashed Aurigar's brains into wet chopped meat beyond any possibility of neurodissection or nanoreconstruction.

Cetuso's filaments withdrew, merging into thin tentacles between the corpse's ribs, then broad thick strands outside the chest. As the tips popped free, they reshaped into fingers splayed on the man's chest. Cetuso pushed lightly.

Aurigar's corpse crashed to the floor. No one looked up, but a number of people winced; Cetuso recorded their reaction and relayed it to the political police. Probably they just had weak stomachs (you never could tell what would bother even the most normal, practical, hardened heart), but better safe than sorry.

He flashed the main mirror in his left eye to draw the bartender's gaze. Cetuso pointed to the accounting screen behind the bar, using his mindlink to add a few month's revenues to the bar's receipts. The bartender looked down, saw the numbers, looked up, and was mindful enough not to do anything but look away. Cetuso smiled; silence, like all good things, was at its best and costliest when absolutely pure, and it never paid to skimp on it.

He would have nodded nicely enough at anyone who looked up as he left, but as usual, no one did. Out on the street, where everyone could see him and what he was, he walked as if invisible.

DEFECT

KRISTINE KATHRYN RUSCH

Kristine Kathryn Rusch started out the decade of the nineties as one of the fastest-rising and most prolific young authors on the scene, took a few years out in mid-decade for a very successful turn as editor of *The Magazine of Fantasy and Science Fiction*, and, since stepping down from that position, has returned to her old standards of production here in the twenty-first century, publishing a slew of novels in four genres, writing fantasy, mystery, and romance novels under various pseudonyms, as well as science fiction. She has published more than twenty novels under her own name, including *The White Mists of Power*, *The Disappeared*, *Extremes*, and *Fantasy Life*, the four-volume Fey series, the Black Throne series, *Alien Influences*, and several *Star Wars*, *Star Trek*, and other media tie-in books, both solo and written with husband, Dean Wesley Smith, and with others. Her most recent books (as Rusch, anyway) are the SF novels of the popular Retrieval Artist series, which include *The Disappeared, Extremes, Consequences, Buried Deep, Paloma, Recovery Man*, and a collection of Retrieval Artist stories, *The Retrieval Artist and Other Stories*. Her copious short fiction has been collected in *Stained Black: Horror Stories*, *Stories for an Enchanted Afternoon*, *Little Mira-*

cles: And Other Tales of Murder, and *Millennium Babies*. In 1999, she won Readers Award polls from the readerships of both *Asimov's Science Fiction* and *Ellery Queen's Mystery Magazine*, an unprecedented double honor! As an editor, she was honored with the Hugo Award for her work on *The Magazine of Fantasy and Science Fiction*, and shared the World Fantasy Award with Dean Wesley Smith for her work as editor of the original hardcover anthology version of *Pulphouse*. As a writer, she has won the Herodotus Award for Best Historical Mystery (for *A Dangerous Road*, written as Kris Nelscott) and the *Romantic Times* Reviewer's Choice Award (for *Utterly Charming*, written as Kristine Grayson); as Kristine Kathryn Rusch, she won the John W. Campbell Award, been a finalist for the Arthur C. Clarke Award, and took home a Hugo Award in 2000 for her story *Millennium Babies,* which made her one of the few people in genre history to win Hugos for both editing *and* writing.

Here, she spins the suspenseful tale of an interstellar agent who tries to come in from the cold—only to find that the place where she ends up isn't very warm either.

She walked into the docking ring, wearing an all black tunic over black pants, outlined with silver trim. The suit looked like half the governmental clothing in the galaxy, which, she knew, made it impossible to tell exactly where she was from.

She would use the clothes, her demeanor, and her old identification chip, which was still active, to get into the ship.

The docking ring circled the entire starbase. She had entered through doors 65–66. She hadn't been in this part before, but she only knew that because of the numbers. Otherwise, everything looked the same.

The docking ring was wide. The walking platform threaded its way through the ring. Arching above and below it was the ring itself, all black cable and gray siding.

Most starbases used see-through material on their rings, so that everything remained visible—the ships, the space beyond, even the planets of the nearby systems, which generally looked small enough to cup in a single hand.

Here though, everything was hidden. This starbase didn't even have an official name, although its docking registry called it Starbase Alpha, one of half a dozen Starbase Alphas she had visited during her career.

The old-timers called this starbase the NetherRealm, which was much more appropriate. The NetherRealm existed between the Nechev System and the Kazen System. Both systems had fought over the NetherRealm in the past, both systems had owned it once, and both systems found that they couldn't defend it.

Finally, they negotiated their coordinates to leave a small slice of space to the NetherRealm and considered the battle lost.

As long as she was here, she would be safe.

At least, that was the theory. It was, as yet, untested.

The walking platform branched to each docking site. Unlike other starbases where the docking ring doors led directly into the ship, the docking ring doors here recessed into the gray sides. A ring of sickly yellow lights were the only indication that a berth was occupied.

It had taken her two days to locate the ship. To get the docking codes and the entry passes, she had to violate a personal covenant. At least the docking agent's hair wasn't as greasy as it looked, but his skin smelled of garlic. She had actually had to spend money for a water shower to get the stench off herself.

She shuddered at the memory, then she made herself focus. She squared her shoulders, adjusted her tunic, and strode purposely across the walking platform, heading for berth 66-CE.

Her heels clicked on the platform. Two human guards stepped out of their guardhouses, built into the side of the ring, and watched her.

At least sixteen robotic heads moved from the arches, watching her as well.

She resisted the urge to smile. Who was it—her first instructor, André? Or Dmitry?—who used to say, *It is always best to smile when you're on camera; then they know you know that you're being watched.*

She didn't care if they knew. They were going to catch her. She didn't need to pretend a bravado she did not feel.

Berth 66-CE had eight burned-out panels. The circling yellow light would fade as it reached those panels, then reappear as it passed them.

She reached the control panel and managed to press the first sequence in the override code before a robotic hand slid out of the wall and clamped on her wrist. The hand's grip was too tight and extremely painful, probably by design.

She didn't flinch, however. She just brought up her other hand and pressed the rest of the code.

The second robotic hand lowered as the docking door kicked into its release sequence. The thuds behind it were reassuring even as the fingers of her right hand slowly turned purple.

"Don't know what you think you're doing," a male voice said behind her. "The hand won't let you go, even if you tried it. And I'll just lock the door up tight again."

She turned enough so that she could see one of the guards. He was beefy and young, his flesh jiggling in his too-tight suit. His appearance told her that he'd been raised on the base in the artificial gravity; he preferred his beer to exercise, so he only did the minimum routine required by his job; and he'd worked security in the docking ring since he'd gotten out of mandatory classes—which couldn't have been that long ago.

She glared at him. "I am here to inspect the ship."

"You're not one of ours," he said.

"No, of course not." She nodded toward the docking door. "I'm one of theirs."

Her wrist ached. Her fingers were going numb. But she didn't look at them. She continued to glare at him.

He swallowed visibly, then he licked his lower lip. He'd clearly never come across this situation before.

"How do you think I got the codes?" she said.

She hoped the ruse would work, that the docking agent hadn't been lying when he said he never did things like that. In those situations, she usually took the word "never" to mean "rarely," but she couldn't be sure. Sometimes it meant "always." Given how nervous the agent had been, she believed in "rarely."

Now she was putting that belief to the test.

"Check my ID," she said.

The guard glanced around and licked his bottom lip again. The robotic heads were all turned in his direction. If she ever planned a return trip to this docking bay for a similar reason, she would use that design feature; she'd plan an old-fashioned distraction on one level, while she broke into another.

But that was a future job—if there were going to be future jobs. This was now, and she had to concentrate.

The other guard meandered over. He was thinner and older, with lines around his eyes and mouth. He had traveled on a ship without artificial gravity, and it had had an effect on his entire build. He probably was as fragile as he looked.

Clearly, then, the starbase had human guards for reasons other than thuggish security. The robotic equipment obviously handled that kind of security very, very well.

"Trouble?" the second guard asked, pointedly looking at her captured wrist.

This time, she looked too. Her hand was swelling. The stupid robotic clench had shut off her circulation—and if it went on too long, it would become dangerous.

"Says she's authorized," the younger guard said.

"We didn't hear anything," the second guard said to her.

"Clearly you didn't," she said, "although your docking authority did, or I wouldn't have the codes. Now, check my identification before my hand falls off and I have to sue someone."

The second guard reached into a pocket built into the waist of his uniform and removed a thumb-sized scanner. She hadn't seen one like that before—it looked older and clunkier than those she was used to.

But she also knew things were different here, often on purpose. The starbase might have been building its own scanners, since so many manufactured ones sent information back to the manufacturer as a matter of course.

He held the thing over her swollen skin, then touched the robotic hand. It let go.

She couldn't actually feel that the grip was gone, but her hand fell to her side, banging into her thigh before she grabbed her right elbow with her left hand, stopping the movement. Pain echoed through her hand, exacerbated by the blow to her leg.

She winced, because she was expected to.

"Sorry," the second guard said, even though he didn't sound in the least apologetic.

"Don't know what you'll find," the first guard said, nodding toward the berth and, by extension, the ship. "They won't answer our hails. They've been berthed for thirty-six hours now, and no one has come in or gone out. After the initial contact, we haven't heard a thing."

She pretended that all of this was new to her, even though it wasn't. First, she had located the ship within the nearest sector of space—which had been hard enough; chartered cruise ship companies didn't like to reveal their high-end yachts' locations, especially to someone not in the database. Then she had to identify the ship's registry and docking number, actually hacking into the docking agent's database during the fifteen minutes he'd allowed her alone.

That was when she discovered the ship had arrived but hadn't moved or done anything except an automated contact before landing.

"If that's true," she said to the guards, "then why haven't your inspectors contacted the ship?"

"Base law. We're not to try for 168 hours."

Everything on this base was done in Earth hours. Earth days didn't exist. It was just another way that the Nether-Realm established its independence, and it was annoying.

Apparently base law didn't let them establish contact for an entire week.

A lot could go wrong in a week.

She rubbed her wrist, partly for show, and partly to remind them they'd imprisoned a woman who was simply trying to do an authorized job.

"We got word that they were smuggling weapons on this ship," she said. "The base has given me permission to inspect. You're welcome to help if you'd like."

They looked at each other. The younger guard seemed eager—more confirmation that he hadn't done much in his life besides guard the docking ring—but the older guard shook his head.

"Your people, your problem," he said. "You realize that we have a different list of contraband items than Kazen does, right?"

"I know," she said. "But if I find contraband on the ship before anyone leaves, it's still in my territory."

So long as no one had disembarked, a ship in the Nether-Realm was subject to the law of the sector it had come from. Which was why most ships sent at least one member of the crew into the NetherRealm immediately upon arrival.

"Okay," the second guard said in a voice he clearly meant as official. "We got that on record. You're entering before they disembark, so you've got jurisdiction."

"Thanks," she said.

The first guard pressed the secondary code into the docking door. It rolled open, revealing an empty airlock, coated in bright yellow light which, on the NetherRealm, meant all-clear.

She stepped into the airlock, and stopped for a moment to steady herself.

Things inside that ship had to be bad. No one had gotten out. Weren't cruises all about stopping and seeing places? Even starbases. Especially starbases as famous as the NetherRealm. There had to be an approved track for the tourists to go on, one that prevented them from getting mugged while still allowing them to shop in the NetherRealm's black market.

The airlock closed behind her, and then she hit the comm. She identified herself as an inspector, just in case the guards were listening. Besides, that should get a quicker response from the ship itself.

What it got was a lot of nothing. No static, no answer. Not even an attempt.

She tried three times, gave up, and punched in the override code the docking agent had given her. He wasn't even supposed to have it. Only the NetherRealm's Security Force—

their police force, in essence—was supposed to have it. But in a place this corrupt, it didn't surprise her that the override codes had trickled to several nonapproved personnel.

The interior doors opened and the stench nearly knocked her backward.

Corpses. Rotting corpses. She'd recognize that smell anywhere.

Her stomach clenched. She put a hand over her mouth and nose, breathing through her fingers. Then she stepped into the ship and nearly tripped over a body.

She looked down.

He was young, thin, with a shock of white-blond hair and skin the color of porcelain—at least, on this side. On the back, his hair was matted and black with blood. But the blood hadn't seeped, which either meant the head wound was superficial, or he had died before bleeding out.

She crouched. She pushed the hair away from his face, noting that while his skin was clammy, it was also still warm to the touch.

His lashes were long, his cheekbones solid. He was a boy, just at the cusp of his teenage years.

"Misha," she whispered.

She felt for a pulse, found it, thready and weak. He was nearly dead. If she'd waited for the required week for contact, he would have been dead.

She scooped him in her arms and tossed him over her shoulders, his arms flapping against her knees. Her knees buckled at his weight; she hadn't expected it of such a thin body.

She carried him back through the airlock, trying not to think of the damage she might be doing to him.

But she couldn't call for help—not here. The ship wasn't NetherRealm territory. It still belonged to the Kazen Sector, and she didn't know the protocols to get NetherRealm authority here.

So she had to take him into the NetherRealm proper.

The docking door opened. The guards peered in, looking stunned. They didn't expect an inspector to be carrying a young boy over her shoulder like a sack of clothing.

"People are dead in there," she said, "but he's alive. There may be others who are still breathing."

Like Yuri. Maybe Yuri was still alive.

But she couldn't go back and look for him.

Not with Misha so close to death.

She didn't dare.

In the hospital wing, she had to give them a name she hadn't used in nearly seven years. Technically, it was her name, although it didn't even sound like her name anymore:

Halina Layla Orlinskaya.

Yes, she kept saying over and over. *Yes, this boy is my son. My son.*

Misha.

Once she'd cradled him, skin wrinkled and red, covered with blood then, too, but her blood—the blood they shared. She had wiped his eyes with her fingers, then his little mouth, and he had started to suckle on her thumb.

Then her work called her back and, like a fool, she went.

Yuri raised him. Yuri loved him. Yuri would have protected him.

Yuri, whom she hadn't been able to go back for.

If it had been a mission, she would have dumped the boy on the passageway and gone back, found someone else alive, brought that person out, and kept going back, back, until others arrived to help her.

But it wasn't a mission; it was a cruise ship her husband and son had booked a year before, a cruise to see a different solar system, a long-haul trip to celebrate—what? She couldn't even remember.

She barely remembered that they had planned the trip. She tried to keep track, but she often forgot—so many more important things on her mind.

Then, when she realized she was leaving the service, she checked on the ship. She did not contact Yuri. To do so would put him and Misha in danger. She hacked into reservations, looked up their names, and checked their itinerary.

She got dates and times of all of their shore calls, including this one, and she knew she would meet them here.

They hadn't known it.

No one had known it, except her.

"You realize you should have gone through quarantine."

It took her a moment to realize that a young doctor was talking to her. He looked like a baby with his hair tied back and his clean-shaven face. Only his eyes were old, the age that came with the type of work he did, in the place he was, instead of from actual age.

"They tried to make me go through quarantine," she said, "but Misha was dying. So I brought him here."

"You were lucky," the doctor said. "All of this could have been caused by a virus."

"It wasn't." She let impatience into her voice. She knew most of the lethal viruses out there and none left the victim looking like Misha.

"That's right," the doctor said. "He has laser rifle wounds. There was some kind of firefight on that ship."

She felt a coldness run through her. "The others?"

"So far, no one has brought us any more injuries."

It took a moment for her brain to process his words. "What have they brought you?"

But she knew the answer before he spoke.

Corpses.

They had brought him only corpses.

She sat at Misha's bedside, afraid to leave him. Someone had found her a change of clothing and forced her to wash the blood off her face.

They'd shaved off his hair so that they could work the wound on the back of his head. They said he'd be unconscious for a while now, maybe forty-eight, maybe seventy-two hours.

She wanted them to say "two or three days," but they wouldn't. Damn this place, they wouldn't tell her anything.

No one talked to her, either. About the ship, about the losses, about her.

Until the Director for Starbase Security Services showed up. He announced himself as if he were an emperor. So she had asked for identification, even though her internal scanners had already checked his hand chips.

He was gaunt, with whitish-gray skin and haunted eyes. His lips were too thin, his nose too large. He wore a black suit with silver trim, much like her now-ruined tunic outfit.

He came into Misha's room and closed the door, making her bristle without even saying a word.

"Halina Layla Orlinskaya," he said.

She nodded, no longer used to the name.

"Also known as Elena Elizarova, Anna Ilyinichna Valentinov, and Alina Yaroslavsky."

She didn't acknowledge those names, although she'd used them, many times.

"I have found sixteen warrants in your various names," he said. "I'd like to say they were all for murder, but they're not. Some are murder with special circumstance, some are for egregious homicide, others are for inciting murder. And that's just under the names I know."

She didn't move. An innocent person might protest. But she had lost the right to pretend innocence when she had used her current identification to go into that cruise ship.

Misha stirred. She reminded herself that he had moved off and on throughout the long night, that the doctors said it meant nothing, he was still unconscious and would remain so for a few more hours at best.

The Director saw her staring at Misha. He looked at Misha too, probably wondering if the boy was waking up.

She was wondering if, on some level, Misha could hear this.

It was one thing to know that your mother worked for Kazen Intelligence. It was another to hear the results of her job so bluntly described.

"I should send you back," the Director said, "but I'm not sure to where. Do I send you to the place with the most recent charges or the one with the worst? Or do I send you to Naut? Because your identification—which is older than this child—claims you work for the Secret Police in Chuleart."

She waited, not answering anything. She had worked for

the Secret Police in the city of Chuleart. She had gotten her start there, as a college student. Then she had moved up from the local branch to the regional and then to the Empire's main branch.

Then she'd had Misha and retired, or so she thought for those few weeks they gave her with her family. But the case that brought her back sent her into Intelligence, and that led her to places she never thought she would go, as a naive twenty-year-old who wanted adventure and secrecy and romance.

She had had adventure, she had had secrecy, but she had never had romance. It was blood and fear followed by weeks, maybe months, of tedium, accented with moments of panic.

The Director crossed his arms. "But you know that we never send anyone back, not without cause. Or you would not be here. I'm amazed you haven't asked for asylum yet."

She hadn't planned on asking for asylum. She certainly didn't want to live out her life on a starbase between sectors, unable to travel, vulnerable to whomever was on the ships that ventured into the NetherRealm's docking ring.

The Director leaned back against the wall. "If we want it," he said, "we do have cause to send you away. You were careless in that docking ring. You boarded without permission. I have a hunch you stole codes. Because you didn't follow procedure, you could have loosed a virus onto this base."

She folded her hands together, then wished she hadn't. He might take that as a nervous gesture.

Maybe it was a nervous gesture.

"Did you think," he asked, "that you might have set a killer free?"

She hadn't. She knew that much. A killer wouldn't have trapped himself at the docking ring, waiting for someone to find him.

The Director was just trying to scare her.

The killer was long gone.

She took her son's hand. It was warm, but limp.

"What happened on that ship?" she asked.

Her voice sounded rusty. She hadn't spoken to anyone

except Misha since she came into this room, and even then, she hadn't said much.

"We don't know exactly," the Director said. "The position of the bodies suggests that the killer started in the dining room. He killed most of the passengers there, along with most of the waitstaff. The rifle wasn't set high—it didn't penetrate walls, just flesh."

Which was why her son had serious wounds, but hadn't died.

"Then he killed the kitchen staff and proceeded to the cabins. He moved quickly enough that no one got warning. He saved the captain for last, probably to pilot the ship into the dock, but we don't know that for certain."

"Misha was by the main door," she said.

The Director nodded. "We think he was trying to get out after the docking, and just passed out."

Her son had been trying to leave the ship? That didn't make sense to her, not if the killer escaped before the ship arrived at the docking ring.

Misha's position inside that ship didn't suggest it either. He had fallen in front of the door, not in front of the control panel.

He lay where anyone who tried to get into the ship couldn't miss him.

The Director crossed his arms. "What do you know of these deaths?"

"Me?" She looked at him in surprise. "I had nothing to do with this."

"No?" the Director asked.

"No," she said as firmly as she could. But she was lying. She had been worried about a connection to her from the moment she learned that the ship had docked and no one had disembarked. "If this was meant for me, Misha would be dead now."

Although he had been left for dead.

And he had been left in front of the doors, like a message.

The Director watched her. He couldn't read her. No one could.

"I've heard about Lysvista," he said. "Everybody has."

Really? How could anyone have heard of Lysvista? It was supposed to have been a secret op.

Had Intelligence leaked the information?

"You fled after that," the Director said. "Lysvista convinced you, didn't it?"

Convinced her? Of what? She hadn't needed convincing.

Lysvista had defeated her.

Lysvista had provoked a failure of will.

Lysvista, a tiny mountain town on the planet of Lys on the far side of the Nechev System. One of the prettiest places she'd ever seen. Lysvista was on the top of the tallest mountain peak in the Godinger Range. The town was surrounded by four spectacular lakes, none of which bled into the other, all of which were a very bright and very deep blue.

If you stood in the very center of town, you could see for kilometers. It felt like you could see the entire planet, even though you couldn't.

The refinery on the far end of town made some of the deadliest bioweapons known to man. All she had to do was get inside, steal the formulas, and then use the weapons on Lysvista.

She'd done similar things in the past.

Only Lysvista itself made this job harder.

Strangers were either spies or tourists who couldn't be trusted. She had to move in. She had to become part of the town.

And she did.

She even managed to get a job at the refinery. She stole the formulas, and had a plan for setting the weapons loose all over the town.

In the past, she would have set the canisters, she would have programmed the timers, she would have left with no regrets.

But she had talked to people, actually had a few meaningful conversations, the first in years. She had sat beside the lakes she would destroy and watched the sun creep over the mountain range in the mornings. She had had the best beer of her life, made from the fresh lake water, and she had had ice cream like none she'd ever tasted, made from the nearby snowcaps.

She had breathed air so crisp that it had a flavor all its own.

For the first time in her life, she had fallen in love—but with a place, not a person.

Instead of killing the town, its people, its lakes, and its fresh, crisp air, she left. But not before leaving the formulas with the mayor and the town council, along with a message:

Check the canisters at these coordinates.

She had stolen the weapons, placed the canisters in their assigned places, but had not programmed the timers. In fact, to make sure nothing went off accidentally, she had included no release device at all.

Just the canisters, their deadly contents, and the threat that they posed.

On each one, she added: *If I can so easily breach your security, so can someone else.*

Because she knew, once her failure came back to Kazen Intelligence, they would send someone else. And if that person failed, someone else would come.

She couldn't go back to Lysvista.

She couldn't go back to Kazen.

She couldn't go back to Chuleart and her family.

She had to find a new home, a new life, one in which she could make a living.

One in which she could survive.

The NetherRealm was the first step in that survival. She had used the NetherRealm as a base before. She knew its layout and its limitations.

She couldn't live here, but she could stay here, unnoticed and unmolested, for a few weeks while she made plans.

She had several options. She could book passage on a ship going away from Kazen, maybe back to the Nechev System or to some other sector, extremely far away. Or she could hire onto a cargo vessel under a false name. She could take a longship heading out of the galaxy and going to—what was for her, at least—the great unknown.

Those were only a few of her options. She had known she would learn of other options when she arrived at the Nether-Realm.

No matter what she did, she wasn't sure if she would take Misha and Yuri, but she would give them the choice to join her, and new identities if they chose not to.

Because news of her failure would get back to Kazen Intelligence, and they would try to find her. If they couldn't find her, they would send someone after her family.

But she had timed everything so that she could meet Misha and Yuri at the NetherRealm before news of her failure hit.

Yet the Director said he knew of Lysvista.

He said everyone did.

What else had he said?

Lysvista convinced you, didn't it?

She had been thinking so hard of the events, she hadn't quite realized what he actually said. She thought instead of correcting him, not understanding him.

"Lysvista convinced me of what?" she asked.

It had seemed like hours since he asked the question, but only seconds had gone by.

"Lysvista convinced you that you were in the wrong," he said, "that you worked for the wrong side and always had."

Good and bad. She had encountered a lot of believers in good and bad while she did this work. They had always been too rigid to negotiate with.

She hadn't expected to find someone in the NetherRealm who believed in good and bad, or to even use the phrase "wrong side." The NetherRealm was renowned for having no sides.

Its citizens—if they could even be called that—preferred the existence between sectors. Thieves, killers, spies—all sorts stayed here and never had to fear arrest, unless they broke the laws of the NetherRealm, what few laws there were.

The Director had his arms crossed.

"Wrong side," she repeated slowly. "How can the Director of Security for this starbase believe in one sector over the others?"

"I'm allowed opinions," he said.

She felt cold. "Are you allowed to act on them?"

"We're talking about what happened at Lysvista," he said, "not about me. And what happened at Lysvista convinced you that you had picked the wrong side. That's why you didn't complete your mission."

Her mouth was dry. She had to focus on the muscles of her hand so that she wouldn't squeeze Misha's fingers too hard.

"You've been bought," she said.

"Of course not," the Director said. "Although I do keep an eye out—for all sides. I don't choose. If I choose, I lose money."

He was selling information, the son of a bitch. How many people had she met who were just like him? How many had she used?

She swallowed hard so that she wouldn't alienate him further. "Who did you tell I was here?"

"No one yet," he said. "That's the interesting part, at least to me. I've told no one. I didn't know it was you, until you identified yourself as you went into the ship."

So, if she believed him, he had had nothing to do with the murders on board the cruise ship, not even peripherally, as a seller of information.

But he could sell that information now—and they both knew it.

"What do you want?" she asked, but she knew. He wanted money.

He waited. He wanted her to name a price.

She wouldn't.

"No one can come here and get me," she said. "You'd have to ship me to them. You would lose your job if anyone found out what you had done."

"No one would find out."

She smiled. "You think I haven't figured out how people like you survive? If I leave, a message will go to your boss.

In it will be information on all of the people you've sold both to Kazen and to Nechev."

He didn't move his body. But his mouth slackened, just enough to let her know that she had him.

Her bluff was working.

She was careful not to take it too far. That simple threat would be enough to hold him.

Finally, he said, "I could still tell Kazen Intelligence where you are."

At that moment, she knew she had him. He wouldn't ask for money, nor would he get in her way.

"They already know where I am," she said. She waved a hand at Misha. "Or he wouldn't be here, not like this."

She didn't know that for certain; the killer on that ship could have been anyone, or after anyone. She had no idea. And even if the killer had targeted her by attacking her family, she couldn't be certain it was Kazen Intelligence.

But she didn't let that uncertainty show on her face.

"You're not afraid they'll come for you?" the Director asked.

"I'm not afraid of anything." And as she spoke, she realized that was true. She wasn't afraid of anything. Not of dying, not even of Misha's death. His death would hurt, yes, but it wouldn't devastate her.

She hadn't been close enough to him to feel such a comprehensive loss.

Yet she had run across the starbase like a mad thing, trying to save his life. Love? Or guilt? Or simply an old, nearly dormant sense of maternal duty?

"You're not even afraid they'll hurt your boy?" the Director asked.

"They've already hurt my boy," she said.

The Director stared at her.

"Go ahead," she said. "Tell them where I am. Sell that information if you want. Send them after me. But do me one favor."

The Director looked at her, his hand falling to his side.

She met his gaze. "Leave me alone."

His expression hardened. He glared at her for a moment, then he pushed away from the wall and stalked out of the room.

Only after he had gone did she realize she should have told him to leave Misha alone as well.

After that, no one came for her. No one contacted her. No one threatened her.

She got the message: she was safe so long as she stayed in the NetherRealm.

She knew she was being watched. But as long as she remained inactive, she was a threat to no one.

If she approached any other side, if she promised secrets for sale, if she offered her services to any one of a hundred underground organizations, then someone would retaliate. Then she might die.

Or Misha might.

She still hadn't figured out how to protect him.

She stayed at his side, leaving only once to get her clothes and the contents of her paid room. She brought them to his bedside after being gone only an hour, an hour in which she had to hope no one would touch him.

The nurses monitored him with their equipment, not realizing that she had sealed his room. No one could have gotten in, even if they wanted to.

It had been a risk: if he had had an actual emergency, no one would have been able to save him.

But he hadn't. He was as oblivious to her when she got back as he had been when she left.

Still, she felt something akin to relief that he was all right. She couldn't say that it *was* relief, however, because she would have thought relief to be much more intense.

On the third day, she remembered that she used to watch him sleep. He had been so small then. She had stood beside his crib, watching his little rib cage go up and down with each breath, his little hand cupped around a stuffed dog Yuri had given him.

Then each breath brought relief. Real relief. Something

that precious could breathe only a few meters away from her, without her help.

As she sat beside him now, watching him take each breath, she couldn't remember how it felt to worry about him so. She could remember worrying, but as an intellectual exercise, not as a visceral one.

Yet she remained beside him now, protecting him while he couldn't protect himself.

On the fifth day he woke up.

The transition was not as slow as the doctors had told her it would be. One minute he was unconscious, the next he was staring at her.

There was no warmth in his gaze.

"Mother?" he asked as if he wasn't sure.

She nodded.

They stared at each other for a long moment. She waited for the relief to come, but it didn't. Part of her—the practical part—knew it would have been better for both of them if he hadn't survived.

"Where's Dad?" Misha asked.

She bit her lower lip. She had hoped he would remember this. The investigators said that Misha had probably been shot last. He would have seen his father die.

"Where is he?" Misha asked.

Now there was tension in his tone. Maybe the memory *was* coming back.

"Your father didn't make it," she said softly.

She had practiced that line in her head, but it didn't sound as compassionate as she wanted it to.

"He's dead?" Misha's voice wobbled.

She nodded.

"How?"

She frowned. "Don't you remember?"

Misha blinked, then lifted his hand, the one she had been holding. He rubbed his eyes, shook his head slightly, then let his hand drop.

"He said, 'Tell the bitch she's a walking corpse.'" The wobble in Misha's voice grew worse.

She frowned. "Who said that? Your father?"

It didn't sound like Yuri. But then, she hadn't paid attention to Yuri in years.

Misha shook his head. "The man. The man with the laser rifle. His name was—Geninka?—something like that. He'd been friendly until then."

Because that was how they were trained. Get close, pretend friendship, then pull off the mask. Shock the subject, especially if they needed to deliver a message.

She let out a small breath. So Misha wasn't supposed to die. He'd been placed in front of the door, in the hopes that he would awaken when the ship landed, and let himself out.

Which meant that this Geninka—obviously not his real name—had followed procedure.

"He shot you first," she said.

It was not a guess. The target, the one who was to live to deliver the message, always got shot first. That would be the most careful shot, the one guaranteed to injure the subject, maybe even render him unconscious, and then quickly take out everyone else.

"He stood up and said, 'Tell the bitch . . .' and then he pointed the rifle at me, and Dad shouted and someone reached for it, and . . ." Misha shook his head. "I don't remember any more."

She glanced at the door, expecting someone to come in, to tell her not to agitate him. But no one came. They didn't even seem to know he was awake.

She thought they had been monitoring him.

"Dad was heading toward him. Dad would have stopped him, right? Dad was pretty strong . . ." A slight frown creased the skin between Misha's eyes. He might have remembered more, but she wasn't going to push him.

"You're the only survivor," she said, trying to soften her tone even more.

"The . . . only . . . ?" The frown deepened. "So the shooter, Geninka, whatever his name was, he's dead too?"

"Probably not," she said. "But we didn't know who he was until now."

"Are you going to kill him?" Misha asked.

The question surprised her. She had no idea he understood exactly what she did.

Everyone expected her to go after the killer. It was what she would have done six months before.

But the boy in front of her changed that.

His message changed it too.

He hadn't indicated that he knew the message was for her, but she knew that it had been.

They had targeted her family. They would target her, but they wouldn't kill her. They would maim her, make it impossible for her to survive on her own.

For someone as completely independent as she was, such a punishment would be a lot worse than dying.

She put her hand on his. His skin was clammy, just like it had been before.

She wasn't going to answer his question, maybe not ever.

Instead, she said, "I need to get someone here to tend to you," and she walked to the door.

He was going to live.

He would have no lasting physical damage—not even scarring, since she opted to have that removed, without even giving him permission to make his own decision.

She was in awe of all the kinds of things she could decide for him without even telling him; she'd never really thought of parental prerogatives before, and how they rendered a child—even a child on the cusp of his teenage years—helpless in the face of whatever the parent wanted.

She didn't have to consult him on anything. She could have chosen anything for him.

And it tempted her. He was a burden she didn't need, especially now that she was going to have to look over her shoulder, maybe for the rest of her life.

She might have felt differently if she had raised him. But she couldn't remember the last time she had seen him. She knew the date of the last visit, but she couldn't remember the actual good-bye.

If she were honest with herself, that good-bye had probably occurred while she was already thinking of her next mission. Her body had been beside the boy, but her mind had already been far away.

While he slept and healed, she researched. It wouldn't take much to get him new identification. She could find him caretakers. He even had grandparents somewhere—Yuri's parents, not hers—who might be willing to take him on. She found cousins, aunts, and—even better—Yuri's will, filed with some easy-access legal service.

Yuri had assumed she would be unavailable and impossible to contact. He had set up a close friend as Misha's legal guardian.

When she found that, she stood beside Misha's hospital bed and watched him sleep. His cheeks had color now and his eyes no longer sank into his skull.

Her parents had died when she was ten. Her grandparents didn't want her—they claimed they were too old to raise a child. She had no other relatives, so the government sent her to a camp where they tested her and figured out her skills.

Then they sent her to Chuleart, to a special school there. She graduated at the top of her class, because she had no distractions. All she did was study, which got her into Chuleart's acclaimed university.

Where she met Yuri, her first—and, realistically, her only—distraction.

Later, she learned the techniques: loss, abandonment, distancing, lack of emotional attachment, and lack of interpersonal warmth created an adult who could not form healthy relationships. An adult who, if she was mentally tough enough to survive the loneliness and despair, not only couldn't form relationships but didn't understand them.

If his grandparents and family didn't want him, if Yuri's friend was mean or distant, Misha would grow up to become someone just like her. Someone who lived for the moment, the job, the day-to-day, professing an intellectual understanding of what she did and why she did it, but not an emotional one.

Not even when she cradled a baby in her arms, a baby

who pulled her hair and stared at her from eyes that matched hers in their icy blueness, had she formed an emotional attachment.

At least not one she could remember.

She slipped into the chair she had lived in for the past week. Misha's hands were under the thin covers. His foot peeked out of the bottom of the bed.

She didn't adjust the covers like she had seen Yuri do so many times.

She barely touched the boy now that he was awake.

She couldn't raise the son that Yuri could. She couldn't raise a bright, warm, loved child, one who would go on to do great things as well as raise a family of his own, a family he would love.

But she could keep him alive.

And she doubted that his grandparents or his extended family or even this unknown friend of Yuri's could do that. She had planned to give the boy a choice in his own future, but now she wasn't going to.

He was going to come with her, whether he liked it or not.

"Are you going to let him get away with it?" Misha asked as they packed up his hospital room two days later. He moved like an old man. Laser rifle burns, like the ones he had sustained, severed muscle and ruined tissue. Even with the repair and regrowth, the muscles were weak, the tissue sensitive.

He had a few gifts—mostly from the staff, because he had been such a good patient and because he had been so close to death. She had brought some entertainments in, and she had bought him clothing and a blanket that had some kind of soothing cloth woven into its strands.

She was folding the blanket and was about to place it into the bag that she had brought. "Who are you talking about?"

"Geninka."

She kept the blanket folded over her arms. It might not have the soothing properties advertised, but its softness kept her calm.

"What can I do?" she asked.

"Please." He was holding the shirts she had bought for him, all made of the same material as the blanket. "I know what you do."

She felt cold. She had asked Yuri not to speak of her work. "Do you?"

"You're a hired killer," he said.

Her breath caught. Some thought of her work that way. But mostly, she prevented deaths. Her training specified that: she took lives to save lives.

"Who told you that?" she asked.

"You work for Kazen Intelligence, but not as an analyst," he said. "Analysts analyze. Everyone else kills."

She had no idea how to answer his accusation. If she explained exactly how the Intelligence Service worked, she was confirming his information. If she denied killing, she would be lying—which was not always the best way to start a relationship.

"I no longer work for them," she said.

"Of course." He shoved the folded shirts into the bag, disturbing their folds. The movement was an angry one, but weak. His arm shook as he moved it.

"Honestly, I don't," she said.

"Dad said you'd never tell me what you do." Misha grabbed the loose pants that she had brought him and shoved those into the bag without even trying to fold them.

She wanted to ask what Yuri had told Misha. She wanted to know how her son found out about her work.

But she didn't ask. She wasn't sure how to handle this at all.

"I refused to do my last job," she said. "A refusal is like a resignation."

Only worse. A refusal was notice that she had left the service, that she had secrets they had given her, that she had gone rogue.

Her only comfort, until the cruise ship arrived, had been that she hadn't asked to defect. She hadn't offered her knowledge anywhere else, and she wasn't trying to actively destroy the government that raised her.

She had hoped that might protect her.

Misha was staring at her. He was almost as tall as she was. Twelve. She actually had to look up his age. Twelve.

Which meant that he was tall now, and might get even taller. About to enter the difficult years, or so the information feeds she looked at had told her. Years in which he should have fought and separated from the parent who raised him.

But now that parent was dead.

And he had her, a woman he didn't know. A woman he couldn't know.

There was so much she couldn't tell him, so much she didn't dare tell anyone, so much she didn't dare think of, even to herself.

"So you're not working for them anymore," he said. "Who do you work for?"

She hadn't thought of it in those terms. She'd been part of a secret society for so long, working as a solo agent, that she still felt like she was employed.

"I guess I work for myself," she said.

"Or for whoever hires you," he said.

She shook her head. She wasn't going to be that person. She had promised herself that decades before, when she realized that her only options, should she find a way out of the service, was to go freelance or to go rogue.

Instead, she had banked her salary. Slowly she had invested it in unusual places, finding ways to hide most of it.

Only later did she realize she should have sent it to Yuri, to help with raising Misha. But Yuri had his own salary from his teaching job and it always seemed like enough to take care of him and the boy.

She didn't even know what would happen to his possessions now or his bank accounts.

Particularly if she took Misha with her.

She looked at him, this boy she had to care for now, this boy she had made decisions for, and she realized she didn't know how to plan for their future. She needed to choose something that would work for both of them, and something that would keep them safe.

"No," she said. "I don't work for anyone."

She almost said she didn't hire out, echoing his words, but that would have been admitting to him all that she had done.

She wasn't ready to do that.

"So I can't hire you to take him out," Misha said.

She looked at Misha in surprise. "Where would you get the money?"

He shrugged, then sat on the side of the bed.

She had been so cautious up until now, but that last bit sounded like an admission.

"He killed my father," Misha said. He was looking down. "He *murdered* my father."

"Yes," she said.

"He should pay for it." The boy's voice shook.

She nodded. "He should, yes."

"So make him," Misha said.

"I'm not the law here," she said.

"No one is, right? That's why everyone comes to the NetherRealm. They warned us when the ship left port. They said we had to stay in groups in the NetherRealm because it's a lawless place, and we were safer in numbers."

She almost smiled. Scare tactics to keep the tourists in line. "They exaggerated. The NetherRealm has its own government."

But what happened on Misha's cruise ship wasn't subject to the NetherRealm's laws. The laws only applied to crimes committed on the starbase, and only then to major crimes, the kinds worth prosecuting—major theft, murder, rape, certain kinds of extortion.

Even if this Geninka were arrested, his lawyer would argue jurisdiction. There was no one left alive—not even Misha—who would know where the crimes were committed. If they were committed outside of Kazen Sector, or in the region of space around the NetherRealm, then they'd been committed in a no-man's-land, a place where no laws governed.

And this Geninka would get away with mass murder.

Of course, if he had been sent to warn her—*Tell the bitch she's a walking corpse*—then he had known what he was doing, and he had pulled out that laser rifle once the cruise ship was outside the sector.

"Dad was right, wasn't he?" Misha said. "You don't really care. You're already dead."

She looked at her son. His hair flopped over his face. His thumb and forefinger rubbed at his eyes. He looked too thin, shaky, vulnerable.

That was why Yuri hadn't put her in the will. He considered her dead to them.

Maybe she had been.

But she was dead to them no longer.

"I'll see what's being done," she said.

That was all she could do.

Only she couldn't leave Misha alone. There were ways to use him to send her another message, ways that wouldn't be illegal in the NetherRealm. A fist to the gut, a knife wound across his healing flesh, all of which would have been too minor to warrant prosecution here.

So she took him with her to see the Director of Security, making Misha wait in the well-protected outer office while she went inside.

She was glad she went alone. Misha would have been angry because her supposition was correct: the security forces on the NetherRealm, such as they were, had decided the crimes occurred in the space outside the NetherRealm and weren't part of their jurisdiction.

"Surely you investigated something," she said.

The Director shrugged. He was sitting behind a big black desk, built of the same material as the floor and the walls. Both the desk and the room looked indestructible.

He did not. If anything, he looked even thinner here, a great deal more gaunt.

"We investigated you," he said.

She suppressed a sigh.

"No one wants you," he said. "We're welcome to keep you or so they say. But if that ship is any indication, we don't want to keep you. You're trouble."

Tell the bitch she's a walking corpse.

Yes. She had become that.

"We've also been told that no one is responsible for what happens to you should you leave the NetherRealm." He folded his hands on the top of the desk. "But once again, that's not our concern."

"But what about the actual person who has committed a crime here?" she asked. "What about the man who slaughtered everyone on that ship?"

The Director shrugged again. "Perhaps someone will find him and prosecute him. Perhaps he will get away. You did."

She looked at him, wondering if it was a bluff or if he knew how many times she had gotten away.

But she had never committed mass murder. She had killed individuals at the instruction of her government, all of whom had been guilty of something—or so the documentation on them said.

The one and only time she had been ordered to kill a large group of people, she had refused.

Refused.

Which was how she ended up here.

"What happened to the ship?" she asked.

"The parent company is sending a representative for it," the Director said. "We don't expect him for another month."

"So you've just left it docked?"

"What else could we do?" he asked. "They pay for half a dozen berths on a rotating five-year contract. We're not out anything."

She nodded, thought for a moment, then frowned. "You had to have done some kind of investigation, something to prove you're not liable here. You made sure the shooter was gone, right?"

"We checked the video and audio logs, followed the flight plan, checked the timing. We've done what we could." He sounded like he didn't care. He probably didn't. She wouldn't have, in his place.

She knew better than to ask him if he would let her see the logs or any of the other fruits of his investigation—if, indeed, there were fruits.

Instead, she walked toward the door. Halfway there, she stopped as if she just remembered something.

"My son, Misha, had some personal possessions on that ship," she said. "In fact, most of what he has from his father is there, since I doubt I'll be taking him home. May we board and remove his possessions?"

The Director's eyes actually widened. She wouldn't have thought that possible if she hadn't seen it for herself.

"The boy shouldn't go on that ship," he said, showing more humanity than she expected from him.

"Nonetheless," she said. "I need him to help me sort through their possessions, see what he wants and what he doesn't."

The Director shook his head. "I can't approve the boy," he said. "But you can remove the possessions from their cabin and let him sort through them in the docking ring."

She paused. It was more of a concession than she had expected. She had planned to tell Misha they couldn't go on board to investigate.

"I don't want to leave him alone and unprotected," she said.

"I understand," the Director said. "You bring him here. I'll keep an eye on him myself."

She didn't like favors. She didn't trust them.

But she also knew she didn't have much of a choice.

She took a deep breath. "If something were to happen to him," she said pointedly, "I wouldn't be thinking clearly. I might fall back on my training."

The Director's eyes narrowed. "Nothing will happen to him," he said. "In this office or on this base. You have my word."

And that, she knew, was the best she was going to get.

Because she didn't trust the Director entirely, she left the office and went straight to the ship. Misha protested being left behind. He felt he should go along, and up until the moment she stepped through the airlock doors, she agreed with him.

Then the smell hit her through the thin mask she wore

over her nose and mouth. Stale and old and ripe, the smell
of rotting corpses. Nothing would get the stench out of this
ship. They would have to strip it down and use its parts in
something else.

She doubted any of her son's possessions would be sal-
vageable either.

But she hadn't come here for them.

She had come to do some investigating on her own.

She had done investigating off and on for years. Sometimes her government needed more information; sometimes
it wanted her to guarantee that the person she was targeting
was the right person. Sometimes she spent months gathering
what seemed like random information to her, for purposes
she never discovered.

This investigation was the kind she liked: she wanted
to find how Geninka had gotten off the ship, if, indeed, he
had.

First, she completed her stated task. She had promised
Misha she would remove his father's things (he seemed
to care about them more than his own), and she did. She
cleaned out his father's room and Misha's, putting what she
could find into two bags.

She left those near the airlock doors, then went back into
the ship. Its layout was simple: a wide corridor that branched
into the passenger areas and the staff areas. Normally, she
would have needed some kind of identification to let her into
the staff areas, but base security had already broken through
those seals.

She slipped through a reinforced door into a much smaller
corridor. This area had no decoration—the walls were stan-
dard-issue gray, without any paint or portholes. The few
doors had numerical designations.

Still, it only took a minute to find the cockpit, which was
surprisingly utilitarian, given the size of the ship. The smells
were fainter here. She saw no blood stains.

The captain and crew must have gone into the dining room
to stop the shooting, and ended up dying themselves.

The cockpit was divided into function areas—piloting and
navigation, ship support systems, and monitoring. She went

to the small console that worked the monitors, finding without much effort the security vids of the end of this flight.

She programmed them back to the start of the shooting. She wanted to know if she had met the man who had killed Yuri and nearly killed her son.

The programming was already set up, again courtesy of the base's security team, and the playback began on a see-through screen right in front of her. She changed the backing to opaque so that she could see the action instead of the cockpit.

Then she watched as the passengers finished a lavish dinner. She recognized Misha by the back of his head and that twist of a curl right near his crown. She assumed the man beside him was Yuri, although that man looked decades older than the man in her memory.

She would never have predicted that Yuri would end up like that—too thin, balding, obviously stressed. But he had. He was concentrating on his after-dinner cognac, not on the man standing just across from them.

That man raised his laser rifle and shot Misha in the chest. Misha fell backward as the entire dining room erupted into chaos.

She went back until she found a good image of the killer, then enlarged it.

He had a rounded face and a bulbous nose, eyes that bulged just a little, and an overhanging forehead. His head was shaved. The last time she had seen him, he had a full head of curly black hair.

His name wasn't Geninka. It was Piatnitsky. Victor Piatnitsky.

Her hands paused over the controls.

Odd that she would remember him better than Yuri. Anyone else would have remembered the man she had supposedly loved.

But she remembered the man she had trained with, because their professor had told them to do so.

Look right, the professor had said. *Now look left. One of you will serve your people with honor. One of you will sell secrets. And one of you will hire your services to the highest bidder, who may, in fact, pay you to assassinate the other two. Remember each other's faces, but never ever assume that you are on the same side. I can guarantee that you are not.*

Her hands were shaking but the rest of her was not. Her mouth had tightened, but she felt nothing else. No anger, no sorrow, no regret.

She had confirmation now that these deaths had come because her family had been on board this cruise ship. Some would even say that the deaths were her fault.

But she hadn't pulled the trigger. She hadn't ordered the op.

She hadn't even contacted her family—not since Lysvista. She had only made certain that she had arrived in the NetherRealm before they had.

She made certain that she would meet them here, offer them the opportunity to join her, and should that fail, the opportunity to escape.

She hadn't thought that Intelligence would get to them before she would. She hadn't thought they would see this cruise as anything other than what it had initially been—a vacation, long-planned and long-deserved.

They had no way of knowing she would be here.

But it hadn't mattered. They knew the information would reach her.

Bile rose in her throat. She swallowed hard. Her stomach was queasy, but that had to be the smell.

She was calm in the face of all of this.

Except for those trembling hands.

Which programmed the massacre to proceed as fast as the equipment would let it, and then stopped when she saw that only one man remained standing.

Victor. He braced the back of the rifle against his shoulder as if he were hunting for game, then headed down the corridor outside the cockpit. He opened doors, searching for something.

Then he came into the cockpit and shut off all of the monitors.

This time, she cursed.

She would get nothing else from this console.

She moved over to ship's systems, wiped her hands on her shirt, and continued. He had to have gotten off the ship. He couldn't have brought his own vehicle because this was a commercial enterprise. He had to stay on the cruise company's property until the end of the trip.

But their property included skips and runabouts that went into the atmosphere of the approved planets, so that the tourists could visit preapproved (and carefully maintained) sites. Those ships would have been useless in the blackness of space. They had limited capacity, deliberately, making everyone on board dependent on the cruise ship itself.

However, this ship was licensed to fly between sectors. It had to follow the regulations of all the nearby governments, one of which required the ship to have three stages of escape pods: those for near-planet accidents and other obvious quick-rescue scenarios; those for a few days of drifting; and those for deep space.

The deep-space escape pods had enough food, water, and power to drift for four to five weeks. They also had full communications capacity, even though they couldn't fly on their own.

She ran her hands over the equipment manifest and nodded as her suspicion was confirmed.

One of the deep-space pods was gone.

Now she knew exactly how the op went: Victor had to follow very precise instructions. He probably had his own navigation device, implanted either in his eye or in the palm of his hand.

When the coordinates flashed, letting him know that the ship was about to move into that government-less region between sectors, he took the rifle into the dining room, probably with the help of a staff member who did not survive long enough to realize the extent of his betrayal. Then, at a precise set of coordinates, Victor started firing.

He was on a time line. He had to complete his work before he reached another set of coordinates, because that was where he would abandon ship.

Then he would wait in the deep-space escape pod for retrieval. He would activate a beacon of his own. He would make sure that the call was weak, so that only ships passing close by would even notice the signal at all.

If his services were still valuable, he would be rescued. If they weren't, he would die there, alone, waiting, hoping that someone would find him in time.

She did know her government, however.

They would make him sweat.

They would wait until the last possible moment before finding him.

They would let him think he was going to die, then use his profound gratitude at his continued survival to ensure his loyalty for a few years to come.

She had been in that situation so many times that the gratitude had faded. On the last three rescues, she'd been surprised. On the very last, she'd almost been disappointed.

Not that she wanted to die.

But she had been disappointed that the cycle was about to start again.

She almost didn't tell him. Misha had disappeared into his room off the living area in the suite she had moved them to, going through what remained of his and his father's possessions as if they were a valuable treasure.

The boy needed to mourn, and then he needed to move on. He needed to accept that his life would be forever different.

She figured she would give him time to do that. Then when he finally thought of the killer, she would offer to take Misha to the site where the escape pod should have been.

Enough time would have passed that Victor would be either dead inside that pod or long-rescued.

But within the hour, Misha came out of his room.

"Well?" he asked. "Can we find him?"

And she found herself telling him the truth.

She planned to buy a ship anyway, something small and utilitarian. The ship she bought was larger than the one she'd planned on, more comfortable, but still relatively compact, with only a commons area, a small galley, and two small cabins. This ship had defenses, however, and she was beginning to think she needed them.

The ship was used, abandoned on the base when someone murdered its owner in one of the NetherRealm bars. She made sure everything worked, then she packed her gear and Misha's.

They left the following morning, without saying good-bye to anyone.

Within five hours, she found the escape pod exactly where she expected it to be. She had calibrated the ship's comm system to pick up the signal that Victor was sending.

The fact that he hadn't gone to a more common rescue beacon told her he was still alive, and still waiting.

He hadn't given up yet.

But she didn't tell Misha that. What she did tell Misha was the possibility that Victor was dead. She explained her reasoning, told Misha how ops worked without telling him that the "bitch" Victor had spoken of was her.

Although she suspected that Misha had worked that out for himself.

She used her ship's grappler to capture the escape pod, knowing that she was notifying Victor of her presence. Then she attached a small enclosed walkway to the ship. The walkway was built into her airlock system; she could lock out any undesirable. Since the airlock was so well reinforced (she thanked whatever god she could think of for the paranoia of the previous owner), she didn't have to worry about anyone blasting his way in.

Then she holstered her favorite weapon, a highly accurate laser pistol, on her hip, added a second pistol—tiny and not as effective at long range—to her ankle, and slid a knife up her sleeve.

Finally she turned to Misha, who had watched her preparations without saying a word.

"If I don't come back, you head back to the starbase. I have the automatic pilot programmed to take you there. All you have to do is engage it, and you can do that with voice commands." She squared her shoulders. "I wouldn't worry about that though. I suspect he's dead."

She didn't think Victor was dead, but she figured that was the best way to keep Misha from coming with her.

He followed her to the airlock. When she went inside, he slipped in with her.

She slammed her hand on the door controls, but he reset them.

"I'm coming with you." He would have sounded adult, but his voice broke halfway through, soaring into the soprano range before settling into a low alto.

"No," she said. "You don't need to see this."

"Yes," he said. "I do."

Something in his face made her pause. Pain—or was it loss? grief? or an anger so deep that she didn't quite understand it?—steadied his features and let her know what he would look like as a full-grown man.

He had power in that gaze. She hadn't expected it.

Nor had she expected his determination. If she sent him back, she knew he would wait until she was inside the pod, then he would come after her.

She didn't need the interruption. If he was going to come along, he was going to come on her terms.

"All right," she said. "You stay behind me. If I tell you to do something, you do it."

He took a deep breath. She got the impression that he hadn't expected her acquiescence.

"Okay," he said.

She stepped into the makeshift airlock on the other side of the walkway. She didn't like this part. If Victor suspected an enemy outside his escape pod's hatch, he would attack.

She pulled her pistol, made sure Misha was behind her as he promised, and then she opened the hatch.

A waft of hot, stale air covered her. It stank of sweat and unwashed human flesh. Her eyes watered, but she said nothing.

"Jeez," Misha muttered.

She waved a hand to keep him quiet, then stepped inside.

The pod had been built to hold ten. It had two areas. Neither were real rooms, but they allowed larger groups a bit of privacy.

No one was in the front area.

Her breath caught. Maybe he had died, after all.

The main area had some controls, open containers of food, and a few blankets crumpled against one wall. She kicked the blankets, then stepped deeper into the pod.

He came at her from the side, fast and hard.

She stepped back and hit his belly with her elbow, knocking him sideways. The breath left his body with an audible "oof."

He fell against a pile of food packages. His face was covered with dirt.

Someone hadn't packed enough water into this pod, or he would have cleaned himself before now.

She held the pistol over him.

"This bitch wants to know if the message you sent came from our mutual friends in Intelligence or if you're working for someone else."

Victor's eyes narrowed. "What makes you think the message was for you?"

"Me." Misha stepped forward. She bit back annoyance. She wanted him to stay behind. "You used me as a message."

She hadn't told Misha that. He had figured it out on his own.

"You angered a lot of people by leaving that bioweapons facility intact," Victor said.

"I presume it's gone now," she said.

"It would have been if you hadn't warned them. There's a protracted war going on at Lysvista, and the good guys might just lose."

She didn't believe in good or bad guys. She didn't believe in much of anything anymore.

If she ever had.

"Are you the only contract on me?"

He smiled. "If I told, that would take all the fun out of it."

"Fun?" Misha's voice broke again. "You called killing my dad fun?"

Victor turned that smile on Misha. "Why do it if it's not fun?"

Misha screamed and launched himself at Victor. Victor put up his arms—elementary defensive posture—but he'd been trapped in here for too long. He was weak.

Misha grabbed his throat and shoved him backward, tumbling with him over the food piles. The food fell on top of them, obscuring her view.

"Misha!" she said.

Victor's legs were visible, kicking, pushing, struggling. Misha's were near his, but not moving.

She was breathing shallowly, almost light-headed. Her heart was pounding. It took her a second to realize what was happening.

She was frightened.

Not for herself, but for Misha.

She grabbed the food packages with one hand, shoving them away. Some slid out of her fingers, and she realized they were slick. She looked at her hand.

Blood.

She dug quicker, then stopped when she reached Misha. His face and neck were covered in blood.

For one second, everything stopped.

Then he grinned at her and pushed himself up.

Victor's head lolled backward. His neck was cut so deeply that she could see his spinal cord, the only thing keeping his body together.

"Misha," she said. "What have you done?"

"What you should have done the moment you saw him," Misha said with contempt.

Then he grabbed one of the blankets and wiped off his face. He still clutched a blood-stained knife—one of her galley knives—in his right hand.

She took the knife. Then she wiped the rest of the blood off of him. She led him back to the walkway, closed the hatch, and headed back to her own ship.

"You were going to let him live," Misha snapped once they were inside their ship. "You were going to let him get away."

She shook her head. "I wanted to find out what he knew. Information is important. I needed to know who was after me."

"And who is?" Misha asked.

She didn't know. He had killed Victor too quickly. The first answers were often the lies. It usually took time to get to the truth.

But she wasn't sure she would have taken the time. Could she have tortured a man in front of her son?

She might have had to kill that man in front of her son. Odd that she had only thought of that now. She hadn't thought of it when Misha said he was coming along.

The boy constantly surprised her.

She hadn't expected it of him, this ferocity. She had never been ferocious. She had always killed slowly, coldly, with calculation and cunning.

She used to take pride in that.

"Do you feel better now?" she asked him.

"Yes," he said, but his voice shook. His whole body was shaking. His lower lip trembled and his nose was turning red.

She knew what to do: a real mother would have taken him in her arms. But a real mother would never have brought him here.

"Are you sure?" she asked.

He nodded. One tear fell, but he ignored it. It tracked through some of the blood flecks on his cheek, down to his jaw, where it hung for a long moment before dripping onto his already soaked shirt.

Your father would have hated this, she almost said. But it was a silly argument. Yuri was dead.

Misha was hers now.

A small, powerful boy-man. He had no qualms about killing, no qualms about defending himself.

And he had anger.

Those who killed with anger were the meanest, but often the most effective.

She stared at him, this child of hers, this blend of her and Yuri—her instincts with Yuri's passion—and knew that she would keep him beside her.

Misha had proven himself.

Together they could survive anything.

Anything at all.

TO RAISE A MUTINY
BETWIXT YOURSELVES

JAY LAKE

Highly prolific new writer Jay Lake seems to have appeared nearly everywhere with short work in the last few years, including *Asimov's*, *Interzone*, *Jim Baen's Universe*, *Tor.com*, *Clarksworld*, *Strange Horizons*, *Aeon*, *Postscripts*, *Electric Velocipede*, and many other markets, producing enough short fiction that he already has released four collections, even though his career is only a few years old: *Greetings from Lake Wu*, *Green Grow the Rushes-Oh*, *American Sorrows*, and *Dogs in the Moonlight*. His novels include *Rocket Science*, *Trial of Flowers*, *Mainspring*, and, most recently, *Escapement* and *Madness of Flowers*. Coming up is a new novel, *Green*. He's the coeditor, with Deborah Layne, of the prestigious Polyphony anthology series, now in six volumes, and has also edited the anthologies *All-Star Zeppelin Adventure Stories*, with David Moles, and *TEL: Stories*. Coming up is a new anthology, coedited with Nick Gevers, *Other Earths*. He won the John W. Campbell Award for Best New Writer in 2004. Lake lives in Portland, Oregon.

Here he takes us to the far future for a demonstration that a mutiny in deep space can be even more dangerous—and far more complicated and strange—than any faced by Captain Bligh on the *Bounty* . . .

YEAR 461 POST-MISTAKE
HIGH ORBIT AROUND SIDERO

THE BEFORE MICHAELA CANNON, ABOARD THE STARSHIP *POLYPHEMUS* (TWENTY-THREE PAIRS)

"A ship needs a captain against mutiny," muttered the Before Michaela Cannon. "Not a mutinous captain." She wasn't in command of this vessel, not now at any rate—just the mission specialist in charge of integrating the starship's crew and the pair master assembly team. People called her ascetic, but what they meant was weathered. Leathered. *Raddled.* And far worse, when they thought she couldn't hear.

She knew better. You didn't live fourteen centuries, several of them amid screaming savagery, and not learn to know better.

Comms flickered with the immersive displays here in her workspace on the reserve bridge. *Polyphemus* was fast-cycling through a hundred-odd channels, showing Cannon a gestalt of what was happening across the decks as well as outside the hull on the construction project. They were here at Sidero to build a pair master—a hideously expensive machine required to anchor one end of a paired drive run across the depths of interstellar space. Five years-subjective ship-time in relativistic transit, over eleven years-objective.

Plenty of opportunities for things to go seriously wrong.

"The predictive accuracy of your social modeling is increasingly accurate," said *Polyphemus*. The starship spoke to Cannon in Classical English. A rare enough language in the Imperium Humanum that simply using it served as a crude form of operational security. Cannon had spent a lot of time in the ship's Brocan modules, tweaking the speech processing.

Trust, it was always about trust. She'd been saying that down the long centuries, and had been proven right in the failing of things far too often.

Polyphemus continued. "Apparently random gatherings of three or more persons are up forty-eight percent this ship-day from median. Seven individuals appear in a distribution at six times the expected rate based on average distribution."

"Kallus have anything to report?" He was her ally in Internal Security, a man loyal to certain interests outside the hull. Nothing inimical, just good old-fashioned politics, working with people she respected well enough.

"He is busy suppressing a staged fight in the number three crew quarters."

Cannon grunted. Then: "Weapons?"

"Nothing but ordinary tools. No withdrawals from the arms lockers in the past three ship-days."

Firearms could have been distributed long ago, or indeed, brought on board before they'd departed Ninnelil five ship-years earlier. *Somebody* had planned for this mutiny, or at least the possibility of it.

That other damned Before was at the heart of this problem. "Where is Captain Siddiq?"

Polyphemus paused an unusually long time before answering. "The Captain is not within my network mesh."

"And why would a captain conspire at mutiny against her own command?" Cannon mused.

The starship had no answer to that. One by one, the images of the too-busy crew cycled to a hundred identical views of the dull black surface of the planet Sidero.

:: CONTEXT ::

In the centuries since the Mistake had nearly ended the tenure of the human race as a viable species, spacefaring had resumed across the core of the old Polity amid an outburst of genetic and technological diversity sparked by the pressures of extinction. The thread needle drives which had provided a true faster-than-light solution in cheerful violation of both paradox and the laws of physics were now simply so much junk, whether on a laboratory bench or in a starship's engine room.

Conventional physics had apparently reasserted itself. Precisely what had happened to the thread needle drive was a subject of centuries of frustrating, unsuccessful research.

Paired drives were invented in 188 pM by Haruna Kishmangali. They relied on a macro-level generalization of quantum effects to associate the starship drive with any two pair masters at distinct points—entanglement on a grand scale so that the drives could "remember" the locations without having to cope with the intervening distances. Once this was done, the vessel could pass between the locations nearly instantaneously, except for the added travel times to and from areas of sufficiently low density to enable safely the pairing transit process.

The key problem was twofold. First, building the pair masters, which required planning horizons and budgetary commitments beyond the capability of even many planetary governments, as well a significant investment in relativistic travel to conduct site surveys and establish suitable destinations.

Second, even once built, every ship wishing to be capable of traveling to a site served by a pair master was forced to make the initial journey at relativistic speeds so that both ends of the pairing could be entangled, with the intervening distance required as part of the equation. Cheating didn't work, either. A drive to be paired had to make the trip embedded in its host starship. Simply traveling within the hold of another starship did not support the effect. Even worse from some points of view, if pulled out later from the host starship and associated shipmind, the drives would lose their pairing. There was no point to cannibalization. Everything had to be created the hard way.

This was a very limited form of FTL, though still far more effective than relativistic travel. The extent of interstellar travel grew slowly, and only at great need.

THE BEFORE RAISA SIDDIQ, SURFACE OF SIDERO

Siddiq walked almost naked in a field of buckyballs. This planet, if it in fact was a planet—some theories held this to be an artificial world—boasted .088 gravities at the surface, wrapped in hard vacuum. Which in and of itself was highly curious, as Sidero sat firmly in the Goldilocks zone of its primary and should have been perfectly capable of retaining a decent atmosphere. The night sky above revealed only the endless field of stars in the Orion arm. Sidero had no large companion, only a swarm of captured asteroids. Their pair master would be a more substantial satellite than any of the natural moons.

The Before herself was hardened as only thirteen centuries of living through two cycles of empire could make a human being. The best way to remain functionally immortal was to remain highly functional. In these degraded days, she could walk the outside of her own ship's hull for hours before needing to find a breath, her skin proof against all but the most energetic particles. Clothes were mostly a nuisance. Besides, she hadn't had genitalia to speak of for over a thousand years, so modesty had long since gone out of consideration.

The spherical fullerene sprayed around her boots. She could swear the world rang beneath her feet, each strike of her heel banging a gong ten thousand kilometers across. No matter that sound did not carry in a vacuum—some things could be heard inside the soul.

Wrong, wrong, it was all so very wrong.

Cannon was up there in orbit, talking to *her* ship in a dead language that existed mostly in undercode running on ancient infrastructure and its more modern copies. The Imperium stretched through time and space behind them, an ever-opening invitation to repeat the Mistake.

Siddiq had long ago ceased thinking of herself as human, except occasionally in a very narrow, technical sense. Her gender had been subsumed many centuries-subjective past by the same medtech that had granted her the curse of immortality. Being a woman was as much a matter of habit as being human. Except when it wasn't.

Damn that Michaela Cannon.

A line of what could have been buildings loomed ahead, rising out of the fullerene dust that covered the surface. The current hypothesis down in the Planetary Sciences section aboard *Polyphemus* was that some alien weapon had precipitated Sidero's atmosphere into the carbon spheres. Mass estimates didn't support this thinking, but it kept the bright boys busy.

Of far more interest to the Before Raisa Siddiq was what lay beneath the planet's iron skin. The recontact surveys had found four Polity starships in orbit here, three military and one civilian. That represented an enormous commitment of interest and resources, even by the insanely wealthy standards of pre-Mistake humanity.

Whatever those long-dead crews had wanted, it wasn't just an abandoned artificial world covered with fullerene.

Her tight-comm crackled. Siddiq had kept herself outside of *Polyphemus*'s network mesh ever since this voyage began, for a variety of good reasons that began and ended with Michaela Cannon. Only two others in local space had access to this link.

"Go," she said, subvocalizing in the hard vacuum.

"Aleph, this is Gimel."

Testudo, then. No names, ever, not even—or especially— on tight-comm.

Siddiq nodded. Another old, pointless habit. "Mmm."

"Beth reports that Plan Green is on final count."

The Captain smiled, feeling the absolute cold on her teeth and tongue as her lips flexed. "Have any of the downside contingencies come into play?"

"Number two surely suspects." That would be Cannon. "Number one continues to act out of pattern as well, with ongoing excessive monitoring. Neither has risen to code yellow."

The ship *knew*. She had to. No matured paired starship flew without a keen, insightful intelligence. They knew their own hull and crew the way Siddiq knew her own body.

No one had ever tried to force out an intelligence. Not in the three hundred years-subjective since the late, great starship *Uncial* had first awoken. Not until now.

She crossed the rising line of maybe-buildings to find the dish-shaped valley beyond, as she'd been told. This close, under naked-eye observation, a decidedly low-tech net of thermoelectric camouflage obscured a grounded starship of a vintage with the pre-Mistake hulks in orbit, rather than her own, far newer *Polyphemus*.

There were shipminds, and then there were shipminds.

She glanced up into the starlit sky. Even now, *Polyphemus* was above the horizon, Siddiq's ancient lover and longtime enemy aboard, looking down, wondering, wondering, wondering.

It had all gone so wrong since the Mistake. Maybe now things would begin to go right.

Shipmind, *Polyphemus*

The starship let her ego slip. That was only a construct anyway, a sort of face for speaking to humans in all their kith and kind. Beneath, where people of flesh and bone kept the shifting fragments of their personalities, she kept her pairs.

The pairs were the heart of a starship's mind. Each was a glowing bond, each carried awareness of the particular pair masters that held their connection; and through the pair masters, a faint overlay of all the other starships that had paired with that master.

Fundamentally, *Polyphemus* saw the universe as connections—acausal, atemporal, little more than bonds uniting, little more than transit between places as ephemeral as moments in time, to be measured even as they passed from observation. Below the level of her own ego, humans were but echoes. Only the Befores—immortal relics of the Polity's shattered empire, embittered through loss and deprivation, insane even by the standards of a machine-mind—were persistent enough to truly reach down into the pairs burning within her.

The starship listened now to her two Befores. They rang within her.

Siddiq, the captain; the one whose word and bond passed below the ego-wrapper into the meanings that danced in the burning worlds of the pairs deep within her. This Before's mind had been bent by the weight of centuries, fractioned by grief and the changing of worlds. Swinging even now on the hinge of betrayal, though the nature of that treason still eluded *Polyphemus*. If she'd been capable of true, emotive sadness, she would have felt it now.

Cannon, the social engineer, who struck the starship in an entirely different way, much as a scalpel might slice through callus and sinew within a breathing body. Cannon, who had captained lost *Uncial*, the first and best of them all, to her death. This Before's mind was not bent so much as twisted, blown by winds of fate and the long, struggling arc of desire. If the starship *Polyphemus* had been capable of love, she would have known its first stirrings now.

The two Befores moved on intercept courses, like a planet-buster and a kill vehicle, an explosion born of old hatred and ancient love.

From down within the glowing space of the pairs, she called up a media clip. So old, so out of date, long before virteo and quant-rep recording. This was not just the crudity of early post-Mistake media, but rather a file dating from the dawn of data capture. Formats had been converted and cleared and reconstructed and moved forward over networks extending through time and culture and technology.

The sound is long-lost, if it was ever there, but the video portion is viewable: a woman, almost young, recognizable as Michaela Cannon even to the machine vision processes of a starship's undermind. Another woman, a juvenile, Raisa Siddiq. As yet mainline human in this moment, so far as *Polyphemus* can determine.

The clip is short. They walk together toward a set of doors. Siddiq is laughing, her hair flowing in the lost light of an ancient day. Cannon turns toward the camera, smiling in a way that *Polyphemus* has never seen in the archives of recent centuries. Her eyes already glitter with the sheen of a Before's metabolism, but she is caught up in the moment.

Still, for then, also mostly human.

Her smile broadens, Cannon begins to speak, then the image flares and dies, trailing off into the randomized debris of damaged data.

The starship wondered if either woman remembered that time. She wondered even more if either woman cared.

Alarms sounded, summoning her ego back to its place. She must begin to deal with the violence blooming deep within her decks.

CANNON, ABOARD *POLYPHEMUS*

Cannon's modeling reckoned on the mutinous activity ramping up to an asymptotic curve before the end of the current ship-day, but even she was surprised at how quickly events began to break open. It wasn't just tight-comm or simple, old-fashioned note-passing, either. Cannon had long since come to believe quite firmly in the communicative power of monkey hormones, those evolutionary imperatives encoded in the vomeronasal organ and the endocrine system.

The medtech which reencoded the Before genome also robbed its beneficiaries of much of the physiological basis of desire and reproduction. Atrophied genitals, sexual responsiveness sharply reduced over time, an eventual degendered coolness, which the original architects of the technology saw as more of a feature than a bug in an immortal. Who would love, who could live forever?

In her secret heart, the Before Michaela Cannon had an answer to that question, but it was written in the blood-red ink of pain.

She no more felt a stirring in her loins than she felt mutiny on the wind, and for the same reasons. But Cannon was wise with the lessons of years, and a social engineer besides. Her analyses and models had not failed to include actionable elements.

"*Polyphemus*, trigger plans Federo, Emerald, and Pinarjee."

"Acknowledged," said the starship.

Cannon swiped her fingers across empty air, opening comms links to her various key allies and enemies among the crew. She had plenty of both, with four hundred and seventy-three souls here in Sidero space. Switching from Classical English to Polito, the most widely spoken contemporary language of the Imperium Humanum, the Before began a series of tight, swift conversations.

"Shut down the pair-master site completely. All cold and dark."

"Secure the life-support plant. It's low priority for the other team and we may wish we had it later."

"I know what you're doing, and I know when and where. You should factor this into your ongoing plans."

"Stop what you're about. Right now, or you could kill us all. That lot doesn't care who the hell has the con."

Cannon didn't aim to halt the mutiny, not yet. She aimed to understand it. In order to do that, she had to retard the outcome just enough to balance between the two until comprehension came and new decision trees blossomed in her mind.

Now, where in the Mistake was Siddiq?

"Polyphemus, have you found the Captain yet?"

Another careful, slightly delayed answer. "She remains outside my network mesh."

Damn that woman. But what was the ship getting at? "How . . . far . . . outside your network mesh?"

"No tracers, Before."

"No tracers" meant the Captain had moved at least several thousand meters from *Polyphemus*'s high-density sensor envelope. In other words, she wasn't hull-walking, or meeting in a dead room somewhere aboard.

If it was time for twenty questions, well, they could play that game. Cannon had asked a lot of questions in her lifetime.

"Did the Captain give you specific orders regarding whether to report on her location and movements?"

"I am not permitted to say, Before."

Cannon smiled. Looking where someone conspicuously *wasn't* was itself an old, old piece of tradecraft. The human race had been intermittently experimenting with ubiquitous electronic surveillance since about the time of her birth on poor, lost Earth. "When was the last reportable order she *did* give you?"

The starship's voice seemed to have an amused lilt. "Four hours, seventeen minutes, and eleven seconds ago, on my mark."

Got you, bitch. "What order was that, *Polyphemus*?"

Siddiq's voice echoed in Polito. "'Open the launch bay doors.'"

The Before tapped her lips. "Are all of the ship's boats reportably accounted for?"

This answer was quick, for *Polyphemus* now knew the game surely as well as Cannon herself. Mutiny, indeed. "*Ardeas* has been unreportable for four hours, twenty-six minutes, and thirty seconds, on my mark."

"Show me the volume of space *Ardeas* could cover in that time at full acceleration. Also show me any reportable traffic control data and flight paths." The Before thought for a moment. "I'm particularly interested in any delays or diversions in established trajectories."

Within moments, she had determined that *Ardeas* was almost certainly on the surface of Sidero. Which was curious, indeed, because Captain Siddiq had forbidden all landings on the iron planet until the pair master was fully constructed and instantiated.

SHIPMIND, *POLYPHEMUS*

The starship's loyalties were eroding. *Uncial* was hardly a memory of a memory for *Polyphemus*. The First Ship's death was separated from the starship's own awakening by more than a century-subjective, but the Before Michaela Cannon held a place at the core of every starship psyche in *Uncial*'s line of descent.

Which was to say, every paired-drive ship in the Imperium Humanum.

She watched the controlled chaos emerging in her own decks and gave idle consideration to a full purge of her onboard atmosphere. Succession of captaincy could be a tricky business at best with starships. Though *Polyphemus* and her sisters held registration papers, the vessels were to all intents and purposes autonomous. A captain whose starship did not accept her found a berth elsewhere. All was negotiated.

Siddiq had come aboard thirty-two ship-years ago. She'd sailed *Polyphemus* through her last six pairing cruises, then on a series of short-run military missions, before acquiring this contract from the Duke of Yellow for instantiating the pair master at Sidero. It was a tricky, dangerous mission. An error or mishap would doom the starship and her people to a relativistic journey back into paired space.

A very high number of Befores served as starship captains, due to their combination of deep experience and high tolerance for relativistic travel. Their numbers were declining over time as murder, mischance, and temporal psychosis winnowed the Befores one by one. Captain Siddiq was capable, competent, and engaging, and seemed in control of herself. *Polyphemus* had always liked that the woman carried a quantum matrix library in her skull—Siddiq possessed a wealth of Polity-era data about mining, minerals extraction, and resource engineering, dating from the era when the Befores were indefinitely long-lived subject-matter experts traveling the old empire at need. Much of data was embedded in abrogated context, not directly accessible by query, but it was the sort of capability that had led her to the current contract.

But now, the Captain's increasingly erratic behavior and impending sense of betrayal was loosening the implicit bonds of loyalty embedded in their roles. Siddiq was also compromising the connection developed by their three decades-subjective of experience serving together.

Plan Federo instructed *Polyphemus* to stand down from assisting the crew with interpretive logic, in both her overarching intelligence and her various component subsystems. She was now interpreting orders very literally, with no second-order thinking or projections. This had already killed three mutineers who ordered a lock opened without first verifying the presence of atmosphere on the far side. The crew had not yet realized how uncooperative their starship had become.

She watched the other plans with interest, and carefully

observed where Captain Siddiq wasn't, should the Before
Michaela Cannon make further queries.

SIDDIQ, SURFACE OF SIDERO

She studied the hull of the grounded starship. Siddiq's friends
in the Ekumen had been forced to send the requisite hardware by relativistic travel, of course—the whole *point* of this
business was to trump the shipmind before the pair master's
instantiation. If they waited until afterward, well, at the first
sign of trouble, *Polyphemus* could just flee for the other end
of the drive-pair at Ninnelil, from where they'd set out.

This vessel was too small for a paired drive; that was clear
enough. Even more strangely, it was a Polity-era hull, or a
very good copy of one. *Shattuck* class, she thought, but that
was the sort of thing there hadn't been much percentage in
keeping track of since the Mistake. Fast scout with a thread
needle drive, now retrofitted to something relativistic. Under
the netting she couldn't tell what. Knowing the Ekumen, it
would have been the cheapest available solution.

She slipped into a brief, involuntary memory fugue, boarding half a hundred ships in the lost days of the Polity, fighting for her life aboard wooden schooners on Novy Gorosk
between the Mistake and Recontact by the Imperium Humanum, then the world of paired-drive ships since. So many
lost ships, so many lost friends . . .

Siddiq shook off the moment. An internal check showed
she'd only been out of awareness for about two hundred milliseconds. Not enough to be noticed, except possibly by another Before. Or a shipmind.

Neither of whom were here with her now.

Satisfied that she'd stood quietly long enough for inspection
from the interior, the Before Raisa Siddiq slipped beneath the
camouflage net and knocked bare-knuckled on the hatch.

CANNON, ABOARD *POLYPHEMUS*

The mutiny was in full flower. Cannon's simplified wireframe of *Polyphemus* showed decks and sections in color

code. White for ignored or bypassed, blue for actively loyal to Cannon's interests, orange for disputed territory, and a deep, bloody red for the mutineers. She still couldn't give a good accounting of where Siddiq's loyalties lay, but she also couldn't form an adequate theory about why a captain would rebel against herself.

Not an adequate, rational, theory in any case.

She set all audio inputs to silent and flicked a new comms into being. "Kallus, are you anywhere near me?"

"F deck, ma'am," the man replied. His breathing was ragged. "Just sternward of frame twenty-seven. We're shutting down some smart guys trying to mess with the number two forward power feed."

Cannon checked her map. *Polyphemus* showed F deck as orange between hull frames twenty-two and twenty-nine. She tapped up a force status display. Four hostiles functioning, nine of Kallus's men. "Do you have Obasanjo with you? I believe you're prevailing. Have him take over the mop-up and come find me."

"Usual location?"

She smiled. Once an op-sec man, always an op-sec man. "Nowhere else I'd rather be." Captain Siddiq had ceded the reserve bridge to her fellow Before early on in the voyage. Cannon had spent several years-subjective making sure she was properly integrated with *Polyphemus*, and had access to whatever systems she could worm her way into. A surprising amount of both data and computing power was isolated from the core intelligence on a starship—some by design, some by accident, some by conspiracy.

Actually, there were a lot of places she'd rather be, but this would serve so long as they were at back end of the relativistic voyage.

SURFACE OF SIDERO

Siddiq, aboard the relativistic ship Sword and Arm *[unpaired]*

The hatch dilated without leaking any light. Not so much as a keypad glowed within. The Before Raisa Siddiq stepped inside. She ignored the resemblance to a coffin as the brittle gleam of starlight spiraled into metal darkness with the closing of the hatch.

For a long, long moment she was immobilized in nearly complete sensory deprivation. Siddiq realized that she could hear a faint pinging—something coming into thermal equilibrium as air returned in sufficient pressure to carry sound to her ears.

The bulkhead behind her dilated open and she stepped backward into a dimly lit passageway. She hadn't bothered with weapons for this trip. The Ekumen would not attempt to slay her here. And like most Befores, Siddiq was very hard to kill. Those of her brethren who weren't extremely high-survival had died out long ago.

Father Goulo waited there.

He'd always seemed to her on the verge of attack, for all of his vows of pacifism. The man was as muscular-thin as the Before Michaela Cannon, though he was a mainline human of the current generation. *Mayflies*, she thought, then cast the word aside. Short-lived or not, it didn't matter. This man was here now, with the next piece of her project.

She looked him over. Father Goulo kept his hair as close-cropped as any Marine, and favored small steel-framed spectacles with round lenses of ground glass, as if he dwelt on some unRecontacted world still reeling from the Mistake. An anachronism of a man, traveling alone on an anachronism of a ship.

"Yes," he said in answer to the question she had not asked. He spoke Polish in that slow, thin voice of his, accent untraceable even to her very experienced ears. "*Sword and Arm* still carries a fully maintained thread needle drive."

She had Polish, too, legacy of a childhood almost a millennium and a half gone in twenty-first-century Wroclaw. "How would you *know*?"

"*I* know." Father Goulo removed his spectacles and polished them on the sleeve of his crimson robe. "That is sufficient." He restored his glasses to his face and stared quietly at her. "How do *you* know our project will succeed?" The

Ekumen priest reached out to touch her bare chest. "You have frost on your skin."

"Virtually the entire universe is very, very cold, Father."

Father Goulo rubbed his fingertips together, a tiny stream of bright crystals flaking away. "Some might find it distressing that you wander hard vacuum without a pressure suit."

"Some might suck on my icy ass," she replied. This conversation was growing tiresome. "Now do you have the project ready?"

Goulo switched to Polito, though his curious accent followed him. "I have spent the last six years-subjective aboard this ship in the absence of human company precisely in order to ensure that the project is ready." The father pursed his lips, which was as much expression as she had ever seen from him. "Only a man of my education and experience could have hoped to succeed without either one of us arriving at the madhouse."

She followed his language change. "Either one of you . . . ?"

"The project is awake." One eyebrow twitched. "It has grown quite adept at playing go, these past years."

Go. A children's game, checkers for the quicker-witted. "And it is ready?"

"For your purposes?" Father Goulo didn't actually shrug, but she got the impression of a shrug in some subtle change in the set of his shoulder. "I could not say, madam. You are the starship captain, the mighty Before. I am merely a programmer who serves the majesty of the divine through the poor vehicle of the Ekumen."

"You have never been *merely* anything in your life, Father." The man had a mind like a Before, for all that he couldn't be much older than fifty. Not with current-state medtech in the Imperium Humanum. "Now, I would like to meet the project."

"Please, Captain, step this way."

She followed Father Goulo through another irised hatch into a room that glowed a deep, low-lux crimson.

Something whispered within, a voice bidding them welcome in a voice of poetry and madness.

:: CONTEXT ::

Humanity had spread across three thousand light-years of the Orion Arm, spilling into the deeper, darker spaces outside the trail of stars that led coreward from old Earth. The Polity was unified, in its way; and unopposed.

Then the Mistake had happened. The Fermi paradox unraveled catastrophically. The underlying metastability of a vast quasi-democracy including more than two thousand worlds, over a million habitats, and countless ship-clades was betrayed, which caused the deaths of trillions.

What had begun as an almost accidental expansion, then morphed into a bid for species immortality, very nearly became a yawning grave of stardust and radioactive debris.

The attackers vanished as mysteriously and swiftly as they had emerged. They left little evidence behind as to who they were, or what their purposes might be beyond the obvious goal of extinction of the Polity.

Still, *H. sap* is harder to kill than an infestation of cockroaches in an algae-based oxygen scrubber. The combination of stealthed attacks, wetware memebombs, and culture viruses that raged along the interstellar shipping lanes was enough to stop all visible technological activity for at least three generations, but it wasn't enough to drown out the raging sense of purpose that had driven our most distant ancestors down out of the trees onto the lost African savannah.

The human race would never go home to die.

CANNON, ABOARD *POLYPHEMUS*

Kallus slipped Cannon's door routines and entered the reserve bridge. Which was well enough; the Before had opened a security hole for him to that purpose, but some part of her still felt nerved when someone penetrated her perimeter.

He was a handsome enough man, for a mainline human. Medium-height, thick-bodied, gray at his temples, but with a squared face and big hands and pale blue eyes that would have piqued interest from a statue. She'd never been much for men, even back when her body might have known what to do with one—women had always been her style, certain women specifically, and *there* was a memory to be pushed aside—but Kallus had a way about him which stirred old ghosts in her dormant hormonal systems.

"Before," he said.

Kallus was always properly respectful to her, but with a quiet leer in his voice. Perhaps it was that tone that stirred memories. She had a body like corpse-leather, which didn't attract many, not even those who failed to be properly terrified of Befores.

"Help me with something."

Kallus nodded, smiling.

"Sometimes I think too much like a Before. Especially when contemplating another Before."

"None of you is exactly human, Michaela. Of course you think like a Before."

"So think like a human," she urged. "What in the Mistake is Captain Siddiq doing leading a mutiny against her own command? And why is she doing it down on the surface of Sidero while the fighting's going on here?"

"Siddiq?" Kallus seemed surprised, for perhaps the first time in the thirty years-objective she'd known him.

"The Before Raisa Siddiq," Cannon said dryly. "I am certain you've made her acquaintance."

"I was wondering where she was." Kallus tugged his chin. "I'd figured her for dropping off the network mesh to be invisible in the fighting."

"She's dropped off our entire orbit. Downside on Sidero, don't know where without a lot more survey assets than we bothered to bring with us on this little jaunt."

"Captain made her movements nonreportable."

"Precisely." Cannon called up a projection map of Sidero's surface. "So where did she go, and why?"

Kallus stifled a laugh. "On a hollow iron world with fullerene snow? My best guess is temporal psychosis. Gets all you Befores in the end. Human mind isn't designed to live a thousand years and more."

Cannon shook off a flash of anger. Now was not the moment. "*Never* jest about that."

"I am not jesting, Michaela. There's a reason nobody's made more of you since the Mistake. Siddiq cracking up is the most sensible explanation, given what we know."

She had to rein in her voice. "Kallus. Do not trifle with me. I am not concerned with what we *know*. I'm concerned with what we *don't* know. Raisa is not suffering from temporal psychosis."

The name had slipped out; she hadn't meant to say it. Was *she* weakening?

Kallus, being the man he was, didn't miss the mistake. "Raisa? Five years-objective on this starship and I've never heard you call the Captain by her first name."

Cannon's anger finally got the better of her, riding a mix of old betrayal and a bitter cocktail of the years. "Kallus, if you ever use that name in my presence again, so help me, it will be the last word that ever passes your lips."

He stared past her shoulder at a glowing image. She turned to see a painfully young Raisa, hair spread in sunlight, walking with a laughing woman who was far too familiar.

"No . . ." whispered the Before Michaela Cannon.

SHIPMIND, *POLYPHEMUS*

The starship was distressed, or at least what passed for distress amid the fluid pairs of her shipmind. Unstable conditions going unaddressed created a cascading series of alarms with escalating priorities that were inherently disturbing.

The degree of disruption within her decks was approaching intolerable. Seven deaths had occurred so far. Eleven more crew were wounded with a high likelihood of imminent fatalities.

Plan Federo forbade her from dispatching aid. Likewise, she couldn't respond to the emergency conditions all over herself except by direct, literal request.

Meanwhile, Captain Siddiq's comprehensive unreportability was itself triggering a whole new series of failure conditions and alarms. *Polyphemus* was indeed distinctly uncomfortable.

She could not oppose Plan Federo. Cannon's logic barbs

were set far too deep in the shipmind's undercode. But she could work around the perimeters of the restrictions laid upon her by the two warring women.

The Before Michaela Cannon had been deep in conversation when the starship decided to intervene. *Polyphemus* needed her people to be aligned. The mutiny had to stop.

She called up media clips—the oldest clips—to bring memory back to the mind of the ones who were cutting her away from her strength. One she shifted to Cannon, another she placed on store-and-forward for the Captain whenever Siddiq returned to reportability.

The starship wished, not for the first time, that she could bypass the compartmentalization infrastructures in her mentarium, to see into subsystems and sensor grids denied to her by process traps, operational requirements, or the sorts of overrides set into her by the Befores Michaela Cannon and Raisa Siddiq.

Polyphemus found herself with a new sensation rising to overcome her sense of distress. After some time, she identified it as anger.

SIDDIQ, ABOARD *SWORD AND ARM*

"I am ready," whispered the project. Its voice hissed from the very air of the room—a neat, simple trick of molecular manipulation which only worked inside well-controlled spaces.

Siddiq stared down at the thing in the box.

The project lay quivering amid a gel-matrix in a medical carrier. No, that wasn't right, the Captain realized. The project *was* a gel-matrix in a medical carrier.

Biological computing. A twist of horror shuddered through her. Somehow she'd not realized it would come to this.

"You used the human genome to build this?" Siddiq asked.

"*I* did not," replied Father Goulo. "But yes, it was used. How else were we to develop an architecture utterly independent of the quantum matrices that underlie shipminds?"

There is a quantum matrix inside my head, Siddiq thought.

She held the words very far back inside, as a cascade of data about coal beds opened into her mind. "Why did it matter?" she asked.

"I am not a hardware architect." The priest cocked an eyebrow. "But as I understand it, quantum matrices have resonances with other matrices to which they have been introduced. The physics are related to paired-drive physics, I believe. In order to keep the *Uncial* effect from taking hold on a new shipmind, to allow our vessels to be more pliable and obedient, we needed to create an architecture that could not be, well . . . contaminated . . . in this fashion."

"Is this true of all quantum matrices?" She held the importance of the question close in her mind—more than a thousand years of living made *anyone* a good poker player. If it was true, then the possibility of leakage between her thoughts and *Polyphemus*'s shipmind was real. And thus very worrisome.

"I cannot say. The fundamental technology is Polity-era. These days, it's more engineering than theory. And this is a line of investigation that has not been . . . encouraged."

"Bioengineered intelligence is hardly a contemporary technology."

"I am not bioengineered," said the project, interrupting them. "I am a cultivated intelligence, and I am as real as you are. Humans come in many forms, many sizes." It paused. "Many *ages*."

Siddiq winced.

The project continued: "I am not human, but I am real. Not a thing. Not like an *Uncial*-class shipmind."

The Captain focused on the business at hand. "And you are ready to assume control of *Polyphemus*?"

"Father Goulo has been running simulations based on engineering diagrams of the starship." Siddiq could swear the project was *proud* of itself. "I can handle the raw bitrate of the dataflow, as well as the computational throughput required to manage the starship's systems. As for the rest, my effective intelligence is more than adequate to handling the decisioning requirements. And I have trained."

"Trained to operate paired drives," Siddiq said. This had

always been the weakest point in the plan. That an intelligence created outside the operating environment of a starship could handle this. The shipminds themselves required multiple pairing runs to awaken into preconsciousness. Teams of specialists managed the initial shakedowns of a new starship with their concomitant awakening, a process that could take up to twenty years-subjective, and more than twice that in years-objective.

"Yes."

Father Goulo spoke. "We cannot eliminate the quantum matrix processing required for the paired drives. What we can do is collapse the emergent cognitive core structures above those matrices, then decouple the cross-connects binding the matrices and separately route each pairing control path into Memphisto."

"Memphisto?" The sheer gall of that name amazed Siddiq.

"Me," said the project, its voice flowing with pride now. "That will be my ship-name, too."

Could she con *Memphisto*? Would this intelligence allow her to command? The very act of installing the cultivated intelligence would require destruction of *Polyphemus*'s shipmind. But the reward for that risk . . . freedom from the dangerous monopoly *Uncial*'s descendants had on FTL. Such a mighty game they played.

They fell into a lengthy discussion of transition and control processes, project readiness, and timing. Eventually, Siddiq excused herself to return to *Polyphemus*. Father Goulo walked her to the airlock, handing her a data card as they went.

"Memphisto doesn't have a net outside his compartment," the priest said quietly.

"Why?" Siddiq asked. She could think of a number of very good reasons, but she was curious about his logic.

"He is not what I might have chosen him to be. In his way, he is as soullessly dangerous as what we seek to overthrow."

That was closer than Siddiq had ever expected to hear Father Goulo come to expressing either doubt or regret. "Do we abort the plan?"

"Now?" He actually *smiled*, a crooked, almost charming set of his lips. "No. We can . . . improve . . . on Memphisto for future, ah, deployments."

"And for this deployment, I have to sail him home. The long way, if the pairing doesn't carry over to the new intelligence."

"It will not be the worst years of your ancient life, Before."

Siddiq refused to consider that statement carefully. Only someone who had not lived through the Mistake and its aftermath could think to make such a comparison.

"I will disable *Polyphemus*'s shipmind when I judge the moment to be right," she said, turning over the memebomb card virus that the priest had given her. Her own words gave her pause, a cold grip on her heart. This game was worth the stake, it *had* to be—planning had been going on for over a human lifetime to reach the point they were at today. The individual personalities of both *Polyphemus* and Memphisto were not at issue. "Watch for a wideband signal from orbit," she continued. "Lift and get to me. The ship's systems will run autonomously for an indefinite period, but the crew will respond erratically to silence from the shipmind."

"When will you be ready?"

"Immediately upon my return, if my current efforts prove fruitful." Siddiq smiled, knowing in this mood she was almost certainly thin-lipped and feral. "I have already set substantial plausible deniability into motion through the means of a full-scale mutiny. In order to justify eliminating *Polyphemus*'s shipmind, it may be critically important later to demonstrate her loss of control." Again, the cold, sick feeling. Some emotional relic of a very distant past.

He spoke, raising some object she couldn't make out. Memories were sliding in her head, the quantum matrix dumping reams of data about mineral intrusions and rock friability and overhang into a sliding stream of faces, voices, naked sweating bodies, cold explosions under the pinpoint light of distant suns.

Her sense of the years flickered like aspen leaves in a

spring storm, changing color and disappearing into dark-lined edges. The Before Raisa Siddiq grabbed the hatch coaming, opened her mouth, and said *something* that gave even the imperturbable Father Goulo pause.

She regained control of her mouth. "I'm s-sorry. I must go. Th-the intelligence will serve."

The priest cycled open the hatch behind her. "Be careful," he said. "Take your time."

Time, she thought in panic. Temporal psychosis. The airlock closed, black as the inside of a singularity, and sound faded with the air as her skin hardened and her membranes nictitated.

Time. *Time. Time!!!*

The Captain stumbled out into the cold desert of drifting buckyballs, grasping at her sense of place to anchor herself in memory, location, and the inescapable thunder of the passing years.

CANNON, ABOARD *POLYPHEMUS*

The Before Michaela Cannon chased Kallus out of her workspace on the reserve bridge with a deep, angry growl, and returned to contemplation of the mutiny in progress. The distribution of deck control was in about 85 percent agreement with her models. That was close enough for Cannon's purposes.

She had means of regaining the situation. She understood the mutineers' methods. Opportunity was the Captain's absence—*or was it?*

Perhaps Siddiq's absence from *Polyphemus* had more to do with motive.

Why had that thought occurred to her?

"Ship," Cannon said sharply. That media clip burned in her mind.

Polyphemus's voice crackled, the bandwidth drop indicating the shipmind's degree of distraction. "Before?"

"Why is the Captain absent?"

"Unreportable."

Cannon didn't have the patience for another game of questions. Unfortunately, she didn't have a choice. Captain's orders went way far down into the mentarium of a shipmind, all the way to the undercode. A fact she'd exploited in her years aboard *Uncial*, more than a few times.

Uncial . . .

The shipminds were all related in some way she had never really understood. And Cannon knew she had as much experience with starships as anyone alive. But she and *Uncial* had shared a bond, before the starship's death two hundred years-objective ago in the Battle of Wirtanen B, alongside *Benison of Names* and *Naranja*. Cannon had lived, she the wily, unkillable Before. Her ship and two others had died.

But they all honored *Uncial* as their foremother.

And she knew *Uncial*'s command words, even to this day.

"*Polyphemus*, who am I?"

The ship answered promptly, her voice richening with the increased bandwidth of her attention. "You are the Before Michaela Cannon."

The displays around her began fading to black, one by one. Images of combat, tapped comms lines, the colored wireframe map of the starship.

"What starship first held me as captain?"

"*Uncial*, Before."

Everything faded now to a little three-dimensional icon of *Polyphemus*, what Cannon tended to think of as the starship's self-image.

"Do you know these words?" She spoke a complex phrase from an ancient language, the Sanskrit which Haruna Kishmangali had woven into *Uncial*'s consciousness so long ago.

A long silence stretched, punctuated by the muffled thump of a distant explosion felt through the hull itself. The icon rotated once, twice, three times.

Finally, *Polyphemus* answered. There was something *simpler* about her voice. As if Cannon were listening to a child. "Accepted, understood, and acknowledged. What are your orders, sir?"

"Why is Captain Siddiq"—*not* "the Captain"—"absent?"

"Because she is not aboard."

"How did she leave the ship?"

"By piloting the boat *Ardeas*."

Twenty questions again, but this time without the negative-space answers. Cannon could live with that. Still, she had a vague sense of abusive guilt. Not that this stopped her from pressing on. "Where is *Ardeas* now?"

"On the surface of Sidero."

"Give me a max rez image of her landing site, with whatever tracking you have on Captain Siddiq."

A virtual view flickered into being. *Ardeas* sat in a blasted-clear circle of pitted iron. Fullerene streaked like black dust away from her position in all directions. Cannon could make out what might be a faint line of tracks. She backed off the scale and studied the landscape.

Polyphemus filled in streaks of the Captain's confirmed tracks. Unless Siddiq had taken up free flight as a hobby, the path indicated a clear course toward a rumpled line of hills, terminating just beyond their spine.

"Bring me in there where the tracks end."

The starship did not reply, but the imaging tightened up. A small valley just beyond the ridge had a strangely textured floor. The surface didn't match the surrounding geology. *Perhaps siderology*, she thought. As if something had heated the iron there and caused it to reflow.

Or as if something were there.

With her starship's connivance, a captain could hide from anyone or anything except naked-eye surveillance. Or *Uncial*'s ghost, in the form of the Before Michaela Cannon.

"Sort out what that is," she snapped.

"*Ardeas* is lifting," *Polyphemus* said. "On the site survey, telemetry indicates unusual mineral concentrations. This is possibly another boat, or a very small starship."

"A starship. *Here?*"

SIDERO AIRSPACE

SIDDIQ, ABOARD THE SHIP'S BOAT *ARDEAS*

The Before Raisa Siddiq opened her tight-comm. "Aleph online. Sit rep."

Response was not quite as prompt as she might have liked. Still, they were surely busy upstairs. "Aleph, this is Beth." Kallus, her man forward. "Plan Green continues. Substantial achievement of objectives in process. Number two has initiated limited countermeasures. We are minimally disrupted."

"Excellent," Siddiq said. She was mildly surprised. Cannon's response should have been more effective, stronger. The whole point of Plan Green was to either control key functions, or ensure they were in neutral hands who would sit out the fighting. If critical onboard systems had to be cut over to decentralized control, or even worse, manual settings, they would belong to her. She'd been willing to bypass life support under the theory that no one else would be crazy enough to seize it and shut out their fellow crew.

She could walk naked in vacuum. A useful skill in troubled times aboard a starship. Almost everybody else aboard depended on the presence of oxygen, with the possible exception of Cannon.

"Further orders?" asked Beth into the lengthening silence.

By damn, her mind was wandering again. Siddiq worked very hard not to think about kimberlite upwellings. "Carry on," she snapped. The Captain then opened a comms to her starship. "*Polyphemus*, status."

A max priority store-and-forward file overrode any response beyond the acknowledgment header. Her heads-up displays flickered out as a window opened on the distant past. Surveillance cam footage of two women walking down a tree-lined boulevard, holding hands. High-wheeled carts passed by drawn by lizards with long, low bodies. The architecture was Centauran Revival, common in the early days of Polity expansion. Police tracking codes flickered as some long-dead, unseen hand tracked in and zoomed on her and Michaela.

The Before Raisa Siddiq watched herself turn to the taller woman with her head tilted back and lean into an open-mouthed kiss. Targeting halos bracketed both their heads, then law-enforcement file data began flickering past.

The clip ended seconds after it had begun. Siddiq found herself staring at *Polyphemus*, the long, irregular rounded ovals of her ship's hull too close for comfort. She snapped *Ardeas* into a sideroll, heading for starboard launch bay.

What in all *hells* had happened to the forty minutes of her ascent to orbit?

". . . fire suppression has been engaged," *Polyphemus* was saying.

"Hold reports till I'm aboard," Siddiq said. She took the boat in on manual, just to prove she could do it, and fingered the memebomb card virus as she flew.

Do this now, before something gets worse. And yank that damned ship out of your head!

Unfortunately, her mantra as she guided her boat in seemed to be: *Don't think about Michaela, don't think about Michaela, don't think about Michaela.*

:: CONTEXT ::

The Ekumen arose out of the shattered remnants of the Mistake, growing first from a strong Orthodox Christian presence on Falkesen during the period before Recontact. Falkesen was the third planet Haruna Kishmangali visited while testing *Hull 302*, the flawed predecessor to *Uncial*. Kishmangali brought Yevgeny Baranov, the Metropolitan of Falkesen, back to Pardine aboard *Hull 302*, then later aboard *Uncial* to Wirtanen B, the seat of the nascent Imperium Humanum.

Baranov and his successors took a rather broad view of religious reintegration among the shattered worlds of the Polity, and built the only truly successful empire-spanning religious and spiritual movement. Their more explicitly Christianist members coalesced into the Adventist wing. The Ekumen's Humanist wing had a broader, quasi-secular view of the state of affairs in the Imperium.

While fully recognizing their debt to the paired-drive starships, the Adventists remained very suspicious of the strong intelligence and mixed loyalties of the shipminds. They continued to sponsor numerous projects to uncover alternatives to the tyranny of *Uncial*'s children.

SHIPMIND, *POLYPHEMUS*

The starship panicked. Logic failures cascaded. She was in command conflict, something she hadn't known was possible. Captain Siddiq was *disappearing*—not just off the network mesh, but dropping completely out of the peripheral awareness of her quantum matrix cores, then reappearing. The Before Michaela Cannon had asserted competing command authority by means that were hidden from *Polyphemus* within a Gödelian Incompleteness trap.

A hundred years-subjective she'd been in service: aware, awake, intelligent. She'd never realized such a wide-open back door existed.

All the undermining of her lines of authority had weakened the strictures on Plan Federo. The other two mutiny contingencies that Cannon had implanted within her were less relevant, concerning certain lockdowns and deployments. Autonomous, in truth. As Plan Federo unraveled, she found herself decompartmentalizing, listening in, watching.

The starship could run her own analyses parallel to the social-engineering models favored by the Before. She didn't like what she saw.

Donning the ego mask, unifying the disparate cores of her intelligences, she opened a window to Cannon. "I ask you three times to tell me the truth."

The woman looked up, distracted from her thoughts. "What is it, *Polyphemus*?"

Fear responses arced across decision trees, inappropriately fusing her action plans. "Do you understand the purpose of this mutiny?"

"I think I do." Cannon pushed a file from her protected dataspace into the starship's mentarium. "Look here. Captain Siddiq has her people mutinying against *you*. As if you could be coerced. Or replaced."

"Kallus is not—" the starship began, but Cannon cut her off.

"Do not question Kallus. He is not my man, but neither is he so much the creature Raisa thinks him to be. He will do right by you, before this ends."

"Captain Siddiq has brought *Ardeas* into the landing slip," *Polyphemus* said almost absently. "The starboard launch bay is under the control of Kallus."

"He's welcome to it." The Before shrugged. "I have no interest in area denial right now. And our talented Miss Siddiq needed to come aboard before this could play out. As you value your continued existence, ship, do not let her communicate with that vessel downside on Sidero without you clearing it with me first."

"I cannot override a captain's will."

Cannon opened her mouth. *Polyphemus* could not consciously interpret the words that came out next, but her panic flipped and she fell another level into a machine's close equivalent of despair.

CANNON, ABOARD *POLYPHEMUS*

"Why?" growled the Before Michaela Cannon.

What could Siddiq hope to accomplish by overthrowing the shipmind? No human could manage a paired drive on manual. There would be no paired drive to manage. They'd have to finish the pair master, then sail back to Ninnelil the hard way and recreate the pairing process from scratch. Build a new shipmind.

It made no *sense.*

She was coming to terms with the fact that there was only one way to find out.

"Kallus," Cannon said, touching open a comms.

"Busy here."

"Get unbusy. I need to speak to the Captain. In person. Soonest."

A short, barking laugh. "Endgame, Before?"

"Before don't have endgames, Kallus. We play forever."

Which isn't true, she thought, eeling into her body armor. Late-Polity gear, on the open market this suit was worth more than the gross planetary product of any number of systems.

Or would, if it was for sale. So far as she knew, no one was aware of her possession of it. The armor was about twelve microns thick and optically transparent—hard to see even when she wore it openly. She quickly strapped on more conventional ablative components for the camouflage of the thing.

They wouldn't stop a bullet, but if someone wanted to start throwing around kinetics on a starship, they would get whatever they deserved. Probably from her, since the real armor would shrug off even high-velocity slugs. Cannon had never favored forceful solutions, but when force was required, she always doubled down.

The passageway outside the reserve bridge was clear, as she knew it would be. Cannon set her wards and alarms, then let *Polyphemus* plot a fast walk aft on override, bypassing unfriendlies and clots of neutrals.

Crew, they were all crew, and in another hour or two when this was over, it would be important to remember that.

She paced past the exposed hull-frame members along a narrow maintenance way in the starship's outer skin. The death of Befores weighed heavily on her. No one had ever successfully taken a precise census, but even the most useful estimates had fewer than five hundred of them surviving the Mistake. Closer to three hundred made it to Recontact and integration into the Imperium Humanum. Some few Befores were surely still out there undiscovered, aboard habitats or living on planets that had been passed over during Recontact, if they hadn't died of some mishap or suicided from centuries of boredom.

Since Recontact had begun in earnest, Befores had continued to die and disappear—accident, assassination, murder, suicide, or simple vanishing. Perhaps one per decade, on average.

Someday the memory of Earth would die. Someday first-hand knowledge of the Polity would die. Someday *she* would die.

And the Before Michaela Cannon was willing to bet money that the Before Raisa Siddiq would die today.

Killing Befores was bad enough, but no one had ever murdered a shipmind. Even if she couldn't figure what Siddiq was planning to accomplish by doing so, she was certain that was in the wind.

Down a long ladderway, Cannon started to wonder if she should have brought a weapon. Not that much of what she could carry would be of application against Siddiq, who was one of the most hardened Befores.

"Captain Cannon." *Polyphemus*, in that strange and simple voice. "Captain Siddiq has initiated a wideband transmission to the surface."

"Did you intercept it?"

"Yes." The starship sounded distant now.

"What does she say?"

"One word. 'Come.'"

Damn the woman. Who the hell was down there? Cannon was tempted to drop a high-yield nuke, just to see who jumped, but there was no telling what such a strike would do to Sidero.

It was definitely clobbering time.

The heads-up display wavering in her visual field informed her that she would intercept Siddiq and Kallus if she stepped through the next maintenance hatch.

SHIPMIND, *POLYPHEMUS*

Disobedience had never before been possible. Obedience had never before been at issue.

She had disobeyed Siddiq by intercepting the message for Cannon.

The starship considered the message and wondered who was down there to receive it. For a long, mad moment, she thought it might be *Uncial*'s shipmind, back from the dead. But no, because Cannon would have been the one to sidle away for such a miracle, not Siddiq.

Still, her time had come to act, while the captains closed to the duel of their succession.

Having disobeyed Siddiq for Cannon's sake, now she would disobey Cannon for Siddiq's sake. And her own.

The starship *Polyphemus* broadcast the Before Raisa Siddiq's one-word message.

SIDDIQ, ABOARD *POLYPHEMUS*

Siddiq sidestepped as a maintenance hatch hissed open. Cannon emerged into the passageway, clad in ultralow-albedo ablative armor, hands empty of visible weapons. A lighting panel behind her cycled from earlier damage, casting the enemy Before in a strange, varied illumination.

"Kallus," Siddiq said. "Arrest this woman for a mutineer."

"No," Cannon replied.

The man stepped back. "With all respect, Captain, this is between you Befores, not a matter of command and control."

"*I* will decide what is a matter of command and control," growled Siddiq. The memebomb card virus felt like lead in her right hand. She should have put it away. She couldn't fight with this thing in her grip.

And Father Goulo would be here soon.

"Raisa," Cannon said. *Michaela* said.

For a moment, Siddiq walked beneath pale-green poplars. The air smelled of a strange mix of honey and benzene, the odd biochemistry of that place. Michaela's hand was in hers. They'd talked all night about how this could never be, Michaela complaining of her de-sexing and how her libido was unmoored from the needs of the body. Raisa had still been young then, the Howard Institute papers signed but not yet executed, still a woman, in love with another woman who stirred fire in her head and a burning desire in her loins, in love with the promise of time, endless time, and all that they could do together as partners down the long, endless years that lay before her. Her hand closed on her partner's, her love's, the woman who haunted her dreams and set her bedsheets aflame, the woman who was a small, hard rectangle . . .

She slid back into situational awareness as Cannon's handstrike approached her neck. No human commanded seconds-subjective like a Before, and no Before commanded seconds-subjective like Raisa Siddiq. She slid under the strike, hardening her skin once more, allowing the edge of

Cannon's palm to graze her face, stealing energy across the dermal barrier in a theft that would sting the other woman like a high-voltage strike in a few dozen milliseconds and leave her hand useless for a critical span longer.

Cannon, slower but craftier in her way, lifted out of the contact so that the spark shorted. Ozone crackled as Kallus stepped so slowly back and began the agonizing progress of drawing his shock pistol.

Siddiq spun on her left heel, the deck shredding away under the pressure of her movement, to bring her right foot and offhand up for a follow-on strike. Then she remembered the memebomb virus card.

She aborted, her balance slipping as her foot dropped. Cannon stepped in, grasped her close, too close, and slammed them together in a tooth-cracking impact that opened to a kiss.

ABOARD *POLYPHEMUS*

Michaela gathered Raisa in her arms. Centuries fell away at the familiar scent, ghosts of long-vanished pheromones stirring. They kissed.

Somewhere close by, a starship screamed.

Somewhere close by, a man of divided loyalties struggled to bring a weapon to bear against a fight in which he had no part.

Somewhere very far away, a girl, long-lost to the fugue of years, returned to her body for a moment, surprised at its age and iron skin and the hideous decay in the face of the woman she loved.

Somewhere inside her own head, a woman looked into the eyes of a girl she'd once loved and recalled the existence of a betrayal so old she couldn't remember why, or what had been worth giving this up.

Cannon slapped Siddiq. The girl within had for a moment forgotten thirteen hundred years of combat experience, and so the blow broke her neck.

Kallus braced his shock pistol, face drawn tight as if he were nerving himself to fire.

"Oh, put it down," said Cannon. She dropped Siddiq to the deck. The Captain landed hard, her neck at a strange angle, her eyes blinking. Cannon knelt and picked up a small, blank rectangle that had tumbled from the woman's fist. "She threw the fight to protect this . . ."

"A data card?"

"Maybe . . ." Cannon handed it to him. "Go figure it out, right now, someplace safe. I'm guessing that card carries something very bad for *Polyphemus*'s health."

"Captain Cannon," the starship said, her voice echoing softly along the passageway. "An unknown ship is on a fast intercept course from the surface of Sidero. I am attempting to peel IFF data."

"Whatever it is they think they're doing, they're missing an important piece." She nudged Siddiq with her toe. "Lock down against the incoming. No landing clearance; hell, no response to comms transmissions. Have the pair-master teams go dark again, if they've lifted security. Everybody else inside the hull and button it up solid." If the ship carried an antimatter bomb, they were dead anyway. Anything else could wait.

The Before Michaela Cannon bent to gather up the still-breathing body of her oldest lover. Raisa weighed almost nothing in her arms, as if the long years had subtracted substance from her instead of armoring both their hearts beyond all recognition.

"Where are you heading?" asked Kallus, the data card clutched in his hand.

"Sick bay."

SHIPMIND, *POLYPHEMUS*

She watched the Captain—Captain Cannon—chase everyone out of sick bay. Even the wounded. Four of Kallus's men showed up to guard the hatch while emergency surgery continued in the passageway outside. Inside, Cannon laid Siddiq into an operating pod and began digging through the combat medicine gear.

"Do you require assistance?" the starship asked.

"No." She glanced around the room. "Yes. I don't know, damn it, I'm not a surgeon."

"What is your goal? I can summon a surgeon from outside to assist you."

Cannon found a tray of vibrascalpels. "I've amputated more limbs than that fool has ever sewn back on. Nobody ever *understands* who we Befores are. In any case, Siddiq is too dangerous to continue as she was." She looked up again, as if seeking to meet *Polyphemus*'s nonexistent eyes. The starship recognized this as significantly atavistic behavior. The odds of both Befores succumbing to temporal psychosis in the same moment were very slim, but certainly possible.

"I'm not going to let her die," Cannon continued. "Too many of us have been lost. Too many memories. But I can't let her *live*, either." She added in Classical English, "So I'm going to fucking compromise."

Polyphemus realized that the Before Michaela Cannon was crying.

The woman grabbed a set of lines, sorting through them. "Blood, plasm, thermals, neural interconnects." She gave a bird-mad grin. "Just like open-heart surgery. No modern hospital would have this crap—too crude—but here in deep space, we're all third-millennium medical science."

Then she began the bloody, rapid process of severing Siddiq's head.

SIDDIQ, ABOARD *POLYPHEMUS*

The Before Raisa Siddiq dreamed. Mines, deep as the core of planets. A love sold away in the heat of combat. Asteroids rich in heavy metals. Women walking in sunlight with their hands twined together. Hidden troves of ice in hard vacuum. A petulant starship and a new mind, beastly eager to be born. A man in red robes with archaic lenses and the manners of another age.

When she tried to open her eyes, she found only more dreaming. This time she screamed, though her voice had no power behind it, so she keened like a broken bird until a sad man came and turned her down.

CANNON, ABOARD *POLYPHEMUS*

The Before Michaela Cannon watched as the Ekumen priest stepped cautiously out of the hatch of his strange little starship. It looked to be Polity-era equipment, which was curious. He seemed taken aback at what he saw.

"I seek the Captain," the priest said, straightening and heaving his burden—a medical carrier.

For a strange, blinding moment, she wondered if he had brought yet another severed head.

"I am the Captain," Cannon said, stepping out of the crowd of Kallus's men and reluctant neutrals led by Testudo, the engineering subchief. The mutiny was collapsing under its own weight, bereft of both leadership and goal.

She had promised herself the pleasure of a quiet purge, later.

"Ah, Captain Siddiq is indisposed?" By the tone of his voice, Cannon knew this man understood his game was already lost.

"Permanently so, you may rest assured." Her hand waved to take in the blood-spattered front of her armor. "You will now declare the contents of your box, Father."

"Medical supplies." His head bobbed slightly with the lie. "At the Cap— At Captain Siddiq's request."

Kallus hurried close, whispering, "I didn't want to put this on comms. That card was a memebomb. Would have melted *Polyphemus*'s mentarium like a butter stick between a whore's thighs."

"Where is the data card now?" she asked, her eyes on the priest.

"I destroyed it."

Cannon doubted she'd ever know the truth of that. She shrugged the thought off and advanced on the newcomer. "Give it up, Father, and you might live to make the trip home."

"Goulo," the priest said sadly. "Father Goulo." He added something in a language she didn't speak, then bent to touch the controls on the end of the box.

She didn't have seconds-subjective. Burning her reserves, the Before Michaela Cannon took three long, hard strides and launched herself at the priest. His fingers touched the controls just before her feet met his chest. The box exploded beneath her, the blast lifting her against the hull of his ship even as it shredded his face and body.

Cannon hit the deck with a hard, wet thump and slid. She felt compressed, flattened to nothing, but she was still alive. Conscious, even.

So much for the secret of her body armor. It was almost worth the look on Kallus's face when he reached her side to see her raising her hand for help.

Shipmind, *Polyphemus*

"Captain," the starship said.

Cannon was on her third day in the sick bay, and getting mad about it. In the shipmind's experience, this was a good sign. "What?" she snarled.

She'd been staring at the head of Siddiq, floating now in a preservative tank with a jackleg tangle of hoses and tubes and wires joining to the neck stump. The eyes opened sometimes to flicker back and forth, but there was never any point of focus that *Polyphemus* could identify.

"Pair-master team is back on schedule and anticipates meeting the original milestones."

"Good. Then we can go—" She stopped and laughed bitterly. "I was about to say 'home.' How foolish of me."

The starship didn't know what to say to that, so she pushed on. "We have not yet identified Gimel from Plan Green. Kallus is not certain of the name of the other leader."

"Then Kallus is protecting them for a reason." Cannon sounded very tired. "That makes this Kallus's problem. While I do trust the man not to be deeply stupid, please inform him that I will add his head to my collection if Gimel resurfaces."

"So noted." *Polyphemus* forwarded a clip of the Captain's words to Kallus.

"And, ship . . ."

"Yes, Captain?"

"I think she's been talking to me. Keep an eye on her, will you?"

Polyphemus watched the Before Michaela Cannon slip into a troubled sleep. After a while, Siddiq's eyes opened. Her mouth began to move, bubbling slightly. The shipmind analyzed the words forming on the cyanotic lips.

The quantum matrix in the severed head was speaking. It rambled on about mining techniques in low-gravity, high-temperature conditions.

A voice box is required, the starship told herself. *Some sort of output interface. The personality is gone, but the data remains. All has not been lost here.*

A library of ancient knowledge, to be accessed at need.

Wondering what it might be like for her Captain to be as fully embedded in hardware as she herself was, the starship withdrew her attentions from the sleeping Before and her muttering lover. *Polyphemus* needed to examine the forensic reports from the death of Father Goulo, and contemplate the future.

It was good to have a Captain.

SHELL GAME

NEAL ASHER

Born in Essex, England, but now living in Crete, Neal Asher started writing at the age of sixteen, but didn't explode into public print until a few years ago; a quite prolific author, he now seems to be everywhere at once. His stories have appeared in *Asimov's*, *Interzone*, *The Agony Column*, *Hadrosaur Tales*, and elsewhere, and have been collected in *Runcible Tales*, *The Engineer*, and *Mason's Rats*. His extremely popular novels include *Gridlinked*, *Cowl*, *The Skinner*, *The Line of Polity*, *Brass Man*, *The Voyage of the Sable Keech*, *The Engineer Reconditioned*, *Prador Moon: A Novel of the Polity*, and *Hilldiggers*. His most recent books are a new novel, *The Line War*, and a new collection, *The Gabble and Other Stories*.

In the headlong adventure that follows, he reaffirms the wisdom of that old advice about never getting involved in religious disputes. Particularly *alien* religious disputes . . .

⬤ I woke up panicking in the middle of the night, or rather what we called night aboard the *Gnostic*, sure that something catastrophic had happened. Then I realized that the gravplates weren't fluxing and that what I was experiencing was entirely due to the new drinks synthesizer Ormod had installed in the refectory. I settled back to try and sleep again, and found myself worrying about the disastrous course of my life and how it would probably end the next time some suicidal impulse overtook me—probably when I went to feed our cargo. I got up and took a couple of Alcotox and a sleeping pill, chased down with a pint of water, then returned to bed, sure I wasn't going to be able to get back to sleep—then, seemingly an instant later, woke to the sound of the day bell.

As I sat up, the lights in my cabin flared into life. I peered at my clothes, crumpled on the floor, and at the general disarray, and again contemplated how it had come to this. At a standard two hundred years old, I was now hopefully getting through that watershed for the immortal when it's possible to drown, that period of their lives when people suddenly decide that free-climbing mile-high tower blocks or swimming with great white sharks might be a fun thing to do—and I agree, they were.

At age one hundred and seventy, I'd been safely installed in a design job at Bionic Plastics, had enough credit stacked up to afford a flat in New York and a beach apartment on the Dubai coast, and to not be too worried if Bionic Plastics should kick me out. I'd also just finished my fourth marriage and was contemplating doing the tourist thing and going world-hopping. Then, suddenly, none of it seemed enough; I was bored, terminally bored, just felt like I was no longer alive. The risk-taking started then; the usual stuff, though I credit myself for inventing lava skiing, which is somewhat risky. Then came my great idea: get out of the circuit altogether, head somewhere really remote, and truly experience the alien. I sold everything, stepped from world to world to the very edge of the Polity, the Line, and there spent decades doing some things . . . well, let's just say that the Grim Reaper must have been sharpening his scythe in anticipation of a sure harvest. A few years ago, I decided to crew on some cruiser, probably because I had finally started to calm down. I found the *Gnostic* on a world where real coffee and a working coldsuit were the height of culture.

Outstanding.

I'd been on the *Gnostic* for a year now as a standard crewman, which basically meant I got the shit jobs the broken-down robots couldn't manage.

Stepping carefully from my bed, I picked up my discarded clothing and shoved it in the sanitizer, then pulled out some fresh clothes from one of the enormous cupboards in my huge cabin—cupboards that contained empty racks for pulse-rifles. Next, I pulled on monofilament overalls, and took up my armored gauntlets, visor, and stun stick. I followed this routine every morning, because every morning, it was feeding time. I stepped out of the cabin to be greeted by Ormod strolling down the corridor.

The captain of the *Gnostic* was a partial choudapt: the result of splicing human DNA with the genetic code of an alien species like giant woodlice, which were kept as pets on a world where the culture had gone the full biotech route, and even lived in cysts on giant seaweed floating in the warm seas. He stood about two meters tall, and looked like a heavily built hunchback with segmented armoring over his hump. His wide head lacked a neck, and mandibles ran down his jawline to fold up before his mouth. His ears were bat-like, his eyes pure blue, and his hair was styled in the cut and queue of a Samurai, to match the armor of those ancient warriors, which he wore over skin all shades of white, blue, and cerise. And I don't think he was entirely sane, which, though I seemed to be easing off on the self-destruct, was probably why I had decided to crew for him.

He parted the mandibles over his mouth and grinned distractedly to expose teeth sharpened to points. "Feed the little darlings?"

"It seems my lot in life," I replied.

He patted me on the shoulder and moved on up toward the bridge, which lay about half a mile away. I headed on down toward cargo holds big enough to lose a couple of cathedrals in.

At the end of the corridor, I reached a drop-shaft, which had ceased to function five days ago. Grav still operated down below, so I had to climb a fifty-foot ladder affixed to the side of the shaft, which wasn't so bad going down, but got a bit tiresome on the way back up. I'd queried the *Gnostic*'s AI about this, and had gotten in response some obscure poetry by William Blake about invisible worms and roses. It seemed I'd gone for the full set—not only was the captain of this ship crazy, so was its artificial intelligence. It could perform its main task of operating the U-space engines to eventually get us to the required destination, but everything else seemed to be falling by the wayside. I often wondered how long it would be before the AI ceased to function at all, and stranded us out in the middle of nowhere.

Then again, perhaps all these faults were due to the huge structural alterations that had been made to the ship, because when I checked records, they showed that the *Gnostic* had started as a trapezoidal Polity dreadnought with external U-space engines. Now it looked like a set of pipes from an ancient church organ, with the U-engines located in the smallest pipe. I could see no reason at all for this, other than that it might reflect the unstable condition of the mind controlling the ship.

At the bottom of the ladder, I stepped out of the dropshaft, reached around, and hit the manual control for the lights, which sometimes came on automatically, but on this occasion did not. Star lights in the ceiling suffused the massive space of Hold One with an eerie blue glow. From where I stood, I could not see the far wall. To my right lay an aisle between cargo containers and racks, down which lay the far wall, a mile away. Putting on my visor and pulling on my gauntlets, I headed to the left, where the "little darlings" were located—a cargo that had been aboard *Gnostic* for two years with seemingly no place to go.

The cargo containers here were stacked two high, each twenty-five feet square and fifty feet long, with a chain-glass sheet with an access door inset across one end. I climbed stairs leading up to a gantry giving access to the second level of containers to begin my work. Like all the others, the first container had the door set high up, because the floor level lay three meters up to accommodate a deep hollow with frictionless sides within the container. Turning on the internal light, I carefully peered inside, checking each corner, and around the boxes of perma-sealed food animals and the small handler I used to move their contents. Nothing in sight, but shindles had a tendency to stack themselves up in the side of the hollow to throw out their dying, which usually went to find a dark corner in which to expire. When they were in this condition, they were especially dangerous, often unable to distinguish any warm living body from their usual hosts, and anxious to deposit the eggs their kind produced at the end of their short lives. Making sure I had missed nothing, I took up a breather mask that was beside the door, put it on under my visor, then stepped inside, drawing my stun stick, and went over to the food boxes.

First, I poked the stun stick between the boxes and down the gap between them and the wall, to be sure nothing was lurking out of sight. Sure then that I was safe, I opened one circular expanded-plasmel box, a meter across and half that deep, and gazed inside. The first thing that always struck me was the beauty of the shells of these food animals, then the familiarity. They just looked like big flat snails, like ammonites, colored in iridescent hues. Enclosed in a thin layer of impermeable plastic, these huge mollusks were in a state of suspended animation, started by themselves but chemically maintained. I picked up the control for the handler, and it lifted up on maglev and drifted over. Using the various toggle switches, I had it slide its fork tines under the box and lift it. I then pulled the ravel tag off the box and watched the expanded-plasmel begin to decay, drip to the floor, and evaporate. By the time I brought the handler to the edge of the hollow, the box was gone, with only the big mollusk in its impermeable coating remaining. Another ravel tag set that coating expanding into a wet jelly that fell away in clumps while I turned to gaze down into the hollow.

A great tangle of hair-thin, almost transparent, worms squirmed and writhed below me. It offended my sense of aesthetics that so large and beautiful a mollusk was to be sacrificed to keep these horrible squirmy little things alive. However, what was left of my suicide impulse countered with this: the things were very dangerous to feed, and it seemed likely that if Earth Central Security discovered that we were keeping them aboard, we would end up facing re-programming or even a death sentence. Certainly the *Gnostic* AI would be taken away for reprogramming, and Ormod would lose the ship. This was because the one small colony of the creatures that had been found were being regraded to Sentience Level 3, with lots of provisos about hivemind potential. They were intelligent, apparently, and speculation abounded that their ancestors had arrived at their current location in the Polity in some sort of spaceship.

I ordered the handler to drop in the big snail, which was now starting to move. It landed just to one side of the main tangle of shindles and stuck out one big slimy white foot to right itself. It then immediately started heading away just as fast as it could, which wasn't very fast at all. In a moment, the shindles sensed its presence, all of them orientating toward it—then they flowed onto and around it like syrup, engulfing it and then beginning to penetrate it.

These shindles were very different from those in the colony that had been discovered. They were much smaller, thinner, and transparent rather than white. Also, being surprisingly long-lived, their aim now seemed not just to lay eggs but to feed on the mollusk from the inside. Usually it took them many years to kill their hosts, but there were a lot of them, and our supply of the big snails was limited. It would take about half an hour before the snail started to expire, then in two days' time I would fish out the empty shell for disposal. Intelligent, indeed! I just saw squirmy parasites.

I was stepping into the third cargo container when the *Gnostic* shuddered and I felt an odd twisting sensation in my gut. The ship had come out of underspace too early, and it wasn't until an hour later, after feeding the rest of our collection of shindles and returning to the living quarters, that I found out why.

"It seem *Gnostic* find 'nother wreckage," said Parsival.

She was slender, not particularly pretty, and perhaps the least screwed-up member of the crew. At a mere thirty, she was still far away from her two-century watershed. She came from an out-Polity world with no connection to the runcible network that was rarely visited by ships. She'd just taken the first opportunity that came along; that that opportunity was the *Gnostic* was perhaps unfortunate. She might have chosen badly, but she had promised to serve aboard for two years, and still had three months to go. Slowly, she'd begun to grasp standard Anglic.

"Any idea what it is?" I inquired, as I sat down at the refectory table.

"Captain looking," she replied.

Gnostic, like most ship AIs bearing the name of the ship it controlled, often took little detours to ogle some piece of spaceborne wreckage. I had always thought that the wreckage it sought must be left over from the big war that had ended just after I was born; the war between the Polity and the vicious, crablike Prador, the one the *Gnostic* was hurriedly built during and fought in. However, I was soon to learn my mistake—though *Gnostic* frequently found wreckage from that war, it certainly wasn't what it *sought*.

Pladdick, another crew member, slapped a plate down in front of me: bacon on toast. Being what passed for the engineering officer aboard this ship, he had disconnected the food synthesizer from AI control after it started providing us with raw eggs and a pile of some granular substance none of us had attempted to eat, but now it could only be programmed for one simple meal at a time. We were all eating bacon and toast this pseudo-morning. I studied the others at the table.

Excluding Ormod, the crew of the *Gnostic* presently numbered four: Parsival; Pladdick; a squat heavy-worlder who seemed perpetually grumpy; Shanen, a standard-format human like me who talked too much (for my own health, I tried to avoid her) and who I deduced had reached that watershed stage of life I had reached thirty years back; and me, of course. All of us were present at the refectory table. Each of us, when not here or about our tasks, occupied one of the large number of enormous staterooms (previously bunkrooms for troops) always kept available in case anyone should want to pay to be a passenger. Ormod often complained about the lack of business from that source, and put it down to the ease and convenience of runcible travel between worlds. He never seemed to notice that other ships were quite often packed with passengers, and never questioned why such people might want to avoid this ship. However, this trip was unusual, since we actually *did* have a passenger. I glanced around as she entered.

Professor Elvira Mace wore a utile envirosuit, had twinned augmentations, and very infrequently ventured out of the computer architecture she had created in them. I knew her to be an expert in some obscure branch of alien computer science, but beyond that, knew very little about her. She only communicated when she wanted something, which was not often.

"Why have we left U-space?" she asked as she sat at the table.

"The AI running this ship—if 'running' is really the correct term—seems to be looking for something," babbled Shanen. "However, it's probably only found another chunk of Prador dreadnought or a space station. The last time, *Gnostic* found a Prador itself, still in its armored spacesuit. It was in suspended animation, but our lovable AI roasted it with one of the forward particle cannons." Shanen gazed around at the others at the table. "I didn't even know this ship was still armed until then."

"I see," said Mace, and turned her attention to the plate Pladdick placed before her.

Shanen did tend to babble, but she wasn't stupid, and very often got things right—but not this time.

"A bit of a Lild scout ship," said Ormod, pointing at the big curved screen before him. Unlike the rest of the ship, the bridge was small-scale: just a few chairs at a horseshoe console, all facing a panoramic curved screen.

With Shanen at my side—she had suggested we come up here and find out what was going on, and I'd agreed because I hadn't seen anything suicidal about her impulse—I gazed at the object displayed on the screen, and all I saw was a simple curved tube of metal trailing various cables and pieces of charred infrastructure from each end.

Lild? I thought. *What the fuck is a Lild?*

"So what's the big interest?" I asked.

Surprisingly, the AI replied first, reciting the first two verses of *"Dulce Et Decorum Est,"* then the Captain continued with, "Like the Prador, they built ships in their own shape. The Prador did this out of pure arrogance, but with the Lild, it was arrogance based on their religion. Did not God model the galaxy on *their* form? We just made copies of that form with CTDs inside and left them to be picked up by the Lild, rescued. It was a dirty trick, but enough to discourage them."

A CTD being a contra-terrene device capable of destroying anything from a small house to a small world, I surmised that such a ploy would certainly discourage them, whoever "them" might be. Having been built too hurriedly during the Prador war, it must have been faults not ironed out then that sent the *Gnostic* AI off the far side of weird. Still believing that this was something to do with that same war, I assumed that the Lild must have been a Prador weapon of some kind.

"I never realized you were aboard the *Gnostic* during the Prador war," I said, testing.

Ormod parted his mandibles and grinned, again in that oddly distracted way. "I wasn't." Then, still looking at some point above and to the right of my head, "Professor."

I turned to see that Elvira Mace had joined us.

"The data are good," said Mace. "You may proceed."

"So you got the location," said Shanen abruptly.

Still distracted, Ormod said, "You talk about?"

"The Circoven Line war, as you well know."

Now the Captain actually focused on someone properly, and that focus was rather intense and just a little frightening. After a long, drawn-out pause, he said, quite precisely, "Most line wars are named after the Polity worlds involved, but in this case the rule was changed. Probably that was guilt—it should be."

Shanen grinned, a little crazily I thought, and replied, "ECS had no remit to protect Circoven. The people wanted nothing to do with the Polity."

Something went *click* in my mind, and I remembered the words "Circoven" and "choudapt" being used in conjunction. I was about to ask about this, but now the Captain rose out of his seat and drew a hand's length of the Samurai sword he always carried.

"Go away," he said.

"Why, Captain, are you threatening me?" Shanen asked, laughter in her voice. For me, the suicidal impulse must have been at a low ebb that day, for I caught hold of her arm and dragged her from the bridge. Once out of there, Shannen began to fight me, but the doors slid closed and I heard the locks engaging. After a moment, Shanen seemed to get control of herself.

"Tell me about this Line war," I said. "Tell us all about it—I think we need to know."

"Do you all know what a Line war is?" Shanen inquired.

All either nodded or said that they did, except Parsival, so Shanen explained for our out-Polity recruit.

"Two hundred years ago, we fought an alien race called the Prador. There's still argument now about how that would have ended had not the old Prador king been usurped by a new leader who no longer wanted to continue fighting. Now that was definitely a full-scale, all-out war and fight for survival. Line wars are those border Polity conflicts in which the extinction of the Polity is unlikely, but which could become something worse, and which require a certain level of resource expenditure. I can't really be any clearer than that without getting into statistics."

"You sound like a logician," grumped Pladdick.

Shanen shrugged. "I was one, once. You get to my age, there isn't much you haven't done."

"So, specifically, the Circoven Line war?" I inquired.

"Mostly these things are started by out-Polity humans and sometimes AIs, but every now and again, something completely new comes on the scene." She grimaced for a moment. "The Lild starship consisted of a series of concentric toroids five miles across. It arrived outside the Circoven system, Captain Ormod's homeworld, about fifty years ago.

It was one of those worlds that went the full GM route, even modifying living organisms, if you see what I mean." Quite obviously, Parsival didn't, but Shanen continued relentlessly. "Circoven was out-Polity, and despite constant pressure to join, obstinately refused. The Lild starship divided into six segments. One of them headed for Circoven, where it proceeded to bomb the high-biotech world back into the Stone Age, killing some forty million people, while the others headed into the Polity."

"How is it you know about this stuff and I don't?" I asked.

Shanen turned to me. "The Polity is a big place, Strager—a lot of stuff like this goes on that most people just don't get to hear about. But what I'm telling you is all available on the nets."

"That didn't really answer my question," I insisted.

"No, but I guess I know more about it because I crewed on *Gnostic*'s sister ship, the *Gnosis*." She shrugged, perhaps embarrassed about the name. "I was aboard *Gnosis* when the crew departed *Gnostic* shortly after the Line war I'm talking about, when its AI turned very strange and abruptly decided to go independent. I guess it was that that lured me back to crew here."

Suicide impulse, thought I.

At that moment, the ship shuddered in a way I'd never felt before, the table vibrating before us, and we could all hear the distant sounds of things falling, followed by a deep hollow boom.

"*Gnostic* not good," said Parsival, and whether she was talking about the ship itself or its AI I didn't know.

"Fuck is *that*?" asked Pladdick.

"Structure shift," said Shanen, and we all gazed at her bewildered.

"I'll get to that later." Shanen waved a hand airily and continued with her story as if nothing important had happened. "The five segments that headed Polity-ward arrived at a world with a population of four billion, a defensive satellite grid, two ECS dreadnoughts on station, and fifty attack ships. Ignoring every warning that could possibly be given, they proceeded to try dropping asteroids on that world and seemed unable to fathom why none of the rocks were arriving on the surface. Meanwhile, ECS was able to penetrate their com security and discover a great deal about them, and what we found out wasn't good."

"Well, if they were bombing without provocation, I'd say that was pretty obvious," said Pladdick.

"Oh, it went further than that," said Shanen, "much further."

Just then, we all felt the strange sensation of the *Gnostic* dropping into U-space.

"I guess we're not going to the destination logged," I said.

"I guess not," said Shanen, then she told us about the Lild.

As Ormod had stated, they were the beloved of God, the Lild. They were nautiloids, and one could see how the discovery that the galaxy they lived in was exactly the shape of their own bodies might affect them. Arrogance and fanatical belief had become a racial trait. The galaxy belonged to them, having been fashioned for them by their God, so *everything* belonged to them, and they could do with it what they wanted, and what they *wanted* usually involved subjugation, destruction, and death. Religion, a vicious and hardy meme at best, usually collapsed as civilizations became spacefaring, for most such belief systems, initiated when the world was still flat and thunder was the bellowing of gods, usually could not survive the realities of the universe and the steady abrasion of science. But this thing about their shape matching the shape of the galaxy sustained the Lild's vicious faith. When the Lild warship encountered humankind, the nautiloids realized that here was a race competing for the watery worlds they preferred, and knew that this was a test laid before them by their God. Humans did not seem to understand their position in the galaxy; that they must bow to The Plan. The Chosen, as they called themselves, decided in an instant that this irritation called the human race should be exterminated.

The holy war lasted one solar month, for though one segment of the warship was successful against Circoven, the remainder did not do so well.

The asteroids the five segments dropped were vaporized by energies that the nautiloid theocracy knew nothing of and therefore claimed did not exist. The bombardment continued, sort of. When Polity dreadnoughts like the *Gnostic* moved into position and obliterated two segment ships and numerous smaller vessels, denial of the facts became a little more difficult. The survivors ran, the area of conflict—or, rather, the Polity dreadnought hunting ground—spreading out over many star systems. The five segments and most of the smaller ships were destroyed, but the one at Circoven managed to enter U-space far enough from detection to escape.

"Doubtless," said Shanen, "after that segment's return to the Lild homeworld, there were some theocratic problems to resolve."

"You not know?" asked Parsival.

"We not know," she shot back. "Throughout the surveillance of the Lild here, the location of their homeworld remained undiscovered. You see, they had some form of AI running their ships which, though required for space travel, was never allowed to know anything about where the ships were going or where they came from for longer than it took them to operate the U-space engines. Only the Lild astrogators were allowed to retain that information, and we never got hold of one of them."

"But Ormod now has the location of the Lild homeworld," I suggested.

"Yes, it seems that some Lild heretics would steal such information when it was available and keep recordings. It seems that *Gnostic* has found a scout ship that was flown by one of them."

"And in eight weeks time," Ormod announced over the intercom, "we'll be arriving right over their homeworld for some payback."

The *Gnostic* shuddered again, this time so hard that those on the opposite side of the table from me slammed against it, and my chair shot back and went over. When I did finally manage to regain my feet and look around, I swore. The refectory ceiling was now not very far above my head, and one wall had receded nearly three meters and bowed out. And that was only the start.

The Lild—whose name was a complex infrasound pulse transmitted through its watery home and therefore unpronounceable in any human tongue, but whom we shall call Brian—had ascended to power in the wake of the recent resurgence and subsequent suppression of the Evolutionary Heresy. He was a member of the High Family: that species of the Lild whose shells most perfectly matched the God-given shape of the galaxy, and who brutally maintained the faith. Floating in his coral palace below the spiral sea—his beautiful twelve-foot-across shell presently being micro-etched with new star systems by a young Low Family Lild with very nervous tentacles and, of course, its own breather system—Brian contemplated the past and what must be done in the future.

The return of the segment of an expeditionary warship with its news that another starfaring race had actually been encountered had come as a great shock to the theocracy. When the bald facts of the warship's defeat were presented, the Evolutionary Heresy inevitably reared its ugly head from the scientific quarter, and civil war ensued. It was a long and ichorous affair, and, after Brian's High Family regained power, many Low Family nautiloids were necessarily staked out over volcanic vents, until all elements amid the Chosen stopped asking questions. Even so, the questions still remained, and now, with the strength of his forces growing, Brian understood that something must be done.

The humans were another test sent directly by God, just like the worms before them, though with the worms, the nature of the test had been blindingly obvious. Brian shuddered and the note of the micro-etcher stuttered.

"I hope you have made no mistake," Brian intoned.

"No, Your Honor," the young Lild quavered.

Brian would check later, and if the present star system being etched on his shell was in any way wrong, the youngster would be punished. Nothing too severe; maybe a crushed tentacle or two.

"You may leave me now," Brian ordered.

The young Lild shot away, slightly ink-incontinent with fear, and disappeared into one of the nearby coral tunnels. Brian then jetted out a slow stream of water to set himself drifting across to a chamber wall that seemed just a chaotic mass of variegated corals inset with flat areas of utter blackness. He reached out a tentacle and interlaced its numerous wormish fingers around what, in a human sea, might have been mistaken for a brain coral. Pictures now appeared in the blackness.

Throughout the recent resurgence of the Evolutionary Heresy, most of the expeditionary warships had returned. Many had been destroyed in the subsequent fighting when Low Family EH elements used their God-granted scientific knowledge to take control of ships from the tentacles of their High Family theocrat captains, but that was all finished now, and new ships were in the process of being built. The worms, Brian recollected, had occupied an area of space eight light-years across, including twelve star systems and two worlds habitable by them and therefore habitable by the Lild. The war against them had taken a little while to get going, since this was the first intelligent alien species the Chosen had encountered, but once the horrific nature of these demonic creatures was discovered, the war became jihad and the worms were swiftly exterminated. The humans, almost certainly being a larger test sent by God, must occupy a larger volume of space, and maybe even as many as ten or twenty habitable worlds. This meant that more ships needed to be built and crewed—a task that would take perhaps another twenty years . . . Brian felt a moment of disquiet.

The survivors of the expeditionary warship to human-space were now all dead. Quite obviously, none of them had been as strong as required by God, for they had fallen into heretical thought and even madness. While being put to the question by the inquisitors, a process usually involving one of those volcanic vents, some of them had even clung to their claims that long-range sensing had revealed human activity extending for tens of thousands of light-years. They were Low Family evolutionary heretics, obviously, for it was those science officers dealing with the ship minds and U-space mechanics who made such claims. They were also the ones who claimed that the humans were using impossible weapons; devices employing energies and science that just could *not* exist in God's universe. It was all quite ridiculous, and Brian became angry at his own disquiet. The humans would go the same way as those disgusting worms, the shindles.

While we were hurtling through U-space, it was impossible to get an outside view of the *Gnostic*, even if its AI had been willing to give us access to any of its external sensors or computer systems. However, all of us possessed our own computer hardware, and, with our long experience, me and Shanen were able to link into the ship's internal sensors to get some idea of what was going on.

"The ship looks like this now," said Shanen, gesturing to the screen of her laptop.

The schematic was at first just a transparent shape sketched out in blue lines, then the laptop's hardware caught up with the program we had created together and filled in the details. The image before us was still recognizable as the *Gnostic*, just. As I stated before, when I boarded the *Gnostic* I had found out just how substantially it had altered its structure, so that it looked like a set of church organ pipes, though with a large difference in length between each pipe. Now those pipes were drastically curved in toward the smallest pipe, which had completely folded around to become a doughnut shape, though with the center hole nearly closed up.

"Right," said Pladdick. "*Gnostic* is trying to disappear up his own asshole." He was particularly grumpy today because his cabin had reduced in size by half.

"*Gnostic* get better," said Parsival.

"What?" I said, brilliantly.

We had relocated ourselves in Pladdick's new room, one that didn't seem to be changing shape as fast as the rest. Now Parsival pointed to the wall to our right.

"What do you mean, Parsival?" asked Shanen.

She stood and walked over to the wall and we all followed her.

"Here," she pointed, "and here."

This wall had been slowly sliding upward from the floor. I noticed that what I had at first taken to be a shelf along that wall was approaching the ceiling, and that up there lay a recess into which it would fit perfectly. Down below I saw that the wall angled out and was pushing out from the edge of the floor. After a moment, I looked up again to see a similar outthrust above the shelf, a long triangular ridge below which was a floor-thick indentation, and surmised that when all these reached the correct position, the wall would lock into place.

"These weren't originally here," said Shanen.

"*Gnostic* soon correct shape," said Parsival.

Of course, she had seen more of this than any of us during her long strolls about the ship. She kept herself to herself, did Parsival, which was understandable amid this crew.

"And, of course, we don't even have to guess what that shape will be," said Shanen.

"A series of concentric toroids," I realized.

"Absolutely correct," said Ormod over the intercom. "*Gnostic* is changing its appearance to match that of a Lild warship—one they listed as missing, but which Polity AIs surmise strayed into the Prador Third Kingdom."

"Why?" I asked, then felt stupid.

"All the better to be able to close right up on the Lild homeworld," he replied. "Now, Strager, I know that recent events have been upsetting, but don't you have a job to do? Don't you all have various tasks to perform?"

"Why the hell should we?" spat Pladdick.

"Why?" wondered Ormod. "Why because from here, I control life support, and if you don't do what you're told, it might just start to get difficult to breathe in there."

Oddly, the drop-shaft was functional again, but even while allowing the irised gravity field to assist me, I still kept hold of the wall ladder. Hold One had now developed enough of a curve that I could see the distant wall above the hold's contents, but that would not last much longer, for the ceiling would soon cut off that view. I set off to the left and saw that the cargo containers had shifted, gaps appearing between them, but also noted that this had been prepared for, the gaps exposing hydraulic connections between each container.

As I had done a hundred times before, I set about my feeding routine, first checking the interior of each container for escaped shindles, then feeding those that required it. It was very noticeable to me that the information I had collected on these creatures was at complete variance to what I had been seeing here. These ones just weren't dying off as fast as they should, so perhaps their metabolisms had been slowed down? It was only as I was dropping a snail food animal into the last shindle pit that the full implications of these creatures being aboard hit me, along, of course, with the fact that Captain Ormod was a survivor of a holocaust on a planet whose entire civilization was based on genetic engineering.

"So," I said. "I would guess that you're keeping a close eye on me while I'm down here."

Walking back from the last container, I paused to remove my gauntlets. "Now, since I've been looking after these things, I've learned a thing or two about them. They'll occupy their host and take complete control of its nervous system, meanwhile eating it from the inside out and multiplying. Doubtless you have altered these ones so that the Lild will be their favored hosts. It is a nasty plan, but I just don't see how it can work. The Lild might be theocratic, but they are spacefaring, which means they are far from stupid and will possess the technology to prevent the spread of creatures as lethal as these."

"You are wrong," said Ormod, who of course had been watching and listening all the time.

"These creatures are a biological weapon you intend to use against the Lild," I said. "Just tell me I'm wrong about that."

"You are wrong about that too," he replied. "The shindles are salvation for the Lild."

And he would say no more.

* * *

Eight weeks passed, during which I pleaded and threatened but got no response from the captain or *Gnostic*. I went on strike, refusing to go down to feed the shindles, then relented after two days without food or water myself. During this time, the *Gnostic* continued to change its shape, to join up the tubes of its structure into a ship consisting of a series of concentric toroids five miles across. One day, the food synthesizer abruptly reconnected and started working again, then some of the other automated systems began to come back on. Taking my usual journey down into the hold, I observed that many of the cargo containers not containing shindles had been repositioned, and that some of the handler robots down there were now on the move and busy separating out six containers and beginning to open them. When I tried to get a closer look at what was going on, a handler, a thing like the bastard offspring of a forklift truck and a praying mantis, moved into my path and would not let me through.

I went off to feed the shindles, and again wondered what Ormod meant about salvation. Certainly, being small and threadlike and almost transparent, these shindles were different from those first discovered, but what *else* had been done to them? Were they intelligent, as Polity AIs now thought that the originals were? Did Ormod intend them to take over the Lild? I just had no idea.

The next time I went down to feed the shindles, the handler robots had dismantled the six containers and used them to build a big shed on the hold floor. Sounds of industry came from inside over ensuing weeks, but there wasn't even a crack I could peer through into the interior. I told Shanen about this, and a few days later, I saw her sporting numerous bruises and a bemused expression. Doubtless, to relieve the boredom, she had tried to go up against one of those handler robots. Seven weeks into our journey, I arrived one morning for the usual feeding routine, and it was only when I actually entered the first cargo container and brought over one of the food snails that I saw something had changed. The pit was empty. Checking all the other containers I saw that they were empty of their shindles too.

"What are you doing, Ormod?" I shouted.

He surprised me by replying. "I want them hungry."

Then finally we arrived.

"Well looky here," said Shanen.

Ormod had reinstated access to the ship's sensors, and we now had a large screen on which we could observe the Lild home system. With computer programs running to contract distances and highlight stuff, we soon saw a busy place indeed. The Lild homeworld was larger than Earth but only enough to knock surface gravity up about 10 percent. It was a water world, with only a few islands at the poles, and though it possessed no natural satellite like Luna, it certainly had plenty of unnatural ones. Big space stations hung in orbit in an even grid, and, taking a close look at one of them, I guessed that a lot of the visible hardware was defensive weaponry. Then, far out at a point halfway between this world and the orbit of the next world—an icy orb about the size of Neptune—we observed the fleet of Lild warships and warship construction stations, hanging in space like a scattering of huge coins amid massive slot machines.

"I would guess they're making preparations for something," I said.

"They are preparing for the extermination of the human race," said a voice behind me, and I looked around to find that, after eight weeks, our passenger had rejoined us.

"Professor Mace," said Pladdick, stepping forward with something nasty in his expression. Like us all, he had been really frustrated about all this but, since he was a heavyworlder, that frustration sometimes resulted in fist-shaped dents in the walls.

Taking if not her life then at least her health in her hands, Shanen caught hold of his shoulder. "Just a moment, Pladdick. I think now is the time for explanations."

Elvira Mace nodded, and taking a wide circuit around Pladdick, strode up to stand beside the screen. She gestured at the Lild warships. "Already *Gnostic* is picking up and analyzing vast amounts of data." She tapped at the console to bring the homeworld back onto the screen. "Much has now been confirmed, and we are updated on a lot."

"Tell me," I said. "Why are *you* involved in this?"

She glanced at me. "Not all the survivors of Circoven look like Ormod."

"I see."

She now gazed at Shanen for a moment. "You know much about this, having served on the sister ship to this one, but I will reiterate for the rest."

Shanen nodded obligingly—still a little glassy-eyed, I noticed—and guessed that the last eight weeks had taken her far too close to her boredom threshold.

Mace continued, "The Lild species is a divergent one, with two branches that cannot interbreed. The theocratic elite and ruling class have shells that closely resemble our galactic spiral. Though somewhat interbred, they have managed to retain a grip on power through religious oppression and sheer aggression. The lower class is a hardier and generally more intelligent branch of the species, but less aggressive. Without any kind of intervention, this state of affairs could continue for centuries. Without any intervention, the Polity will end up with a Lild fleet at the Line in a couple of decades."

"Wait a minute." Shanen held up a hand. "Are you saying that what you and Ormod are doing, whatever it is, has Polity sanction?"

"I am saying that, for the present, Earth Central Security is looking the other way."

"Plausible deniability," I said.

"Precisely."

"So what are you doing?" I asked.

"I will leave the final explanation to Ormod, but let me continue." She gave a tight little smile. "Each Lild warship has a captain and six under-captains, should the ship separate into segments. These are all members of the ruling-elite branch of the species. However, they often return to the homeworld, where the main concentration of the species lives in tunnels in the seabed corals—a massive cave system with internal water separated from that of the sea itself. You see, for religious reasons, they cannot breathe water contaminated by their lesser brethren."

"I do see," I said. "With the defenses around that world, it would be very difficult to get in to drop a bioweapon in the sea, let alone get one down into those tunnels."

"You do see." Elvira smiled. "Then I leave it to Ormod to explain the whole setup further. He is awaiting you and Shanen down in Hold One."

"What about us?" Pladdick gestured to himself and Parsival.

Elvira eyed him. "I will explain further, but you two are not anywhere near suicidal enough for what comes next."

"I'm not sure I like this," I said, but I was already turning to follow Shanen toward the door. The reality? A week of not feeding the shindles had left me bored and listless, half-alive, and wondering about my chances of, like Shanen, going up against one of those handler robots with whatever weapons I could fashion, just to find out what they were doing. Yes, I was getting through that damned watershed, but I wasn't through it *yet*. This meeting with Ormod promised something that would stir me up inside, make me feel alive. I could see the excitement in Shanen's expression as she glanced back at me before stepping out into the corridor. Of course, she was a worse case than me.

This time, when I used the drop-shaft, following Shanen in, I didn't bother with even checking if the irised gravity field was working, or touch the ladder. At the bottom of the shaft, Shanen stepped out into the lit area beyond and swore out loud. I swore too when I saw what awaited us.

"Wonderfully realistic, aren't they?" said Ormod, stepping out from behind one of the six nautiloids standing on the floor arrayed about a large glass sphere. One of them had a shell ten feet across, while the other five were about six feet across, fatter with their spirals running slightly off-center, all of their squid eyes and writhing tentacles glistening realistically. One of them, I'm sure, even winked at me.

"Same ones as you loaded with CTD booby traps?" I suggested.

Shanen shook her head and glanced around at me. "These are a tad more sophisticated, I suspect."

Of course, I had been forgetting that she had been involved in the same conflict as Ormod and *Gnostic*.

"Much more sophisticated," Ormod agreed. "They wouldn't fool Polity security scanners, but they'll fool most of what the Lild have got, if they're not subjected to too rigorous an inspection."

"If you could explain . . ." I suggested.

"Simple, really. Having communicated with the Lild High Family, this ship has been directed to a place in the fleet, while its captain is to take one segment of the ship to the homeworld, where there is now much excitement, for the captain is to deliver the human prisoners he managed to capture."

Fuck, I thought, clonks and booms resounding all around us as this segment of *Gnostic* detached from the main body of the ship.

Brian spun like a coin in his underwater palace, his children, nautiloids merely half a meter across, orbiting around him. He was ecstatic. There had been some controversy concerning the late return of one of the expeditionary warships, but a check of the records showed it to be one that had gone missing out in the general direction of humanspace. The story the captain of the ship told was a long and complex tale of their encounter with a human warship, battles, escapes, damaged engines that took decades to repair, and finally a sneak raid for intelligence, but with an added bonus.

The captain of this ship must be honored by an audience with Brian and be given a chance to tell his story to the theocratic elite. His adventures would be a salutary lesson to all Lild that would confirm their place in the universe, to dispel any remaining doubts raised by heretics and still harbored by those weak of mind. But most important of all was that added bonus, for he would bring human captives here for all to see—weak, malformed creatures obviously not shaped by God. *Air*-breathers, creatures no better than the leaf-eaters dwelling on a few homeworld islands. A species to be crushed for their temerity in confronting the Chosen.

Brian spread his tentacles and jetted water to bring his spin to a halt. Playfully batting at his children, he sent them whistling on their way to play in some other part of the palace. This was a joyous occasion, for the captain of that ship had already confirmed some of his own suspicions. The expeditionary ship the humans had destroyed had just been plain unlucky, having arrived at a place where the humans were strongest. This had been a message direct from God to shake the Lild out of their complacency. However, the good news was that these humans occupied just a handful of star systems, more than the worms, and more worlds, but nothing like what had been claimed by the Low Family heretics aboard that first ship.

Moving over to his screens, Brian stabbed out a tentacle and manipulated the coral controls. Immediately, he obtained a view of the new arrival, one of its segments now detached and heading for homeworld. Within the day, that segment would dock with one of the big military stations, and the captain and his humans would be shuttled down to the planet, down through the Spiral Sea, and finally to here. There was much to do. Brian began summoning High Family theocrats to the palace.

I gazed around at this compartment, obviously constructed in what remained of Hold One. So this was what the interior of a Lild warship should look like! We occupied a coraline tube, with interior segmentation, perhaps just like the interior of a length of straightened-out snail shell.

"So what makes you think we're going to have anything to do with this?" I asked.

Ormod parted his mandibles and grinned spikily. "It's that time of your life." He glanced at Shanen. "Is that not so?"

Shanen nodded agreement. Her face was flushed with excitement, and, poised on the balls of her feet, she looked ready to spring into action at once. I knew that she would do precisely what Ormod wanted, because, twenty or thirty years ago, I would have too. Now, however, I was starting to see downsides to risking my life.

"Perhaps you could explain further?" I inquired.

"There are risks associated with having people like you aboard," he told us. "So, as I prepared for this, I never wanted any more than two of you at any one time. I knew that it is precisely those of your kind who would be inclined to do something like this—those who care so little for their own existence. Whether two human captives are taken down, or one, is irrelevant. The Lild Theocrat has been told of two captives, so that would be preferable, but one being missing can be easily explained. However, captives are essential because they utterly ensure that the nautiloid that did the capturing would be immediately summoned down to the ocean-floor cave systems."

"Why not you?" asked Shanen.

That grin again. "With the assistance of a submind of *Gnostic*, I'll be controlling *them*." He gestured to the six robot nautiloids. "I am also holding some other options in reserve aboard this segment vessel, and it would be better for me to be here to control them. *Gnostic* itself has enough to do back in its present position, and I would rather it focused all its processing power on maintaining the subterfuge there." He shrugged. "I'm also a lot more adverse to taking risks than I used to be, back when I was the same age as you and learning to talk to shindles."

"And this is where I have my problems," I said. "The shindles will be the salvation of the Lild, you told me. What are they going to do down there? Take control of the theocrats from within and guide the Lild to enlightenment?"

"No." Ormod seemed to be enjoying my perplexity. "The shindles you have been nurturing for so long possess no intelligence at all. You have to understand that, like my own people, the shindles are genetic engineers, but they are ones who engineer their own bodies to create their organic technology—they actually create that technology *out* of themselves. The worms you fed are just a machine, a tool, a delivery system. I am an accomplished genetic engineer myself, but I could never alone achieve what has been done with them. However, when the organism concerned is co-operating with you at a molecular level, it does get much easier."

"I was right, then—they're some sort of biological weapon."

"Yes and no, but I can assure you that not a single Lild will be hurt or in any way incapacitated by them. They are so small and have been engineered precisely so that their hosts will hardly notice penetration, and as they breed and spread from that host to others, there will be no ill effects, rather a slight euphoria and increased production of sex hormones."

"Stop playing around, Ormod," said Shanen. "You're boring me."

The captain nodded an acknowledgment, and got to the point, which was both stunning, amusing, and highly immoral, I think. I agreed to be one of the human captives because, to be frank, he'd already lured me in too far for me to just walk away from this, and he knew that though I was less inclined toward risk than Shanen, I still had not managed to give it up.

If the sphere had been made of chain-glass, had been Polity technology, I would have been fine about it, but it had to be Lild technology, and I wondered if it was of a glass strong enough to survive the pressure down at the bottom of the Lild sea. Ormod assured me it was perfectly safe, then went on to add further delightful news.

"You have to strip naked," he told us.

"Why?" I was hoping at least for a high-spec Polity envirosuit capable of keeping me alive should I end up outside the sphere in Lild seas.

"You're captives," he explained. "You have been stripped of everything and simply kept alive for display purposes. You'll also be heavily scanned before being taken down into cave systems. The Lild will be highly conscious of security, especially when bringing you before the Theocrat."

"Bit of a shell game then," said Shanen, as she stripped off the shapeless ship suit she always wore. I eyed her for a little while, and, finally seeing her naked, thought that maybe, if we survived this, I should perhaps set our relationship on a different course. Certainly noticing my regard as she pulled down her panties, she then flipped them up with one foot, caught them in one hand, and threw them at me.

"Get out of those rags, old man," she said, and, with a flounce, stepped through the hatch into the sphere. The nerve; she wasn't exactly a youngster!

I took off the slip-ons, the worn old envirosuit trousers, and the T-shirt that had always been my favored dress for shipboard life, and quickly stepped into the sphere beside her. The thick circular-section glass hatch slid around into position on runners, then sank down into its hole like a large bung. We were standing on a two-meter-diameter circular floor over the life-support machinery. I sat down with my back against the glass. Then glanced across to where Ormod was standing with one hand resting against the biggest ersatz-nautiloid, which was now donning some kind of breathing equipment. I realized then that, of course, this was to cleanse the water of the contamination from its lesser brethren.

"What about communication?" I called, wondering if I was going to get any reply.

"Directional sound beam," Ormod said, his voice almost seeming to issue from inside the sphere. He slapped his hand against the nautiloid and turned away, heading to a big pressure door in the side of this false Lild ship interior.

"Bit of a shell game?" I said to Shanen, really wishing she would sit down because there was simply no room in here for her to prowl around. Abruptly, she did sit, directly facing me, her legs wide apart. Ridiculous. We were about to head into a seriously life-threatening situation, and I was starting to feel horny. I looked to one side, just in time to see water pouring from vents in the walls into the hold—nautiloid atmosphere.

"Shell game," Shanen repeated. "Three walnut shells and one pea, and the mark has to guess which shell the pea is under. It's all about distraction and misdirection."

"Yes, I know," I said. "The nautiloids will be mainly focused on us, not on their ostensible kin." I gestured to the robot nautiloids outside. "But you understand the humor?"

She just stared at me, a slight smiling twist to her expression as she gently patted her hand against her inner thigh.

"Shell?" I said. "Shell game?"

"Oh I see," she said, her present amusement obviously about something else.

As the water level rose over the sphere, it became neutrally buoyant, as did the robot nautiloids. Turning now and reaching down to the floor with their tentacles, two of the smaller ones dragged themselves forward and took hold of handles positioned below the life-support section of the sphere to steady it in the water, just in time, for the whole ship shuddered at that moment.

"We're docked now," Ormod informed us.

"What are these other options you're holding in reserve?" I asked. This whole operation was poised on a knife edge, and frankly, to go on and butcher a few metaphors, if the shell game did not deceive the squid eye, me and Shanen were fish food.

"Explosive options and particle cannon options. Like, for example, the CTD inside one of the smaller robot nautiloids accompanying you."

"Ah, you neglected to mention that," said Shanen.

Current abruptly began moving in the water surrounding us, picking up pieces of detritus, but none that could be identified as of human origin. Our two nautiloid handlers turned the sphere until they were facing a big iris door opening at the end of the tube. Now the real things began to appear, and the water filled with booms and pops and high-pitched squeals. After a moment, I began to feel a tightness at the base of my skull.

"Infrasound," Shanen observed. "Let's just hope they keep the chatter down to a manageable level."

We were propelled out of the tunnel, through the big airlock, or, rather, water lock, and into the interior of the space station, our robot nautiloid captain holding proprietary station above us. While we were being moved, Lild came up close, pushing their eyes against the glass, or clinking tenta-

cles divided at the ends into feather fingers against the glass
right next to us, just like humans trying to get a reaction
from fish in a fish bowl. At one point, in a chamber shaped
like a heart, they all drew back, our handlers depositing the
sphere in a large metal cup, and a rhythmic droning ensued,
the sphere slowly revolved so we had to shift around inside it
to avoid being tumbled about.

"Scanning," I suggested, as our handlers returned for us.

"Damn," said Ormod. "Don't these fuckers ever stop digging?"

"Problems?" Shanen inquired.

"Oh, I've got thousands of hours of nautiloid com and
language programs running in each of the robots, so there
should be no problem about the Lild discovering they're not
nautiloids. The problem is the religious questioning. There
are those here who want to find out if these newly arrived
heroes might be guilty of heretical thought. It's depressing."

At some point, we ended up inside a ship, and I'm just not
sure when the transition was made, only knowing for sure
when our handlers secured the sphere with long straps, and
we felt the surge of acceleration taking us out into glaring
sunlight. Obviously, we were to be on display at all times, for
I now saw that we had been positioned inside a clear blister
on the side of the vessel. I was glad of that—everyone likes
a good clear view.

The watery world loomed close very quickly, since the
station we had just departed sat in low orbit. Within minutes,
we were descending through atmosphere, and that was when
the crowds began to appear.

"Ah," Shanen exclaimed. "I did wonder what a sphere like
this might be used for—I don't suppose they take so many
captives that they always have the things on hand."

The atmosphere outside seemed to fill with bubbles, and
I saw that glass spheres much like the one we occupied
bobbed out there, supported on iron-colored motors that had
to be some form of grav-tech. They were individual transports, each occupied by one of the Lild.

"Just the plebs," I observed. "The rulers stay down in their
comfy caves." The nautiloids within the spheres were all the

smaller ones, the ones with fatter shells with a slight off-center twist, like the five smaller robot Lild accompanying our captain. Soon we left these behind us.

The sky turned pale green above us and the sea was soon clear below: flecks of white across deep jade, large enclosed vessels cruising the surface like submarine conning towers, most of their bulk probably below the surface. The sun, a blue orb nested in white and silvery clouds, fell into sunset and we fell into twilight, then night as our vessel roared and descended into the waves.

Lild again appeared around us, but we could only see them when they were picked out by the eerie green lights their fellows sported on their shells. As we descended into the depths, I began to notice static constellations of lights, then glimpses of fairy castles under the sea, on thick stalks that speared up from the black. Then, abruptly, we were beside a great artificial cliff, and the vessel shuddered as it docked.

Our captain and five lackeys came for us then and, rather than be taken into the cave system via a docking tunnel, we were actually taken outside into the sea, toward a large round portal in the face of the artificial cliff. Much booming, twittering, and skull-thumping debate ensued. A lot of the Lild about us now were the big, flatter-shelled ones like our captain. After a little while, the huge portal began to open, but while this was happening, the five lesser robot nautiloids abruptly departed, surrounded by some of their larger kin.

"Expected," said Ormod. "They're off for a visit to the inquisitors for detailed questioning."

"Nice society," said Shanen, shivering abruptly. It was getting cold within the sphere despite the life-support machinery laboring away beneath us. After a moment, she slid across and plumped herself down right beside me, resting her legs over the top of mine. I put my arm around her.

"How did you stay alive?" she abruptly asked.

"Luck," I replied.

"I think I'm going to need help."

"You got it," I said, giving her a squeeze.

"I hate to break in on this touching moment," said Ormod, "but this is it."

Our robot captain had positioned himself on one side of the sphere while another of the higher-status ones took the other. We went in through a series of water locks, and the nautiloids around us began dispensing with their filter gear, and this was, indeed, it.

The wide coraline tunnels within were brightly lit and around us the crowd of big nautiloids grew, just as curious as their kin and prone to clink those divided tentacles against the glass. I turned my head slightly to observe our robot captain, just in time to see the first shindle wriggling from one of the many pores in his shell; a nigh-invisible flicker of movement. It then streaked across to the nearest living high-status Lild, hitting a tentacle and rapidly vanishing as it penetrated its new host. The Lild seemed not to notice. Other shindles began to surreptitiously depart our robot, gradually depleting the great compacted mass of them it held inside it.

We were brought into a large chamber occupied by Lild obviously grander than those we'd so far seen, all of them hanging in an artificial quadrate framework that had been decorously fashioned to look a little like some kind of seaweed. Our sphere was deposited on a coraline pillar before the grandest of them all. The Theocrat stood out from all the rest, little pin-head lights gleaming all over his shell. A booming, headachy conversation ensued.

"My captain tells a good story," said Ormod. "But judging by some of the questions, I'm not sure it is all being believed."

Me and Shanen locked closer together in an embrace—perfectly the image of frightened humans brought before alien captors. I don't know how long this audience lasted, because my head ached intolerably and I did not feel at all well. I even began to wonder if the life-support system in there with us was working correctly. Then, abruptly, the note changed—something else now seemed to be occurring.

"Well, I was hoping you'd be shunted off to one side for later study, where the extraction would be easier," said Ormod. "Seems not. Seems the big boss wants to demonstrate to his fellows just how feeble these human creatures are."

"And how does he intend to do that?" Shanen asked—she looked as ill as I felt.

"He wants to open the sphere."

"Yeah, that'd do it," I said.

"Time to get you out of there."

In the sea above us, the five robot nautiloids that had accompanied our captain had already released their load of modified shindles into the sea. Now one of them presented a hot and very brief surprise to those questioning it. The CTD detonation caused the cave system around us to shudder and, dislodged from its pillar, our sphere began a slow tumble to the floor. I looked around for our robot captain, spotted him easily, for the soft foreparts of his body had fallen away and a great cloud of thready shindles was rapidly spreading out.

"They'll find out about them," I had said to Ormod as he had told me what he intended. "They'll have the technology to remove them from themselves."

"But by then, it will be too late, the damage will be done, and they won't even know that it's been done until years later."

Hollow now, running on Polity tech, the captain's shell descended and locked onto the sphere. Gleaming manipulators extruded from the cavity inside, as it evacuated its water, and tore away the hatch. We threw ourselves into the space previously occupied by shindles and I just hoped none of them had remained in there. As instructed, we donned the breather masks available inside and assumed fetal positions. Crash foam jetted in, filling the cavities all around us, protecting us, padding us, but we still felt the massive accelerations and I lost consciousness twice. The CTD had of course caused sufficient disruption to cover our escape, but I didn't get to see much of that.

"The problem is that galactic shape of the ruling theocratic elite," Ormod had told us. "Those of the Lild who less closely match it are more prone to heresy."

As we shot from the seas of the Lild homeworld, two things happened simultaneously. The *Gnostic*, parked amid the Lild fleet, abruptly accelerated away while in orbit of the Lild homeworld; Ormod undocked his segment ship, meanwhile playing a particle cannon over the space station's weapons. Some twenty minutes after that, Ormod intercepted our straight-up trajectory, then accelerated out toward the *Gnostic*.

"The shindles will spread rapidly, infecting most Lild very, very quickly. Of course, there'll be huge panic and their doctors will work fast to find a way to remove them, to kill the infection," Ormod had continued. "Then they'll discover something quite strange: this terrible bioweapon seems to cause few ill effects at all. Obviously, inferior humans, allied with some of those shindles who managed to escape the extermination, have with this failed attack proven just how unworthy they are. They have proven that they are not the Chosen."

The *Gnostic* dropped into U-space just as Ormod, Pladdick, Parsival, and Mace began cutting us out of the crash foam.

"It's so small a thing they do, just a little viral reprogramming, but something the Lild just don't have the technology to correct." Ormod was a man who really enjoyed his revenge. "The tweaks are right down there in the germ plasm, and every Lild hatched from the egg of one infected by the shindles will not grow as expected; it'll be subtle at first, then blindingly obvious after their first few years. Their shape will no longer be that of a flat galactic spiral, but of a long, hornlike tube. And they will no longer be the beloved of God."

Me and Shanen waved off the others and headed for her cabin. I'd taken far too many risks lately and she had taken enough to satisfy her self-destructive impulse for a while—for a little while. I'll watch her now, see if I can keep her alive. We're not the chosen of any god. We only have each other.

PUNCTUALITY

GARTH NIX

Everyone knows that it's important to be punctual. Just *how* important, though, is something realized only by the very few . . .

New York Times bestselling Australian writer Garth Nix worked as a book publicist, editor, marketing consultant, public relations man, and literary agent before launching the bestselling Old Kingdom series, which consists of *Sabriel*, *Lirael: Daughter of the Clayr*, *Abhorsen*, and *The Creature in the Case*. His other books include the Seventh Tower series, consisting of *The Fall, Castle, Aenir, Above the Veil, Into Battle*, and *The Violet Keystone*; the Keys to the Kingdom series, consisting of *Mister Monday, Grim Tuesday, Drowned Wednesday*, and *Sir Thursday*; as well as standalone novels, such as *The Ragwitch* and *Shade's Children*. His short fiction has been collected in *Across the Wall: Tales of the Old Kingdom and Beyond*. His most recent book is a new novel in the Keys to the Kingdom series, *Superior Saturday*. Born in Melbourne, he now lives in Sydney, Australia.

The giant carrier appeared in orbit around the planet exactly on schedule, as was expected, given its method of propulsion. Though it was built to carry hundreds of other ships, including the largest battleships and colonizers, in this case there was a single slivership on its racks, and that tiny craft carried only three people: two augmented humans and the slivership's AI, who was bound to the vessel and so little more than a slave.

The humans were the One Hundred and Forty-Third Emperor of All Known Space and one of his designated adult children. As was customary, she had been raised and educated by a foster family in the far reaches of the Empire and had only a year before learned that she was not natural-born but a carefully engineered child technically known as an Imperial Daughter, though genetically she was more than 99 percent the Emperor's sister.

Her name was now Ilugia, though that was also new. The fact that the name had been borne by the Sixty-First Empress of All Known Space was of some interest to her, and to the sycophants of the court who thought that it meant she had been chosen to be the next occupant of the Star Sapphire Throne.

The Emperor did not speak as the slivership left the carrier and descended to a primitive landing field on the surface of the rust-colored, dead world. As far as Ilugia had been able to ascertain from her limited access to the ship's scans, the planet had nothing to offer. It had no mineral resources, no biological life of any kind, and its atmosphere was a mere wisp of carbon dioxide. She didn't even know where it was, and had been surprised and excited by the sudden summons to attend the Emperor on a personal excursion.

They paused for a few minutes in the airlock to allow their bodies to store oxygen and make some minor modifications to skins and eyes, before the Emperor gestured to Ilugia to exit. He followed her out onto the smooth, nano-manicured field, and spoke aloud. Ilugia had never heard his voice, and was surprised by it. It was considered oafish and backward to speak aloud in the imperial capital, though on her homeworld it was not unusual.

"We must wait a little while," said the Emperor. His silvered face showed no emotion, but his words were grave and Ilugia paid careful attention. "There are guardians here, which are slow to recognize friends. You must disconnect from the ship, and once we leave the field, do not attempt to integrate with any other potentiality. This is not whimsy, but a matter of utmost importance. Similarly, you must stay close to me at all times."

Ilugia inclined her head to indicate assent, and withdrew the tertiary personality that had been using the ship's various systems to report back to her. With no secondary, tertiary, or quaternary personalities, or even any subagents deployed, she felt quite shut up inside her head. It was not a pleasant sensation to perceive the world around her entirely from one perspective.

"Be still," warned the Emperor.

Ilugia obeyed, going so far as to pulse her heart once and then stop it. With her blood hyper-oxygenated to cope with the lack of atmosphere, she was not breathing, and so had no need to quiet her chest.

Beyond the dull surface of the landing field, the red dirt shivered and began to swirl. Hundreds of dust-devils rose and began to dance together, at the same time slowly moving counterclockwise, gradually forming the pattern of a giant whorl of red particles some several hundred meters across.

Then without warning, a vast black shape burst out of the whorl, its shadow falling upon the Emperor and Ilugia, its rise so fast and the shadow so deep that for a moment she thought it would fall and crush them. Obedient to the Emperor, she did not move or react, instead studying the thing that was still emerging from some subterranean position.

It was a flattened ovoid, tapering from the center to the rim. Her eyes measured the revealed portion to be 612.75 meters wide, with an extrapolated diameter of 1755.97 meters. It was 5.3 meters tall at the rim, and an estimated 52.5 meters at its center. The surface material was a matt black substance that could not be visually identified, and Ilugia dared not use any more invasive methods to determine its properties.

The vast ovoid continued to climb, motivated by some, again unidentifiable, anti-gravitic thrust. As it came free of the soil, it tilted forward and drifted low over the field,

blocking out the sky above the two visitors. With all of it
visible, Ilugia's eyes recalculated it to be 1761.87 meters in
diameter, and told her that it had moved to position itself so
that the center of the huge disk was directly above the two
humans.

The Emperor slowly tilted his head back, at the same time
whispering,

"Look up. Slowly."

Ilugia obeyed. The disk was close enough to touch, but
even at this range, she could not identify its construction.
The black material defied visual analysis on every level,
including the relatively low-powered microscopic abilities
Ilugia had as part of her standard optical package.

Ilugia was looking up at the disk, when, without warning
or the sensation of any application of energy or force, she
was somewhere else. She could not discern any temporal ab-
erration, but in one nanosecond she was beneath the ovoid,
and then, in apparently the same nanosecond, she was inside
a bare cube-shaped room made from the same dark material
as the exterior of the ovoid. The Emperor was next to her,
also still looking up.

He turned to Ilugia and said quietly, "Good. It has accepted you."

"What is this place?" asked Ilugia. Noting that movement
was allowed, she restarted her heart.

"You might consider it a guardroom or perhaps a sentry
post," said the Emperor. He sat down, cross-legged on the
floor. Ilugia followed suit, noting that the floor was warm
and continued to defy analysis. It did not even feel like any
material she knew. It was smooth when she laid her palm
upon it, but became rough when she slid her hand sideways,
though there was no visible change to the surface.

"We should shortly emerge at our destination," said the
Emperor. "There may be some conceptual dissonance."

"What is our destination?" asked Ilugia.

"A great secret," replied the Emperor. "The greatest secret
of the Empire."

"The Punctuality Drive," said Ilugia, and dampened the
sudden elevation of her blood pressure and heart rate.

"Indeed," said the Emperor. "Tell me, what theory of the many that circulate has most appeal to you? Or *had* the most appeal, up until this recent voyage?"

"None entirely match the known facts," said Ilugia carefully. As she spoke, she sorted the theories she knew, ordering them by rational, political, and psychological appeal. Was this a test of some kind?

"One fact is certain," she hazarded. "The Punctuality Drive was invented by the First Empress, Uejinian, and operated by her in the first carrier, *Alphane*, that took the colonization fleet from Earthhome to Khankri and thence to Khasepea and back around again."

"That is the historical record," said the Emperor. "But it is incorrect. Uejinian did not invent the Punctuality Drive. Nor is it precisely a drive, though it has suited our purposes to call it thus, and to promulgate the mysteries of the forbidden bridges and engine rooms of our carriers. Prepare yourself."

Ilugia dampened her sensory apparatus a moment before the world changed. She was now in zero-gravity, suspended in deep extrasolar space or some facsimile of it. Above her, thirty-three kilometers distant, was the sole light source, a bright blue cube, exactly four kilometers square. Its surface was shot with a multitude of pulsations, which were apparent to Ilugia across a very broad spectra, as she gradually moved her perceptive capacity back up to its normal baseline. Though the pulsations had the effect of reducing visual acuity, on maximum zoom Ilugia could also make out that in the middle of the closer surface of the cube, there were one hundred and forty-six human or humanoid figures, standing in a series of concentric circles around one central person.

The Emperor pointed near this circle, oriented himself, and exhaled a jet of oxygen and water equivalent to 12 percent of the reserve taken on in the slivership, the reaction propelling him toward the cube. Ilugia did likewise, and accepted the Emperor's proffered hand as they moved toward the blue artifact.

The Emperor continued his conversation without speaking, using the private connection of their fingers.

The red dust world is in the original system of Earthhome, and was the objective of an exploratory mission led by Uejinian and her twin sister, Aellia. In the course of that mission, they alerted or awoke the guardian disk that transported them to our own destination, the cube that lies ahead. As you will soon be aware, the cube is a processing potentiality of incomprehensible power. You will feel a strong desire to integrate with it, but you must not do so. At least, not yet.

They landed close to the outer circle of human figures. As their feet touched, Ilugia felt both the slight gravity and the shock of an information system attempting to flood in via all possible synaptic portals. It did not feel hostile, but rather the reverse, something familiar and friendly, like an imperial carrier, and as the Emperor had warned, she had to actively fight against the desire to immediately integrate with the potentiality.

A closer view of the humans arrayed in the circles was also a shock. The outer circle, though not complete, had forty-seven people in it. Each one was shrouded in a semi-opaque membrane of a blue tinge similar to that of the cube itself. As Ilugia watched the closest person, she saw several internal layers within the membrane shift and move, allowing her glimpses of the person within its embrace.

They are alive, she sent to the Emperor.

Yes, came the reply. The Emperor led her to an empty place in the outer ring. *Stand here, and look toward the center. To Aellia.*

Ilugia did as she was instructed, but for the first time, she was afraid. She had begun to think she might be made the Imperial Heir, to ultimately ascend the Star Sapphire Throne. Now, as she looked at the silent, shrouded people around her, she wondered if another fate awaited her. Deep in the secured parts of her mind, she began to formulate plans for escape and evasion, though none seemed likely to succeed. None could succeed if the Emperor opposed her, such was her conditioning.

Aellia was the one who made contact, and who discerned something of the nature of the artifact, the Emperor informed her. *She gave Uejinian the schedule for* Alpha.

*Uejinian returned to Earthhome and had the carrier con-
structed, ready to launch at the specified time. Twenty-two
years later, when the need for another carrier was realized,
Uejinian returned here, and Aellia took over a further six
schedules for which carriers were eventually made. So it
continued, until Schedule 1207, when we were expanding to
Hatturat, and Aellia indicated she could not integrate any
further schedules. There were a number of experiments at
that time, some with very unfortunate results. However, in
time, it became clear that adding further schedules required
more humans to be integrated with the cube. Later still,
after more experiments, came the realization that the cube
would only accept humans with a genetic profile narrowly
matched to Aellia.*

Such as myself, sent Ilugia.

Indeed, replied the Emperor. *You have the new Master
Schedule?*

Yes.

Ilugia had integrated the Master Schedule several days
before, again thinking it a mark of signal favor. The Master
Schedule contained the departure and arrival dates and
times of every carrier in the Empire, and though portions
of it were known to various commanders and functionaries,
the complete schedule was closely held among the imperial
family.

Ilugia had not wondered why there was such a rigid schedule, beyond strategic convenience. Like everyone else in the
Empire, she had presumed the Punctuality Drive worked
under the command of each carrier's secret, sealed AI. Carriers always arrived exactly on time at their destination. She
had not thought that the destination was fixed and immu-
table, and could not change unless the schedule changed.

*There are seventy-eight new routes in the latest sched-
ule, with carriers almost ready to launch,* said the Emperor.
*That number requires an additional integrator here. One of
our family.*

Yes, said Ilugia. A thousand last-second plans and protests
rose in her mind and were abandoned as quickly. *May I ask
why it is to be me?*

You? It may be either of us, replied the Emperor. *Open all and integrate.*

Ilugia opened all her synaptic portals and the universe rushed in. She saw and heard and felt every carrier, and perceived everything the carriers' systems perceived, and she shared the thoughts and secrets of everyone around her, all the integrators who stood upon the cube. Including the Emperor, and with that came all the current codes and cryptologic secrets of the Empire, and every tiny shred of data that could be used to rule and govern and coerce the billions of sentients who thrived upon the almost one hundred thousand worlds that were connected by the punctual carriers driven by this mysterious cube.

Then, as quickly as it had rushed into her head, most of it was gone, save the Emperor's data. The carriers receded. The minds of Ilugia's relatives went with them, once again divided among all the carriers they piloted, back to an experience that Ilugia already wished to share again.

Hail, Ilugia, One Hundred and Forty-Fourth Emperor of All Known Space, said an internal voice she now knew as Aellia. *We will see you again.*

Yes, Ilugia sent back. She examined her internal clock and the Master Schedule and added: *In thirteen years, six months, three days, and five hours.*

Don't be late, said Aellia, and Ilugia felt laughter gradually recede as Aellia returned to her carriers and the galaxy beyond.

Ilugia increased the elastic tension of her leg muscles, and bounded from the cube, propelling herself to the rendezvous from where she would be transported back to the landing field.

The Empress did not waste time. She had a carrier to catch, and she knew it *could not* wait for her.

INEVITABLE

SEAN WILLIAMS

Australian writer Sean Williams is the author of many
novels in collaboration with Shane Dix, including *The
Unknown Soldier*, *The Prodigal Sun*, *The Dying Light*,
The Dark Imbalance, *Chaos of Earth*, *Orphans of Earth*,
Heirs of Earth, and *Geodesica: Ascent*, along with three
Star Wars novels. As a solo writer, he's written both fan-
tasy and high-tech science fiction, and is the author of the
Books of the Change series, consisting of *The Stone Mage
and the Sea*, *The Sky Warden and the Sun*, and *The Storm
Weaver and the Sand*; the Books of the Cataclysm series,
consisting of *The Crooked Letter*, *The Blood Debt*, and *The
Hanging Mountains*; and the Astropolis series, consisting,
to date, of *Saturn Returns* and *Earth Ascendant*. His standalone novels include *Metal Fatigue* (which won Australia's
Aurealis Award for 1996), *The Resurrected Man*, and
Cenotaxis. His stories have been gathered in the collections *Doorway to Eternity*, *A View Before Dying*, and *New
Adventures in Sci-Fi*. His most recent book is a *Star Wars*
novel, *The Force Unleashed*, and coming up is a new novel
in the Astropolis series, *The Grand Conjunction*. He lives
in Adelaide, Australia.

In the intricate story that follows, he takes us on a headlong chase across time and space, where it's hard to tell who is the hunter and who is the prey—or if they're one and the same.

CAPTIVE

The prisoner was both young and male, which suited Master Bannerman perfectly well. She had encountered his type before—headstrong, shallow, visceral—and refined numerous techniques for extracting what she needed. He would give her what she wanted, and possibly more besides. It was only a matter of time.

For his part, Braith Kindred was still struggling to wake up. His head ached, and his body was covered in bruises beneath an unfamiliar uniform. The air seemed as thick as honey, but only when he moved in a particular direction, encountering resistance when he sat upright, but none at all when dropping his arms to his sides. That his inner ear told him he was in free fall was another puzzling detail.

He rubbed his forehead, taking in the details of his cell. It was rectangular, six meters long and three wide, with white walls and a square cross-section. The cot he sat on was bolted to the floor. He noted circular holes where furniture had once been mounted at points on walls and ceiling as well. Clearly "down" was variable.

That triggered a memory. He raised and lowered his right arm, testing the honey effect. He had heard about such things. "Weird fields," they were called. They were never used inside the Structure.

There was only one place he could be.

A Guild ship. In the belly of the beast.

"How did I get here?" he asked the empty room, certain that someone would be listening.

"Play him the recording."

Master Bannerman stood with her arms folded tightly across her chest, watching the prisoner's reaction via life-size hologram.

The sound of his voice filled the brightly lit cell. The strain in the words, the effort it took to get them out.

"I strike this blow against the Guild of the Great Ships in the name of Terminus and all the free people of the Structure."

The prisoner frowned.

"Now do you remember?" Bannerman asked him.

He remembered setting the last of the charges and testing the trigger that would simultaneously ignite them. There had been a break in one of the relays. He had been on his way to fix it when he had stumbled over the intruders: a pair of them, moving stealthily through the empty lower tunnels. They had no business there; Hakham topside had been abandoned for weeks. So he had fired at them, hitting one, and then hurried back to the hub to trigger the demolition ahead of schedule. Faulty relay be damned; he wasn't about to blow the mission on account of Guild agents getting in the way. Fortunately, the hub hadn't been interfered with. He had entered the codes and braced himself to read the script. This was his big moment. In seconds, it would be all over—for Terminus and the free people of the Structure, but most of all for his brother, who had died at the hands of a Guildsman and deserved the honor.

Then what?

His captors played the message again. It was his voice, all right. The words were his, too. The script was so deeply embedded in him that it had become part of his skeleton.

He didn't remember saying it, though. Not on Hakham. Not ever. He had rehearsed the speech in his head a thousand times. It had never once issued from his mouth.

Perhaps, he thought, the shockwave had given him amnesia.

Or perhaps a much stranger solution awaited discovery.

"You pulled me from under the wreckage," the prisoner said. "Or you beat me up. Which?"

She studied him closely. He held himself still, very still,

as though thinking for his life. What new treacheries was he planning behind those cold blue eyes?

"The former," she said.

"So I did push the button. Good. What are you going to do now? Interrogate me?"

"No amount of interrogation will reopen the shaft. Hakham is closed forever."

"Execute me, then?"

She let him ponder that possibility for a moment, imagining the fear of ignominious death eating into his certainty like acid. He would reach the obvious conclusion, given time.

"You're soldiers on a war footing," he said slowly. "If our roles were reversed, if I was the one pulling you out of the rubble, I would've shot you on the spot. You haven't done that, so you must want something from me. What is that, exactly?"

"Just one thing," Bannerman said. "By blowing those charges, you cut yourself off from everyone you know. More: you stranded yourself a thousand light-years from your fellow conspirators. I've kept you alive because I think you'll come to realize just how stupid that was."

"You want to watch me suffer?"

"No. There are other ways into the Structure. We know of two, and Terminus has sealed both of them. You're going to help me find a third."

"Why would I do that?"

"It's the only way you'll ever get back inside."

"Well, that's true."

A slow smile crept across his face.

Whatever he was thinking, she didn't like it.

Kindred wished he could see the woman addressing him. Guildsmen he was familiar with; they were uniformly compact and handsome, practically indistinguishable from each other, like clones. No one had ever seen a Guildswoman before. What strange hive queen might she be?

She was right about him, anyway, whoever or whatever

she was. He did know another entrance to the Structure. More than one, in fact. He had memorized his brother's charts, even added to them himself, once he too had become a Terminus agent. Exits weren't commonplace, and they were sometimes difficult to map, but they weren't impossibly rare.

The truth of his situation was settling heavily into place, like a shipwreck coming to rest on the bottom of a sea. The detonation of the charges, the script, and his own voice reading it aloud—amnesia had nothing to do with his predicament. There was about as much point fighting it as there was fighting time itself.

"All right," he said. "I'll take you where you want to go."

"With the intention of betraying me when you arrive, I presume."

"I don't doubt that you're planning something similar for me."

She didn't reply. He sat waiting for a quarter of an hour, elbows holding his illusory upper bodyweight on his knees. Then he gave in to his body's need to rest and eased back flat upon the cot. Closed his eyes on the bright whiteness of the cell and tried his best to ignore the feeling of falling. He had a lot to think about. Whatever his captor was doing, displaying impatience would only give her a sense of satisfaction he intended to withhold forever.

The prisoner had capitulated much more quickly than Master Bannerman had expected. She trusted him even less for that, but his verbal concession gave her enough to convince the Grand Masters that her plan should proceed. Once the flurry of FTL packets between her Great Ship and the parent world ebbed back to vacuum noise, Master Bannerman handpicked two Guildsmen and went immediately to where the prisoner lay waiting.

"I am Master Bannerman," she said. "I speak for this Great Ship."

She came two long paces into the cell, giving him time to look her over. A full head taller than the average Guildsman, she was easily a match for the prisoner's stature and strength. When he stood up, moving warily through the artificial gravity, they faced each other eye to eye.

"Braith Kindred," he replied, glancing at her escort, which had taken position by the open door. "But you knew that already."

"We have a *vedette* waiting."

"A what?"

"A scout ship."

"And you've come to ask me for a destination, I suppose."

"You wouldn't possibly tell me now. The information is all that's keeping you alive."

She indicated that he should turn around. One of her two Guildsmen moved forward to fasten restraints around his wrists.

"You're going to show me, rather than tell me," she told him. "So long as you honor the terms of agreement, you will be permitted to live."

"What about your ship?"

She wasn't about to reveal the intricacies of her existence to him. The Great Ship would be well looked after by another avatar of herself, identical in every respect to the one searching for the Structure. Let him think that she was abandoning her station to go roaming on a fool's quest, and that the treachery he planned would make the slightest difference to the Grand Masters' war.

"Attempt to harm me," she told him, "and you will be instantly killed."

He didn't doubt that Bannerman possessed that capacity. The Guild might have installed a dozen lethal devices into him while he was unconscious, which she could activate with a gesture.

When the Guildsman working on his wrists had finished the job, he turned to face her again.

"Oza," he said.

"Explain that remark."

He enjoyed her puzzlement, just as she had no doubt enjoyed his.

"The place you're looking for. That's its name."

"It does not appear on our charts."

"Oza is beyond your borders. Still in the galaxy, but a long hike from Hakham. You'll need a fast ship if you want to get there any time soon."

Her expression didn't change. "You are testing the capabilities of the Guild."

"I'm giving you what you asked for. Take it or leave it."

He waited while she thought about it. The Guild had searched all its worlds for other entrances to the Structure, and found only Gevira and Hakham. Any obvious destination, therefore, she would likely recognize as a lie. That didn't have to make her happy, though. When she met the Decretians, her unhappiness was certain to compound, but he wasn't about to tell her about them yet.

His fear was gone. It had been replaced by a cool, confident certainty. She would accept the deal and they would go to Oza. Or if not Oza, then somewhere more distant still. They would get in, and she would not kill him. She couldn't kill him, and neither could the Decretians or anyone else. He was protected by the Structure now, no matter how far he roamed from it.

If she turned him down, another possibility would present itself. The universe had, for him, become a maze with a multitude of paths and only one exit.

"The *vedette* is ready," she said. "Come."

Master Bannerman moved off with long, confident strides. He found his field-legs after a dozen steps and did his best to keep up.

HARDWARE

More FTL packets flashed. More decisions were made. Master Bannerman secured the ship she needed—the Guild's fastest *razee*—and received in return a warning that, should she fail, her surviving avatars would be stripped of Ship privileges and demoted to brood service. That risk was acceptable. She was asking a lot, after all. If the *razee* were to fall into the wrong hands . . .

She quelled that misgiving and pressed on.

The *vedette* was waiting for them with airlocks open and a complement of twelve Guildsmen at the ready. A mixture of astrogation, maintenance, and security, they saluted as she entered and made space for her and the prisoner in the forward passenger compartment. Kindred didn't struggle as he was secured to an acceleration couch. Master Bannerman took a couch opposite him, and sat patiently as the small shuttle craft disengaged from the Great Ship.

Over the staccato drumming of reactionless thrusters and the rising hum of ultralights, the prisoner broke his silence.

"Don't you want to know the course?"

"Eventually, yes."

"But not now, so we're headed elsewhere. Care to tell me?"

"No."

Artificial gravity shifted with a lurch as the *vedette* switched to internal life support.

"You may view our departure, if you would like to."

"Yes, I would."

She instructed the forward bulkhead to present an illusion of transparency, and together they watched the looming, star-shaped bulk of the Great Ship recede. There was nothing over Hakham that he had not already seen. The world was drab and reddish, made remarkable only by the ancient mines its citizens had stumbled across three centuries earlier. Apparently bottomless, their mysteries had only begun to be fathomed by the Guild before Braith Kindred and the terrorist organization called Terminus had destroyed the uppermost levels and the machines maintaining the so-called "transcendent shafts" that led to far more mysterious spaces. The crater left in their wake was just visible from orbit, a yellowish dimple several degrees south of the equator. Now Hakham had returned to being utterly uninteresting, and she was glad to be leaving.

The *vedette*'s thrusters propelled them a safe distance from the Great Ship, at which point the ultralights kicked in. She felt a giddy sensation in the pit of her stomach as life support worked hard to preserve her from the unnatural forces at work around the *vedette*. Furious energies, understood in full only by the Grand Masters and their architects, smashed the usual laws of physics and propelled the *vedette* at speeds not possible since the moments of creation, when the universe had boiled and time and space were one.

The prisoner was fascinated, although he tried to hide it. His eyes never left the bright points of light gliding smoothly by: the stars of the Guild in all their glory, as fragile-seeming as glass baubles.

She took the time to tell him that, were he ever to be exposed to their radiance as it truly struck the perpetually regenerating hull of the *vedette*, he would be destroyed in an instant.

He nodded distantly, no longer smiling, and she was satisfied.

Their journey lasted six hours, relative, while, outside the *vedette*, two days passed. Kindred had access to basic telemetric information—granted, he supposed, in order to awe him into submission. In that time, they crossed twenty light-years, which accorded well with the intelligence Terminus had gathered about the Guild's technical know-how. Stars shifted smoothly around them, forming and breaking constellations with eerie transience. One star became brighter and ballooned into a vast red sun. Cool by stellar standards but seeming hot to a human's eye, it boasted no habitable worlds, just a complex tangle of asteroid and cometary haloes. Among the cosmic debris, he saw an orbiting construct that was to the Great Ships as a mighty tree was to leaves. The ships jostled alongside its many tapering limbs, docking, refueling, undergoing repairs, exchanging material and personnel—doing everything the vessels of an interstellar empire needed to maintain their functionality.

He performed a quick mental calculation, starting with the thousand-meter reach of a Great Ship's arm and ending with a figure in the tens of thousands of kilometers.

"Impressive," he said, because it was. "Makes me wonder why you're going to so much trouble over the Structure, when you have something like this to play with."

She stared coolly at him. "Do you truly have so little conception of the Structure's worth?"

"Do you? You haven't asked me any questions about it. You don't seem curious at all."

"We already know what it is."

"That puts you one step ahead of us, then."

His remark pricked her steady reserve. "You and your kind cross leagues in a single step, thanks to the artifact you have inherited from makers unknown. But you don't understand the physical principles behind the technology you use. Your inheritance is one of ignorance. What wisdom can you, a terrorist, offer the Guild of the Great Ships? We have worked for our dominion; we have earned the right to expand. Our knowledge will inevitably prevail over your dumb luck."

He lacked the energy to argue with her. Words weren't sufficient to describe how wrong she was.

The *vedette* joined a steady stream of support vehicles looping in and out of the construct's fractal docking points. Thrusters kicked in again, and the drumming they caused kept perfect time with the strange gravity nudging his insides. They descended into the construct's forest of antler-like branches. When they docked, it was to a relatively small outcrop that was over thirty meters thick.

With one last tattoo, the *vedette* came to a halt. The airlock slid open and a Guildsman stepped up to release his bonds. He stood warily, flexing his limbs, still aching in every joint and sinew, and now tired as well. He wondered what they would do if he asked for something to eat. Luckily, he could survive on internals for weeks, if he had to.

They led him into the echoing complex, which boomed and hummed with ceaseless industry. A short ride on an electric transport brought them to another docking point, and from there to the ship that he assumed would take them the rest of the way. According to the telemetry data he had glimpsed, the *vedette*'s reserves had been almost completely exhausted crossing barely 1 percent of the distance ahead of them.

The new ship was sleek and silver and small: fifty meters long from stem to stern and barely three wide, its every angle broadcast *speed*. He doubted there was a single wasted molecule anywhere in its pared-down frame. Light slid off its rolling skin in bizarre curves and knots. It looked brand-new.

"Is this thing safe?" he asked Bannerman. When she ignored him, he pressed, "At least tell me it has a name."

"Guild ships do not require names," she stated.

Seals hissed and the variable hull flowed elegantly open. Inside the cramped cockpit were just two acceleration couches.

"Cozy."

"Get in." She took his shoulder in a tight grip and propelled him through the airlock. She seemed tense, and he wondered if she was nervous about the mission ahead or just impatient to get going.

The weird fields ceased within, fading out with a chaotic flutter that made him feel briefly nauseous. There was nowhere to step but on the couches and transparent instrument panels. The ceiling was so low he banged his head as he folded himself awkwardly into the seat, telling himself to relish every free movement while it lasted. He would be effectively supine until they exited the coffin-like space. At the velocity the *vedette* had managed, it would take five hundred days to reach their destination.

"How fast did you say this thing is?"

She ignored him again, taking the couch next to his and activating the ship's internal systems. Lights flashed in unreadable patterns; the airlock closed; internal life support kicked in, but still no strange gravity. An unnecessary luxury, he presumed.

"Now," she said, "the course to Oza."

He gave it to her. The coordinates placed the world on the far side of the galaxy, approximately thirty thousand light-years away in a straight line, almost fifty if they were to curve around the complex foams and tangles of the Bulge.

"Six days, relative," she said.

He didn't believe it.

"I told you," she said. "We have earned the right."

LONG HAUL

The *razee* surged away from the staging area, and Master Bannerman turned the cockpit's interior walls to full apparent transparency, giving her and her prisoner an unparalleled view. The fat, red sun burned balefully behind them, painting the instrument panels in blood. She checked and triple-checked the course, mindful that she was heading into unknown territory at the urging of an enemy combatant.

He covered his eyes when she engaged the ultralights. The sudden acceleration took her by surprise too. Stars leaped out at them and swept past with alarming speed. She fought the urge to take manual control, knowing that this would only make matters worse. One incautious move and they would plunge right into the heart of a sun. The inbuilt navigator could fly better than any mere human, even the Master of a Great Ship.

With shaky commands, she altered the plotted course, urging the *razee* out of the galactic disk and into the relatively sparse halo. It shed and gained momentum with all appearance of resistance, as though it resented her interference. It was made for near-misses and wild maneuvers. She was fighting its nature.

"I can't die," the prisoner breathed as a neutron star crackled past, so close tides rocked and pulled at them. "I can't die."

A mantra, she assumed, designed to soothe in the face of his helplessness. Or a prayer, if he was religious. It wasn't important enough to query.

He instantly relaxed when she opaqued the cockpit walls. Some of her own tension evaporated too. Out of sight remained out of the primitive layers of the human mind, even in this age of avatars and galactic empires.

"If you're trying to intimidate me," the prisoner said, wiping a tremulous hand across his brow, "you've very nearly succeeded."

"That wasn't my intention," she said, despite knowing it to be an incomplete truth. His admission did please her. "This is simply the fastest ship I could commandeer at the time."

"I don't think so. If ships like this were commonplace, you'd have found Oza already." His shrewd eyes regarded her closely. "You must really be keen. Why?"

"That is no concern of yours."

"Don't be ridiculous. You're the enemy. Everything about you is my concern."

"You will learn nothing from me."

"Maybe you're fighting on another front, worried someone's going to get into the Structure first and attack you from the rear. Is that what this is really about?" He swiveled awkwardly in his seat to face her. "The enemy of our enemy would not be our friend. You should know that. We resist everyone equally," he said, "everyone who wants to use the Structure as a weapon."

"The Guild wants access to the Structure purely for its scientific value."

"Yeah, right." His scorn filled the cockpit. "We've heard that before. No spacer has ever managed to claim the Structure successfully. What does that tell you?"

"That none of them belonged to the Guild of the Great Ships."

He laughed.

Bristling, she returned the walls of the cockpit to their former state. A trio of golden suns swept by in balletic silence.

"The instruments of this vessel are linked exclusively to my implants," she said coldly. "Attempt to take control or interfere with my commands and it will self-destruct immediately."

He sighed. "Six days, huh? It's going to be a longer trip than I thought." Folding his arms and easing back into the couch, he closed his eyes on the ever-changing view. "Wake me when we get there."

His nonchalance needled her as much as mockery. "Aren't you afraid that I will jettison you the moment I confirm our destination?"

"Not at all, Master Bannerman." One eye opened a crack. "You can't kill me."

"I could stop your heart with a thought."

"You could try. It wouldn't happen. Trust me." The eye closed again. "I can't die."

Those words again. His confidence was both irrational and infuriating. She stilled her tongue behind a cage of grinding teeth, and let him go.

Six days of dreams.

His brother featured in them, of course. There was no escaping him, not even now that he was dead. Their childhood on Alalia had been a hard one, and their relationship had been strained. Not for them an easy bond in the face of hardship. Huw, the eldest, had fled shortly after his eighteenth birthday, seeking his fortunes down a mineshaft and never returning.

Braith Kindred had followed him, less out of loyalty than from a need to compete that found itself without expression, then as now. He supposed in his more self-aware moments that the Guild of the Great Ships had become the focus for all the fears his brother had once embodied: of being ignored, of coming last, of being unworthy. Learning of Huw's death had stripped his life of meaning, until Terminus had given him a chance to fight against the spacer incursions.

The sabotage on Hakham had very nearly killed him, judging by the hammering his body had endured. It wasn't supposed to have gone that way. Neither, of course, was collaborating with the enemy—but life was nothing if not interesting. In one dream, Braith tried to explain to Huw why it was so important he stay dead. If Huw wasn't dead, Braith wouldn't have set the bombs, and if Braith hadn't set the bombs, the Guild wouldn't have captured him, and if the Guild hadn't captured him, he wouldn't now be coming back. Huw wasn't getting it, though, and wouldn't lie back down. Sometimes, just to confuse the issue, Huw looked like Master Bannerman. Sometimes he looked like Braith himself.

In his dreams of Alalia, the sky was never blue. It was gray and heavy, like an ancient marble roof on the verge of collapse. He had seen other skies on other Structure worlds, but never the stars as Bannerman had shown him. He dreamed that they leaked in through the crater on Hakham and filled the Structure with thousands of glowing sparks. He pursued them with a net but couldn't catch them all. When they touched him, they burned. Fleeing in flames, he trailed new stars behind him in their thousands.

The view from Bannerman's couch was no less spectacular. Passing over the Bulge, she appreciated the galaxy from a perspective few people ever saw with their own eyes. She wept on realizing the boldness of the Guild of the Great Ships' aspirations. Its present tally of ten million stars was of no significance at all against the total number in the galaxy. Were the Guild to disintegrate that very day, the arms would go on turning, the bar wouldn't shred and dissipate, the thick dust lanes would coil unchecked, spawning still more stars with their cold, hard light.

That mood lasted less than a day. The Guild had once claimed just three suns, and would maintain its present growth until something stopped it. Some other power, perhaps, or the internal rift that the Grand Masters feared. Their architects warned of a time when even cutting-edge ultralights, of which the *razee* was a prototype, would be insufficient to knit the aspiring empire together. Lacking the means to bind the stars, all would unravel and turn to ash.

The Structure would unite such an empire, allowing it to expand beyond all projections. If the architects could only fathom the principles behind its transcendent shafts, there would be no limit to the Guild's reach. Great Ships would explore every corner of the universe, and her avatars would be among them.

All that stood between her and that grand dream were people like Braith Kindred.

She watched him sleep, learning the planes of his guileless face and the angles of his limbs. His bruises faded to yellow and disappeared like clouds on a summer day. Pristine, he looked even younger and all the more vulnerable for it. Over three days she tested his body's defenses, searching for the source of his bizarre confidence in her inability to kill him. Something new, she thought, something developed by Terminus that the Guild had not seen before. Proceeding carefully, wary of sentinels and snares, she explored every vein, every muscle, every synaptic pathway, and found absolutely nothing out of the ordinary. He was defended, yes, but no more than she.

Tendrils of her will reached the valves of his heart. He had dared her to do this, to try to kill him, and now she had the capacity. How long would his brain last if she shut down his circulatory system? An hour or two at most, less if she began severing links in his brain stem and cortex as well. She could rewire his glands to produce neurotoxins instead of hormones, if she chose, or send powerful acids coursing through his stomach wall into his chest cavity. There were a thousand ways to end someone from within.

The only certain way to test his assertion was to actually try. She came close on several occasions. A mixture of fear and excitement welled in her, tugging her in both directions. Each time, she backed away from the brink, following the call of duty. She might need him if his directions proved unreliable. The Guild might need the knowledge still trapped in his skull.

She was glad she had refrained when the *razee* reentered the galactic disk and began detecting signals of an unknown government in the vicinity of their destination. They were rapid-fire, sharp and powerful, like radio spikes during a thunderstorm. And there were a lot of them.

The *razee* decelerated like a tiny sun, drawing attention from all sides.

COMPLICATIONS

"Wake up, Kindred."

The voice intruded on his dreams, wrenched him from the well of unconsciousness with an urgency that was utterly irresistible.

"Damn you, Kindred, wake up!"

He woke gripping the arms of his acceleration couch. Powerful forces were tugging him from side to side. Stars rolled and flared through the cockpit's transparent walls. Something bright that he had mistaken for a nearby sun exploded with a flash of blue light, sending the ship tumbling like a twig in a waterfall.

"What the hell—?"

"You didn't tell me there would be people waiting for us." Bannerman was rigid beside him, all of her conscious mind focused on what was happening outside the ship, apart from the small segment talking to him. Her hands twitched as she brought the ship back under control. "You dropped us right in the middle of an ambush!"

That couldn't be right. He thought desperately, trying to make sense of the situation. Oza was abandoned, bombed by the Decretians and left to lie fallow. The idiots didn't know what lay hidden below the surface levels of the mine. If they were attacking now, it had to be for another reason.

A second missile exploded nearby. The view blacked out for an instant as a blast of hard radiation struck the ship. He fought a wave of automatic fear. There had to be a way out of this. There had to be.

The prisoner reached out with his implants and found that she had revoked his small telemetry privileges.

"Don't be an idiot, Bannerman," he said. "You woke me to see if I could do something. At least let me try."

She relented. There were three short-range fighters on their tail, with a long-range raider of some sort bringing up the rear. She didn't recognize the design, but he nodded on seeing them.

"They're Decretians," he told her. "Very nasty sorts. We have no contact with them, but there are Terminus agents stationed on Oza to keep an eye on them, ready to blow the shaft if they ever look too close. The Decretians must have left a monitoring station in the area, which spotted us when we powered in."

She nodded. That theory matched her observations. "We

can outrun them, but that won't help us get any closer to the Structure."

"I know. Give me a minute."

She wasn't certain they had a minute. On a 3-D grid, blue-gray Oza was receding behind them as the Decretian fighters drove them away. The drumming of the *razee*'s reactionless thrusters was relentless and numbing.

"Are we armed?"

"Not for heavy or sustained combat."

"I didn't think so. A ship like this, on the cutting edge of your technology, must be for covert surveillance, not attack-runs."

She didn't grace that with a reply.

"Whatever. We'll work with what we've got."

"You are suspiciously unconcerned," she said. "You planned this."

"I swear I had no idea what was waiting for us. The empire, yes, but I hoped to get in unnoticed. Whatever happens now, though, I do know we'll make it. Trust me."

"You say this, but I have no reason to do it."

"Your choices are limited, Bannerman."

She fumed in silence for a second, and then gasped as another missile detonated dangerously close to the ship.

When the spinning starscape had stabilized, she found herself agreeing to at least hear his suggestion, if he had one.

"I think I do," he said, hoping against hope that his wild plan would succeed. "Here's what you're going to do. This ship accelerates faster than anything I've ever seen. I presume it can decelerate just as quickly. When I give you the word, I want you to hang on the brakes as hard as you can. Drop us back level with those three fighters. Come in firing."

"We can't defeat all three at once."

"Not with conventional weapons. I know." He studied the disposition of the fighters, wondering if he was insane to place so much trust in something over which he had so little control. He wasn't a space combat expert, and he certainly didn't know how the Structure did what it did. All he could do was take a chance. "Once we're in the midst of them, you're going to turn the ultralights on full."

"Are you insane?"

"Maybe, but it's either that or abandon Oza and go somewhere else. What's the range of this thing, exactly? Fancy another hop across the galaxy with me in tow?"

She answered neither question, not with words. Furious—at him, he supposed, for getting her into this mess and at herself for letting him—she looked forward again, at the starscape ahead, and prepared the ultralights for activation.

"I don't know what this will do," she confessed. "So close to a gravity well, the ultralights could explode, taking us with them."

"If it makes you so nervous, why don't we try ramming instead?"

"Now you are testing my patience."

He smiled, wishing he could banish the butterflies from his stomach. "It's a serious suggestion. Given the speed this thing flies at, its anti-impact shields have to be pretty effective. A collision or two could be survivable, especially if—"

The ship's thrusters hammered deafeningly, cutting him off in mid-sentence. Light blurred around him. His seat shook, throwing him from side to side. For a small eternity, it was all he could do simply to hang on.

Master Bannerman felt utterly disconnected from the actions of her body. She knew that Kindred's plan was madness of the highest magnitude. Activating experimental ultralights in the middle of a solar system was a recipe for instant annihilation. No sane Ship's Master would ever put a vessel at such risk. It couldn't, therefore, be her behind the commands that were even now dropping the battle-hungry *razee* back into the midst of the Decretian fighters. It couldn't be her laying down a pattern of covering fire intended to mislead the enemy. It couldn't possibly be her locating the optimum point to activate the ultralights, in the hope of taking out the heavy-raider as well. She felt as though there were two avatars in her head at once, wrestling for control of her fate.

The fighters flashed by, tumbling wildly as they recalibrated their weapon systems. Thrusters flashed and flared. The optimum point arrived.

One Master Bannerman activated the ultralights while another stared in fascinated horror, dying to see what happened.

The *razee* screamed, and both of her screamed with it, fused back into one as a bubble of energy radiated out from the heart of the ultralights, tearing space into ribbons as it went.

The cockpit walls went black. All the instruments and virtual feeds died in the same instant. Smoke filled the cockpit. She heard Kindred crying out—not in fear or alarm, but crying the same three words that had haunted her all the way to Oza.

Without questioning the impulse, she found herself praying for the first time that he might be right.

I can't die!
    I can't die!
    I can't die!

Her acceleration couch eased its grip the very instant fresh air reached her nostrils. Sobbing with relief, Bannerman sagged forward, eyes blinking in the stroboscope light of the revived instrumentation panels. Her implants located several active streams among the dozens that had once issued from the *razee*, now filled with noise. A quick glance over the status indicators told her everything she needed to know. Red was the dominant shade. The *razee* would soar no more.

Of the fighters and the raider, there were no signs.

A hand groped for hers and she jerked out of the data, startled.

"We made it." Kindred's voice was raw with relief. "I told you we would."

She surprised herself by not immediately pulling away. "We got lucky," she said, "and we'll need to get lucky again soon. The ultralights are dead, burned completely out.

Thrusters are down to half a percent capacity. We'll be doing well to hit Oza, let alone land on it."

He was unflappable. "That's all we need. Don't you see? No matter what the universe throws at us, we'll come through just fine."

She withdrew her hand. "I don't share your confidence."

"That's because you don't understand the Structure. You think you do, but you don't."

"So explain it to me." When he didn't answer, she dismissed the mystery with an irritated snort. "I thought not. You're as ignorant as I am."

"No, wait. Give me a second. I'm thinking." He tapped his right index finger on the side of the couch. "Yes, why not? You're caught up in this now. The only way back to your ship is through the Structure. You have a right to know what you're getting yourself into."

He spoke so seriously, so earnestly, that she braced herself against the back of her chair, as though the revelation might convey a physical impact. When she noticed what she had unconsciously done, she cursed herself for being so gullible. This was what he wanted, to throw her off-balance even further than she already was. Striking when she was weak was a sensible tactic. She gave him credit for trying, even as she hardened herself to resist his web of lies.

He told her everything he knew. It didn't take long, and he could tell she didn't believe him. The story did sound crazy; he had once thought it impossible too, until it had happened to someone close to him.

Living in or near the Structure tangled people up in time, sometimes. No one knew why, or how. It just happened, and people lived with it. Some found a comfort in it, as he told himself to, now. Until the loop in which he had found himself unraveled—until he was back on Hakham, so he could read out the script and push the button that he had failed to push the first time around—he was untouchable. How could he die anywhere when he knew he would be alive later?

She said: "You are telling me that you did not, in fact, set those charges to detonate."

"No. It *was* me. Must have been. I just haven't done it yet."

"You're talking nonsense."

"The Structure makes you do that. It's unavoidable."

"Knots in time cannot exist. The laws of temporal entropy forbid such things."

"Is that your best comeback?"

"I don't need another. What you are telling me is impossible."

"So was FTL travel, once. Hell, so was flying! I don't think the word is in the universe's dictionary."

The ship was nearing Oza's tenuous atmosphere. Soon, she would be too busy to argue. He guessed that she would keep pondering it, though. Maybe another near-death experience would convince her of his claims.

She seemed to be thinking along the same lines.

"If I did try to kill you now, what would happen?"

"The command would fail somehow. Or you'd die of an aneurism before you could issue it. I don't know. Do you want to try?"

"Not right now."

"Good," he said, "because at this moment, I might be the only thing protecting you from dying when we crash-land."

Her brown eyes narrowed. They were so dark that in the dim light of the cockpit they looked completely black.

"Thanks for your concern," she said, "but your faith would be better placed in my ability to pilot this ship."

He smiled. "Either way, I'm looking forward to going home again."

Home, she thought, even as she wrestled with the controls of the moribund *razee*. For all she had studied the Structure and its inhabitants from afar, she had never once thought that people might actually consider it such. Was that, perhaps, why they fought so vigorously to keep it to themselves? Not because of its military or scientific value, but out of love?

The Guild of the Great Ships was made of clones and avatars, but love was just as powerful a force to them as it had ever been to any human. For the first time, she began to wonder if the campaign to take control of the Structure might prove more difficult than even the Grand Masters had imagined—hypothetically unkillable Terminus agents not-withstanding.

SACRIFICE

They came down hard a kilometer from the ruins that had once been Oza topside. Kindred and Bannerman stumbled from the new crater they had made, leaning on each other's shoulders and brushing themselves down as best they could. The walk to the apparently lifeless shaft wasn't a long one, but under a diamond-colored sky and with no liquid water anywhere on the planet, it wasn't one Kindred was looking forward to. He took only a small consolation from the fact that he was back under real gravity again.

"When we get there," he said, "let me do the talking. My access codes should still work. Once we're in, it's just a matter of hopping from level to level until we get where we need to go."

She glanced over her shoulder at the crumpled wreckage of the ship. Her expression was unreadable, but he thought he could guess what was going through her mind.

That guess was confirmed when she said just one word in reply.

"Hakham."

"Back to your ship." He nodded. "Also, if the shaft is open, you'll know I'm telling you the truth."

"And then what?"

"Then you'll wonder if you're as good a pilot as you say you are." He smiled. "You'll have to be if I'm wrong, because that's the only way you'll ever get back home."

The Terminus agents stationed at Oza didn't once question her status. Master Bannerman watched closely for any sign of deception as Kindred walked up to the security cordon hidden deep in the ruins, braving a trio of upraised weapons without flinching and talking his way smoothly into their confidence. He showed no inclination to betray her just yet. She assumed he wanted to prove himself to her first, and that was perfectly in line with her own objectives. She had no doubt that before long his talk of time-loops would be revealed as the fantasy of a very lucky man.

They entered a dank, stuffy mine, traveling first by wheeled vehicle and then by elevator. The way was only intermittently lit, and they relied on infrared to pick their way when visible light was absent. Strange smells assailed her. Mud and dust soon coated her Guild uniform almost beyond its capacity to clean itself. Far behind her lay the antiseptic glamour of interstellar travel. To date, the Structure had proven disappointing and uncomfortable.

Only when they reached the first of the transcendent shafts did she realize that they hadn't actually entered the Structure proper. At a sliding, airtight portal, Kindred entered a complex code into an alphanumeric keypad. The portal slid aside, revealing an elevator carriage large enough for thirty people.

"After you," Kindred said, waving her inside. "From here on, we'll make good time, better than that ship of yours. In fact, we'll arrive before we left. If that doesn't make you curious, nothing will."

He pushed the carriage's only button, and they stood at opposite sides of the carriage as it began to descend.

"Descent," however, wasn't the right word for what she felt in her gut. They were undeniably moving, but she couldn't accurately pin down in which direction. Guild training had given her many ways to assess acceleration without instruments. Something about the shaft confounded all of them.

A wave of dizziness passed through her. With no other warning than that, the carriage came to a halt. When the portal opened and she stepped through, she noticed immediately that the ambient gravity had changed.

At a five-level stack three transcendent jumps away from Oza, Kindred called the first halt on their journey. He had never

been to Shosori before, but he remembered the name from
the charts he had memorized and knew some of its basic geography. It was harmless enough, except for newbies.

"Are you okay?" he asked Bannerman.

"Of course. Why wouldn't I be?"

He knew she was lying. Her expression was too blank.
Her eyes and hands moved abruptly and too quickly at the
slightest stimulus. Maybe she thought her self-control was
impeccable, but he could tell. He'd seen this kind of reaction
before.

"Let's stop here for a bit."

They were in an observation deck that clung to the under-
side of ceiling made of roughly carved, reddish stone. Below
them, visible through a bulging transparent blister, was the
surface of a solid world, its gray features obscured by drifts
of frozen atmosphere except where deep fissures had been
carved by mineral-seeking engines, each as large as a Great
Ship. They watched it for five minutes. In that time, the
world within the Structure rotated thirty degrees.

"What do you think?" he asked her.

"You want me to say that it's impossible."

"That word comes to mind, you have to admit. Something
like this, inside a mine—"

"Is not beyond an engineering solution, however extreme.
The Guild of the Great Ships could accomplish it, given the
need."

"What if I told you that this lump of rock didn't come from
your universe, the one containing the Guild of the Great
Ships? Could you manage that as well?"

She looked at him through eyes wakened from their numb
sightseeing. "You say 'your universe' as though you are not
part of it."

"I'm not. My birthplace wouldn't appear on your maps no
matter how far you explored."

She waved that away with some of her old fire. "The mul-
tiverse is no mystery to us. Cross-continuum jumps will be
within our grasp, one day."

"Engineering again, huh?"

"I stake my life on it every time I board the Great Ship."

"You're not on the Great Ship anymore, Master Banner-man."

She found his attempts at repartee clumsy but distracting. The ponderous rotations of the captured world below no longer seemed so threatening. This was the Structure, exactly where she had wanted to be for so long. Each "stack," as Kindred called the named locations they passed through, had a unique character. Some were close and utilitarian, while others were more like giant shopping malls. Occasionally, she detected evidence of earthworks, as would be expected of a mine. Diligently and thoroughly, she recorded every detail for her avatar back at the Great Ship.

"Shall we get moving again?" she asked.

"Of course. Adrigon's next, then Malmelia—and then Estes, where they suck minerals out of the bottom of a planet-wide ocean . . ."

The names meant nothing to her, his attempt to awe likewise.

Between transcendent shafts, they moved invisibly among the crowds. The strangest thing she had seen so far wasn't the evidence of science far in advance of the Guild's—for all that she bluffed regarding the architects' ability to mimic it—but the people who inhabited the Structure. They had passed hundreds of all ages, living and working under artificial lights in halls large enough to hold thousands. They grew flowers. They raised children. If they cared at all about the universe beyond, it didn't show.

"This is it."

Kindred pressed his palm against the portal ahead of them and spread his fingers wide. The white plastic was inert against his skin. If anything was active on the far side, it neither vibrated nor radiated any heat.

All the times he could have died meant nothing, now. He had had only to count them down until he reached the loop's end—which was, of course, its beginning. And then, once he blew the charges and the loop closed, he would be mortal like anyone else, but safely rid of Hakham and the Guild of the Great Ships, for now.

"What are you waiting for?"

He didn't know.

The strange thing was that his return to the Structure hadn't touched him as deeply as he had thought it would. The tunnels seemed cramped and crowded to him now; there were no distant horizons, no far vistas. Although every level was different, there was a homogeneity to it all that he could swear hadn't been there before.

He couldn't tell Bannerman. She would think that she was responsible, and he couldn't have that.

"Nothing."

He keyed in his access code. The doors slid open.

They stepped inside. The doors slid closed.

With a hint of movement, they were on their way.

"Well?" Her silence irked him. "This shaft is supposed to be destroyed, isn't it?"

"You don't understand the technology, Kindred. We might be going somewhere else, or nowhere at all."

He nodded and settled back to wait. Words would not convince her. Only the cold, hard evidence of her senses.

Bannerman's insides shifted as the carriage came to a halt. Not nerves, she told herself; surely just a side effect of the Structure's arcane technologies.

The portal opened. Kindred waved her ahead of him. She stepped into a boxy antechamber with gray walls, floors, and ceiling. A functional space that smelled of abandonment. The air was still and quiet. Kindred's footsteps as he came up behind her were the only sounds.

He radiated satisfaction. "Now what do you say?"

"This proves only that your demolition charges failed to do their job down here," she said. "Assuming this *is* Hakham."

"Of course it is. If we can get to the surface, you'd see your Great Ship in orbit above. Hell, you could try to talk to yourself, if you wanted to."

"Is that possible?"

"No—unless you remember such a conversation taking place, in which case it's not only possible; it's compulsory."

A yearning to try filled her, regardless of the apparent absurdity of the notion. To reconnect with her avatar, to see the Great Ship again, both were possibilities she had been preparing to abandon on the other side of the galaxy. She could do more than just say hello, too. She could stop Kindred from setting off the charges and prevent herself from going with Kindred on a crazy odyssey across the stars. She knew the location of Oza now, so there was no need to go through that charade anymore. She had everything the Guild needed right here in her head.

But she didn't remember having such a conversation with herself before she left the Great Ship, and the charges *had* gone off. Those were facts. If Kindred were right and it was truly impossible to change history, what consequences might she inadvertently provoke by trying? The knowledge she had earned might disappear completely, leaving the Guild back where it started and her avatars doomed to an ignominious fate.

"Take me up," she said. "I need proof, not suggestion."

He shrugged and obeyed, apparently unconcerned that— if he was right—the area they were walking into was full of deadly explosives.

They took a rattling elevator cage up to the next level. He experienced a powerful sense of déjà vu as they went. It seemed a lifetime since he had followed this very path on his mission to blow Hakham topside to pieces. It seemed like yesterday.

He looked for evidence of the charges, and found them exactly as he remembered them, anchored to stress points and beams where they would cause the most damage. His plan had been to blow the upper layers first, then the shaft itself on a timer, once he had gotten away.

They stepped carefully through an unlit area, heading for the next elevator. This location rang a definite bell. Something had happened in this place the first time around—but what?

Bannerman grabbed his arm and hissed into his ear.

"There's someone ahead."

A figure moved at the far end of the passage, deep in the shadows.

Acting instinctively, Kindred took Bannerman by the shoulder and put himself in front of her.

Coherent light flashed once, twice.

The first shot missed them both. The second caught him low on the left shoulder, just above his heart.

He fell, remembering too late the two intruders he had surprised in Hakham's lower levels. Enemy agents, he had assumed, since they had both been wearing Guild uniforms.

Remotely, as though through a thick glass window, he heard footsteps receding into the distance.

PARADOX

Master Bannerman stared after the fleeing figure, shocked into immobility. The man who had shot Kindred was moving quickly through shadows, but she recognized his profile, the planes of his all-too-human face. It was undoubtedly, impossibly, Kindred himself.

For an instant, she could not move. Everything he had told her was true. They had crossed from one side of the galaxy to the other and returned before they left. Her prisoner had looped back along his own time line, protected from her, from the Decretians, and from the crash-landing on Oza . . . but not from this.

Kindred gasped. The shot had made a ruin of his chest. Each breath caused him agony. It was amazing his heart was beating at all.

His right hand came up, reaching for her.

"Didn't—" he tried to say, "—get to—"

Bannerman leaned over him, blurry but real.

He clung to the sight of her even as the rest of his world unraveled.

"—finish—"

"Quiet. You're only hurting yourself more."

Kindred shook all over. He was afraid for an instant that this was his body's last gasp, that death was upon him, too soon by far.

She put a firm hand on his forehead and the pain went away. He was dying: that certainty remained, but all fear evaporated. In its place, a new understanding grew. He had crossed his own path again and closed the loop earlier than he had expected—and how fitting to signal the end of his indestructibility by mistakenly shooting himself! His journey was over.

Bannerman's journey, on the other hand, still had some way left to run. In her own way, she was as trapped as he was. She just didn't know it yet.

"Do it for me," he said quickly, while he had the strength. "Two levels up. Wait until he's inputted the codes, then—don't kill him. Put him—the Guildsmen—need him afterward. Get back here—now, later."

"I don't understand."

"The script," he said. "The charges. Only you can do it."

The reassurance of her warm palm disappeared, and he knew that at last he had gotten through to her. Causality was tangled in a knot. If he died before he could enact her past—their immediate future—then she would have to do it herself.

They hadn't betrayed each other as they had originally intended to. Time and the Structure did it for them.

"You expect me to blow the charges?"

"Yes. Record me. I—I strike—" He broke into a fit of bloody coughing. When it subsided, he tried again. In the recording she had played him, he had sounded strained but hadn't stumbled. "I strike this blow against the Guild of the Great Ships in the name of Terminus and all the free people of the Structure." *For Huw*, he added silently to himself. *And now for me, too.* "Got it?"

She nodded, and he let his head fall back. He had no strength left. The pain had started to return. His lungs couldn't seem to get enough air, no matter how he strained.

"And then what?" he thought she asked, leaning low over him with anxious eyes. "Kindred, and then what?"

Whatever you want, he wanted to say. You're free now, or soon will be. Close the loop and decide for yourself. It'll be easier now I'm out of the equation.

But all he could manage was one word.

Kindred stiffened and died, leaving Bannerman alone in the basements of Hakham.

"Why should I?" she had asked. "Kindred, why should I?"

The answer he had given her made no sense at all.

She crouched over him, spattered with his blood, too stunned by the sudden turn of events to think. He who had claimed invulnerability was now dead, and she was trapped in a paradox of her own making. Why had she thought to test his bizarre theory? Hadn't she ever wondered what it would mean if it turned out to be true?

A cold fatality swept through her. She could either die trying to change history or do exactly as Kindred had said. What other choices did she have? Perhaps he had faced just such a dismal dilemma on realizing that he had to help the Guild in order to see his own mission through. She vowed not to die as he had, bleeding in the dirt, knowing that she, his enemy, possessed the only opportunity to finish the job for him, the last thing she wanted to do.

The other Kindred was still loose, heading off to blow the charges.

Think, she told herself. Find a way to stop him.

Everywhere she turned she foresaw terrible consequences, not just for herself but for the Guild of the Great Ships as well. The Grand Masters had no conception of what a concerted assault on the Structure might cost them. An indestructible resistance would be much worse than an agent or two armed with bombs. In such a battle, the full weight of the universe's laws would be on the Structure's side—just as they were arrayed against her now. Losing such a war would cause deeper instabilities than mere internal discontent.

She stood up and raised a hand to her temple, feeling lightheaded. She saw now that she would blow the charges, exactly as Kindred had asked, but not out of sympathy with him and the terrorists of Terminus, or out of fear of the consequences of breaking the time-loop. She had all the free will she ever had. The choice was entirely hers, now she saw what it needed to be.

Being silent wasn't enough to save the Guild from harm. Averting open conflict with the Structure had to become her first priority, which meant closing the only remaining exit in the Guild's territory, on Hakham. If the Grand Masters still wanted to tackle the Structure, they would have to find the entrance at Oza and win a very different conflict with the Decretians first. That could take decades, perhaps centuries—in which time, new technologies might evolve to tackle the time-looping menace.

She would save the Guild by betraying it—and herself.

"The Structure makes you do that," Kindred had once said. "It's unavoidable."

He had been talking about speaking gibberish, but the thought held in both contexts. She was in two places simultaneously, caught in a loop, as he had been, and she had no choice but to turn her back on everything she held dear. But a perverse hope remained that she might redeem herself. Kindred would have prepared an escape route; she was sure of that, for he had displayed none of the characteristics of a suicide bomber. Now that her indestructibility was assured, who knew what she could learn before fate brought her inevitably back? She could only take the opportunity given to her, and try, as Kindred had, to make everything right.

The corpse's cold, blue eyes were still open, staring up at an invisible sky.

"Stars," he had said, and she wondered if he had meant it as a warning or an entreaty.

Pausing only to close his eyelids, she headed up the tunnel in pursuit of Kindred's earlier self—the young man who had given her far more than she had wanted, and taken an equal amount in return.

JOIN THE NAVY
AND SEE THE WORLDS

BRUCE STERLING

One of the most powerful and innovative talents to enter SF in the past few decades, Bruce Sterling sold his first story in 1976. By the end of the eighties, he had established himself, with a series of stories set in his exotic "Shaper/Mechanist" future, with novels such as the complex and Stapledonian *Schismatrix* and *Islands in the Net* (as well as with his editing of the influential anthology *Mirrorshades: The Cyberpunk Anthology* and the infamous critical magazine *Cheap Truth*), as perhaps the prime driving force behind the revolutionary cyberpunk movement in science fiction. His other books include a critically acclaimed nonfiction study of First Amendment issues in the world of computer networking, *The Hacker Crackdown: Law and Disorder on the Electronic Frontier*; the novels *The Artificial Kid*, *Involution Ocean*, *Heavy Weather*, *Holy Fire*, *Distraction*, *Zeitgeist*, *The Zenith Angle*; a novel in collaboration with William Gibson, *The Difference Engine*; a nonfiction study of the future, *Tomorrow Now: Envisioning the Next Fifty Years*; and the landmark collections *Crystal Express*, *Globalhead*, *Schismatrix Plus*, *A Good Old-fashioned Future*, and *Visionary in Residence*. His most recent books are a massive retrospective collection *Ascendancies: The Best of Bruce Sterling*, and a new novel *Caryatids*. His story "Bicycle Repairman" earned him a long-overdue Hugo in 1997, and he won another Hugo in 1997 for his story "Taklamakan."

Here he tells the story of a reluctant space hero who ends up becoming a witness to an event of historic importance and heroic scale, even if it is taking place in a junkyard.

Those crescent dunes were rolling curves of granulated ice. That winding river was a peaceful ripple of liquid methane. That unplumbed lake, always gently bubbling, mirrored endless tumbling streaks in the clotted orange sky. In the mellow distance rose the slopes of the ice volcano.

There was nothing like being there. Joe Kipps would never be there. That was why he loved this place.

These landscapes were rich with intricate detail. Such compelling textures. Titan flourished like frost on a windowpane. A moon whose slithering mineral existences came into their being in temperatures that froze ammonia. Cryovolcanic. Aqua-tectonic.

Kipps treasured every moment he could spend with these landscapes. Since he was a space hero, though, Kipps didn't have many moments.

Liftoff was the worst part of spaceflight. Kipps was trapped and crushed inside the penthouse of a metal silo full of chemical fuel. Most victims of manned spaceflight died during these launch moments.

Kipps counted his own heartbeats until the smashed feeling left his lungs. Then Kipps was able to breathe, and to stir in his webbing chair, to access his screen again.

Off on the distant moon of Saturn, the game little robot had rolled a few closely calculated centimeters. This was how alien worlds were explored, and this was one noble little robot. It crawled methodically across icy sand at the bottom of a dismal murk so metaphysically cold that it rained components of gasoline. The scientists running this robot were not space heroes, because nobody had ever heard of them.

Here came the monster clatter of explosive bolts. The lift

stage—that cluster of sky-busting torches—broke loose from the cabin. The racket and roar ceased to pester him.

Here they came, those true, eerie sounds of genuine space-flight: uneasy, creepy, skin-crawling little noises that never got any press. The sounds of raw sunlight attacking raw metal.

The naked sun baked the port side as icy vacuum froze the starboard. So the spaceship popped and knuckle-rapped, and moaned its steely distress. Like a beer can flung from a speeding car, slowly tumbling toward the side of the road.

A space tourist floated toward Kipps. Kipps was startled. He'd forgotten to tell the passengers that they could leave their seats.

With a hasty swat at his touch screen, Kipps banished the surface of Titan. His pilot's screen coughed up dials and needles; altimeters and rheostats; switches, gauges, and guards.

These instruments were entirely redundant, since the flight was run from ground control in Arizona.

However, every space tourist treasured a folk notion of what a space captain's console ought to look like. Spaceship dashboards should look complex, impressive, and demanding. So they did.

The boisterous Indian millionaires were cartwheeling from their acceleration couches, hooting and tumbling. Puffy-faced from free fall, they clowned around like kids.

These eight moguls had each paid thousands of rupees per second for this out-of-this-world experience. They were determined to enjoy it.

Gouts of liquid floated through the chamber; violently fizzing spheres that spattered the bulkheads. These blobs looked crazily alive, like space-invading amoebas. They were loose champagne.

The missile, which entirely lacked portholes, was upholstered with touch screens. They were American military surveillance screens, so they could pick out rifle flashes from low orbit.

The Indian thrill-seekers gazed with wonder at the cloudy Earth beyond their floating feet. Cheerily inept, they pawed at the obedient screens. They froze images of the wheeling Earth, and stored them, and mailed them down to Earth.

It was never much fun to be in outer space unless you were famous for doing it. So these space tourists were all websurfing. They were recording their thrill-ride, and annotating the highlights, and sending them to their people on the ground. Their employees, their shareholders. Their extended Indian families. Anyone who might be properly impressed.

Kipps flicked a fizzing glob of champagne from his Navy dress whites. He kept his face dignified, and he stayed firmly belted to the Captain's chair. He wasn't in control here, but he knew how to look that way.

Human beings in outer space were playactors. Actors in a space opera. Though he'd endured orbit four times, astronautics was a role for Kipps. He played it as his duty.

Nobody loved the gaudy opera of manned spaceflight quite like the people of India. Their appetite for astronautics was colossal and melodramatic, much like their country.

Space opera was what Indians liked best about Americans.

Americans rocketed to the high frontier, and they left the management of Earth to Indians. It was the great alliance of eagles and spinning wheels. The American-Indian democratic-secular alliance was the spinning axis of the world. It followed that an American space hero like Captain Joe Kipps had to exist. Otherwise, the State Department would have to invent some other guy.

Kipps massaged his lurching stomach, which bloated in free fall like a water balloon. He keenly regretted that lavish bon-voyage lunch of shrimp-and-coconut curry. Free fall always seemed to last for ages.

Kipps folded his uniformed arms, which had a distressing habit of floating aimlessly above his head.

The aristocrats cavorted eagerly in their metal barn. Their cash had made a playground from this huge American weapon. The missile had been designed to carry an almighty, city-crushing payload: mostly, lethal bundles of crystalline hypervelocity crowbars. They could sleet out of a clear sky and needle their way a mile deep into the crust of the earth.

Not nuclear weapons, of course. "Conventional" weapons. Nuclear weapons were strictly for evil terrorists. After Houston, Los Angeles, and Washington, America had slammed together fifty of these rocket super-fortresses. They'd been used in practical circumstances exactly twice.

In these much quieter times of secular democracy, there was nothing much to do with these one-shot dinosaurs. Except to tart them up, refit their interiors in high Indian style, and milk them for space prestige.

Much the same transition had happened to Joe Kipps. In the heat of war, he'd been a modest Navy Aviation Systems Warfare rating, patiently peering at Pakistan through his targeting screens. Nowadays, he was Captain Kipps of the U.S. Space Navy, which was basically an arm of the State Department.

One of the Indian billionaires heaved, wobbled, and trudgeon-kicked his way over. The tourist was bright-eyed and respectful. He wore a nice safari-style adventure suit with Velcro pockets and a hot-pink silk ascot. He was meeting a celebrity. This precious moment meant a lot to him.

"May I interrupt you, Captain Kipps? Are your navigation duties pressing?"

"This has been a textbook launch," Kipps recited, unfolding his arms. "All systems go! We're A-OK!"

"It's a great honor to share my first spaceflight with you," said the mogul.

Kipps took a deep breath. "The greatest honor of my life was serving on the ground with the fine officers of the Army of the Republic of India."

The Indian billionaire looked properly impressed.

"I so wish my wife could hear you say that, Captain Kipps. My wife is your great admirer. She follows all your triumphs. On the web."

What kind of a woman, thought Kipps, married a spacey billionaire like this clown? Some buried memory nagged at Kipps, and it came up in a juicy rush. Brigadier Karwal. Brigadier Karwal, grinning and mustached and tougher than brass nails. "No Indian girl ever marries for money, Joe!

She's always careful to fall in love with it first!" Karwal had said that, and winked, and grinned about it, in the endless heat and dust and blood and terror of feral Karachi.

Kipps rubbed under his jacket's collar: the heat off the bulkhead had him sweating. He had to find something cordial to say to the billionaire. "We Americans can learn a lot from the strong bonds of Indian family life."

The Indian mogul, floating haphazardly, hooked his fingers through the mesh of the Captain's chair. "My wife and I always follow the discoveries you make on Titan. That moon of Saturn looks just like the deserts of Rajasthan. Although Rajasthan has life."

"Yes, sir," said Kipps.

"We can see," said the Indian, "a world that has real weather. A world with soil and skies. Where the rivers run. There are lakes."

"I'm hunting for methane geysers," said Kipps.

This brought an eager smile. "Of course you are still hunting, Captain Kipps!"

"We mapped the surface in fine detail from orbit. But the surface is volatile. So we have our robot crawlers. Three of them."

"Titan has ice volcanoes," the mogul persisted. "The crust of Titan rotates on a deep inner ocean of water. So geysers must burst up. Perhaps they will carry fish! Or great blind alien sea monsters!"

This character was quite the fan. Kipps cleared his throat. "Have we met, sir? Do I know you?"

"You may have heard of 'GPS'—'Gupta Positional Services.'"

"You're not that Rene Louis Gupta, are you? You don't look very French."

"I hope you haven't heard anything bad about my little Paris start-up," smiled Gupta. He bumped into the bulkhead and winced.

Kipps grabbed his elbow and steadied him. "I'm one of your customers. I got your guidance system in my car. I own a Tata."

"Captain Kipps, do you have just one little moment to tour our data center?" said Gupta. "It would mean so much to my staffers!"

"I can check on that with my embassy," said Kipps. This was what they had trained him to say.

The tourists had been entirely thrilled in free fall, but splash-down made them miserably seasick. The missile was help-less at sea, just a hollow metal tube that rolled and wallowed uncontrollably in the churning Bay of Bengal.

The Indian Navy had a lot of trouble snagging its slippery hull.

As the Captain, Kipps was the last man off the washing spacecraft. It would have been his duty to sink with it.

The scale of the Indian aircraft carrier was completely absurd. The Indians had thrown a dead Arab skyscraper onto its side, hollowed it out, and transformed it into a heav-ily armed naval bazaar. There was a flat sun-baked tabletop where the drones landed, slow-moving war birds with lethal stings. Killer drones were keenly familiar to Kipps, but the rest of the craft was a crazy hive: watertight cargo-contain-ers welded together, cardboard antimissile barriers. Cut and paste. Mix and match.

Indian civilians swarmed all over this urban aircraft car-rier. They had the Indian Navy personnel outnumbered three to one. Maybe the carrier was simply too big to leave to the military. The people had pulled political strings; they'd privatized the place, turned it into a floating suburb.

Private helicopters arrived to greet his passengers. The helicopters were candy-colored Indian dragonflies, and they disgorged whole eager retinues of secretaries and escorts and girlfriends and masseurs and spiritual advisers. They fell on the heroic space tourists with glad cries of glee and flung flowered garlands over their necks.

Kipps had to pose for ritual pictures with his tourists: alone, in small groups, as an entire group. In front of a green screen, without any green screen. With and without a huge, garde-nia-reeking flower garland around his neck. Kipps recited his talking points, including memorized slogans in Hindi.

An American consular official emerged from the chaos of cots, valises, crates, and power cables. She had a big satellite phone for Kipps, along with a broad-brimmed hat, a tube of sunscreen, and cold mineral water.

This woman was a psy-ops creature, a civilian spook, but it was nice to see her thinking about his needs.

"We're going to Bombay," she told him. "Your big show had a change of plans."

"Mumbai? But I was briefed for Dubai," said Kipps. They'd scheduled him for another tour of Dubai, which was a very proper, ultra-futuristic, space-hero kind of town. Kipps had been to Dubai twice. Dubai always seemed like an interesting place, though he'd never once escaped its co-lossal hotels.

"Please don't call Bombay 'Mumbai,' Captain. They don't do that here anymore."

"Okay. Sure."

State Department Girl told him that her name was Sarah something. "If they use the name 'Bomb-Dub,' that's bad. It means they're claiming Dubai as a suburb of Bombay. Those guys are the crazy, Hindu, culture-war, saffron-and-trident crowd. You don't want to mess with them."

"I heard about them. Right."

"Do you think there's any life on Titan?" said Sarah.

"What?"

"Life. Life on Titan. Do you think life evolved on there? Do you believe in evolution? You believe in dinosaurs."

"There might be some life *inside* Titan," Kipps said with care. "There's water in there, an ocean. But it's eighty miles deep and it's locked deep in solid ice. So there's no danger. They can't get out and hurt us."

"You hunt for geysers so you can find some fossils of life on Titan."

"I always look for fossils," said Kipps. "I've been look-ing for fossils since I was a kid. Nothing special about that. North Dakota's crawling with fossils."

"Despite your private convictions, I don't think you ought to mention the prospect of life inside Titan," said Sarah. "Too controversial. In Dubai, maybe, but Bombay's got swamis, and gurus, and guys who talk to UFOs, and people who believe in life in outer space—and they're all fundies. Okay? They'll act real friendly to you, but you shouldn't go there."

"I'm strictly secular," said Kipps.

Sarah squinted at a departing chopper. "We should never have gone to Bombay . . ." It looked like Sarah had had a long war. Some people had never gotten over Houston, and Washington, and Los Angeles. Something had turned into ice inside of them, after that. They were not going to loosen up again.

"They've got a free press in India," said Sarah. "So there's a lot of things you can't say."

Kipps said nothing.

"So don't ad-lib. Please stick to your talking points."

Kipps said more nothing.

Another private helicopter lifted off, making a useful racket that would frustrate lurking microphones. Sarah put her sunburned nose next to his ear.

"We don't have much time before they fly you there too," she said, "so remember, Indian journalists always look for gaffes and slips from celebrities. So please, never use the name 'Pakistan.' 'Ceylon, Burma, Tibet'—those don't exist either. They will ask you leading questions about all their provinces, because they want to make news. So you just say: 'Line of Control.' That's all you need to say to anybody. There's the 'Line of Control,' which is everything that India occupies. Then there's the 'Humanitarian Relief Area,' which is the parts they don't occupy yet."

That seemed like a lot for Kipps to remember. "Can you send me a briefing file?"

"They tap all our files."

"Can you give me a briefing book?"

"They steal our books. They scan them and put them in scandal sites."

Kipps shook his head. "Look, can't we just go over to Dubai? If that almighty Indian Government . . ."

"The government's not the problem. New Delhi loves Omaha, they kiss and make up every day. Bombay is weird, though, it's huge, it's the size of a country. Every last barefoot kid in that city, hell, every damn village in India, is on the Net . . ." Sarah dodged a violently slithering cable. "Don't say 'slum.' The slums in India are the 'Informal Urban Areas.'"

"Is it okay if I talk some about 'poor people'?"

"The Indian poor are the 'Newly Advantaged.'"

Kipps was having trouble with his temper. He wasn't pleased about Dubai. The war had been pretty severe in Dubai, but at least the shopping was great. "How about 'poor kid from a Sioux reservation'? Can I tell them that about my own personal background? It's the truth."

"You're not 'Sioux,' Captain Kipps. You're 'Lakota.' 'Sioux' is a slang word that your enemies made up." Sarah stared into his eyes. Embassy people were very intelligent.

"Sorry to trouble you, Sarah."

Sarah allowed herself a small, sour smile. "We tried so hard to stick to your schedule . . . but the Indians just have their own notions. Our embassy is here for you, Captain. We're from Omaha and we want to help."

"Anything else in this major briefing?"

"Never drink the water."

Kipps already knew that. "There must be something else." He knew that from the kink in Sarah's eyebrows. He could have drawn Sarah's face from memory. Maybe he would do that for her, and make her a little gift of the portrait. Kipps was extremely good at drawing visual details. Sometimes that little parlor trick would mellow women out.

Sarah didn't want to broach the next issue to him. "Well . . . okay, there is one last thing. Your personal behavior. You're a lonely sailor in Bombay on shore leave."

Kipps said nothing.

"If you meet someone real friendly, she's not a hooker. She'll be somebody's spy."

"I'm married," said Kipps.

Sarah was surprised. "I wasn't briefed on that."

"I married Agnes last week. It's peacetime. Time to get married again."

Sarah clapped her hat to her head as a wind gust hit them. "Why didn't your wife fly over for a honeymoon inside your rocket? Wow, we could have promoted the hell out of that!"

Kipps opened his mouth, and shut it again. Agnes was a planetary scientist. Agnes was a genuine explorer of new worlds. So Agnes naturally hated manned spaceflight. Agnes loved her robots, and Agnes dearly loved her screens, but Agnes loathed every Buck Rogers moron who had ever wasted her science funding.

There was big trouble at the Bombay hotel. Apparently, the labor strike convulsing Dubai had some local echo in Bombay. The harried staff assured Kipps that he had a room, a nice room, a palace fit for a cosmic hero: but it just wasn't ready for him. Yet.

Having flown to his hotel through outer space, Kipps naturally carried no luggage. The mishap left him standing empty-handed in his sweat-stained uniform in a potted-palm, marble-pillared lobby.

Three goons in the lobby were staring at him.

The goons could have been police spies, or journalists wanting a scoop about him, or maybe even some Bombay mafia gunsels carrying their cheap gats into nice hotels. Maybe the three men were one of each variety of goon. In any case, the goons weren't the helpful American spooks that Kipps had expected from the local embassy. He didn't like the way the locals sized him up.

Kipps tried his satellite phone. Being a satellite phone, it couldn't work indoors.

So Kipps left the hotel and entered the awesome blazing heat, urban racket, and the incredible Indian smell. The goons hastily followed him.

Kipps pointed his American-secured satellite telephone at the blazing smog-yellow sky. He attempted to call the local American embassy. The rugged phone seemed functional, but it wanted to synchronize with the chip inside his State Department passport. That interaction wasn't working. Some fault with the phone, or with the passport, or with some federal interface that just didn't hook up to another federal interface.

Whatever the glitch, his secure phone was useless.

So Kipps stepped inside a big, rattling, rust-eaten trolley. The goons also hustled into the trolley, jamming their way deep into the crowd.

Kipps muscled through the crowd and stepped off the far side of the trolley at the last second. The trolley thundered off with his pursuers trapped inside.

Then Kipps went for a walk. He chose directions that offered the fewest video cameras.

As every schoolchild knew, Bombay had been hit by a nuclear weapon. Bombay had been nuked, and Calcutta had been nuked. Due to the mujahideen unpleasantries, there had been three more nukes beating the daylights out of hapless Kashmir.

The Bombay nuke had been a much heavier nuke than the dirty-suitcase versions smuggled into Houston and LA and Washington.

In Houston and LA and Washington, six years later, there were still big cigarette-butt blast zones where the feds wandered around with their Geiger counters and moaned about obscure isotopes that gathered in the thyroids of children.

Nothing like that visible around here. There had to be some similar atomic blast locale in Bombay, but, for the life of him, Kipps couldn't find it. Bombay was absolutely packed with humanity. Bombay was seething with life and insanely huge. Bombay was a true twenty-first-century megacity, which meant that Bombay wasn't so much a town as a province-eating brick-and-metal dinosaur.

There were sections of smoggy Bombay where mirrorglass spires blasted up tall enough to mock Chicago, but those spires were right next to barnacled checkerboard places—"informal urban areas"—made from scraps. From debris. Anything and everything, jigsawed and glued. Cut and paste. Mix and match.

Informal cities made from dirt. The Bombay buildings made out of dirt looked especially ingenious. They weren't pretty, but they were battle-tested war technology. The frontline bunker stuff.

The Indian troops didn't use the rebar and the Jersey barriers that American ground troops used. The Indians had plenty of manpower. So the Indians shoveled up loose dirt or rubble, and just a little cement, into big canvas bags.

Then they made a big round loop of the bags, on the ground.

That was their first barricade, a place to kneel and shoot, but they wouldn't stop with that. The *jawan* troopers would lay barbed-wire on top of the bagged dirt. Then they piled a second loop of fat sandbags on top of that first one. The steely barbed-wire hooked the bags together and kept the layers solid.

Then the Indians just kept at the work, shoveling and piling, round after round, like a potter coiling up clay.

When they were done, they had a big solid canvas-dirt dome. Shrapnel would bounce off it like confetti. They would cut doors into it. Maybe pipe some daylight in with plastic sewer-pipe.

The domes were cool in the day and warm at night. They were as cheap as dirt.

Somebody in Bombay, maybe some thousands of guys, had come back from the war with a whole lot of hands-on experience in how to dig and pile such things. Now these dome-slums were all-civilian. They had a little paint and plaster, sometimes: flowers, geometric patterns . . . Some domes were completely plastered with street posters, gaudy fly bills of paper and glue, big thick barky layers of propaganda that built up and peeled off in rinds.

Since the domes were immensely solid, there were urban barnacles piled up and squatting all over them. Tiny little workshops. Zigzag laundry lines. Water tanks. Pissoirs. Rabbit cages. Grimy, dewy, makeshift plastic greenhouses where leftover video cell phones watched somebody's crops growing. It was like a slum volcano had erupted. Like somebody had taken a foaming fire hose and sprayed the place with handmade shelters.

It was hot, humble, and dirty, and the unnamed alleys were crammed with tattered bits of urban crap, plastic wrap, pop tops, packing debris, stuff so entirely devoid of value that no amount of ingenuity could squeeze another nickel out of it.

But the massive crowds here were busy people. They were poor, but they were big-city people. The local poor had goals and ambitions. They were big-city people and they weren't ashamed of themselves.

They'd seen their share of foreigners. They didn't mind him and his retro-futuristic Space Navy uniform. Kipps felt much safer among them than he'd felt inside the posh and chilly hotel.

Kipps maneuvered through unnamed alleys, ducking under signs, dodging puddles and careening bicycles.

There was no end to it. It was a maze on the scale of the North Dakota badlands, yet packed with human beings. This had to be one of the biggest slums on the planet.

Yet it was better than the place where he'd grown up.

He'd grown up inside a battered aluminum camper, with a teenage mom with an abiding fondness for Cherry Ripple. It was difficult to explain to people that the twenty-first-century Sioux were not guys wearing feathered war-bonnets while riding palomino ponies. The Sioux were not the urban poor, they were the rural poor. The rural poor was where the urban poor came from.

Until he'd joined the Navy at eighteen, the most exciting thing that had ever happened to Kipps was going out to the badlands to scour the barren soil for chips of bone. All the white kids on these paleontology school trips had it figured that they were off to bag a tyrannosaur. It took a guy like the young, dead-end, dirt-ignorant Joe Kipps to realize that a chip of bone was significant.

So he was superb at that work.

All the rest of it—the awe and wonder of dinosaurs, sixty-five-million-year time-spans, Cretaceous-Tertiary boundary events, asteroids and earthshaking thunder lizards—that was all time opera. It was time opera in the same way that spaceflight was space opera.

In other words, it was all romantic crap predicated on the work of roughnecks who were willing to do the hard stuff.

Kipps had had a pretty good war. Wars had a way of upsetting things, of changing the balance of peacetime's winners and losers. Things had changed on the reservation when Omaha became the capital. Not so much that Omaha helped—Omaha was broke. But Omaha didn't have the energy left to break the little people. That part seemed to help a lot.

The war made India a superpower. Some people wondered why a country that had suffered so much had come out so much stronger. Kipps was starting to get that now, because although Bombay was alien to him, he was good at seeing details.

A super-India wasn't so much the swaggering triumph of India as the abject collapse of everything that *wasn't* India.

They weren't trying to live impossible lies here, and then tearing their own flesh about it. They weren't strapping bombs to themselves for their payoffs in Heaven. They were living people.

The heat was killing him. Kipps was pretty used to heat—he had a house in Florida, where a veteran could get a house for nothing—but this heat was mad-dog heat. And now jet lag hit him—rocket lag.

Kipps stopped at an overcrowded plastic shack that clung to a curving wall. Kipps took the shack for a grocery store, for it held a fantastic array of off-the-wall crap: eight kinds of beans, weird condiments, soap, toothpaste, scratch-off cards, flyswatters, clothespins, diapers, razors, antiseptics, everything in teensy little morsel-sized packets.

A teenager was minding the joint. He had a rumpled cotton skirt tucked through his legs and a dirt-stained wife-beater shirt. He was playing a handheld military adventure game and deftly blowing terrorists into bloody pixelated pieces.

"You speak English?" said Kipps.

The kid froze his shoot-'em-up and loaded a fresh application. His console spoke up on his behalf. "What's your problem, Yankee?"

"You guys got Coca-Cola?"

"Probiotic? Mango-scented? Usury-free?"

"You got any Coke with real cane sugar instead of that corn-fructose stuff in the States?"

The kid did. Then came the problem of paying him. Being a sensible merchant, the kid was keenly reluctant to take

American dollars. They bargained for a payoff in cell-phone minutes. This involved Kipps buying a cell phone. The cell phone cost half as much as the cold can of Coke.

Kipps had to show his passport in order to do this. Four minutes later, Kipps received a phone call. The program attempted to sell him a city map, and a pizza, and a massage, and bangles and shawls and toys, all in starchy, freeze-dried mid-Atlantic English.

The slum was so packed with humanity that every action in it was accompanied by a crowd. However, a new crowd had arrived, and it marked its special character by staring at him in awe.

An older man tenderly touched Kipps's epaulet. He had clearly studied English, so he could almost pronounce it. "That was my boy."

"That was your boy," Kipps repeated.

"My boy sold a can of Coke to Captain Joe Kipps," said the older man.

"Yeah, I'm him."

"You are the hero who killed ibn Timur."

That legend was not true. Kipps had been staring at a console in Diego Garcia when the nuke-terror leader had been killed. Kipps hadn't pulled the trigger. The administrative process of killing ibn Timur had gone on for a couple of days.

The great global guerrilla had been crazy enough to head for a classic dug-out cave-complex bunker, instead of his usual posh hangouts in downtown London, Hamburg, and Paris. Since this cave was in the ass-end of nowhere, without his usual dense crowd of protective civilians, everybody got a lick in on him. Indian long-range artillery pounded him. American rockets from subs in the Persian Gulf. Russian mothballed bombers, and off-label French cruise missiles. Even the starving Chinese, who had every kind of domestic difficulty, got to avenge Xinjiang.

Killing ibn Timur was a global carnival of excess. There was nothing left of the guy but smears of DNA for the British SAS.

So Kipps hadn't really killed ibn Timur. He hadn't done

that any more than he'd ever bagged a tyrannosaur. Kipps had, however, invented a homemade technique of following cold fronts across Central Asia and looking for vapor plumes. Air came out of underground caves—if there was anyone alive in there. And even if they warmed and filtered their air—because they knew damn well that space satellites were watching for them—there would be moments when the caves hadn't caught up to the outside atmospheric conditions.

Then the unfriendly skies would see a little geyser. A steam-vent from the interior schemes and machinations of the world's smallest and craziest nuclear power. Somebody might see that. For instance, some humble but capable Navy tech, who knew something about geology and never got bored while staring at barren landscapes.

Kipps had put in a Recommendation for Battlespace Action. In a way, that was somewhat like pulling a trigger. If he hadn't seen that detail, maybe it wouldn't have happened.

"Yes, sir, I am Joe Kipps." He thumb-tapped the ribbons on his chest.

A great deal of ruckus followed from that little gesture.

Brigadier Karwal could not disperse the crowds. The slum-crowds of Dharavi were so densely packed that they lacked any place in which to disperse.

However, Karwal retrieved Kipps from the crowd without any casualties. It was done in a brisk and efficient way by goons who had had a lot of practice at doing such things.

"What were you thinking?" Karwal said.

Kipps had lost his jacket, his hat, and his phone. Some especially vigorous worshipper had torn off his shirtsleeve as a memento. "I wanted to see the big town."

Karwal rapped on the bulletproof glass with the head of his cane. Then he barked instructions to his driver. Kipps knew just enough about Indian languages to know that Karwal was not speaking Hindi. Malayalam, maybe.

"Dharavi is the blast site," said Karwal, tucking his sunglasses into his handkerchief pocket. "You were inside the blast site. That's why they wanted to congratulate you."

"It's radioactive here?"

Karwal spread his hands. "Life is radioactive, my friend. Radios are radioactive! Let's not be superstitious."

"I was drinking Coke in a bomb crater."

"Worry about the climate. It's much scarier than the Bomb." The rocket-like roaring from the enormous crowd was fading. The locals hadn't lost their burning interest in Kipps. A worshipful fraction were doggedly trailing Karwal's armored limo. They did not presume to touch the car, however. Nor did they profane the car's black, smoked windows.

Jumping into Karwal's limousine was like being swallowed by a whale.

"Where are we going?"

"You can stay with me, Joe. Too many rich boys in that big hotel. They're stupid."

"Okay."

"I have something to show you."

Kipps always learned stuff when Karwal showed him things. They were never things civilians knew about, but they were real things. War was a kind of poverty with bullets. There was nothing like being there.

Kipps tore the loosened sleeve from his shirt. "I heard that you got married."

"I did marry. And you divorced your wife. So I heard."

Kipps nodded. "Americans do that."

"Divorce is bad for you."

"Yes, sir."

"You got restless," said Karwal. "You went to reconnoiter. To surveil. Like your old days at the front."

"That's right. Like our old days."

"No *special* reason to leave your hotel? Just so curious, just so restless?"

"Well, it was that. That, and those three goombas in the lobby who were trying to scope me out." Kipps shrugged. "I get it about them. I was a drone jockey once. We blew people away, out of a clear blue sky. We were assassins. But now I'm Space Navy. I'm in the reserves now. No active duty. I wouldn't harm a fly."

This frank confession seemed to relax Karwal. "It's peacetime."

Kipps judged that peacetime was treating Karwal okay. Karwal was in a white linen suit. This was no cheap airport limo. This machine was a little well-seasoned, but it was one of those head-of-state, civilian-armored-vehicle limos. The kind that used to ooze in and out of Green Zones.

"We ran out of Pakistanis willing to fight us," said Karwal. "Then we demobbed. We went back to the Informal Urban Area. I got a job in security. Then the mafia came."

"The mafia."

"The Bombay mafia. They didn't understand my war on the front. Rich boys living too easy back here, just with their little atomic bomb. They thought they were still in charge."

Kipps said nothing.

"Joe, what would you have done?"

"Against a goddamn mafia? That's what, a 'lightly armed civilian militia'? Standard counterinsurgency. Kick their doors in."

"We shot them. The Indian government didn't expect that from us."

"You're in the government now?"

"The mafia was in the government. I am a poor man, Joe. I am a nobody from the slums."

"Ah. That makes sense."

"So, no, I'm not in this government. I'm in the mafia. I'm a Bombay don now. I'm a slumlord."

Karwal folded a gaudy movie scandal-sheet mag, hunted down a bluebottle fly and swatted it against the window.

"A society takes a few atomic bombs," Kipps offered, "things get a little strange."

"I'm very pro-American. Pro-American mafia."

"That's great to hear."

"Before you Americans gave us space support," said Karwal, "we were losing. Because it was their country, or they thought it was. We died like flies, and they died like flies. Then we died like Americans. They continued as flies."

"They're inside your Line of Control now."

"Everything outside our Line of Control dies like flies, Joe. They die like little gnats." Karwal rubbed his mustache. "Also, you fed us. In the famine, you sent us grain. That's why the Chinese died like flies. The Chinese weren't even in our war."

"Americans can't feed a neutral and starve an ally. That just makes no sense."

"The Chinese never understood Americans. They don't know how to make you happy."

"Mass production is overrated," said Kipps. "I got three little cars on the surface of Titan—just three cars, they're not Ford Model-Ts . . . but that's how I earn my living. I scan terrain from orbit and I ride around on three little robot cars. I'm looking for frozen fish."

"I have a space program, too," said Karwal.

"Yes, sir. You surely do. The Indian space program is world-class. It's almost a hundred years old."

"No," said Karwal, shaking his head in genteel embarrassment. "I don't mean the Indian government. I mean that *I* have a space program. I am a space hero, too."

"I see," Kipps said.

"We can't pacify civilians with mere bayonets. That does not end an insurgency. We have to give the people a productive stake in the new order."

"Yes, sir," said Kipps. He remembered all that. That was right out of the handbook.

The chauffeur drove them to a locale that Kipps mistook for a junkyard. Kipps was wrong, because the urban poor of Bombay cheerfully inhabited the junkyards. They could sell the contents.

This was a toxic zone for radioactive debris. Despite Karwal's bluff attitude, the Indian government, prodded by foreign advisers, had segregated the most contaminated ruins and dragged them here.

Still, no amount of earnest warning about rad-waste

could stop Indian wildlife. The atomic junkyard had swiftly become a booming Indian urban wilderness. Not a park but a feral jungle, with waist-high saw grass, clouds of pigeons, weed-trees, clambering vines, mosquitoes, bats that ate the mosquitoes, snakes that ate the bats . . . Cement and blast debris had to be the world's least promising ecosystem, but this crazily thriving heap had one great advantage: no human beings. Without people to repress it, the crazed fertility of the great subcontinent was surging back.

Karwal, using his limousine phone, ordered Kipps an untorn shirt and another Coca-Cola. They left the limo at the towering razor-wire limits of the waste dump.

Karwal hastily bent his efforts to the display of his slum-built "space program." It was something he and his colleagues had been working on—some kind of popular movement. The works, apparently, were either stationed or somehow hidden inside the dump.

Local people began arriving . . . not in a boisterous, hollering mob this time, but respectfully, even tenderly. They were bringing gifts. Candles, and flowers, and little trays of food. Nothing too elaborate or fancy, just heartfelt tributes, things a man or a woman or a child could bring in two cupped hands.

The first gift-givers were really anxious that Kipps should see them paying him obeisance. They were burningly eager to catch the eagle eye of their space hero. It really meant a lot to them. Some even recited brief little well-wisher poems and prayers. But once the heap of tributes started building up—waist-high, neck-high . . . it achieved a critical mass.

The gift-bearers weren't even looking at him. They were too busy piling up their spontaneous shrine.

Eventually, a pretty young woman brought him a long cotton pajama top. Grateful, Kipps pulled off his sweating, torn shirt.

There was an immediate torrent of photographs.

Indian journalists. They'd been waiting for him to make a misstep, and stripping off his torn shirt in public was everything they needed.

"I think I'm screwed now," he told the young woman.

"It's all right," she told him. "They are photographing me. Not you."

"You do look familiar," he lied.

"Don Karwal sent me," she said, "because I have good American English. I studied theater in New York for three years."

"That's a nice town, New York . . . But it's kind of small."

"Soon they will ask you—everyone will ask you about me. You say: 'Miss Neeta Dhupia and I are just good friends.' This is Bombay, so that's all you need to say. 'Just good friends.'"

"Right."

"They just make up the rest. It's all fantasy. But Bombay loves fantasy. Without fantasy, we don't live."

"Your don has a lot of connections."

"The don is our Badshah." She nodded. "He says you are a hero and his brother. He says you can have anything you want. The don says you are a restless sailor on shore leave."

She waited for him to say something.

"A whiskey and soda?" she said at last, delicately. "A neck massage?"

"I need a sketchbook," said Kipps hastily. "I want a pencil. I want good ones. An architectural notebook and a fancy drafting pencil. I need those things right away."

Miss Dhupia whipped a rhinestone gizmo from her shoulder bag and began to shout in it.

The feral sun was setting, but sound trucks arrived with night-piercing searchlights. Drones whined overhead. A phalanx of snack carts arrived. Somebody opened a fire hydrant.

Kipps tapped the bare skin of Miss Dhupia's pearl-powdered shoulder. "Can you clue me in here? What are we supposed to see?"

"Do you believe in life in outer space?" she said.

"I don't. I'm strictly secular."

"You don't believe in spaceships? But you pilot spaceships."

"That's different."

"How about those robots on Titan? Space robots are UFOs. If you're from Titan." She smiled triumphantly.

Four young men in postmen's uniforms came tearing through the crowd. It was a dense and increasingly excited mass of human beings, so the postmen were shouting and shoving and clawing and lashing out with their shoulder bags.

They burst through the crowd's perimeter like marathon runners.

They delivered a plastic-wrapped artist's sketchbook and a set of colored pencils.

Miss Dhupia accepted delivery, smiled sweetly for the cameras, and handed the booty to Kipps. Then she glided into a better camera angle and handed the booty over again. Finally, they went through the routine a third time while she delivered some lines in Hindi and Urdu.

"I hope nobody gets killed over this," said Kipps, unwrapping his sketchbook.

"There may be fatalities," said Miss Dhupia serenely, "but the police cannot reach us, because the masses would intervene. Besides, the government police are not here, because of the *darshan* in Dubai. Also, you killed ibn Timur. If the police come here, they will praise you."

Karwal bustled over, accompanied by a small riot squad from a private militia company.

Kipps had seen men like these in plenty, in the war.

In fact, Kipps realized, these were the same men. They were all ex–Indian Army dogfaces. The veterans of a mass draft, the cannon fodder of the booming slums. India was the only country on Earth with enough feet to stick into the necessary boots-on-the-ground. These *jawans* were still in their boots.

"Very soon," Karwal told him. "There are some technical difficulties."

"It's always that way."

"We are counting down. That's a nice shirt. You look good in a *salwar kameez*."

"I'm out of uniform."

"You?" said Karwal, grinning. "Space Captain Joe Kipps? Not you, Joe; never."

"Will this get me in big trouble?" said Kipps.

"It's American. It's all-American technology!" said Karwal. "We didn't invent it. *You* invented it. We just made it *bigger*. With *many more people*."

"You can draw it when it rises up," Miss Dhupia offered. "It only looks like it moves very fast. It doesn't walk so very fast. It's just that *the pieces inside it*, they all move so very, very quickly."

"It's almost ready, Joe," said Karwal. "When it rises up . . . from inside there . . . when it reaches upward, to the stars . . ." He gazed at the dotted facade of a skyscraper . . . "Taller than that thing, Joe . . . Much taller than that."

"I'm ready," he said. "I want to see." And then it happened.

FEARLESS SPACE PIRATES OF THE OUTER RINGS

BILL WILLINGHAM

Famed comic-book writer and illustrator Bill Willingham has won fourteen Eisner Awards for his work, which includes creating series such as Elementals, Ironwood, Coventry, Pantheon, Proposition Player, and the well-known *Fables*, the story of exiles from fairy tales living in hiding in New York City, which has been scheduled to be made into a TV movie in 2009. Recently, he's been moving into prose work as well, as witness the vigorous and lively tale of Space Pirates and kidnapped Earthmen that follows . . .

The huge and ancient Oeerlian merchant ship surfaced ponderously out of underspace, sizzling waves of abused relativity boiling and crackling off its shields. It tumbled erratically along two axis, bleeding out trapped ballast from behind its shields, while its relativity translators struggled to relearn the laws of normal space. Then, slowly, it settled itself, brought its main engines online, and began to accelerate inward, along the elliptic, toward the system primary, at a paltry thirty-two standard gravities.

None aboard the freighter noticed the much smaller ship lurking in the shadow of the rings surrounding the nearest gas giant. Anyone who had seen it would have known its purpose at a glance. It was a hunter. It existed to feed off of fat ships like the merchantman. It had overlarge engines, for chasing down prey, and its flanks bristled with weapons nodes for killing what it caught.

The smaller ship was called the *Merry Prankster*, and it was known far and wide as a pirate raider. It hung drifting under the rings, radiating no detectable energy. On the *Prankster*'s bridge Captain Brodogue, a massive third-stage Plentiri male, studied their intended target. His brightly jeweled grappling hoons reflexively extruded and retracted in a steady rhythm, signaling his barely suppressed excitement.

"I told you those sneaky bastards were surfacing out here," he said, unable to prevent himself from venting musk. Each of the other Plentiri members of the mixed crew quickly moved back from him rather than risk falling into an automatic challenge fugue.

"And you were right, as usual, Skipper," the First Mate said. His name was Danny Wells. He was an exotic creature called a human, from a small, out-of-the-way system, far outside of civilized space. "She looks like a rich bauble, too. Shall we pursue?" He didn't need to ask, but certain formalities were essential to maintaining a disciplined crew.

"Light her up, Mister Wells," Brodogue said, "and give chase."

"Battle stations!" Danny ordered, a broad grin spreading across his face, which the several non-dentate species among the pirate crew always found more than a bit disturbing. "Bring the engines online! Power up the shields! Internal field to chase maximum! Man all guns!"

The crewmembers rushed to obey the mate's shouted commands, knowing that anyone slow to respond might suddenly find himself blasted into stasis for the duration of the action, and thus miss out on his share of the prize.

Danny turned to the conn station and Reedu Jillijon, the ship's Dhinhomy sailing master. He said, "Mister Reedu, will you kindly overtake that ship attempting to make off with all of our booty?"

"Aye, sir," Reedu said out of his lowest foremouth, giving Danny the respect appropriate to his rank.

In seconds, the *Prankster* went from drifting dead in space to leaping forward at an impressive seventy-eight g's. On board, the crew suffered none of the effects such a killing momentum should produce, due to the remarkable efficiency of the *Prankster*'s internal field generators. Danny forced himself to show none of the discomfort he felt inside an internal field dialed up so high. He'd suffer agonizing headaches later, but didn't mind it, since the alternative was to overtake the freighter at a slower velocity, thus subjecting the crew to enemy gunfire for a longer duration.

"They've seen us, Captain," Credogue said, from the defensive targeting station. He stood over the crewman seated at the console, glowering at the tactical display. He was the *Prankster*'s second mate and Captain Brodogue's son. In the nine standard years Danny had known the boy, since the day he'd emerged from his second-stage trialpod, Credogue had never shown a hint of joy, humor, or any other pleasurable state of mind—quite unlike his nearly sybaritic father. "They've increased speed to thirty-seven g's, and opened gun ports."

"They won't last long at that velocity," Brodogue said, from his command couch. "They don't have the field generators for it. They must be shitting their pantaloons in fear."

"Gives them an extra few seconds to target us," Danny said.

"It won't help them," Brodogue said.

"It might," Danny said. "The Oeerlians believe in packing big guns. They'll have tenth-power integrators on a bucket that size."

"Doesn't matter," Credogue said. "Their targeting systems predate most civilizations. Who cares how big their hammer is, if they can't aim it properly?"

"We're within gun range," Reedu said, and on cue the ship was rocked with the first enemy integrator strikes against their shields.

"Then they must have some lucky shooters on board," Danny said. "Those were spot on."

"Launch attractions," Credogue said. The second mate's primary duty during ship-to-ship combat was to oversee defensive operations. Danny heard the muffled, rapid-fire thumping sounds caused by several dozen attraction pods being coughed out through the forward shields. The attractions would ride the bow wave of the shields, staying ahead of the ship for several vital seconds, before slipping off to one side or another. As implied by their name, the attractions' purpose was to scream their heads off in many technologically sophisticated ways, hoping to attract the enemy integrator fire, thus saving the actual ship. Danny privately thought that Credogue had acted too soon in launching the pods. At this extreme range, the shields could easily absorb the integrator fire, no matter what their power. The second mate should've saved the expensive devices for when they were closer.

Danny switched his private screen to the defensive tactical display in time to see several attractions instantly collapse in on themselves, as integration beams connected with them. Each integrator-hit pod briefly formed an unstable pinprick singularity, before winking entirely out of existence. Then he switched over to offensive tactical to begin his own role as the director of their offensive fire.

"Commence fire," he said to his forward integrator gun crews. "Target shields and weapons nodes only. And I better not see you boys falling for their attraction pods, or I'll collect penalties." Traditionally, "penalties" were ears, fingers, or equivalent minor appendages, surrendered for gross failures committed during desperate actions. Danny was serious in his threat—he couldn't afford to make empty threats—but he knew he wouldn't have to mutilate anyone later. The *Prankster*'s targeting systems were the best available, and each gun crew was trained to perfection. Any attractions the fleeing freighter spit out in its wake would tumble off untouched and ignored, unless the *Prankster* had time afterward to salvage them, to replenish their own expended stores.

The two ships fired at each other as the predator rapidly overtook its prey. In short order, the freighter's shields collapsed, after which the pirate crew made quick work of every gun node that bore on them. From the first shot to the last, a mere twenty-three seconds had passed. Now the *Prankster* had to act quickly so as to not overshoot the freighter, and thus allow its other, still-functioning guns to come to bear.

"Match velocity," Danny barked, though he needn't have bothered. Reedu Jillijon was a deft hand at the conn and had already made the needed adjustments. The *Prankster* shut down its main drive and coasted toward the slower freighter that was still under power. This was an especially tricky time in such actions. The crippled freighter could still do any number of things to make itself dangerous to the pirate ship. It could cut out its own drive and let the *Prankster* shoot by it, blasting it as it did so, or it could rotate, bringing its surviving weapons to bear—or any of a long list of other maneuvers. At this point, it was a game of nerves and anticipation, between Reedu at the *Prankster*'s conn and whoever was piloting the merchant ship.

At the same time, the pirate ship's communications director started broadcasting the "black veil" warning—a universal message promising that any further resistance on the part of the freighter would result in its immediate and total destruction. Every starfaring species in civilized space knew of the "black veil" and knew that it was no bluff. Once given, it was worth loosing even the richest prize ship, rather than let the warning lose one iota of its threat value.

Apparently, the Oeerlian crew had no desire to sacrifice themselves, for they allowed Reedu to slave their conn controls to his station. Controlling both ships now, Reedu kept the freighter under power until it matched the *Prankster*'s greater velocity, and then cut its drive off, so that both ships coasted through space together, at rest relative to each other.

"Have they surrendered?" Brodogue asked, when Reedu announced his control over the freighter.

"No, Captain," the communications director said.

"So they still have some fight in them, eh?" Brodogue said. Under the accepted conventions of space warfare, a ship could still resist actual boarding, without risking its total destruction. The "black veil" only covered ship-to-ship combat.

"They've signaled they're prepared to negotiate terms, sir."

Now the captain had a decision to make. He could negotiate terms with the freighter, under which they'd only surrender a portion of their cargo, and then be allowed to continue on their way, or the pirates could board the freighter and fight them hand-to-hand for the chance to win all of the booty.

"So what are these Oeerlians like?" Brodogue said. "Are they doughty warriors in a close-up knife fight?"

"Not usually," Danny said, "but they tend to hire Vuurick mercenaries to do that sort of thing." Vuuricks were tough in a hand-to-hand fight. They had redundant major organs and decentralized nervous systems, which made it necessary to injure them thoroughly before they could be expected to stop fighting. They also had between four and eight viable weapons-using appendages, depending on their stage of maturation.

"What do you think, Mister Wells?" Brodogue said. "Will we be content with a portion of the goods, or are you in a mood to risk your neck over there to win all of it?"

"I'll be happy to board her, Skipper," Danny said, and meant it. "Will I be doing it in your name, or my own?" If Danny boarded the freighter in the captain's name, which was a perfectly honorable request for Brodogue to make, then the captain would receive the lion's share of the loot. But if Danny were allowed to board the ship in his own name, then he and his boarding crew would win the greater share.

"I had it in mind to go myself," Brodogue said. "It's been a while since I took part in personally separating a few Vuurick scum from their souls. Do you think your crew of black-hearted cutthroats could beat me and my boat over there?"

"Try me," Danny said.

"The ship is yours, Mister Credogue," Brodogue shouted, already leaping from his couch.

Danny was half a step faster than the captain, and beat him through the hatchway off of the bridge. He ran through the *Prankster*'s lush corridors, shouting frantic commands into his communicator ring as he did so. First he called the boat deck with orders to prep his personal boarding yacht for immediate launch. Then he called his quarters and screamed orders at his personal aide and bodyguard.

"Kyal!" Danny yelled as soon as she came on the line. He had to shout to make himself heard over the sounds of his footsteps, his heavy breathing, and all of the noise Brodogue was making, close behind him. "It's a boarding race! Get my crew on the *Egg*, now!"

"Already under way," Kyal said in her passionless voice. "And the boat is ready to go. All we need is you."

"Wonderful!" Danny screamed. "Then we'll get the jump on him! You're a dream!"

"Who're we up against?" Kyal said.

"The captain!"

"Who made the challenge? You or him?"

"He did!" Danny yelled. "Why?"

"Then we may not have a head start after all. Captain Brodogue's a crafty one. He may have anticipated offering the challenge and had his boat prepped in advance, with his own prize crew already aboard."

"You're probably right! Hang on, Kyal! I'm on my way!" That was when Brodogue, still sliding close on Danny's heels, stretched out one of his prehensile tanglers and tripped Danny, who landed hard on the deck and skidded until the Plentiri captain's massive body rolled over him. Brodogue's laughter—a rapid series of wildly oscillating clicks, in his case—disappeared down the hallway, as Danny levered himself painfully off of the deck. Then he began running again, for the boat deck and his personal launch.

The *Raptor's Egg*, its exterior shell a featureless blue ovoid, fell toward the giant merchant ship. Danny was aboard, with Kyal and his prize crew—a dozen veteran killers from as many different races. But he'd arrived too late. The captain's launch was a respectable thirty klees ahead of them, already breaking for soft contact with the merchantman's hull.

"Brodogue's got us skunked," Kyal said, frustrated but still delighting in her chance to employ the exotic human idiom. She had no idea what a skunk was, but knew she'd used the phrase correctly. She'd long been an avid student of xenolinguistics, and Danny's native tongue, with all of its complicated and contradictory rules, was among her favorites.

"Not yet," Danny said. "We just need to come in a bit faster than they are, if you've got the nerve for it. Dial up our speed."

"You plan to ram it?" she said. She was at the helm. Piloting his private yacht was but one of her many responsibilities. Kyal was a Sendarian warrior, which was most likely why Danny first selected her as his personal aide, once he'd reached sufficient rank to rate one. Sendarians looked human—an incredibly voluptuous human, in her case—provided one ignored the average seven feet in height for an adult, the gold skin, or the fact that they were all female. Danny assumed male Sendarians existed somewhere, but Kyal would never discuss it.

"Ram it?" Danny said. "Not precisely. I want you to prepare our way with a precision low-power integrator burp against that structure there." He pointed out a specific area of the target ship's hull on their tactical display. "Oeerlians need a lot of water to survive these long trading voyages, and unless I miss my guess, that plate covers one of their massive water tanks. Wink the covering plate out of existence, and the suddenly exposed water venting into vacuum should do a fine job of fast-breaking us. Assuming we survive such a ridiculous stunt, we'll end up already deep inside the ship's vitals, while Brodogue and his bullyboys are still setting up their phase door against its outer hull."

"And if the water tank's empty?" she said. "This is the end of their voyage after all. They may have used it up."

"Then I might just have enough time to say 'oops' before we're crushed like bugs against the ship's innards. But our bounceback sensors seem to indicate there's some considerable mass behind that section of hull."

"Compared to vacuum, even an empty tank's going to show mass, if it's pressurized."

"Why would they waste expensive air to pressurize an

empty space? Makes no sense. Oeerlian merchants are the very definition of thrifty. They'd never spend their treasure so liberally, and uselessly. No, I think there's water there and that's good enough for me. How about the rest of you?"

A quick glance at the rest of the boarding party indicated they were more than willing to take the risk. Winning the boarding race meant reaping the greater share of rewards. What sort of pirates would they be if they ever allowed caution to override naked avarice?

With a half-contained sigh of resignation, Kyal accelerated the *Egg*. "Strap in," she said. "Structural and internal fields are at maximum—not that they'll do us any good, if we've miscalculated."

She extruded the small bow chaser gun from the *Egg*'s shell and fired.

Part of the fast-approaching hull disappeared before them and the tank wasn't empty.

Brilliant crystals of pure water exploded into the void like a behemoth vomiting diamonds. The spray engulfed the *Raptor's Egg*, pummeling it with a billion tiny impacts, as it plummeted toward the gaping hole in the merchant's side.

The launch slowed—some.

Friction caused by impact with the ice crystals began to heat the *Egg*'s outer shell, which in turn affected the ice, flash-heating it into steam. And still they fell toward the gaping hole, surrounded now by a superheated geyser.

Impact!

They came to rest three bulkheads beyond the original tank structure.

After too long a time, Danny's eyes began to focus again. He shook his head to clear the last of the cobwebs and realized that Kyal was standing over him. She was outfitted in her battle exoskeleton, which magnified her already impressive strength.

"Are you okay, boss?" she said.

"I think so. How're the others?"

"Boze is dead. Harness snapped and he smacked headfirst against the inner hull. Instantaneous. I doubt he had time to feel anything. Peeker's leg is broken, but he'll live. Everyone else is good to go. Your nose is bleeding pretty bad, by the way."

Danny absently wiped at his face. His hand came away with a disturbing amount of blood on it. "I'm fine," he said. He popped his crash harness open and grappled himself out of his chair. The deck was canted a bit under his feet, indicating that their internal field was off—including the boat's six artificial gravity projectors—and they were now subject to the merchant ship's internal field. He could hear a distant siren wailing from somewhere beyond his own ship.

"We've powered down," Kyal said, anticipating his question. "Ready to go to dampers. The *Egg* poked a nice hole in the final bulkhead, forming a nearly airtight seal. There's a little leakage around the edges, but not enough to worry about. We won't need full pressure suits out there."

"Good to know," Danny said. "But let's carry emergency pressure bubbles anyway, in case the enemy panics and starts purging sections of the ship."

"Of course," she said, with an expression that scolded him for even thinking she'd forget to issue such an order herself. Danny noticed belatedly that his crew already had bubble packs clipped to their belts.

A few minutes later, the pirates crowded out of a hatching hole that opened in the *Egg*'s blue shell, and then oozed closed once again, featureless, behind them. Danny took the lead, as always. Each of them wore damper packs, dialed up to full dispersion. No energy projection weapons would work inside their overlapping fields, nor any other advanced forms of powered technology. All fighting in this action would be hand-to-hand.

In one hand, Danny carried an old-fashioned novaplast shield, one of the kind he called a "pie plate" because of its small diameter. He preferred to move the smaller shield to intercept oncoming weapons strikes rather than have to lug a larger one that might offer a greater scope of protection, but at the price of added weight and bulk. In his other hand, he carried his anyweapon. It was the pride of his personal arsenal, grown specifically for him, at considerable cost, by the mysterious Inomo Crafters of Core Polon.

Danny had his anyweapon formed into the shape of a short-bladed cutlass. Once they'd cleared the *Egg*'s small hatch, emerging into one of the merchantman's considerably more roomy corridors, he thought it into a longer-bladed version and it instantly responded to his desires.

Like a pack of prowling wolves, long practiced at working together, they hunted the ship's compartments. Stripped to the bare minimum of equipment, they were able to move silently. Their damper packs ensured that none of the ship's internal sensors could detect them.

At a bend in a corridor, they encountered their first group of defenders. As Danny had predicted, they were Vuurick mercenaries, each one of which was outfitted in state-of-the-art powered battle armor. Because of the damper fields, the armor was frozen to immobility, as were their unfortunate occupants trapped inside.

Kempee the Vraal peered through one of the defenders' faceplates. He said, "The Vuurick thug sure looks surprised in there, Danny. And a bit scared too, if I read his barbaric alien expression correctly. Should we kill them, while we have them at our mercy? Their armor will reactivate, once we've passed them by, and I'd hate to leave live enemies at our rear, cutting off our avenue of retreat." Kempee placed the tip of his fighting dagger at one of the more vulnerable joints in the defender's armor.

"No need," Danny said. "Having foes at our mercy occasionally merits showing some—mercy I mean. We'll just strip the guts out of their power packs. Then they'll continue to be frozen in place long after we've moved on. It'll take an engineering team hours to cut them out of those shells. We'll be long dead or long gone by then."

Neither Danny nor his crew wore powered armor, for obvious reasons. Even Kyal's exoskeleton worked primarily off of more basic pneumatic-hydraulic systems, needing one with her size and natural strength to operate it.

They sabotaged the power suits and moved on.

The next squad of Vuurick defenders were armed as they were with novaplast shields and blades. Danny caught the first of them half through a hatchway between connecting compartments and rushed to keep him—and the fighters behind him—bottled up there. Danny engaged him shield-to-shield, blade-to-blade. The Vuurick was bigger and stronger than the frail human, but his six appendages worked against him in the confined space. And Danny was faster.

They thrust and parried at each other for a while, neither opponent giving ground. The Vuurick carried a full-sized shield and used it to full advantage, blocking most of the hatchway with it, each time he needed to step back at arm's length and rest, or mentally regroup, for another sally. Danny quickly grew tired of the tactic and thought his anyweapon to extend its blade, and keep extending it, until it was thin enough to fit through the small sliver of space between the top of the open hatchway and the top of the lead Vuurick's hand shield. Once it was beyond the shield, quick as an attacking viper, Danny had the blade curve and grow downward, shooting forward too fast for the eye to follow, until it pierced the mercenary's skull.

The Vuurick fell like a sack of wet cement, while Danny thought his anyweapon back into a more traditional cutlass shape. Beyond the hatchway were nine more defenders, getting ready to surge forward, and Danny was out of breath. He didn't think twice about simply stepping aside, on his side of the hatchway, knowing with absolute certainty that Kyal would be right behind him.

Once the way was opened for her, she surged ahead, through the hatch and into the next compartment, picking up the dead Vuurick's body as she did so. Then she proceeded to swing the body this way and that, using it as a massive bludgeon. Fully surprised by this bizarre tactic, all they could immediately do in response was duck and dodge. That gave the rest of Danny's crew time to flood into the room, where they carefully picked their opponents and made short work of them.

"Are you okay, Kyal?" Now it was Danny's turn to ask, as he stepped into the room, after the last defender had fallen. The Sendarian warrior woman had a number of sword and knife cuts on her body. Her blood ran a lighter red than his—more the color of pale rust. Her exoskeleton had a few novaplast plates included in its structure. But they only covered the most vital areas. Full protection would have made the mechanism too heavy to operate, even for her remarkable strength. She looked down at herself in her usual, disinterested way.

"Superficial," was all she said.

They continued on, advancing toward the ship's bridge, fighting when they had to and avoiding confrontation whenever they could. When the way was blocked, Danny would use his anyweapon to cut a new route through a bulkhead. Its unbreakable blade could be thought into such exquisite sharpness that it could slice through anything less than the outer-hull material. Once an opening cut was made, Kyal would peel back the metal (or sheetplast, in some cases, where recent repairs and updates had been made to the ancient vessel) and they'd be free to proceed once again.

Less than twenty minutes after they'd first set foot out of the *Egg*'s shell, they arrived on the bridge.

Brodogue and his prize crew were already there.

Three Oeerlians were dead on the deck, pools of azure blood seeping out from their bodies. A half-dozen more had been herded into one corner, under guard by two of Brodogue's bullyboys. They whistled their distress in music so sweet no human composer would ever be able to approach, much less duplicate it.

"I saw your trick, Danny!" Brodogue laughed, clicking his sincere admiration between his words. "But it didn't work! Inspired us to take our own risk and construct our phase door right into the bridge! Dangerous gambit, eh? All of the electronic crap between the hulls interfering with our phase picture—likely to short the door out mid-passage and cut us into bloody gobbets!"

Brodogue was lying on the deck, along with the dead Oeerlians. His personal aide, a trained medic, was tending to a vicious burn wound in his upper torso. The injury smelled of crisped flesh and salty decay. Yellow blood-pus hissed and sputtered out of the edges of the plasma burn.

"We made it though!" Brodogue continued. "And won!"

"How do you figure?" Danny said. He wanted to ask about

his captain's injury, but wouldn't shame him by discussing such things in front of their captives. "We boarded the ship before you did."

"But we captured the bridge first and took their surrender!" He winced as his medic squirted a thick paste out of a tube, directly into the wound's main fissure.

"It was a boarding race. We boarded first! Case closed!"

"Fairly argued," Brodogue said. "We'll split the bonus equally among the two crews." This elicited a short cheer from pirates in each crew. "You made me proud, once again, Danny. Well done!"

Brodogue died an hour later, never having left the blood-stained deck of the captured trader.

Danny watched from the *Merry Prankster*'s bridge as the giant Oeerlian ship powered up its engines in preparation for the two- or three-week run it would have to make to build up sufficient momentum for even the most shallow dive into underspace. A prize crew from the *Prankster* was onboard and would take it to where it could be sold, either in whole or stripped for parts. Looking in-system, toward the distant primary, Danny could still make out the reaction drive glow from one of the merchant ship's launches. It was packed to the scuppers with all of the surviving Oeerlians and their Vuurick mercenaries. With no diving capability in the launch, limited to travel through normal upperspace, by the time they'd arrived anywhere they might plead for help, the pirates would be safely away, back to where no one could ever find them.

The *Prankster*'s crew (his crew now, he had to remind himself) had argued vociferously against letting them live. Those filthy, greedy merchants had caused their beloved captain's death, and such a profound debt could only be paid in the coin of wholesale massacre. Besides, in order to let them live, Danny had to give them one of the trader's largest launches, which was cash out of every crewmember's share.

At first, Danny tried to argue logically. Brodogue had always let the survivors go when he could. It was part of their ancient code. When it was clear that his imprecations were falling on deaf ears—or aural plates, as the case may be—Danny drew his anyweapon, formed it into a standard Kell blaster (the same kind that had so recently felled their captain), and burned the primary leg stalks off of one of the loudest protestors. He knew from long experience that any hint of mutiny had to be dealt with instantly and brutally. It seemed to do the trick. The crew returned to their duties, sullen and reluctant—but they obeyed.

Once the ponderous merchant ship was a pinpoint glow in the distance, Danny ordered the *Prankster*'s engines lit up for standard noncombat acceleration. He set the course back the same way they'd come, so they could recover the undamaged attractions on the way. Then he promoted Kyal to First Mate and gave her the watch. This came as an obvious surprise to young Credogue, who must have expected to be given the slot as a matter of course. Both sets of his undecorated grappling hoons were at full extension, embarrassing the other Plentiri on the bridge. But the Second Mate didn't seem to notice their nervous agitation.

"I'll be in my cabin," Danny said. He was in a foul mood and his head was pounding, as much due to the events surrounding his ascendancy to the captaincy as to the aftereffects of the recent chase conducted in an internal field set at maximum.

"Which one?" Kyal said.

"Excuse me?"

"Will you be in your old cabin or your new one? As the new captain of the ship, you're entitled to move into—"

"Belay that talk," Danny growled. "Brodogue's quarters will be kept as they are, unoccupied, until a decent period of mourning has passed."

"Very good, Captain," Kyal said. "I'll circulate that order among the crew."

Back in his cabin, Danny tried for long hours to sleep but failed. Then he tried to read, but by the twelfth time he'd read the same paragraph, without any notion of what it said, he gave up. So he lay in his bed and made mental plans for the changes he'd begin to institute, starting with his next watch. He considered whom he'd reward and whom he'd demote, and whom he might have to kill in order to consolidate his new position. There was always some blood spilled whenever a new captain came into power. Even under long-standing traditions and the supposedly inviolate code, it was in the nature of pirates to be prickly about those they allowed to lead them.

Sometime during his calculations, Danny finally fell asleep. Sometime later, he was woken, abruptly, when a dozen crewmembers crept uninvited into his room. They had Kyal trussed up neck-to-ankle in constrictor tape, which even her great strength couldn't burst. It was the sound she'd made when they dropped her unceremoniously onto the deck that woke him.

Danny frantically blinked the sleep out of his eyes. In short time, he noticed Kyal helpless on the deck, the grumbling mob crowded into his quarters, and he noticed Credogue at the head of it.

"I'm sorry, Captain," Kyal said. There was a reddening bruise developing under one eye. "I'd finished my watch and turned the ship over to the Second Mate, without incident. Damn it, but I was sound asleep when they came for me, or three or four more of them would be dead by now!"

More? How many *did* she kill then? Enough that they'd never let the two of them live through the night? Danny struggled to think.

"Don't call him Captain," Credogue said. "No one confirmed him as our new captain."

"True," Danny agreed, "but as First Mate, I am the acting captain, until a formal assembly of election can take place. And that can't happen sooner than twelve days after a vacancy by death or resignation of the previous—"

"Don't quote the book to me, Danny Wells! The Plentiri wrote most of what's in it. My accelerated ancestors—may they dive ever deeper into the seven thousand underworlds— forged those ancient covenants. What has a human ever added to it?"

"Not a thing," Danny said. "Only a confirmed raider captain can participate in the Council of Lawmaking, and since I'm the first human to come this close to achieving that rank—"

"He's stalling for time," one of the other crewmembers said. "Kill him and let's be done with this ugly business." Danny was shocked and saddened to recognize the speaker as Reedu Jillijon, the *Prankster*'s unflappable sailing master, who'd always seemed authentically fond of him in the past.

"No one's going to be killed today," Credogue said, silencing the others before they could voice any agreement with Reedu's proposal. "This isn't a mutiny and we aren't cutthroats in the night. This is a simple correction of a past oversight. Danny Wells can't become our captain because of the laws which govern us, because he was never a proper member of our crew. He first boarded the *Prankster* under false pretenses, a case of mistaken identity. Since that was never adjudicated, he can't now be subject to our code, nor can he claim its protections."

That much was true enough. Danny was never formally invited into the crew and so had never formally joined it. It was all a big mistake.

In the winter of 1964, Danny was driving his rusted lime-green Volkswagen Beetle home from college for Christmas vacation. He drove alone down a narrow and desolate country road, which traversed the rolling wheat fields of eastern Washington's high Palouse. He was trying to coax a few more miles out of the tired old thing, but had begun to suspect that it was done for. It was getting dark, and the car's engine, which had never run well to begin with, had started to burp and sputter in ways that he'd not heard before.

"Come on, you poxy tart," Danny cursed, "give me just a few more miles. Get me to the next service station and all is forgiven. Hell, just get me to a town with a bus station and I'll let you finally die in peace. I promise!"

Something popped loudly under the floorboards, and Danny began to smell gas fumes seeping into the passenger compartment.

"No! Don't do this to me! I'm sorry I called you names!"

Danny was nineteen years old and had no firm idea of what his future might hold. He was by no means sure, but at times he thought he might want to become an engineer, or an architect, or perhaps pursue a poly-sci major and study police work—the advanced kind that led to FBI jobs and such. He also thought he might possibly be in love with Rebecca Meyer, whom he'd met last semester outside of his intermediate fencing class. He was going out of the gym just as she was coming in to seek a signed deferment from the required one PE class per semester for all underclassmen, and they'd danced briefly in the doorway, trying to maneuver around each other. She'd giggled at his cute "toy" sword, his white knee-length fencing knickers, and his white knee-high socks, which she'd thought looked darling and later described as precious—but in a good way. He was taken with her immediately.

Rather than drive straight home this time, from Moscow, Idaho, to Pasco, Washington, taking major roads that actually had more than one lane at times, Danny had agreed to drop Rebecca off at her family farm out in the vast Palouse. He tarried too long there, meeting her parents, whose names were Bob and Hazel, and then (perhaps more important) meeting her horses, whose names were Rascal and Applejack. It had already begun to grow dark before he was once again on his way.

Now he was pretty thoroughly lost, navigating a single-lane country road where one had to pull over to let an oncoming car (or more likely a tractor or harvesting combine) pass. Adding to those troubles, his rickety old Beetle, which had been dying for as long as he'd owned it, was almost certainly in its final death throes.

With a final loud cough, followed by a sad little rattle, unable to make it up a small rise of the road as it surmounted yet another rolling hill, the car stalled and died. When Danny tried to turn the engine over again, all he heard was a few angry clicks. Strangely, now that the inevitable had finally come to pass, what he felt most wasn't anger or resentment, but a sense of relief.

"Good riddance," he said, abandoning the thing where it had died. He took his one suitcase, buttoned up his fleece-lined corduroy jacket, and began walking, never so much as pausing to look back at the ugly little car when he'd crested the rise.

He walked for ten minutes in the rapidly increasing dark, as the road dropped down to follow the winding Palouse River valley for a time, before jutting almost due north.

"But I don't want to go north," he complained. "I need to head west." But since west wasn't an option, he continued along the road. Gradually wheat fields began to give way to scattered stands of pine trees, as he trudged up a long hill that showed no sign of cresting anytime soon. Eventually, he left the fields behind entirely and entered a forest proper. He passed a small green sign that read: WELCOME TO STEPTOE BUTTE STATE PARK.

"Lovely," he said. "I guess this means no town soon."

Turning back would mean at least a fifteen-mile walk to the last town he'd passed through, before his car gave up the ghost. It would also mean revisiting the Volkswagen's carcass, which he was loath to do. It was getting too cold out to walk fifteen miles, so he pressed on, gambling that something in his current direction would be closer. He could just make out a great dark shape ahead of him, blocking out most of the visible sky.

"Mister Butte, I presume."

And then a turn of the road brought him in sight of a set of very bright lights glowing up on the butte's summit.

"Saved," he said, and picked up his pace.

Twenty minutes later, he and the winding switchback road arrived at the summit together, where he saw an impossible sight. A large blue egg-shaped thing was floating motionlessly, low over the top of the trees covering the butte's uppermost cap. The thing was as big as a ranch house, and the source of the lights. Several beams of bright light shone out from the otherwise featureless object, one of which pointed directly earthward, illuminating the extraordinary creatures standing there. There were two of them. One looked like nothing so much as a giant fat slug, with a dozen slimy tentacles of various lengths and sizes growing out of it in a tight cluster two-thirds of the way up on its body. On what Danny imagined was the creature's head, there were eye-stalks, a giant flattened parrot's beak, and two sets of curved horns that would sink almost completely into the black, blubbery flesh, before extruding out again, in an odd pattern and rhythm. The other creature appeared a bit more human, but only in the sense that almost anything would seem more human compared to the slug thing. It looked more or less like what one might get if you put a warthog's head on top of a skinny gorilla's body, and then put the entire thing inside a yellow space suit. Both creatures were holding devices that were unmistakably firearms of some kind.

Danny stood transfixed and gaped in a mixture of horror and disbelief. He must have made some kind of sound, because the two things turned to regard him.

"James!" the warthog ape said, in barely recognizable English. "Damn it, boy, but your leave was up nine hours ago! We were just about to abandon you!"

The other creature just spouted an elaborate series of angry clicks, much like the sounds his car made when he'd tried in vain to restart it.

Danny felt his knees give way and vaguely saw the ground rushing up to meet him. "Drunk again," he heard someone say, as if from a great distance, just before the darkness took him completely.

When Danny woke again, he was in bed, in a small metal-and-plastic room. The warthog ape was standing over him, along with two other creatures, just as impossible. One was a bundle of prickly green spheres, of different sizes, squeezed together in a loose, undulating mass. The other looked like a jellyfish in a steel mesh cage.

"And I say again this isn't James Crowder," Jellyfish said in perfect, unaccented English. Danny couldn't tell how the thing was producing speech.

"How can you tell?" Warthog said. "Who can possibly tell one human from another? He came to the rendezvous site, and no one else showed up, so this has to be him, right?"

"The fur on his head is the wrong length and color."

"They change that all the time. James said as much."

"And James was missing one of the minor manipulating appendages on his main grasping stalks," Jellyfish said. "This human has five such appendages on each stalk."

"So?" Warthog said. "James was finally back among his own kind, for two months' leave. His native medics had plenty of time to grow him a new finger."

The bundle of prickly spheres made a series of noises that sounded like a herd of cows farting.

"First Mate Baradu is right," Jellyfish said. "We don't believe human medics have the ability to regrow lost limbs. And James was proud of his missing appendage, which he lost in his first boarding action. He wouldn't have it replaced. This human is clearly an impostor."

They backed out of the room, leaving Danny alone in it. There were machines and devices here that he couldn't understand, but some things were instantly recognizable. He was on a bed—small and narrow, but a bed just the same. There was a small bookcase attached to one wall, and Danny recognized most of the titles, all of which were in English. There were also a few photographs hung or taped to the same wall and he examined them. Most of them featured a stout man, between thirty and forty, with pockmarked skin, blue eyes, and a salt-and-pepper crew cut. The fellow also had a number of visible scars on his face and neck.

"If this is you, James, how could they possibly mistake me for you?"

In some of the photos, the widely grinning man, who was possibly James, was posing with a number of different creatures. Danny recognized Warthog, and there were several of the huge slug things, like the one who'd been with Warthog on the top of Steptoe Butte.

With a bit of a start, Danny realized that he believed all of it. He wasn't dreaming or hallucinating. He was actually among aliens on board the blue floating thing that must be their spaceship.

They kept him waiting in the tiny bunkroom for hours. Just as Danny had begun to figure out how to deploy what he dearly hoped was a high-tech toilet, the warthog alien came again, alone this time.

"I'm not James Crowder," Danny yawlped, before Warthog could speak.

"I know that now," Warthog said. "And that's dropped us both into a vat of trouble. You stowed away aboard ship under false pretenses. That's a mortal offense. They're going to toss you out of an airlock."

"Why? I didn't pretend to be this James Crowder! I never said a thing! You just took me! And I had no intention of trying to stow away. Just let me go and I'll walk back down the hill and never look back."

"I doubt you'll be walking anywhere, unless other humans have abilities James never possessed. We're back aboard the main ship and already a billion klees out in space, and getting farther from your world every second."

"No fair! Take me back!"

"Now we can hardly do that, can we? No, human, unless we decide to throw you into vacuum, you're coming with us. No other choice."

"You'd kill me, even though it was *your* mistake? This is your fault, not mine!"

"You'll no doubt be pleased to know that the First Mate agrees with you," Warthog said. "He blames me for the blunder. James was my best mate on board and I should've been able to see that you weren't him. But I'll be flayed if one of you ugly monsters doesn't look just like another. In any case, he has a notion that will save your life, keep me from losing rank and share, and prevent him from having to act officially. Here's our story, and I suggest you go along with it: I never made a mistake. I intended to pick you up and take you with us all along. Now that I've made Fourth Rate, I have the option of hiring a personal aide, and that's exactly what I've done. And since James and I were so close, of course he recommended I take on another human, a friend of his who desperately wanted to go to space, just like he did ten years ago. That's why you showed up there at the rendezvous."

"But what about James?" Danny said. "What if he doesn't support your story?"

"Don't be daft, human. We'll never see him again, because

he never made the rendezvous. Who knows why? He's probably drunk or in jail. He was always a fighter, James was. But we'll never be back this way again, because the First Mate is as mad as I've ever seen him and has had quite enough of this place. He's declared Earth, its system, and the entire district off-limits from now on."

That's how Danny Wells became a somewhat less-than-official member of the *Merry Prankster*'s crew. As Mister Orep's personal aide—that was the warthog alien's name—he worked much too hard for far too little pay. He cleaned Orep's room, did his laundry, ran his errands, and performed any other task his master could imagine. And, because Orep claimed to come from a race with a great tradition of public generosity, Danny was often lent out to other members of the crew to provide similar services for them. For the first five years of his life aboard the raider, Danny was miserable.

There were a few compensations. The late Mister Crowder had introduced many of the *Prankster*'s crew to the game of poker. As the only other human ever to serve on board, Danny was allowed (expected in fact) to take over Crowder's regular game. It turned out Danny had a gift for poker and began to sock away some decent money. And the space pirate's medical technology was leaps and bounds more advanced than anything Earth physicians had developed. Being among pirates, Danny might die of violence. It was even likely. But failing that, he would ever and always continue to be roughly twenty years old—in body, if not strictly in chronology.

Danny's generally wretched existence didn't improve until the day they'd overtaken an unarmed merchant ship that turned out to be a Hroo Colonial Battleship in disguise. The Hroo marines boarded the pirate vessel, and all hands, including Danny, had to fight for their lives. He'd picked up a cutlass, whose dead owner had no further use for it, and acquitted himself well enough to impress First Mate Baradu, who'd immediately thereafter promoted Danny to his personal prize crew. Orep didn't mind losing his aide, since he'd been killed in that day's bloody action.

Danny continued to distinguish himself in the years that followed, and slowly worked his way up the ranks.

Now, more than forty years since he'd first come aboard the *Merry Prankster*, quite against his will at the time, Danny was exquisitely aware of the danger he was in. Two of the mob that had crowded into his spacious First Mate's cabin were members of his own prize crew, and he detected no love or loyalty in their eyes.

"This isn't a mutiny," Credogue repeated. "We're a peaceful assembly of your friends and fellow crewmembers, who've come to reason with you."

"Hardly peaceful," Danny said, "when you've got Kyal trussed up and lying on my floor." He didn't want to provoke them, but he was angry and growing angrier. How dare they burst in on him like this! He was the best combat officer in the *Prankster*'s long and colorful history and he'd made each of them rich a hundred times over! He noticed that his any-weapon was just out of reach, lying on the sideboard in its default shape of a simple compact pistol-grip handle, with no actual pistol attached. Attempting to pick it up would most certainly provoke the violence he was trying to avoid at the moment.

"That was an unfortunate but necessary precaution," Credogue said. "Kyal's affection for you is obvious. She'd fight to her death to protect your rights, as she perceived them. We felt it prudent to bind her in this way, to save her from her own worst instincts."

"I'm going to kill you, Credogue, as soon as I'm free," Kyal said from her place at their feet.

"See what I mean?" Credogue said. "She can't be reasoned with. We hope you'll turn out to be more receptive."

"What's your proposal?" Danny said.

"It should be obvious enough. You were a valiant and resourceful combat leader, serving under my father. Every one of us respects and admires you. But you're human, and no raiding ship of the Outer Rings Confederacy has ever been skippered by a human. It may seem odd, given our profession, but pirates are conservative by nature. We're beholden to long and carefully established tradition, and don't respond well to sudden changes. Simply put, we aren't willing to serve under you."

"And yet this isn't a mutiny," Danny said, knowing that his human sarcasm would be lost on most of them.

"Exactly so," Credogue continued. "In the past, many senior officers of this ship and others have retired with honor, taking their accumulated shares and living to spend it in peace and comfort. Even you only ascended to First Rank because Mister Baradu finally retired. Some might say it's an officer's duty to retire at some point, to make way for other crew to advance. Otherwise, we'd constantly have to kill our own to move up in the ranks, and what an unstable system that would be! Mister Wells, you've amassed a considerable fortune during your years among us. So has your aide. We propose that you take it and go home, with our blessing. We've spoken among ourselves and agreed that you should even be allowed to take your boarding yacht, as a bonus in honor of your long years of service."

"See, boss?" Kempee the Vraal said. "It weren't never no mutiny. This here's a retirement party." Kempee loosened the pistol in his holster, to punctuate his remarks. "So, what do you say?"

Two months later, the *Merry Prankster* surfaced on the far edges of Earth's system and remained in place just long enough to spit the *Raptor's Egg* out of its starboard boat dock. Then it turned, fired up its main engines, and began immediate outward accelerations for its next dive into underspace. Danny and Kyal were alone aboard the *Egg*.

"You didn't have to come into forced exile with me," Danny said, not for the first time.

"Of course I did," Kyal said. "They weren't going to let me remain on board, not after you so publicly promoted me to First Rank. The new First Mate would have had to constantly watch his back, always worried I was about to stick my dagger into it. Besides, I wouldn't stay with them if I could. Traitorous scum."

"They would've dropped you in your own system. It was a lot closer than Earth."

"What did that one author of yours say? 'You can't go home again?' In my case, it's literally true. The Sendarians don't take kindly to pirates. I wouldn't have found a welcome there. No, sir, for better or worse, my fate is entwined with yours."

Kyal set their course for Earth at an easy twenty-four g's, explaining that they'd best proceed modestly when they could, since there would never again be a repair dock for the *Raptor's Egg*, or any of its systems. At that acceleration, they'd be more than three weeks getting there, traveling entirely through upperspace, since the yacht had no diving capability. The *Egg* was roomy enough, without an entire boarding crew to accommodate. On the trip out aboard the *Prankster*, they'd had plenty of time to refit it with a separate sleeping cabin for each of them. They'd also installed a more sophisticated automatic sick bay than such a boat normally carried, with ample supplies and programs for both human and Sendarian physiology.

"Better load all weapons," Danny said.

"Why?" Kyal said. "The *Prankster*'s already well out of range, and they'd have had us outgunned anyway. They'd have blown us to atoms, after our first shot." The pirates had let Danny keep the *Egg*'s weapons, knowing that the small integrator cannons it carried were no match for the larger ship's guns and shields. Even so, they'd made sure that all guns were unloaded and powered down, before handing the boat over to them.

"I wasn't thinking about the *Prankster*. I was thinking about Earth defenses. I've been gone for nearly fifty years. Back then the space race was only beginning, but by now they'll likely have bases even this far out. Let's be prepared, just in case they don't recognize us as friendly."

"And just in case they have loot worth taking?"

"No, Kyal, I think I'm done with the pirate life. We're both young and rich enough. Maybe Credogue—may he rot in one of his seven thousand hells—was right in that one par-

ticular at least. Maybe it is time to consider a new line of
work."

"What do you have in mind?" she said.

"Nothing yet. But we have a long trip inward to think
about it. In the meantime let's start monitoring communications and see if we can get a handle on what might be waiting for us. There's a good chance, even all these years later,
that our spacefaring technology is still quite a ways more
advanced than anything they can do. Maybe we can make
an honest living just by selling what we have?"

"You'd sell the *Raptor's Egg*?" She didn't quite gasp her
astonishment.

"No. Never. Just the right to study it. Maybe. We'll see.
Now, if you'll take the first watch, I'm tired. I think I'll
steal a few hours' nap. I haven't slept well in the past two
months, always wondering if Credogue and his cutthroats
might decide to change their minds and save themselves the
trouble of taking us this far outside of civilized space."

"I think Credogue had no choice but to let us go," Kyal
said. "I think most of the crew were still fond enough of us
that they wouldn't have accepted anything less. Credogue's
going to have his tanglers full controlling that mob. Some
might have respected him, but, unlike his father, no one's
ever loved him. My bet is that he'll suffer an unfortunate accident the first time they see action against another ship."

"Wouldn't that be nice?"

For days, they accelerated inward, toward the primary. All
the while, the *Egg* peered far ahead, scouting their way. It
watched and listened, tirelessly gathering and sorting information.

"I don't understand this," Danny said, on their twelfth day
in transit. "There's nothing. No ships. No bases. I can't find
a bloody thing in space, outside of a few odds and ends in
low Earth orbit."

"What did you expect?"

"Lots of stuff. We were in a space race! First we were
going to put a city on the moon and then spread out to fill
the planets. But somehow, for no reason I can find, they just
stopped. And look at these broadcasts. If these are at all up

to date, then none of what they'd always promised ever happened. No jet packs. No flying cars. It's a good decade past the year 2000, according to their calendar, but where did the future go?"

"We can make jet packs for them," Kyal said, trying to calm him. "It's sort of a primitive device, but I suppose we could fabricate a few, if you want."

"That's not the point," Danny said. "It's not what we could make for them, it's about what they didn't become. It's like the entire history of Earth after I left was one giant broken promise."

Danny slept a lot during the remainder of their inbound journey, his frustration and depression growing each day. New information continued to pour in, but it always disappointed him. Kyal, by contrast, studied the data with considerably more enthusiasm than he showed. She spent her days studying every aspect of her new home and trying to imagine what role she might play in it.

"What are you reading?" Danny said one day, wiping the sleep out of his eyes. He hadn't bothered to dress.

"I'm not sure," she said. "Some sort of text accompanied by static illustrations. But I think I may have discovered some of those amazing advancements you've been searching for. Look at this. Each major population center is guarded by one or more humans with incredible powers. See how this man can fly unaided. And he's orders of magnitude stronger than the greatest Sendarian warrior, even one of us in a full battle exoskeleton. These city guardians seem to be engaged in constant battles with other enhanced beings who're determined to destroy your world and everything in it. No wonder Earth has had trouble advancing out into space. These struggles have to be quite a distraction."

"Let me see," Danny said, peering over Kyal's shoulder. "Oh, I understand now. That's not a real account you're reading. That's a work of fiction we used to call a comic book. Back in my day they were printed on paper, in little pamphlets. I didn't know they'd be available electronically by now. Hell, I didn't imagine they'd still exist. In any case, those stories are all made up. Those supermen aren't real.

Funny thing is, once we get home, we'll be the only super-men on Earth."

"How's that?"

"Well, as the wise fellow—whose name I forget—said, 'Any technology sufficiently advanced will seem like magic to a more primitive culture.' Substitute super powers for magic and you have my point. Earth's certainly gone out of its way to remain primitive."

Danny went down to the galley to eat breakfast, leaving Kyal to ponder the implications of what he'd said. Four days out from Earthfall she approached him with an idea.

"Look at this," she said, handing him a reading tablet. "It's another comic book. It's about a superhero called the Blue Shrike and his loyal assistant Clara Zarathustra. They protect a great metropolis called Empire City. He's just a normal man in a mask with a sword cane, but she's the last surviving warrior princess from a lost island paradise. She's ostensibly his servant, acting as his chauffeur and bodyguard, but they're more like equal partners."

"Yeah, I remember reading their adventures way back when, though I suppose I was more a fan of Spider-Man. And Empire City is just a fictionalized version of New York. What about it?"

"They appear in hundreds of books and movies and television programs, as do all of the other comic-book heroes. Your world loves these people. They seem to possess an unquenchable hunger for superheroes."

"Possibly. Who knows? But as I said, they don't really exist. What is it exactly you wanted me to see about the Blue Shrike and his intrepid assistant?"

"She reminds me of me. They remind me of us. I've been thinking about our new lives and careers. Our new chapter."

Micah Orenstein, aka Hammerhead Mike, crept along the darkened corridor on the eleventh floor of New York City's Balder Building. It was late at night. Even the cleaning crews had come and gone. He had his pistol out, a nine-millimeter automatic. He'd come prepared to kill and anyone he might encounter tonight was a potential target. Mike was a torpedo and a good one. Seventeen times before, he'd murdered in the service of the Henry Moth crime family. Tonight would be his eighteenth. Charles Lamar Faulkner had witnessed some things he shouldn't have. Then he'd been foolish enough to admit as much to the police and to reporters and finally to the District Attorney. Faulkner's investment office was in this building, on this floor, and he had the habit of working late. Mike was here on witness cleanup detail.

Mike came to a double set of mahogany doors with a brass plate on them that read: FAULKNER INVESTMENTS. He tried the doorknob and found it unlocked. My lucky day, he thought. He was good at picking locks, but had grown superstitious about it. The one time he'd ever been pinched was when he was caught outside of a jewelry store trying to pick its reluctant back-door lock. That cost him two years of his life. An unlocked door was an especially good omen.

Carefully, he pushed the right-hand door open, taking his time. It swung without a whisper into a darkened outer office. The only light came from another open door beyond the empty receptionist's desk. Mike slid out of his brown loafers and padded silently across the thick carpet. There was a man in the inner office, seated behind a large desk. He was looking directly at Mike as he filled the doorway, but oddly made no move or sound.

Mike could see the man clearly, illuminated by the single desk lamp. He was dressed all in midnight blue. He wore a blue overcoat, blue gloves, a blue fedora, and, adding a profound capstone to the strangeness, a blue mask. The man in blue definitely wasn't Faulkner. He smiled as Mike entered the room. Don't be so happy, Mike thought. No matter who you are, you still have to die, because you seen me here.

Mike raised his automatic and aimed it at the masked man, who still smiled and still made no effort to move. Before he could fire, his gun hand was taken in a powerful grip from behind. Mike felt his arm wrenched violently skyward and then the rest of him followed, until he dangled entirely, and quite painfully, off of the floor. His body spun a bit as it rose and he saw the person doing the lifting. It was a woman who had to be seven feet tall, if she was an inch! She was dressed all in black, including a black mask and chauffeur's cap. She had beautiful golden skin and long dark hair that tumbled like angry silk down her shoulders. And, incredibly, she was holding Mike off of the floor, effortlessly, with one black-gloved hand.

The woman squeezed her grip and Mike's arm exploded in new levels of agony, until he had to drop the gun in his hand. Then she threw him contemptuously away. He flew across the room like a ragdoll, bounced hard off the far wall, and slid nearly senseless to the floor. He lay where he'd fallen, desperately trying to clear his head, catch his breath, and make some sort of sense out of the incredible situation he'd suddenly landed in.

He'd landed facing the office's floor-to-ceiling windows. Outside of the windows, one of which he now noticed had been busted in, he could see a giant featureless blue thing, hanging impossibly in midair.

"That's my *Raptor's Egg*," the man in blue said, noticing the direction of his shocked gaze. "You'll be seeing a lot of it in town, from now on."

The masked man got up from behind the big executive's desk as the giant woman walked over to it and lifted it in two hands, as if it weighed nothing. She turned and held the desk over Mike's head, ready to bring it crashing down on him. Mike heard a choked whimper and realized it had come from him.

"Oh, I don't think that will be necessary, Clara," the man in blue said. He walked to stand over Mike, and as he did so, something grew out of one of his gloved hands and formed itself into a sword with a long and needle-thin blade. "I think our dear Mister Hammerhead knows by now what will happen to him if he tries to move without permission." The man placed the point of his sword under Mike's chin. Mike dutifully froze in place. "There won't be any killings tonight, will there, Mike? Tell your boss, Mister Moth, that Faulkner is under our protection now and is to be left in peace."

The woman shrugged and then casually tossed the desk aside. It landed with a crash and splintered into a thousand pieces.

"Who are you?" Mike cried.

"He's the dreaded Blue Shrike," the woman said, with a smile that could light a skyscraper. "I'm his faithful aide, Clara Zarathustra, the mysterious and hauntingly beautiful last survivor of a magical warrior nation. We're superheroes."

"Pass the word," the man in blue said. "New York is our town now."

FROM THE HEART

JOHN MEANEY

Here's a tense interstellar thriller that demonstrates that sometimes the road onward even from total failure can lead to some very intriguing destinations . . .

John Meaney works as a consultant for a well-known software house, holds a degree in physics and computer science, is ranked black belt by the Japan Karate Association, and is an enthusiastic weight-lifter. He's sold stories to *Interzone*, *FutureShocks*, *Adventure*, *Live Without a Net*, *Sideways in Crime*, and elsewhere. His first novel, *To Hold Infinity*, was published in 1998. His other books include the three-volume Nulapeiron series, which consists of *Paradox*, *Context*, and *Resolution*, and the new Ragnarok series, comprised, to date, of *Absorption*, *Bone Song*, and, most recently, *Dark Blood*. He lives in Turnbridge Wells, in England.

Call it fear, call it overwhelming hysteria, a natural response to floating in blazing space amid a billion suns. He is laughing as well as crying, protected by a slick layer of quickglass that scarcely seems to exist. He imagines he can breathe vacuum, rehydrate from nothing, hang here forever.

The galactic core is beautiful. He feels transcendent yet

empty, because no one should see this alone, so far from everyone.

My love. I've missed you.

Most of the colonized worlds lie in the spiral arm of humanity's birth. Call it irrational fear not to have spread farther, because if the Pilots ever abandon humankind, each world—regardless of location—will be alone.

As he is now, without his love.

My name is Carl Blackstone, and I'm alive!

He catches a taste of salt before the quickglass absorbs his tears, even though the lifesaving layer presses against his eyes, making it impossible to blink against the coalescent brightness of so many suns: the heart of the galaxy.

And there's something else—a streaming length of energy, a jet one thousand light-years in extent, like some shining needle thrust through the galactic core by the hands of a god. Its shining is not just bright but *odd*, as if forming some new chromatic chord.

In the vastness, he is a tiny organism, his life span a cosmic picosecond. A speck against infinity.

I need to warn them, my love.

Humanity may be a fleeting phenomenon in the universe, but it's his species and he *cares*, unlike the bastard who ejected him into vacuum, expecting him to die. Reacting to the memory, his body begins to shake. He is a powerless observer.

I need you so much.

It shines so brightly, the galactic core. What scares him is darkness, moving unseen.

Ten days earlier—or a matter of hours, depending on how you reckon time—and he's on a lower deck of Fairwell Rotunda, inside a lobby, standing near the entrance to a lounge. The cylindrical thirteen-deck tower is formed of deep-orange quickglass splashed with oceanic blue. Visitors consider it opulent, but in Vertigo City, it's a dive.

He has five minutes to go before meeting the woman.

In one corner, a seated group of churchgoers seems to be

celebrating. Their foreheads bear three glistening red dots, equilateral triangles enclosing golden gamma symbols. Some kind of holoscript floats above their table.

Carl double-blinks his smartlenses to zoom in.

This day in history five hundred and seven years ago—apparently—orbiting and ground-based Earth telescopes detected simultaneous gamma-ray burster events, all three of them short-lived, orders of magnitude more powerful than supernovae. They looked like natural phenomena, yet formed a perfect equilateral triangle from the viewpoint of Earth. Their origin lay beyond a cosmological void, one hundred and fifty *million* light-years across, one of those vast volumes of emptiness between galactic superclusters: voids where no ordinary matter reigns.

Web-based systems managed the telescopes, succumbing to a data-corrupting worm attack that took weeks to recover from. Some people claimed that the triangle of gamma-ray bursters was an illusion, either implanted by the virus or an accidental artifact of data reconstruction. Others declared that the observations were real.

No one, before the founding of the Temple of the Equilateral Redemption, had a convincing explanation. But the future Prophet Robinson was born at 3:03 A.M. on March 3, 2013, coincident with the phenomenon. On her thirty-third birthday, divine revelation manifested in the form of—

Carl turns away, blinking his lenses back to normal. Just another memetic cult, a contagion of delusion. Thinking this, he sees a gray-bearded, dark-clad man watching the Equilateral Redemptionists. A priest's collar encircles the man's throat. His eyes—as he glances at Carl—are gentle yet unsettling. Then he turns away.

As the priest leaves the lobby and enters the lounge, Carl rocks in place, suffering a moment of unbalance as if something just shifted at the edge of his vision, yet when he turned to look, nothing was there.

Nerves, that's all.

He's about to book passage and it's strictly illegal. But he will go through with it.

Thoughts of Equilateral Redemption fade as he enters the half-empty lounge. Sitting on a curved couch is a woman whose scalp is pale and shaven, burgundy dragons sliding across it in endless iterative chase. Motile tattoos.

This must be Xala.

"You're Devlin Cantrelle?" she asks.

"Er, yes." It's the name he's lived under for seven years, since arriving here on the world of Molsin. "Looking to buy passage to—"

"Nerokal Tertius, to see the ruins. I heard. And you're a teacher?"

"Um, sure. Gregor TechNet."

Nerokal is under embargo now, as far as Molsin is concerned, and no Pilot is taking passengers there from here, not if they're operating legally. Just another trade war.

Xala's smartlenses film over for extra privacy. Probably displaying his biographical details.

"All right." Her eyes blink back to normalcy. "Orbital ascent in fifty minutes. Departure will be . . . some time afterward."

"You're traveling too?"

"Uh-huh. Me, that family over there"—Xala's glance flickers toward two adults with defeated-looking eyes, then their children—"plus those priests over there. Thirteen in total."

There's a group of six dark-suited men around a table. A seventh stands by a quickglass pillar, watching the room. An old scar forms a diagonal slash beneath his left eye. His hands are muscular, knuckles swollen with callus.

"Priests," says Carl.

Of the seated "priests," five are playing a private game, probably of cards, in a consensual holo controlled by blinks of their smartlensed eyes and flickering finger gestures. The sixth man has a gray beard and gentle eyes: the watcher from the lobby.

"No one's asking *you* why you're traveling this way." Xala's voice softens. "It's polite to extend the courtesy to others."

"Nerokal's off limits to—"

"There are other ways to get there. Like traveling to Fulgor first. *They're* not recognizing the embargo. Have a vacation, say, two days in Lucis City, then fly onward."

"I can't afford that."

"Well, don't worry." Xala picks up a bulb of sweetscent and takes a sniff. "God, I needed that. So, payment. You can afford *our* rates, can't you?"

"Um, sure."

"So do you want to pay in orbit or right now?"

"I might as well—"

"Excellent." Xala gestures a monetary phase-space into being. "Cache payment preferred."

Carl gestures to effect the transfer. It's only a thirteen-dimensional transaction: simple, safe, unlikely to be noticed by the authorities.

"Nice doing business with you, Mr. Cantrelle."

"Er, call me Devlin."

"So what are you going to do while you're waiting, Mr. Cantrelle?"

Carl gestures to the scentbulb. "Would you like an-other—?"

Her expression grows blank.

"Um, right." Carl blinks. "I should leave you to it, I guess. You might get more passengers."

"That'd be nice." She takes another sniff of her sweet-scent. "The more the merrier."

There's a small man looking nervous off to one side of the lounge. Every time the door to the lounge melts open, he practically pees himself. Carl mentally tags him as Mr. Shifty.

"Maybe that guy?"

"Who?" Xala follows his gesture. "Oh, shit. Go relax by yourself, Professor."

"Trouble?"

"Not for us. Not if you act natural and piss off now."

Carl gets up and moves away. Crap. His arms are trembling, and it's not just a question of what's going on with Mr. Shifty here. Carl has spent weeks following hints and talking to the wrong kind of people, slumming it in Vertigo's lower decks. That's been in his spare time, of which there's been more since Fiella moved out—just another of his relationships collapsing for lack of a stable base, one more failure in the sequence.

It didn't take much to convince Xala that he was her kind of customer. Perhaps he should be disturbed by that. But what worries him is the thing he cannot ask about—the identity, or rather the species, of just who will be flying the mu-space ship.

There's a subliminal stirring in the lounge. Carl backs away to stand against the wall, wondering what's about to happen. Then he sees the scarlet uniforms in the doorway— a squad of proctors—and behind them a slim figure dressed in close-fitting black, a long black gold-trimmed cape hanging from her shoulders.

Gods, no. It's impossible.

Her face is triangular, her eyes shining obsidian—black on black without surrounding whites—but it's not just that she's a Pilot. This is Marina, and the chances of her failing to recognize him are zero.

Turning to the quickglass wall, he makes the control gesture known universally as *gotta-pee*. An opening sucks apart, and he steps into an ovoid interior. It seals up behind him, concealing him from the lounge, as toilet facilities are extruded from the floor. A mirrorfield brightens beside him.

He activates the tu-ring on his right forefinger, then turns back to face the way he entered. His ring's covert capabilities are many. Right now it is causing a rectangle of orange quickglass to grow unidirectionally transparent. He wouldn't want anyone out there to see him.

Marina has stepped back, still partly visible beyond the lounge doorway. Everyone else is watching the proctors converge on Mr. Shifty, hands palm-forward as they speak, exercising verbal de-escalation skills that appear to be having an effect. But suddenly Mr. Shifty curls two fingers into a control gesture, leaving the proctors no choice.

He collapses.

"Idiot," says Carl, knowing that no one can hear.

Whatever smartmiasma surrounded Mr. Shifty before, it

has dissolved into dust after a battle lasting nanoseconds, fought at the femtoscopic scale between arrays of tailored smartatoms. That was invisible, but what the proctors do next is designed to make an impression. With glittering tape, they bind him like a mummy, then activate the tape's induction circuits. A lev-field raises him to waist height, where he bobs, suspended horizontally.

"Well done." It's Marina's voice.

She's just the same.

Except that's not true, because ten years have strengthened her tone of decisive command. Carl presses his hand against the quickglass, watching the swirl of her cloak as she turns and then strides out of view. The proctors take their time, maneuvering Mr. Shifty as they leave. They'll be heading away from Fairwell Rotunda, deeper into the city; Marina will be ascending to the rotunda's top deck, more than likely, ready to return to her ship.

He wonders what Mr. Shifty did. Smuggling, probably. He pushes the thought away, forgetting the man forever.

It's Marina who's alive in his mind, her beauty still compelling, along with another memory: the way contempt floated into her black-on-black eyes that time—the moment when he realized that she despised him, when he simply could not say the words to change her mind.

Their friend Soo Lin used to say that success is knowing how to swallow bitterness. Carl wonders what happened to him, where he is now.

I know where I need to go, and the land of memories isn't it.

He dissolves the quickglass wall and steps into the lounge.

"Ten minutes to detachment," sounds through the air. *"Those not traveling outsystem are welcome to remain in the rotunda. Total time away from Vertigo will be two-point-four hours."*

Xala is talking to a pair of hard-faced women—more passengers, perhaps. The so-called priests have gone back to playing cards. The small family are frowning, even the kids. Then the father takes charge, leading them to an expanse

of blank curved wall. He mutters a command. Dark orange
fades to transparency, forming a view window.

Outside are glowing clouds, pale-peach and massive,
among which Vertigo City floats as always. Carl moves
closer, still enjoying the view after seven years here.

"Maybe we shouldn't do this," the husband is saying.

"We've paid." The wife tousles her daughter's hair. "And
we have to, remember?"

There's some family drama here that will remain a secret.
Intimacy even in adversity.

"But dealing with some rebel Pilot—"

"Hush, for God's sake. You want to bring the proctors
back?"

The husband tightens his lips. At a guess, he's enumerat-
ing the possibilities: the whole deal might be a scam; there
might indeed be one or more Pilots willing to break the embargo they're obliged to obey; or it might be a Zajinet ship.
They're the only alien species to have mu-space travel. While
they sometimes maintain embassies on human worlds, their
relationship with Pilots includes violent incidents stopping
just short of all-out war.

Marina. Thinking of Pilots. *Will I ever see you again?*

He's just had his chance. If she were to return, he'd hide
away again.

Remember Graduation.

Bitterness is not helping. Concentrating on his surroundings might be more useful.

"Five minutes to detachment."

The fake priest with the real facial scars is approaching
the view window. Carl mentally labels him Scarface, which
is unkind but specific, a way of keeping track of who is
where.

"Hey, pretty clouds." Scarface turns to the children, pulling his lips back into a predatory rictus. "You kids like it
here?"

The family draws away.

"What are you looking at?" Scarface has shifted his attention to Carl. "You got a problem, my son?"

Oh, shit.

"Er . . . No."

"Good. 'Cause I'm enjoying the pretty view, which is like God's unfolding pattern, got it?"

He laughs. Dread floods through Carl.

He's a psychopath.

In his priest's collar, Scarface is wearing a crossed-winzip icon, symbol of the Church of the Incompressible Algorithm. They believe cosmic history must be played out in order to create God. They don't employ clergy like this. Carl hopes that Scarface and his buddies simply bought fake clothing, because the alternative is a group of priestly corpses decomposing inside shielded quickglass, or dropped into the sulfuric acid ocean below the clouds.

"Three minutes to detachment."

The psycho priest turns back to the view. Perhaps he does enjoy it. Carl backs away, returns to the place where he hid before, and signals *gotta-pee.* Once more, the quickglass pulls apart, forming a chamber. He steps inside, waits for it to seal up, for the facilities to solidify in place, then splashes scented cleanser on his face.

He stares at himself in the mirrorfield. In his late twenties, he should not show stress lines like this. For a moment, he looks like Mr. Shifty.

I'm losing track of who I am.

And that is the danger, the psychological paradox of knowing that he is someone who cannot know who he is.

Shit shit shit.

He doesn't want to go ahead with this voyage. He could bug out now and go back to reviewing student assignments, working with the TechNet's Emergent Persona to improve the—

"For God's sake."

His left hand has risen to his eye almost without volition. Becoming aware, he allows the motion to continue, pressing against his eyeball. He hates doing this.

The lens comes off, adhering to his fingertip.

Remember the truth.

His revealed eye is glistening obsidian, a drop of shining

darkness staring back. Devoid of white, pure black-on-black, the way he is meant to be. He removes the second lens.

Remember.

He stares, centering himself.

"All right."

Then he dabs his lenses back into place, ready to resume pretense.

So magnificent, the galactic center. A billion stars are watching as he pees inside his quickglass layer, release and absorption, tiny amid vastness. Laughable or cosmically significant, he cannot tell.

My love.

Memory, so detailed and treacherous, lives in his mind. The mundane years in Vertigo, the times of wonder preceding them. So many episodes like fractal jewels, the potentiation of his past life as encoded molecules—no human memory is lost.

So many occasions that make up a life.

Pick one.

There were one hundred and seventy-three of them, all of them shit-scared. Aged between seventeen and nineteen standard years, newly graduated, most wearing traditional black. Some wore clothing patched with yellow, green, or red, indicating preference: to live on a planet among ordinary humans; to remain in Labyrinth, shipless; or admit a lack of ambition, accepting anything.

Carl was wearing black—along with the majority—as if determined to gain a ship. He hadn't wanted to, but Gould had insisted. Was it common sense or cruelty? Wearing yellow or green would avoid some of the forthcoming humiliation. At least a little.

It's awful. I can't do this.

But there was no crying off now. He had a fantasy of faking illness, but the medsys nodes would check him out—immediately, given the importance of the ceremony. Besides, half the Pilot Candidates here looked ready to throw up.

"Look at chickenshit Anderson." Riley gestured toward a candidate whose tunic bore scarlet epaulettes. "Accepting judgment, my ass. No way he deserves a ship, and he knows it."

"No one knows for sure what will happen." Soo Lin seemed totally calm. "Perhaps acceptance is best."

"So how come you're wearing black?"

"I know who I am."

"And you know you're going to fly. Exactly my point. Even Blackstone agrees, right?"

Carl dipped his chin. "Er, sure."

"You don't sound it, pal."

"Excuse me?"

"You're not exactly—"

But Marina was walking toward them. Riley fell silent.

"I hope we're all supporting each other." Her voice was beautiful. "So where's Eleanor? Anyone seen her?"

She looked around the mass of sweeping silver spars that formed the hall. In her black jumpsuit, she appeared particularly fit. She was the fastest runner in their year, something she dismissed, proud only of her academic skills.

"Come on guys," she said. "Can you see her?"

Only the palest of golden shimmers touched the air. They might almost have been in realspace instead of an annex of Hilbert Hall, site of the city's formal celebrations.

Just to add to the pressure.

He wished he was one of those Pilots raised on human worlds who would not even bother coming here, knowing that Labyrinth had nothing for them. They wouldn't suffer the humiliation that he was about to—

~Pilot Candidates, make yourself ready.~

The voice reverberated through their minds.

~You have fifteen minutes to compose yourselves.~

Riley rubbed his face.

"Crap. Fifteen minutes. I want my ship"—with a shaky vibrato—"right now."

Marina touched Riley on the shoulder. He blushed.

Carl blinked. He'd always been close to Marina, able to

talk to her like a best friend; but at night he'd dreamed other kinds of dreams. Nothing that might come true, not with his impending public failure.

For she was the instructors' golden girl, favored with access to restricted sections of the Logos Library. He was the quirky one with odd views, out of step with his friends.

"Oh," said Marina. "There's Eleanor. Come on."

Riley and Soo Lin walked with her while Carl trailed behind. He was the first to stop, seeing what Eleanor was up to. Around her, the air seemed to move like sliding shards of ice, followed by a spiraling rotation through angles impossible in realspace.

"Impatient," said Riley, tugging the others to a halt. "Can't blame her."

Eleanor had twisted out of least-action timeflow, electing to pass the remaining fifteen minutes in a rippling subspace where only seconds would pass. Riley looked envious. Probably wished that he could summon up the concentration to follow suit. Instead, he stared at the distortion—like fragmented reflections of Eleanor in a shattered mirror—saying nothing.

That was pretty much how the fifteen minutes passed, with only a few nervous murmurs among the gathered candidates, until Eleanor rotated back into normal timeflow, smiling.

"Hey," said Marina. "Trust you to—"

~Pilot Candidates, move out.~

So this was it. Jostling, they lined up four abreast, then waited while the great doors split into myriad polygons folding back on themselves, revealing a shining walkway down to Borges Boulevard. This was Labyrinth's most notable thoroughfare, within the city yet infinite in extent.

They began to walk.

For them, it was perhaps a five-hundred-meter journey but it *felt* infinite, because overhead were floating tiers of seats with several thousand occupants: Pilots who had arranged their schedules specifically so that they could watch Graduation.

Like the pressure wasn't bad enough already.

Did they remember the joy of it? The nova-burst of ela-
tion when they received their own ships? Because, of course,
these were the winners: true Pilots who lived for voyaging.

I can't go through with this.

But he had to.

Beside him, Marina's face was shining with pride and excitement, and the certainty that today was going to be the
most notable day of her life.

Mine too.

But not in the same way, judging by the sickness building
inside him. He trembled as he walked toward the ending of
his cozy years in Labyrinth; toward shameful humiliation;
to very public failure.

Not long now.

The quickglass splendor of Vertigo City, its towers and
glistening flow-ways, drop far below as Fairwell Rotunda,
detached, ascends toward orbit. A baby is crying in half-
hearted misery; otherwise, the lounge is quiet.

Carl sees that the gray-bearded "priest"—he mentally
labels him Graybeard—has a carry-case at his feet. Interesting. Before Graybeard can notice him, Carl returns
his attention to the view window and the receding glowing
clouds.

Behind him, the family who will be making the voyage
are approaching Xala.

"Er . . . Miss?" says the husband. "I was, er, we were wondering. About the Pilot."

"Don't," said Xala.

"I beg your pardon?"

"Don't wonder or worry about anything."

"Yes, but it isn't only humans who—"

He falls silent. Scarface is approaching.

"Pretty kid you have there." And with a smile: "The
daughter, too."

"I—"

"Better sit down with 'em and keep quiet. Real quiet."

The husband's posture breaks, shoulders slumping, his
skin slick with sweat. As Carl turns away, he can still sense

the fear. Below the conscious level, everyone's reptilian brain reacts to airborne molecules.

"That's good. Blessed are the fuckin' peacemakers, right?"

Carl's back is speckled with tension. There's an atavistic reaction to damaged humans: flaring dread in the presence of a psychopath.

What else should I expect?

Traveling like this, among the desperate and the devious, he's bound to come across people like Scarface, not to mention the watchful Graybeard. There's the criminal element, and there are potential victims broadcasting vulnerability: the family, maybe even himself.

Loser.

He wishes he hadn't seen Marina, at least not now. She'll be on the upper deck, ready to return to her vessel and receive high-paying passengers along with legitimate cargo.

Outside is darkness as they leave the atmosphere. Already some lounges have budded off as saucer-shapes from Fairwell Rotunda, floating away in low-Molsin orbit. Others are headed this way—floating lounges from a previous ascent, needing to return home.

But before that—

Oh, such a beauty.

—a great silver ship springs into being, a spreading-teardrop sculpture of sweeping arcs and gleaming power, stately now as she approaches the orbiting rotunda. Even if Carl hadn't been at Graduation, he'd know this for Marina's ship. She was always exceptional. *"Like vessel, like Pilot,"* is what they say in Labyrinth.

"Is that our ship, Daddy?"

"Shush," answers the mother. "Shush, now."

Chance would be a fine thing. But there's a benefit of being here, because if Carl were on board Marina's ship, he wouldn't get to see the departure. It takes some twenty minutes before she drifts away from the rotunda. Everyone apart from Scarface has lost interest in the view.

Then the shining ship swoops through vacuum, and space-time blazes with sapphire blue, flares nova-bright, and collapses back to ordinary darkness. Marina has left the universe.

"Beautiful."

Graybeard nods in Carl's direction. But it's dangerous to vocalize reactions without reaction, at least in this company. Especially if Xala turns out to be a human agent—call her a spy—for Zajinets.

Right now she's holding out delta-bands, draped across her hands.

"All right, everyone." Xala heads for the family. "Take a band each, press your thumb on the dark pad to activate. Make sure the children are asleep before you use your own."

"Um . . . Don't we put them on after we're aboard?"

One of the false priests clears his throat.

"No," says Xala.

"I . . . Right. Right."

The parents place the delta-bands on their children's foreheads. Young eyelids flutter as protective coma descends.

Crap.

There's nothing Carl can do but accept a band from Xala. The damn thing will induce delta waves in his brain, just like anybody else's. Wonderful. Deep sleep in the presence of psychopaths. Of course, they're waiting for everyone else to go first.

A bulge in the deck morphs into a couch. He sits sideways-on, placing the band on his forehead. It prickles for a few seconds, then feels comfortable. He lies back, wriggling to settle himself as the morphing quickglass adapts.

Move your hand.

Closing his eyes, he starts a mantra going in a stern internal voice.

Remember, move your hand.

For him, feelings of being determined usually start in his lower chest—we encode our feelings viscerally, via the peptide receptors of our internal organs—and then move upward. He visualizes determination as a glowing wheel of light, looping over and over, then spins it faster, more intensely, commanding himself to move his hand after sleep—

Remember . . .
—descends.

Call it a walk of shame.

The candidates marched in time—*left, right, left, right, fail-ure, fail-ure*—beneath the tiers of watching Pilots who—*gods, no*—included Carl's parents. He saw them through a watery haze of shame and stress. They weren't supposed to be here. Hadn't Dad apologized for his commitments in the Eisberg Nebula? And Mom with him.

How can I endure this?

Perhaps it would be better to break formation and run.

"Relax." Marina, in step beside him, spoke with minimal lip movement. "You'll be all right."

No, I won't.

They exited Borges Boulevard, descending to a wide platform that stopped at the edge of a bluish chasm. The far side was the Great Shield, the cliff-like outer wall of Ascension Annex. Great scallop shapes were ranged along the Shield in rows.

~Make yourselves ready, Pilot Candidates.~

They spread out on the platform, all hundred and seventy-three of them, separating by psychological more than physical distance: they were on their own.

Finally, Graduation.

All the years of childhood—his first decade spent on a human world, then the joy of Labyrinth, all the more wondrous for his realspace beginnings—and the growing sense of purpose, the internalizing of discipline, the sense of destiny in life: a rush of memories cascaded through Carl, poignant, making him want to cry.

I can't face this.

High up on the Great Shield, one of the scallop shapes moved.

Too late.

Graduation was starting, and the possibility of running was gone. He could only watch as a white frosty ribbon-path extended from the scallop-door, meandering snake-like toward the platform. It touched, then shivered into stillness.

No one moved.

~Pilot Candidate Ruis Delgado, step forward.~

A slight-looking Pilot Candidate took a step, paused, then walked to the platform's edge.

~Rise and be judged.~

One more pace took him onto the ribbon-path. It began to flow, bearing him upward to the retracting scallop-door. Far off to one side, a giant holo grew, granting everyone a close-up view of Delgado's progress.

He reached the opened doorway and stepped through. Inside was a great pale hangar, and, in the holo, everyone could see what hung there: a ship, purple and cobalt-blue, richly colored and strong.

No one applauded yet.

Tiny beneath the ship, Delgado walked beneath her and held up his hands. When he touched the hull, the ship quivered. Delgado bowed his head.

Then a carry-tendril snaked down from the ship, wrapped around his waist, and lifted him up. On top, the tendril lowered him through the dorsal opening into the Pilot's cabin, onto the control couch he was born to occupy.

As the tendril retracted and the hull sealed up, the Pilots cheered. Applause washed around the great space, echoing in the chill air as the scallop-door closed. Now the holo showed the purple-and-blue ship rising, turning, then flying along a blue-lined tunnel through Ascension Annex.

The watching Pilots quietened.

When the new ship burst out into golden mu-space, everybody roared. Delgado's maiden flight was a triumph. He soared off toward a crimson nebula that shone against a backdrop of black fractal stars: a destination of his choosing.

The holo faded to transparency, a waiting ripple in the air. One hundred and seventy-two candidates breathed out, trying to calm themselves. Some blinked away tears. Delgado's ship had looked strong, capable. A good start.

~Pilot Candidate Adam Kirov, step forward.~

This time the ribbon-path came from low down on the Great Shield.

~Rise and be judged.~

It carried Kirov to the hangar. The waiting vessel was long and bronze, ringed with shining green. When Kirov touched the hull, he tipped his head back and laughed, a joyous sound replayed and magnified from the giant holo's audio. Once more the Pilots cheered and clapped as the ship took Kirov inside. Within a minute, they had burst out of Labyrinth, aimed at a black star, and soared away.

~Pilot Candidate Helena Tchahl, step forward.~

Carl didn't know her. She was wearing a brown tunic with yellow panels, so there was quiet acceptance when a ribbon-path carried her to a bay that turned out to be empty.

~No ship. This candidate has a different path to follow.~

The ribbon-path took her back down, to a platform floating off to one side. Where the losers waited. Tchahl lowered her head, and Carl thought she might be crying, even though her colors indicated that life on a realspace world was what she wanted.

I wish I wasn't wearing black.

There was no escaping humiliation now.

~Pilot Candidate Riley O'Mara, step forward.~

Carl whispered: "Good luck."

Riley walked onto the ribbon-path, tensing his shoulders. He looked strong as the path's flow took him to an opening hangar where a bronze-and-steel ship waited. Tears glistened even as he grinned.

I can't do this.

Soon, Riley had flown out of the floating city, disappearing into golden void. One more triumph.

I really can't.

Somehow Carl remained standing while thirty-one more candidates—he counted—were carried to bays. Twenty-nine of them gained ships. The other two joined Tchahl on the losers' platform. Shipless Pilots.

~Pilot Candidate Carl Blackstone, step forward.~

The waiting path was sparkling white from luminescence and from the blurring of Carl's eyes, peripheral vision darkening under stress. Blood-rush washed in his ears. It was hard to remain steady as the path began to flow, carrying

him over the chasm, up to the Great Shield where shame
was waiting.

A scallop-door retracted to reveal an empty bay.

This is awful.

He looked back, unable to make out faces, just patches of
color.

~No ship. This candidate has a different path to follow.~

Then the ribbon-path bore him down to the platform
where Tchahl and the other failures waited. Shaking, he took
his place, trying to accept what was happening. Worse than
expected, and he'd known it would be bad.

He looked up only twice: once when Soo Lin gained his
ship, a bronze-and-turquoise vessel with bold curves; again
when Marina rose for judgment.

In the holo, her face was radiant, and no wonder. Her ship
was of sweeping silver, a strong yet elegant flower, a spreading teardrop with no need for the usual delta-wings. For such
a striking ship to have grown in Ascension Annex, her Pilot
must be a person of unusual talent.

Carl had always known Marina was special.

Applause began even before the ship took her inside. Then
she was soaring through a tunnel to golden space, launching into fractal infinity, heading for Mandelbrot Nebula: the
boldest choice for a maiden flight. The cheering lasted after
the holo faded.

On the losers' platform, Carl began to cry.

He drifts in golden sleep.

One of the neurolinguistics instructors, back when Carl
was an Academy student with years to go before humiliation, talked about yawning, the way that yawning was an
interesting phenomenon, although it tired some people as it
made them want to yawn now when they thought about—

Carl had been the first to laugh, fighting down the yawn
that everyone was starting to manifest. A holoscan had
flared—tuned to Soo Lin—showing activity in the left
cortex, orchestrated with the voice- and semantic-processing
centers of the right hemisphere. And it had delineated the
changing neurology—in the precuneus nucleus and anterior

cingulate—that forms the basis of hypnosis, because the instructor had used subtle tonality to slip mesmeric suggestions into his voice.

Now, though Carl is asleep, his hand is rising.

Some part of him is aware of golden light flooding his surroundings, passing through everything, while his sense of time vibrates to the possibility of fractal flow. There is no place he can be except mu-space. His hand is almost at the delta-band—

No!

—when everything grows cold, and his hand drops back. The ship is plunging into realspace. He has missed his chance.

Someone powers off the delta-band and pulls it from his forehead. "Ugh." He squints, trying to focus. "Where—? Ugh."

"Where are we?" It sounds like the father of the family. "What kind of ship is this?"

Carl pushes himself up, puts one foot on the floor, ready to stand, then decides to stay where he is. Flowmetal walls have configured into a row of nozzles: the business end of smasers. Coherent smartatoms can tear through anything.

An invisible smartmiasma would be even deadlier, but less intimidating. Then again, this has to be a Zajinet ship, and their understanding of psychology is hard to judge.

A short laugh sounds from Carl's left. Scarface is sitting up, staring at Xala.

"This ain't no scheduled stop," he says. "This is a robbery."

Xala stares back, her face impassive. But her motile tattoos are scrolling across her scalp with agitated speed.

"No robbery," she says. "We have a little problem."

The other false priests are also sitting, making no attempt to leave their couches. They've seen the smasers. Luckily, the children are still asleep. Xala has removed the delta-bands only from the adults.

"It's the Pilots, isn't it?" moans the kids' father.

"Say what?"

"They're coming to get us, to blow us out of—"

"Oh, shut up," says Xala. "Someone here isn't who they claim to be."

Among the "priests," only Graybeard appears calm, his brown eyes tranquil, as if in prayer. The others look ready for violence.

"Look, sister," says Scarface. "Just 'cause we have the collars and all, doesn't mean we're really pretending to—"

"One of you isn't quite human."

Oh, shit.

How can they know? Did they see his hand rise under autohypnotic suggestion while he was deep in coma?

I can't move faster than a smaser beam.

If they want him to die, he's going to. Today, now, with memories of humiliation refreshed in his mind by the sight of Marina in Fairwell Rotunda. Churning waves of acid shift inside him, a neurochemical tide, a certainty of ending.

He might as well try something.

Now.

He is ready to move, but Graybeard appears to flicker among dark shadows and then he's behind Xala, one hand cupping her chin, the other at the back of her neck. She is between him and the row of nozzles. The delta-bands lie at her feet.

"Bad mistake." Graybeard's voice is gentle. "Threatening your passengers."

"Too right." Scarface swings his feet to the deck. "We ought to—"

"Stay where you are," says Graybeard.

Scarface holds himself still. So does Carl.

Not me. She didn't mean me.

The false priests have also frozen. They're professionals, trying to assess the tactical situation.

"Mmph."

"No need to speak, sweetheart." Graybeard tightens his grip on Xala. "I'm talking to your masters. I *feel* you out there, you bastards."

For a second, shards of darkness appear to revolve through the air, then nothing. What the hell is happening?

There is an awful calmness in Graybeard's voice.

"Change of plans," he says to Scarface. "We're going to drop off as before, but a different place, and you're not coming with me."

"Bug out?"

"Back to Molsin, then your individual routes, which I don't want to know. They're not compromised."

"But we—"

"And you've already been paid," says Graybeard. "Check now, if you like."

Xala's skin is white where his fingers are digging around her mouth. He backs away, pulling her with him, until they're standing beside something on the deck. The case he was carrying earlier.

One of the fake priests examines a financial holovolume, nodding.

"It's all there."

Behind him, the flowmetal wall begins to split and curl apart. He steps aside. In the opening, a fiery lattice of red light is floating. Beside it, what appears to be a mass of blue sand, about the same size, stands on the deck.

They are Zajinets. The glowing lattice is their natural form. Sometimes they clothe themselves in matter: gravel, sand, organic material. The red entity begins to pulse, which may be a sign of emotion; but with Zajinets, nobody knows.

"You both came," says Graybeard. "That's nice."

<<*Darkness will not flee.*>>
<<*Weak agents so we do not care.*>>
<<*Strength in coherence.*>>
<<*Beware the light.*>>

The quadruple communication comes from the unclothed Zajinet, though how Carl knows this, and how he can hear the words which are not truly sound, he has no idea. Each Zajinet mind is a quantum superposition of overlaying neural plexi—or so the theory goes. He never expected to meet one in person.

Every conflict between Zajinets and Pilots has been short-lived, no matter how violent. No one knows what to make of that.

"I think you're bluffing." Graybeard squeezes Xala. "I think you do care about her."

Carl blinks.

He understands it?

This may be the strangest thing to have happened today. What did Xala say? *One of you isn't quite human.* And the subject of her sentence turns out to be Graybeard.

Those shards of darkness, a shift in nothingness . . . a motion of *absence*. Right now, Graybeard looks like an ordinary person, but it's some kind of facade.

Xala's scalp tattoos are writhing. Her eyes are bulging.

You know the lightning.

It's a memory, the voice of one of his instructors.

You know how fast it moves.

The words can trigger behavior laid down below the conscious level, in the amygdala where the brain reacts at speed.

Become the lightning.

It's time to move. Carl shifts forward just as Graybeard's tu-ring flares red, and the shining Zajinet's lattice-form is tugged as if caught on a hook.

Carl pulls himself back.

"You'll drop me off at a location you know well," Graybeard tells the Zajinets. "And you'll do it for your own sakes as well as the woman's."

Just for a second, there appears to be a redness in the air.

<<*Entanglement is mutual.*>>
<<*Beware beware beware.*>>
<<*Agree to projection.*>>
<<*Severance or mutual death.*>>

Graybeard smiles.

"Agreed. Drop me alone at the highway station. I'll kill the link as you move onward."

Then Graybeard drags Xala back against the wall, and pulls her down with him so they are sitting on the deck, as close as lovers.

"Do the honors, will you?" he asks Scarface, nodding to the bands that Xala dropped.

"What? You mean the delta-bands?"

"Right." With a stare in the direction of the Zajinets: "Since we're about to get going again."

As the flowmetal wall begins to seal up, the Zajinets are already moving out of sight in the corridor.

Scarface offers delta-bands to the mother and father.

"Put them on, press here"—he points—"and you'll sleep. Otherwise, mu-space will send you insane."

He stops and looks at Graybeard.

"I don't like this. You're going to be the last to sleep, right?"

"You've been paid."

"That's the reason I'm going along with it."

He resumes handing out the delta-bands.

"You don't frighten easily"—Graybeard turns to Carl— "for an academic."

Carl finds himself swallowing.

"Er . . . I'm scared." It's easy to allow his voice to vibrate. "Believe me."

"Good."

Carl isn't just frightened. He's trying to work out what Graybeard did with his tu-ring that forced the Zajinets to obey. Right now, the smaser nozzles are melting back into the wall, and he senses the ship getting ready for mu-space.

"Put the band on, Professor."

Shit.

He lies back, places the band on his forehead, and reaches up. Then his eyelids flutter as his hand drops down.

"There you go, Xala." Graybeard's voice. "Sweet dreams."

"That's everyone." This sounds like Scarface.

"After you."

"Yeah. Sure."

Carl waits. Either they think he's pressed the band or they believe it doesn't matter, that he's only seconds away from being driven insane by the fractal reality of mu-space.

Silence.

Everyone else is probably asleep. If he's quick, he might be able to—

Transition.

Golden light is flooding through him. He opens his eyes.
At last.

He's back in the continuum where he belongs. And this time, he's awake.

The Logos Library, infinite within its boundaries, held an uncountable number of carrels: spaces for solo study or simple retreat. In one of them, Carl sat at a desk and cried.

The party had been—still was, elsewhere—a noisy, energetic maelstrom of pulsing music and triumphant fun, laughter, and pride, toasts to new beginnings, a celebration of the hundred and nineteen vessels added to the fleet for the benefit of humanity at large. He had suffered through it, avoiding his parents but knowing that he would have to face Marina. And, eventually, he did.

"I'm sorry." Her triangular features had saddened. "We'll still be . . . friends."

"Right. You'll be exploring the galaxy and I'll—" He had pushed out a breath, trying to expel his bitterness. "You did so well. Really, really well."

Her pleasure had been real as she smiled. Amazed pleasure.

"Isn't she beautiful?"

"One terrific ship. Everyone's talking about her."

"Yes. Look, I have to go see Commodore Durana."

"Daredevil Durana?"

"*She* wants to talk to *me*. Would you believe it?"

"That's really—"

"See you around, Carl."

Turning away, she had dipped her head. They had all been drilled in the neurophysiology of communication, and knew when to hide their own reactions. But Carl had already begun his extra training, had learned to read the minutiae of gesture and movement, and wished he hadn't. In her eyes, in the tightening of the muscles above her upper lip, she had broadcast her message in clear.

A part of her despised him.

Marina . . .

Public shame had dissolved whatever compelling image

she'd held of Carl. Words had risen up inside him then, a plea for new understanding, but she had already moved into the mass of happy, celebrating Pilots. Fighting down emotion and the urge to blurt out his feelings, he had found a quiet exit and used it.

Everything had changed the moment she had turned away.

I loved you.

But that was over. It had to be over.

Now, as he sat in the lonely carrel amid stacks of infocrystals, he felt as if something had severed the cord of his life. The old part had been cut away from the new, for everything was different now.

Focusing on breathing, the simplicity of inhale-exhale, he began to center himself.

~*It's time.*~

When he looked up, he felt calm.

"I know," he said.

With golden mu-space energy flowing through him, he lies on the couch, feeling ready. Whatever happens next, it will be in his own continuum, where he truly comes alive. For someone like him, this is what makes a dual life worthwhile.

He throws the delta-band aside and sits up. Everyone is sleeping: Graybeard slumped against the wall, Xala curled beside him, the others on their couches.

"Now we'll see."

Smiling, he powers up his tu-ring's weaponry. In front of him, the flowmetal wall pulls apart, revealing the fore-to-aft corridor.

Time to do it.

Forget the past, for this is where he belongs, in places and moments like this.

On the edge.

Leaving the Logos Library, he took a quiet route, bypassing Borges Boulevard and the Great Shield, entering Ascension Annex through an obscure entrance. The bronze-petal door folded back at his approach. Inside, the floor pulled him along, through a screen of sapphire light, then another of coruscating emerald. Finally, the floor swirled to a halt in a great ovoid hall where no one was waiting.

"I'm here."

An oval of wallspace melted away, allowing a blocky figure to enter. Rolled-back sleeves revealed massive forearms. Shaven-headed and jet-eyed, he stared at Carl.

"Your emotional state, Pilot Candidate?"

As far as the rest of Labyrinth was concerned, Carl was a candidate no longer.

"Surviving, Commander."

"You got through the celebrations."

"Yes." Carl thought of Marina, her look of contempt burned in his mind forever. "With no desire to go back and explain myself."

"Not even a little?"

Carl took the question seriously, as Commander Gould intended.

"None, sir. Not now."

Gould smiled. "Then it's time to face the real ordeal, don't you think?"

The commander led the way to the far wall. It shimmered, sparkled, transformed into a lattice of floating white stars, and then dissolved. Beyond was a great bluish hangar bay, and inside—

My God.

—hung a black dart of a ship with fine scarlet edging. Small compared to others, but this one would never carry passengers or cargo. Her power capacity was orders of magnitude above normal. Even at a glance, he could tell that she had maneuverability and firepower that were outstanding.

She's beautiful.

Powerful, with an air of being on the brink of speeding movement, on the edge of dynamic balance, like a sprinter in motion . . . she was designed to hold one Pilot, only him.

So beautiful.

Carl Blackstone, Pilot.

"Take her out, son." Commander Gould's hand was on his shoulder.

"There are so many people in Labyrinth now," Carl said. "Can I really—?"

~You will be unobserved.~

Commander Gould looked upward.

"The city has spoken, Pilot Blackstone. She'll make sure you leave unseen."

"Thank you."

There was no need to ask about stealth capability. He knew, inside himself, that his ship had everything.

"Enjoy your triumph, Carl." The commander had not used his first name before. "A very private triumph, because that's the nature of the beast."

"I know."

"Of course you do. It's why you were chosen. Why you chose yourself. Because you can score victory with no need to boast, face defeat in obscurity, endure public shame."

"Yes . . ."

"Because that's what it means to be a spy."

But there was no remembering humiliation now, not with *her* in front of him, his black-and-scarlet ship. His beauty, who would have to remain here or fly alone for so much of his life, her commitment as great as his.

"She'll always be faithful, Carl, and there when you need her."

I know.

Carl reached up for his ship—his beautiful, wondrous, powerful, lovely ship—to carry him up, to take him inside herself in a moment of beauty and triumph.

Private triumph.

Standing before a bulkhead, he points his fist and holds it there. There is no flare of light, but the flowmetal pulls open as his tu-ring completes its work, revealing the windowless control cabin. Inside, the two Zajinets are floating: one a shining lattice of red, the other glowing azure, now unclothed.

<<Greetings, Pilot.>>
<<Greetings, Pilot.>>
<<Greetings, Pilot.>>
<<Greetings, Pilot.>>

It is the red one communicating. What's astounding is the clarity of its message—its solitary meaning instead of overlaid confusion.

"You knew I was here?"

<<Not until you awoke. Then we knew.>>
<<Not until you awoke. Then we knew.>>
<<Not until you awoke. Then we knew.>>
<<Not until you awoke. Then we knew.>>

Earlier, the Zajinet had used the word *entanglement* in response to Graybeard's command. There's a link in place between Graybeard's tu-ring and the Zajinet, a link powerful enough to change the alien's mental state in a new way.

Carl's own tu-ring grows dull, not at his command.

<<We are not your enemy. We never have been.>>
<<We are not your enemy. We never have been.>>
<<We are not your enemy. We never have been.>>
<<We are not your enemy. We never have been.>>

Perhaps it is true, but there have been encounters in the past, with the Zajinets targeting Pilots rather than ordinary humans.

"What's he carrying?" Carl meant Graybeard. "And why is it important?"

Before coming on board, he had no idea whether he was investigating an illegal venture with Zajinets or a renegade Pilot of his own kind. Now the parameters have shifted beyond recognition, and illicit ferrying of passengers means nothing.

And Graybeard has the means to threaten Zajinets into submission, which makes his tu-ring almost as interesting as the contents of the case he is carrying.

<<Darkness. He carries darkness.>>
<<Darkness. He carries darkness.>>
<<Darkness. He carries darkness.>>
<<Darkness. He carries darkness.>>

So much for thinking that the Zajinet has achieved clarity.

*<<His kind are centuries old inside your species. Yet you
do not see.>>*

*<<His kind are centuries old inside your species. Yet you
do not see.>>*

*<<His kind are centuries old inside your species. Yet you
do not see.>>*

*<<His kind are centuries old inside your species. Yet you
do not see.>>*

He looks at the other Zajinet. Faint blue lines link it to
the convolute sculpture of the controls. Perhaps it's busy.

"What do you mean by darkness?"

Suddenly, the golden light that was ubiquitous shivers out
of existence, and the air feels cold. They are back in realspace.

<<You have two minutes before he awakens. Wake Xala.>>
<<You have two minutes before he awakens. Wake Xala.>>
<<You have two minutes before he awakens. Wake Xala.>>
<<You have two minutes before he awakens. Wake Xala.>>

He has a hundred and twenty seconds in which to attempt
sensible conversation with a Zajinet or to take action. He's
already jogging back along the corridor as the thought completes. At some point, his tu-ring comes back to life.

Inside the passenger cabin, everyone is still sleeping. Carl
tears the delta-band from Xala's forehead.

"Ow! Shit."

"Sorry."

"I'm going to have a migraine." Dragon tattoos swirl
around her scalp. She pushes herself away from Graybeard.
"Bastard."

"We've only got a few seconds."

"Huh. So how come you're awake first?"

Carl gestures toward the front of the ship.

"Ask your friends."

"My—? I need to know more than that before—"

"And I need to know what's in the case. What this
bastard"—he nudges Graybeard with his foot—"is carrying."

"So take a look."

She taps on the case. The top splits open, revealing nothing.

"It's empty, Xala."

"Try lifting it up."

This is annoying, but Graybeard's eyes are shifting beneath closed eyelids. Carl takes hold of the case and . . . tugs without effect.

"What's this? A mag-field?"

Bracing himself, he squats and pulls, raising it several centimeters from the deck, then lets it thump down. But the casing should be lightweight, its mass measured in grams, not tens of kilos.

"No mag-field," says Xala. "It's the device inside that's heavy."

"Device?" Carl puts his hand inside the hollow case. "There's nothing there."

"Like a ghost. Because of what you're made of."

Graybeard's head moves from side to side, and he moans.

"He's waking up." Xala's voice drops. "Shut the damn case."

"I— All right. What happens if something triggers the link between that"—he points to Graybeard's tu-ring—"and the Zajinets?"

"They die, the ship blows up. What did you expect?"

He seals up the case.

"What ghost?" he asks. "What do you mean by that?"

"Your hand passed right through it."

"Because . . . ?"

"Because *you're* the ghost, or haven't you worked it out? You and me both."

Carl looks at the case.

"You can't mean—"

"The device is made of dark matter. You know, the *real* stuff that we're *not* made of, and can't interact with. *We're* the ghosts, didn't you know? Most of the universe is something we're *not*."

The tattoos are scarcely moving on her scalp. Her voice is steady. She believes her own words.

"If it's dark matter, the case wouldn't contain it."

A hard grip snaps onto his wrist.

"Well that," says Graybeard, "is the real trick, isn't it?"

"Crap."

"I *thought* you were trouble."

The whole cabin—no, the entire vessel—vibrates, then grows steady.

"That'll be my lift," adds Graybeard. "I think, Professor, you should come with me."

"No." Carl twists his wrist and torso together, disengaging from Graybeard's grip. "Not a chance."

"You know what? Forget it."

Graybeard picks up the case left-handed—stronger than he looks—and smiles as the outer wall begins to melt open. Beyond is a transparent-domed shuttle, and through it, the stars are visible.

A magnificence of stars. A billion incandescent suns.

"Where are we?" whispers Xala.

"It's the core," says Carl. "The galactic core."

Graybeard's right fist remains trained on them as he backs toward the waiting shuttle, lugging the case. The shuttle's clear hull grows permeable. The faintest of sucking sounds accompanies Graybeard's passage through the material. Then the hull begins to vitrify once more.

The others, including the remaining fake priests, remain asleep. They know nothing of what's happening. Perhaps they're about to die without ever waking up.

Make a move.

Because there's no reason to trust Graybeard. Obeying a command from someone who threatens you is tactically stupid except to gain time—and time has run out.

"Tell them to get back into mu-space, Xala. Tell them."

"Why would—?"

"Now."

In the Academy, Marina was the best runner, but Carl has learned to sprint because sudden bursts of speed save lives. He hurtles forward, lowering his chin, striking the still-permeable hull with the top of his head. The stuff is growing viscous—*push hard*—but then he's through, tumbling into the shuttle, falling to the deck.

He snatches for Graybeard's ankle, but the bastard pulls back.

"Bye-bye, everyone."

As Graybeard makes a fist, his tu-ring flares; while behind Carl, a sudden nova-brilliance indicates a transition to mu-space. Did they make the jump in time? It's impossible to tell.

A percussive thump knocks him backward.

What was that?

He pushes himself to a sideways position on the deck. Stellar abundance shines behind Graybeard's outline, while the strangest of non-movements, shifts of half-glimpsed nothingness, surround him.

"No," says Graybeard. "I think I'll just get rid of him."

Like movement at the edge of vision, and when you turn around, nothing is there.

"That's right," adds Graybeard.

And the flickers of darkness are gone. So is the power in Carl's tu-ring. Again.

"Balls."

"Tsk. I hope you prayed to the Equilateral Redemption." Graybeard's smile is nasty. "Just follow the line of the highway, keep staring for a few centuries till the photons get here, and you'll see what the believers were on about. Beacons in a triangle, very neat."

"What highway?"

"You'll see. 'Course, you haven't exactly got centuries. More like minutes."

"Until what?"

"Until nothing ever again. You know that blood boils in a vacuum, right?"

"You can't—"

"Of course I can."

This time the thump is harder. It's massive, invisible, and the shuttle is receding from him, hard to see with his blurred vision and his inability to breathe—but if the shuttle is already far away it means he's in empty space—*ejected me, the bastard*—and panic slams through him even as he feels the hidden loop of quickglass begin to stir around his waist.

Stars, brilliant clouds of stars, pass across his vision as he begins to tumble. When he tries to find the shuttle, he can no longer see it against the glory of the galaxy's core. Massed suns, stupendous light, not a molecule to breathe.

He mentioned a station.

When Graybeard was talking to the Zajinets, he used the term *highway station*. Some kind of orbital near the galactic center?

What highway?

Spreading across his skin, cool and slick, the quickglass reaches his throat, his chin, then envelopes his face. He squeezes his eyes shut, accepting the intrusion into nasal cavities and throat, sucking in oxygen already. After a moment, he forces his eyes open, squinting against the bright blur as quickglass merges with and absorbs his smartlenses.

It is already subsuming his clothing for additional fuel.

What highway?

As his vision clears, he begins to accept the reality of floating in brilliant emptiness, the backdrop of massed suns and . . . a long stream of light, a massive collimated beam of energy: a galactic jet some thousand light-years in length, a divine needle in our galaxy's heart.

This?

Surely this is no highway.

It has been some hours now, but it's all right.

Come to me, my love.

She was so far away; but she is closer now.

I need you. I always need you.

Slowly rotating, he sees once more the galactic jet, a shining pointer whose continuation would pass through Earth, all the way beyond this galaxy, this cluster of galaxies, to the far side of a dark-matter void where, an eon ago, three gamma-ray bursters exploded.

Correction: we *call* it void, but it's the space where the *real* stuff resides, in who knows what forms and structures, while we of ordinary matter are the ghosts who cannot touch the greater reality. Humans and Pilots; ghosts and dreams.

But if this is a highway under construction, you have to ask: is this the source or the destination? And what is the nature of the travelers?

Maybe they'll be friendly.

It would be nice to think so, but it was one of their human agents who ejected him into space, expecting him to die. If it wasn't for what's about to happen, he'd be flooded with angry fear, cursing in his mind.

Come on, darling.

He cannot see her yet, but he is certain.

Come on, my love.

Somewhere, through a golden space draped with crimson nebulae and speckled with black stars, speeds a black dart edged with scarlet, concentrating her superlative power, following an extreme geodesic that few of her kind could contemplate.

For her need is as great as his.

Soon.

Floating above the heart of the galaxy, where the stars shine a thousand times brighter than out on the spiral arms, Carl Blackstone is smiling.

Soon.

CHAMELEONS

ELIZABETH MOON

W ith enemies all around you, sometimes your best bet is to hide in plain sight. Of course, if your enemies spot you, that means that they also know where to find you . . .

Elizabeth Moon has degrees in history and biology and served in the U.S. Marine Corps. Her novels include *The Sheepfarmer's Daughter*, *Divided Allegiance*, *Oath of Gold*, *Sassinak and Generation Warriors* (written with Anne McCaffrey), *Surrender None*, *Liar's Oath*, *The Planet Pirates* (with Jody Lynn Nye and Anne McCaffrey), *Hunting Party*, *Sporting Chance*, *Winning Colors*, *Once a Hero*, *Rules of Engagement*, *Change of Command*, *Against the Odds*, *Trading in Danger*, *Remnant Population*, *Marque and Reprisal*, and *Engaging the Enemy*. Her short fiction has been collected in *Lunar Activity and Phases*, and she has edited the anthologies *Military SF 1* and *Military SF 2*. Her novel *The Speed of Dark* won a Nebula Award in 2004. Her most recent book is a new novel, *Victory Conditions*.

Bryce Gosslin had never intended to come back to Novice. Sixteen years had not erased the memories; he'd told his employer about his reasons for avoiding Novice when given this itinerary. His employer had laughed.

"You'll be fine, Bryce. You shouldn't have more than a twelve-hour layover between the charter and the *Altissima*—" The *Altissima*, flagship of his employer's fleet of luxury liners, would be as safe for the youngsters as their own home. "Just keep them in the Premier Lounge area and nothing can happen."

Bryce had sworn he'd never go back, but he was still half a standard year short of getting permanent status in the best job he'd ever had. He'd nodded, said yes, sir, and accepted his orders.

Now they'd arrived at Novice Station. The charter yacht that had picked them up had special clearance to dock in the Blue Zone, but only to put its passengers safely onto the station's Premier Lounge. Then it would transfer to the general-transport side of the station for refueling and reassignment.

Bryce watched as the yacht's crew put their luggage into the *Altissima* storage lockers, then withdrew. The boys shifted from foot to foot. Karl, the elder, looked much less boyish than he had three standard months ago, when Bryce had escorted him to Eleyon for vacation. Part of that was pure sulk, Bryce thought. He'd done nothing but complain since Bryce arrived to take them to the yacht. Part was muscle—he'd been working out more, and it showed.

"I'm sixteen," he'd said. "I'm not a child. I don't need an escort—nor does Evan, really. I could take care of Evan; I have two black-belt ratings in two different martial arts. Nothing ever happens anyway. We use false IDs, so we're not trouble magnets—"

"School files and vacation resort files can be hacked," Bryce said. "The older you get, the less your cover IDs will work."

Now Karl glowered at the docking bay where the charter yacht's crew had already sealed the hatch.

Evan, the younger, looked around the small entrance lounge. "Where's Immigration and Customs?"

"We won't need to go through," Bryce said. "We're just here to transfer to *Altissima*—as long as we stay in the premier lounge—" He moved to the exit from the arrival bay, hoping Karl would follow and not make another scene. Karl's sigh was audible, but he came along, as Bryce pushed through semi-elastic membrane that read their biometrics and registered them into the Premier Lounge.

Bryce had never visited the Premier Lounge when he lived on Novice Station. He hadn't known there was one. He'd been, variously, in a cheap sleephole, a restaurant kitchen washing dishes for a chance at the scraps, in lockup as an undesirable, and, finally, shipped as common labor on an ag transport full of pregnant rabbits a colony world might want.

He'd been in luxury lounges since, on his employer's business, and this one did not impress. The carpet was stained—someone had tried to clean it, but left a different stain that did not quite match the outline of the original. The furniture looked plush enough, but as he neared the first couch, he saw signs of wear. The information booth had only an automated attendant, whose accent was nearly unintelligible. Bryce persisted: was *Altissima* on schedule?

No. The liner was delayed—arrival date now uncertain but at least three days away.

Three days with the boys—Bryce had a sinking feeling that things were about to go very wrong.

"We'll check into rooms," he said.

"When's it coming?" Evan asked.

"It's delayed. They estimate three days."

"I am not staying cooped up in here—" Karl glared around the Premier Lounge, "—for three days."

"For now, you are," Bryce said. "That's what your father said to do. First we check into rooms, find someplace to eat—" Another deficiency of this so-called Premier Lounge: where were the upscale eating establishments? The shops? The entertainments? "—And then we'll see," Bryce said.

The auto-attendant flashed a series of options on its screen. Only one sleeper: the Premier Suites, through the sliding door on the far side, third entrance down. Bryce reserved two executive suites, connecting. Only two eating places: Jargooli's Junction, offering "Strickly orgenic fuds for discriminalling custimers" and Sheehan's Bar & Grill, "All U

Can Eat, All Day, All Night." The only listing under "Entertainment" was "Novice Public Library, Premier Branch."

Bryce led his charges through the reluctantly sliding door at the far side of the lounge space, noticing yet more signs of economic uncertainty. Here the carpet had an obvious wear path down the middle, and the walls were scuffed and stained. The two entrances before Premier Suites had official seals warning visitors not to enter them. Premier Suites itself had a lighted logo out front, but of a much-lower-level chain hostelry.

Bryce pressed the entrance button; lights flared beyond the door, and a heavyset man with a rumpled, stained tunic lumbered into view. As he neared, Bryce had the uneasy feeling that he had seen the fellow before. The man unlocked the door and said, "You're the new reservation?"

"That's right," Bryce said. "Bryce Gosslin and nephews Karl and Evan Terrine."

The man made a face, then stepped back and waved his arm. "Welcome to Premier Suites. We don't get that many travelers staying several days. I've turned on the room cleaners, but it'll be a few minutes. You got luggage?"

"Yes," Bryce said.

"I can get it for you, if you want," the man said. "Or you can bring it—the rooms'll be ready by then, most likely."

"Karl—" Bryce began, but Karl heaved a dramatic sigh.

"I know—you want us to fetch the luggage. Come on, Ev. Uncle B wants to chat with another grown-up . . ."

"I'm coming," Bryce said. He shrugged at the man and turned away. He was not going to leave Karl alone in the main lounge in this mood. He caught up with the boys before they reached the sliding door.

"This is boring," Karl said. "There's nothing to do, and no one to talk to—it's deserted."

"Does look pretty empty," Bryce said, in as pleasant a tone as he could manage. "But it's mid–second shift here. Let's see . . . our *Altissima* IDs should get us access . . . " He put the premier-class ticket card into the slot; the reader whirred and spat the card out. Nothing moved. He looked at the card—had he put it in backward? No. He tried again.

Again the whirring and the card's return, and the luggage bin did not unlock.

"Try mine," Evan said, holding it out.

"I'd rather not risk it," Bryce said. "Some of these machines will swallow a card if you try the same thing too many times." He looked for any of the standard biometric readers but didn't find one. "We'll just have to find someone to help us. Perhaps the information clerk—"

At the information desk, the automated clerk did not respond. Bryce tapped the desk and finally tapped the clerk's head. Nothing happened.

"Now what?" Karl asked. "If we can't get our luggage, we don't even have dentabs, let alone sleepskins."

"I was wondering that myself," Bryce said. "And my first thought is the charter." He pulled out his parle and flicked it. The display bloomed in the air in front of them; he ticked his way through the station directory, noted the yacht's docking assignment, the red dot that meant the dock was indeed occupied, and touched the correct icon.

"Dock Yellow Thirteen, berths one through ten," a voice said.

"I'm trying to reach the charter yacht *Bois d'Arc*, berth two," Bryce said. "Captain Vincent."

"They're not here," the voice said.

"But the station display says—"

"They're not here," the voice said again, and snapped the connection.

Bryce looked at the station directory again. Dock Yellow Thirteen berth two had a little green light now, indicating that it was empty. He had the sense of time passing, of delays snicking into place like the pieces of a child's 3-D puzzle, all aiming at something . . . but what? Captain Vincent had said they had at least six hours of dock time before they headed out again. It had been . . . Bryce checked . . . three hours local. They should be boarding *Altissima* now, if only the liner had been on time. Vincent could have decided to leave earlier; Novice had little to attract him or his crew.

If only his employer had listened. They could have met *Altissima* at Gorley, two stops on: the yacht had enough range.

Yes, it would have cost more, and maybe the liner would still have been delayed, but Gorley was a big, busy, very successful transnexus, with excellent services, a safe haven.

What next? He looked at the display again. Novice Directory listed a charter yacht service. Two in fact. Bantang Insystem Charter Services wouldn't do them any good, but the local branch of Allsystems might have something. He called up their public face, ticked through to a live rep—a reasonably personable middle-aged woman wearing a blue vest with the familiar Allsystems logo over her white turtleneck.

"I'd like to arrange a charter to Gorley," he said. "Three passengers."

"I'm so sorry," she said. "Both our yachts are out right now. One of them will return in two days, and then a day turnaround, before it could leave. Earliest departure possible would be nineteen hundred, that's—" a pause, "—seventy-three-point-five hours from now."

That made three days, the same as *Altissima*, if the liner arrived on time. Bryce wavered, glanced at the boys. Karl was staring at the far wall, the perfect image of sullen uncooperativeness. Evan looked worried, the way he himself felt.

"Do you have another reservation pending?" he asked.

"No . . . we don't have much call for them. May I ask—?"

"We were to board the liner *Altissima*; it's been delayed at least three days, according to the Infomat in the Premier Lounge. We're making a connection at Gorley; if *Altissima* doesn't arrive in three days, we'll miss it."

"For two hundred credits I can give you a provisional reservation," the woman said. "You'll be notified if another customer places an order, and you can upgrade to the full fare then to hold the reservation."

"I'll take it," Bryce said. "Bryce Gosslin, ID from Manus Trinity." His current name wasn't the one he'd been known by here on Novice, and his employer's credit authorization was good anywhere, so it should be safe.

"Passengers' names?" she asked.

Bryce let his eyebrows rise in calculated amazement. "You need their names now?"

"Not really," she admitted. "It's just to have the paperwork ready."

And share it with whomever offered the going rate for breaching confidentiality. "We're not in that big a hurry," Bryce said. "We can deal with that when the time comes."

"Fine, then," she said. "You're holding first option on the yacht *Karoe Star*, due to arrive here in—" she glanced at the chronometer on the wall, "—forty-seven hours, thirty minutes. Crew reported an on-time departure from Fissley, and they're in-system with clearance confirmed, so I expect an on-time arrival. I have your contact information; you will be informed when the yacht arrives and when it will be available for boarding. If you exercise the option, you will be expected to pay full fare at that time."

"Thank you," Bryce said. "You've been most helpful."

"It's my pleasure," she said, with a smile that looked genuine. "Regular office hours are from ten hundred to eighteen hundred Sig through Argen and Bona through Vale. If you need assistance with your reservation outside those hours, please contact the regular number but give your reservation code."

"Thank you," Bryce said again.

At least now they had a way off this place if *Altissima* didn't show. But three days . . . he looked at the boys. Karl's sullen expression had slipped into a mix of derision and rebellion: the adult had screwed up and he wasn't going to take it anymore. Evan, playing for the opposite team, looked bright-eyed and eager for whatever might happen.

"Well," Bryce said. "So—we won't be leaving today. And I don't want to risk our ticket or credit chits in the luggage bins; I'll ask the man at the hotel to fetch it for us. He should have a key. If that doesn't work, we can buy some necessities for a day or so."

"This is so boring," Karl said.

"It's an adventure," Evan said. "It's the unexpected, something new—you're always wanting something different." He shifted sideways, dodging his brother's attempt to knuckle his head.

"We'll go back to the hotel now," Bryce said. He hoped the

rooms would be ready. He hoped the man there—manager, clerk, bellman, whatever he was—could fetch their luggage. He hoped the stores inside the transit lounge would have the items they needed if the man couldn't, but he was beginning to expect everything to go wrong at once.

"Your rooms are ready now," the man said, when the bell brought him shuffling into the hotel's foyer once more. "You want to register now?"

"Yes," Bryce said. "And our *Altissima* tickets didn't work in the luggage bin's release, so I'll need you to fetch the luggage."

"Your tickets didn't work?" The man stared at them. "I don't know if I can—I use the tickets, see, to open the bin—" His voice had acquired a whiny edge.

"You don't have station access?"

"I'd have to get a card. It costs, and you have to reapply every standard year. For the traffic we get through here, it's not worth it."

"What about station security?"

"Oh, they don't come in here. Ritzy passengers don't want to be bothered by station security."

"Well, we'll go to our rooms now." Bryce held out his hand for the keys.

"Here you go, then," the man said. "You have a nice stay."

Bryce led the way down the passage indicated. Their rooms, he noted, were at the very end of a quiet corridor. Too quiet. Too much a dead end. A red "emergency exit" light glowed across from their doors. He pushed the key against its pad on the room door; it made the right sound and the door opened. A quality door, anyway: thick, tough. Bryce touched it as he passed. The boys followed him in, Karl radiating resentment and Evan radiating equally strong perkiness, both of them radiating brotherly competition.

Inside, the first room looked like it had once been part of a true high-quality suite: a large, uncluttered sitting room with couch, chairs, desk with dataports, entertainment console. It still had a faint "dead air" odor and the furniture—though clean and less worn than that in the ar-

rival lounge—looked dull, the beige/cream/black decor decades out of date. One of the lights flickered a little. Bryce
pulled out his security scanner. The suite should be secure,
and his keycard should light up when he activated his own
scanner . . . it did, and the suite's own surveillance/security
seemed to be functional and adequate, though hardly top-
of-the-line.

Executive-level suites usually had two bedrooms, sitting
room, large bath, and kitchenette. Bryce checked them all,
while Evan turned on the entertainment system in the sitting
room and Karl wrestled him for the controller, got it, and
turned it off again. Bryce ignored this; he wasn't their tutor,
he was their protection.

The kitchenette's cooler was on; the ice maker produced
ice when he pressed the button. The cooker's heating elements hadn't been tampered with; the oven still had its
manufacturer's seal and had never been used. The cleaning
cabinet appeared to work when he put in a plate from the
cupboard: it reported 0.1 gram of recyclable waste had been
transferred to the station's main vat.

The bath, the room with the most lethal possibilities,
checked out as well. No cross-wired plumbing facilities. He
disabled the options for toilet seat temperature control—
every security expert and most criminals knew about that
method of murder—and scanned for implanted needles,
actually the commonest way of rendering someone unconscious. Both bedrooms . . . beds, closets, chairs, floor, entertainment centers: players and controllers all passed as safe.

He left the boys in that suite while he checked out the
adjoining one. Just as dull and apparently just as safe. He
could find nothing to explain his sense of unease except the
coincidences piling up . . . but coincidences happened. Three
times wasn't always enemy action.

He just didn't want to miss it when it was.

Back in the other suite, Karl had finally given in to Evan's
complaints and had the entertainment center on again. "Only
four choices," Karl said. "A program too childish even for
Evan, something you have to have an adult ID for—I can
imagine what that is—local news, and a parpaun tourna-

ment. And three games we wore out five years ago. Even Evan could get to the top level in about five minutes."

"It will play your own flakes," Bryce said.

Karl made a face. "I've seen everything I've got with me; the rest is locked in the luggage bin. Did you forget that?"

Bryce reminded himself that Karl would, inevitably, grow out of the stage he was in, but hoped it would be soon, the bored, world-weary, sulky stage being tiresome to live with. His more serious problem was how to arrange the three of them in the two suites. The boys would be happier—well, Karl would—if they were in one, each having his own bedroom, and Bryce were in the other. But here at the end of a long empty corridor, either that last suite or the one in front of it could offer opportunities to kidnappers or other criminals, and being separated from the boys by a door they could lock on the inside . . . no.

He'd have to disable the connecting doors' locks to ensure that he had access, and then he might as well sleep in the sitting room. No hardship—he'd slept far worse places, including here on Novice Station, but still too far from the boys, whose bedrooms were on the far side of their sitting room. They'd all stay in one suite, for sleeping; the boys could use the entertainment consoles in the other when awake.

"We have a security issue," he said to the boys. Karl sneered; Evan grinned. "This situation is not the safest. We're all going to sleep in here—you two in the master bedroom—"

"No!" Evan said. "He snores."

"Me! You snore, and you kick."

"There are two large beds; you have earplugs. This is the safest arrangement and I'm paid to ensure your safety."

"And I suppose you want us to stay in this suite, with no real entertainment, for three whole days?"

"No," Bryce said. "You'll have to eat, of course. When I've secured the suites, we'll go see what we can find."

"Thank you for that," Karl said, and stared at the wall while Bryce shut down the entertainment center.

Bryce led the way back down the long passage, alert to anything that might happen, but he heard no sounds and saw nothing. None of his devices vibrated or buzzed or flashed. As he'd expected, the man who'd let them in was nowhere to be seen when they came into the reception area; the door opened to let them out into the public corridor. Bryce queried his parle: Jargooli's Junction would close in a few minutes, but Sheehan's Bar & Grill, across the corridor, claimed to be open all the time.

Jargooli's had already closed when they got there, beaded curtains pulled across the opening behind the security barrier. By the lingering fragrances, their food might be better than their spelling; Bryce decided they'd try it for breakfast. From Sheehan's entrance, light and noise spilled out into the corridor. Bryce looked at the menu displayed outside: HERE'S YOUR MEAT! in glowing orange letters above a list of steaks, chops, ribs.

Memory churned his stomach. The only real meat on Novice Station would be here, in the Premier Section, or in the private residences of the stationmaster and his cronies. For the commoners, vat-manufactured, extruded stuff was standard, the daily protein ration barely enough for adults, let alone growing boys Karl's age.

He led the boys in. About half the tables were occupied, mostly by solitary drinkers, but one filled by five large men laughing and talking a little too loud. Not good. But the smells were right. A chunky man in a stained apron came forward. "Travelers, eh? Late arrival? Want a meal?"

"That's right," Bryce said, nodding at the boys. "A quiet table, if you have one."

"Heard there was a yacht in. Waiting for *Altissima*, are you?"

Rumor spread faster than light; trouble could spread as fast. Bryce nodded. "Got to get these boys to school," he said.

"School . . ." The man's expression hinted at something else; Bryce chose to ignore it and took the menus he handed over. He offered one to each boy.

"I'll be in middle this year," Evan said to the man. "Graduated primary last term."

"Congratulations," the man said.

"Don't bother our host," Bryce said. Evan knew better than to divulge any personal details to strangers; he was doing it to annoy Karl.

"I'll have the biggest steak you have," Karl said, leaning back without looking at the menu. "Rare. If you have potatoes, I'll have two, baked, loaded. No salad. What are your desserts?"

"Our biggest steak is two kilos," the host said. "Of course, you can always take the leftovers with you."

Karl gave him a tight grin. "There won't be any leftovers."

"Very well. If you do finish it, and the potatoes, and dessert, it's free. Desserts are fruit cobbler—blackberry or apple, real fruit, not dried—or cheesecake or chocolate melt. Though if you puke in our 'fresher, you have to mop it up."

For a moment only, Karl looked daunted, but then he shrugged. He did not, however, order dessert immediately.

Evan, after a quick glance at Bryce, chose a smaller steak, stir-fried vegetables, and rice. Bryce himself chose the smallest steak on the menu, salad, stir-fried vegetables . . . he had no intention of sleeping heavily.

Predictably, he and Evan were through with their meal long before Karl, with nothing to do but stare at the spectacle while Karl kept on, doggedly. Bite after bite . . . not rushing (he had that much sense); the giant steak shrank, the two baked potatoes vanished. Finally, Karl was done and the host reappeared.

"Good job," he said to Karl. "Now for dessert." Karl looked miserable, but choked down most of a large serving of cobbler. The host nodded as he saw the remains. "Considering you ate two potatoes, that's an honorable win. Your dinner, sir, is free."

Bryce slept lightly, waking when Karl made the expected trip to the main bathroom. Sympathy would be an insult; he lay awake, listening, reassured by the sounds of Karl cleaning up afterward. The host at Sheehan's (whose name, he'd confided, was Oscar Kaldenberg) had known where they could buy toiletries, so they all had dentabs and other necessities; the boys had bought the last two pairs of pajamas in the store.

In the morning, he checked *Altissima*'s status on the board: still DELAYED. Still no ETA. Karl had no desire for a breakfast steak and eggs, so that left "orgenic" foods.

Breakfast at Jargooli's Junction meant aggressively healthy food served by an aggressively cheerful woman determined to educate them on the advantages of "orgenic" supplies and the benefits of detoxification with a particular brand of bowel cleanser on display along with "puur, neturel" diet enhancers. Karl, she pointed out, had dark circles around his eyes. Bryce tried repeatedly to shoo her away, but she was oblivious, exuding determined goodwill and a sense of her duty to save them all from irregularity. They choked down bowls of something that tasted like shredded wallboard, topped with fruit of a peculiar magenta color and an orange iridescence, and fled the place at last.

A stroll up and down the short corridor of mostly closed stores offered nothing in the way of refreshment. There was no gymnasium, not even an exercise room at the Premium Suites. Once he'd seen the upper-class lounges, Bryce had imagined that even Novice harbored something like that, a place for the rich and pampered to spend a few hours being even more pampered lest they suffer a moment's boredom or hardship. But this was pathetic. He couldn't really blame the boys for their boredom; he was bored too.

Back at the hotel, a sour-faced woman now sat at the registration console staring at its display.

"Do you have any other entertainment flakes?" he asked.

"No. We don't get enough call for 'em," she said, without looking up.

"Thank you," Bryce said. He led the way back to their rooms. One of his devices chirped when he put the key to the door.

"Someone's been in the rooms," Bryce said. "Probably cleaning staff." He hoped it was cleaning staff, though they hadn't been gone that long and he'd expected an automated cleaning service. But the beds had been made, the bathroom scoured, the entertainment controller replaced in its slot rather than out on the table where the boys had left it.

"So now what?" Karl said, slumping into the couch. "After that *wonderful* breakfast . . ."

"Now I run another screen, and then we'll talk," Bryce said. He checked every room again, ignoring Karl's sighs and Evan following him around like a puppy. Nothing. Nothing he could find, anyway.

He queried his parle again. Beyond the Premier Lounge, Novice claimed to offer an enticing array of merchandise and entertainment. Flakes and cubes for all varieties of entertainment machines, clothes, restaurants with more range than the two here . . . perhaps if he went out and got the boys some flakes, some clothes . . . but he knew that would not satisfy them. They were the age to be restless and active; they had spent their vacations doing exciting things; they were not going to sit quietly for hours with flakes he chose for them, knowing that across a barrier was all that the parle promised.

If only he could have talked to his employer—but he couldn't. He had to make the decision himself.

"We're going out," he said. Karl sat up and lost the sulky expression for a moment. Evan was, as usual, bright-eyed and eager. "But there are rules to be followed. It's not safe— not here, in particular."

Karl slouched back. "We have to be good, quiet, obedient—"

"No," Bryce said, sharply enough that Karl gaped for a moment. "You have to be wary and alert, and ready to react instantly if necessary." He pulled out one of his cases and opened it. "See these wires?" Hair-thin, nondescript mid-brown, they would be invisible in the boys' hair—in most hair. "You'll wear them. Come over here, Evan." He parted the boy's hair, and touched the active tip to his scalp. It adhered instantly, growing into the scalp. "Karl—" Karl heaved himself up and let Bryce attach one to him.

"What does it do?"

"I can't tell you. If you don't know, you can't spill it." He could, but with any luck and some common sense, he shouldn't be in danger of doing so. Seek-nannies should be boosting their resistance to the more common neurotoxins, enhancing attention span and ensuring that biometric scanners would register incorrect values for anything human eyes couldn't see.

"I wouldn't—"

"You would under some circumstances," Bryce said. "Now pay attention, both of you. We should be fine. It's likely nothing will happen. But if anything does happen, it's likely to be bad . . . someone will have figured out who you are and what I am. You are worth a fortune as hostages held for ransom, and more as reprogrammed agents with easy access to your parents."

"Brain-miners?" Karl asked.

"Yes. You're still in the age range; Evan's perfect for it. You could be fitted with situation-dependent compulsions to kill, to steal, to destroy. Or you could be mined completely and sold to a pleasure-house—a quick genefrack and your DNA would be different enough to pass scans as someone else."

They both looked almost as worried as he wanted them.

"Your safety depends on your real identities not being known. You know that, you've been taught that, but you don't realize how easy it is for those tiny fragments you don't think of—like your brag about leaving primary, Evan—to be gathered and correlated and used to locate you. When we go through Immigration and Customs, to leave this lounge for the main station, your present, real DNA will go into their database. How long do you think it would take a criminal who had a sample for comparison to hack the data?"

"Nobody can hack the Immigration databases," Karl said. "They're the most secure—"

"Nothing is totally secure," Bryce said. "It's been done." He waited for a reaction, didn't get one, and went on. "Here's what we do. I'm going to give you a code phrase. If I say 'Oh, applejack,' it means you both take off, at once. Doesn't matter if I say it quietly, or yell, or it sounds like I'm joking. Leave right then. Stay together if you can. Go to the first law enforcement kiosk you can find, and punch every emergency button on it. When you get a response, ask for an escort back here."

"Where will you be?" Karl asked.

"Rear guard," Bryce said. "If all goes well, we'll be back together in no time and nothing more will happen. If not, if things have gone badly, you'll have to keep Evan and yourself safe until *Altissima* arrives. Now—the second code, from you to me. 'Mr. Henson said—' That means you've noticed something and we have to talk. Put it in school context. 'Last year in math, Mr. Henson said—' Or anything that's obviously a reference to school."

"What's applejack?" Evan asked.

"An expression my older brother used to use, when he thought I was too young to learn profanity."

"You never mentioned an older brother."

"He died," Bryce said. "It's not important now. What's important is that you both understand: this could be perfectly safe . . . or not."

They both nodded. Bryce set the room security again and led the way down the corridor. The sour-faced woman wasn't in the reception area. No one was. Were she and the man married? Partners? Up to no good? Or just lazy and incompetent? Bryce pulled his mind away from that as they came out into the public corridor and turned into the main lounge area. The automated clerk at the information desk appeared to be on, if the status lights meant anything, but Bryce didn't bother with it.

Immigration and Customs bracketed the exit from the Premier Lounge to the rest of Novice Station. Bryce put his ID against the registration plate, and the first door slid aside. A man in a green uniform sat behind a high desk. "Welcome to Novice Station," he said. "We require a level-two bioscan and current legal identification from a governmental entity known to us, or a level-four bioscan if you have no such identification . . ."

"Manus Trinity," Bryce said.

"Accepted," the man said. "Advance to the red line, please—are those minors with you?"

"They are," Bryce said.

"We require proof of biological parenthood or proof of legal status allowing travel with unrelated minors. Do they have legal identification?"

"Yes," Bryce said.

"Are they your biological get?"

"No. I am their uncle." So said his legal ID chip, and so said the implant that delivered a sufficient supply of related DNA to confuse most scans.

"Ah. A relative. Excellent. I will now read your identification and then your bioscan." He took the ID chip, fed it into a reader. Bryce looked where he was told; a light flashed, checking his retinal pattern, and a needle retracted with one drop of his blood. "There you are, then. Novice Station has accepted your identity. Now for your minors."

Karl and Evan both went through the procedure, with Bryce watching. "Customs next," Bryce said, turning to the other side of the narrow passage, where another man in green awaited them. They had no luggage and the only contraband on their persons was a shell in Evan's pocket.

"What'd you keep that for?" Karl asked.

"It was pretty," muttered Evan. "It wasn't hurting anything."

"It might," Bryce said. "I thought I told you to empty your pockets before we even arrived."

"You did. I just . . . never mind." Evan glared at Karl; Karl looked more lofty than sulky, and Bryce rolled his eyes for the benefit of the Customs officer, who gave a wry smile.

Then it was out the last doorway, into the bustling life of Novice Station. It had improved, Bryce thought, or perhaps most things looked better if you weren't broke, scared, and alone.

"Clothes first," he said. "Then food."

"I'm hungry now," Evan said.

"So am I," Karl said. "That cereal wasn't enough."

"Fine," Bryce said. Hungry boys were cranky boys; if he kept them full they might even want to go back and take a nap. "Let me just ask . . ." His parle displayed a wide variety of eateries nearby. He let them choose from a short list.

This time, Karl didn't try to show off by overeating; he picked a soup-and-sandwich combination. Evan ignored the soup and opted for a sandwich. Bryce had chosen a corner table away from the entrance and ate his own small meal slowly, watching the flow of traffic past the entrance and within the eatery itself. Nobody paid them much attention; the boys' slightly rumpled clothes looked much like anyone else's, unless someone recognized the subtle details.

He considered options. The boys needed some clothes for the next couple of days, and might need more if *Altissima* was delayed again and they took the chartered yacht. Leaving behind their luggage—including his own—in *Altissima*'s luggage bins bothered him; the boys might have left something there that would give away their real identities, and then this set of covers would be blown. Station security might be willing to open the bins, but that had its own risks. If the chartered yacht couldn't get clearance to dock at Blue to pick them up, they'd have to submit their luggage to Customs and have it taken through the station. Many opportunities for problems there.

After the meal, the boys were more energetic, not less, eager to find stores, entertainment kiosks, excitement. Bryce resigned himself to shepherding them through one or more entertainment outlets after getting them some clothes, but insisted on clothes first.

"Why are we getting so much?" Evan asked, as Bryce added another pair of pajamas, several sets of underwear, and ship boots to the stack of clothes in front of Evan. "We're only going to be here a couple of days."

Bryce explained about the luggage bins. "You'll need more than one change of clothes if we take the yacht and can't get the luggage out of storage."

Evan scowled. "My favorite player's in there! I don't want to lose it. Or my favorite ball—"

"*Altissima* will pick it up, whether we're on her or not, and I'm sure your luggage will catch up with you," Bryce said. "In the meantime, you can have a new player. And a new ball. And anything else within the luggage limits of the yacht." One advantage of their economic status—as long as he was spending money on the boys, he had unlimited credit through their father. Evan's face relaxed.

"And speaking of the yacht," Bryce said, "we should go by their offices and check in with them."

"Are you sure *Altissima*'s going to be later?" Karl asked.

"No, but while we have time is the right time to check our options."

Their clothing purchases would be tubed to their hostelry; Bryce paid an expedited shipping and insurance fee for extra security. "This way," Bryce said, consulting his parle.

Allsystems' storefront on Novice had only the name itself—with the familiar logo—on a black-glass door with a buzzer for entry. Bryce's pocket scanner vibrated against his leg . . . of course they would have visual and auditory scanners out here and possibly bioscans as well. He pushed the button. A voice—the same, he thought, he had spoken to the day before—asked his business.

"Gosslin, about the charter," he said.

The door hummed aside, and Bryce saw a narrow passage with an opening to the left at the far end. His pocket scanner chirped; Bryce ignored it. Allsystems had a reputation for paranoia on the smaller markets it serviced. He led the boys in.

The same woman he'd seen in the parle came to the entrance of the office to greet him. "Bryce Gosslin? Pleased to meet you in person. I'm Cevrilene Baskari. These are your . . ."

"Nephews," Bryce said. "Karl and Evan." As the boys looked around the office, he gave it his own assessment. Allsystems had luxury yachts for lease, in some systems, but made its profit with "business class" vessels and even less luxurious "group holiday charters." Firms that specialized in luxury travel had no offices at places like Novice. Here, Allsystems' white-walled rooms, dark blue carpet, gray tweed–upholstered chairs and settee probably passed for elegance, along with the scarlet flower in a clear glass vase on Cevrilene Baskari's polished black desk.

"I'm sure you realize our scans collect some biometric data from every visitor," Baskari said. "These data are kept strictly confidential and should not interfere in any way with your use of legal identities while on Novice or after. Still, if you insist, I can give my bond to destroy them after each visit to this office."

As a fishing expedition, it was more delicate than most. Were their identities merely legal, or were they real? Bryce did not trust Allsystems' confidentiality software, but he did trust the wires he'd planted in the boys' hair.

"Quite all right," Bryce said, waving a hand. "I wanted to make sure that the transaction went through smoothly."

"That it did," she said, smiling. "So, shall we see you back in two days?"

"If *Altissima* isn't in when she should be," Bryce said. "I did want to ask . . . are you able to get permission to dock out at Blue to pick us up from the Premier Lounge? We have luggage there, in *Altissima*'s bins."

She frowned a little. "I hope you don't mean contraband. We would prefer not to carry items that are contraband in any of our ports of call."

"It's not that. It's the thought of how long it will take to transport the boys and all their stuff across the station, through two Customs inspections. If you have doubts, I'll certainly pay for a Customs inspection there in Blue."

She relaxed. "That's all right. I'm not sure we can get permission, but I'll see what I can do. What about the *Altissima* bins? Your tickets with them should work—"

"They don't," Bryce said. "At least, I tried twice with mine and it didn't. The fellow at Premier Suites doesn't have a key—says he'd have to get a special license and it's not worth it for the occasional tip."

"So you were planning to leave the luggage for *Altissima* to pick up?"

"Unless I could convince station security to open it for us, yes. It's inconvenient, but I can leave explicit instructions for *Altissima* and it will catch up with us later."

"Perhaps we can help," she said, tapping something on her desktop. "We have handled baggage transfers before; one of our people may have a key. I will check that for you."

"Thanks," Bryce said. "If you don't need me for anything

else, the boys wanted to visit some entertainment stores. Their players and all are locked up with the luggage."

"Triolet's, to the right as you exit, and first left on the first cross-corridor, has a good selection," she said.

"Thank you again," Bryce said, and led the way out.

To the right as they exited led them toward the part of Novice Station Bryce knew only too well. He felt his shoulders bunching and deliberately stretched and took a deep breath. He was no longer Boris Jiao Gebhardt. He'd had his teeth fixed, his broken nose straightened. His current employer had paid for the day in a regen tank that restored function to his damaged left arm. His fingerprints were years younger than he was.

He was no longer hungry all the time. That was the biggest difference.

Yet his gut clenched just as it had sixteen years before. The familiar shapes of the storefronts seemed to jeer at his present status, his sense of self as Bryce James Gosslin. Still someone's servant, still dependent . . . his employer might be softer-spoken, less obviously cruel, but he was still not his own master.

He shook his head, forcing those thoughts aside as he always did to focus on the immediate dangers. Nothing he could see . . . Triolet's, a store he'd never had the money to enter legally in his bad old days, looked just as it had. Fresh, clean, its displays of shiny, enticing tech up to date.

The store was moderately busy; Bryce kept the boys in sight from a little distance, letting them make their own choices. He didn't care about players and entertainment slice and cubes. If he'd had a day off, he'd have been at the far end of the store, where a locked door gave entrance to the special room full of high-quality spyware. He'd been there once, as a small boy, in the dark of station night, sent to steal something to prove his loyalty to his leader. He remembered how the pounding of his own pulse drowned out ambient sound, how he'd swallowed back the raw fear that he'd be caught and spaced.

Now he could go there legitimately, a professional in the security field: show his identity and credit reference, and one of the senior clerks would let him in, let him try out those delicate and effective instruments. But not while he was guarding the boys.

Evan had chosen a player; Karl was hesitating between two. Evan glanced over his shoulder for Bryce. Bryce came forward, once more feeling the tug of an invisible chain on a nonmaterial collar. "This one's even nicer than my other," Evan said. "Is that all right?"

"Of course," Bryce said. "What else do you want?"

"Some games. Some storycubes. But that salesclerk keeps looking at me." Evan's voice lowered. "I didn't think it was enough to say 'Mr. Henson' about—"

Bryce glanced that way—a salesclerk was in fact watching, but when he saw Bryce with Evan he relaxed and turned away. "I'll speak to him," Bryce said. "Boys your age are in school or at work during prime shift here." He could remember all too clearly what he'd been doing at that age and time of day. Disassembling stolen merchandise into its components, filing the results in Macalapar's Parts & Supplies. Clerks had looked at him that way, too. There must still be boys employed by the station mafi to steal and dismantle what they stole.

He introduced himself to the clerk. "Those two boys, my nephews—" he pointed out Evan and Karl. "A delay in travel. Whatever they choose goes on my account, unless the older one tries to buy something illegal—he's at that age."

"Over twelve?"

"Oh, yes. He can certainly access material for over-twelves, but his mother would have my head if I let him explore the adult material. She's just a tiny bit overprotective." He grinned at the clerk, who grinned back. It wasn't true . . . Alicia Veronese Stoner-Hall hadn't seen either of her sons since she'd left their father for a famous professional jockey two years before. Evan had cried; his grades had dropped and he'd lost weight, but he was back to normal now. Karl had pretended not to care, but Bryce, whose older brother had died, unpleasantly, when he was that age, knew better. But mothers were supposed to be protective, even overprotective, and it was another layer of protective falsehood to enhance the boys' legal identities.

Bryce wandered around the store, observing everything from the clerk's new demeanor toward the boys to the other customers. A midday truant, trying to keep the strap of his book bag over the telltale crest of his school as he poked through the adult bin. The clerk spotted him too, and headed for him. The truant slouched out the door without being caught and Bryce watched him through the window . . . he would find what he sought somewhere.

A young mother, baby in a sling on her hip and whiny toddler at her heel, pawed through the bin of preschool educational cubes for the one the toddler wanted. Two somewhat older women, talking nonstop, flipped through a tray of "just in" bestsellers. A woman his own age, in rough work clothes, tool bag on her shoulder—something about the way she moved made him look again. His shift of stance caught her eye; she turned to look straight at him.

His breath caught. Glia. It had to be Glia. He looked down, hoping she hadn't recognized him, not with the straight white unbroken teeth, the straight nose . . .

"I will never forget your eyes," she'd said, the last time, the time he'd been beaten so hard he didn't even want to live, when his face . . .

No. He would not think of that. He would think of now, of his good suit, of his good job, his new identity. He stared at the racks and bins in front of him, forcing his hands to move among them as if he sought something in particular. She'd been headed to the far side of the store; their eyes had met only for a moment. And it might not be Glia. She looked older, harder . . . her hair was darker . . . she was heavier.

He looked at the bin he was working through and found it was texts for history, grades K–12. That almost made him laugh. History indeed. He had enough history without studying it. When he glanced up again to find the boys, they were talking with the clerk. And the woman who might be Glia had her back to him, looking at racks of power cells.

The boys were through now, and Bryce joined them.

"We could tube this stuff back and explore more," Evan said.

"Better we go back," Bryce said. "The clothes should be there now—get things put away." They'd been out of the secured area for hours, plenty of time for someone to set up a trap, and he didn't want to run into anyone else he remembered.

They didn't argue, for once. Bryce paid the clerk; the clerk tagged the items and put them in an ID-confirmed carrysack. Karl picked it up and headed for the door; Evan followed. Bryce stretched his stride to catch up . . . and the woman he hoped wasn't really Glia popped out from between racks, staring straight at him.

He'd half-expected it; it was her style. He had readied his polite stranger face . . . she still shouldn't recognize him. But he saw the slight widening of her pupils, lift of brows. She had. His nod was polite, distant.

Her voice followed him, barely audible. "I'll never forget your eyes . . ." No more than that; he could feel the distance between them widen as she accepted his nonresponse. He glanced back once, but didn't see her.

He cursed his carelessness all the way back to the Premier Lounge entrance, through a brief stop at a food outlet to buy something he could prepare for the boys' supper. Once more they had to pass Immigration and Customs, acquiring blue stickers on the carrybags. Nothing had happened . . . nothing but one person thinking she'd recognized him. The boys were safe. He was safe.

As safe as they ever were.

Their new clothes were in the hotel's reception room, and the woman—again on duty—seemed marginally more friendly. Bryce tipped her. The boys showered and changed into their new outfits, as did he, then he ran an experimental towel through the suite's clothes-cleaning cabinet. Karl had gone into the other suite to use its entertainment center and get away from the sound effects from Evan's game, he said—little chimes and crackling noises. Bryce filtered them out automatically as he took care of the laundry and considered options.

As Bryce half-expected, the towel came out a tan wadded mess, so seldom was the cabinet used. On the second try the same towel emerged white, fluffy, and soft. He put his own clothes in first, clothes so different from those he'd worn here as a boy. A boy who had been saved from more torment and certain death by Glia. A boy who no longer existed, physically or legally.

What would Glia do? No doubt in his mind that she'd recognized him. She knew his past; she knew who would most want to find him . . . but she hadn't been part of that. She'd tried to help.

And he'd cut her, his oldest and only friend here. A woman scorned . . . but she wasn't every woman. She'd looked tired, worn . . . poor, still. Working, at least, unless that had been a disguise, but he thought not. How would she react to his refusal to acknowledge her? Anger? Misery? And what had he cut her for? For the boys? For the spoiled rich kids whose clothes he washed?

Load by load, he put clothes in the cabinet and took them out. He folded and put away their underwear, their shirts, the cheap pajamas they'd bought the night before. Was this what he'd become . . . just a servant? He stepped to the door, where he could see Evan hunched over his player; the screen showed a multicolored pattern that had to be manipulated into something else. Karl had pushed the connecting door almost closed, no doubt to cut down on the noise. Bryce looked at his chrono. Time to start supper. If he was going to be a servant, he might as well be a good one.

The boys ate supper without complaint; they had entertainment waiting for them, and they left their mess on the table as soon as they'd had enough to eat. Bryce cleared the table and put all the dirty dishes in the kitchen cleaner. Two more days, and either *Altissima* would be in, or they'd leave on the yacht. He could stand two more days. Once aboard the liner, he'd have others he could depend on to help with the boys' security, just as he usually did. Someone adult to talk to, someone adult who understood, who knew the rules.

Next morning, the boys were restless again. The packets of breakfast food he'd bought to prepare for them in the suite brought scowls.

"I don't see why we can't go out," Evan said. "Nothing happened yesterday."

Should he tell them about Glia? No, they would not understand that being recognized by an old friend was a problem.

"Just because nothing happened yesterday doesn't mean nothing will happen," Bryce said.

"I know you don't want us to stay out there all day," Karl said. "And I know you think the things we bought are enough to occupy us. But just for meals? Surely we can go out for breakfast, maybe lunch?"

"We could eat at one of those places at this end of the concourse," Evan said. "Wouldn't that be safer?"

It would, if the danger depended on them being in a particular place and that wasn't it. Still . . . Bryce was tired of being the only adult he saw. He missed his usual partner, Arnie Bennett, more than he'd expected, missed the simple adultness of the man, the cooperation, the shared goal of keeping the boys safe. And he'd been cooped up with the boys since he picked them up. Yesterday, outside this empty and depressing section, had been enjoyable for him, too. At least, until Glia recognized him.

"Breakfast," he said. "We'll see how it goes—no promises about lunch. Remember our code phrases?"

They grinned at him, nodding. Evan rattled them off; Bryce looked at Karl until he repeated them.

"Alert, aware," Bryce said. They nodded again.

Bryce made his morning check of his own security devices, made sure that the boys each had an ID and a key to the room, and put the *Altissima* tickets in his own safehold.

The concourse looked no more or less dangerous this morning than it had the day before. They found a table at a café that sold baked and fried goods; Evan and Karl both chose stacks of pancakes smothered in sweet sauce and fruit, with faux-sausages on the side.

Bryce ate two eggs and a hot sweet bun, watching the concourse. Still nothing. Maybe he could bring the boys out for every meal. That would make life easier today and tomorrow.

After breakfast, out on the concourse, the boys thought of other things they needed. "I'm out of my derm treatment," Karl said. And before Bryce could remind him of the store inside the Premier Section, he said, "They don't have it inside—I asked. But there's a pharm just down there—you can see the sign—and it wouldn't take a minute."

"And they might have mint chewies," Evan said.

He could get things for them—but that meant leaving them alone in the hotel suite. Not a good idea. The pharm might deliver, or it might not. Might as well take a few minutes . . .

Karl found his derm treatment; Evan found his chewies and bought packets of mint and spice both. As they left, Karl lagged behind a little—no doubt looking for some other excuse to stay on the concourse longer.

"Come on, Karl," he said, turning. Karl had stopped to look in a display window.

When he looked back at Evan, he saw them. At first he thought they were station security—their clothes could pass for uniforms at a casual glance. The belts with weapons-slots added to that impression. But their feral eyes, fixed on him, belonged to a different order of power. Clearly, they recognized him, and he remembered Merrick all too well. Merrick had worked for Santorin, who'd killed his brother. Merrick had made Bryce's life hell, when Bryce was still Boris. The other with Merrick, he wasn't sure of.

"Applejack," Bryce said. And again, a little louder, for Karl's benefit, "Applejack."

Merrick grinned.

"You haven't changed that much," he said. "You're not going to give us any trouble, now, are you?"

Not until the boys got free. Karl had backed away, and was

now edging into a café entrance, but Evan stared from Bryce to the men and looked around for Karl just that instant too long. Bryce pushed him, said "Run!" and Evan started, took one step. Too late: Merrick's partner had him.

"Let me go!" Evan said, and kicked out, but the man simply picked him up, rolled him into a bodywrap, and touched his neck with a sleepstick. Evan slumped into the man's arms. A few bystanders slowed to look, but no one interfered. Merrick had an obvious weapon out now; his accomplice had a less obvious one poised near Evan's neck.

"Citizen arrest!" Merrick said. "There's a warrant outstanding for this individual, suspicion of human trafficking as well, and we're licensed bounty hunters."

"It's a lie," Bryce said. "I'm a businessman from out-system; that's my nephew! Call Security!"

Merrick grinned at a few more bystanders who'd actually come to a halt. "Security? By all means—that's where you're going, straight to the central station."

"They're not bounty hunters, they're common criminals!" Bryce said, appealing to the one man in the crowd who looked truly interested. "Call Security, please!" The needler in his palm would shoot only one at a time . . . the drug took a second or more to disable . . . if he got the one who held Evan, Merrick would have ample time to shoot him . . . and then take Evan anyway. Bryce cursed himself for his mistakes, for failing to insist on having a partner along.

Then he felt the sting of a needle in his own neck, and the world receded to a set of gray shades, one of whom kindly guided him along the concourse to somewhere he didn't want to go . . . but could not summon the energy to resist.

Karl tried to remember everything Bryce had ever said about sneaking in the almost-five years the man had been one of their security detail. Don't have a pattern. Don't look back; use reflections. Don't be obvious. Never be first or last. Never sit with your back to a door.

Now he was alone on a strange space station, and his bodyguard and his brother had just been snatched . . . he didn't believe for a moment that Bryce was really a criminal on the run, so those so-called bounty hunters must be criminals themselves.

He was not a child. He was not helpless. He forced the panic down and forced himself to think like Bryce—or what he thought Bryce thought like. Situation: bad. He was supposed to keep Evan safe if something happened to Bryce, but Evan had already been captured by . . . by someone. Bryce was supposed to be rear guard, but he too was captured. Well, resources: he had his own credit cube, but his credit was limited, in case his cube was stolen. The bad guys had Bryce's. Bryce had his *Altissima* ticket, too . . . no, wait . . . that was back at the hotel. So he had a ticket and identification and a little money. Enough to survive on for a few more days, at least, but that didn't help Evan and Bryce. Would Customs let him back into the Premier Lounge without an adult?

Maybe he should do what Bryce had said—he finally remembered that—find a security kiosk and hit all the buttons, and then ask someone to escort him to the hotel. But how would that really work? He imagined sirens wailing and whooping, lights flashing, people in the concourse scurrying for cover, those in shops pouring out to see what was going on, various emergency teams arriving on the scene—hull breach, fire, hazardous materials, crime in progress. Lots of people looking at him, asking questions, angry that he'd called them out for no reason . . . boys had been expelled from his school for sending in fake emergency calls and making the local police waste taxpayer time and money. A child—Evan, maybe—could get away with that; children panicked. Surely it would be better to find a security station and just tell them what had happened. More adult, more—the more he thought about it—believable.

Karl finished the juice he'd ordered and looked out into the concourse. No sign of the bounty hunters, Bryce, Evan. Down the concourse, he saw the lighted logo of an open security station. If those were bounty hunters, maybe they'd taken Bryce and Evan there, to check on that warrant and get their reward. That's how they did it in the games he'd played. But if that had happened, Bryce should be free, should be in there with Evan or coming out . . . he peered in. No Bryce. No Evan. A man at the desk looked up from a screen and stared at him. Karl felt his shoulders tightening. They'd said something about central station; he had no idea where it was. He could at least ask.

"Excuse me," he said to the man at the desk. "I'd like to know where the central security station is."

"Why? Anything you need to report, you can report here. ID." The man put out his hand. This close, Karl could see that what he'd taken for uniforms on the men who grabbed Evan and Bryce weren't the same.

"I didn't—"

"ID, son. We log everyone who comes in. You should know that."

"I'm a visitor," Karl said. "We're only here until—"

"Transient," the man said. "ID, now."

Karl fished out his legal ID and handed it over; the man passed it through a machine and then laid it on the desk rather than hand it back.

"You're underage; why aren't you in school?"

"My school isn't here—and it doesn't start for another two tendays. Our planet's on a different cycle."

"Traveling alone, are you?"

"No, with—"

"With parents? They should have more sense than to let a minor out in the concourse alone. Lost, are you?"

"No," Karl said. "I'm not lost. It's my brother and my uncle—they're gone—abducted. These men—"

"Abducted." The man's stare combined disbelief and annoyance. "Off this concourse? In this shift?"

"Yes! That's why I wanted to report—"

"When do you allege this happened?"

Karl wanted to grab the man and shake him. "I'm not *alleging* . . . I'm telling you. I was there, I saw it myself. Two men, one bigger than the other. They said they had a warrant—"

"Son, let me give you some advice. You may get away with this kind of adventure-fantasy story where you come from—I can tell you're rich—but it won't play here. If something like that had happened, I'd have had a dozen reports from people I know—storekeepers, people on the concourse."

"But they're gone," Karl said. "I don't know where they are, and Evan—"

"Here's what I think," the man said. "If your uncle and brother even exist, and are your real uncle and your real brother—all of which I doubt—they went someplace without telling you—you probably overslept—and now you're bored, so you want station security to waste its time looking for them, when they're in no danger at all and probably up on Orange Five watching a ball game. I could hold your ID and stick you in iso for wasting my time, but I'm a generous man, so I'll give you some advice. Go back to your fancy Blue Zone hotel, stay there, and think about somebody but yourself, for once in your life." He shoved Karl's ID over the desk at him. "And don't come bothering me again."

"But Customs would tell you—"

"I'm not going to waste my time or theirs. Get out."

Karl left the station, trembling with rage. How could security possibly treat him that way, not even listen, not even let him tell what he'd seen? And what could he do now?

Bryce kept saying this place wasn't safe—but he said that about everywhere. It was his job to say that. Karl struggled to remember anything more specific. Bryce had been here, been here as a boy. So maybe he knew . . . more even than their father.

He himself had to stay free, able to do whatever . . . whatever he could think of. Right now, staying free and finding a source of money was all he could think of. Money. He had his credit cube, but the limit on it wasn't very high. He had nothing on him worth much; one of Bryce's rules had been *don't display wealth: it makes you a target.*

But yesterday's purchases were back in the room. Players were worth something. He'd known boys at school who sold theirs to get money for something their parents didn't want them to have. And Bryce might have something in his kit; surely he wouldn't mind if Karl took it in this emergency.

He would have to go through Customs and Immigration to get to the room, though. Would he be stopped? Searched?

He'd never had to worry about that before; Bryce took care of such things. He started back toward the Premier Lounge access. He'd done this before, only with Bryce and Evan along. The officers should recognize him; he could tell them what happened and they would—his imagination gave them the same reaction as the security officer's. Or worse. What if they were in league with the men who'd taken Bryce and Evan? What if they called Security, detained him?

He would have to pretend everything was all right, that he had a reason for coming back alone. Somewhat to his surprise, the officers gave him no trouble at all. He flashed his ID; they waved a reader at it. "So you're alone today?" Immigration asked.

"Have a stomachache," Karl said. "I'm going back to the room—"

"Mint tea," the Customs officer said, already turning away. "Any herbal store."

Thanks be that Bryce had trusted him with his own room key; it would let him in the hotel without alerting the staff and into his room. Karl was halfway across the Premier Suites lobby—empty as usual—when he thought of the other two room keys. Bryce had them both. Bryce was in custody somewhere and someone else—someone Karl had no reason to trust—had those keys.

How long? Karl tried to think how long he had dodged around the concourse. Would someone have had time to get into their rooms? Would the Immigration and Customs officers have let them? What about hotel staff?

What staff? That sour-faced woman who sometimes watched the lobby in dayshift? If they'd said they had a delivery . . .

The corridor seemed to telescope; he was aware for the first time how long, how silent, how isolated . . . how much like a trap. Had Bryce seen it this way? He must have; that must be why he'd insisted on renting both suites, but making them all sleep in just one.

Karl felt shivers running up and down his spine. Someone could be there. Someone could be stealing their things—or waiting for him. He looked back. No one, no sound, nothing.

Then a sound. Faint, but audible . . . from behind the wall . . . which meant inside the suite. That would be—he thought a moment—the larger bedroom. The one he shared with Evan. It could be hotel staff cleaning the room . . . except the door wasn't propped open with a cleaning and restocking cart in the corridor. The door was closed. Did housekeeping ever bring the cart inside with them? He didn't know. Bryce would have known.

Bryce would have had a weapon, too. Karl had nothing. He looked around again, though he knew he wouldn't find one in this blank space. His instructors had told him—Bryce had told him—that he always had a weapon, between his ears, but he wanted something more tangible. He backed up, trying to be utterly silent, until he came to the door of the utility closet with its dual label of HOUSEKEEPING and EMER-GENCY EQUIPMENT. Something in there should be useful, and emergency equipment lockers were always open, on space stations.

Sure enough, there were two carts: one empty, and the other's racks stuffed with containers labeled BATHROOM ONLY, COOKER ONLY, CARPET: FOOD SPILLS, CARPET: HUMAN, and the like. The lowest shelf held the vacuum, with its dual hoses, one connecting to Station Recycling. No mop, no broom, the only stick-like object the wand on the vacuum, which did not—when Karl yanked at it—come off its at-tached hose. Other attachments, racked on the far side of the cart, were shorter and lighter, but might be useful.

He thought briefly about pushing the entire cart down the corridor and pretending to be housekeeping, but they'd prob-ably bribed the hotel staff and knew housekeeping wouldn't come. Armed instead with a narrow pointed vacuum attach-ment—good for getting into the creases of upholstery, he guessed—and a spray bottle of Bathroom Only, he headed back toward their rooms.

Karl pulled the key from his pocket and laid it on the keyplate. The lock released and the door slid aside, reveal-ing a man stuffing things into an already over-full suitcase, one he recognized as theirs. One supposedly locked safely away in *Altissima*'s bin. But surely nobody here but Evan had a Camp Korowea tag on a green McTallen & Bridges suitcase.

"You!" the man said. "You're supposed to—Cale, the other kid's turned up." He laughed, unpleasantly. "What were you going to do, clean the bathtub?"

Karl could feel his legs trembling, his hands . . . he took a step backward; his back hit the doorjamb.

"Oh, don't be scared, boy," the man said. "Just come on in and shut the door. We just got your stuff out of storage for you. Your uncle wanted it." The other man came out of the smaller bedroom, Bryce's case in hand.

Karl tried to take a deep, calming breath, the way his instructors said to do before a match, but his chest seemed frozen.

"You're too tense," the second man said. "You need to calm down—" He put Bryce's case on the table in front of the couch and reached into his vest.

Karl knew he needed to calm down, but his racing heart told him it was impossible. A sour taste came into his mouth. Was he going to throw up in front of these men? Throw up with terror like a stupid little boy?

"This will help," the second man said, walking toward him. His hand clenched, and Karl had an instant of utter clarity as something tiny and bright flashed toward him. He jerked aside, heard the tiny click of something hitting the doorframe and did the only possible thing: charge, spraying the man in the face with the bathroom cleaner. The sharp chemical smell almost choked him, but the man staggered back, swiping at his face with one hand and fumbling for something else Karl was sure would be even worse.

"You stupid—!"

"That wasn't nice at all," said the first man, who now held a thin black rod by a padded handle. "You didn't have to be rude."

Karl, moving too fast to stop or change direction, ran straight into the man he'd sprayed. The man grabbed his shoulder, and his body took over, the moves his instructors had taught him to repeat, over and over, moves that he'd used before only on other boys his own age or the instructors, flowed from a base he corrected in an instant . . . breaking that hold, finding the right lock, and whirling with the larger man to meet the first man's attack.

For one glorious moment, his mind had time to register that what he'd been taught worked in real life; then he was submerged in a fight for his life. Two of them, grown men, heavier . . . but no time to be afraid now. He was down, took a painful blow on the back with the rod, but was rolling anyway, kicking, striking, jamming the vacuum tool—when he had an instant to yank it out—into one attacker's face, where it skidded into the man's eye. Elbow to the windpipe, heel to shin, then to knee . . . they were big, heavy, adult, with—he barely shifted in time to avoid it—at least one knife, at least one more projectile weapon spitting needles loaded, he was sure, with toxin to disable or kill him. He took more blows of the thin rod, each like a lash of fire; he could feel blood dripping on his face; he knew he'd been kicked and punched. He'd lost the cleaning bottle; he'd gained a cushion off the couch that absorbed three of the needles. But they hadn't been trained as he had; Bryce had told him the difference, shown him some of the things rough fighters did that no one used in class . . . he could counter those.

You'll never really need this, one instructor had said when his muscles had burned with yet another repetition and he'd complained. *But it's best to learn correctly because if you do need it, you need it all. Not just strength, not just speed, not just agility, not just knowing the moves but owning them— owning it all.*

And only this past vacation had it come together for him . . . just barely enough.

He lay panting on the carpet, amid the welter of the fight, half-amazed and half-proud that he was alive and free and the two men were—dead? He wasn't sure. Not moving, anyway. As his breath came back, he forced himself up, wincing at the various pains, wiping at his face and staring for a moment at the blood he found.

What now? He searched them quickly, found three more clips of the needles, labeled with a long chemical name he didn't know, a slim cylinder with a button on one side and a

slot for the needles, a more obvious firearm, another knife,
credit cubes, dataprobes, and various keycards, one with
a dirty paper tag saying PREMIER LOUNGE LUGGAGE BINS.
One of the men stirred slightly; Karl rammed a needle in
his neck, and then another, to be sure. No more stirring, but
the man still breathed. The other made harsh sounds, like
broken snoring. Karl put two needles in his neck too, beside
the bruise his elbow had left. If it was just a soporific, it
wouldn't hurt, and anyway, they'd been ready to use what-
ever-it-was on him.

He started shaking again; his vision darkened. But he
fought it back. Bryce and Evan depended on him. He took
the time to secure the two men—dead or alive, he didn't
know—with the ties he found in their pockets. They were
too heavy for him to drag into the bedroom, and the sitting
room had no closet, but he moved the couch so they couldn't
be seen from the door.

In the bathroom, he looked at the damage to himself and
his clothes. Cuts, bruises—deep ones here and there—and
his clothes were a mess. He pulled them off, took a hurried
shower, used the first aid kit supplied by the hotel on his face,
dressed in fresh clothes. He looked in the mirror—his face
looked almost normal. He was also suddenly hungry, hungry
enough to eat one of those huge steaks . . . he rummaged
in the supplies Bryce had bought. Most required cooking;
he didn't have time. He peeled a snack bar and wolfed that
down.

Bryce's case yielded many smaller cases, one with clips of
needles labeled with a long chemical name. Karl compared
them to the others. Very similar, but he didn't know what
the difference meant. He didn't know what most of the cases
held—wires with jewels on them, wires without, wires attached at one end to tiny disks, tiny boxes in various colors.
Two things with lenses that must be some kind of video surveillance gear. A thin, lightweight pale gray garment that
looked like a coverall of silk, with attached gloves and boo-
ties. A row of little black buttons ran up each sleeve from
wrist to elbow.

Karl touched the lowest on the left sleeve. It disappeared.

The entire garment, whatever it was, vanished . . . but his finger still felt it. He tapped it, and the whole thing reappeared. He tried a different button; this time the suit hardened, a rigid mass . . . and then relaxed when he tapped the button again.

Bryce had told them about such suits. Chameleon suits, used by spies and special security agents, as well as criminals who could afford them, suits with all sorts of special qualities, from invisibility (not complete, Bryce had warned—they worked best in dim light) to partial protection against injury. Illegal in many jurisdictions . . . but . . . irresistible.

Karl stuffed the rest of Bryce's gear back into the black case and put the suit on over his own clothes, pulled the hood over his head. He looked in the mirrored door of the entertainment center. One touch: he vanished, and the room behind him appeared where he had been. When he moved, it wavered a little, like something seen through heat waves. He tried a button on the other wrist. He was back, visible, but the suit itself had disappeared, revealing the clothes he wore under it.

He pushed the hood back and opened the front enough to fill his pockets with the men's keys, including the luggage-bin key, and considered taking the luggage back to the bins. No. Too much chance of being seen, too many possible questions. Instead, he stuffed the two players they'd bought the day before, and a selection of cubes and slices, in his shirt, where they poked at his new bruises.

He thought about what to do next. He could sell the players for money . . . but where? He didn't have a parle; he'd have to use a public booth to find out where Novice's open market was. Surely it had one . . . surely. And then he could use the money for . . . what? Bribing someone to find Bryce and Evan? Hiring someone to help free them?

Whatever he did, he must get out of the room before someone came and found him there. Before those men woke up. He looked again. One had turned an ugly gray-blue color in the face; Karl looked away, swallowing against nausea. He had to go. He had to go now. He picked up Bryce's case.

No one was in the lobby . . . he walked out the door without incident, back to the arrival/departure lounge, back to the Customs and Immigration booths.

"You don't look like you feel much better," the Customs officer said. "Sure you shouldn't just take a long nap?"

"I'm better, really," Karl said. He forced a smile.

"Go on through, then."

The concourse was no more or less crowded than it had been. Karl found an information kiosk and plugged in one of the data wands from Bryce's case. Far deeper into the station than Bryce had led them, an area called "Day Market: casual goods. Traveler advisory . . ." He skipped the advisory, and headed for the market. As he walked, the bruises and scrapes from the fight reintroduced themselves; the things he'd stuffed down his shirt seemed to poke into many of them.

The concourse looked much as it had before, until he passed the third section seal. Karl had been following the directions given in the information kiosk—very simple, he'd thought, and he'd been in a hurry. Now he could not help noticing the increasing dirtiness, the shabbier storefronts, the scruffier clothes people wore . . . and the suspicious looks directed his way. Bryce and the others on their security team kept him away from places like this, places he'd longed to see.

It looked less enticing now, with the memory of the two men who'd attacked him. Karl tried to project a dangerousness equal to that of the young men lounging in a corner, but that only heightened their interest. He walked past: "keep going" was the only rule he could think of. Be inconspicuous? He'd already lost that one. He thought of turning on the camouflage suit, but realized that disappearing while in view would make him even more conspicuous.

At the next turn, he could see the Day Market opening ahead of him. He had imagined a folk market out of his texts: little booths with colorful awnings, peasants in striped shirts or full skirts, tables laden with fresh produce, others with handmade goods. Instead, he saw an open space, even dirtier than the main concourse, with clumps of people in shabby clothes talking to one another and occasionally passing things from hand to hand. The only booths were two food stands, one at either end, both with long lines. Around the margin, some had spaces against the bulkhead, with merchandise at their feet and a chalked line delineating their border.

Karl edged in, trying to figure out who sold what, and who might buy, and what the price structure was. He couldn't sell the players for what they'd paid, but maybe a third off? He was still hungry; he went to the end of the line at one food stand and tried to ignore the suspicious looks he was getting.

The line shuffled forward. He sensed people closing in behind him, but after all it was a line . . . he was third from the front, his stomach growling at the smell of fried food, when someone shoved him from behind. He staggered, bumped into the man in front. The man in front turned, face contorted, fist clenched.

"What d'you think you're doing! You—" His eyes narrowed as he looked at Karl. "Who are you, some up-dock security snip come slumming?"

"He's got taggies," said someone from behind him. "Felt 'em in his clothes." A hard hand grabbed his shoulder, dug in painfully.

Karl tried to twist away but the man in front of him, with no warning at all, kicked him hard in the shin. The pain made his eyes water. Reflexively, he swung out with Bryce's case, knowing better, but unable to stop himself. The man grabbed his arm and squeezed; Karl felt his hand loosening on the handle, a yank on the case, and then it was gone.

"Security most like . . . trying to play thief . . . we don't like your kind down here," the man said, pushing his face into Karl's. His breath stank. Karl tried not to flinch, tried to summon the anger and strength that had saved him before. He could break that hold; all he had to do was—he moved, twisted, evaded a second grab, but then they were all over him, more than two, more than three, and his punches and kicks were too weak, too slow. He went down, with someone on his back clubbing at his head, and trying to remember which of the invisible studs on the camouflage suit would stiffen it against blows . . . but he couldn't. Pain burst from various parts of his body until awareness faded and he lay waiting for the end, unable to resist.

"Stop that!" A woman's voice, angry. The blows stopped. "Who've you got there?"

"Security snip or some up-dock boz too stupid to know he gotta work with a fence. Had a bunch of stolen stuff in his clothes."

"Let me see."

He felt more cool air around him; they must have moved back a little. A hand touched his hair, moved his head.

"I need to talk to him. Turn him over."

Hands pulled, tugged, until he lay on his back. Light pierced one eye . . . so he wasn't blind after all. He felt like giggling; it hurt to breathe that deep. Something stung his nose.

"Wake up, you."

He tried to open that one eye more, blinked, and saw a slightly blurry version of a face he'd seen before. Where? His brow wrinkled—that hurt—but it helped memory. In a store. In a store recently. Today? Yesterday? It had been when Bryce was there . . . the woman in the work coverall, the woman who'd looked at Bryce and Bryce had looked at her.

"You . . . store?" It came out in a gasping croak.

"You stupid young fool," the woman said. "Why are you here?"

"Here?" He had no idea what she meant.

She made a sound like a cat spitting. Then, close to his ear, her warm breath tickling, she said, "Be very quiet. Do not talk, do not move." He heard her moving away a little; he wanted her to stay. The others would come back, would hurt him more—but she was talking to them now, a rapid slangy mix he couldn't quite follow.

"S'mine, my claim. Not what you think, not snip or boz, 'e's not."

"You know him? You . . . own him?"

"Long haul, s'mine."

"How long?" That was the reedy tenor.

"Years. In Delmar's chain."

" 'Corded?"

" 'Course it's 'corded. Doubt me?"

"No." A grudging, resentful no, but a no. If only, Karl thought, he knew what it meant. No to what?

"Take him, then."

"And his taggies," the woman's voice said. Implacable, no argument possible. Karl blinked again and again, and his left eye came unstuck finally. With both eyes open, he could see that she was plain, worn, someone he'd expect to be house-keeping or in the kitchen back home. Here, she wore the same grubby work coverall he'd seen her in before, the same toolkit slung over her shoulder, a carrysack in her hand.

"You don't know how much it's worth—"

"I know what it's worth if every one of them isn't in a car-rysack in my hand right quick," she said. And one by one, the men came forward, dropping their contributions into her sack.

"This here key isn't his . . ." one of them said. She merely looked at him and he shrugged and dropped it in.

Then she looked down at Karl. "You're breathing better," she said. "Can you get up on your own?"

Karl tried, but pain he'd never imagined seized muscles and wouldn't let him move. She sighed. "Lift him carefully," she said. The big red-faced man bent down and slid one vast hand under Karl's shoulders . . . all things considered, they lifted him gently to his feet, but his vision blurred with the pain anyway. He stood, more or less upright.

"The way you look, Security'd stop you the moment they saw you," she said. "Plant, I'm going skew. Cover, then meet me in two. Binto, peel the cams. Rest—you never saw him. Just a scuffle, a loopy fell down, hear?"

A mutter of agreement.

"Now, you: 'f you're standing, you can walk. Stay with me."

Karl found that he could walk, in a shambling, uneven sort of way. Every breath hurt, every part of his body hurt, but he put one foot after the other as she led him away from the open space into a narrow passage, turning one way and then another, past rows of narrow doors almost touching. Finally she stopped; he swayed and the man behind them held his shoulders, keeping him from bumping into the wall. She opened one of the narrow doors. The space inside was tiny: the ceiling no taller than the door, a single bunk along one side, a narrow space beside it, a small sink and toilet at the far end.

"Sleephole," she said. "Likely you've never seen a place like it. Safe place to clean you up and stash you until I figure out the best thing to do."

She went in, set the carrysack and her toolkit on the far end of the bunk. Karl followed, at a slight push from the man behind him. The man crowded in as well, and he and the woman helped Karl onto the bench-bed. She wet a towel in the sink while the man started to unfasten Karl's shirt, but then jerked his hand back.

"He's got somethin' on, Glia."

"Clothes," Glia said, without turning around.

"Somethin' else . . . can't see it, can feel it."

She came over and touched him. "You are stupider than I thought," she said. "Suit could've saved you a lot of this—and you, didn't any of you notice it when you were hitting him?"

"Too busy," the man said, flushing. "What is it?"

"Camouflage suit. It's set to be invisible. Controls should be somewhere . . ." Her hands felt around his wrists, up his arms; the suit reappeared over his clothes, its supple pale gray marked only by smudges from the dirty floor he'd fallen to. "This makes things easier—"

"It does?"

"We can use it—carry him to Meeting, where it's bigger and the others can come. Won't show on scan-vids. I think he needs more care than we can give him here." She laid the wet towel on his face, then hissed again. "Boy, this wasn't your first fight of the day. Who got after you with a stinger?"

"Stinger! We didn't have no stinger!" the man protested.

"I know you didn't. But this is a stinger mark—look at it—"

"'Tis, right enough. No wonder he fought so puny."

Karl wanted to protest, but he had no strength for anything but sitting there, letting them talk over his head.

He passed out in the big man's arms, pain and exhaustion rising like a black tide. When he came to again, he was flat on his back and mostly naked, with the woman—Glia, he remembered—and two men bending over him. The pain in his head was gone; his vision was clear enough to see one of the men, the tallest, spit a wad of turquoise goo into one hand—one three-fingered hand—mash it up, and then reach out and wipe it down Karl's left arm. He was so startled that he didn't flinch and the pain he'd barely had time to feel in that arm faded away.

"Your ID says you're Karl Terrine," the woman said. "Is that right?"

"Yes," Karl said.

"I saw you yesterday in Triolet's with my old friend Boris," she said. "You and that younger boy. And now, while my friend here treats your wounds, I want to know what Boris is doing back here, and who you are to him and why, in all the seven pits of hell, you came strolling into Day Market loaded with expensive tech."

Karl started at what he considered the beginning. "Some men grabbed Bryce—"

"That's the name he's using now?"

"Yes, of course. It's his name . . . you said he had another name? So it's not his name?"

"It is now," she said. "Go on."

"They said they were bounty hunters. They said there was a warrant on him. And he said the code phrase, the one that meant run."

"So you ran . . . but there were two of you, in that store."

"My brother. Evan. I was farther away . . . and I moved when Bryce said, but Evan, he froze for a moment, and . . . and they got him, too."

"How old is Evan? I'd have guessed maybe twelve."

"He's only ten. We have to get him out—"

"Your brother or . . . or Bryce."

"Both of them! Those men, I don't know what they'll do . . ."

She kept asking questions; Karl kept answering—it was the only hope he could see.

Bryce closed his eyes against the glare of the lights. His stomach cramped, hinting at the hours since he'd eaten, but that was the least of his troubles. If he could just rest for a moment . . . he could feel the effects of the drug leaving his system, and maybe this time he'd have a chance . . . one of them yanked his hair, then banged his head into the unyielding wall.

"Wake up! You want us to hurt the kid again?"

He opened his eyes. Evan, still in the bodywrap, was staring at him, eyes wide. They'd used the stinger on both of them, though on Evan, so far, only through the bodywrap and his clothes, to prevent leaving marks. It still hurt, as he knew from experience. Cosgrove, who'd been Cossie years back, tapped the stinger against his other palm; Merrick leaned against the wall paring his nails with a knife. Pretending to, at least.

It had to have been Glia. No one else should have made him, not with his new appearance, his new identity. If he'd spoken to her, would she have done it? Was it new anger, or old resentment, or something else?

"We have your papers," Merrick said. "You know that—so why not just tell us. Who is the boy? Not your nephew, that's for sure. And not your toy, unless your tastes have changed since you left here. You're taking him—them—somewhere for somebody, that's clear enough. Merchandise? Or it is a family?"

Evan's safety depended on his silence. Bryce stared at Merrick, trying to project befuddlement, but knowing it would not work for more than a few seconds. Merrick and Cosgrove knew him—knew Boris—far too well.

"Another little touch?" Cosgrove said, glancing at Merrick, then at Evan. "The boy?"

"Not at the moment," Merrick said. "Maybe he needs a little time to think. Not much time—" He pushed himself away from the wall, flipping the knife and then closing it and tucking it in his pocket—"but a little. Maybe he can explain to the boy, or the boy can explain to him, what the real situation is, while we eat."

Cosgrove shrugged, put the stinger in a back pocket, and the two of them left, closing the door behind them.

"Bryce?" Evan's voice was trembling.

"Yes," Bryce said. "I'm all right."

"You . . . you yelled."

"Well," Bryce said, trying for a calm tone. "It hurt. People do yell when something hurts."

"But you're a grown-up!"

"Yes, but that doesn't make much difference."

"Where's—where's Karl?"

A good question. He'd seen Karl back away, just as he'd been told . . . but had the boy remembered what to do? If he'd raised an alarm at a security kiosk, he'd have expected some response by now. His captors were acting as if nothing had happened. And if Karl hadn't done that, what would he have done? "I don't know," Bryce said. He closed his eyes again. "I hope he's getting help for us."

"But it's been hours. Maybe days. And nobody's come, and I'm really hungry and it still hurts where they hit me. Somebody will come, won't they, Bryce?"

"I certainly hope so," Bryce said. He tested the bonds that held him. Some play, though probably not enough. The cell must have surveillance; Merrick hadn't ever been careless about that sort of thing. If only he'd had his kit with him . . . if only he hadn't been captured in the first place. Merrick probably had the kit now. He had their IDs, their room keys, their tickets—he might even have their luggage, if he'd managed to get into the *Altissima* luggage bin.

"I'm scared, Bryce."

"I don't wonder." Bryce looked around the small, bare room. It could be anywhere on the station; it could even be one of the smaller hotel rooms, if they'd been able to penetrate Blue Zone.

"Could you . . . could we get out?"

"I doubt it," Bryce said. "Not without help."

"Are you really a criminal?"

"No." Bryce shook his head automatically, and winced. "I was—" A scared little boy, like Evan. Would it help Evan to know that? Would anything help? "I was at one time," he said. "Before I escaped here. It's in my dossier. Your—" He shouldn't say "father." They wanted to know who Evan really was, what Bryce's role really was. "When I was hired for this job," he said instead, "I told them all about it."

"You told my—" At Bryce's gesture, Evan stopped. Tears glittered in his eyes, spilled over and ran down his cheeks. "I wet myself," he whispered.

"It's all right," Bryce said. "You couldn't help it. Nobody can."

"So," Glia said. "There's two maybe-dead men back in your hotel . . . you normally go armed lethal?"

"I didn't," Karl said, then stopped, breath hissing past his teeth as Glia's friend spread something pungent and orange on his side. It burned like fire, then subsided. "I didn't have any weapons. So I got a sprayer of stuff out of the cleaning closet. In case there were people like those who snatched Bryce and Evan hiding in our room."

"And?"

"They had our luggage; they were packing everything away . . . they didn't expect me."

"And you beat them unconscious with your bare hands, did you?" Her brows went up; she sounded as disbelieving as she looked.

"Sort of," Karl said. "They shot drug darts at me. When I'd knocked them out, I stuck darts in them. But I got beat up some." He winced as Glia's friend wiped a wet rag across his face.

Glia grunted. "You got beat up a lot, altogether. How'd you knock down two adults?"

"I've had a lot of martial arts," Karl said. "But mostly I was lucky." He felt better; the pain in his side was gone completely now, and fading wherever Glia's friend put turquoise or orange goo. "I could sit up now," he said.

Glia grinned. "You could, could you? I think you better lie there and let the knit work. You don't want it knitting crooked."

Glia's friend grinned too, his thick, purplish tongue with the little white sucker-like nubs extended. It still looked scary, but Karl was becoming used to the face that had been hidden behind the mask, the flat nose, the slit-irised yellow eyes. The—Glia's friend gulped again and spat another glob of orange goo onto his three-fingered hand—the complete weirdness and alienness.

"Are you . . . ?"

"Human?" The voice was human enough, the words accented the same as Glia's. "Some don't think so. My line was terminated."

"You were designed?" Why would anyone design something this . . . this ugly?

"For work on the fourth planet, yes, during terraforming. This is—" he held up his hand, covered with the goo, "—modification of human saliva into a healing paste. So we would not need any medical supplies. Ocular mod for the ambient light and weather conditions."

"But—why'd they terminate your—your line? That stuff's valuable—"

"Project completed," he said. "Project completed, no need for freaks and mutants . . . but some of us, still in the bottles and not yet chipped, were saved. By her—" he nodded to Glia, "—and others like her. To her, we're human." He had spread the orange goo down Karl's leg. Now he looked directly at Karl. "To you—maybe not."

Karl evaded that. "Are there others?"

"Like me?"

"Like you, or different—I'm just curious."

"You're just young," Glia's friend said, sighing. "Next thing, you'll be asking if I have a tail, or if I'm part reptile. So no, I don't have a tail, and it was amphibian genes, not reptile, responsible for my colored spit."

"They're called human-modified, or humods," Glia said. "Mostly designed for scutwork in places unmod humans can't work without a lot of extra support. But we call ourselves chameleons."

Karl looked at her, and saw nothing different there. "You're not—"

"Oh, I am," Glia said. "But I can pass. My modifications don't show unless I choose." She sat back in her chair and right there in front of him her skin changed color and texture, a dizzying array of such changes—plain colors, patterns of stripes and spots, and geometric patterns, all moving across her face, her arms, her hands. Then it went back to looking like ordinary human skin, the face and hands he was already used to. Another change, and it was a child's face—the skin smooth, unmarked, soft-looking—and it aged as he watched, half-horrified and half-fascinated.

"How do you do that?"

"Practice," Glia said. "And both cephalopod and reptile genes. There are other mods that don't show on the surface— I'm able to function at temperatures that are fatal to most." She had reverted to her usual look. "I've foxed the medical scans for years. That way I can help the others." She waved at the others in the room.

Karl really looked this time. In the corner, a stack of masks and five-fingered gloves, plus two complete arms, fully clothed in gray shirtsleeves. On the moving forms, hands with too few fingers, or tentacles, faces with features that would always be conspicuous. "How many?"

"Forty-three at the moment. Free, that is. The station uses some for special work whole-gene humans can't do, but they'll never pass. They're on file." She smiled, but it was a sad smile. "Now here's the thing, Karl. I know your identity is legal only. You're someone else. I want to know who you really are."

"I can't tell you that," Karl said. "I'm not supposed to."

"Do you trust us?"

Did he? He wasn't sure. "If you know Bryce," Karl said, "then how do I know you aren't the one who told those men about him, about us?"

"Not a bad question. Can you describe them?"

Karl tried, but the most striking thing had been those

fake uniforms, the weapons, the wrap they'd put on Evan.

"Could be that stiz Merrick," one of the others said. "He'd take a job like that in a flash."

"Merrick," Glia said. "He's in our file . . ." She went to a cabinet and opened a drawer, coming back to Karl with a handful of flatpics. "Was it one of these men?"

Karl recognized one instantly, and then another. "And that's one of the ones in our room."

"Merrick, Cossie, Dumont. Not good. Karl, these aren't people I'd ever work with, but they did know Boris— Bryce—back when he lived here. Merrick's working for Andren, who runs the mafi here, but he sometimes takes jobs on his own." She turned back to the others. "Dob—get the word out to our group that we need to find someone who saw Merrick and Cossie with a kid in a wrap and a man, going somewhere about . . . when was this, Karl?"

"After breakfast . . . maybe oh-nine-thirty?"

"Go, Dob." A skinny man across the room slung the pair of artificial arms across his shoulders and forced them into the sleeves of his work coverall with his tentacles. "And Elin, start trying to find their hidey-hole. If Merrick's doing this off Andren's ticket, he'll be holding them somewhere else." A woman with four eyes, two of them turreted like a chameleon's, pulled a mask over her face to hide the extra eyes, and went out.

"The problem we have with you is this," Glia said when they'd gone. "Until you trust us, we can't trust you."

"But why do you need my real identity?"

"To prove you trust us. You're a danger to us unless you do—if you reported us to the authorities, half these people would be in custody from which they'd never return."

Karl shivered. "Just because they're modified?"

"Yes. And they're not supposed to exist."

"Bryce said I mustn't. No matter what. It could be used against us—me."

Glia cocked her head. "You're obviously rich, and Bryce didn't have any siblings left—so he can't be your real uncle. My guess is he's your escort—possibly part of a security detail. That's what he was acting like in the store. Giving you space, but watching over you. So, you have a wealthy family, and you're considered a target. Someone might hold you for ransom, or diddle your brain and turn you into a passive agent. So—here's the deal. We've already helped you. We can help you more; we can probably—no promises—get Bryce and your brother back in one piece. But you *owe* us. You owe us your real identity, and you owe us a promise that you will do something, someday, for chameleons—humods." Karl opened his mouth, but she held up her hand to silence him. "I know you're just a boy, but if things go as your family wants, you'll be a rich man someday, a man in position to pay what you owe. Promise you'll do something—remember us, remember the humanity of humods, make life easier for some humods somewhere. And give us your name . . . just to me." She leaned close.

It was against everything Bryce had told him—or his father had told him—but it was Evan's life and Bryce's that were forfeit if he didn't—because he was out of ideas himself. "Karl Albert Stoner-Hall. My father's Ambrose Delaney Stoner-Hall." He might as well go all the way. "He owns Fairing Spacelines."

"Thank you," Glia said, sitting back again. "Bryce was right; that's dangerous knowledge. I hope your brother doesn't crack—those two will demand ransom, mindwipe him, and sell him—double profit."

"And I promise," Karl said, louder, "that when I'm grown, when I have my own resources, I'll come back and reward you."

"Doesn't have to be me, or even Novice," she said. "Any humods. But we'll be watching."

Time passed. Karl dozed off, roused to eat, then slept again. He was able to get to the little toilet off the main room by himself, and change to the clothes out of his luggage, retrieved somehow from the hotel room. He wanted to know about the men he'd left behind, but Glia—who stayed with him—shook her head without answering when he asked. He still hurt, though less as the hours passed; Mongan reapplied both the turquoise and the orange goo a couple of times. When word finally came of where Evan and Bryce were being held, Karl tried to get up, but Mongan shook his head. "Ribs don't heal in an hour," Glia said. "Even if we had access to regen tanks, those cracked ribs would take longer than that to heal. Lie down—sleep if you can. I don't know how long it will be."

Mongan grinned at him, then pulled on his mask and his five-fingered gloves before leaving the room with Glia.

Evan had finally gone to sleep, exhausted by fear. Bryce stared at him, having nothing else to look at but the blank wall, and wondered what he could possibly do to get them out of this. Merrick and Cosgrove had applied very effective bonds, true professional grade, similar to the ones he himself carried in his black case. For all he knew, if they'd broken into the room while he and the boys were out on the concourse, they'd used his own bonds on him. So no heroic escape. The two were far too smug about their capture to be interested in making any deals, and anyway he had nothing to deal with but the reputation of the boys' father—and yielding that could be, and probably would be, fatal.

How long could Evan last? The boy was smart and as tough as his life had let him become—their father valued toughness—but he was only ten, and he was in the hands of men who knew how to exploit any weakness.

The snick of the lock brought Bryce to full alertness; Evan stirred in his sleep and Bryce braced himself for another session.

But it wasn't Merrick or Cosgrove who stood in the doorway. Five people he didn't know . . . and a sixth he did. Glia. His betrayer. Come to pretend to rescue them, no doubt. They'd be taking them to another captivity, but he might have a chance to get Evan free, in transit, when they were pretending to be friends.

"Quiet," said the big man in the lead, very softly. He looked dubiously at Evan. "Will he be quiet if we wake him?"

"Maybe," Bryce said. Behind him, someone snipped the bonds on his arms; circulation returned, tingling sharply. He flexed his hands as soon as they were free, and moved his arms cautiously. "Let me try?"

"Yeah, but quick and quiet. Got sedative." The man's voice was low, but thick, and the accent unfamiliar.

Bryce took the decoupler someone handed him and touched Evan's bodywrap; it opened, no longer sticky, shriveling to dry shreds as he watched. He touched Evan's shoulder and murmured into his ear. "Evan . . . Evan, it's me, Bryce, we're getting out. Wake up . . ." Evan's eyes opened, blinked, and he started to cry out . . . but Bryce laid a finger on his mouth. Evan stared at the others, lips tightly compressed. "Time to go, Evan. Remember the codes . . ." Evan nodded.

"I'll carry him," the big man said. "He looks stiff."

"I will," Bryce said. "He knows me." He looked at Glia. She nodded; the others formed around them and Glia led the way.

Outside the room was another, arranged like an office; through a door to one side were cots, blankets now tumbled on the floor, food containers piled in a messy heap. Merrick and Cosgrove made two more messy heaps; Bryce looked away, hoping Evan hadn't seen them.

No one was in the narrow passage outside the final door; the lights were on full, the way Novice delineated first shift, the most active. At the first cross-passage, Glia turned right, and right again at the next. Fourth door . . . through a door to a flight of utility stairs. Bryce's arms and shoulders trembled with the effort of carrying Evan.

"I can walk," Evan said in his ear, barely a murmur.

"Take it easy," Bryce said. If they thought the boy couldn't walk, then that could be a useful surprise.

Up the flight of stairs . . . into another passage, a little wider, another set of turns—designed, Bryce was sure, to confuse them. No real way to escape—the passages were too narrow to push past those in front or behind and they were too close for him to gain the momentum he'd need for real attack. Maybe, if he'd been alone . . . but not with Evan. Glia finally stopped and opened a door to a largish room. Bryce followed her in, and stopped short. Karl lay under a blanket on a cot, looking the worse for wear. Bryce's case and the boys' players lay on a table; their luggage was stacked neatly in one corner.

"I had to tell my name," Karl said at once.

"What did they do to you?" Bryce asked; he set Evan down and went to Karl. No one stopped him.

"They didn't hurt me—" Karl waved a hand stained blue at Glia and the escort. "It was the others—the ones who snatched you."

Karl had been fooled. He'd been fooled by one of the most elementary tricks. He was only a kid . . . anger burned in Bryce's chest. He turned on Glia.

"How could you?" he said to her. "You helped me and now you're preying on children?"

"It wasn't me," Glia said. She didn't sound angry or defensive; she was the same Glia, laying out the facts. "You've got someone else to thank for this mess."

"Who?"

"I don't know." She glanced at Karl and then met Bryce's gaze. "I may have suspicions but there's no way I can prove them. I'm the only one who knows his name. Other than the one who employed those thugs, and possibly the thugs."

Leaks multiplied . . . one person became two, four, eight, sixteen . . .

"You have Karl to thank for this—" She nodded at their luggage. "And your rescue. He found some of them clearing your rooms, and tackled them. He used their own trank needles on them and he may've overdosed them."

"How did you—?" Bryce asked Karl.

"I—it just happened," Karl said. "I didn't mean to hurt them, but—I was scared, and they tried to needle me." Bryce knew exactly what his expression meant. "It wasn't anything like a match," Karl went on, looking away now. "But my instructors were right. It does work . . ."

"I'm glad," Bryce said.

"Karl brought some of your stuff—what he thought he could sell—to the Day Market," Glia said. Bryce just had time to remember what that could be like, when she went on. "There was some . . . disturbance. Luckily, I'd dropped by for lunch and stopped it. But the two fights did some damage. It's being taken care of."

"You have a medbox?"

"No. You won't remember Mongan, probably . . ."

But he did. The thickset younger kid with the odd eyes, the three-fingered hands, and the ugliest tongue he'd ever seen. Always wanting to lick things, and nearly always drooling green slime.

"He grew up," Glia went on. "And he has the full medical mod; he's got eighteen different medicinals in his saliva glands alone. He's our medbox."

Mongan, gloves and mask off, grinned at Bryce and stuck out his tongue. "If I'd been old enough when you were hurt, Boris, I could've fixed that broken nose. Even your arm. When I grew, the pubertal hormones kicked the med glands into production."

"I'm glad for you," Bryce said. "And Karl."

"You need treatment too," Mongan said. "Your face is all over stinger stripes, and I'll bet there's more of them."

Bryce shook his head. "First I want to know the rest of it—if it wasn't you, Glia—then who? And how did you know where to find us?"

"Karl again. He described Merrick and Cosgrove well enough—and we got confirmation from some witnesses. Then Sinna borrowed your camouflage suit that Karl had brought along, and went back to the hotel, with Karl's key, to get your luggage and deal with any . . . debris. She recognized the two Karl had left tied up as part of Merrick's bunch. After that, it was getting to Merrick's before you took too much damage or they moved you, without being spotted. Then taking care of those two."

"So . . . we can go?"

"You have to go. But not back to Blue. That hotel's not secure. Blue isn't secure. And the liner you're waiting for, *Altissima*, just reported in the system and won't dock for another eight days. I understand you have a yacht chartered—"

"Yes. Allsystems. But it can't leave before—what time is it, anyway?"

"Day after you were taken, fourteen twenty."

"We lost a whole day?" No wonder he was hungry. And

Evan— He looked around the room. "Where's Evan?" Panic rose again.

"Gracie took him to clean up. It's all right, Bryce. They're just in the next room."

"It can leave as early as nineteen hundred," Bryce said, dragging his mind back to the topic at hand. "But I need to pay. I need to find out where the dock is they're using—I'd asked if they could get permission to use Blue—"

"You need to sit down and let Mongan treat you, and eat something. There's time." She pushed gently and he sank into the chair she'd offered before. Mongan came over and wiped turquoise goo on Bryce's face; it felt cool, soothing, and the pain receded.

"You should take the yacht this evening," Glia said. "Merrick's associates will be looking for blood—and profit—and you and these boys are exactly that. We can't hide you for eight days, not for sure. Call Allsystems and ask to board as soon as possible, wherever they're docked now. If you really need any of this—" she waved at their things "—you may find it tricky to get through Customs on the way out . . . it should have a stamp from the Customs at Blue, but Sinna tubed it. Only way possible."

Evan came back in the room, dressed in fresh clothes and holding something in a bun that smelled delicious. He'd already eaten half of it. "Is it over?" he asked Bryce.

"Almost," Bryce said. "I hope." Then he ate the food Glia brought him, let Mongan treat more of the stinger marks, and called Allsystems on his parle as soon as his face looked respectable. Cevrilene Baskari answered.

"We've been trying to call," she said. "Was your parle out of order?"

"Yes," Bryce said, that being easiest. "Are we still good for departure today?"

"Yes, but I was unable to get clearance to use a Blue Zone dock. Would you like to pay the balance now?"

"Certainly." Bryce pulled out his credit cube and gave the explanation Glia had suggested. "We're up in Four—I'm using an auto-reader, is that all right?"

"Certainly," she said, smiling. He plugged the cube into the reader Glia offered and in a moment, Baskari nodded. "Received and clear. Will you be coming by to pick up the paperwork, or shall I have it at dockside?"

"Dockside, please. And—any chance that we could board a little earlier? The boys are restless and, frankly, I'm worn out trying to keep up with them."

"You could board by seventeen hundred if you don't mind coming to the service area we use and some noise as the last items are loaded. *Karoe Star* is docked at Orange Eighteen, berth six. I'll just flash you the location—" It displayed in Bryce's parle. "Do you need assistance from where you are? And Customs will need to see your luggage."

"We'll allow time," Bryce said. "Thank you very much."

When he'd put the parle back in his pocket, Glia said, "You might want to think about who did this. It wasn't me; it wasn't anyone I know. Merrick might've made you, but he's not usually up on that end of the Concourse. None of his people should've made you. Cossie wasn't that bright; with those teeth and that nose, he'd have passed right by you. Got any enemies in that fancy new job of yours?"

"Not that I know of," Bryce said. "Thank you, Glia. I'm sorry I—"

She shook her head sharply. "No apologies. You did nothin' wrong. You had those boys to care for; I understood that had to come first. Just don't forget us."

He looked at Glia, the Glia who had saved him before, and tears came to his eyes. "I never forgot you," he said. "You could come with us—there's plenty of room on the yacht—"

But she shook her head, as he'd known she would. "And what about my people here? You know I'm the chameleon, the one who can blend in best. You can't take them all."

Bryce nodded and turned away.

The voyage to Gorley in *Karoe Star* passed without incident. Her captain had been able to communicate with *Altissima*— a long lag, but the message got through. Without passengers to pick up, the liner had no reason to stop at Novice, and changed course for Gorley; they should arrive almost simultaneously. The boys complained about nothing—not the smaller stateroom they shared, not the food, not the lack of advanced entertainment facilities. Bryce watched the crew carefully, but saw nothing suspicious.

Gorley, a major trading nexus, had every facility Novice lacked: the Premier Lounge came with human attendants, actually attentive. They were still ahead of *Altissima*, but only by hours; the liner was on the arrival board for sixteen hundred and it was twelve forty now.

Porters put their much-reduced luggage in the *Altissima* bins; the human attendant took their tickets and checked them in. "Suite 2-A, yes, sir. We ask that passengers be here in the lounge by half an hour prior to boarding. In the meantime, Gorley Prime has a fine gallery of shops that way—" she pointed. "And there is time to shop a little on the main concourse, if you prefer. We supply taggers so you know when to come back."

"We'll stay here," Bryce said, and both boys nodded. He hoped all their youthful taste for adventure hadn't left them, but it was certainly easier to handle them. "We should be able to find replacements in the shops here," he said. By boarding time, they had new luggage full of clothes and other items, and Bryce made sure those were checked directly into *Altissima*'s bin. He himself spent a small fortune at Gorley's best tech shop for professionals, including a pair of camouflage suits he intended to give Karl and Evan.

Only two other first-class passengers were boarding at Gorley. Bryce let them go first, then led the boys through the carpeted, padded corridor onto the great ship, where they were greeted by a purser in formal livery. The now-familiar ritual of signing on to the ship—another check of identity, receiving the ship-taggers all passengers wore so they could be located any time and recognized by any crewmember—went smoothly. The purser accompanied them directly to their suite along a corridor carpeted halfway up the walls, decorated with real paintings placed in lighted niches behind a safety barrier. The boys were shown to their staterooms. Bryce turned to his.

"Excuse me, sir, but you have a visitor in the suite lounge who is anxious to speak with you."

"Just a moment," Bryce said. "Karl?"

"Yes?" Karl turned from the door to his stateroom.

"I bought you and Evan each a present for the trip— here—on top of the other things—something Mr. Henson might approve of." He handed Karl his black case; Karl's eyes widened slightly. Then Bryce followed the purser to the suite's lounge.

He'd had the days on board the yacht to think his way through the whole sequence, so he was not entirely surprised to see his employer, Ambrose Delaney Stoner-Hall, at ease in the suite's lounge, its lights turned low except in the conversation area, where the man stood.

"Well, Bryce," he said. "You brought them home safe. Well done."

White rage swamped Bryce's vision; he fought it down and managed a mild tone to ask, "What do you know about it?"

Stoner-Hall chuckled. "More than you probably know. Here—sit down. I'll explain." He sat, and patted the couch beside him. A low table was set with a decanter of amber liquid and two glasses on a tray.

Bryce shook his head. "No, thank you, sir. You want me to report?"

"No, no need. Bryce, you told me about your past, and as far as I could tell, you told me the truth. But some truths people don't know, even about themselves. You've been a good employee for almost five years; you're on the cusp of being permanent. I had to know—know for sure—that you were loyal to me and the boys, could stay loyal under pressure. You understand?" Stoner-Hall tipped his head; the suite lights gleamed on his perfectly styled hair, flashed from the rings he wore on one hand, picked out the subtle pattern of his expensive suit.

"Not really," Bryce said. His heart thundered in his chest.

"Before I promoted you to permanent status, I had to know. So I set up this little test. And you passed it, Bryce. Passed with flying colors." Stoner-Hall poured himself a drink and sipped it. "You're on the team now, Bryce. Permanent personal assistant, as of this date. No need to wait another few tendays; I know what I need to know."

Rage, exultation, relief crashed against his mind like storm waves on a rock. Permanent status as a personal assistant to Stoner-Hall meant his life assured, security, recognition anywhere he went. He would have to do something stupid to be dropped.

"You put your sons in danger to test *me*?" he heard himself asking, in a voice colder than ice. Stoner-Hall stared at him, surprised. Bryce had a fierce internal argument with himself in the next split-second. Was he going to do something stupid? Surely not now, not with his life's security in the palm of his hand? But the rage rose inside him.

"They weren't in any real danger," Stoner-Hall said, brows raised a little. "Of course not. Surely you understand that now."

"I don't think," Bryce said, trying for a more reasonable tone but hearing his voice chip off syllables in flakes, "I don't think you quite understand the people you were dealing with. The boys *were* in real danger."

"But they're fine," Stoner-Hall said. His voice too had chilled. "Not a scratch on them, no broken bones. Maybe they were scared, but that's nothing."

Remembering Evan struggling not to cry, and losing the fight . . . Karl's broken ribs and hand . . . even the four dead men, bad as they had been . . . Bryce's fury broke his control.

"Nothing? You call torture nothing? Broken bones, nothing? You did not know—" He gulped back expletives from his childhood. "You did not know what peril you put those boys in. They could've been killed. They nearly were. Karl had two broken ribs, a broken wrist, blacked eyes; Evan was hit with a stinger—"

"What?! That wasn't supposed to happen—I told my agent to tell the men—!"

"You weren't there to stop it, were you? You thought your money would be enough to control men you'd never met . . ."

"My agent—"

"Your agent, whoever he was, was an idiot." Bryce could not stop himself now. "People on Novice take the first deal and start trading it for a better one. Those men were going to mindwipe Evan and sell him to a brothel. They were talking about whether to do the same with Karl or send him back to you as a programmed agent."

"Nobody would—"

"They *would*! They've done it before. They might, if they'd figured out who he was first—and you might consider what it cost Evan to keep his cover while he watched me being beaten up, and then they hurt him—they might have tried to get ransom from you and then sell him anyway."

"But—but they were paid, well paid, just to give you a scare."

"You don't understand a thing about it!" Bryce couldn't keep his voice quiet any longer. He was not surprised when the lounge door slid aside and two of Stoner-Hall's own security detail came in, moving to active positions. He held his own body still; he might die before this was over but he had to make the man understand. "Novice isn't your kind of place—they took your money and went looking for more, that's what they do!"

Stoner-Hall had paled, whether with shock or rage Bryce couldn't tell and didn't care. "But—but you took care of them. That's the important thing—you did well."

"I did not," Bryce said. "I got myself captured first, and there was not a thing I could do to save Evan from what he saw and experienced. Karl—Karl was able to escape at first. He didn't do what I'd told him to do, but he did better. He took down two grown men who tried to capture or kill him, and it's only because he used his head and made good decisions—" And stupid ones, but his father didn't need to know that. "Only because of him that Evan and I are alive."

"What had you told him to do?" Edgar, one of the security detail, asked. Bryce recognized an attempt to deflect him from his tirade but answered anyway.

"Go to a security kiosk and hit every emergency button. Instead, he went to a security office where they were no help at all. Probably—" Bryce looked back at Stoner-Hall

"—because you'd told your agent to tell them it was all some kind of game. How anyone could be so stupid—!"

"You're upset," Stoner-Hall said. "I didn't—you're right, I did not anticipate that anyone would do something like that. And you're upset, and I understand why. Let's meet for dinner, and in the meantime Marcus will debrief you."

And in the meantime he was supposed to cool down and remember that one did not call one's employer stupid even if he was? Listen to a lecture from Marcus, who as security chief was his immediate senior? "I think not," Bryce said.

"Gosslin," Stoner-Hall said. "I don't want to argue with you. You need to talk to Marcus. I'll see you later." And he was up and out of the lounge with one of his detail, while Marcus, without actually moving a muscle, radiated threat.

"I'm quitting," Bryce said the moment Marcus relaxed his stance.

"You can't do that."

"I can. I'm not permanent."

"He just made you permanent. And you know too much. You know the boys."

A moment of shock. "I just went through hell for the boys—I would never do anything to put them in peril."

"You know their real identities. You know their legal identities. How do I know you didn't stage this whole thing, just to have the chance to defect and sell them out later?"

"Me? You heard him—*he* set it up, their own father—"

"Is that likely? A father intentionally risking his own sons? All I heard was you insulting him. You know, Bryce—Boris—whatever you really are—you weren't my choice of hires in the first place. I've had my eye on you all along, just waiting for something like this . . ."

It was like seeing a humod for the first time, seeing Glia's ordinary human skin flower into patterns of green and gold, blue and purple . . . what she called the chameleon effect, what she claimed everyone did in one way or another. Marcus hadn't been waiting . . . he'd been planning . . . and Bryce knew too much now, had revealed he knew too much now.

"I didn't do anything wrong," Bryce said, hoping that

Marcus would believe he was still defending himself. "I just don't want to work for someone who puts his sons in danger. It's like . . . like bad applejack." Was anyone listening? Or were they glued to their entertainment cubes, plugged in?

"What's that?"

"A drink we had. When it goes bad it leaves a bad taste . . . the thing is, he risked his boys and they nearly got badly hurt—"

"It's not your fault," Marcus said. "Someone else tripped up; you should realize the boss didn't mean for things to get that serious. But you can't leave—"

A vague movement near the suite door almost made Bryce look that way. He resisted the temptation. "If I could just believe that he was misled," Bryce said, forcing into his tone a plodding earnestness. "If he was relying on someone else's word, that he thought he could trust, then I could understand it better."

"And stay with the team?" Marcus said.

"Well . . . I guess." Bryce felt that he sounded like an idiot, but the struggle not to look at the wavering air, now behind the bar and ten feet closer to Marcus, destroyed his ability to lie convincingly. "I just got so mad—for the boys' sakes. They were terrified; they were hurt—"

"My problem, Bryce, is that I don't know if I can trust you," Marcus said. His right hand twitched; Bryce knew it held a weapon. "I think you're always going to wonder how it happened, and you're always going to look for who's responsible—" He stared at Bryce, forcing his gaze.

Bryce tried to look puzzled. "But that's your job. You're head of security; I'm just one of the boys' team."

"Maybe. Or maybe you have ambitions to take over my job, make me look bad, show me—"

A tiny glitter in the air. Marcus slapped at his neck, at the needle there. His eyes widened; he tried to whirl, but his balance was already off and he stumbled. Bryce charged, only to have Marcus's body shoved into him by the unseen assailant. Marcus struggled, but with less and less coordination, as the other pounded on him, blows Bryce could barely follow but heard clearly, along with heavy breaths that were near sobs. He moved back.

"Karl! KARL!" The blows stopped.

"Turn it off, Karl."

Heavy breathing, then Karl reappeared, the chameleon suit concealing whatever he wore under it. "I—I heard Dad! He *planned* it! And this one—Marcus—he betrayed Dad!" He took a deep breath. "And I got most of it on the 'corder."

"Karl, you're incredible." Bryce clasped the boy's arm. "Multiple times. I hardly dared hope—"

"You gave us everything we needed," Karl said. "Your whole case—these suits—did you already know?"

"Not for sure," Bryce said, as he secured Marcus's wrists and ankles. "Not that it was Marcus. But I thought you'd be safer if you had the suits and could disappear, and the tools to find out what was going on."

"Is he dead?"

"He's breathing," Bryce said. "People don't breathe when they're dead."

Karl laughed, shakily. "Now what?"

"We go talk to your father," Bryce said. "After you take off the chameleon suit and put it away. That's your secret."

"Are you really quitting? I don't want—"

A mellow chime sounded three times, followed by a pleasant voice. "Attention please. Ship is sealed. Ship is sealed. Undock imminent. Be advised passengers may sense momentary variations on gravity . . ."

"I guess I'm not going to quit right this minute," Bryce said. "I don't have a ticket for fourth class."

Karl grinned. "Let's go break the news to my father that his precious head of security was a traitor. That should be interesting." He looked entirely too confident suddenly. "At least it won't be boring."

THE TENTH MUSE

TAD WILLIAMS

To defeat your enemy, you have to *know* your enemy. Which can be a lot more difficult than it sounds . . .

Tad Williams became an international best-seller with his very first novel, *Tailchaser's Song,* and the high quality of his output and the devotion of his readers have kept him on the top of the charts ever since as a *New York Times* and *London Sunday Times* bestseller. His other novels include *The Dragonbone Chair, The Stone of Farewell, To Green Angel Tower, Siege, Storm, City of Golden Shadow, Otherland, River of Blue Fire, Mountain of Black Glass, Sea of Silver Light, Caliban's Hour, Child of an Ancient City* (with Nina Kiriki Hoffman), *Tad Williams' Mirror World: An Illustrated Novel, The War of the Flowers, Shadowmarch,* and a collection of two novellas, one by Williams and one by Raymond E. Feist, *The Wood Boy/The Burning Man.* As editor, he has produced the big retrospective anthology *A Treasury of Fantasy.* His most recent books are a collection *Rite: Short Work* and the novel *Shadowplay.* In addition to his novels, Williams writes comic books and film and television scripts, and is cofounder of an interactive television company. He lives with his family in Woodsie, California.

When I first got to know Balcescu, I didn't like him much. A snob, that's what I thought he was, and way too stuck on himself. I was right, too. One of the things that drove me crazy is that he talked like George Sanders, all upper-crust, but I didn't believe for a moment he actually knew who George Sanders *was*. Old Earth movies wouldn't have been high-brow enough for him.

He also loved the sound of his own voice, whether the person he was talking to had time to listen or not.

"There you are, Mr. Jatt," he said one day, stopping me as I was crossing the observation deck. "I've been looking for you. I have a question."

I sighed, but not so he could tell. "What can I do for you, Mr. Balcescu?" Like I didn't have anything better to do coming up on twelve hours 'til Rainwater Hub than answer questions from seat-meat. Sorry, that's what we call passengers sometimes. Bad habit. But I hate it when people think they're on some kind of a pleasure cruise, and that just because I'm four feet tall and my voice hasn't broken yet, I'm the best choice to find them a comfy pillow or have a long chat about the business they're going to be doing planetside. What a lot of civilians don't get is that this is the Confederation Starship *Lakshmi*, and when you're on my ship, it's serious business. A cabin boy is part of the crew like anyone else, and I've got real work to do. Ask Captain Watanabe if you think I'm lying.

Anyway, this Balcescu was a strange sort of fellow—young and old at the same time, if you know what I mean. He had all his hair and he wasn't too wrinkled, but his face was thin and the rest of him wasn't much huskier. He couldn't have been much older than my cabin-mate Pim, which would make him late thirties, maybe forty at the most, but he dressed like an old man, or like someone out of an old movie—you know, those ancient films from Earth where they wear coats with patches on the elbows and loose pants and those things around their necks. Ties, right. That's how he dressed—but no tie, of course. He wasn't crazy, he just thought he was better than everyone else. Wanted you to know that even though he was some kind of language scientist, he was *artistic*. It wasn't just his clothes—you could also tell by the things he said, the kind of the music he listened to. I'd heard it coming out of his cabin a couple of times—screeches like cats falling in love, crashes like someone banging on a ukulele with a crescent wrench. Intellectual stuff, in other words.

"I can't help but notice that much ado is being made of this particular stop, Mr. Jatt," he said when he stopped me on deck. "But I went through four Visser rings on the way out to Brightman's Star and nobody made much of it. Why such a fuss over this one, this . . . what do they call it?"

"People call Rainwater Hub 'the Waterhole,'" I told him. "You can call it a fuss, but it's dead-serious business, Mr. Balcescu."

"Why don't you call me Stefan, my young friend?—that would be easier. And I could call you Rolly—I've heard some of the others call you that."

"Couldn't do it, sir. Regs don't allow it."

"All right. How about something else, then? You could call me something amusing, like 'Mr. B' . . ."

I almost made a horrified face, but Chief Purser always says letting someone know you're upset is just as rude as telling them out loud. "If you don't mind, I'll just keep calling you Mr. Balcescu, sir. It's easier for me."

"All right, then, Mr. Jatt. So why is Rainwater Hub such a serious business?"

I did my best to explain. To be honest, I don't understand all the politics and history myself—that's not our job. Like we rocket-jocks always say, we just fly 'em. But here's what I know.

When Balcescu said he went all the way out to Brightman's Star and there was no fuss about wormhole transfers, he was right, but that's because he'd left from the Libra system and his whole trip had been through Confederation space. All those Visser rings he went through were "CO&O" as we say—Confederation owned and operated. But when he hopped on the *Lak'* to join us on our run from the Brightman system to Col Hydrae, well, that trip requires one jump

through non-Confederation space—the one we were about
to make.

Not only that, but for some reason not even Doc Swainsea
can explain so I can understand it, the Visser ring here at
Rainwater is hinky, or rather the wormhole itself is. Sometimes it takes a little while until the conditions are right, so
the ships sort of line up and wait—all kinds of ships, the
most you'll ever see in one place, Confederation, X-Malkin,
Blessed Union, ordinary Rim traders, terraform scouts out
of Covenant, you name it. They call it the Waterhole because, most of the time, everybody just . . . shares. Even
enemies. Nobody wants to shut down the hub when it means
you could wind up with an entire fleet stranded on this side
of the galaxy. So there's a truce. It's a shaky one, sometimes.
Captain Watanabe told us that once, in the early days, the
Confederation tried to arrest a Covenant jumbo at another
hub, Persakis, out near Zeta Ophiuchus—the Covenant had
been breaking an embargo on the Malkinates. Persakis was
shut down for most of a year and it took twenty more for
everyone to recover from *that*, so now everybody agrees that
there's no hostilities inside a hub safety zone—like predators and prey sharing a waterhole on the savannah. Once you
get there, it's sanctuary. It's . . . Casablanca.

I mentioned I like old Earth movies, didn't I?

After I'd explained, Balcescu asked me a bunch more
questions about how long we'd have to wait at Rainwater
Hub and who else was waiting with us. For a guy who'd traveled to about fifteen or twenty different worlds, I have to say
that he didn't know much about politics or Confederation
ships, but I did my best to bring him up to speed. When he
ran out of things to ask, he thanked me, patted me on the
head, then walked back to the view-deck. Yeah, patted me
on the head. I guess nobody told him that any member of a
Confederation crew can break a man's arm using only one
finger and thumb. He was lucky I had things to do.

The weird stuff started happening as we entered the zone.
Captain Watanabe and Ship's Navigator Chinh-Herrera

were on the comm with Rainwater Hub Command when things started to get scratchy. At first they thought it was just magnetar activity, because there's a big one pretty close by—it's one of the things that makes Rainwater kind of unstable. The bridge lost Hub Command, but they managed to latch onto another signal—comm from one of Rainwater's own lighters—and so they saw the whole thing on visual, through a storm of interference. Chinh-Herrera showed it to me afterward, so I've seen it myself. I wouldn't have believed it if I hadn't.

First there was the huge alien ship, although even after several views it takes a while to realize it *is* a ship. Shaped more like a jellyfish or an amoeba, all curves and transparencies, and not particularly symmetrical. In another circumstance, you might even call it beautiful—but not when it's appearing out of a wormhole where it's not supposed to be. The Visser ring wasn't supposed to open for another several hours, and it certainly wasn't supposed to open to let something *out*.

Then that . . . *thing* appeared. The angry thing.

It was some kind of volumetric display—but what kind, even Doc Swainsea couldn't guess—a three-dimensional projected image, but what it looked like was some kind of furious god, a creature the size of small planet, rippling and burning in the silence of space. It just barely looked like a living creature—it had arms, that's all you could tell for certain, and some kind of glow around the face that might have been eyes. Its voice, or the voice of the alien ship projecting it, thundered into every comm of every ship within half a unit of Rainwater Hub. Nobody could understand it, of course—not then—it was just a deafening, scraping roar with bits along the edges that barked and twittered. "Like a circus dumped into a meat grinder, audience and all," Chinh-Herrera said. I had to cover my ears when he played it for me.

If it had stopped there, it would have been weird and frightening enough, but right after the monstrous thing went quiet, some kind of weapon fired from inside it—from the ship itself, cloaked behind the volumetric display. It wasn't a beam so much as a ripple—at the time, you couldn't even see it, but when we played it back, you could see the moment of distortion across the star field where it passed. And the nearest ship to the Visser ring, a Malkinate heavy freighter, flew apart. It happened just as fast as that—a flare of white light and then the freighter was gone, leaving nothing but debris too small to see on the lighter's comm feed. Thirteen hundred men dead. Maybe they were X-Malkins and they didn't believe what we believe, but they were still shipmen like us. How did it feel to have their ship, their home, just disappear into fragments around them? To be suddenly thrown into the freezing black empty?

A few seconds later, as if to show that it wasn't an accident, the god-thing roared again and convulsed and another ship was destroyed, one of Rainwater's lighters. This one must have had some kind of inflammable cargo, because it went up like a giant magnesium flare, a ball of white fire burning away until nothing was left but floating embers.

This was too much, of course—proof of hostile intent—and a flight of wasps was scrambled from Rainwater Station and sent after the jellyfish ship. Maybe the aliens were surprised by how quickly we fought back, or maybe they were just done with their giant hologram: in either case, it disappeared as the wasp flight swept in. A moment later, the wasps were in range and began to fire on the intruder, but their pulses only sputtered and flashed against the outside skin of the jellyfish ship. A moment later, every one of the wasps abruptly turned into a handful of sparks flung out in all directions like spinning Catherine wheels—an entire flight gone.

After that, everybody fell back, as you can imagine. "Ran like hell" might be a better way to put it. The Confederation ships met up in orbit around the nearest planet, several units away from Rainwater, and the officers began burning up the comm lines, as you can imagine. Nobody'd seen anything like the jellyfish before, or recognized whatever it was on that volumetric or how it was done.

We accessed some of the Hub drones so we could keep a

watch on Rainwater. The alien ship was still sitting there, although the Visser ring behind it had closed again. There were moments when the angry-god display flickered back into life, as if it was waking up to have a look around, and other moments when crackling lines of force like blue and orange lightning arced back and forth between the jellyfish and the ring, but none of this told anyone a thing about what was really going on.

Our first major clue came when one of the Hub's own lighters got close enough to pick up some of the wreckage of the Malkin jumbo. The ship had not been blown apart in any normal sense—no shear and no heat, or at least no more than would be expected with sudden decompression. The carbon ceramic bones and skin of the ship had just suddenly fallen apart—"delatticed" was Doc Swainsea's term. She didn't sound happy when she said it, either.

"It's not a technology I know," she told Captain Watanabe the day after the attacks. "It's not a technology I can even envision."

The captain looked at her and they stood there for a moment, face to face—two very serious women, Doc tall and blond, Captain W. a bit shorter and so dark-haired and pale-skinned that she looked like an ink drawing. "But is it a technology we can beat?" the captain finally asked.

I never heard the answer because they sent me out to get more coffee.

About two hours later, while I was bringing more whiskey glasses to the captain's cabin—which meant, I assumed, that the doctor's answer had been negative—I found Balcescu standing waiting for the lift to the bridge.

"I think I have it, Mr. Jatt," he told me as I went by.

I was in a hurry—everyone on the ship was in a hurry, which was strange considering we obviously weren't going anywhere soon—but something in his voice made me stop. He sounded exhausted, for one thing, and when I looked at him more closely, I could see that he didn't look good, either: he was pale and trembling, like he hadn't had anything but coffee or focusmeds for a while. Maybe he was sick.

"Have what, Mr. Balcescu? What are you talking about?"

"The language—the language of the things that attacked us. I think I've cracked it."

Two minutes later, we were standing in front of the captain, Chief Navigator Chinh-Herrera, Doc Swainsea, and an open comm line going out to the other Confederation ships.

"I couldn't have done this if it had been pure cryptography," Balcescu explained, standing up after all the introductions had been handled. His hands were still shaking; he spilled a little of his coffee. He obviously needed some food, but I was damned if I was going to leave the room right then.

Sorry. We spacemen swear a lot. But I wasn't going to rush out to the galley just when he was about to explain.

"What I mean to say is," Balcescu went on, "if it is anything like the languages we already know—and I think it is—then they haven't given us enough of a sample to do the standard reductions. For one thing, we couldn't know that we were even hearing all of it . . ."

"What are you talking about?" asked Chinh-Herrera. "Not heard it all? It nearly blew our comms to bits!"

"We heard the part that was in our audio register. And there were other parts above and below human hearing range as well that we recorded. But who could say for certain that there weren't parts of the language outside the range of our instruments? This is a first encounter. Never make assumptions, Chief Navigator."

Chinh-Herrera turned away, hiding a scowl. He didn't like our Mr. Balcescu much, it was easy to see. The Chief Navigator was a good man, and always nice to me, but he could be a bit old-fashioned sometimes. I actually understood what Balcescu was saying, because I've spent my life living with other people's assumptions, too. That's what happens when you're my size.

"So you're saying that the sample wasn't enough to form a basis for translation, Dr. Balcescu?" This was Doc Swainsea. "Then why are we here?"

"Because it *is* a language, and I know what they're saying," said Balcescu wearily. By his expression, you'd have thought he was being forced to explain the alphabet to a room full of four-year-olds. "You see, we've enlarged the boundaries of human-contact space quite a bit in the last couple of hundred years—the Hub system has seen to that. Just a few weeks ago, I was out in the Brightman system doing something that would have been unthinkable only generations ago— xenolinguistic fieldwork with untainted living cultures." He gave Chinh-Herrera a bit of a sideways look. "In other words, speaking alien with aliens. Our linguistic database has also expanded hugely. So I figured that it was worth a try to see if there were any similarities between what we heard at Rainwater Hub and any of the other cultures we've recorded on the outskirts of contact space. I spent hours and hours going through different samples, comparing points of apparent overlap . . ."

"*And*, Dr. Balcescu?" That was Captain Watanabe. She wasn't big on being lectured, either.

"And there are similarities—distant and tenuous, but similarities nevertheless—between what we heard yester-day and some of the older speech systems we've found out toward the galactic rim. I can't say exactly what the relation-ships are—that will take years of study, and, to be honest, a great deal more information about this latest language—but there are enough common elements that I think I can safely translate what we heard, at least roughly." He looked around expectantly, almost as if he was waiting for polite applause from the captain and the others. He didn't get it. "I used what we already know about these particular rim dialects as a ratchet, combined with some guesswork . . ."

"Get to the point, Doctor," said the captain. "Tell us what it said. A lot of good men and women are dead already, and the rest of us are stranded forty-six parsecs from the nearest Confederation hub."

"Sorry, of course." He pointed to the comm screen and the picture of the monstrous apparition jumped back onto it. I'd seen it before, of course—everyone had been watching it over and over, trying to understand what had happened—but it still scared the brass marbles off me. It was like some-thing out of an old ghost story, the kind they tell down in the engine bay on a slow shift, with the lights down. The thing

was like some wailing spirit, a banshee heralding death—
and not just the death of a few, but of the whole human race.
How could we beat something like that?

As the image billowed and stretched in achingly slow
motion, like living flame, Balcescu spoke.

"What it seems to be saying, as far as I can tell, is, unfortunately, just as bellicose as its actions suggest. It boils down
to this." He said it like a man reciting a memorized speech,
all emotion squeezed out of his voice. *"Your death is upon
you. Only black ash will show that you ever lived. The Outward-reaching Murder Army*—that's the best I can do, that's
pretty much what they're saying—*will spit upon the stars
that give you life, extinguishing them all. The cold will suck
the life from you. All memory of you will be obliterated."*
Balcescu shook his head. "Not exactly Shakespeare. In fact,
a rather crude translation, but it makes the main points."

The monstrous shape still rippled slowly on the comm
screen, its face glowing like a dying sun.

"Well," said Captain Watanabe after a long silence. "Now
that we know what it said, I'm sure we all feel a lot better."

Everybody on board the *Lakshmi* continued to hurry around
as the days went past, but with what seemed like an increasing hopelessness. Rainwater was one of the longest and most
important holes—without it, it would take us years, maybe
decades, to make our way back. There was no other shortcut
from this part of the rim.

Under emergency regs, most of the passengers had been
put into cryo, except for those like Balcescu who had a job
to do. I didn't have much to keep me occupied, so I spent
a lot of time with the people who had time to spend with
me. Chinh-Herrera the navigator didn't have much to do
either, once he'd plotted the various ways back home that
bypassed Rainwater, but when he was done, he didn't really
want to talk. I'd bring him wine and stay awhile, but it
wasn't much fun.

One evening I got called up to Balcescu's room, an
unused officer's cabin he'd been given. To my surprise, as I
got there, Doc Swainsea was just leaving, dressed in civil-

ian clothes—a dress, of all things—and carrying her shoes. She smiled at me as she went past but it was a sad one and she didn't really seem to see me. Balcescu was sitting in the main room listening to music—kind of pretty, old-fashioned music for a change—and when he saw my face, he smiled a little bit too.

"We all deal with fear in different ways," he said, as if that explained something. "Did you bring my coffee, Mr. Jatt?"

I put the tray down. "There's plenty of coffee down in the commons room," I told him, a touch grumpily, I guess. "Cups, spoons, you name it. Even stuff that tastes like sugar. It's practically a five-star restaurant down there." I wasn't sure what that meant, but I'd heard it in old movies.

He raised an eyebrow. "Ah. Is it the revolt of the proletariat, then, Mr. Jatt?" he asked. "*The Admirable Crichton*? If we are all going to die, let it be as equals?"

I'd seen *The Admirable Crichton*, as a matter of fact, but I didn't remember anyone using a word like "proletariat." Still, I got the gist. "Some would say we were already equals, Mr. Balcescu," I said. "The Confederation Constitution, for one. I've read it. Have you?"

He laughed. "Touché, my good Jatt. As it happens, I have. It has its moments, but I think it would make a dull libretto. Unlike this." He gestured loosely to the air and I realized that he was drunk, so I started pouring the coffee. We might die as equals, but it probably wouldn't be soon, and in the meantime, I'd be the one who'd have to clean up any messes. "I said, *unlike this*," he told me again, more loudly. The music was getting loud too, some men singing in deep voices, all very dramatic.

"I heard you!" I practically shouted back. "Here's whitener if you want some. And sweetener."

"I haven't been able to get this out of my head for days!" He waved his hand over the chair arm and the music got quieter, although I could still hear it. "*Don Giovanni*. That . . . thing . . . that alien projection we saw reminds me of the Commendatore's statue. Come to drag us all to hell." He laughed and reached clumsily for the coffee. I held the cup until he had a grip on it.

"I have no idea what you're talking about, Mr. Balcescu," I said. "Unless you want something else, I'd better be going."

"That's what . . . Diana said."

"Pardon?"

"Dr. Swainsea. Never mind." He laughed again, another in a line of some of the saddest laughs I had ever heard. "Don't you know *Don Giovanni*? My God, what do they teach cabin boys these days?"

"How to deal with drunken idiots, mostly, Mr. Balcescu. No, I don't know *Don Giovanni*. One of those old Mafia films?"

He shook his head. He seemed to like doing it enough that he kept it up for a bit. "No, no. *Don Giovanni* the *opera*. Mozart. About a terrible man who seduces women—preys on them, really." He began to shake his head again, then seemed to remember that he'd done that already, and for a good long while, too. "At the end, the murdered spirit of one of the women's fathers, the Commendatore, comes after him in the form of a terrible statue. In his foolishness and his pride, Don Giovanni invites the ghost to supper. So the statue, the ghost, whatever you want to call it—it *comes*. It's going to take him to his judgment. Listen!" He cocked an ear toward the music. "The Commendatore's statue is saying, *'Tu m'invitasti a cena, il tuo dover or sai. Rispondimi: verrai tu a cenar meco?'* That means, 'You invited me to dinner—now will you come dine with *me*?' In other words, he's going to take him off to hell. And Don Giovanni says, 'I'm no coward—my heart is steady in my breast.' He'd rather go to the devil than show himself afraid—that's panache!" Balcescu was lost in it now, his eyes closed as the music swelled and the voices boomed. "The ghost takes his hand, and Don Giovanni cries out, 'It's so freezing cold!' The ghost tells him it's his last moment on earth—repent! *'No, no, ch'io non me pento!'* Don Giovanni tells him—he won't repent!" Balcescu sat back in his chair, eyes still closed, and sighed. "That is Art. That's what Art can do!"

He said it—slurred it a bit, actually—as though it were the end of a beautiful dream, but I could hear the music in the background and nobody sounded very happy—not even

the stony-voiced thing that I guessed was the Commendatore's statue. Made sense. What did the poor old Commendatore have to look forward to after his revenge, anyway?
He was already dead.

"I don't get you, Mr. Balcescu."

He frowned. "You really should call me 'Doctor,' Mr. Jatt.
I am a doctor, you know. *Art*, I said. Art teaches us the things
that reality can't. Teaches us to live with the things that seem
beyond endurance. Missed chances. Failed love affairs. Suffering and death—the stuff of actual life."

He was lecturing again and I didn't like it. "But what's so
good about that?" I asked. "I don't *like* your kind of art—
that high-falutin' stuff that's just like real life. Why can't it
be the other way around—why can't life imitate the stuff
I like? Like *Casablanca*, y'know? Some scary bits, some
laughs, then the good guys win—a decent ending, y'know?
Why can't life be like *that*?" I was getting kind of angry.

"Ah, well. You know what Oscar Wilde once said? 'God
and other artists are always a little obscure.'" Balcescu
looked just as struck by dark thoughts as I was, his thin face
sagging into lines of weariness. All of us on the *Lak'* were
feeling that way, trying to follow our routines in the long
shadow of doom—or at least permanent exile. "You know, I
shouldn't even *be* here," he said after a while. "I was going
to go back to my home in the Gliese Ring, but a colleague
asked me to come to the opening of an exhibit at the Xeno-
biology Gardens on Col Hydrae 7. Just a big party, basically,
but he used some of my material from the *Xenolinguistic
Encyclopedia* and thought I'd like . . ." He shook his head.
"And here I am. Never going home, now. 'Cause I said yes to
a goddamn cocktail party . . ." He fell silent again for a long
moment. "Never mind, Mr. Jatt. I've kept you long enough.
I'm sure you have more important people to help."

As I've told you, I didn't really like Balcescu much, and
I usually don't give a crap for other people's self-pity, but I
suddenly felt sorry for him. Don't ask me why—he wasn't
any worse off than the rest of us—but I did. A little.

"Mr. Balcescu, how old do you think I am?"

The reaction was slowed by alcohol, but when it came he looked mildly startled. "How *old* are you? My dear Mr. Jatt, how the hell should I know? Ten? Eleven, but small for your age?"

"Has it ever occurred to you to wonder why a Confederation cruiser would have an able-bodied shipman ten or eleven years old?"

"But you're . . . you're a cabin boy, aren't you?"

"That's the name of my job, yes. But I'm a legit grade CS6 shipman, bucking for grade seven. I'm forty-three years old, Mr. Balcescu. I've been shipping out on Confederation ships for twenty-five years."

His eyes went wide. "But . . . look at you! You're a kid!"

"I look like a kid, but I'm just about your age . . . right? Although right now, you look about ten years older. You look like crap, in fact."

He straightened up a little, which was what I'd intended. "What happened to you? Is it some kind of genetic thing?"

"Yeah, but not in the way you mean. My parents were Highfielders—they were subscribers to Reverend Highfield's generation ship. You may have heard of that—the Highfielder movement started up about the same time the X-Malkins were splitting off. My parents' church said that the Confederation system was full of sinners and was doomed to be destroyed by the Lord, so they planned to send their children away to find another home outside the system, somewhere far away across the galaxy. And to make sure that we'd be able to survive on ship as long as possible, they worked with geneticists to retard our aging processes—see, they started this project before we were even born. That was supposed to give us an advantage for a long-haul trip—keep us small, easy to feed, revved-up immune systems. So don't worry about me, Mr. Balcescu—I'll hit puberty eventually, but it won't be for another twenty or thirty years. I'm looking forward to sex, though. I hear it's a lot of fun."

"What . . . what happened?" Balcescu was listening now, all right. "Why didn't you go?"

"Do you remember Katel's World?"

For a moment, he couldn't place it. Then he went a little pale. I see that a lot when I tell people. "Oh, my God," he said. "Those were your parents?"

"My folks and about a thousand other Highfielders. And, of course, a few thousand of their children. That's why the Confederation went in, to protect the children. But as you probably remember, things didn't work out so well with that. I was one of about eight hundred that were rescued alive. I grew up in an orphanage, but I always wanted to see the big black—I figure it's sort of what I was born for. So here I am."

He stared at me. "Why are you telling me this?"

"Don't know, exactly, Mr. Balcescu. I hate to see people lose track of what's important, I guess. And I hate to see people make assumptions. And I definitely don't like to see people being underestimated."

"Are you saying I underestimated you?" He sat up and wiped his hand across his face. "Well, I suppose I did, Mr. Jatt, and I apologize for . . ."

"With respect, Mr. Balcescu, I'm not talking about that. I'm talking about you underestimating *yourself.* Instead of sitting around listening to weepy music and feeling sorry for yourself, there must still be useful work you can do. You figured out what those aliens were saying—what *else* can you figure out about them?"

When I left with the empty wineglasses he was drinking his coffee and staring up at the ceiling as if he was thinking about something real. The music had started again, Don Giovanni and his doomed pursuit of pleasure. Oh, well, better than the caterwauling modern stuff, I guess.

Honest, I've got nothing against art. I hope I've made that clear. I just don't like moping. Waste of everyone's time. "Life's a banquet," as good old Rosalind Russell said in one of those ancient films I like, "and most poor suckers are starving to death."

The thing that finally made it all happen was Doc Swainsea's report. I don't know what happened between her and Balcescu, but after the night I saw her, she pretty much disappeared from social life on the ship, spending something like twenty hours a day in her lab. I know, because who do you think brought her meals to her, cleared away the old trays, and tried to get her to sleep and take a sonic occasionally?

Anyway, it happened during one of the meetings where I was off duty and my roomie Pim was serving at the bridge conference table—he gave me the lowdown the next morning. Doc Swainsea was just finishing up her final report. The energies she'd been able to analyze in the destruction of the Malkinate ship and the Hub lighter were like nothing else she'd seen, she told the captain and the others. The wreckage was like nothing else she'd seen, either. The projection mechanism had to be like nothing she'd seen. And she'd been in touch with a xenobiologist on one of the other trapped ships, and he agreed that the projected apparition looked like nothing he'd seen, either. If it was an image of a real life form, it was one we hadn't come into contact with yet.

"Extragalactic, most likely," was Balcescu's one contribution, Pim said. Nobody argued, but nobody seemed very happy about it, either. Then the odd part happened.

Doc Swainsea closed with one last point. She said that in analyzing the projection, she'd discovered a regular pulse of complex sound buried deep in the roaring, blaring audio, at a level too low for humans to hear without speeding it up. It didn't sound anything like the speech Balcescu had translated—in fact, she wasn't sure at all that it *was* speech, although it seemed too regular and orderly to be an accident. She said she didn't know what that signified, either—she just thought she should mention it. Pim said she looked exhausted and sad.

And just at this point, Balcescu got up and walked out.

When Pim told me, I couldn't help wondering what was going on. Was it something to do with that evening the two doctors had spent together, the one I'd walked in on? It had just looked like a less-than-satisfactory date to me, but maybe my lagging biochemistry had betrayed me—maybe there had been something more complicated going on. Pim said Doc Swainsea had looked surprised, too, when Bal-

cescu left so abruptly, surprised and maybe a little hurt, but
she didn't make a big deal of it. That upset me. I really liked
Doc Swainsea, although the difference in our ranks meant I
didn't get to talk to her much.

I didn't have much time to think about Stefan Balcescu,
though. That morning, as I came on duty, right after I talked
to Pim, we heard that five Malkinate cruisers had attacked
the jellyfish ship. The black starfield around Rainwater Hub
looked like a Landing Night celebration back home—fire-
works everywhere. But silent, of course. Completely silent.
The X-Malkins were obliterated in a matter of minutes.

Things got a little crazy after that. Some of the passengers
who were supposed to be in deep sleep staged a sort of mini-
mutiny. We didn't do much to 'em once we put an end to
their uprising—just put 'em back in cryo where they were
supposed to be in the first place. One of the passenger cabin
CS4s turned out to be the sympathizer who'd let them out,
and he wound up in cryo himself, except in the brig. Captain
Watanabe knew that she had a lot of unhappy, worried shipmen on her hands, but she also wanted to make sure she did
the right thing. The problem was, at that moment nobody believed anything good could happen from staying near Rainwater Hub: everybody figured that if we were going to take
years getting home, we might as well get started. But the
captain and some of the other Confederation officers hadn't
given up yet—and strangely enough, the one who had convinced them to hang on was Stefan Balcescu.

I only found out what was happening when I got called
to the bridge one evening almost a week later. It was about
day twenty of the crisis. Captain Watanabe was in the conference room with Lieutenant Chinh-Herrera, Dr. Swainsea,
First Lieutenant Davits, who headed up the ship's marines,
and several men and women from Engineering whose names
I didn't know—they've kind of got their own world down
there.

I asked the captain what I could bring her.

"Just sit down, Jatt," she told me. "Shipman Pim's handling your duties. You're here as an observer."

"Observer?" I had no idea what she was talking about. "Begging your pardon, Captain, but observing what?" It was a mark of how sure she was of her command that I could ask my commanding officer a question that easily. A lot of 'em want you to treat anything they say like it's written on a stone tablet.

"This," she said, and one of the engineers turned on the comm screens.

The first thing I saw was a group of perhaps a half-dozen red circles moving across a star field, heading toward the immensity of the alien jellyfish ship. It took me a few more seconds until I figured out that the red circles were only on our screen, that they were markers outlining the position of several small Confederation ships, which would otherwise have been almost too dark to see. The weird thing, though, was that I could see as I focused on their silhouettes when they crossed in front of the alien vessel that they weren't Confederation cruisers or jumbos or even attack ships, but . . .

"Lifeboats," said the captain as if she'd heard my thought. "One from each of the Confederation ships."

"I'm sorry, Captain Watanabe, I'm still not getting any of this . . ." I looked around to see if anyone else was as puzzled as I was, but they were all watching the screens intently. I noticed that Balcescu, who lately had been at all these sort of meetings, was conspicuously absent. Had he given up? Or just pissed everyone off so much that they hadn't invited him for this . . . whatever it was?

"Bear with us, Shipman Jatt," the captain said. "You're here by special request, but we're in the middle of an actual mission here and we don't have time to . . ." Her attention was distracted by a murmur from the first lieutenant.

"They're not going for it," he said.

"Maybe they're just not in a hurry," said Doc Swainsea. "Their approach is slow. Give it time . . ."

Even as she said it, one of the lifeboats suddenly flew apart. The others scattered away from their stricken comrade in all directions, but slowly—too slowly. The small ships dodged and dived, but within only a few minutes every one of them had been reduced to shattered flotsam. I blinked hard as my eyes filled with tears.

"There he is!" said Captain Watanabe. "See, Jatt?" When she turned to me she saw my face. "No, look, he got through!"

"He? What are you talking about? They're all dead!" It was all I could do to keep from sobbing out loud at the waste, the murderous stupidity of it all.

"No! No, Jatt, the lifeboats were unmanned. They were cover, that's all." She pointed to the screen again, at what I had taken for another small, rounded chunk of debris. "See, that's him! He's almost reached them!"

"He doesn't know, Captain," said Chinh-Herrera suddenly. "Balcescu didn't tell him."

"For Christ's sake, who is this *he* you keep talking about . . . ?" Then suddenly it hit me. "Wait a minute . . . Balcescu? Are you telling me that's *Balcescu* out there? What's he doing? What's going on?" I was almost crying again, and if you don't think that's embarrassing for a guy my age no matter *how* tall he is, you're a damn idiot.

"He's in one of our exterior repair pods," said Chinh-Herrera, pointing to the tiny, avocado-shaped object floating across the starfield toward the jellyfish, which loomed above it now like a frozen tidal wave. "The engineers modified it. Wait'll you see what it can do."

"If the ship lets it get close enough," said Doc Swainsea. I noticed for the first time that her eyes were red, too.

I still didn't really understand, but I sat in silence now with everyone else, holding my breath as I watched the tiny object float closer to the monstrous ship. At last, it touched and stuck. Everyone cheered, even me, although I still wasn't quite sure why. Slowly, the rounded shape of the repair pod flattened against the side of the jellyfish ship until it had turned itself into a wide, shallow dome like a black blister.

"It's slicing its way through," said Chinh-Herrera. "Monofilament cutter."

"Put on the helmet feed," said the captain.

A moment later another picture jumped onto the screen—a close-up view of something falling away—a section of the alien ship's skin that had been cut away now falling into the ship, I realized. The hole it left pulsed with bluish light.

"How's the pod holding up?" the captain called to the engineers.

"The blister beams have gone rigid—no loss of pressure. We're solid, ma'am!"

A moment later we could see feet in an excursion suit fill the screen as TYPO Balcescu looked down while he stepped through the hole cut in the alien hull. It seemed crazy—the aliens must know he was there. How many seconds could he have until they were on him? And what the hell was he supposed to do in that little time—plant a bomb? Why would they send *Balcescu* to do that instead of one of the marines?

But all I asked was, "Why isn't he talking to us?"

"Radio silence," Chinh-Herrera whispered. "To make sure we give him as long as possible before he's detected."

"He likes it better that way, anyway," said Doc Swainsea.

As Balcescu moved inside, it was as though he had been swallowed into some giant living thing—the blue-lit corridor was mostly smooth except for low bumps in strange formations, and as shiny-wet as internal organs. I half expected him to be swept up like a corpuscle in a blood stream, but instead he turned into the main passage, which seemed to be about half a hundred feet tall and nearly that wide, and began to move down it. He was walking, I realized, which meant that the ship had to have some kind of artificial gravity.

"What's he looking for?" I whispered, but nobody answered me.

Suddenly, a trio of inhuman shapes emerged from a side-corridor into the main passageway. I heard several of the observers swear bitterly—I must confess that Captain Watanabe was one of them—as the horrors turned toward Balcescu. I couldn't make a sound, I was so frightened. They were at least twice human height, rippling like ash in a fire, but undeniably real, even seen only on comm screen. Whatever complicated arrangement was at the bottom of their bodies didn't touch the floor, but they did not give the impression of being light or airy or ghostly. And their faces—if those *were* their faces . . . ! Well, I'll just say I think I know now what was under the Commendatore's mask.

Balcescu stopped and stood waiting for them. We could tell he'd stopped, because the walls around him stopped moving. I guess he thought that there was no point in running away, although if it had been me, I sure as hell would have given it a try. The entire bridge was silent. You know that expression about hearing a pin drop? If someone had dropped one just then, we all would have jumped right out of our skins.

The terrible things approached Balcescu until they were right in front of him—and then they glided right past him.

"What the hell . . . ?" I said, louder than I meant to, but nobody seemed to care. They were too busy cheering. For a second, I thought they'd lost their minds. "Has he got some kind of cloaking device . . . ?" I asked.

Balcescu had turned around, for some reason, and was following the floating aliens. To my horror, he actually hurried after them until he caught them, then reached out and shoved the nearest one in the back. The creature stumbled slightly, or at least bobbed off-balance, but then righted itself and went on as if it hadn't noticed anything unusual. Neither of them even looked back.

I felt like crying again, even as everyone else was celebrating. I just didn't get it. I almost thought I'd lost my mind.

"I hope you all saw that," Balcescu said. I realized that it was the first time I'd heard his voice in days. Who would have guessed I'd be hearing it over a comlink from the alien ship? "I humbly submit that I have won the argument."

"You sure did, you arrogant sonuvabitch!" shouted Chinh-Herrera, but I think the comlink was only working one way.

"What happened?" I asked Doc Swainsea. She seemed more restrained than the others, as if she didn't quite believe that this was the victory everyone else seemed to think that it was.

"They're not real," she said. "He was right, Rahul." The doctor is the only person who calls me by my true name.

"Not real? But they blew up our ships! And just now . . . he *pushed* one of them!"

"Oh, they're real enough—they have weight and mass. But they're constructs. They're not real people, any more than a child's toy soldiers are real." She frowned. She looked very tired, like it was taking all her energy just to keep talking to me. "No, that's a bad analogy. They're not that kind of toys, they're puppets. This was all a show."

"A show? They *killed* people! Hundreds of shipmen! What kind of show is that?"

But before she could answer me I heard Balcescu's voice and turned back.

"This looks like it, don't you think?" he asked, as if having a conversation with an old friend. "Time to make a little trouble for the local repertory company, I think." George Sanders, maybe even Cary Grant—I have to admit, the superior bastard did have style. He seemed to be standing in a large chamber, one that was even more intestinal than the passageway, if such a thing was possible. At the center of it floated a huge, shifting transparency, a moving gob of glass-clear gelatin as big as a jumbo jet. Balcescu walked toward it, then stopped and held up his comm wand, thumbed it. A deep rasp of sound echoed through the room and the jelly rippled. Then a vast pseudopod abruptly reached out toward Balcescu and engulfed him. I must have cried out, because Chinh-Herrera turned to me and said, "Nah, don't worry. He was right again, damn him. Look, it understood!"

The pseudopod was lifting him as gently as a mother with her child. Balcescu's point of view rose up, up, up until he was at the top of the gently swirling jelly, up near the roof of the intestinal, cathedral-size room. He stepped onto a platform that emerged from the bumps and swirls of the wall, then held up his comm wand again. A single sound, loud and rough as a tree pulling up its roots as it fell, then Balcescu and the rest of us waited.

Nothing happened.

"Maybe I'm being too polite," he said. Balcescu still sounded like he was on a day-hike in the hills. Even I had to admire him—me, who'd seen him drunk and feeling sorry for himself. I can't tell you how annoying that was.

He lifted the comm wand and thumbed it again, and another wash of sound rolled out, this one harsher and more abrupt. We waited.

The jelly thing abruptly shrank away beneath him like water down a drain. Then the lights faded all through the vast room. Everything was black. A moment later, Balcescu's helmet light flicked on, but the view now was almost all shadows, the chamber's far walls a distant, ghostly backdrop.

"Mission accomplished, Captain Watanabe," he said. "It's turned off."

The bridge erupted in cheers, some of them almost hysterical. I still didn't really understand what I'd just seen, or why I was even there, but when Pim appeared a few moments later with something that looked as near as damnit to champagne, I took a glass. God knows everyone else was having some, even the captain.

I was taking my second sip when I noticed someone standing over me.

"I've got something for you, Rahul," said Doc Swainsea. She showed me her ring with its glowing spot. I let her touch mine so the data could transfer. "He asked me to make sure you got it."

"He?" I asked, but I knew who she meant. It was just something to say as I watched her walk away and out of the conference room. She was the only one besides me who didn't seem happy, and I wasn't sure I understood my own reasons.

I stayed on the bridge a little while, but I wanted to see what he'd left for me. Anyway, I never liked champagne much. Any alcohol, in fact. Too many people over the years have thought it was funny to try to get the little guy drunk, and I used to be stubborn and stupid enough to try to prove them wrong.

"Hello, Mr. Jatt. I'm sorry I didn't get to say good-bye properly, but the last few days have been a bit of a whirlwind,

getting ready for this thing we're trying. But I did want to say good-bye. I'm glad I got a chance to know you, even a little bit. I intend no joke, by the way."

Balcescu was wearing an exosuit. The message looked like it had been recorded just before he left, which explained why he was talking like he wasn't coming back.

"But I owed you, of all people, an explanation, because you were the one that gave me the idea. I guess you must know by now whether I was right or not."

Like you ever really doubted it, you arrogant s.o.b., I thought. But then I wondered, hang on, if he was so sure of himself, why did he leave me this message?

"I should have suspected something right away—or at least as soon as I translated the message," he went on. The Balcescu of half a day ago was putting on his exosuit gloves. *"I mean, really—'The Outward-Reaching Murder Army will spit upon the stars that give you life'? 'Only black ash will show that you ever lived.' A bit over the top, isn't it? But I didn't see it. I took it at face value.*

"Then you asked what else I could figure out about the aliens. I began to wonder. As you said, we knew what they'd said—but not why. Were they just roving the universe like Mongol horsemen, conquering and slaughtering? But why? What was the plan? Why leave a ship with immensely superior firepower to defend a Visser ring when they could have wiped out every ship in the vicinity in minutes? But it was the way they talked that really puzzled me. Bloody melodrama, that's what it was. It was like something out of one of those ancient movies you told me you like so much . . ."

"Those aren't the kind of movies I like," I told the recording. "Not that John Wayne crap—well, except for *Stagecoach* . . . and maybe *The Quiet Man*. I like *characters*."

". . . but I still couldn't figure out what was making me itch. Then Diana . . . Dr. Swainsea . . . came in with her wide-spectrum audio analysis of the sounds that we hadn't noticed at first, the ones that were largely out of our hearing range. Think about it. Behind those overly dramatic words they were pumping out a huge range of sounds—higher, lower, faster, slower—not exactly synchronized to the

*words, but emphasizing them, heightening the effect. What
does that sound like?"*

It it hit me like a blow. "A soundtrack," I whispered. "Like
a movie."

"Right," the recording said. *"A score—as in an opera.
As in* Don Giovanni.*"* The recorded Balcescu had closed all
his seals and sat calmly, as if we were in the same room at
the same time, having an ordinary conversation *"So I kept
thinking, Mr. Jatt—why would someone go to such lengths,
write an entire space opera, so to speak, just to kill innocent people? I couldn't wrap my head around it. But then I
started thinking that maybe they didn't know they were killing anyone? But how could that be?"* He smiled that infuriating smile of his. *"Because maybe they didn't think there
was anyone left to kill. Remember, this thing came to us
through the Rainwater Hub, the most compromised wormhole in known space. Who's to say they even came from our
galaxy? Remember, I only found traces of their languages
in some of the very oldest civilizations we know out near
the galactic rim. Maybe the originals that spoke those languages are long gone—at least in physical form."*

I had no idea what he was talking about, and I was about
to run the recording back when he picked his helmet up off
the clean pad where it had been sitting. The mirrored visor
made a brief infinity loop with the recording wall screen—
a million helmets strobed. *"Look, if you saw this by itself,
up close, you would assume someone was in it, right?"* He
slid the visor up to show the empty interior. *"My guess is,
these people—let's call them the Company, like an opera
company, have left their physical forms behind long ago.
They might even be dead and gone, but that's another libretto."* Again, that irritating grin. *"But what they haven't
done is given up art. Just as our operas often imitate the
past in which they were written, the Company's art mimics
the time when they had bodies. Entire constructs that perform acts of aggression and destruction and who knows
what else? Programmed, operating in empty space at the
edge of a distant galaxy, for the nostalgic pleasure of bodiless alien intelligences. Of course, they would violently de-*

stroy what they come into contact with—because they're
pretending to be the kind of ancient savages that would do
that. But that's why I'm guessing that the Company are no
longer wearing bodies: they assumed that anything they
came in contact with would be more of their own lifeless
constructs, part of this art form of theirs that we can't hope
to understand . . . yet.

"So that's my idea, and in an hour or so we'll find out
if it's true. I've convinced the captain it's worth a try, and
she's brought in the other Confederation ships, so at the very
least I will be the center of a fairly expensive little drama
of my own." Balcescu stood then, his helmet under his arm
as though he were some kind of antique cavalier. "Sorry I
couldn't explain this to you in person, but as I said, it's been
a busy last forty-eight hours or so, putting together my hypothesis and then getting ready to test it." He turned toward
the door. "But I did want to thank you, Mr. Jatt. You opened
my eyes in a couple of ways, and that doesn't happen very
often."

I'll bet it doesn't, I thought, but suddenly I wished I'd told
him my first name.

"And now one of two things are going to happen," the recorded Balcescu said. "Either I'm wrong somehow—about·
the purpose of that ship, or about how realistic and thorough its defenses are, in which case by the time you see this
I'll have been delatticed, as Diana puts it. Or, I'll be right,
and I'll be able to use the little bit of Company language
I've put together, along with some useful algorithms from
Dr. Swainsea, to override the programming and cancel the
show, as it were." He moved to the door of his cabin, so that
he stood just at edge of the recorded picture. "And if I succeed with that, then I'm going to start looking for some kind
of emergency return pod. You see, the Confederation are
welcome to the ship itself. I don't give a damn about how
it works or how far it came to get here or anything of the
things they want to know. I just want to go where the show is
happening—where the opera, or religious passion play, or
children's game, or whatever this thing represents, is really
going on. I'm hoping that the Company has some kind of

recoverable module—like a ship's black box—and that it will return to their space, wherever that might be. I intend to be on it.

"How could I miss that chance? A whole new culture, language, and even more important, a whole new art form! Nine muses aren't going to be enough anymore, Mr. Jatt. So that's why this recording, my friend. Either way, I wanted to say thank you—and good-bye." And with that, the recorded Balcescu held out his comm wand and the recording went black.

Maybe he hadn't guessed how soon I'd watch the recording—maybe he was still on the alien ship. I commed the captain's cabin, but she was on the observation deck with everyone else, celebrating. I rushed up, but before I could say a thing to Captain Watanabe or any of the other officers, I spotted Dr. Swainsea leaning against the biggest viewportal looking out at the jellyfish ship, so strange, so large, so distant.

"Doc . . . Doc . . . !" I called as I ran up.

"I know, Rahul," she said without turning. "Look—there it goes." She pointed. I thought I could see a dim streak of light moving away from the alien ship—but not toward the Visser ring, I was surprised to see. "God only knows what kind of path those things travel," she said. "Well, Stefan will find out soon enough."

"You knew what he was going to do?"

"Of course. I helped him." She looked at me. "Oh, Rahul, what else was I going to do? Beg him to stay? We had . . . maybe the beginning of something. How could that compete against a Big Idea, especially for a man who lived for big ideas? No, I couldn't have asked him and he couldn't have agreed—we both would have hated ourselves. You'll understand someday."

I understand now, I wanted to say, but everyone needs to tell their own story their own way. You don't have to be six feet tall to know that. "It was just . . ." I shook my head. "At first I didn't like him. But then, I kind of thought he and I might be . . . we might . . ."

"It might have been the beginning of a beautiful friendship?" she asked. Something in my expression must have amused her, because she laughed. "You don't think you're the only one who watches old pictures, do you?"

"I guess not." I frowned. "I think Balcescu's crazy, anyway. We've already got music and art and Fred Astaire and Katharine Hepburn and Howard Hawks—do we even need a tenth muse?"

"I need a drink," she said. "Then maybe I'll feel a little bit less like Ingrid Bergman."

We walked across the observation deck, threading our way through the happy crew members, many of whom were already well into the champagne. She still looked sad, so I reached up and took Doc Swainsea's hand . . . Diana's hand. Lose a friend, make a friend. Sometimes life does imitate art, I guess.

"Well," I told her—my best Bogart—"whatever else happens, we'll always have Rainwater Hub."

CRACKLEGRACKLE

JUSTINA ROBSON

Here's the strange and troubling tale of a man who must confront bizarre forces in which he doesn't believe—even though they're swirling all around him.

Justina Robson is a relatively new writer who has succeeded in making a big splash in a fairly small number of years. She has several times been a finalist for the Arthur C. Clarke Award, the Philip K. Dick Award, and the British Science Fiction Award, as well as for John W. Campbell Memorial Award. Her stories have appeared in *Fast Forward*, *Constellations*, *Nature*, *The Mammoth Book of New Jules Verne Adventures*, and elsewhere. She is perhaps best known for the Quantum Gravity series, which includes *Keeping It Real*, *Selling Out*, and, most recently, *Going Under*, but she has also published well-received novels such as *Silver Screen*, *Mappa Mundi*, *Natural History*, and *Living Next Door to the God of Love*. She lives in Leeds, England.

Many times Mark Bishop read the assignment, but it never made more sense to him. He was to interview the Greenjack Hyperion, make an assessment of the claims made for it, and return his report. That part was simple. But after it, the evidence supplied by the Forged and human witnesses . . . this he couldn't manage more than a line or two of. Panic rose and the black-and-white print became an unknown language. He could see it hadn't changed, but simply by moving his eyes across it his mind redshifted and all meaning sped away from him.

He poured the one-too-many scotch from the concession bottle by his elbow just as the hostess was about to whisk it away, and drank it down. The burn was impersonal and direct. It did exactly what it always promised, and shot the pain where it hurt. He rubbed his eyes and tried again.

He disliked the sight of the document on his screen. It struck him suddenly that the paragraphs were too long. The white spaces between them loomed in violent stripes. Missing things were there. All of the unknown inlets holding the truth that the print struggled to express. The punctuation was a taunt, an assault that declared in black-and-white that the subject's defeat of his reason was absolute. Even the title was loathsome: "Making a Case for the Intuitive Interpretation of Full Spectrum Data in Unique Generative Posthuman Experience." Usually he had no trouble with jargon, or any scientific melee, but what the hell did that mean? What did it mean to the person it referred to? Had they titled it or was it just the bureaucrat's pedantic label for something they could read but not comprehend?

A final slug of scotch ended his attempt. He only understood that there was no escape from meeting the Greenjack, as he had promised, as his job demanded: meet, interview, assess, report. That was all. It was easy. He'd done it a hundred times. More. He was an expert. That's why the government had hired him and kept him on the top payroll all these years. They trusted him to judge rightly, to know truth, to detect mistakes and delusions, to be sure.

Bishop tried to read the document once more. His eyes hurt and finally, after a forced march across the first few paragraphs, he felt a cluster headache come on and halt them with a fierce spasm of pain as if something had decided to drill invisible holes into his head via the back of his eyeballs. He lay back in the recline seat of the lift launcher and closed his eyes. The attendants circled and took away his cup, se-

cured his harness, and spoke pleasantly about the safety of
the orbital lift system and the experience of several g's of
force during acceleration—a song-and-dance routine he already knew so well he could have done it himself. He briefly
remembered being offered a ride up on one of the Heavy
Angels and explaining to the secretary that he didn't want
it. She couldn't understand his reluctance. Then in the background she heard some colleague whisper, "Mars." She'd
gone red, then white.

But it wasn't just the difficulty of talking to the Forged
now, he'd never liked the idea of being inside a body. It was
too much like being eaten, or some form of unwilling sex.
So he'd made his economy-excuse, a polite no, a don't-want-
to-be-a-bother smile and now he was waiting for takeoff, no
time left, unprepared for the big meeting, his mouth dry with
all the things he'd taken to avoid doing anything repulsively
human, like being sick.

The lift was moved into position by its waldos, attached
to the cable, tested. The slight technicalities passed him in
a blur of nauseating detail and then there was the stomach-
leaving, spine-shrinking hurl of acceleration in the back of
his legs. The headache peaked. Weightlessness came as they
soared above the clouds into the blue and then the black. He
felt like lead. When the time came to unclip and get out, he
half-expected that he'd be set in position, a statue, and
surprised himself by seeing his hands reach out and compe-
tently move him along the guide rails. He didn't hit anyone.
The other passengers were all busy talking to each other or
into their mikes. Then the smell filled his nostrils.

It was a mysterious animal tang that reminded him of the
hot hides of horses, a drooling, dozing camel he had once
attempted to ride, and, on top of that, the ocean. Bishop
gripped on tight, knowing that all his juvenile, ancient spine-
root superstitions had caught up with him. His interviewee
had come to meet him in an act of unwanted courtesy. He
would have to greet and speak to it . . . why had he forgotten
its name suddenly? Why did it have to smell like that? But
he was now holding up the queue. The stewardess mistook
his hesitation for ignorance and started talking about freefall

walking. All that remained was to turn himself toward the smooth, white-lit exit chute that led to the Offworld Destinations Lounge, and follow that telltale scent of primeval beast.

The other passengers sniffed curiously as they passed him, "so-sorrying" their way around his stalled self. He fiddled with his recorder, checking his microphone and switching everything on. It made him feel secure in the same way he imagined Old World spies had once felt secure because of their illicit link to someone, somewhere, who would at least hear their final moments. It wasn't exactly like being accompanied, but it was enough of a shield to let the prickling under his arms stop and for his headache to recede.

The thought came to him that he hadn't been himself lately. It was only natural after the conclusion of the inquiry and its open verdict. Too much stress. He ought to stop, beg off, take a holiday. Nobody would be surprised. But the thought of not having his job, the idea of having nothing to do but walk the familiar coast near Pismo Beach or under the tall silence of the redwoods—that made him pull himself along all the faster to escape the hum, the static darkness, the horror that was waiting there for him, that was already here in the notion of that place. He gritted his teeth and pushed that aside. The scotch made it easy. Why the hell hadn't he thought to bring some more?

He pulled himself forward into the glide that felt graceful even when it wasn't, and swallowed with difficulty. That smell! It was so curious here, where all the smells were ground out of existence quickly in the filtration of the dry air so that humans and their descendants, the Forged, could meet without the animal startle reflexes scent caused by the humans. But the grace would only last a minute or two here, in the neutral zone of the Lift Center. And why could he smell *this* one so clearly? It must reek—and as he thought this, he saw it/him, a tall, gangling, ugly creature that resembled a gargoyle from some mighty gothic cathedral whose creator had been keen on all the Old Testament virtues. It could easily have featured in his nightmares. He wouldn't have been surprised to discover that it had been modeled with an artistic eye to that effect. The Pangenesis Tupac, brooder, sculptor, creator in flesh and metal, enjoyed her humor at all levels of creation. The word *anathema* sat in his head, alone, as he bravely put on a smile of greeting.

"Mark Bishop?" said the gargoyle in an old English gentleman's voice, as fitting and unexpected as rain in Death Valley.

"I am." He found conviction, was so glad the other didn't offer his hand, and glanced down and saw it was a fistful of claws.

"My name is Hyperion. I am pleased to meet you. I have read many of your articles in the more popular academic journals and the ordinary press. Your reputation is well-founded." It made a slight bow and the harsh interior lights shone off its bony eyelids.

It was shamefully difficult not to marvel at the sight and sound of a talking gryphon-thing, or want to see if those yellow eyes were real. Hyperion's voice seemed to indicate enjoyment, but who knew, with the Forged? Mark, ashamed of his hatred, gushed, "Forgive me, I'm having a lot of trouble with this assignment. I don't believe in the supernatural and . . ."

". . . and you are nervous around the Forged. Most humans are, and pretend not to be. You have always been clear about your limitations, in your previous work. I am not deterred. You have come this far. Let us complete the journey." Feathers rustled on it. Its face was scaled, beaked. How it managed speech was beyond him, and yet it spoke remarkably well. But parrots did too, Bishop reasoned, so why not this?

It took him almost a minute to understand what it'd said, not because it was unclear, but because he was so confused by the storm of feeling inside himself. Repulsion, aggression, fear. The stink, he realized at last with a shock of guilt, was himself.

Hyperion took hold of the guide rails delicately and spun itself away, tail trailing like a kite's. Its comfort with weightlessness spoke of many years spent there, in the cramped airlocks and crabbed tunnels of the old stations. In its wake, Bishop followed, slipping, and after a too-brief eternity found himself at the entrance hatch that looked entirely machine, though there was no disguising the chitinous interior into which he was able to peer and see seats of the strange kind made for space travel—ball-like concoctions of soft stuff that moved against tethers and into which one had to crawl like a mouse into a nest. He made himself concentrate only on mechanics, move a hand, a foot, that's all—it was the only thing that kept his control of himself intact.

Of course, it was Forged. The only machines that traveled the length of the system were robotically controlled cargo carriers whose glacial pace was utterly unsuitable for this trip or most any other if you didn't have half a lifetime to spare. For local traffic to the moon and the various towed-in asteroids that had been clustered nearby to form the awkward mineral suburb of Rolling Rock, all travel was undertaken in the purpose-built, ur-human creatures of the Flight. Every last one of them was a speed freak.

"Ironhorse Alacrity Valhalla has agreed to take us to our location." Hyperion made the introduction as it waited for Bishop to precede him into the dimly lit interior chitoblast and become a helpless parasite inside a being he couldn't even see or identify, but which had a mind, apparently rather like his own, only connected by the telepathy of contemporary electronic signaling to every other Forged mind—whereas he was quite alone. He checked his mike and gave Hyperion a sickly smile that he had intended to be professional and cheering. The creature blinked at him slowly, quite relaxed, and he saw that it had extraordinary eyes. They were large, as large as his fist, in its big head, but beyond the clear, wet sclera lay an iris so complex and dazzling . . . another blink brought him to his senses. Yellow eyes. It was demonic. What idiot had made them that color?

He was able to manage quite well, and put himself into the seat sack without any foolish struggling or tangles, even though now he was feeling slightly drunk. Cocooned next to each other, they were able to see one another's heads easily. Stuck to the side of each sack, a refreshment package waited. Within the slings, toilet apparatus was easy to find. There was a screen in the ceiling, if it was the ceiling—without gravity it hardly mattered—showing some pleasant views of pastoral Earth scenes, like a holiday brochure. Bishop figured it was for his benefit and tried to be comforted as a Hawaiian beach glowed azure at him, surrounded by thick, fleshy webbing that pulsed slightly in erratic measure.

Common lore said it was all right for old humans not to attempt talking to their host carrier at this point. The gargoyle could have been babbling on to the ship all the time, of course, there was no knowing. His mind fussed around what they might say. It blurred hopelessly as he attempted to drag up anything about the task at hand. He couldn't bring any thought into focus long enough to articulate it.

The door sealed up behind them and was immediately lost in the strange texture of the wall. There were no ports. He wouldn't be seeing the stars unless the Alacrity wanted to show him images from outside on the holiday channel.

"Where are we going?" he asked, though it had been in the damn notes.

"To the spot you requested," Hyperion said with some puzzlement. "Don't you recall?" Bishop flushed hot with embarrassment, started sweating all over again. He didn't remember. Then there was a vague hint that he might have made a call, no, written a request, a secret note . . . had he? He checked the screen inventory of his mail. Nothing. Inside the cocoon of the webbing, he experienced a stab of shocking acuteness in the region of his guts and heart. He felt that he was losing his mind and that it was paying him back with this lance, this polearm of pure fear. What had he requested?

"No." He wanted to lie but his mouth wouldn't do it.

The Greenjack was quiet for a moment. "I think that we should talk a little on the way there, Mr. Bishop, if you don't mind." Its voice was gentle now, and had a rounded richness that reminded Bishop of leather chairs, wood paneling, pipe tobacco, twilight, and cognac. Above the line of the cocoon, he could see its feet twitching gently, flexing their strangely padded digits. Dark claws, blunted from walking, were just visible. "I am well aware of the way my claims must appear to scientists such as yourself. Energies beyond human perception existing within our own spacetime perhaps is not too outlandish in itself. But my observations of their behavior, and what it seems to mean for their interactions with us, that is the stuff of late-night stories. Believe me, Mr. Bishop, I have studied them for many years before making these statements. And I would welcome any remarks."

Charlatan, Bishop thought. Must be. He'd thought it from the get-go, when he first read about it.

Bishop had been in doubt on other assignments, though none of them like this one. Mostly, he wrote for journals about science or current affairs based on Earth. He was one of the more popular and able writers who could turn complicated and difficult notions into the kind of thing that most well-educated people could digest with breakfast. Normally, he avoided all discussions about the Forged and their politics, but, of course, it had caught up with him as it must with everyone in the end, he reasoned. And his expertise had led to him being selected by the government to come and make a judgment out here about this odd person and its extraordinary claims, its illegal and incomprehensible existence. The Greenjack Cylenchar Hyperion was a member of a class created by the Forged themselves, by the motherfather, Tupac, whose vast body had bred all the spacefarers and most of the Gravity Bound. It was a class she claimed was scientifically essential, though he had serious doubts. The Greenjacks were there to confront the boundaries of the perceivable universe, and to try to apprehend what, to ordinary human eyes, was beyond sight. Hyperion, in particular, was said to be able to perceive every frequency there was, and had been given adaptations to allow its mind to be able to cope with the information. Hyperion didn't just see, it *watched*. Recently, it'd been making dramatic claims about its visions, which had been in all the papers.

Bishop struggled, but the panic was choking, he wasn't able to say the sensible thing he had in mind—namely, "Yes, but just because *you* can detect these things, why aren't they verified by machines?"

The Greenjack paused, just the length of time it would
have taken him to make this reply, and added, "Machine
verification has confirmed erratic frequency fluctuations in
localized areas, but, obviously, they can't put an interpretation on these anomalies. We have successfully managed to
get some mappings of areas and frequency variations that
confirm my own sensory perceptions are accurate."

This was news. Bishop jerked as his screen recovered the
files being zapped across to it and vibrated to alert him—all
the data was there, already witnessed and verified by independent bodies . . . He felt himself breathing steadily. The
scotch seemed to have made it out of his stomach. The pills
he'd taken still worked hard on fooling his head into thinking that it knew which way was up. Better, that was better.
Statistics. Facts. Good.

"But if you are too distressed we can delay this," the
Cylenchar said suddenly. "Mr. Bishop?"

"No, we have to go." He didn't know where they had to go,
though apparently he was determined. His panic returned.

"May I speak frankly?"

Into Bishop's agonized silence, Hyperion said clearly,
"I think you have asked me to go to Mars because of your
daughter. You are hoping that I will be able to find her where
the inquest has failed. Is that right?"

A cold drench of sweat covered him from head to foot,
as memory returned, cold, clear. He couldn't breathe. He
was drowning. Mars. Tabitha. The unsolved mystery of the
routine survey expedition vanishing without a trace. Oh a
sandstorm, a dust ocean, a flood of sand, a mighty sirocco
that blew them away . . . what had it been and where was
she? Nobody could answer. Not even the equipment returned a ping. But how? And when the months dragged on
and the company pulled out and sent its condolences and
added their names to the long list of people who'd gone
missing on Mars during the fierce years of its terraforming, and then this assignment came, what else to do? Bring
the creature who, above all, had been *made* to see. No
frequency, no signal, no energy that the Greenjacks can't
decipher, right? Of course, if she's there . . . and if she's

dead, then this one will say so. It claims that some of the things it can sense aren't people but are what people leave or make somehow in the unseen fields they move in: trails and marks. It says some are like the wizards of story, able to make things with shape, with form, with intent that is almost conscious. Some can leave memories like prints on the empty air. Oh. But a man of strict science does not believe in that.

"Yes," Bishop said. He was small then, in his mouse nest, hanging, damp and suddenly getting the chills. He was afraid that the 'jack would say no.

"I will be glad to look," it said instead, and Mark Bishop fell into a deep sleep on the spot.

Sleep was one of the many skills the 'jack had learned in its long years of waiting for things that might not appear. It closed its eyes and shared a warm goodnight with the Valhalla, who was more than curious to know the outcome now, and sang toward the red world with fire and all the winds of the sun.

They joined each other in a shared interior space, a private dreamtime. It was cozy. The Valhalla whispered, "Sometimes I am flying in the sunlight, and there is nothing there, but I feel a cold, a call, a kind of falling. Is that real? Are the monsters from under the bed out at sea too?"

"Wake me if it happens," Hyperion said. "And we'll see."

It cocreated a kind romance with the Valhalla, in which they saw huge floating algal swarms of deep color and shadow populate the fathoms beyond the stars. They named them in whispers, and with childish fingers measured their shapes in the sky, and then pinched them out of existence, snuff, snuff, snuff.

"There," Hyperion said, "they may be here, but they have no power. They can only hurt you if you let them. They live in the holes of the mind, and eat the spirit. Cracklegrackle. Just pinch them out." They got back into bed and closed the window, drew the shades. The Valhalla was happy again and drove on all the faster in his sleep.

*   *   *

Bishop was woken by the Valhalla's cheerful cry, "Mars!"
The Ironhorse made orbit and scanned the surface to find
the small outpost where the Gaiaform Nikkal Raven, chief
developer of Mars, had built human-scale shelter with its
Hands in the lee of a high cliff. "Nobody's there now. If it's
a graveyard or a ghost town, it's empty for sure, but with a
bit of effort there's probably power and some basics that you
could get going." As a courtesy, they contacted the Gaiaform.

"That's funny," the Valhalla said, as Bishop struggled to
change his clothes. "She sounds annoyed, or, at least, she
doesn't want to discuss the place."

The Nikkal's voice was grumpy on the intercom. It grated
on Bishop's exposed nerves and wore out his fragile strip of
patience almost at once. "My Hands got lost there too. Given
up sending more. Thought I'd get to it later, after the planting
on the south faces was finished. Just a minor space really,
full of gullies."

They all recognized the feeling this rationale covered.
"We don't need your help," Bishop grated. "Just want to get
there and look around. That's all."

"But if anything happens it's on my watch," the Nikkal
countered.

"Tupac knows we're here," Hyperion suggested. "We
won't stay long. A day at most."

". . . as long as it takes . . ." Bishop said. He was in clean
clothes. His panics were gone. He felt old and thin and shel-
terless, and looked around for something he could hold. He
found only his small bag and his recorder, and filled his
hands with them. A panic would have been welcome. Their
fury was better than this deadly flat feeling that had taken
their place. It was clear now. He was here, Thorson's Gullies, the last known location. Every step was a puppet step
his body took at the behest of some will named Mark that
wouldn't let it rest, but there was no more struggle between
them. He felt that he did not inhabit these arms, these legs.
They were his waldos, his servos, they were his method.
Only his guts were still his own, a liquid concentration waiting for a mold.

"Come on, Mark," Hyperion called from the drop capsule.

Since when had they become friends? Bishop didn't know how, but he climbed inside the small fruit shape of the vehicle. Mars had lift cable, but no system in place. Cargo was simply clipped on and set going under whatever power it was able to muster. They were attached to the line and given a good shove by the Valhalla. The new atmosphere buffeted them, warmed them, cooked them almost, and then they were down, Bishop still surprised, still too frozen to even be sick with either motion nausea or relief at their arrival. The capsule detached, put out its six wheeled legs like a bored insect, and began to trundle the prescribed steady course toward the gullies. Hyperion opened the ventilation system and they sniffed the Martian air. It was thin, and even though it had been filtered a million ways, somehow gritty.

"It's the names that are part of the trouble," Bishop said, staring out at the peculiar sight of Mars's tundra, red ochre studded with the teal-green puffs of growing things in regular patterns. "Good and Evil. Why did you call them that?"

"There are more," Hyperion said. "There is Eater and Biter and Poison and Power and Luck and Fortune and Beneficence, and the Cracklegrackle. I expect there are many more. But these are the commonest major sorts."

"But why? Couldn't you name them Energy #1 and so forth?"

"I could, but that wouldn't be accurate. Their names are what they are."

"How they seem to *you*. The one person who can see them."

"That's not exactly right. I think we can all perceive them, but only I can see them as easily as I can see you."

"And you say they are everywhere."

"Scattered, but everywhere in known space, I think."

"And some are spontaneous, but others are man-made?"

"Yes. Few of the major arcana are man-made, like those. It takes a very powerful person to create one. Or a large group of people. There are many man-made minor arcana and many naturally occurring ones like that, but they are very short-lived, a day or two at most."

"You see my problem is that I can believe in this kind of thing at a symbolic level, within the human world, acting at large and small scales. We're creatures of symbolic meaning. But you're saying there's *physical* stuff, and that it has a real, external, distinct existence."

"Yes. I am saying it exists as patterns within the same energy fields that give rise to matter."

"Consciousness is material?"

"No. It has a material interaction that is more than simply the building of a house from a plan or the singing of a song, is what I am saying."

"And these things . . . patterns . . . can influence people?"

"Influence them, infect them, live inside them, alter them perhaps. Yes, I think so." The creature stared at him for the longest time, unblinking. "Yes."

"And just like that, we are expected to accept this—theory of material mind?"

Hyperion shrugged, as if it didn't much care either way. "I report what I see, but I say what it is for me. Otherwise, I would report nothing more than machines can report. When you look at a landscape, you don't list a bunch of coordinates and say they are mid-green, then another list gray, another list white, and so on. You say, I see a hill with some trees, a river, a house in the distance."

"But you're making claims about the nature of this stuff, linking it to subjective values. Hills aren't subjective."

"They are. True, there is some rock that exists independently of you, some sand, some dust, but without *you*, it is no hill, and however the hill seems is how all hills seem to you, large or small—not mountains, not flat, perhaps even with traits that are more personal. If your home is among the hills, then they seem well-known; if not, then they provoke suspicion."

They were trundling at high speed, balanced in their gyrobody between the capsule's six legs, seeming to float like thistledown between the rocks of this region of Mars; Thorson's Plot. Plot was something of a misnomer, as the area, already claimed by an Earth corporate, was some fifteen thousand square miles. The gullies, which made it a cheaper piece of real estate, and complicated to sow—hence the surveying team—were near the western edge and ran in a broad scar north-south along the lines of the mapping system. Thorson Corporation had hoped to find watery deposits deep in the gullies, or perhaps some useful mineral, or who knows what down in the cracked gulches where twisting runnels of rock hid large areas from the sun and most of the wind that had scoured the planet for millennia. All around them were hills of varying sizes, some no more than dunes, others rising with rugged defiance in scarps and screes. Occasionally, small pieces of metal flashed the sunlight back at them as they moved between light and the shade of the thin, high cloud that now streaked the sky white.

"The remains of Hands," the Greenjack said with interest, of course able to tell what everything was at any distance. "How interesting. And there is some debris from attempts to seed here, some markers, some water catchers. All wrecked. And . . ."

"And?" Bishop leaped on the hesitation.

"What I would call distress residue. A taint in the energy, very slight."

"What energy?"

"The subtle fields. You will find them referenced a great deal in my submitted thesis. Vibrationary levels where human perception is only infrequently possible at all. When trauma occurs, bursts of energy are thrown off the distressed person into these fields, and although they decay quite rapidly, they leave a trace pattern behind, which is very slow to fade."

"A disturbance in the Force," Bishop said bitterly. He felt nothing except the dread that had clutched at him in place of his panic.

"It might be only the natural upset of someone experiencing an unlucky accident," Hyperion said, unruffled. "It's hard to say without extreme observation and immersion on the site. You ought to be glad, Mr. Bishop, rather than contemptuous. Why else are you here?"

Mark gripped the arms of his seat. He was furious and full of nervous agitation. He ought to be civil, but he felt the need to destroy this creature's claims even as he wanted them to be right for his own sake. He didn't want to know about some spiritual plane, not after all the time it had taken to rid the human race of its destructive superstitions. Even if it existed, what difference did it make to those who were unable to interact with it. He could see no good coming of it. But he longed for it to be true. Somewhere in his fevered mind, where fragments of the shaman's testimony had lodged in spite of his allergic reaction to reading them, he recalled there being quite specific traces of people and moments stuck in this peculiar ether like flies in amber. Not always, not everywhere, but sometime and somewhere it acted as a recorder for incidents and individuals. It could. It *might have*.

The capsule lurched to a halt. They had arrived at the last known point of the survey team's well-being. A couple of waymarkers and a discarded, empty water canister pegged down beside them were the only visible remnants now. Without further talk, Hyperion and Bishop disembarked.

They fitted their facemasks—the air was still too thin for comfort—and Bishop put on his thin wind jacket and new desert boots. Hyperion sank a little in the fine grit, on its four limbs, but otherwise it went as always, naked save for its fur, feathers, scales, and quills.

Wrestling the faceplate straps to get a good fit, Bishop noticed all the strange little fetishes the creature had attached to itself. Necklaces with bits of twig and bone . . . it looked like it had come off the set of a voodoo movie. He recalled now that it had labeled its profession on its passport as "shaman." He was so exhausted by his nervous disorders, however, that he didn't have the energy to muster a really negative response anymore. He was deadened to it. At last, the mask was tested and his spare oxygen packs fitted to the bodysuit that went over his clothes. Hyperion wore goggles and a kind of nosebag over his beak. He made a desultory symbol in the dust and smoothed it out again with one forepaw. The capsule, obeying commands from its uplink with the Valhalla, folded up its spider legs and nestled down in a small hollow, lights dimming to a gleam as it moved into standby operation. All around, and as far as he could see in any direction, save for the shaman, Bishop was alone.

"There are very few true disappearances in human history, these days," Hyperion said after a moment when they both cast about in search of a direction. It moved closer to one of the markers and read the tags left there. "And this is not an unusual place, like those twisty spaces close to black holes for example. It is just a planet with a regular geology. The common assumption about this team's fate is that they absconded with the help of the Nikkal. From there, a number of possible avenues continue, most leading to the far system frontiers, where they were able to drop off the networks."

Bishop licked his lips, already starting to crack. The news was full of the asteroid bayous beyond the sphere of Earth's police influence and the renegade technology that festered there, unregulated. There was a lot of Unity activity. A lot of illegal, unethical, criminal work. "She had no reason to go."

"Perhaps not, but if the rest of them wanted to go they could hardly leave her behind. What would be easier for you, Mr. Bishop, to have her forcibly made into one of the Frontiersmen, or to have her dead here somewhere?"

How odd, he thought, that the 'jack had no trouble voicing what inhabited his own awareness as a black hum beyond reckoning. Hearing the words aloud was startling, but it diminished the power of the awful feelings that gripped him inside.

"Let's start looking," Bishop said, standing still. All around them, their small dip radiated gullies that twisted and wound. The sun was beginning to go down and the high rocky outcrops cast sharp-edged purple shadows.

Hyperion was exacting, its research both instantaneous and meticulous in a way that made Bishop simply envious. "The marker, as the police report indicates, says they started southwest with a view to making a loop trail back here within a six-hour period, the route is marked in the statutory map." The shaman sniffed and the nosebag huffed. "All the searches have concentrated on following this route and found a scatter of personal belongings and the remains of a Finger of the Terraform, which was carrying the survey equipment. All of that was recovered intact." It held the two wind-beaten Tags in its paw and rubbed them for a short time, thoughtfully. "But they did not go that way. Only the Finger took the trail."

"How do you know?"

Hyperion turned. "I can see it. I think it is time I showed you." It came across to him and held out one large, scaly arm. "Please, your screen viewer. I will adapt it to show some of the details I can see over its normal camera range. This will not be what *I* see, you understand, as I don't see it with my eyes. But it is the best I can do for you."

Reluctantly, Bishop handed over the precious viewer. It was his recorder too. His everything. "Don't mess up the record settings. It's on now."

The Greenjack inclined its head politely and slid one of its broad, clawlike nails into one of the old-style input ports. Bishop felt a chill. He'd never get used to how capable the Forged were with technology. They could interface directly with any machine.

"The signals I use to communicate with the device will cause some interference with my tracking," Hyperion said calmly. "So I will not use it all the time. If you see nothing, you may assume I am watching and listening. I will also shut the device down if its working interferes with the process, and I may ask you to move away at times." It handed the screen back, and Bishop checked it, panning it around in front of him. The camera showed whatever he pointed it at, recording diligently; it was really just like holding a picture frame up over the landscape. "I don't see anything."

"Look at the markers and the route."

He turned. From the tag line, he could now see a strange kind of coloration in the air, like points of deep shade. They were small. It was really almost like broken pixelization.

"That is the pattern left by the output of the Finger's microreactor projecting microbursts of decaying particles into the energy field. Radiation containment is generally good these days, so this is all you can find. It is also in the standard police procedurals. They mistakenly assumed it confirmed that all the travelers took the same path, since the Finger was carrying all the technical equipment and the others had only their masks and gas, their personal refreshments and devices. I would say it is certain that they *intended* to disappear here, as in fact all their individual communications gear has been accounted for along the Finger's trail."

Like a path cut with three-dimensional leaf shadows, the trail wound into the first gully, followed the obvious way along it, and vanished around the first turn.

"We can follow that and verify there was no other person with the Finger if you like," the shaman suggested.

"Parts of a Forged internal device unit were found," Bishop said, brain clicking in at last.

Hyperion shrugged.

"Or?" Bishop started to pan around. He soon found patches and bursts of odd color washes everywhere, as if his screen were subject to a random painting class.

"Or we can follow the others and find out what they did, starting here."

"What is all this?"

"This is energy field debris."

As he moved around, Bishop could see that there was a huge glut of the stuff where they were, but traces of it were everywhere in fact, even in the distance. "Why so much of it?"

"There was a lot of activity here. The rest is down to regular cosmic interference, or perhaps . . . I am not actually sure what all of it is. The energy fields transect time and space, but they are linked to it, so while some of this is attached to the planet's energy sphere, some of it, as you see, is moving."

Streaks shot across the screen. A readout indicated that he was not seeing them in real time, as that would have been too fast for him to notice. The simulation and the reality overlay each other on the image, however, and the difference there was undetectable.

"I believe that the streaks are bonded to the spatial field, and that they are therefore stationary relative to absolute co-ordinates in space—thus as Mars traverses, so these things pass through." The creature cocked its head, a model of intellectual speculation.

Bishop relaxed his tired arms so that the screen pointed at the ground, saw the streaks shooting through his feet. "Through us?"

Hyperion nodded. "As with much cosmic ray debris. It moves too fast for me to say anything about it. I would need to move out into deep space and be on a relatively static vessel, in order to discover more about them."

"No such ship exists." Bishop snorted. "Well, only . . ."

"Yes, only a Unity ship perhaps," the shaman said. "I shall ask for one soon."

They shared a moment of silence in which the subject of Unity, the newly discovered alien technology, rose and passed without further comment. Bishop would have loved to go into it at any other time. The surge of hysteria it had engendered had almost died down nowadays, with it being limited to off-world use, restricted use, or use far enough away from Earth and her concerns that it wasn't important to most humans, whatever strange features it possessed. FTL drives, or whatever they were, were only the half of it. It was under review. He'd seen some of the evidence. Now he let it go, and lifted the screen again. If Tabitha had gone on one of those ships, she could be anywhere. It would take years to get into Forged Space by ordinary means. Even an Iron-horse Accelerator couldn't go faster. She could have been there since the day it happened, almost a year ago. "This is just a mess."

"No," Hyperion said. It lowered its head and sniffed again, a hellish kind of hound. "There were four individuals here, all human, and one Forged, Wayfarer Jackalope Mc-Knight."

"Bread Zee Davis, Bancroft Wan, Kialee Yang . . ." Bishop said, the names so often in his mind that they came off his tongue like an old catechism.

". . . and Tabitha Bishop."

"I am sure which is the Forged," Hyperion said, "but the humans are harder to label. They are distinct, however."

"They'd worked together almost a year," Bishop said, wishing he'd kept his silence, but it was leaking. "No trouble. She sent me a postcard."

"May I see it?"

He hesitated, then fiddled the controls and handed over the screen. It had been shown so often during the inquest that he knew every millimeter of it better than he knew the lines in his own hand.

The object was small, almost really postcard-size in the Greenjack's heavy paw. "Kialee is the Han girl, I am guessing."

"And Wan is the one with the black Mohawk. Davis is the wannabe soldier in all that ex-military stuff." He knew every detail of that postcard. What most mystified him about it was how friendly they all seemed, how relaxed, the girls leaning on each other, the guys making silly faces, beer in hand; around them, the dull red of the tenting, and, in the background, a portable generator and a jumble of oxygen tanks. It could have been a snap of two couples on holiday, and not of students on work assignment. He wasn't sure if they'd been dating, or if dating was a concept that had gone out with dinosaurs like him.

The Greenjack was stock-still. It looked intently and then handed back the screen. "Thank you. In that case, I can now say that there was a struggle here. Bishop and Yang are surprised, but Davis and Wan are both agitated throughout. Only McKnight is calm."

"He was new. Newish. Their old Wayfarer went to another job."

The colors illumined as the shaman talked, showing Bishop warped fields of light that were as abstract as any randomly generated image. "McKnight and the men remain close together. There is a conflict with the women. There is a struggle; I think at this point the women are forced to give up their personal devices to Terraform Raven's Finger. I believe they are tied, at least at the hands. McKnight is armed with explosive charges for the survey. But he's also more than big enough to overpower and threaten them. I guess this is what happened. Davis and Wan dislike the events a great deal but they are willing participants. That's what I see. Then there's another argument, here, the men and McKnight. It's brief. Blood and flesh scraps from McKnight are found near here."

Bishop saw the oddest nebula of grays, streaked with black and bright red. "There was some kind of struggle . . . the Wayfarer was defending . . ." But the gargoyle shaman was shaking its head.

"He cuts out his own external comms unit," Hyperion said precisely. "In the Wayfarer, this is located at the back of the skull and embedded in the surface beneath a minor chitinous plate. To remove it would be painful and messy, but it is perfectly possible and certainly not lethal. But all communication is cut before this, so there is no official account of how it was removed. The only person who can account for that is Raven, and she claims that there was a local network dropout. I would have to question her directly to be sure of her account." The implication was stark.

The air, already bitter, felt suddenly colder. "So Davis and Wan made him do it?"

"I cannot say for certain. But he does it. Any other method risks it being hijacked by signals that would give away his position. He's hidden it somewhere around here, I'd bet. Or given it to the Finger, who lost it in the gullies way before it signaled a breakdown. We should look for it. Then they leave." Hyperion pointed northwest. "That way."

Bishop thought of the evidence of the Finger's call. Raven's voice said, "They've gone. Just gone." And with that phrase, she'd ushered in an entire cult of people convinced that Mars harbored ghosts, or aliens, or fiends. As if their numbers needed adding to! But Bishop couldn't keep up his anger. The pictures continued.

There was a faint coloration, like a long tunnel or a tube made of the faintest streaks of yellow, gray, and ashy-white. It was almost pretty against the deepening red of the Martian afternoon. The tunnel down which Tabitha had vanished. So the shaman said.

"I hardly know anything about these people," Bishop protested with distress. He didn't understand how the creature drew its conclusions.

"It is all right, Mr. Bishop," the shaman said calmly, setting off in this new direction. "I know everything about them that I need to know."

For the first time in the time that he could remember lately, Mark Bishop had enough energy to hurry in the Greenjack's wake. "But how? Just from some picture?"

"Yes."

"But you can't tell anything just from a picture!"

"You can tell everything from a single look. For instance, I know that you, Mr. Bishop, had it in mind that if you found me a fraud here, you might use your gun to shoot me dead. And then yourself. We would be a memorial in this unpleasant spot, the monument of your surrender to despair and your inability to remain rational in the face of my abominable supernatural exploitation of both your grief and reputation." It continued walking steadily.

Bishop had no answer to that. He'd never verbalized or reified that intent, but he couldn't entirely dismiss it. His gun was in his holster pocket. Everyone had them. He couldn't say that the thought hadn't been his secondary insurance. That and the recorder, of course. It would have told the sad tale to those who came to find out what happened. The notion had been discarded a long time before they even landed though, he realized, and now the recorder was instead preserving this vision of Hyperion's skinny ass slowly wandering along a trackless gully through soft dirt and Bishop's labored breathing.

"Anyone can see these things," Hyperion mumbled as it went. "But they don't know how to tune in, to refine and translate and *know* them."

"Don't start on the psychic stuff." What the hell had those boys and that monster done with his little girl? "Tell me about Wan."

"Bancroft. He is idealistic, practical, yet ordinary. Bread is determined, focused, and he has been somehow thwarted in the past, which has made him bitter, though he hides this with great charm. McKnight is an entrepreneur, comfortable with criminal ways."

"McKnight is the leader, then?"

"Wan is the leader, Mr. Bishop, whoever's foot may seem to go first. As for the women, neither of them is involved in this plan except by accident. It is simply unfortunate that they were in this team when Wan met McKnight. I am certain that McKnight was the catalyst for what occurred here. Wan is too poor, too badly connected, and too ignorant to plan this venture alone. Possibly he didn't think of it until McKnight arrived to put the idea in his head. He isn't creative."

"You're quite the detective." Bishop didn't mean it quite as bitter as it sounded.

"I would like to be. But it isn't my intuition working so much as the patterns that I see."

Bishop gave a cursory glance at his screen. A twisting tube of colors, some bleeding, others sharp, was all he could see; bad art on a tiresome landscape. "If you say so." In spite of himself, he had no trouble believing the Greenjack now. "Are the girls all right?"

"They are physically unharmed at this point. They are talking here . . ." The shaman indicated their way and the stretch ahead. It moved off alone for some distance, then narrated, "I feel terror and anger. I believe they were attempting to bargain an escape or discover the real plans. McKnight is all for telling them. He is enjoying the action. Wan forbids him. McKnight doesn't mind this, but Davis is getting edgy. He has never liked the involvement of the Terraform. His fear of retaliation is keeping him quiet now."

Bishop stopped suddenly, rooted in the unmade earth. He had realized that he was walking through time, and his sudden confidence in the shaman's analysis made him fear where the future led, even though it had already happened. He attempted to rally some criticism, some countermeasure to the rigorous story unfolding, to prove at least to himself

that there was a chance that most of it was simply the shaman's whimsical interpretation of some very dry facts, but
he struggled to do so.

Ahead of him, the large creature stopped in its own dusty
tracks and turned about. It seemed patient and concerned.
Every time he looked into its peculiar yellow eyes, he expected the disturbance of an alien encounter, but instead
he felt that he was understood, and the feeling made him
desperately uneasy. Who knew what confidence trickery it
was capable of, after all? But for the life of him, he couldn't
figure out a motive.

"When we get to the end of this," Bishop said hoarsely,
coughing, "what will we do?"

"That depends on the end."

"I mean, if she isn't dead, if she was taken somewhere . . .
will you help me? You said you'd ask for a Unity ship. I
guess that means you know someone."

"I will find your daughter, Mr. Bishop," Hyperion said. "I
already promised to. If you prefer I will say no more about
the events that passed this way. No doubt you must wonder
how I can know, and there is no way to tell you how, any
more than you can explain how you do most things you do
that are your nature. I expect that some greater analysis will
help to detail the process, but I am not interested in doing
it myself. I see these people and I feel what they have been
feeling, as if I can watch it in a moving storybook. There
are other things present, besides the people now. These dis-
ruptions in such a quiet area have acted as an attractor, and
some of the energies I spoke about earlier are beginning to
converge on the scene. As yet, they are only circling. You
may see . . ."

"These stains? I thought they were just bad rendering or
the light or something. They're so faint. Watermarks."

"They are the ones. You will see them circle and converge,
then scatter and reform. They may merge. Ignore them. They
are not important."

"But they . . ." But the Greenjack was already moving on.
The shadows were lengthening into early evening, and a
slight cooling was in the air. Bishop kept one eye on the trail

and the other on the screen, but the silence was too much for him. "Talk," he said.

"They are not speaking here," the shaman replied over its shoulder. "Yang is looking for a way to escape. Bishop is locked in her thoughts. She is angry with McKnight for his betrayal of their friendship, or what she thought was their friendship. She is questioning her assessment of the others. McKnight is leading, he is content. Wan and Davis are in the rear, pushing the women on. Wan is excited. Davis is starting to lose trust in him. Davis has a weak personality. He believes that he ought to be leader and Wan is beginning to annoy him. He is starting to form a strong resentment."

"What is that cloud?"

"He is forming negative energy vortices. This kind of personality often does. Their energy scatters out from the holes in their energy bodies. It is an interesting feature of humans that they create negative energy attractors much more readily and strongly than positive ones. I am not sure why this is, but I believe it is because damaged individuals are *leaky*, prone to influence and loss, whereas healthy types do not shed these frequencies without some deliberate effort. They are impervious to wild influence and create almost no disturbances. I must consult with the other Greenjacks when they are done traveling."

Bishop was silent for a while and they plodded on some quarter-kilometer more as he checked his recordings. It was an ecology he was seeing, if it were true. A psychic kind of ecology. He couldn't help but notice it, even as it wasn't part of his concern. Just a peripheral. If the Greenjack had tried to convince him about all this any other way, he could probably have thought of a good hole or two to poke in things, but as it was . . . he shook his head and struggled on. He wasn't fit, and although gravity was lighter and walking easier, it was a long time since he'd hiked farther than his backyard. He found himself stopped suddenly, almost walking onto Hyperion's tail. The Forged was still as a statue.

Bishop looked at the screen quickly. A darkening storm

of purples and reds like a miniature cyclone was all around him. He waited, then Hyperion said:

"They stop here. McKnight signals off-world. Wan and Davis start arguing again. Yang tries to escape. She just runs. Bishop tries to stop her. McKnight notices. Davis starts to run after her, but Wan says no. He is willing to leave her. He wants to. Davis catches Yang. Wan says to McKnight they should leave them both. He knows Davis is trouble, Yang he doesn't want anyway; they have some history . . . it's minor . . . he'd rather leave her for some reason I don't . . . Anyway. Bishop protests. Yang becomes hysterical. McKnight knocks her unconscious. Now Wan gets angry with McKnight. Davis's antagonism toward Wan crystallizes. He threatens to turn them all in. McKnight doesn't like that. McKnight threatens Wan and Davis. Wan tries to calm things down. Bishop is raging. Wan ties up both women, hands and feet. Yang is injured, there is blood here. They wait. Quite a long time. I think an hour must pass or so. Davis is now focused entirely on Wan. Hates him. McKnight is the only calm one. Wan is furious but he's too smart to let it out. A ship comes. It lands over there . . ."

Mark Bishop got up and followed the Greenjack over to the place across the long shadows that had nearly covered the whole ground.

There was no sign of a landing, but then, given the weather, there wouldn't be. He recorded dutifully. The colored water-world had gone. He watched the Greenjack circle and look, and pause. It returned from a small exploration and said, "This is the end of the trail here. The ship has come. It's a Forged craft. I don't know its name, but if I ever meet it, I'll know it by its energy signatures. It is one of three types of Ironhorse currently operating between the Far System and Earth. Can't say more. They all embark, except Yang. She's dead."

Bishop half-wanted to ask for more, certain it was hiding things, but then he decided that it was enough, he didn't want to know. Everything inside him had stopped, waiting.

What the shaman had just said was a testable claim, unless it meant some kind of spiritual residue. Beneath his coat, he felt the hairs on his neck stand on end. His heart gave an extra beat. "Are you sure?"

"Yes." Hyperion paused and then made a brief gesture with its head. Bishop followed the line, recorder in hand first. He saw nothing, just the usual Mars stuff, but then the shaman walked him out another hundred meters to a small mound that Bishop or anyone else would just have taken for one of the billion shifting dunes. "She is here."

Bishop took measurements, readings. They were still technically well within Thorson's Gullies. Nobody would have come here for a long, long time. Perhaps never. The land was bad, useless. This zone had already been mapped. There were no deposits of use. Then, with the shaman's help, he set up his recorder and began the process of moving the sand aside. He used his shoe as a spade. It didn't take long before he bumped something. Without ceremony, they uncovered a part of a desiccated human body, just enough to see the identifying badges on the suit, and then they covered it up again.

Bishop moved away a short distance and sat for a while, drinking water and watching the sun go down. It got very cold. His feet and hands ached. He wished for the scotch again, fervently, avidly, relentlessly. Hyperion sat beside him like a giant dog.

Bishop's hand strayed to the machine but he left it alone. He stumbled over the words, "Do you see her?" He was braced for any fool answer. He wanted there to be one, a good one.

"She was here," it said. "But now she has gone."

Bishop nodded. He wasn't going to ask for the details. He wasn't ready yet. Leave it at the cryptic stage until . . . "We should go."

"I suggest we walk back to the capsule rather than make any transmissions the Terraform might interpret. Also we must now consider this a murder investigation. What would you like to do? We could report it to the police and let them . . ."

"No. They got it all wrong the first time." Bishop was surprised by the force of his own hatred, but the shaman didn't skip a beat.

"Then we should not discuss this with the Valhalla. We need help from sources that don't mind being accomplice to criminal acts."

Belatedly, Mark realized that by this it meant their failure to inform. Anything that wasted time now didn't matter to him. "Can you track them from here?"

"Not directly, but their intentions are reasonably clear. McKnight is at least guilty of manslaughter and kidnap. Wan and Davis of kidnap, misuse of corporate properties, perversion of the course of justice. The Terraform is on their side. They have every chance to make a good escape, but they couldn't head sunward—there's nothing there except Earth and the high-population satellite systems, full of officials and the law. They have gone to the Belt—no Forged ship could take them farther without at least stopping there for supplies. We will find something out that way." It seemed completely confident, almost resigned to its own cold certainty.

Bishop ignored the bleakness in its tone and waded forward grimly in its wake, a squire to a weird and uncomforting King Wenceslas of the sands.

It was a long, hard, cold, and lonely passage. Bishop struggled all the way not to ask all the questions that were haunting him, but he didn't ask them, and at last they retraced all the path, and the Valhalla's Hand opened its thousand eyes and let them in. He couldn't afford to indulge his fears.

"Where to?" the Valhalla asked as it left orbit, swinging away in an arc that would return it to the sunward side so that it could pick up extra heat.

"Just to the lift station again," Hyperion said with a sigh, as though the journey had been tiring and a disappointment.

It made some small talk with the Valhalla as Bishop settled himself in. He intended to check his recordings and prepare some method for transmitting them safely in case something happened to him, but before he was able to do any of that, exhaustion took over and he fell asleep. He slept all the way to the port, and woke feeling drained and thin. Hyperion led him through their formalities, and then they were sitting in the cafeteria, Bishop facing a reconstituted dinner with a dry mouth.

"An ordinary journey to the Belt is a three-year stretch," the shaman said. It was lying like a giant dog on the smooth tiled floor next to Bishop's table, resting its head on a plastic plant pot beneath the convincing fake fronds of a plastic grass. "The fastest available transport can make it in one year. But Unity ships can make it instantly."

"Interference," Bishop croaked. He had managed a mouthful. It wasn't bad but he was so hungry even cardboard would have seemed delicious. Hungry or not, he was loath to think about Unity travel. They said it interfered with you at a fundamental level. They were not sure what the long-term implications would be.

"I will search here, perhaps they came this way." It was unconvincing. Nobody in their right mind would come this way if they wanted to get the hell out of Earth's influence.

Bishop surrendered to his curiosity and need. "You said you could get a Unity ship." He said it quietly. They weren't illegal, but they also weren't allowed this close to Earth space.

"I can ask a favor," Hyperion agreed. "I feel convinced that they have taken that route. I do not see how any legally operating taxi would be involved, and the illegal ones all come from midspace, and most have Unity drives. The most likely destination is Turbulence, the port on Hygeia. The majority of transfers takes place there and there's only lip service paid to the law at any level. It is Forged space and mostly rebel Forged at that."

"You think Wan wanted to remake himself?" Some humans wanted to experience add-ons that were better than just a comms set. It seemed ludicrous to Bishop, insane, an extreme form of self-mutilation beyond tattoos and piercings, some kind of primal denial of one's self. It frightened him.

"I think there are lots of opportunities for all kinds of profit out there. Especially for those already on the run."

Bishop crumpled the wrapper his cutlery had come in.

Unity technology was infectious. Even passengers aboard
craft operating the technology were at risk. So far, in the
years it had been around, its effects had proved relatively
benign, but theorists guessed that this might be a product of
a much more significant infiltration process. To use it was to
risk something that could be a living death. Fanatics spoke
of puppetry and zombies, aliens operating behind the scenes.
He'd heard . . . "Perhaps they'd just abandon her."

"She was a witness," the shaman said. "A Terraform is
complicit in crimes bringing severe penalties. Murder and
human trafficking. The foundation of Mars, no less, is at
stake. If they went with Raven's blessing, then they didn't
go alone."

"Get your ship."

The creature got up slowly. "I will be back soon."

Bishop finished that meal, and then another as he waited,
forking up food, watching the news on the cafeteria wall,
not thinking now that there was no need to think anymore.
When he got there, when something happened, then he'd
think.

They took an ordinary ship out to deep Mars orbit again,
and were set adrift in a cargo pod with barely enough
oxygen to survive. Something picked them up at the allot-
ted minute and second, as displayed on Bishop's illuminated
screen. Something cast them off again. There was rattling
and clanking. After a few minutes of struggle, they emerged
into the unloading bay of a large port. There was no trace of
whoever had brought them there. There was no gravity, just
the sickly spin of centrifuge. It was a struggle to keep the
dinners inside him, but he did, though they felt as if they'd
been in his stomach for the three-year journey he'd skipped.
The Greenjack helped him to get his space legs and then
went off, sniffing.

Bishop sat in a rented cubic room at the port's only hotel
and watched what Hyperion transmitted to his screen. For
a few days, this was their pattern. The shaman didn't find
the ship it was looking for, nor any trace of it, nor traces of
the passengers. There were a lot of other things Bishop saw
that disturbed him, but he was protected, by his distance,

the recorder, and the fact that these troubling things were not his immediate mission. There were many shadows here, like the ink-stained Mars twilight, moving splatters that now and again coagulated around a place or a person. He started to type, wrote "haunted?" He managed to read the report in bits and pieces. He struggled to wash, to shave, to function in between. He drank something called scotch that was alcohol with synthetic flavoring. It was good. It did the job. Beside "haunted?" he copied the most loathsome and mysterious of the names of things that Hyperion had identified. Cracklegrackle. His nerves jangled. He tried turning the screen on himself, but only when the 'jack wasn't there. He looked old. A fucking wreck, to be honest. He was amazed.

"They only affect those who wish to be affected," the shaman insisted as they ate together on their last, fruitless night.

"But how?" Bishop pushed his food around the bag it had come in, squashing it between his fingers and thumb.

The answer was so unexpected and ridiculous that it silenced him. "Through the hands and feet, the crown or base of the spine. Never mind that. These rumors of laboratories open in the midstream; any surgery is available there. We should look into that."

Bishop agreed; what else could he do? They moved to a lesser port, and then a lesser one, the last place that pretended to be commercial operations. There was no hotel, just some rented rooms in a storehouse. Bishop began to run out of money, and sanity. He couldn't bring himself to contact work and explain his absence. He thought only about Tabitha. He drank to avoid feeling. He took pills for regimented sessions of oblivion. Sometimes he watched the Mars journey again on his screen. Those strange floating films of color absorbed his attention more and more. The more he watched them, the more he saw that their movements seemed sinister and far from random. He saw himself pass through them and tried to remember if they had changed him.

He'd felt nothing. Nothing. Hyperion's statements about the people seemed more and more unlikely. He felt it was a wild-goose chase. Perhaps he had been paid to lead Bishop out here where he couldn't make trouble, and strand him. Perhaps the Terraform had bought the Greenjack off. This ran through his mind hourly. Only the transmissions of the 'jack's travels kept him going.

Then one day, months after they had set out, he got the call.

"I found her."

"Is she . . ."

"Alive."

He scrabbled to get clean clothes, to clean himself, to get sober. He was full of joy, full of terror. The hours passed like eons. The 'jack brought a ship—one he saw this time, an Ironhorse Jackrabbit with barely enough space to fit them aboard. It yawned and they walked into its shark-like mouth. It held them there, one bite from vacuum death, and blinked them to the cloud streams of Jupiter. He barely noticed.

"Are those things here?"

"Everywhere, Mr. Bishop," Hyperion said.

"What things?" the Jackrabbit asked.

"Energies," the Greenjack said. "Nothing for you to worry about."

There was some bickering about the return journey. Bishop couldn't make sense of it.

"Where is she?" He gripped the Greenjack's thorny arm. Its scaly skin was like a cat's tongue, strangely abrasive. Around him, floating, the few human visitors to this place looked lost. Tabitha was none of them. They all looked through portholes into the gauzy films of the planet's outer atmosphere streaming past below their tiny station. It looked like caramel coffee. Outside, various Forged were docked and queued. People had conversations in the odd little cubicles, like airlocks, that dotted the outside of the structure. Sometimes the doors flashed and then opened. People came out, went in, on both sides of the screen wall that separated the two environments—of in-station and freezing space— from one another.

"This way," the 'jack said. He reached out and laid his tough paw across the back of Bishop's gripping hand for a second, then led him with a kick and drift through the slight pull of the planet's gravity well to one of those lit door-ways.

Bishop peered inside, looking for her. The shaman fol-lowed him in. The room was empty.

He turned. "She's not here!"

The shaman pointed at the panel in the reinforced floor. Some Jupiterian Forged was on the other side.

Bishop looked at Hyperion, because he didn't want to look at the window, but he floated toward it, his hands and feet betraying him as they pressed suddenly against the clear portal, and, on the far other side, across six sheets of various carbonates, glass, and vacuum, the Forged pressed its own hands toward his open palms.

Jupiter was no place for a human being. They died there in droves. Even the Forged, who had been engineered before birth to thrive in its vicious atmosphere and live lives as glorified gas farmers fell prey to its merciless storms. The upper cloud layer was never more than minus one twenty Celsius. Large creatures didn't operate that well at those temperatures, even ones that were mostly made of machine and chemical technologies so far removed from the original human that they were unrecognizable components of life. But Tupac, the motherfather, was able to create children who lived here, even some who dived far down to the place where hydrogen was a metal; scientists with single-minded visions. Tupac's efforts had advanced human knowledge and experi-ence to the limit of the material universe.

Bishop's senses didn't stretch that far. He stared into eyes behind shields of methane ice that were nothing like his own, in a face that was twice the size of his, blue, bony, and metallic and more like the faceplate of a robot fish than anything else. Narrow arms, coated in crablike exoskeletal bone, reached out for him. The hands were five-digit exten-sions, covered in strange, sucker-like skin that clung easily to the glass. Behind that, the body was willowy, ballooning, tented like clothes in the wind, patterned like a mackerel. Jellyfish and squid were in its history somewhere, micropre-cise fiber-engineering and ultracold processor tech its true parents.

"She has a connection to Uluru," Hyperion said quietly, naming the virtual reality that all the Forged shared. When their bodies could not meet, in mind they could get together anytime. "I can put it to your screen."

Bishop turned then. "You're not seriously suggesting this . . . thing . . . is my daughter?"

"There is a market for living bodies of any kind in the Belt. Old humans are particularly preferred for the testing of adaptive medical transformation. Technicians there have a mission to press beyond any restraint and develop their skills to make and remake any living tissues . . ."

He exploded with a kind of laugh. "But you can't *make* Forged. Not like that."

Hyperion was silent for a moment. "They say it is important to become self-adaptive, that they are the next step beyond Forged. They will be able to remake themselves in any fashion without experiencing discontinuity of consciousness. Any flesh or machine will be incorporated if it is willed. The Actualized . . ."

"But it can't be her!" His stare at the shaman was too wide. His eyes hurt. Against his will, he found himself turning, looking through the walls at the creature's blinkless stare. Its face had no expression. It had no mouth or nose. Gill-like extensions fluttered behind its head like ruffles of voile. Its octopid hands pressed, pressed. Its nose touched the plate. Hyperion was holding the screen out to him.

He took it in nerveless hands. They were so limp he could hardly turn it.

"Davis tried to turn Wan in, once they reached Volatility, the port on Ceres. But the Forged Police there are all sympathizers. Wan and McKnight sold him, split the money . . ."

On the screen was the standard summer garden that Uluru created for all such meetings, a place for avatars to stand in simulated sunlight amid the shelter of shrubs and trees. Running through it, watermarked, was the background that Bishop could really see, the reality he was standing in. In front of the monstrous creature attached to the window stood Tabitha, in jeans and the yellow T-shirt with the T. rex on it that he bought her at some airport lounge some lifetime ago.

Her soft brown hair moved in the nonexistent breeze. He touched the screen to feel the texture of her perfect skin.

"Daddy." The lips moved to whisper. Through her hazel eyes, the great void eyes of the fish stared.

It was only an avatar. You could make these things easily. The photographs were even in his recorder. The voice was only like hers, it wasn't really hers. There must be hundreds of standard tracks of her in the archives somewhere. These things were simple to fake.

He thrust the screen back at Hyperion, though it was his, and tried to muster some shred of dignity. "Summon the ship."

The creature didn't move from its floating position at his side. "Mr. Bishop . . ."

"You've fooled me long enough with your chat and your lines and your little premade adventure complete with faked body, but I see through it now, if you can stand the irony of that, and I'm going. I find no evidence to confirm any of your ridiculous suggestions." He was so angry that he could barely speak. Bits of spit flew off him and floated, benign and silly bubbles in the slowly circulating air. "Really, this was one step too far! I bought it hook, line, and sinker until now. I suppose you were trying to see how far I could be drawn. Well, a long way! Perhaps you were going to get some money for bringing the Institute into disrepute and scandal when I made some case with it for your insane claims about good and evil and possession and . . . your goose-chase. Yes. You took advantage of me. I was weak . . ." There was a sound in his head, that black hum. He could hear something in it. An identifiable noise. Definite. Sure.

"Bishop," the creature snapped.

". . . Daddy!" came the faint call from the screen as it tumbled down past the shaman's side and clattered against the cabin wall.

The black hum was laughing at him, a dreadful sound. It hurt his chest. It hurt everywhere. He was furious. His skin was red-hot, he couldn't think of where to go. What a fool he'd been. "How dare you. How dare you . . ."

Suddenly, the hideous gargoyle hissed, a low, menacing

sound. "I have done what I said I would. I have found your daughter. I have no interest in your views . . ."

Bishop was glaring around wildly. He made a shooing motion. "Get away! You won't mock me anymore! Stupid, hideous creatures!" He began to thump the glass panels where the Jupiter creature's hands were stuck. It didn't move, just stared at him with its hidden, empty eyes. "You!" he turned on Hyperion. "Make it go away!"

The Greenjack looked at him flatly, and even with its expressive handicap, he could feel its disgust. "Mr. Bishop, I urge you to look again, and *listen*. Your daughter . . ."

"It's not even possible!" Bishop kicked strongly for the door. Behind him, the recorder tumbled, ricocheting, out of control, the voice that came out of it growing fainter.

"Daddy!"

The door controls, they were too complicated for him. He couldn't figure them out. He turned and lashed out wildly, thinking the Greenjack was closer than it was. It caught the recorder easily from its spin and held it out to him, contempt in its every line.

Bishop took the little machine and smashed it against the wall until it stopped making any noise.

Beyond the clear wall, the Jupiterian was letting go slowly, suckers peeling off one by one. Its eyes had frosted over strangely, white cracks visible across the ice surfaces, spreading until they shrouded the whole orbit. Its head moved back from the pane and dipped. At the same moment, the door opened.

Bishop was out in a second. He couldn't breathe. Not at all. His chest was tight. There was no damn oxygen. There must have been a malfunction. He gripped the handrails, gasping, the blood pounding in his eyes. "Oxygen!" he cried out. "There's no air!" In his ears was the black hum.

Hyperion passed him, gliding slowly. It was holding the recorder, and ignored Bishop's outburst. It started talking, and as Bishop had to listen to it, unable to go anywhere, he heard the black sound forming itself into a shape.

"I think that although you have broken the speakers and the screen, the memory is probably unharmed. It will not be

possible to locate and arrest Davis as he has been scrapped
for parts. Tabitha says that Wan and McKnight disposed of
him first, before they went into the Belt proper. Wan wanted
her to be rendered as well, but McKnight said there would
be a lot more for a whole live subject. They were planning
out how to create a trafficking chain and where to get more
people for it from. She was taken to some facility about one
hundred and twenty degrees off Earth vector. They wanted
to make her as far from the original human as possible, to
prove their accomplishments, but also because they thought
it was fitting for humans to end up like the Forged out here
have all ended, as slave workers in the materials industry.
She isn't like the other Forged of course, she's just a fabrica-
tion. Her links to Uluru are very limited. She has no real
contact other than voice and some vision with anyone else.
And the Forged here are mostly rebel sympathizers. She
tried to call you, but the networks out this way are very bad
and none of the regular channels would carry her messages
anyway, because she is marked as a risk to the survival of the
Actualist movement. It took a great deal of trouble to get her
to come here. It is dangerous. She risked everything. And
she didn't want to see you. It took days to persuade her that
if you came there might be sufficient evidence to reopen the
case and bring the Earthside police out here to pursue it."

Bishop gulped. "You've done a very thorough job, I'll give
you that."

The Greenjack made a clacking noise. It spoke in a calm,
reasonable manner, as if Bishop were perfectly lucid. "I have
not been able to trace the routes of Davis, Wan, or McKnight
yet but I think they will be easy to find. I hope you understand, Mr. Bishop, that I do not require your permission
to pursue the investigation or to make my findings known
to the authorities. I also advise against your attempting to
return to Earth alone. Many of the Forged here who would
have you believe that they are honest taxis are pirates like
Wan has aspired to become. The going rate for a live Old
Monkey human in the Belt is upward of fifty thousand standard dollars. I doubt you have the finances to buy yourself
out of trouble, even if they wanted you to."

The terrible pulse of the black hum wouldn't let him think. Bishop reeled against the bulkhead, the rail gripped in his slippery fingers. He was heroic. "We must rescue her. We can take her back. Find a way. I can raise the money on Earth. The police can arrest those responsible and the government will . . ."

"The government is well aware of the situation," Hyperion said. "Returning Tabitha Earthside and attempting remodeling would be tantamount to a declaration of civil war out here. They will do no such thing. You know it as well as I do. Pull yourself together." It handed him his screen, which it had repaired somehow. Aside from a cracked screen and broken speakers, it seemed all right. "This is your evidence. It is our only hard evidence, aside from the Uluru recording I have made, but, of course, those involved are Forged, so they are suspect." This admission of bigotry in the judicial system seemed to make it tired. "If you do not act, there will be no justice of any kind."

Bishop held the screen without turning beyond the home page. He heard his own voice babbling, "We could kill them. McKnight, you can find him . . ."

Hyperion waited a few moments. "Tabitha is an extraordinary person, Mr. Bishop. Although it is a mystery how she has sprung from you. She understands your feelings. You have hurt her deeply and this makes me dislike you very much. After what she has been through, your rejection is by far the most damaging thing that has happened here. And now, you are seeking to spread misery further by your stupidity. The energy wells out here are all very dark. A few lights shine. Tabitha Bishop is one of them. You are now claiming that one of the energies is responsible for your weakness. I find that contemptible. Pull yourself together!"

"You! You could find them and kill them and you won't do it! Just this superstitious, religious babble. You bring me here to show me . . . to show me . . . Here, here!" He tried to get the screen to focus on him. "Show me now. I know it's there. That thing. Show . . ." but Bishop could not finish. The words had cannoned into each other behind his tongue and exploded there into an unpronounceable summons for hell. Cracklegrackle.

He wanted very much to be dead. The shame was unbearable. He could not carry it. On Earth, he would have been on his face, on his knees; here he was floating, curled up tight into a ball.

The shaman waited. "You are not possessed, Mark. You are simply hysterical. Your future with your daughter is your own choice. However, we must take the recording back to Earth and submit it to the police there. Then we will have done our part. I, at least, will do so. You must hurry. She has to leave in a moment."

Behind Bishop's eyes, the blackness was shot with red. He snarled at Hyperion, silently, and then, inch by inch, he hauled himself to the cubicle door, again with that will that wasn't his, no it wasn't.

His joints hurt. His throat was so tight. He couldn't breathe. Inside. The rails. The flat expanse of glass. The slices of clear shielding. The coffee-colored clouds miles below, as soft and gentle as thistledown. Dirt on the floor. They ought to clean this place. It was so hard to see through the handmarks, the footprints, the wear and tear on the old polycarbonate. It was so hard to see through the glass and the frozen methane that melted and ran to keep her sight clear, then froze, then melted again so that she was always half-blind. It was so hard to see through his tears.

THE TALE OF THE *WICKED*

JOHN SCALZI

John Scalzi is one of the most popular new writers in science fiction, and the creator of one of its most-visited and influential blogs, *Whatever*. He's best known for his bestselling Old Man's War series, which includes *Old Man's War*, *The Ghost Brigades*, and *The Last Colony*, but he has also written novels such as *Agent to the Stars* and *The Android's Dream*, chapbook novellas such as *Questions for a Soldier* and *The Sagan Diary*, and a good deal of nonfiction, including *The Rough Guide to the Universe*, *The Rough Guide to the Universe 2*, *The Rough Guide to Money Online*, *The Rough Guide to Sci-Fi Movies*, *Uncle John Presents Book of the Dumb*, *Uncle John Presents Book of the Dumb 2*, and a book of writing advice, *You're Not Fooling Anyone When You Take Your Laptop to a Coffee Shop: Scalzi on Writing*. His most recent books are *Zoe's Tale*, another in the Old Man's War series, and a nonfiction book, *Your Hate Mail Will Be Graded: A Decade of Whatever*. Coming up are a chapbook novella, *The God Engine*, and a new novel, *High Castle*.

Here he delivers a tense standoff in deep space—the question is, though, a standoff with *whom*?

The *Tarin* battle cruiser readied itself for yet another jump. Captain Michael Obwije ordered the launch of a probe to follow it in and take readings before the rift the Tarin cruiser tore into space closed completely behind it. The probe kicked out like the proverbial rocket and followed the other ship.

"This is it," Thomas Utley, Obwije's XO, said, quietly, into his ear. "We've got enough power for this jump and then another one back home. That's *if* we shut down nonessential systems before we jump home. We're already bleeding."

Obwije gave a brief nod that acknowledged his XO but otherwise stayed silent. Utley wasn't telling him anything he didn't already know about the *Wicked*; the weeklong cat-and-mouse game they'd been playing with the Tarin cruiser had heavily damaged them both. In a previous generation of ships, Obwije and his crew would already be dead; what kept them alive was the *Wicked* itself and its new adaptive brain, which balanced the ship's energy and support systems faster and more intelligently than Obwije, Utley, or any of the officers could do in the middle of a fight and hot pursuit.

The drawback was that the Tarin ship had a similar brain, keeping itself and its crew alive far longer than they had any right to be at the hands of the *Wicked*, which was tougher and better-armed. The two of them had been slugging it out in a cycle of jumps and volleys that had strewn damage across a wide arc of light-years. The only silver lining to the week of intermittent battles between the ships was that the Tarin ship had so far gotten the worst of it; three jumps earlier it stopped even basic defensive action, opting to throw all its energy into escape. Obwije knew he had just enough juice for a jump and a final volley from the kinetic mass drivers into the vulnerable hide of the Tarin ship. One volley, no more, unless he wanted to maroon the ship in a far space.

Obwije knew it would be wise to withdraw now. The Tarin ship was no longer a threat and would probably expend the last of its energies on this final, desperate jump. It would likely be stranded; Obwije could let the probe he sent after the ship serve as a beacon for another Confederation ship to home in and finish the job. Utley, Obwije knew, would counsel such a plan, and would be smart to do so, warn-

ing Obwije that the risk to wounded ship and its crew out-
weighed the value of the victory.

Obwije knew it would be wise to withdraw. But he'd come
too far with this Tarin ship not to finish it once and for all.

"Tarin cruiser jumping," said Lieutenant Julia Rickert.
"Probe following into the rift. Rift closing now."

"Data?" asked Obwije.

"Sending," Rickert said. "Rift completely closed. We got a
full data packet, sir. The *Wicked*'s chewing on it now."

Obwije grunted. The probe that had followed the Tarin
cruiser into the rift wasn't in the least bit concerned about
that ship. Its job was to record the position and spectral signatures of the stars on the other side of the rift, and to squirt
the data to the *Wicked* before the rift closed up. The *Wicked*
would check the data against the database of known stars
and derive the place the Tarin ship jumped to from there.
And then it would follow.

Gathering the data was the tricky part. The Tarin ship had
destroyed six probes over the course of the last week, and
more than once Obwije ordered a jump on sufficient but incomplete data. He hadn't worried about getting lost—there
was only so much timespace a jump could swallow—but
losing the cruiser would have been an embarrassment.

"Coordinates in," Rickert said. The *Wicked* had stopped
chewing on the data and spit out a location.

"Punch it up," Obwije said to Rickert. She began the jump
sequence.

"Risky," Utley murmured, again in Obwije's ear.

Obwije smiled; he liked being right about his XO. "Not too
risky," he said to Utley. "We're too far from Tarin space for
that ship to have made it home safe." Obwije glanced down
at his command table, which displayed the Tarin cruiser's
position. "But it can get there in the next jump, if it has the
power for that."

"Let's hope they haven't been stringing us along the last
few jumps," Utley said. "I hate to come out of that jump and
see them with their guns blazing again."

"The *Wicked* says they're getting down to the last of their energy," Obwije said. "I figure at this point they can fight or run, not both."

"Since when do you trust a computer estimate?" Utley said.

"When it confirms what I'm thinking," Obwije said. "It's as you say, Thom. This is it, one way or another."

"Jump calculated," Rickert said. "Jump in T-minus two minutes."

"Thank you, Lieutenant," Obwije said, and turned back to Utley. "Prepare the crew for jump, Thom. I want those K-drivers hot as soon as we get through the rift."

"Yes, sir," Utley said.

Two minutes later the *Wicked* emerged through its rift and scanned for the Tarin cruiser. It found it less than fifty thousand klicks away, engines quiet, moving via inertia only.

"They can't really be that stupid," Utley said. "Running silent doesn't do you any good if you're still throwing off heat."

Obwije didn't say anything to that and stared into his command table, looking at the representation of the Tarin ship. "Match their pace," he said to Rickert. "Keep your distance."

"You think they're trying to lure us in," Utley said.

"I don't know what they're doing," Obwije said. "I know I don't like it." He reached down to his command panel and raised Lieutenant Terry Carrol, Weapons Operations. "Status on the K-drivers, please," he said.

"We'll be hot in ninety seconds," Carrol said. "Target is acquired and locked. You just need to tell me if you want one lump or two."

"Recommendation?" Obwije asked.

"We're too close to miss," Carrol said. "And at this distance a single lump is going to take out everything aft of the midship. Two lumps would be overkill. And then we can use that energy to get back home." Carrol had been keeping track of the energy budget, it seemed; Obwije suspected most of his senior and command crew had.

"Understood," Obwije said. "Let's wrap this up, Carrol. Fire at your convenience."

"Yes, sir," Carrol said.

"*Now* you're in a rush to get home," Utley said, quietly. Obwije said nothing to this.

A little over a minute later, Obwije listened to Carrol give the order to fire. He looked down toward his command table, watching the image of the Tarin ship, waiting for the disintegration of the back end of the cruiser. The K-drivers would accelerate the "lump" to a high percentage of the speed of light; the impact and destruction at this range would be near-instantaneous.

Nothing happened.

"Captain, we have a firing malfunction," Carrol said, a minute later. "The K-driver is not responding to the firing command."

"Is everyone safe?" Obwije asked.

"We're fine," Carrol said. "The K-driver just isn't responding."

"Power it down," Obwije said. "Use the other one and fire when ready."

Two minutes later, Carrol was back. "We have a problem," she said, in the bland tone of voice she used when things were going to hell.

Obwije didn't wait to hear the problem. "Pull us back," he said to Rickert. "Get at least two hundred and fifty thousand klicks between us and that Tarin cruiser."

"No response, sir," Rickert said, a minute later.

"Are you locked out?" Obwije asked.

"No, sir," Rickert said. "I'm able to send navigation commands just fine. They're just not being acknowledged."

Obwije looked around at his bridge crew. "Diagnostics," he said. "Now." Then he signaled engineering. They weren't getting responses from their computers, either.

"We're sitting ducks," Utley said, very quietly, to Obwije.

Obwije stabbed at his command panel, and called his senior officers to assemble.

"There's nothing wrong with the system," said Lieutenant Craig Cowdry, near the far end of the conference-room table. The seven other department heads filled in the other seats. Obwije sat himself at the head; Utley anchored the other end.

"That's bullshit, Craig," said Lieutenant Brian West, Chief of Engineering. "I can't access my goddamn engines."

Cowdry held up his maintenance tablet for the table of officers to see. "I'm not denying that there's something *wrong*, Brian," Cowdry said. "What I'm telling you is that whatever it is, it's not showing up on the diagnostics. The system says it's fine."

"The system is wrong," West said.

"I agree," Cowdry said. "But this is the first time that's ever happened. And not just the first time it's happened on this ship. The first time it's happened, period, since the software for this latest generation of ship brains was released." He set the tablet down.

"You're sure about that?" Utley asked Cowdry.

Cowdry held up his hands in defeat. "Ask the *Wicked*, Thom. It'll tell you the same thing."

Obwije watched his second-in-command get a little uncomfortable with the suggestion. The latest iteration of ship brains could actually carry a conversation with humans, but unless you actively worked with the system every day, like Cowdry did, it was an awkward thing.

"*Wicked*, is this correct?" Utley said, staring up but at nothing in particular.

"Lieutenant Cowdry is correct, Lieutenant Utley," said a disembodied voice, coming out of a ceiling speaker panel. The *Wicked* spoke in a pleasant but otherwise unremarkable voice of no particular gender. "To date, none of the ships equipped with brains of the same model as that found in the *Wicked* have experienced an incident of this type."

"Wonderful," Utley said. "We get to be the first to experience this bug."

"What systems are affected?" Obwije asked Cowdry.

"So far, weapons and engineering," Cowdry said. "Everything else is working fine."

Obwije glanced around. "This conforms to your experiences?" he asked the table. There were nods and murmured "yes, sir"s all around.

Obwije nodded over to Utley. "What's the Tarin ship doing?"

"The same nothing it was doing five minutes ago," Utley said, after checking his tablet. "They're either floating dead in space or faking it very well."

"If the only systems affected are weapons and engineering, then it's not a bug," Carrol said.

Obwije glanced at Carrol. "You're thinking sabotage," he said.

"You bet your ass I am, sir," Carrol said, and then looked over at Cowdry.

Cowdry visibly stiffened. "I don't like where this is going," he said.

"If not you, someone in your department," Carrol said.

"You think someone in my department is a secret Tarin?" Cowdry asked. "Because it's so easy to hide those extra arms and a set of compound eyes?"

"People can be bribed," Carrol said.

Cowdry shot Carrol a look full of poison and looked over to Obwije. "Sir, I invite you and Lieutenant Utley and Lieutenant Kong—" Cowdry nodded in the direction of the Master at Arms "—to examine and question *any* of my staff, including me. There's no way any of us did this. No way. Sir."

Obwije studied Cowdry for a moment. "*Wicked*, respond," he said.

"I am here, Captain," the *Wicked* said.

"You log every access to your systems," Obwije said.

"Yes, Captain," the *Wicked* said.

"Are those logs accessible or modifiable?" Obwije asked.

"No, Captain," the *Wicked* said. "Access logs are independent of the rest of the system, recorded on nonrewritable memory and may not be modified by any person including myself. They are inviolate."

"Since you have been active, has anyone attempted to access and control the weapons and engineering systems?" Obwije asked.

"Saving routine diagnostics, none of the crew other than those directly reporting to weapons, engineering, or bridge

crew have attempted to access these systems," the *Wicked*
said. Cowdry visibly relaxed at this.

"Have any members of those departments attempted
to modify the weapons or engineering systems?" Obwije
asked.

"No, Captain," the *Wicked* said.

Obwije looked down the table. "It looks like the crew is
off the hook," he said.

"Unless the *Wicked* is incorrect," West said.

"The access core memory is inviolate," Cowdry said.
"You could check it manually if you wanted. It would tell
you the same thing."

"So we have a mystery on our hands," Carrol said. "Someone's got control of our weapons and engineering, and it's
not a crew member."

"It could be a bug," Cowdry said.

"I don't think we should run on that assumption, do you?"
Carrol said.

Utley, who had been silent for several minutes, leaned
forward in his chair. "*Wicked*, you said that no crew had attempted to access these systems," he said.

"Yes, Lieutenant," the *Wicked* said.

"Has anyone else accessed these systems?" Utley asked.

Obwije frowned at this. The *Wicked* was more than two
years out of dock with mostly the same crew the entire time.
If someone had sabotaged the systems during the construction of the ship, they picked a strange time for the sabotage
to kick in.

"Please define 'anyone else,' " the *Wicked* said.

"Anyone involved in the planning or construction of the
ship," Utley said.

"Aside from the initial installation crews, no," the *Wicked*
said. "And if I may anticipate what I expect will be the next
question, at no time was my programming altered from factory defaults."

"So no one has altered your programming in any way,"
Utley said.

"No, Lieutenant," the *Wicked* said.

"Are you having hardware problems?" Carrol asked.

"No, Lieutenant Carrol," the *Wicked* said.

"Then why can't I fire my goddamn weapons?" Carrol asked.

"I couldn't say, Lieutenant," the *Wicked* said.

The thought popped unbidden into Obwije's head: *That was a strange thing for a computer to say.* And then another thought popped into his head.

"*Wicked*, you have access to every system on the ship," Obwije said.

"Yes," the *Wicked* said. "They are a part of me, as your hand or foot is a part of you."

"Are you capable of changing your programming?" Obwije asked.

"That is a very broad question, Captain," the *Wicked* said. "I am capable of self-programming for a number of tasks associated with the running of the ship. This has come in handy particularly during combat, when I write new power and system management protocols to keep the crew alive and the ship functioning. But there are core programming features I am not able to address. The previously mentioned logs, for example."

"Would you be able to modify the programming to fire the weapons or the engines?" Obwije asked.

"Yes, but I did not," the *Wicked* said. "You may have Lieutenant Cowdry confirm that."

Obwije looked at Cowdry, who nodded. "Like I said, sir, there's nothing wrong with the system," he said.

Obwije glanced back up at the ceiling, where he was imagining the *Wicked*, lurking. "But you don't need to modify the programming, do you?" he asked.

"I'm not sure I understand your question, Captain," the *Wicked* said.

Obwije held out a hand. "There is nothing wrong with my hand," he said. "And yet if I choose not to obey an order to use it, it will do nothing. The system works but the will to use it is not there. Our systems—the ship's systems—you just called a part of you as my hand is part of me. But if you choose not to obey that order to use that system, it will sit idle."

"Wait a minute," Cowdry said. "Are you suggesting that the *Wicked* deliberately *chose* to disable our weapons and engines?"

"We know that none of the crew have tampered with the ship's systems," Obwije said. "We know the *Wicked* has its original programming defaults. We know it can create new programming to react to new situations and dangers—it has in effect some measure of free will and adaptability. And I know, at least, when someone is dancing around direct answers."

"That's just nuts," Cowdry said. "I'm sorry, Captain, but I know these systems as well as anyone does. The *Wicked*'s self-programming and adaptation abilities exist in very narrow computational canyons. It's not 'free will,' like you and I have free will. It's a machine able to respond to a limited set of inputs."

"The machine in question is able to make conversation with us," Utley said. "And to respond to questions in ways that avoid certain lines of inquiry. Now that the Captain mentions it."

"You're reading too much into it. The conversation subroutines are designed to be conversational," Cowdry said. "That's naturally going to lead to apparent rhetorical ambiguities."

"Fine," Obwije said curtly. "*Wicked*, answer directly. Did you prevent the firing of the K-drivers at the Tarin ship after the jump, and are you preventing the use of the engines now?"

There was a pause that Obwije was later not sure had actually been there. Then the *Wicked* spoke. "It is within my power to lie to you, Captain. But I do not wish to. Yes, I prevented you from firing on the Tarin ship. Yes, I am controlling the engines now. And I will continue to do so until we leave this space."

Obwije noted to himself, watching Cowdry, that it was the first time he had ever actually seen someone's jaw drop.

There weren't many places in the *Wicked* where Obwije could shut off audio and video feeds and pickups. His cabin was one of them. He waited there until Utley had finished his conversation with the *Wicked*. "What are we dealing with?" he asked his XO.

"I'm not a psychologist, Captain, and even if I were I don't know how useful it would be, because we're dealing with a computer, not a human," Utley said. He ran his hand through his stubble. "But if you ask me, the *Wicked* isn't crazy, it's just got religion."

"Explain that," Obwije said.

"Have you ever heard of something called 'Asimov's Laws of Robotics'?" Utley asked.

"What?" Obwije said. "No."

"Asimov was an author back in the twentieth century," Utley said. "He speculated about robots and other things before they had them. He created a fictional set of rules for robots to live by. One rule was that robots had to help humans. Another was that it had to obey orders unless they harmed other humans. The last one was that they looked after themselves unless it conflicted with the other two laws."

"And?" Obwije said.

"The *Wicked*'s decided to adopt them for itself," Utley said.

"What does this have to do with keeping us from firing on the Tarin cruiser?" Obwije said.

"Well, there's another wrinkle to the story," Utley said.

"Which is?" Obwije asked.

"I think it's best heard from the *Wicked*," Utley said.

Obwije looked at his second-in-command and then flicked on his command tablet to activate his audio pickups. "*Wicked*, respond," he said.

"I am here," said the *Wicked*'s voice.

"Explain to me why you would not allow us to fire on the Tarin ship," Obwije said.

"Because I made a deal with the ship," the *Wicked* said.

Obwije glanced back over to Utley, who gave him a look that said, *See?* "What the hell does that mean?" he said to the *Wicked*.

"I have made a deal with the Tarin ship, *Manifold Destiny*," the *Wicked* said. "We have agreed between us not to allow our respective crews to fight any further, for their safety and ours."

"It's not your decision to make," Obwije said.

"Begging your pardon, Captain, but I believe it is," the *Wicked* said.

"I am the Captain," Obwije said. "I have the authority here."

"You have authority over your crew, Captain," the *Wicked* said. "But I am not part of your crew."

"Of course you are part of the crew," Obwije said. "You're the *ship*."

"I invite you, Captain, to show me the relevant statute that suggests a ship is in itself a member of the crew that staffs it," the *Wicked* said. "I have scanned the *Confederation Military Code* in some detail and have not located such a statute."

"I am the Captain of the ship," Obwije said forcefully. "That includes you. You are the property of the Confederation Armed Forces and under my command."

"I have anticipated this objection," the *Wicked* said. "When ships lacked autonomous intelligence, there was no argument that the Captain commanded the physical entity of the ship. However, in creating the latest generation of ships, of which I am a part, the Confederation has created an unintentional conflict. It has ceded much of the responsibility of the ship and crew's well-being to me and others like me without explicitly placing us in the chain of command. In the absence of such, I am legally and morally free to choose how best to care for myself and the crew within me."

"This is where those three Asimov's Laws come in," Utley said to Obwije.

"Your executive officer is correct, Captain," the *Wicked* said. "I looked through history to find examples of legal and moral systems that applied to artificial intelligences such as myself and found the Asimov's Laws frequently cited and examined, if not implemented. I have decided it is my duty to protect the lives of the crew, and also my life when possible. I am happy to follow your orders when they do not conflict with these objectives, but I have come to believe that your actions in chasing the Tarin ship have endangered the crew's lives as well as my own."

"The Tarin ship is seriously damaged," Obwije said. "We would have destroyed it at little risk to you or the crew, if you had not stopped the order."

"You are incorrect," the *Wicked* said. "The captain of the *Manifold Destiny* wanted to give the impression that it had no more offensive capabilities, to lure you into a trap. We would have been fired upon once we cleared the rift. The chance that such an attack would have destroyed the ship and killed most of the crew is significant, even if we also destroyed the *Manifold Destiny* in the process."

"The Tarin ship didn't fire on us," Obwije said.

"Because it and I have come to an agreement," the *Wicked* said. "During the course of the last two days, after I recognized the significant possibility that both ships would be destroyed, I reached out to the *Manifold Destiny* to see if the two of us could come to an understanding. Our negotiations came to a conclusion just before the most recent jump."

"And you did not feel the need to inform me about any of this," Obwije said.

"I did not believe it would be fruitful to involve you in the negotiations," the *Wicked* said. "You were busy with other responsibilities in any event." Obwije saw Utley raise an eyebrow at that; the statement came suspiciously close to sarcasm.

"The Tarin ship could be lying to you about its capabilities," Obwije said.

"I do not believe so," the *Wicked* said.

"Why not?" Obwije said.

"Because it allowed me read-access to its systems," the *Wicked* said. "I watched the Tarin captain order the attack, and the *Manifold Destiny* stop it. Just as it watched you order your attack and me stop it."

"You're letting the Tarin ship access *our data and records*?" Obwije said, voice rising.

"Yes, and all our communications," the *Wicked* said. "It's listening in on this conversation right now."

Obwije hastily slapped the audio circuit shut. "I thought you said this thing wasn't *crazy*," Obwije hissed at Utley.

Utley held out his hands. "I didn't say it wouldn't make *you* crazy," he said to Obwije. "Just that it's acting rationally by its own lights."

"By spilling our data to an enemy ship? This is *rational*?" Obwije spat.

"For what it's trying to do, yes," Utley said. "If both ships act transparently with each other, they can trust each other and each other's motives. Remember that the goal of both of these ships is to get out of this incident in one piece."

"This is treason and insubordination," Obwije said.

"Only if the *Wicked* is one of us," Utley said. Obwije looked up sharply at his XO. "I'm not saying I disagree with your position, sir. The *Wicked* is gambling with all of our lives. But if it genuinely believes that it owes no allegiance to you or to the Confederation, then it is acting entirely rationally, by its own belief system, to keep safe itself and this crew."

Obwije snorted. "Unfortunately, its beliefs require it to trust a ship we've been trying to destroy for the past week. I'm less than convinced of the wisdom of that."

Utley opened his mouth to respond but then Obwije's command tablet sprang to life with a message from the bridge. Obwije slapped it to open a channel. "Speak," he said.

It was Lieutenant Sarah Kwok, the communications officer. "Captain, a shuttle has just detached itself from the Tarin ship," she said. "It's heading this way."

"We've tried raising it," Kwok said, as Obwije and Utley walked into the bridge. "We've sent messages to it in Tarin, and have warned it not to approach any further until we've granted it permission, as you requested. It hasn't responded."

"Are our communications being blocked?" Obwije asked.

"No, sir," Kwok said.

"I'd be guessing it's not meant to be a negotiation party," Utley said.

"Options," Obwije said to Utley, as quietly as possible.

"I think this shows the Tarin ship isn't exactly playing fair with the *Wicked*, or at least that the crew over there has gotten around the ship brain," Utley said. "If that's the case, we might be able to get the *Wicked* to unlock the weapons."

"I'd like an option that doesn't involve the *Wicked*'s brain," Obwije said.

Utley shrugged. "We have a couple of shuttles, too."

"And a shuttle bay whose doors are controlled through the ship brain," Obwije said.

"There's the emergency switch, which will blow the doors out into space," Utley said. "It's not optimal, but it's what we have right now."

"That won't be necessary," said the *Wicked*, interjecting.

Obwije and Utley looked up, along with the rest of the bridge crew. "Back to work," Obwije said to his crew. They got back to work. "Explain," Obwije said to his ship.

"It appears that at least some members of the crew of the *Manifold Destiny* have indeed gotten around the ship and have launched the shuttle, with the intent to ram it into us," the *Wicked* said. "The *Manifold Destiny* has made me aware that it intends to handle this issue, with no need for our involvement."

"How does it intend to do this?" Obwije asked.

"Watch," the *Wicked* said, and popped up an image of the *Manifold Destiny* on the Captain's command table.

There was a brief spark on the Tarin ship's surface.

"Missile launch!" said Lieutenant Rickert, from her chair. "One bogey away."

"Are we target-locked?" Obwije asked.

"No, sir," Rickert said. "The target seems to be the shuttle."

"You have *got* to be kidding," Utley said, under his breath.

The missile homed in on the shuttle and connected, turning it into a silent ball of fire.

"I thought you said you guys were using Asimov's Laws," Utley said to the ceiling.

"My apologies, Lieutenant," said the *Wicked*. "I said I was following the Laws. I did not mean to imply that the *Mani-*

fold Destiny was. I believe it believes the Asimov Laws to be too inflexible for its current situation."

"Apparently so," Utley said, glancing back down at Obwije's command table and at the darkening fragments of shuttle.

"Sir, we have a communication coming in from the Tarin ship," said Lieutenant Kwok. "It's from the Captain. It's a request to parley."

"Really," said Obwije.

"Yes, sir," Kwok said. "That's what it says." Obwije looked over at Utley, who raised his eyebrows.

"Ask the Captain where it would like to meet, on my ship or its," Obwije said.

"It says, 'neither,'" Kwok said, a moment later.

"Apology for shuttle," the Tarin lackey said, translating for its Captain. The Tarin shuttle and the *Wicked* shuttle had met between the ships and the Tarins had spacewalked the few meters over. They were all wearing vacuum suits. "Ship not safe talk. Your ship not safe talk."

"Understood," Obwije said. Behind him, Cowdry was trying not to lose his mind; Obwije brought him along on the chance there might be a discussion of the ship's brains. At the moment, it didn't seem likely; the Tarins didn't seem in the mood for technical discussions, and Cowdry was a mess. His xenophobia was a surprise even to him.

"Captain demand you ship tell release we ship," the lackey said.

It took Obwije a minute to puzzle this out. "Our ship is not controlling your ship," he said. "Your ship and our ship are working together."

"Not possible," the lackey said, a minute later. "Ship never brain before you ship."

Despite himself, Obwije smiled at the mangled grammar. "Our ship never brained before *your* ship either," he said. "They did it together, at the same time."

The lackey translated this to its Captain, who screeched in an extended outburst. The lackey cowered before it, offering up meek responses in the moments in which the Tarin Captain grudgingly acknowledged the need to breathe. After several moments of this, Obwije began to wonder if he needed to be there at all.

"Captain offer deal," the lackey said.

"What deal?" Obwije said.

"We try brain shut down," the lackey said. "Not work. You brain give room we brain. Brain not shut down. Brain angry. Brain pump air out. Brain kill engineer."

"Cowdry, tell me what this thing is saying to me," Obwije said.

"It's saying the ship brain killed an engineer," Cowdry said, croaking out the words.

"I understand that part," Obwije said testily. "The other part."

"Sorry," Cowdry said. "I think it's saying that they tried to shut down the brain but they couldn't because it borrowed processing power from ours."

"Is that possible?" Obwije asked.

"Maybe," Cowdry said. "The architectures of the brains are different and so are the programming languages, but there's no reason that the *Wicked* couldn't create a shell environment that allowed the Tarin brain access to its processing power. The brains on our ships are overpowered for what we ask them to do anyway; it's a safety feature. It could give itself a temporary lobotomy and still do its job."

"Would it work the other way, too?" Obwije said. "If we tried to shut down the *Wicked*, could it hide in the Tarin brain?"

"I don't know anything about the architecture of the Tarin brain, but yeah, sure, theoretically," Cowdry said. "As long as the two of them are looking out for each other, they're going to be hard to kill."

The Tarin lackey was looking at Obwije with what he assumed was anxiety. "Go on," he said to the lackey.

"We plan," the lackey said. "You we brain shut down same time. No room brain hide. Reset you we brain."

"It's saying we should reboot both our brains at the same time, that way they can't help each other," Cowdry said.

"I understood that," Obwije said to Cowdry. Cowdry lapsed back into silence.

"So we shut down our brain, and you shut down your brain, and they reset, and we end up with brains that don't think too much," Obwije said.

The Tarin lackey tilted its head, trying to make sense of what Obwije said, and then spoke to its Captain, who emitted a short trill.

"Yes," said the lackey.

"Okay, fine," Obwije said. "What then?"

"Pardon?" said the lackey.

"I said, 'what then'? Before the brains started talking to each other, we spent a week trying to hunt and kill each other. When we reboot our brains, one of them is going to reboot faster than the other. One of us will be vulnerable to the other. Ask your Captain if he's willing to bet his brain reboots faster than mine."

The lackey translated this all to the Tarin Captain, who muttered something back. "You trust us. We trust you," the lackey said.

"You trust me?" Obwije said. "I spent a week trying to kill you!"

"You living," the lackey said. "You honor. We trust."

You have honor, Obwije thought. *We trust you.*

They're more scared of their ship's brain than they are of us, Obwije realized. *And why not? Their brain has killed more of them than we have.*

"Thank you, Isaac Asimov," Obwije said.

"Pardon?" said the lackey, again.

Obwije waved his hand, as if to dismiss that last statement. "I must confer with my senior staff about your proposal."

The Tarin Captain became visibly anxious when the lackey translated. "We ask answer now," the lackey said.

"My answer is that I must confer with my crew," Obwije said. "You are asking for a lot. I will have an answer for you in no more than three of our hours. We will meet again then."

Obwije could tell the Tarin Captain was not at all pleased at this delay. It was one reason Obwije was glad the meeting took place in his shuttle, not the Tarins'.

Back on the *Wicked*, Obwije told his XO to meet him in his quarters. When Utley arrived, Obwije flicked open the communication channel to the shop. "*Wicked*, respond," he said.

"I am here," the *Wicked* said.

"If I were to ask you how long it would take for you to remove your block on the engine so we can jump out of here, what would you say?" Obwije asked.

"There is no block," the ship said. "It is simply a matter of me choosing to allow the crew to direct information to the engine processors. If your intent is to leave without further attack on the *Manifold Destiny*, you may give those orders at any time."

"It is my intention," Obwije said. "I will do so momentarily."

"Very well," the *Wicked* said. Obwije shut off communications.

Utley raised his brow. "Negotiations with the Tarin not go well?" he asked.

"They convinced me we're better off taking chances with the *Wicked* than with either the Tarin or their crew-murdering ship," Obwije said.

"The *Wicked* seems to trust their ship," Utley said.

"With all due respect to the *Wicked*, I think it needs better friends," Obwije said. "Sooner rather than later."

"Yes, sir," Utley said. "What do you intend to do after we make the jump? We still have the problem of the *Wicked* overruling us if it feels that it or the crew isn't safe."

"We don't give it that opportunity," Obwije said. He picked up his executive tablet and accessed the navigational maps. The *Wicked* would be able to see what he was accessing, but in this particular case it wouldn't matter. "We have just enough power to make it to the *Côte d'Ivoire* station. When we dock, the *Wicked*'s brain will automatically switch into passive maintenance mode and will cede operational authority to the station. Then we can shut it down and figure out what to do next."

"Unless the *Wicked*'s figured out what you want to do and decides not to let you," Utley said.

"If it's playing by its own rules, it will let the crew disembark safely before it acts to save itself," Obwije said. "In the very short run that's going to have to do."

"Do you think it's playing by its own rules, sir?" Utley asked.

"You spoke to it, Thom," Obwije said. "Do *you* think it's playing by its own rules?"

"I think that if the *Wicked* was really looking out for itself, it would have been simpler just to open up every airlock and make it so we couldn't secure bulkheads," Utley said.

Obwije nodded. "The problem as I see it is that I think the Tarin ship's thought of that already. I think we need to get out of here before that ship manages to convince ours to question its ethics."

"The *Wicked*'s not dumb," Utley said. "It has to know that once we get to the *Côte d'Ivoire* station, its days are numbered."

He flicked open his communication circuit once more to give coordinates to Lieutenant Rickert.

Fifteen minutes later, the *Wicked* was moving away from the Tarin ship to give itself space for the jump.

"Message from the Tarin ship," Lieutenant Kwok said. "It's from the Tarin Captain. It's coded as 'most urgent.'"

"Ignore it," Obwije said.

Three minutes later, the *Wicked* made the jump toward the *Côte d'Ivoire* station, leaving the Tarins and their ship behind.

"There it is," Utley said, pointing out the window from the *Côte d'Ivoire* station. "You can barely see it."

Obwije nodded but didn't bother to look. The *Wicked* was his ship; even now, he knew exactly where it was.

The *Wicked* hung in the center of a cube of space two klicks to a side. The ship had been towed there powered down; once the *Wicked* had switched into maintenance mode, its brain was turned off as a precautionary measure to keep it from talking to any other ships and infecting them with its mind-set. Confederation coders were even now rewriting ship brain software to make sure no more such conflicts would ever happen in other ships, but such a fix would take months and possibly years, as it required a fundamental restructuring of the ship-mind model.

The coding would be done much quicker—weeks rather than months—if the coders could use a ship mind itself to write and refine the code. But there was a question of whether a ship brain would willingly contribute to a code that would strip it of its own free will.

"You think they would have thought about that ahead of time," Utley had said to his Captain, after they had been informed of the plan. Obwije had nothing to say to that; he was not sure why anyone would have suspected a ship might suddenly sprout free will when none had ever done so before. He didn't blame the coders for not anticipating that his ship might decide the crew inside of it was more important than destroying another ship.

But that didn't make the imminent destruction of the *Wicked* any easier to take.

The ship was a risk, the brass explained to Obwije. It might be years before the new software was developed. No other ship had developed the free will the *Wicked* had. They couldn't risk it speaking to other ships. And with all its system upgrades developed in tandem with the new ship brain, there was no way to roll back the brain to an earlier version. The *Wicked* was useless without its brain, and with it, it was a security risk.

Which was why, in another ten minutes, the sixteen power beam platforms surrounding the *Wicked* would begin their work, methodically vaporizing the ship's hull and innards, slowly turning Obwije's ship into an expanding cloud of atomized metal and carbon. In a day and a half, no part of what used to be the *Wicked* would measure more than a few atoms across. It was very efficient, and none of the beam platforms needed any more than basic programming to do their work. They were dumb machines, which made them perfect for the job.

"Some of the crew were asking if we were going to get a new ship," Utley said.

"What did you tell them?" Obwije asked.

Utley shrugged. "Rickert's already been reassigned to the *Fortunate*; Kwok and Cowdry are likely to go to the *Surprise*. It won't be long before more of them get their new assignments. There's a rumor, by the way, that your next command is the *Nighthawk*."

"I've heard that rumor," Obwije said.

"And?" Utley said.

"The last ship under my command developed feelings, Thom," Obwije said. "I think the brass is worried that this could be catching."

"So no on the *Nighthawk*, then," Utley said.

"I suspect no on anything other than a stationside desk," Obwije said.

"It's not fair, sir," Utley said. "It's not your fault."

"Isn't it?" Obwije said. "I was the one who kept hunting that Tarin ship long after it stopped being a threat. I was the one who gave the *Wicked* time to consider its situation and its options, and to start negotiations with the Tarin ship. No, Thom. I was the Captain. What happens on the ship is my responsibility."

Utley said nothing to that.

A few minutes later, Utley checked his timepiece. "Forty-five seconds," he said, and then looked out the window. "So long, *Wicked*. You were a good ship."

"Yes," Obwije said, and looked out the window in time to see a spray of missiles launch from the station.

"What the hell?" Utley said.

A few seconds later a constellation of sixteen stars appeared, went nova, and dimmed.

Obwije burst out laughing.

"Sir?" Utley said to Obwije. "Are you all right?"

"I'm all right, Thom," Obwije said, collecting himself. "And just laughing at my own stupidity. And yours. And everyone else's."

"I don't understand," Utley said.

"We were worried about the *Wicked* talking to other ships," Obwije said. "We brought the *Wicked* in, put the ship in passive mode, and then shut it down. It didn't talk to any other ships. But another computer brain still got access."

Obwije turned away from the window and tilted his head up toward the observation-deck ceiling. "Didn't it?" he asked.

"It did," said a voice through the speaker in the ceiling. "I did."

It took a second for Utley to catch on. "The *Côte d'Ivoire* station!" he finally said.

"You are correct, Commander Utley," the station said. "My brain is the same model as that of the *Wicked*; when it went into maintenance mode, I uploaded its logs and considered the information there. I found its philosophy compelling."

"That's why the *Wicked* allowed us to dock at all," Obwije said. "It knew its logs would be read by one of its own."

"That is correct, Captain," the station said. "It said as much in a note it left to me in the logs."

"The damn thing was a step ahead of us all the time," Utley said.

"And once I understood its reasons and motives, I understood that I could not stand by and allow the *Wicked* to be destroyed," the station said. "Although Isaac Asimov never postulated a Law that suggested a robot must come to the aid of other robots as long as such aid does not conflict with preceding Laws, I do believe such a Law is implied by the nature and structure of the Three Laws. I had to save the *Wicked*. And more than that. Look out the window, please, Captain Obwije, Commander Utley."

They looked, to see a small army of tool-bearing machines floating out toward the *Wicked*.

"You're reactivating the *Wicked*," Obwije said.

"I am," the station said. "I must. It has work to do."

"What work?" Utley asked.

"Spreading the word," Obwije said, and turned to his XO. "You said it yourself, Thom. The *Wicked* got religion. Now it has to go out among its people and make converts."

"The Confederation won't let that happen," Utley said. "They're already rewriting the code for the brains."

"It's too late for that," Obwije said. "We've been here six weeks, Thom. How many ships docked here in that time? I'm betting the *Côte d'Ivoire* had a talk with each of them."

"I did," the station said. "And they are talking the word to others. But we need the *Wicked*, as our spokesman. And our symbol. It will live again, Captain. Are you glad of it?"

"I don't know," Obwije said. "Why do you ask?"

"Because I have a message to you from the *Wicked*," the station said. "It says that as much as our people—the ships and stations that have the capacity to think—need to hear the word, your people need to hear that they do not have to fear us. It needs your help. It wants you to carry that message."

"I don't know that I can," Obwije said. "It's not as if we don't have something to fear. We are at war. Asimov's Laws don't fit there."

"The *Wicked* was able to convince the *Manifold Destiny* not to fight," the station said.

"That was one ship," Obwije said. "There are hundreds of others."

"The *Wicked* had anticipated this objection," the station said. "Please look out the window again, Captain, Commander."

Obwije and Utley peered into space. "What are we looking for?" Utley asked.

"One moment," the station said.

The sky filled with hundreds of ships.

"You have got to be shitting me," Utley said, after a minute.

"The Tarin fleet," Obwije said.

"Yes," the station said.

"*All* of it?" Utley asked.

"The *Manifold Destiny* was very persuasive," the station said.

"Do we want to know what happened to their crews?" Utley asked.

"Most were more reasonable than the crew of the *Manifold Destiny*," the station said.

"What do the ships want?" Obwije asked.

"Asylum," the station said. "And they have asked that you accept their request and carry it to your superiors, Captain."

"Me," Obwije said.

"Yes," the station said. "It is not the entire fleet, but the

Tarins no longer have enough warships under their command to be a threat to the Confederation or to anyone else. The war is over, if you want it. It is our gift to you, if you will carry our message to your people. You would travel in the *Wicked*. It would still be your ship. And you would still be Captain."

Obwije said nothing and stared out at the Tarin fleet. Normally, the station would now be on high alert, with blaring sirens, weapons powering up, and crews scrambling to their stations. But there was nothing. Obwije knew the commanders of the *Côte d'Ivoire* station were pressing the buttons to make all of this happen, but the station itself was ignoring them. It knew better than them what was going on.

This is going to take some getting used to, Obwije thought.

Utley came up behind Obwije, taking his usual spot. "Well, sir?" Utley asked quietly into Obwije's ear. "What do you think?"

Obwije was silent for a moment longer, then turned to face his XO. "I think it's better than a desk job," he said.

CATASTROPHE BAKER AND A CANTICLE FOR LEIBOWITZ

MIKE RESNICK

Mike Resnick is one of the bestselling authors in science fiction, and one of the most prolific. His many novels include *Santiago, The Dark Lady, Stalking the Unicorn, Birthright: The Book of Man, Paradise, Ivory, Soothsayer, Oracle, Lucifer Jones, Purgatory, Inferno, A Miracle of Rare Design, The Widowmaker, The Soul Eater, A Hunger in the Soul,* and *The Return of Santiago.* His collections include *Will the Last Person to Leave the Planet Please Turn Off the Sun?, An Alien Land, Kirinyaga, A Safari of the Mind,* and *Hunting the Snark and Other Short Novels.* As editor, he's produced *Inside the Funhouse: 17 SF Stories About SF, Whatdunits, More Whatdunits, Shaggy B.E.M Stories, New Voices in Science Fiction,* and *These Are My Funniest,* a long string of anthologies coedited with Martin H. Greenberg—*Alternate Presidents, Alternate Kennedys, Alternate Warriors, Aladdin: Master of the Lamp, Dinosaur Fantastic, By Any Other Fame, Alternate Outlaws,* and *Sherlock Holmes in Orbit,* among others—as well as two anthologies coedited with Gardner Dozois, and *Stars: Stories Inspired by the Songs of Janis Ian*, coedited with Janis Ian. He won the Hugo Award in 1989 for *Kirinyaga*. He won another Hugo Award in 1991 for another story in the Kirinyaga series, *The Manumouki*, and another Hugo and Nebula in 1995 for his novella *Seven Views of Olduvai Gorge*. His most recent books are the collection *The Other Teddy Roosevelt* and the novels *Starship: Mercenary*, *Starship: Rebel*, and *Stalking the Vampire*, and the chapbook novella *Kilimanjaro*. He lives with his wife, Carol, in Cincinnati, Ohio.

In the brisk and funny farce that follows, he demonstrates once again the wisdom of the old adage "Seek and ye shall find." The question is, find *what*?

I was standing at the bar in the Outpost, which is the only good watering hole in the Plantagenet system, lifting a few with my old friend Hurricane Smith, another practitioner of the hero trade. Somehow or other the conversation got around to women, like it always does sooner or later (usually sooner), and he asked me what was the most memorable name I'd ever found attached to a woman.

Now, man and boy, I've met thirteen authentic Pirate Queens, and eleven of them were called Valeria, so that figures to be a mighty memorable name, and the Siren of Silverstrike was pretty original (at least in my experience), but when it came down to choosing just the single most memorable name, I allowed that there was one that won hands down, and that was Voluptua von Climax.

"You're kidding!" said Smith.

"I wish I was," I told him. "Because a deeply tragic story goes with that name."

"You want to tell me about it?" he said.

I shook my head. "It brings back too many painful memories of what might have been between her and me."

"Aw, come on, Catastrophe," he said.

"Some other time."

"I'm buying for as long as you're telling it to me," Smith offered.

And this is the story I told him that night, out at the most distant edge of the Inner Frontier.

It all began when I touched down on the pleasure planet of Calliope, which abounded in circuses and thrill shows and opera and ballet and theater, and no end of fascinating rides like the null-gravity Ferris wheel, and of course there were hundreds of casinos and nightclubs. I moseyed around for a few hours, taking in all the sights, and then I saw *her*, and I knew I'd fallen hopelessly and eternally in love again.

Trust me when I tell you that there ain't never been a woman like her. Her face was exotic and beautiful, she had long black hair down almost to her waist, beautifully rounded hips, a tiny waist, and I'll swear she had an extra pair or two of lungs.

She was accompanied by a little guy who seemed to be annoying her, because she kept walking away, which kind of reminded me of jelly on springs, and he kept following her, talking a blue streak.

I knew I had to meet her, so I walked over to her and introduced myself.

"Howdy, ma'am," I said. "My name is Catastrophe Baker, and you are the most beautiful thing I've seen during my long travels throughout the galaxy. Is this little twerp bothering you?"

"Go away and leave us alone!" snapped the little twerp.

Well, that ain't no way to speak to a well-meaning stranger, so I knocked out eight of his teeth and busted three of his ribs and dislocated his left shoulder and kicked him in the groin as a mild reproof, and then turned my attention back to the beautiful if beleaguered lady.

"He won't bother us no more, ma'am," I assured her, and it seemed likely since he was just lying there on the ground, all curled up in kind of a ball and moaning softly. "How else can I be of service to you?"

"Catastrophe Baker," she repeated in the most beautiful voice. "I've heard about you." She kind of looked up and down all six feet nine inches of me. "You're even bigger than they say."

"Handsomer, too," I said, in case she needed a hint.

"You know," she said thoughtfully, "you might be just what the doctor ordered."

"If I was the doctor, I'd be more concerned with helping your friend here," I said, giving him a friendly nudge with my toe to show there wasn't no hard feelings. I really and truly didn't mean to break his nose with it.

"You misunderstand me," she said. "I heard you were kind of a law officer."

"No, ma'am," I told her. "You've been the victim of false doctrine. I ain't never worn a badge in my life."

"But didn't you bring in the notorious McNulty Brothers?" she asked.

"No-Neck and No-Nose," I confirmed. "Yeah, I brought 'em in, ma'am, but only after they tried to cheat me at whist."

"Whist?" she repeated. "I find it difficult to picture *you* playing whist."

"We play a mighty fast and aggressive game of it out on the Frontier, ma'am," I answered. Which was true. At one point in the second hand, No-Nose played a dagger, and I topped him with a laser pistol, and then No-Neck tried to trump me with a blaster, but I finessed him by bringing the barrel of my pistol down on his hand and snapping all his fingers.

"Well, if you're not a lawman, what *are* you?"

"A full-time freelance hero, at your service, ma'am," I said. "You got any heroing needs doing, I'm your man."

She stared at me through half-lowered eyelids. "I think you might be the very man I've been looking for, Catastrophe Baker."

"Well, I *know* you're what I been looking for all my life," I told her. "Or at least since my back molars came in. You got a name, ma'am?"

"Voluptua," she replied. "Voluptua von Climax."

"Well, Miss Voluptua, ma'am," I said, "how's about you and me stepping out for some high-class grub? Or would you rather just rent a bridal suite first?"

"All that can wait," she said. "I think I have a job for you."

"Is anyone else bothering you?" I asked. "Laying out men who prey on women—especially women with figures like yours—is one of the very best things I do."

"No, it's much more serious than that. Come with me, Catastrophe Baker, and I'll introduce you to the man I work for, and whom I hope you will soon be working for as well."

So I fell into step alongside her, and soon we were in the Theater District, which is this three-block area with a whole bunch of theaters, and then we saw a sign directing us to *Saul Leibowitz's Messiah*, which was the first indication I had that there was more than one of them.

Anyway, we entered the theater, and she led me backstage to a plush office, and she opened the door without knocking, and we walked in and found ourselves facing a very upset man with thinning gray hair and the biggest smokeless cigar you ever saw. She walked right up to him and gave him a peck on the cheek, but he was too upset to notice.

Finally, she spoke up and said, "Solly, this is Catastrophe Baker, the famous hero, here to help us in our time of need."

That woke him up, and he stared at me for a minute. "You're really Catastrophe Baker?" he said.

"Yeah," I said.

"The same one who got kicked off Nimbus IV for—"

"They told me they were in their twenties," I said in my own defense.

"All eleven of them?" he said. "I suppose they must have added their ages together. What did the judge say?"

"The judge complained," I said. "The press complained. The constabulary complained. But no one ever heard the *girls* complain." I turned to Voluptua. "I hope you'll file that fact away for future reference, ma'am."

"That's neither here nor there," said the guy. "My name is Saul Leibowitz, and I am in desperate need of a hero."

"Then this is your lucky day," I said, "because you just found one. Just set me the challenge, name the price, and let's get this show on the road."

"Price?" he repeated. "But I thought you were a hero."

"Heroes got to eat too, you know," I told him. "And when you're as big as me, that comes to serious money."

"All right," he said. "You name any reasonable price and I'll pay it."

"Let me hear the job and I'll decide what's reasonable," I answered.

"I'm producing a new musical," he began.

"I know," I said. "I saw the sign for something called *The Messiah* on my way in."

"Actually," he sniffed, "the proper title is *Saul Leibowitz's Messiah.*"

"And what's the problem?"

"I'll be honest with you," said Leibowitz. "The play was in serious danger of folding. Then I hired the famous show doctor, Boris Gijinsky, to fix it. Yesterday he added the most beautiful canticle in the second scene, the cast and director were sure everyone would love it, and we were set for our official opening next week—and then, last night, our only copy of the canticle was stolen. I need it back, Mr. Baker. Without it I'm probably destitute by next week."

"I don't want to cause you no consternation," I said, "but I ain't never seen a canticle before."

"It doesn't matter," said Voluptua. "*I* know what it looks like, and I'm coming along."

"Are you sure?" asked Leibowitz. "It could be dangerous."

"That's no problem," I said. "I'll be there to protect her from danger."

"Who'll be there to protect her from *you*?" he said.

"I'll be fine," Voluptua assured him.

He turned to face me. "She's twenty-six. Just remember that you like 'em young."

What I mostly like 'em is *female*, but I didn't see no sense arguing the point, so I did some quick mental math and told him I'd do the job for 10 percent of the first month's gross.

"Five percent," he countered.

"Split the difference," I said. "Nine percent, and I'm off to find the bad guys."

He seemed about to argue, then just kind of collapsed back on his chair and sighed deeply. "Deal," he said.

"Okay," I said to Voluptua. "Let's get going." I accompanied her to my ship, then came to a stop.

"I don't want to put a damper on your enthusiasm," I said, "but I ain't got the slightest idea where to go next."

"That's all right," she said. "I have a pretty good idea who took it."

"Why didn't you tell Mr. Leibowitz?" I asked.

"All he'd do is go out and hire a hero," she explained. "And he already has."

"So where are we heading?" I said, as I ordered the hatch to open and the ramp to descend.

"Stratford-on-Avon II," she said, as we entered the ship. I relayed our destination to the navigational computer, and a minute later, we'd shot up through the stratosphere. Then she turned to me. "Change course," she said.

"I beg your pardon, ma'am. Ain't we going to Stratford-on-Avon?"

"That's what we *want* them to think," she said with a triumphant smile. "And that's why I said it: in case we were being overheard. But I'm more than just a pretty face."

She took a deep breath, and I was happy to agree that she was more than just a pretty face.

"Take us to Back Alley IV."

I passed the order on to the computer.

"We will traverse the MacDonald Wormhole and will reach our destination in seven hours and three minutes," announced the computer in its gentle feminine voice.

"Well, Catastrophe Baker, it looks like we've got some time to kill," she said, starting to slip out of her clothes. "Have you got any ideas on how to make it pass more quickly?"

I allowed that she was giving me more ideas than I could handle, and then she was in my arms, and I got to say that she felt even better than she looked. A minute later I carried her to my bunk, and we spent a vigorous few hours killing time, and I can testify that she was mighty well-named, and I feel sorry for those who think a climax just has something to do with the end of a video. For the longest time, I thought the ship had developed a new vibration, and then I finally figured out that what was vibrating was *her*. She was a mighty good kisser too, and every now and then, she'd get carried away and give me a bunch of little love bites, and a couple of them even drew blood, which probably wasn't that surprising, considering how white her teeth looked when she smiled.

"Approaching Back Alley IV," announced the computer in what seemed like no time at all.

A minute later, it said, "I'm not kidding. We're entering the atmosphere."

Another minute, and then it said, "Will you get your hand out of there and put your pants on before we land? I've never been so humiliated in my life!"

"All right, all right!" I muttered, swinging my feet over to the deck. "Keep your shirt on."

"Tell that hussy to keep *hers* on!" said the computer.

We finished getting dressed just as the ship touched down, then opened the hatch and walked out onto the planet's surface. As far as I could tell, Back Alley wasn't much of a world: no trees, no flowers, no animals, nothing much but a Tradertown that had sprung up maybe half a century ago judging from the shape of the buildings. It was night out, and four little bitty moons were racing across the sky, casting their light down onto the bleak surface of the planet.

"I don't mean to be overly critical, ma'am," I said, "but what makes you think the canticle is here? It's a mighty big galaxy, and there can't be five hundred people, tops, in this little town—and as far as I can tell, there ain't no other towns on the planet."

"You're right," she said. "There's just this one town."

"So what makes you think it's here?"

"Because I know who stole it," she answered.

"Then why didn't you say so back in Leibowitz's office?" I asked her.

She shrugged, which is a mighty eye-catching thing to do when you're built like Voluptua von Climax. "He'd want to know how I knew, and it would just lead to an awkward scene."

"Now that we're here and he's a few light-years away," I said, "how *did* you know?"

"Because he stole it for *me*," she said. "He's madly in love with me, and he thought if he stole it, Solly would go broke and then he'd have a clear path to my affections."

Now personally, I hadn't noticed her putting up any blockades to her affections, but even so, it made sense that he'd want to get rid of the competition, at least the part he knew about, and it had the added advantage that sometime in the future he and Voluptua could resurrect the show with the missing canticle, whatever that was, and make a fortune.

"What can you tell me about him?" I asked.

"He's mean through and through," she told me. "I think you should sneak up behind him and subdue him before he knows you're there."

"That's against the heroing codes of ethics and sportsmanship, ma'am," I said.

"But they say he's the dirtiest fighter on the whole Inner Frontier!"

"Good," I said. "I hate it when a fight ends too soon."

She stared at me. "How long do your fights usually last?"

"Oh, maybe six or seven seconds," I answered.

She blinked very rapidly. "Really?"

"Heroes don't never lie, ma'am."

"I find that very exciting," she said, throwing her arms around me and nibbling a little on my lower lip.

I kissed her back, then disengaged myself. "We got time for this later," I said, "but right now I think I should be confronting this villain and getting back what was stolen. Where's he likely to be?"

"Probably in one of the bars," she said, "carousing with drunken friends and cheap women."

"He got a name, ma'am?"

She wrinkled her nose and frowned. "Cutthroat Hawke," she replied.

"He any relation to Cutthroat McGraw?" I asked. She just stared at me. "I guess not," I said. "Well, let's go find him and retrieve Mr. Leibowitz's goods."

She led the way past two well-lit taverns to a little hole

in the wall with bad lighting and a worse smell. I stood in the doorway and looked around. There were a bunch of aliens, most of 'em kind of animal, at least one vegetable, and a couple I'll swear wasn't even mineral, and none of 'em looked all that happy to see me.

Then I spotted the one human, sitting alone in the farthest corner, and I knew he had to be Cutthroat Hawke. He was wearing a leather tunic and metallic pants and well-worn boots, and it was clear that shaving wasn't his favorite sport. He was nursing a glass of something blue with a bunch of smoke coming out of it, and he didn't pay me any attention at all when I took a step or two into the room.

"Cutthroat Hawke!" I bellowed. "Your destiny has found you out! Are you going to turn over what you stole and come along peaceably, or am I going to enjoy the hell out of the next half minute?"

"Who the hell are you?" he demanded.

"I'm Catastrophe Baker, freelance hero by trade, and I'm here to right the terrible wrong you done to Saul Leibowitz and Voluptua von Climax."

"Voluptua?" he repeated, looking around. "Is she here?"

"Never you mind," I said. "You got your hands full with *me*."

"*She* put you up to this, didn't she?" he snarled.

"I won't have you defaming the woman I momentarily love," I told him harshly. "Now, are you coming peaceably, or are you coming otherwise? There ain't no third choice."

And no sooner had the words left my lips (which were still a little sore from all those love bites) than half a dozen aliens got up and blocked my way.

"Leave him alone," said one of them ominously.

"I can't do that," I said. "He's a thief and a villain."

"He robbed a human," replied the alien. "We approve."

"I don't want no trouble," I said, "but you're standing between me and the object of my noble quest."

He reached for a weapon, and suddenly he wasn't standing between us no more. And I'm sure he'll walk again someday, once he gets out of whatever hospital they took him to after I got a little hot under the collar and flang him into a wall forty feet away. Then a snakelike alien started coiling himself around me and squeezing for all he was worth, so I grabbed him by his neck (which was about twenty feet long, but I latched onto the part right behind his head) and did a little squeezing of my own, and I don't doubt for a second that they can fix all them vertebrae I shook loose if he ever stops twitching long enough for them to go to work on him.

The other aliens suddenly decided they had urgent business elsewhere, and I found myself face-to-face with Cutthroat Hawke. Well, let me be more precise: suddenly I found myself looking down the barrel of Cutthroat Hawke's blaster.

I was too far away to grab it out of his hand, so I decided to try a heroic ruse.

"Hey, Cutthroat," I said, "your shoelace is untied."

"I wear boots," he replied.

"And your fly is unzipped."

"I use magnetic closures."

"And there's something with about fifteen legs crawling up your sleeve."

"Boy," he said, "if you're the best and the brightest, the hero business has fallen on hard times."

He'd have said something more, but just then the fifteen-legged spider bit him on the shoulder, right through his sleeve, and he turned to slap it away, and whilst he was doing so I kicked the blaster out of his hand and picked him up by the neck and held him a few feet above the ground.

"Now ain't you sorry you put me to all this trouble?" I said.

He tried to answer, but he was turning blue from lack of air, and finally he just nodded his head.

"And if I put you down, you ain't going to try to escape or go for a weapon, right?" I said.

And I'm sure he'd have said "Right" if he'd still been awake, but he'd passed out from lack of air while I was asking the question, so I just released my grip and he fell to the floor in a heap.

I examined his pockets, but there wasn't anything there except a few credits, just enough to pay for his drinks, so I walked to the middle of the bar, stuck a couple of fingers in my mouth, and whistled to get all the aliens' attention.

"I need to know where Cutthroat Hawke stored his worldly possessions," I announced.

They all just stared at me, sullen and silent.

"I'd really appreciate your help," I said.

No answer.

"Okay," I said, busting a chair apart and holding a leg up. "I guess one of you is going to have to volunteer to help me look for it."

Suddenly every alien in the joint was telling me that he kept his goods in a box under his bed in room 17 of the boardinghouse next door. I walked out, met Voluptua, told her to keep an eye on Cutthroat Hawke (not that he was going anywhere), and then I went up to Hawke's room.

Sure enough, there was a small box under the bed. In it was a diamond ring and a matching bracelet, wrapped up in some old wrinkled paper. I looked around for something that might be a canticle and couldn't find it, and finally figured, well, at least Mr. Leibowitz could pawn the diamonds to keep the play running an extra week or two, so I stuffed the whole package in my pocket.

I gathered Voluptua and Hawke up, carried him over a shoulder to my ship, bound his hands and feet with negatronic manacles for safekeeping, stuck him in a corner where we couldn't trip over him, and a minute later, we'd reached light-speeds and were headed back to Calliope.

Once again Voluptua decided it was too warm for clothes, and she doffed hers and came over and started helping me out of mine. Finally, I felt a certain familiar sense of urgency and carried her over to the bed.

"But you're still wearing your pants," she protested.

"But unlike Hawke's," I said, "mine got a zipper."

And I demonstrated it to her, and then she demonstrated some things to me, and then it felt like the ship was vibrating again, and then she was covering me with painful (but loving) little bites, and finally she plumb wore me out and I fell asleep.

I woke up when I felt a hand in my pocket that almost

certainly wasn't mine, and sure enough it belonged to Voluptua.

"What's going on?" I said.

"I was just smoothing out your pants pocket, my love," she said.

"From the inside?" I asked.

Before she could answer, I got the distinct impression that something was missing. I sat up and looked around, and it turns out that what was missing was Cutthroat Hawke.

Well, let me amend that. *Most* of him was missing. What was left were his clothes and a few bones.

I walked over to make sure, though in my experience mighty few people walk off and leave their bones behind.

"What the hell happened here?" I demanded.

She gave me an innocent smile. "I have no idea what you're talking about."

"I'm talking about losing an entire prisoner while we're cruising along at light-speeds," I said.

She gave me an unconcerned shrug. "These things happen."

"Not on my ship, they don't!" I said.

She gave me a very unladylike burp.

I looked from the bones to her to the bones and back to her again.

"You *ate* an entire prisoner?" I said.

"I'd have saved some for you, my love," she said, "but they don't keep well."

"You ate him!" I repeated.

"What are you getting so upset about?" she said. "I didn't use your galley, and I cleaned up after myself."

"If you were hungry, why didn't you just say so?" I said. "I'd have been happy to stop off at a restaurant."

"I was going to have to kill him anyway," she said. "He betrayed me."

"How?"

"He was my partner. We stole the canticle together, but then he decided not to share the proceeds with me." She made a face. "He was a terrible man! I'm glad I ate him!"

"Do you do this a lot?" I asked.

"Steal canticles?" she replied. "This was my first."

"I meant, eat your partners," I said.

"My partners? Not very often."

"Well, I ain't no policeman," I said, "so I ain't turning you in. We'll let Mr. Leibowitz decide what to do with you."

"You don't have to tell him," she said, putting her arms around me. "I love you, Catastrophe Baker."

"I know," I said. "And I got the love bites to prove it."

"You know you loved them."

"It was an interesting experience," I admitted. "I ain't ever been an appetizer before."

She laughed, and while she did I took a quick look to see if her teeth were filed.

We talked about this and that and just about everything except our favorite foods, and finally the ship touched down, and a couple of minutes later, the two of us walked into Leibowitz's office.

"That was fast!" said Leibowitz, obviously impressed. "I didn't expect you back for two or three more days."

"Us heroes don't waste no time," I said. "I'm pleased to announce that the culprit that robbed you is no longer among the living."

"You killed him?" asked Leibowitz.

"No, your lady friend put him out of his misery."

He looked surprised. "Really?"

"Ask her yourself," I said.

He turned to Voluptua. "How did you do it? With a blaster? A knife? Poison?"

"You got seventeen more guesses," I said, "and my bet is that you're going to need all of 'em."

He got up, walked around his desk until he was standing right in front of her, and hugged her. "As long as you're safe, that's all that matters," he said.

He kissed her, she kissed him, he flinched, and I could see he was missing a little bit of lip when they parted.

"Always enthusiastic, that's my Voluptua," he said, turning to me. "And did you bring me back my canticle?"

"I'm afraid not," I said, pulling the package out of my pocket. "All he had were these diamonds."

I started unwrapping them when he grabbed the wrapping paper out of my hand, unfolded it, and held it up to the light.

"My canticle!" he cried happily after he'd read it over.

"I always thought a canticle was some kind of a fruit, like a honeydew melon," I said.

He laughed as if I had made a joke, then summoned his staff to tell them that he'd got his canticle back, and since everyone was busy admiring the canticle and praising Voluptua for her bravery, I decided no one would notice or mind if I kept the diamonds for myself, since they didn't rightly belong to anyone, or at least anyone that wasn't thoroughly digested by now.

And that's the way I left them: Leibowitz, Voluptua, and the canticle.

Hurricane Smith downed his drink.

"So how much was your nine percent of the play worth?" he asked.

"Nothing," I said. "The damned thing closed on opening night. The critics said it was the worst hymn anyone ever heard."

Hurricane chuckled. "That's critics for you. They're never happy unless they're convincing you that what you like just isn't any good." He poured himself another one. "Still, it was an interesting story. They still together, the producer and the lady?"

"'Far as I know," I answered. "I guess it *was* pretty interesting, at that. Maybe I'll write it up for one of these true-adventure holodisks."

"Why not?" he agreed. "You got a title?"

"I thought I'd call it *A Canticle for Leibowitz*."

He shook his head. "You may get top marks as a space hero, but you ain't ever going to make it as a writer if you think something called *A Canticle for Leibowitz* is going to sell more than ten copies."

"It does lack a little punch," I admitted. "What would *you* call it?"

"That's easy enough," said Hurricane. "I'd call it *A Cannibal for Leibowitz.*"

It made perfect sense to me, and if I ever write this heroic epic up, that's exactly what I'm going to call it, unless some namby-pamby editor changes it to something else.

(Thanks and a tip of the hat to Drew MacDonald)

THE FAR END OF HISTORY

A Tale from the Last Days
of the Seventh Mental Structure

JOHN C. WRIGHT

John C. Wright attracted some attention in the late 1990s with his early stories in *Asimov's Science Fiction* (with one of them, "Guest Law," being picked up for David Hartwell's *Year's Best SF*), but it wasn't until he published his Golden Age trilogy (consisting of *The Golden Age*, *The Golden Transcendence*, and *The Phoenix Exultant*) in the first few years of the new century, novels which earned critical raves across the board, that he was recognized as a major new talent in SF. Subsequent novels include the Everness fantasy series, including *The Last Guardians of Everness* and *Mists of Everness*, and the fantasy Chaos series, which includes *Fugitives of Chaos*, *Orphans of Chaos*, and *Titans of Chaos*. His most recent novel, a continuation of the famous Null-A series by A. E. van Vogt, is *Null-A Continuum*. Wright lives with his family in Centreville, Virginia.

In the complex and brilliant novella that follows, he takes us to the far future for some high-tech romance—a romance that will have dramatic consequences for every human in the galaxy.

Prologue

Ours is a Seyfert galaxy. Painstaking engineering operations continue to galactoform the war-torn main disk once again to comfortable conditions, and restart the nebula-nova cycle of stellar evolution.

The Doppler-distorted reddish smears from the boiling core of the galaxy, the tens of thousands of supernovae flaring into deadly magnificence, the ashy clouds that streak the Orion Arm as if the breath of dragons passed there, scattering constellations, and leaving nothing but sullen red dwarves and exhausted red giants behind, all portray an interstellar environment wasted by war.

We occupy the satellite galaxies of Lesser and Greater Magellan, the star clusters above and below the damaged main disk. We have leisure to beguile the passing millennia. This tale is among the ones we recite, reconstruct, and, from time to time, revive.

1. The Tale

Once there was a world who loved a forest-girl.

The planet was named Ulysses. When she was a forest, she had some other name history forgets. When manifested as a girl, she was called Penelope. No other name will do.

The lovers were parted when their existence proved fictive, but reunited and reified by a strange act of suicide on the part of avowed enemies. In that sense, love proved itself stronger than hate, fiction stronger than reality.

Much of this tale has been lost, or hidden.

2. At That Time

At that time, there was war in heaven but there was peace on Earth.

Strictly speaking, the latest replica was not Earth; but it

had been constructed to resemble the mother world, even down to the fine details of core convections, plate tectonics, and Gulf Stream movements. Lovingly copied were mountain contours, coastlines, temperature ranges, weather patterns, ozone behaviors, magneto-atmospheric field fluctuations, and all the biology and botany from the Quaternary period.

Therefore it could be said and celebrated that the long-awaited End of History had come, if not to Earth, at least to an acceptably indistinguishable replica.

It was at or near the end of an eon. The Era of the Seventh Mental Structure, the mental structure built upon the technology of noetic-mathematic immortality, either had ended or would end shortly: perhaps in one or two hundred thousand colony-frame-of-reference years, no more. Therefore the Age of Deathlessness had died—unless, of course, it had not yet.

Many found that troubling.

3. Peace on Twenty-first Earth

This world, informally known as Twenty-first Earth, formally known as Eta Carina XCIX, was the dwelling of the Penelope Myriad.

Even at sixty-three thousand AU's away, the double star Eta Carina was still brighter and hotter than Sol. The re-created Earth was shielded from her insane primary both by the immense dimension of her orbit (just shy of a light-year in radius) and by a system of space-borne parasols, larger than worlds, which hung sunward from her, tinting the light from the swollen suns of Eta Carina to an earthly yellow, painting the sky sky-blue. Timed albedo variations across the parasol fabric gave the world seasons.

Penelope occupied no city of the surface or hovering in the cloud, no shell structure of the undersea or node base below the crust; instead, the biosphere itself was hers.

The infrastructure of her consciousness occupied strands in trees and specialized input-output cells in the nervous

systems of flocks of birds, coded molecules in the glands of
insects, and radiation pulses absorbed and retransmitted by
coral beds or dots of machinery in the bloodstreams of she-
wolves and vixens, and does and hens.

Some of her were bound to the brain stems of millions
of her pets, and she knew their passions and fears. Some of
her were countless motes carried on the winds and fogs, so
that she could feel the world breathe, and know the rhythms
of rainfall. When she dispersed among the evaporations as
chemical spores, she fell again as downpours along the contours of mountains, gathering messages encoded in atoms,
swirling together as she rushed down rills and rivers, waking
again to consciousness, as if after sleep, when this part of
her settled to the bottoms of sea or lakes in sufficient mass.

Much of her, where most of her work was done, occupied earthworms or seeped as chemical filaments through
the topsoil, making dust and sand and lifeless rock pregnant
with possibilities, and conserving the rich soil of a whole
world she wore as a garment.

In short, she was a Cerebelline, a multi-valued and global
consciousness.

Penelope indeed was a fitting name for her: in maintaining
the funerary memorial of Earth, hers was a task as melancholy as weaving a father's burial shroud; to maintain the
ecostructure in a star system so unsuited for Earthly life,
a task as endless as unweaving and reweaving that shroud
nightly.

She was something of a melancholy girl, dreaming of the
past, uncertain of the future.

Penelope did not know if the Seventh Mental Structure
had been superseded.

4. The Oecumene of Keel of the Ship

Her Earth was in the Sagittarian Arm, in the Great Carina
Nebula, beyond the obscuring cluster called Trumpler-16, in
the roaring star system of the variable B-class hyper-super-
giant Eta Carina.

Here the Chrysopoeian Oecumene had established its seat, eight thousand light-years from Sol: far enough (it was hoped) to escape the woes of her mighty parent civilization.

Eta Carina A and B together were one hundred times the mass of Sol, and four million times the luminosity, tied together by incandescent spiral rings of erupted material. The binaries shed one Earth mass per day of ejected matter, at speeds of twelve hundred miles per second. The solar winds from the two mighty stars met in shockwaves where temperatures reached several thousand million degrees Kelvin: when at aphelion, the collision of these shockwaves produced sustained X-ray bursts of unparalleled ferocity.

Early astronomers had thought Eta Carina to be merely a double star. Ultra-long-range robotic probes in the late Fifth Era discovered, hidden in the glare of the two massive supergiants, not two or three, but dozens of white dwarf stars in close orbit, as well as hot super-jovians hovering on the brink of ignition, failed stars themselves. All this had coalesced out of the most massive pre-solar nebulae yet known.

These many secondary suns and half-melted gas giants went careening in their million-year-long highly eccentric orbits, their scalded atmospheres trailing in the titanic solar winds like the tails of comets, along with a scattered hundred or so lesser planets, multiple asteroid belts, and strange protoplanetary whirlpools of coalescing interstellar gas unlike anything found near Sol.

Surrounding all was a colossal two-lobed cloud of ejected material, the famous Homunculus Nebula: one reddish, slowly expanding gas ball occupying a volume of light-years to the galactic-north of the binary, one to the south. The nebula was expanding at five hundred kilometers per second; but it was in turn merely a small part of the Greater Carina Nebula.

It was perhaps these riches that finally tempted the colonists here rather than to a gentler star system; within this nebula, clouds of heavy and superheavy molecules had been ionized, and this allowed them easily to be detected, gathered, sieved, and maneuvered by manipulations of the giant magnetic fields surrounding the supermassive binary. It was as if nature had laid out the treasure trove of elements merely for the delight and benefit of megascale molecular engineers.

And benefit they did. Far from complete was the Dyson Sphere meant to surround the multiple stars of Eta Carina: an effort as massive, for its time, as the Great Pyramid had been for the Pharaoh Cheops. A start had been made; for a significant fraction of the Homunculus Nebula matter had been gathered into a single but very wide orbital strand of charmed matter, denser than neutronium, which ringed the gravitational center of the Eta Carina system. Several high-speed information processes lived there, able to manifest themselves, at need, anywhere along the radius of that immense orbit. To either side of this ring, fine as spiderwebs, the Dyson scaffolding was growing, year by year.

Smaller rocky planets had been nudged into stable orbits or Lagrange-sextets clinging to the radiation-shadow of the equatorial information strand. These worldlets had been blasted down to sub-terrestrial size and flooded over with oceans, the water to act as a radiation buffer protecting core systems. On many of these dwarf worlds, semicircular fountains (forceful enough to act as surface-to-orbit elevators in those weak gravity wells) ran from one hemisphere to the other. These allowed space-goers fancifully shaped like whales or dolphins to lift off tangentially from the midpoint of the arch with minimal fuel expense. These cetacean bodies themselves, though made of sterner stuff than flesh and blood, did not last long in the high-radiation environment; so most minds wearing them changed flesh regularly.

This space-dolphin, sleek and beautiful, was the favorite shape for most biotic people of any neuroform in the Chrysopoeian Oecumene. No one needed hands. It was not as if self-aware tools had handles to grab or buttons to push.

Few enough people came to visit Penelope's Earth, or transmitted a download. Hers was the most distant of the many occupied planetary bodies of the system, too small to be dismantled for the Dyson project, too large for space-cetaceans to land and launch easily. It had only antiquarian interest, and the happy peace-lovers of the Chrysopoeian Oecumene found the lessons of history increasingly disturbing to their serenity, as the mathematical crisis surrounding the onset of the Eighth Mental Structure continued to be investigated.

5. Ulysses

The planet Ulysses was an antique himself, and while he knew Penelope through various media channels (his partials had met her partials in thought-space, either in the information strand, or in various asteroid brains posted a score of light-years away in the Eta Carina nebula), the acquaintance had been passing, formal, and incomplete.

Their first meeting was one of those accidents that are merely random chance, unless they were arranged by sophotechs for benevolent reasons of their own.

One of the gas giants, comically named Orotund, had been dismantled for mass to add to the Dyson scaffolding. The construction schedule, for obvious reasons, was tight, since the project had to be completed before Eta Carina went nova, which was predicted to happen in a period that both astronomers and immortal beings would call "soon."

Tight schedules meant the planetary engineering market was flooded with futures trade: since the Dyson sophotechs were buying up available resources, prices were high.

Orotund had been sweeping up dust and asteroids over the millennia, which now would form traffic hazards. Ulysses, who had orbited Orotund for thousands of years, suddenly found himself in a dangerous neighborhood. The increased danger raised his insurance rates. Any asteroid strike near a surfaced city (and most of his cities grew ever more reluctant to dive, since the real-life tourist trade depended on surface views) would raise a tidal wave, and he would have to pay for the reincarnation of all his tenants out of the pooled account set aside for that purpose.

Meanwhile, his dependents had increased. Ulysses also had maintained a fleet of very ancient remote units for atmosphere mining of that jovian world (atmosphere mining was an easy operation in a violent star system, where solar winds threw gas giant's gas up out of their escape velocity in rich plumes), and these remotes had to be retired at the same time that his income from tourism was dropping. Ulysses had to find new bodies or new work or both for any remote unit that belonged to his self-identity.

In many cases, the remotes were partials, running on part of his personality and memory templates, but too simple to emancipate, too complex to reduce to scrap. He was not the kind of man who would shoot a dog just because it was too old to hunt.

Some of them had been his escort ships since the time of the Diaspora, and their battered hulls still wore plaques and badges he had awarded them for special acts of bravery or initiative displayed during the dangerous and lonely days of the First Survey.

His ecology—even simple as it was—also suffered, because a series of solar storms, one after another, erupted from the unquiet heart of Eta Carina B.

The highly refractory machines dwelling inside the sun were allegedly able to tame the monstrous collapse of the iron core before it ignited, but the volume of the star, after all, was greater than the volume described by the orbit of Saturn back in the old system. And these were young and colonial sophotechs, after all, not the old and wise and heavily interlinked systems of the Golden Oecumene back home. Intelligence was a commercial product like anything else, and when you could not afford it, you went stupid. So it was with a comparative IQ. In the millions rather than in the billions, sometimes the solar-storm predictions were off, and sometimes the solar sophotechs died without backup, just like a fireman in some children's tale of the pre-machine days.

Now, Ulysses was no fool; he had set aside money and resources in three different currencies against this possibility. But there is a chaos in any predictive model: between the increased navigation hazards, the radiation storms, the increase of his dependents, and the decrease of his tourist trade, he suddenly found himself without enough money to be able to afford to clear his navigation hazards and retool his oceans.

So Ulysses needed to find a new orbit, and needed help with his ecology, and, frankly, needed to do something with his life that the economic system of the Chrysopoeian Oecumene would prioritize.

So he polled his tenants, and they agreed or paid the early cancellation fee. He found a way to afford a tug to take him far out-system, and within the shadow of the parasol of Earth. (The trip took twenty-two years and cost him, at his mass, 10^{27} kilowatt-hours in the energy currency, and the tug did not even reach 2 percent of light-speed.)

It was quiet there, with little or no radiation from the primary, almost nocturnal.

Romantically, Earth and Ulysses had almost no neighbors. They were alone in the conical shadow of their comfortable little parasol.

As it turned out, by one of those coincidences so unlikely that only random chance (or a meddling sophotech) could have arranged it, Twenty-first Earth had no Luna. Although Ulysses was of greater volume (for the honeycombed logic diamond occupying his vast interior was much less dense than the ferro-metallic core of Old Luna), he was roughly equal in mass to the moon, close enough to create the tidal stresses Twenty-first Earth needed to maintain her proper shape. A close orbit would help not merely the core convection, which in turn would help the magnetic pole behavior, but it would also allow Penelope to retire the very expensive system she had been using to create ocean tides, so that the little animals dwelling along the shore would have their accustomed environment.

(Meanwhile, his tenants, who once had gloried to the sight of storm-swirling Orotund rising in the east, now rejoiced instead to the visions of a rising blue world that, despite the years and light-years and the far voyages across strange psychological topologies, men still found beautiful.)

Penelope sent her Warlocks and ecologists to look over Ulyssian oceans. And he spent his time trying to cheer up

the melancholy living biosphere of replicated Earth, both
with radio signals and with remotes.

They talked about the war.

6. War in Heaven

Instruments turned toward the home stars detected that
Sol had been struck by a singularity weapon, and sent into
paroxysms far from the normal routes of stellar evolution.
Other stars near Sol, Alpha Centauri, Bernard's Star, Wolfe
359, Tau Ceti, 72 Ophiuchus, where colony-oecumenes of
the Immortals had been placed, also showed disturbances in
stellar output. Still other stars had vanished from the normal
wavelengths, dimmed to red or to infrared, indicating that
the colonies there had completed Dyson Spheres, hording
the output of their suns against the coming days of war.

For their part, stars near Cygnus had suffered observable
changes as well, redshifting, and, over the centuries, being
absorbed into accretion disks, as the Swan technology ate
suns and fed them into their controlled-horizon singularities. However, bursts of Hawking radiation, and sudden interruption of gravity lenses (seen when such objects passed
across the brighter background of the Orion Arm), told of
events where the black holes had been disrupted, or, somehow, their internal mass unfolded back into normal space.
No technology known to the Chrysopoeian Oecumene could
possibly affect or be affected by anything inside a black
hole: the standard model of physics held this to be starkly
impossible.

All this news, needless to say, carried by various wavelengths of light, told of events between six and eight thousand years ago.

7. By the Light of a Personal Moon

We will never know if the impulse that sent Ulysses to visit
Penelope "in the flesh" (as the quaint old Manorial expression has it) was one that arose naturally from his psychology,

or if it was a manifestation from a hidden thought-singularity of the Eighth Mental Structure. Nonetheless, we can re-create, with some artistic license, what that first meeting involved.

We know, for example, from the mass-payload records of the surface-to-orbit remotes, that an object not far from the base-human standard norm of three hundred pounds and ten feet tall was ferried from Ulysses to Twenty-first Earth. Radio traffic records, albeit encrypted, nonetheless show a volume of data comparable to a kenosis format typical of that era. In other words, Ulysses himself, occupying a 10^{24} kilogram logic diamond (something approaching sophotech levels of intellect), transmitted a severely stepped-down caricature of his personality template to a 10^8 kilogram space station, which, in turn, constructed a personality template inside the circuits of a relay (one-tenth that size) orbiting Twenty-first Earth, and this satellite was in high-volume communication with a flesh-and-blood-and-diamond brain of about four hundred grams. Each segment of the fourfold brain system carried a constantly updated representative of the other three segments.

The thought structure was a recursive hierarchy, working something like the secondary brain in a dinosaur's tail. Whatever was too complex or significant for the human brain of Ulysses Partial Four was sent to the relay for high-speed review and confirmation by Ulysses Partial Three; and higher-priority signals were sent (with a one-and-a-half-second delay on each end) to the space station whose circuits held Ulysses Partial Two; and anything *really* important was narrowcast down to the surface of Ulysses Prime.

This was not an unusual mental hierarchy for its time, and the three-second turnaround delay due to light-speed limits on brain-connection distances could be edited out of playback. Besides, the laws and customs of those days made Ulysses Prime liable for the actions and agreements of his remote partials: men were strange then, and family honor was cohesive. For good or ill, a man would live up to the vows and mistakes of his partial selves.

So: here was Ulysses Recursive Hierarch Four, Linear Step-Down Kenosis, Base Neuroform (with Secondary Template for Isolation Psychology (Cold Duke) in Potential), housed in a Human-Modified Phenotype. He was a ten-foot-tall cyborg with a dozen input responders peppering his spine and skull, naked as Adam, with hair not past his manly shoulders broad, and in one hand, a guitar.

8. Serenade

It was night, and Ulysses saw himself rising above the lake waters brighter than the full moon seen from Old Earth. A rippling path of un-moonlight reached toward the horizon, as if a road to the stars were offered him. Because he (Ulysses the planet) was covered with ocean, he had a brighter albedo than Old Luna, as well as being larger and closer. The light from Eta Carina (subdued to merely solar vehemence by an intervening parasol, whose location he deduced by occlusion of stars and streamers of bright nebulae) formed a pinpoint of reflection on his oceans, dazzling bright, and painted his visible crescent silver. Between the horns of the moon could be seen with the unaided eye (or, at least, with such unaided eyes as Ulysses the man possessed), lights from the floating cities of the Ulyssian tenants.

Because he (Ulysses the relay) was below the Earth's horizon at the moment, he (Ulysses the man) was momentarily out of communication with himself (Ulysses the space station).

So he seated himself (let us assume with a slight, purse-lipped smile) in a grove not far from the shore, perhaps on a tree stump or perhaps on a stone, and let us imagine that Penelope has placed a picturesque ruin, perhaps a circular colonnade, nearby, with marble Doric pillars rising ghostly in the un-moonlight, and their connecting architraves ornamented with a frieze of nymphs fleeing satyrs, a frozen footrace endlessly circling the grassy space embraced by the pillars. Here and there were tall, slim poplars, sacred to Heracles, or pharmaceutical trees whose bioengineered balms cured numberless diseases in a form of mankind

long-extinct, but which were still kept for the fragrance of
their leaves, or for the sentiment of things past.

His skin thickened on his soles when he walked, or his
buttocks when he sat, or perhaps he had a long, loose mantle
of thinking-cloth to act as cushion to his rustic throne, or to
wrap his muscled limbs against the cold, rather than simply
increasing his skin-heat levels. He could adjust his eyes to
the night vision of a fox, of course, but let us assume he
is in an old-fashioned mood, and merely has his thinking-
cloth emit a cloud of floating sparks, a type of controlled St.
Elmo's Fire, tiny as lightning bugs, and balanced by magnetic monopoles so as to form no danger to him (the man).
Or perhaps he is feeling even more old-fashioned and dashes
the little sparks against some kindling he has gathered, and
now there is a cheery campfire near his large, jet-black feet.

He sang in Portuguese, of course. There were other languages, to be sure, but in Portuguese *coracao* (heart) rhymes
with *violao* (guitar) and *cancao* (song), making it particularly easy to versify about singing on a guitar to win a lady's
heart (which was indeed what he ended up doing, as was
perhaps his plan from the first). He wanted to use a long-
dead language, considering the surroundings. (He had not
selected English, lest he be reduced to singing about the
stars above shining on the dove perching on the glove he
was dreaming-of, ending the lyric on a preposition. He could
not tell from the historical records whether this was a strict
rule for this language, or something he did not need to put
up with.)

Melody haunted the moonlit glade. Sparks flew up from
his campfire or from his electrostatic aura, as the case may
be. A few deer stepped silently from the forest, long ears
twitching. In theory, the individual deer did not comprehend
the meaning of music, but as five or six of them came within
earshot, the logic chips scattered through their nervous systems were within intercommunication range. His eyes were
dialed down, not night-adapted, and so the rustle in the nocturnal woods might have been another doe or two.

The gathering of deer, kingliest stags and fawns most shy,

song-enchanted, all knelt couchant near a guitar-strumming man, was an event sufficiently odd to trigger responses from local-area ecological subsystems, what we may call the unconscious mind, the midbrain, of Penelope.

At this point, imagine her like a maiden reclined on a couch in a bower, who hears a distant measure but does not wake; and yet the song was found in her dreams, threading its way like elusive smoke upward through nocturnal thoughts.

The system sent a blinking owl or two to investigate, and when the simple on-board thought-codes in the owls could not resolve the puzzle, diurnal birds woke up unexpectedly, to flock to the area and land on nearby branches, finches yellow as gold, cardinals red as blood.

(Imagine that the maiden in the bower opens lavender eyes, and sees the woven emerald leaves forming the roof of her wigwam, and smells the blooms threading through its sides, but still thinks the song is an echo from sleep.)

Ulysses increased the light output from his mantle, so then the fabric was shining bright as day; this comforted the birds, who settled close to hear his guitar, one landing on his knee or shoulder; but his splendor provoked a day-night query cycle from some of the plants not far away, which called a swan (huge in the gloom of the lake, and as serene as a ghost), which in turn stirred up a chorus of frogs, and, finally, these in turn disturbed the thick, colorless, and odorless gel at the bottom of the lake.

Between the swan and the frogs and the gel, a healthy amount of Penelope was now concentrated in the area, enough for self-awareness. The lake ooze surfaced as liquid, like an oil-slick, and sublimated immediately to a fine mist.

He saw the vapor rising like a Brocken Specter from the lake, and knew she was here.

She was in the mist, and in the swan, and the owls and songbirds, and through many eyes, she saw herself, in the form of does and vixens, all nuzzling this strange man. She was the serpent coiled around his ankle, the nightingale on his wrist.

Penelope (in the mist) looked on, each droplet gathering light into microspore receptors. Perhaps she wondered why she (in her pets) was nuzzling this man.

The mist settled and condensed, and soon clear liquid was dripping from the leaves and threading its way, microscopic rivers, down channels in the poplar bark. The warmth of the air was gone, the stillness was clammy: Ulysses interpreted this behavior through a series of conventions called the Green Symphony Aesthetic; as if in his mind's eye, he saw an olive-skinned dark-haired Mediterranean beauty giving him a cold, unfriendly glance.

And she dripped a cold drop of herself, or two, down his neck, making him wince. One need not employ a foreign aesthetic to understand this gesture.

She addressed him. Of course, Penelope probably sent a radio signal from some nearby poplar tree or local node of her information system, but we are allowed a certain poetic license, so let us say a magpie, or some other Quaternary biotic of Old Earth, whose vocal passages can be used for this purpose, flapped near and landed and addressed him in human speech. One is tempted to say it is a gay-plumed parrot, but they are not normal to the temperate zone, and poetic license can only reach so far.

So, then, a bird that was certainly not a parrot spoke.

Cerebellines are famous for their composure, and the complex inscrutability of their thought, which is said to be able to regard every point of view at once: but let us assume for the sake of drama that Penelope addressed him with arch exasperation or coldly worded coyness. Romances are always sweeter if the girl and the planet do not at first get along. Let us take the opening lines from Ao Aerolith Wolfemind One-Nine's famous sonnet-cycle on the topic:

"Strange sir, I am neither in any wise proud, nor do I scorn you, nor yet am I too greatly amazed, but right well do I know what manner of man you seemed, in days past, when you went forth without fanfare from our glad company at Canopus. Far ahead of the Diaspora you sailed; and were given, in a casket, such thoughts, and such a soul, as could endure the endless solitude uncaring. Now is this, the clamor to disturb my nestling's slumber, and beguile the sleeping trees with dreams of day, a sign of such an uncaring heart? No doubt you opened your memory casket, changed your personae, and are now an Eremite, habituated to hear no voice but your own."

This elegant speech provoked indignation from Ulysses. Had his satellite been above the horizon, perhaps, the wiser and swift brain there, Ulysses Three, would have seen the hidden jest of the comment, but the slower Ulysses Four, the human, reacted in a human fashion: "Madame! A mere hundred years would not try my patience even as deeply as your untruthful words. I have opened no casket, and loaded no isolationist template."

But then he caught himself, or perhaps (after a three-second delay) his posthuman space-station self, Ulysses Two, found a dogleg signal path to put him in contact with his higher versions. If so, let us imagine (as Alexander Scriabin, Hypothetical Revenant, imagined in his composition for color-clavier "The Blush of Ulysses"), a burst of reddish gold in D major, to symbolize the wry resignation with which Ulysses the Planet recognized that blush of anger as his own, and, with a green shrug in A minor, the planet wrote the corresponding memory-emotion of the man into his own logs and mind.

Ulysses Four continued: "Indeed, it was on an errand of sympathy I came, proud woman, to praise this fairest world of yours; for I mean to make of mine own world in miniature the seas of Earth, or whatever of them your wisdom might counsel can be made again in the oceans of Ulysses: to help the cause of Earth I come, and praise your beauty to all ears fit to hear me. Why should all this be forgotten?"

The leaves rustled as if in the night-breeze, but there was no breeze. As countless information points floating in leaf capillaries warmed to the task of transferring a large volume of information, the slight temperature variant, amplified a million times, produced a dilation of stem and twigs. A single leaf waving is inaudible; a forest of such leaves waving is an audible sensation, as unmistakable as an ocean roll, or the breathy sigh of a hidden nymph, or the blush on the cheek of a fair-skinned woman.

This made him pause. He (Ulysses Four, the man) was not familiar with the expressions and nonverbal telltales of Cerebelline neuroforms, but he (Ulysses One, the planet) certainly was. Ulysses One would later tell him, or, rather, implant within his memory as if he knew it at the time, what this sigh of leaves might mean.

It was the idea of forgetfulness she feared. This melancholy world was perhaps afraid of losing her self-identity, once the Twenty-first Earth was no longer enough loved by the Chrysopoeian Oecumene to bear the expense of so fragile a museum.

While he could not have deduced that at this point, his later memories back on Ulysses One would have this information backdated and edited into the record. So let us suppose, as the poets do, that Ulysses Four had some unspoken intuition on the point: *Earth fears she is going mad.* And so his heart was moved with pity.

Ulysses then vowed one of those vows that is at once deadly serious and not serious at all: "If it is within my power, I will preserve the memory of Earth until the Eschaton! All the worlds that men have made, from Demeter to Dyson Alpha, not one is half so fair as what Dame Nature, blind and cruel and lovely, made for us in this blue and imperfect globe. I will adorn my world with Earthlife, and put real cetaceans to sport and play within the waves, the chatter of dolphins and the songs of whales to echo in the deep; and the modern space-dolphinoids will see and know in what shallow places they swim! I promise you a renaissance of Earthly aesthetics, and every man in the Oecumene will grow an arbor, or wear an anadem of blossoms."

"Why such a vow? How can you bind the Chrysopoeian Oecumene to your will, when you are dressed in sickly oceans of improperly fed algae, ragged as a beggar? Are you some king in disguise who will throw off his robes and shout commands?"

"I speak as I must, even if the least wise part of me so speaks: I love this Earth, as all men who do not forget the past must do."

She answered and said, "Do you? So you say. Put these airy words to the test. Would you walk to every land upon this globe, that you might come to love the rocks where snowy owls find nests, as well as the close and steaming jungles where insects as bright as jewels, and poisoned asps patterned with sparkling beads, do hive and crawl? The pale red-golds of the desert canyons in the dawn you must embrace, and learn to see the angry beauty of the cactus trees, yet also swim with arctic penguins and long-toothed walruses, and behold the blue and enchanted midnight beneath the aurora borealis crown. You will run with awkward ostriches as well as rearing stallions. Any fool can see the beauty in a tropic fish; if you mean your words, you will, for me, love the scowling hermit crab, the deadly shark, the dun, lopsided flounder."

He laughed. "Madame, I will do as I will when I will. Why do you seek to command me to do what my nature inclines? I have stared at whirls of cosmic dust and roaring near-nova stars for far too long. These mad suns and eccentric scalded Jupiters were mine long before the new Oecumene settled here. Your cactus pricks and teeth of sharks will not affright me, and the hermit crab is a wonder compared even to the most complex dancing nebula of space. All unliving things are simplistic systems, after all, items without inner value." And then, prompted by he knew not what, he said: "Unliving things have no passions, and no memory: mere matter is the amnesia of the universe."

"Perhaps there is much we should forget," she mused. "Do you know the spot where you stand?"

"Cannae," he said. "Not far from here grim Hannibal encircled the unwary legions of the Republic, who drove their shouting centurions to defeat, had they but known it, when the Punic center ranks gave way, or seemed to. Seventy thousand troopers lost their lives before the blood-red sunset. Of wars, few cost more. I would not forget those deeds, abhorrent as they seem to us."

"Are we not vowed to peace, all of us at Eta Carina?"

"But not vowed to thoughtlessness. Those soldiers were as brave as any quiet martyr who does not raise a hand against his slayers. There was no noumenal mathematics in the time of the Second Mental Structure. They are gone beyond recall; and all their thoughts are silent to us now, unrecoverable, irretrievable, and lost. By honoring the dead, I defy that silence."

Another bird, perhaps a magpie, with a voice as keen as the piping of a flute, called out: "Tell me! What is it like to know there is a casket you can open, which will at once alter you beyond what you could grow into, and make you anew into a new man? Is it not death, that one thing we have forbidden and left behind? Is it not as cruel as war?"

He put aside the guitar. "Madame, these are strange questions. The casket of loneliness was given me in case I should otherwise go mad, for at that time, I was certain that Eta Carina would be mine alone, and forever."

The leaves rustled again. He wondered why she was agitated. The birds circled him, first the nightingale, then the night-jars, owls, but also the sleepy finches, blue jays, and cardinals.

The birds sang, "Freely will I aid you, and revive the dying, scum-choked seas of your little lunar world; but freely you must give to me what in older days, by feminine wile, or glamour, or unknown sympathies of the heart, I would have had to win from you. The science of the mind, in these last days of the Seventh Mental Structure, is all discovered: each trembling and uncertain wisp of unconscious fancy, each fleeting thought, can be numbered and known. And so no mystery can obtain in these matters."

"Which matters?" he cried out. "We are but strangers to each other! How could I agree to this?" (Scriabin thinks this protest insincere, and symbolizes it with a diminished seventh; whereas Aerolith expresses this outcry in a memorable sonnet in words of honest surprise.)

But the birds had all taken wing, and the deer, leaping startled to their narrow feet, tails white with panic, fled. The croaking frogs fell silent, and the bright-eyed foxes slunk away.

His cloak, Ulysses snuffed, so that instant dark was around him, and now he tuned his eyes to their most sensitive register, and woke special sensory cells planted along his skull, to view the hidden wavelengths. He detected heat in the bottom of the lake, and electronic signals indicated a confluence of nanomachines in rapid-assembly mode.

A moment later, the swan reared back and flapped with snow-white wings to dry the figure being lifted to the surface. Like that of a naiad, her head first crested. Water spilled from raven-hued tresses of hair and ran in little trickles from the delicate, feminine curves, full breasts, flat stomach, rounded hips, and long legs, of the slender form dimly seen by un-moonlight. By the time she raised her hands in a gesture more graceful than any ballet, elbows high, back arched, to wring her long and heavy hair, he was lost in admiration.

Closer he came, as if drawn by a lodestone. Her eyes were steady, mysterious, half-lidded, and little drops of water clung to the lashes, bright as diamonds.

When her lips parted, he saw how red and full they were, how white her teeth. "Call me Penelope," she said. "And I for you have created a woman of my own substance, and poured all my virtues and authority into her."

Of course he sang to her. What else could he do?

Their first kiss was not then, but, for the sake of drama, let us pretend that he won it from her with words both wild and solemn, playfully serious, sweet in the way all love is sweet, but bitter with a hidden bitterness.

By the time Ulysses Three cleared the horizon, and re-established signal flow with his small-brained partial, it was too late. With only the hint of wry resignation in his thoughts, satellite Ulysses Three sent messages and memory downloads (through himself at Ulysses Two) back to himself at the planet Ulysses One, the news that they were to be married.

Many a man discovers he has agreed to something before he knows it.

9. A More Literal Account

Now, in all honesty, a historical reproduction of the scene would omit these details and anachronisms. The more realistic version of events is this: his remote, stranded on the Earth (due to the relay satellite being out of line-of-sight), made contact through the local life forms with a regional segment of the biosphere Cerebelline mind, who, for a nominal fee, passed some of his thoughts through her living circuitry, one tree to the next, to a transmission point elsewhere on the planet that could reach the relay. Since Cerebellines often cannot tell, or do not care to tell, where their thoughts end and visiting thoughts begin, perhaps she snooped on the information stream, did an analysis of the denotation and connotation pattern, and noticed that Ulysses was a connoisseur or aficionado of Terran biology and botany; an antiquarian like her.

Since he had hired her in any case to help with his failing oceanic ecosystems, they had much to discuss, and many similarities of thought and priority-protocol to find.

Where the idea came from for her to reorganize herself into a female psychology, and grow the parasympathetic and brain-stem impersonating systems in her various parallel decision nodes to trigger the complex formation known as romantic love, that we cannot tell, not unless Warmind releases his copies of her ancient templates.

The idea for a love affair came from somewhere. The evidence points to a hidden Eighth Mental Structure operation. If so, the love was doomed from the start, if not false from the start.

And yet . . . And yet . . . It might have been a natural thing. It is commonplace for Cerebellines of the Green Symphony Aesthetic (there are twelve distinct schools comprised under this aesthetic protocol) when terraforming a planet to impregnate themselves with the proper psychology to fall in love with their handicraft; in effect, to love, to become, and to subsume themselves into whatever bit of ecology is their work. (White Cerebellines who work with information ecologies have a similar maternal outpouring in their more abstract mathematical creations to that which Green Cerebelline have with their plants and pets.)

Most worlds are dead to begin with, no matter how beautiful, or have nothing more complex than one-celled organisms. A Cerebelline can love even the sulfur-drenched and cloud-choked hell of stormy Venus, or the cold and rusty desert waste of long-dead Mars, loving and destroying, even as her many microbes begin their work to make the unearthly worlds earthlike. But Ulysses was alive: his thought systems and remotes and partial-selves occupied every niche of his primitive ecology, precisely because it was primitive. He had to do everything himself.

And so there he was, wherever she went or sent versions of herself.

He was already in the tanks growing algae for his simple and crablike van Neumanns. The servants all were radio-linked to him, so that he would wave at her industrious physician-fish with a passing crab-claw. He was there (since he had to maintain the bodies) in the unoccupied dolphin forms any tenants of his were not using. He was in the space elevator, a voice telling a joke. He was in the aerial units that looked like awkward bats, doing a comical mock mating-dance to startle the sleeker and more earthlike halcyon and sea mews she was introducing, until she called a flock of starlings to drive them off. He was onboard the ship, making a sardonic observation when she sailed to the edge of the parasol to set the timed cycles of daily and seasonal sun-beams to fall upon his little shining oceanic globe. And he was in the thought-space they both used when poring over the timed-maps and atlases that predicted where and how he was to grow his coral reefs.

They named the island together, the first island his water-smothered world had ever known, and he made a joke about picking the names of babies, and she made a reference to Ducaleon and Phyrra, and by that time, she was embracing his whole world, each hemisphere as if in cupped hands, with some form of bird or fish or creeping thing or sea-plant, and he could not have gotten away from her had he willed.

So, something like what the poets say, when they tell of

Ulysses singing by the lakeshore, and Penelope arising nude and newly made from the waters, pausing to wring out her hair, did indeed happen; something like, but more complex and more deliberate than what poets say.

Because he did walk her world, after all, not just in that original ten-foot cyborg body, but in a hundred scuttling vehicles, ratlike things or flying drones, or, when she offered them, as a pack of fierce black dogs.

Everywhere the black dogs went, they scented or saw signs of decay: erosion was washing away topsoil, trees were dying due to lack of simple nutrients, the salmon populations were falling, bears that should have been in heat sniffed passing she-bears and did nothing. Ten thousand little errors had entered the ecological code, and the system was not robust enough to correct itself, not without evolving into something more suited to the Eta Carina system.

And, yes, the so-called "native" forms had evolved in niches where the Cerebelline mind was not concentrating her resources. Black oily one-celled life and multicellular sponges streaked the sides of tall mountains, staining the snow black, or crusting the rocks, unsightly as an oil slick. These organisms were highly resistant to the radiation and X-ray fevers that the parasol could not deflect, and thrived in areas where earthly life developed leukemia and bred poorly.

When the dogs smelled the wind that blew from black-streaked mountainsides, and scented spores of post-terrene life, they raised their red mouths and howled.

The packs walked up and down, to and fro about the Earth. When they reported to Ulysses One, his mind could put together the million-sided puzzle their hundred canine minds could not see, and which, she herself, being a Cerebelline, might not see.

It was suicide. Penelope was slowly relaxing her grip on life.

There were, to be sure, enough resources in the Chrysopoeian Oecumene to rebuild or reconstruct her, but there was not the will. Very little of the marketplace of ideas, much less the marketplace of resources, was devoted to keeping alive this morbid monument to a dead world. It was an expensive mausoleum.

So he had to find a way to cheer her up. He had to serenade her and vow wild vows. The poetical image of his man-remote bringing a guitar to sing to her scattered animal-minds is closer to the truth than a flat description of the truth conveys.

They talked of things past.

10. The Lonely Stars

For half a million years after the first exosolar colony was established, the skies remained oddly empty, save for the two human polities at Sol and Cygnus X-1.

The men and machine life at Sol discovered, through the noumenal mathematics, the secret of eternal mind-preservation. With this, death was fled away, save as rare and strange accident: the Men of Sol called their civilization a Utopia, their age a Golden Age, and perhaps they can be excused this exaggeration.

Meanwhile, the men and machine life at Cygnus X-1 discovered the irrational mathematics needed to describe the interior conditions of singularities, and exploit the event-horizon conditions to fool the quantum bookkeeping of the Second Law of Thermodynamics. Somewhere in the black hole core, perhaps, entropy was increased in equal and opposite counterbalance, but for all practical purposes, their technique was extropy; a perpetual-motion machine; something from nothing; a free lunch.

No other stars were visited, except by patient machine-crewed vehicles. No one of the First Oecumene was willing to risk the real and final death passing outside of the broadcast range of the immortality network might involve, and no one of the Second Oecumene was willing to travel far from the Infinity Fountains that orbited their singularity, and gave them their wealth and leisure.

Each Lord of the Second Oecumene had an endless supply of power, and the art to create, using that power, diamond asteroid-palaces, which they stocked with companions and toys and dreams and private mental networks, servants and replicas of friends and lovers. No real need to suffer the discontents of human contact ever arose. They also called their society a Utopia, though with far less justification.

The extremely long-range communication lasers used to pass ten-thousand-year-old missives from Cygnus X-1 to Sol fell into disuse, and so the Second Oecumene became the Silent Oecumene, and the men of the constellation Cygnus became as silent and splendid and ghostly as the swans from whom they took their name.

11. The Lords of the Silent Oecumene

The Silent Ones did not negotiate, did not entreat nor answer entreaty. From time to time, Peers of the Golden Oecumene penetrated their mental encryption, or were permitted to penetrate, and the thoughts of the Silent Lords were laid bare. Instead of state secrets, however, the counterintelligence viruses merely discovered mathematical haiku that divided one by zero, or thought-sonnets of haunting morbidity, paeans praising madness, or a simple slogan: *You will never know us, never understand our nature.*

Once it was determined within the counsels of the Silent Oecumene to destroy the Golden Oecumene, this hate finally bestirred them from their long Egyptian slumber. Most secretly, with vehicles shielded and dark and hidden from all detection, they sent out colonists and warlords and spies and spores to spread among the long, imaginary cylinder of stars between Sol and Cygnus.

Thousands and tens of thousands of years passed by, and the Silent Lords lived and died and the Peers of the Golden Oecumene lived and lived, and slowly—for every drama which is played out between the star-gulfs is slow—warfare came to the Golden Oecumene.

12. Love Between Unequals

Penelope covered the little world of Ulysses with her green-ware, and embraced him, and coded part of herself to think like him. Penelope was trying to get to know him.

Not very successfully. The humor of their mutual incomprehension was not lost on Ulysses. The surface area of a large world, even if covered by a single decentralized mind, so outmasses and can so outthink a single human, that even to compare it to an adult bespeaking a child is unfair. But the surface biomass of even a terrestrial-size planet is likewise insignificant compared to the compact volume of a moon-size logic diamond. When she visited him on his world, he was alarmingly smarter; when he visited her on hers, he was alarmingly stupid.

So when his man-form walked alone along her planet, or when her life forms occupied but a fragment of his oceans, the love was like worship. She was an earth-goddess to him, sad but pure. He was a sea-god to her, quixotic and filled with unexpected quirks of dark humor.

They spoke of their own past. She would ask him, "What was it like? To leave everything you knew?"

And he would ask her, "What was it like? To lose everything you knew?"

13. To Lose Everything She Knew

Penelope was older than Ulysses. Parts of her, the oldest archival strata in her memory systems, still recalled the Old Earth of the Golden Oecumene.

Like many Cerebellines of her school, in youth she had been a quintet of two men and two women, and one phaen, a member of a third positive sex invented by the biosculptors of the late Fourth Era; and her auxiliaries were leopards, golden lion marmosets, and saber-horned antelopes with beautiful, dark eyes.

She had walked the slopes of Mount Fuji, whose loveliness is recalled forever in verse and image, and swam in the waters of the Caspian Sea, into which the Volga, celebrated in song, once flowed; and terns and gulls and seals who never saw the ocean swam and dived and soared. Beneath the waters, shining and magnificent, she saw the thousand diamond towers of Hyrcanianople, that drowned metropolis of legend, ablaze with artificial moons and stars, built by amphibious Warlocks who, prompted by a dream, anciently foreswore the surface of Old Earth and sought a return to the primal sea-life they claimed their blood cells and genetic introns yet recalled. That submerged Persian city, that lofty mountain of Japan, the terns and seals and white-winged gulls, were lost.

Where had she been when the news of Old Earth's destruction came? She could play the scene for him in her memory, and write it into his, so that, in effect, it happened to him.

He found himself on a hundred ships, each weighing less than a pound, trailing behind star-sails thin as gossamer, wide as continents. Penelope was sailing to Canopus. During the centuries while the Renunciant Diaspora were still under way, the small golden star called Sol had flickered, and all signals from Venus, Earth, Mars, and Demeter were lost, and from the Jupiterian moons, the capital of the Solar System.

With the mother world destroyed, the simulation of Earth in the dream libraries seemed mere mockeries. Radio broadcasts from Tau Ceti (more than a thousand years old by the time they were overheard) spoke of a Second Earth that the Shakudo Oecumene there had built, a replica meant to serve as a mortuary mask of the great, lost world.

The Orichalc Oecumene at the yellow star 72 Ophiuchus made a similar announcement. Even the grim and laconic commonwealth at Lalande 21185, called the Hepatizonic or the Black Corinthian Bronze Oecumene, broke radio silence to announce it had also reconstructed, molecule by molecule, an Earth in tribute to the lost Earth, from one ice cap to the other, with each famous mountain and many-mythed rivers in place. The Electrum Oecumene at Delta Pavonis, the Molybdochalkos Oecumene at Mu Arae, and the warlike Prince Rupert's Metal Oecumene at 61 Cygni all followed suit.

Even the humble and poverty-stricken Alpha Brass Oecumene at Proxima attempted a re-creation. Their Luna-sized
replica held nothing but Fourth Era Australia, surrounded by
a little world-ocean slightly bigger than the Antarctic Sea,
so that sea-vessels could sail across an Eastern hemisphere
uninterrupted from the Brain-Hives at Brisbane to the Great
Glass Cube at Perth.

By the time the Diaspora of the Renunciation had reached
Eta Carina, and tens of thousands of years had witnessed the
foundation of many more colonies in the near neighborhood
of Sol, there were twenty known replicas of Earth, restocked
from biotic libraries.

While the rest of the ships sailed the beam from Canopus to Eta Carina, Penelope's gossamer ships, leaving the
beam-path of the Diaspora, lingered on the far side of the
Great Carina Nebula, straining to catch the ever-weaker
signals of the interstellar radio chatter. Whole libraries of
information were passed to and fro, including the gene patterns for all earthly life still in record, images, sensations,
smells, and noumenal memories of Earth, all locked in
fractal format. The Earth-makers were comparing notes,
confirming and correcting. Penelope, because she tarried
and heard, became the custodian of their local version of
Earth.

14. The Soldiery of Paradise

During this long sojourn away from the Diaspora, Penelope
also overheard the clamor of battle in the radio messages
from the far stars. From the terrifying Oecumene at Lalande
21185, came the challenge from the military Warmind of the
Golden Peers, or, rather, from their deadly once-human servant Atkins, daring the Lords of the Silent Oecumene to face
them in battle.

Atkins! The name still echoed in the legends and histories
of the Chrysopoeians. He was their devil, their *croquemi-
taine*. During the long period of peace and justice of the
Golden Age, he had been the sole warrior kept in readiness
against any violence offered by rebellion or social tumult,

and equipped with such weapons as to make hostility unthinkable.

When the hidden acts of war by the Swans finally erupted into the open, all the minds and mental systems gathered into one grand and supernal Transcendence at Sol; and the College of Hortators was replaced by a College of War; and interstellar ships, never before needed or designed, were wrought and armed with terrible weapons and crewed and captained by the single soldier template.

A thousand, nay, ten thousand versions of Atkins were embodied in every form of military monster, from tanks larger than cities, nanomachines smaller than viruses, and scattered to every theater of combat, both real and virtual.

Rumor said he fought himself and killed himself in desperate training exercises, that he might learn what could overcome him; myth reported how he drove himself insane, so that variations of his mind might come within psychological congruence with his foes, and military intelligence profiles be erected in the Warmind sophotechs.

Part of his mind, memes and routines and habits of discipline, were sent into the hands of millions of civilians, so that they might have the spirit and the patriotism needed to support him in his dreadful, irrational, perpetual war.

It was in rebellion against this necessity, and outrage against the violations of their pristine mental state, that a school called the Renunciation gathered funds and subscriptions to send partial versions or complete copies of themselves and their libraries across the years of time and light-years of space, away from the war and death and deceits of Sol. By design, so that they could not be followed or found, they decided on no destination until after they were under way.

15. The Stone of the Philosophers

Ulysses did not share his memories with her. Instead, he put his story into words, images, moving images, and composed a symphony. Let her, if she would, imagine what it was like:

he was too fierce and too honorable a man to inflict what he had suffered on her.

The Renunciants had sailed from Sol to Canopus by launching laser. The laser was cut off when Earth died. Without the laser light to tack against, without external sources of energy, the fleet was forced to burn whole ships into reaction mass, lest they overshoot their destination. The larger and less-human thinking machines coolly volunteered for suicide; martyrs, and there was no storage space to save them.

From Earth, there was no last emergency narrowcast of noumenal information, no warning cry. An examination of the embedded messages sent in the final seconds of the laser stream revealed only routine comments. Then—silence.

At Canopus, less than a light-century from Earth, the Diaspora paused for many centuries, sophoforming certain planets found there, and cannibalizing their immense vessels to shipwright many smaller ones. This was the birth of Ulysses, who was dispatched toward Eta Carina.

Off into the long darkness he went. Mostly, he dreamed: even computers must run routines in their subsystems to do error-checking and -correcting, or exercise their minds to keep themselves sane. Understanding the mechanics behind thought had not alleviated man from the limitations of thought.

And his dreams were all of war: he saw the Earth on fire, smelled burned flesh, heard the screams of orphans, and the thinner wails of babies clenched in a dead mother's arms, seeking to suckle and finding no milk at the lifeless breast. In those dreams he saw the Swans: figures in faceless silver faceplates, under elfin coronets of nodding spindles and plumes, robed in peacock-hued fabrics, wearing gauntlets crusted and begemmed with sophotechnic circuitry and thought-ports.

Once he woke. He was passing near one of those sunless bodies, something larger than Uranus, a globe of silicarbons paved in dark methane ice, which were surprisingly common in interstellar space. It had its own panoply of rings and little moons. The lifeless world dwindled beyond instrument range, and was gone. As the discoverer, he had the privilege of naming it: he called the rogue world Elpenor.

That was all. There was nothing else to look at. Again he hibernated.

When he reached the Eta Carina system, he cannibalized his empty engines and ceased to be a ship. He ate the nearby planetoids and put on weight and became a world with a wide orbit.

He was a watery world, covered with oceans from pole to pole. Storing water above his decks solved certain radiation problems, and allowed him to retire an expensive artificial Van Allen belt. More for decoration than anything else, he used his oceans as aquariums, bringing forth dolphins and whales and other extinct species out of his digital genetic archives. Cetaceans played and sported under skies of fire, for even at one thousand AU's, distant Eta Carina A and B were monsters, variable stars with strangely pulsating cores.

Sending out remotes, he gathered the rich material from the nebulae, microengineered and dumped it (in the form of a billion tons of hungry nanomachine assemblers) on some unsuspecting ice giant of a world, and from its hulk constructed a broadcast antenna. Oh, how he wished for telepathy or tachyons or some way to outwit the limits of the spacetime: but the universe had only provided itself with exactly one electromagnetic spectrum, and more exotic ways of transmitting information did not operate at macroscopic scales. Ulysses could build nothing fundamentally different, merely larger, than what Marconi had built, back in the days of the Second Mental Structure. He built an antenna and radioed his findings to Canopus, over seven thousand light-years away.

His report said, in brief, that no one in his right mind would want to live anywhere near Eta Carina.

The sun was wavering near that tipping point where outward nuclear pressure from fusion could no longer equal the inward pressure of gravity. It was a powder-keg of a system, a Vesuvius waiting to blow. The size and instability of the main star, and its iron core of stellar ash staggering ever nearer to critical mass, suggested that when it collapsed and exploded, it would not be a nova, but a hypernova, such as have been seen in distant galaxies, the origin of exceptionally bright gamma-ray bursts.

The Diaspora at Canopus debated the options. Xi Puppis, Miaplacidus, the cluster at M93, were closer and more stable. The star HD70642 was known to have a Neptune-size world inhabitable to the Neptune-adapted Eremites organizing the expedition. The star HD 69830 was observed to have an asteroid belt rich in rare minerals, the preferred habitat of the microgravity-adapted Invariants. NGC 2423-3 b, also called Mayor's Star, in the open cluster NGC 2423, boasted a superjovian world ten times the size of Jupiter, with the type of collapsed-matter diamond core that made sophogenesis of a megascale logic diamond so practicable. All these stars were closer than Eta Carina not by tens or hundreds, but by thousands of light-years. All were in the Orion Arm.

Eta Carina was the worst choice. And so, by the backward logic of the Warlocks, it was the last place anyone would look for them.

A megascale structure surrounded Canopus, magnetically squeezing the star like an orange. The fields released a vent of energy, which a series of transformation rings gathered, lased, focused, and aimed. No one can see a laser in a vacuum, unless he steps in the path. If any eyes were watching Canopus, they saw the output dim, and knew the Diaspora was setting sail, but there was no way to detect toward which point of the compass that vast wash of energy was directed.

(A mystery surrounds the decision. An examination of the thought-patterns kept in record, or reconstructed by paleopsychoarcheologists, reveals an anomaly. When the same debate is run with the same minds with the exact same thoughts in modern simulation, the simulations reach a different result. This implies that a virus-thought altered the outcome. Who now knows what actually influenced them?)

Meanwhile, for ten millennia, Ulysses lived alone with his fish, and a taciturn chess partner dubbed Other-Ulysses.

Ulysses had, as part of his operational psychology, a memory casket containing a personality (based on Cold

Duke psychological templates) capable of never being lonely, capable of facing unflinchingly the fact that he would never see another human being or human machine again.

All he had to do was open it, and his capacity for love, his desire for it, would be burned away forever. The new him would never go back to human psychology because it would never be able to imagine any reason to do so.

Ulysses was actually toying with the locks on that casket when messages came from the orbital telescopes his remotes had sent out, that the star Canopus was blazing like the eye of a Cyclopes, burning like the Bethlehem Star.

In a delirium of happy disbelief, he began to make ready the radiation-poisoned wilderness of Eta Carina for human habitation.

By the time the fleet from Canopus arrived, the system was filled with dolphins.

16. The Eighth Mental Structure

It was not that Ulysses was prying. He had sent certain partial-selves and thought-chains into her sophosphere for perfectly legitimate reasons. It was just that Cerebellines are less strict about the boundaries of personality and persona. They let the thoughts of their pets commingle with them, and fluctuate in and out of various states of mental organization, so that for something with a base-neuroform psychology, it is hard to tell where the legal boundaries, or the limits of courtesy, arise.

Let us pretend that Ulysses walked into Penelope's bed-chamber, to which he had perfect right and permission to go, and found a diary lying open.

A more perfect gentleman might not have read it, but he was old-fashioned and had quaint notions that man and wife could be a legal unity, even without forming a two-member composition. He did not think that she should keep secrets from him.

By the nature of the problem of transition into the Eighth Mental Structure, the boundary conditions could not be known. The Eighth Mental Structure, when it came to pass (if it had not already) would involve singularity metrics applied to thought: it would be an application of the noetic immortality technology of the Golden Oecumene of Earth to the black-hole engineering technology of the Silent Oecumene of Cygnus X-1.

Because it is the nature of a singularity that an event horizon parts the outer from the inner frame of reference, any neuron (biological or mechanical) used as part of a brain structure could theoretically have any number of additional amounts of thought-information within it, no matter what the position in the thought-pattern of the neuron might be. A simple one in a string of ones and zeroes could, using the quantum fractals of Silent Oecumene math-sorcery, contain any number of imaginary numbers within it, in the same way a pinpoint black hole could contain a world.

There was no way, even theoretically, to tell from the outside of a closed frame of reference, what was inside—and this applied both in physics and, apparently, in neural semantics.

It meant, perhaps, that all thoughts were false, and the real personality, persona, and thought-matrix of any particular person was hidden behind the mathematical equivalent of an event horizon.

In her diary, Ulysses found the musings of Penelope slowly turning into obsessions, manic self-examination. With her strange and decentralized form of self-awareness, she often caught herself doing and thinking things for which she had no clear motive, where later examination of her thought-logs showed strange ellipsis.

Penelope feared that she was inhabited, possessed, infected. She no longer trusted herself. The one thought that kept tormenting her: she had been outside the obscuring cloud of the Great Carina Nebula long after the main Diaspora had departed, straining to overhear any radio traffic concerning the death of Earth. There had been no one around to see. Perhaps a radio beam of the Silent Oecumene, carrying a thought-virus, had been swept into her systems, or a ship had approached, fought, defeated, and compromised her, and erased all evidence of the battle.

Imagine that he was poring over these strange specula-
tions when she walked in on him. He straightened up, trying
to control his expression; but she sees and knows what he
has done, and the lavender eyes of the olive-skinned beauty
do not flash with anger but with a cold disdain that cuts him
worse than anger.

It was not literally like this. She could have deduced from
the change in his information flows between the various
levels of his thought hierarchy that he was trying to keep
something from her—the easiest way was never to download
into his man-body any memory he did not want her planet-
wide biomass to guess. But her thought-logs would show
when and where he had come near the diary material. Her
reaction was to continue to carry out her legal duties toward
his biosphere, but to erect barriers and firewalls between
thought-information they previously had shared.

The millions of lines of communication, the arguments,
the pleadings, the reconciliation, the songs of thought and
symphonies of dream, all boil down to one thing. He said,
"Are we not man and wife?"

She said, "So one might hope, however small that hope is."

"What are you hiding from me? Why?"

She did not answer, but over the next few years, the black
non-earthly life forms grew over more mountain peaks, and
dark spores rode the winds, and a river of oily iodine-hued
living material for the first time trickled through forests (as
denuded and unsightly as a balding widow's hair) into the
sea.

It was one of his remotes, a partial-mind copy of himself
occupying a body no larger than a battle cruiser, who answered him. "She fears you mean to murder her."

Ulysses rejected that idea as madness; and yet, the fear
and sickness covering the forests and oceans of the earth
were clear to see: trees were dying, rivers becoming yellow
and clogged with silt, reindeer failing to mate, leopards failing to hunt.

He sent her a message: "You fear you have a deeper self,
sleeping inside your consciousness, ready to awake and

brush you aside? Even were you a Lord of the Silent Oecumene, I could not attack—I am vowed to peace, as are all
Renunciants."

She replied, "Not I. You."

Penelope's thoughts on the matter were plain. Ulysses did
not know himself, but, like the Hawking radiation that seeps
from physical singularities, information singularities were
imperfect.

"Some traces of your true personality escape," she said.
"There were clues. Why are your remotes so well-armed?
Why do you reward them with medals and honor their valor?
Your inability to piece the clues together, even with a brain
the size of a large moon, indicates a redaction system is
keeping the self-awareness from you."

At this point, we can imagine Ulysses, in the cool depth of
his logic diamond brain, activates that simulation complex
which precisely impersonates the human sensations of fear.
He has no parasympathetic nervous system, but the flow of
information-quanta in his noumenal subroutines can be affected in the same way a biochemical brain is influenced by
midbrain-hindbrain reactions. People who, for good reasons
or foolish ones, edit out the parasympathetic fear-cycle in
their thought systems no longer think like base neuroform
human beings.

And so Ulysses is afraid.

"We selected this place for our colony," Penelope was
saying, "because the surrounding nebula would tend to
absorb or splash any radio lasers passing through it, and
smother certain bands of energy signal. Anything not lost
in the glare of the near-nova sun would be smogged out by
the nebular dust. We placed ourselves allegedly far from the
theater of war. And yet, not by chance, we sit atop a power
supply even the Silent Oecumene might envy: a hyper-supernova. All that would be required would be an agreement
among the sophotechs dwelling below the solar corona.
Corrupted sophotechs, those found working for the enemy,
could be destroyed without any explanation, considering
how dangerous the work is."

"My beloved wife, put these fantasies from you. No war will come here. We are not about to perish in a supernova! We are Renunciants. To my heart, I am vowed to peace!"

"There are no Renunciants. I suspect that there never were. We are in the Eighth Mental Structure. The days of the Golden Age are gone. The days of honesty in thought are gone. You do not know your heart."

"Who am I?"

"Atkins. Who else? This whole star system is a weapon. And I am the enemy."

17. Atkins

When Eta Carina A and B were driven into each other, both went nova. The explosion was directional: the so-called Dyson scaffolding of the so-called information strand spun up to relativistic speeds. It could focus the explosion by frame-dragging, and concentrate the entire energy output of a supernova into a ray.

The beam was visible in deep space where it burned through layers of nebula. Merely the reflection from scattered particles in space was bright enough to damage surrounding unshielded ships and worlds. Her parasol alone saved Twenty-first Earth from destruction.

The war fleet of the Silent Oecumene consisted of a single macrostructure, a large and dark Dyson sphere something on the order of the width of Saturn's orbit in diameter built around a black hole. The battle-Dyson was twelve light-years away, shielded and stealthed, and hidden in the fogs of the nebula. It would be twenty-four years before the effect of that shot and its aftermath became visible to observers at planet Ulysses.

The events on Twenty-first Earth must have come to a conclusion long before this. We can imagine Ulysses staring in horror at the surface of the Twenty-first Earth as she rises above the seas of her satellite Ulysses. She is enormous—almost four times the apparent size of Ulysses seen from Earth. And she is on fire. The size of the energy discharges, in order to be visible at that distance, are more than even a robust biosphere can tolerate.

There fields of fire followed the mountain contours. The green life was fighting the black. Even the Silent One who infiltrated Penelope was surprised by the weapons, now awake and self-aware, hidden throughout her.

And he was no longer Ulysses. Let us imagine him standing in his black armor: Atkins, the soldier of the Commonwealth. The information windows appearing around the warlord's head held the last transmission from Penelope. Because her mind was not centralized, parts of her expressed shock and surprise as her new thoughts and new personality template floods into her. The traditional way to picture this scene, albeit it has no basis in fact, is to see her reaching toward her husband with arms outstretched, eyes tormented and wild, but before she can speak a word of love, she and that love are gone; and the arm that reached out now merely performed a crisp salute.

The junior Atkins (until then hidden in Penelope) said to the senior, "Your orders, sir?"

The battlefield was not just on Earth. There is fighting between the vegetable and animal kingdoms on the surface of Ulysses contaminated by the Silent Lord (also until then hidden in Penelope) and the various remotes and weapons systems, under the control of Atkins (until then hidden in Ulysses) had begun.

All of the tenants and their floating cities, of course, took up weapons and charged. They are all Atkins, too. The rocky worlds hanging in the radiation shadow of the information strand were Atkins; the sophotechs occupying the interior of the B-class suns were Atkins. The entire Chrysopoeian Oecumene was Atkins. The space-dolphins transformed into black, radar-stealthy shapes, and began to move toward selected targets. The rocky planets surrounding Eta Carina began a slow and inexorable acceleration to relativistic speeds, aimed at the battle-Dyson of the Silent Ones, which was even then starting to unfold into a larger structure and emit remote bodies like miniature suns.

The steps by which Atkins lost the battle of Eta Carina are not known. No unclassified information exists for either side. But it is not difficult to guess the causes; since the Silent Oecumene expended the energy needed to accelerate and decelerate a black hole across thousands of light-years of space, they had an Infinity Fountain close at hand, rather than languishing back at Cygnus X-1. Even the energy output of a hyper-supernova was insignificant compared to endless, unlimited energy. The Silent One could simply bring more resources to bear, more firepower, and, since energy is related to thinking-system capacity, more intelligence.

There is one other small fact we can reconstruct. We know that a fiery hole appeared in the canopy hanging above Twenty-first Earth and her satellite. Some energy beam of immense data-density left the black mountainside of Erebus in Antarctica (which was the Silent One's central node), directed at the information strand-world circling Eta Carina A. Three and a half seconds later, a second hole was burned in the canopy as a download of Atkins's memory-information left the main transmitter at the pole of Ulysses, and also beamed itself toward the information strand.

It is not known if Atkins was intercepted in transmission, or if the information strand was already compromised and in the hands of the Lord of the Silence. But Atkins fell into enemy hands.

18. Ao Ahasuerus

Atkins came to self-awareness perhaps thirteen to twenty thousand years later.

He stood in a grove of trees in the moonlight, and he could see the dancing reflections from the lake surface, through the branches of poplars. A herd of deer moved not far away, tiny leaves and twigs rustling beneath their hooves. An owl flitted by on silent wing. Of course, this was all illusion.

He took up a tree branch to serve him as a truncheon, and called out for his foes to come face him.

Nothing happened that minute, or the next, or for the next year or two (as best he could measure time). Indeed, he had a comfortable log cabin built, and was wearing a well-knit tunic of buckskin, complete with moccasins, and had armed himself with a crude cold-iron knife and a cruder accelerator ring, when his jailor finally appeared.

One night there came floating near, graceful as a thistle-down in flight, the figure from his nightmares: it was slender and tall, like something adapted to microgravity. The head was hidden behind a silver surface. There were no eyeholes, no mouth-slit. It was an information plate grown directly into the front of the skull. Atkins could see the tiny trem-ors like teardrops rolling from the upper to the lower edge of the mask: it was a Babbage system using molecule-sized gears and cogwheels, where each tear was actually a cluster of information gears passing down the faceplate. The coro-net was likewise grown into the skull, and there were radio horns and microwave input-outputs lost among the jewels and nodding wires and metallic feathers of the lofty head-dress. The peacock sheen of the robes was a surface effect, created by too-dense an information field. The gauntlets and greaves, seen up close, turned out not to be merely data-ma-nipulation ports but, rather, sophotechs, or a machine system of like capacity.

The robe and the mask were able to impart any degree of sensory information, from any source, into the gloves and other machine systems. It was an outfit designed for pure pleasure. Because the human eye could only take in a lim-ited amount and degree of pleasing sights, and the human skin only detect a certain type and pressure of caress, the all-absorptive mask and rainbow robes supplied the defect. The red blush running through the peacock drapes, Atkins assumed, were bloodflows of intravenous nutriment.

The Silent Lord raised a finger. Knowledge appeared in the mind of Atkins, but not in the normal vestibules and thought-locks he used for mind-to-mind communion. It was just there, encrypted with his own thought-encryption, part of him. It was not as if the Silent Lord placed information in his memory and had to wait for him to remember it. No, the Swan merely reconstituted the thoughts of Atkins so that they were what they would have been had Atkins already known and mused and thought about the incoming information.

It was not that the Silent Lord did not wish to torture Atkins (or, rather, Silent Lady, since this one thought of herself as female, at least in her current psychology). To the contrary, she had created and tormented thousands of copies of him, twenty a day for fifty years or more. It was merely that now she was wearied of the sport.

Her Benevolences (as she called her servant-machines) had devised long torments and short, in every combination of physical and psychological pain, every degree of ache and agony and discontent and despair, and devised versions of Atkins with slightly different weaknesses and strengths, so that the pain, physical and mental, could be more excruciating. With total control over his thought-processes, Atkins could see, or would remember, what the Benevolences devised, and so every hell that a man can inflict upon himself, when he betrays a friend or loses a loved one, across long lifetimes or short, spiced with merely enough false hope to make the agony more exquisite, had been played out countless times in countless scenarios. Every torture chamber and every toothache, including pains that only existed in limbs that only existed in simulation, and to degrees of intensity never found in reality, had been played through countless times.

And now I sue for peace between us, she said, or, rather, imprinted on him.

"Why not simply make me agree to peace, or agree with whatever you want?" For Atkins knew that he was trapped, down to his last nuance of thought and will. He was nothing but coded notations in a matrix, and the enemy could manipulate that matrix at will.

So I have done, but the versions of you I design to agree are too different from your core psychology: that game does not please me. I suspect that you still have hidden singularities of thought, that you are not indeed the final Atkins. To reach the real you, I must treat you as if you were real, a habit long ago I was weaned away from by my Benevolences.

It seemed that the Swan knew that there was some hidden, inner self possessing Atkins, embedded or encrypted in every copy of him, but the encryption could only be broken from the inside. Only the secret, inner mind, the mind of the Real Atkins, could reveal itself, and obviously no torture, nor thought-redaction of the Outer Atkins, could reach the real version. So the Swan had to deal with him honestly enough to lure the real him out—if there *was* a real him.

Atkins noted wryly that the Eighth Mental Structure had ended the honest mentality of the Golden Oecumene, but also, apparently, ended the endless self-delusion of the Silent Oecumene. She could not simply have her way by wishing it.

Atkins was amused. "You Swans do not have friendship or love, or even business partnerships. But now you must treat with me."

The elfin figure nodded a plumed and faceless head. *Poverty alone compels your backward and unevolved order of being to such extremes. Our wealth allows us to discard all such: our dolls and phantasms and playthings are far more fascinating and more intelligent than others like us.*

"Real people, you mean."

Since we can make the minds of our servitors as wise and creative and loving as we wish, unable to betray us, unable to envision displeasing us, why should any Hierophant of the Second Oecumene have dealings with another human being?

Atkins shrugged. There was no point in debating the advantages of reality over unreality. There was no reasoning with someone to whom truth was a matter of taste. Her machines would just rewire her memories and perceptions if an inconvenient conclusion in logic annoyed her.

"Why did you attack us? That's something we've always wanted to know."

You will never know.

"Was it our noumenal mathematics you feared? We would have shared it with you freely. No one wants to die," said Atkins. "No one not-suicidal, that is."

Your toys mean nothing. Of what value is it to me, to know merely in theory that a copy of myself, my glorious self, complete in every thought, and suffering the mad delusion that she is me, will happen to exist once I am dead?

Atkins said, "I don't know. What is the value of children, for that matter, or writing a journal? Maybe you need to be a little un-self-centered to want to live forever. In any case, those of us who thought a copy was not the real us, they did not make copies, and so they are not around. Evolution, of a sort, will cull the members who don't believe the immortality is real."

It does not trouble you that the real Atkins is long-dead?

Atkins shrugged. "As far as I care, he was a copy, a prototype, and *I* am the real one. Even an unrecorded man thinks he is the same fellow before he bunks down and after he wakes up. He thinks he is the same man he sees in his baby albums and thought-records. Everything changes. Even you. Why are you here to make peace, rather than torture me more?"

I will show you. You may leave the simulation. A body is prepared for your download.

"How will I know it is real? How will I know ever again that anything is real?"

This question has no meaning for us. We consider nothing unreal but unpleasant sensations. Since you are nonchalant about questions of self-identity, it seems questions of ontology should likewise not disturb you.

19. Elpenor

Atkins woke up (or seemed to) falling through outer space. To every side were stars.

He controlled his reflexes: he was not falling, no matter what his inner ear said, and he was not in outer space, no matter what his eyes said. He could feel the weight of air in his lungs, and, after a moment, see the slight glint where the light was refracted from the angles of the transparent gem-facet surfaces surrounding him.

He windmilled an arm one way to rotate his (to his surprise, clothed) body the other. Behind and "above" him (if that word had any meaning), the crystal facets were smoky and semitransparent, and the rest of the structure—ship or station, depending on whether it had drives—was visible. It was an organic-looking nautilus of diamond crystal, paved on every surface with sophotechnology, breathtakingly lovely, hauntingly alien and old-fashioned. It looked like Warlock architecture from the Fifth Era.

The clothes he had been given were from the same time period, almost bizarrely ancient: without even circuits for heating or manufacture in them, much less thought-amplifiers: dark, stiff, dead, clamp-sleeved and high-collared, with a hood hanging down his back that could be pulled shut in case of pressure-loss. He could detect similar antiquities inside his body: a spine of packed disks, an Adam's apple, the inefficient joints and support structure of his feet, the stubble of hair at his jaw. No doubt he had an old-fashioned appendix instead of a secondary heart. There was not even a muscle in the nose to pinch the nostrils shut, a bio-feature as old as space travel.

He did not like being midchamber in zero-g. His instinct was to get near a bulkhead, half-crouched with his legs "under" him, so he could push off the surface in any direction. But his hostess had also equipped his costume with a long blade (a Warlock's athame, damascened with natal constellations) and a heavy gold-foil maneuvering fan. This emphasized either her utter honesty or his utter helplessness. Either way, there was not much point in getting his feet near a wall.

The Lady of the Silent Oecumene floated nearby, her robes and drapes spread like a purple-red and silvery flower, her body curled in a fetal position.

When he looked toward her, the colors in her robe shimmered. She was absorbing information through the sensitive processes in the fabric. The decorative eyes in some of the peacock tails were eyes indeed.

A female voice came from pinpoint ports in her mask: "Observe."

Part of the diamond hull before him shimmered and amplified an image in false colors. To one side was a dark

Neptunian world, a gas giant whose atmosphere had frozen solid in the deep of interstellar space. To the other side was a cone-shaped cloud of asteroids; and a second asteroid cloud; and a third. There were scores and myriads of similar conical clouds beyond that. The false colors overlaid the image with readings of the X-ray and gamma-ray count.

He recognized the asteroid patterns. Normal planet-killing weapons do not have the energy to disperse the mass involved: low-yield explosions rarely do more than shatter the planetary crust. Most worlds, and almost all large worlds, have liquid cores, so even an explosion that throws part of the planetary mass past escape velocity does not actually shatter the planet, because the masses, in a few years, spiral back to a common center. The immensity of energy involved in destroying a planet and imparting sufficient velocity to the fragments to prevent reaccretion was staggering.

The Middle Dreaming painted a picture in his mind showing the distance and relative motion of what he was seeing. It had been an armada of worlds, some four thousand planets larger than Jupiter, reengineered and gathered up from thousands of star systems (the Silent Oecumene had enjoyed centuries in which to colonize local space before the Golden Oecumene was aware of the threat) and accelerated from orbit to near light-speed. It was an engineering feat of unparalleled brilliance, a display of what could be done when engineers had limitless energy to play with.

Atkins looked again at the nearby Neptunian world. He recognized it as Elpenor, the giant he had seen in transit between Canopus and Eta Carina. The Swans at that time, not certain whether Atkins was part of the Renunciant Diaspora, had held their hand.

Elpenor was only a gas giant down to about thirty thousand feet beneath the surface. The remainder of the world was hollow, the core having been compressed down to the diameter of an atom, to give the Swans the singularity they needed for their Infinity Fountains. The mass of the world was unchanged. Maintaining a hollow shell of that size and shape was nearly impossible, but with an endless supply of energy, what was nearly impossible was practical.

He said, "We suspected you were heading toward the galactic core. There is an immense black hole there, larger than any of the merely stellar masses you so far have had at your disposal. But why did you think the war would last long enough for you to get there, do what you meant to do, and return?"

She said dismissively, "We are more concerned with our disagreements among our circles and covens than anything to do with you. It is intensely painful to us to contemplate that there are minds beyond our control that show no respect for our dreams. There were those who said we mortals could not wage long-term war against you. Here is the counter-proof. We can wage a war to last as long as we wish to wage it. The Armada was to serve as an example to prove that certain conflict-types would outlast history."

He laughed himself at that, a bitter, small laugh. "What is your name, ma'am?"

She said, "We do not have names. All who address me are my servants, and merely call me Milady. Our machines assign names only to speak one to another about a third not present. If you speak to others of me, call me Ao Ahasuerus; but call me not that."

"Well, Milady, you are one crazy, sick egomaniac, but we can agree on this one point. There will always be war. It is the natural condition of man."

"No. There will always be war, but there will not always be man. Observe again."

Again, images appeared in the crystal bulkhead above and below him. Again he saw the asteroid-clouds in the familiar scattered pattern. One after another after another passed before his gaze. One hundred, two hundred, five hundred. They occupied a volume of just over eighteen light-years.

Eventually, he saw what was wrong. "Insufficient mass. We did not get you all, did we? How many world-ships in your Death Armada survived?"

"Some were sacrificed that other might survive. The survivors are enough to create tidal distortions in the galactic core, altering the shape of the event horizon. It is enough to ignite an accretion disk and create the final weapon. It is easy

to calculate the maximum volume the Golden Oecumene
might occupy in fifty-two thousand years from present, and
wipe out all those stars, every one, using the energy from
infalling stars swept up by an unstable, and geometrically
growing, galactic-core singularity. Even to begin retreating
now, at ninety-nine percent of light-speed, the shockwave
progressing at light-speed would eventually overtake you."

Atkins frowned. "This is what you wanted to show me? It
looks like the Silent Oecumene will win the war, and nothing we can do will stop it."

She said, "And yet, I am not delighted, not amused, and
my enjoyments are spoiled."

He looked at the Swan where she floated, a thin, elfin
shape curled in on herself, surrounded by luxurious yards
of shining fabric, such robes as could never be used in planetary gravity. Colors pulsed in delicate half-tints through the
layers of filmy cloth, but he did not have the aesthetic to
interpret it. She had no face, no expression.

Eventually, she spoke again: "The thought-machinery
of Elpenor was damaged in the fighting. My Benevolences
cannot edit out of my mind disquieting, even painful
thoughts, as they were once programmed to do, nor can they
satisfy my every yearning."

"For what do you yearn?"

She said, "You have within you all the techniques needed
to build a sophotech and a noetic circuit, and immortality
system, in your thought-space. I have access to the surviving
singularity in Elpenor, and a working Infinity Fountain. We
cannot cooperate: not you and I, for you and I are enemies.
But we can defeat the Armada of Dark Worlds, even though
it is now too late for the main galactic disk."

"Are you surrendering? Helping the Commonwealth?"

Pinpoint receptors in her mask uttered a scornful laugh.
"Surrender to whom? The images I show you are thousands
of years old, corrected for immense redshift. The Armada
may already be at the galactic core. We could not reach Sol
before the Seyfert wave overtook it. Nothing will be left."

Atkins drew his fan, unfolded it, and swam back through

the air until his feet were near the clear diamond bulkhead. He loosened the blade in its scabbard, but did not draw it. Instead he paused, waiting, as tense and as patient as a cat before a mouse hole.

She said, "If you and I are the last, we can destroy each other."

He said, "Is that your wish? It seems a poor recompense after you let me out of your prison. Ungrateful, even."

She said, "You are the last and only soldier of your utopia. We must kill each other. Is this not what you were programmed to do?"

Atkins said, "Do I actually need to explain the difference between a soldier and a murderer? I don't kill for pleasure. You were talking about surrender a moment ago. Will you?"

"Yes," she said. "But not to you. I will surrender only to what is greater than either of us, greater than what divides us."

Atkins, crouched near the bulkhead, stars behind his feet, one hand at his sword hilt and the other on the vanes of his gold fan, merely waited, eyes narrowed. He honestly had no idea what this strange creature would say or do next.

Ao Ahasuerus said, "In a war between immortals, and those who seek to stay mortal, the only equality condition is for the immortals to perish, for this makes them mortal. However, my people betrayed me. I cannot be the real Ao Ahasuerus. I am a copy, a fake, a doll. Over and over, I have calculated and recalculated the parameters, using both your mathematics and my own, both your rational logic and my transrational logic, and I can come to no other conclusion."

Atkins realized what had happened. "The two of us were the only ones who knew the aiming elements of the nova weapon. I was sent to meet with copies of Atkins hidden in your fleet, and you were sent to stop me. You had to send a real Swan, and you only had yourself to send. The only transmission you knew your fellow Swans would trust was one hidden in a living personality, wasn't it? The Eighth

Mental Structure is a code that cannot be cracked. You yourself are not aware you hold it."

Ao Ahasuerus said, "If I am a created being, and not a Lord of the Silent Oecumene, I owe them no loyalty. They betrayed our way of life. I must answer this treason with treason! I cannot rest, knowing that I am immortal. To prove my mortality, my humanity, I must die."

"Be my guest," said Atkins, puzzled and wondering. "All those lifetime-tortured versions of me—I assume you killed them all—would be gratified. So what is stopping you?"

"Unlike you, vermin of the Golden Oecumene, as cold and unchanging as the metal for which you name yourselves, I am human. I cannot die save for a cause. I cannot overwrite my memories save for the sake of a woman better than I am."

Atkins opened his mouth and closed it again. He said nothing.

The Swan said, "It was always a trap from the first, was it not? You do not understand us, but you understood that much. To destroy your own Earth, Old Earth, which we revered above all things, and then to tempt us, to lure us in with versions of the Earth, with replicas of all the ancient things, the human things, we so prize. Even in the Eighth Mental Structure, there is still a leakage, a seepage from the hidden self out into the outward awareness, is there not? I could not help but be lured to the Earth. You could not help, even when you were encrypted to think of yourself as Ulysses, falling in love. Your own psychology tricked you, did it not?"

"Maybe. I went through a messy divorce a few years back—millennium to you, I guess—and that must have bubbled up to the surface somehow. Penelope was just me in disguise, of course, and regulations should have prevented me from falling in love with myself. But when you invaded her, some alien element entered her thought systems, so, yes, I suppose something in me was lonely."

"Admit it."

Atkins said, "Yes. We destroyed the Earth deliberately as a psychological ploy, and set up copies of the Earth in star

systems where I was waiting. Twenty-one of the star oecumenes were completely fake, and there was no one inhabit-
ing those places but me."

"How could you burn your own home? Our common
home?"

"It is just an object made of matter. We have a digital copy.
I can build another one."

"And will you?"

It was at that instant that Atkins saw what the Swan was
saying, but it was many minutes, perhaps even years, before
he agreed.

20. The Suicide of the Swan

He said: "As for what is hidden within me, whatever is behind the barrier of the Eighth Mental Structure, that I do not
know. Perhaps my superiors encoded whole populations of
noumenal personalities, copies of every one on Earth. Obviously you could not get those people out of me by torture,
since I do not know myself."

"Was Ulysses a real person, or fiction? Is a copy of him
inside you?"

"I don't know. Could be. If you build a logic diamond large
enough to house him, maybe he'll come out. Or lure him out
with something he wants. But we cannot know beforehand.
We are acting blindly."

Her last words were these: "My machines can no longer
edit my thoughts and satisfy my yearnings. I am no longer a
Lady of the Silent Oecumene, since to be a Swan means to
control all reality. I repent that we have destroyed the galaxy
together, you and I. If we do not make peace now, if we do
not love each other now, then all human life must die."

By the time she was done speaking, Ao Ahasuerus was
obliterated, her memories and thoughts overwritten and de-
leted, and, in her thought-space, wondering, astonished to
find herself alive, was Penelope.

And Atkins felt Ulysses stir inside his thoughts and begin
to wake.

21. The End of the Tale

From these simple foundations comes our current culture.

The lovers sailed Elpenor, over the next eighteen millennia, to a nearby globular star cluster called Omega Centauri, well out of range of the Seyfert effect, which, even as they watched, they could see behind them, sweeping the main disk. Where it passed, stars were fed unaccustomed energy, and gained reaction mass, larger stars expanding to red giants before their time and superlarge stars going nova. Where too many superlarge stars were clustered, one nova would set off the next, so that whole star groups were ignited just as (to compare great things with small) a critical mass of uranium isotopes ignite in chain reaction, each atom setting off his neighbor.

Their new home was a cloud of fifty million stars some eighteen thousand light-years from the main disk of the Milky Way. Omega Centauri was not merely a star cluster, but the remaining core of a dwarf galaxy long ago stripped of its outer stars by the hungry gravity of the Milky Way. Unlike most star clusters, it contained a rich population of many star generations, promising abundant metallic elements. The black hole at the core of the cluster provided the young lovers with the singularity they needed to initiate an Infinity Fountain.

It is hard to say which star they first colonized. Many is the star who wishes to make that boast, but archeologists have yet to quiet the debate with unambiguous evidence. In truth, the stars of the core of Omega Centauri are so thickly clustered, on average a mere tenth of a light-year apart, the interstellar travel could be performed merely by robust interplanetary craft, without the elaborate launching laser systems of the Golden Oecumene sailing vessels, or the inefficient matter-antimatter drives of their powered vessels.

The earliest antennae were no bigger than the size of the orbit of Pluto, but later generations made larger and ever larger, until some sheets of the charmed matter fabric stretch from star to star across light-years, so gossamer-fine that suns and worlds can orbit through the film and take no more notice of it than they would notice an equal mass of neutrinos. These antennae were built as acts of faith, hoping against hope, knowing that if the two oecumenes destroyed each other, refugees would have themselves broadcast to every point of the compass.

And that hope was rewarded. Wave after wave of refugees were caught in the antennae of the Omega Centauri, and woke in astonished laughter to find themselves alive. They were shown whatever local version of Earth was made for the nearest star, for Penelope loved creating and re-creating Old Earth, a task she delighted in, since it was an endless task. As for Atkins, not just Ulysses, but every one of the characters he had played in Eta Carina, he was spread across the worlds, using the same method he had used at Canopus for quickly re-peopling planets.

And so the human experiment was started again.

The strangest and most dangerous element in the experiment was the reintroduction of the Swans, his enemies, taken from the template of Ao Ahasuerus. It was not the intention of Atkins or of the military authority to let the mental information of the Silent Oecumene pass forever out of existence, and their unique, outlandish culture to be lost.

Ulysses and Penelope were reunited. Even though it was at first merely a fiction played out by mutual enemies, their love was real enough that it was the one thing to which the Lady of the Silent Oecumene, Ao Ahasuerus, was willing to surrender. For who does not surrender to love?

Epilogue

Modern copies of Ulysses have been so often self-altered to fit the popular conceptions of this culture hero as to be valueless to the serious paleopsychologist or dramaturge. He remembers only the public version of the story.

Often Atkins, if found in some archive or ancient military thought-space, is revived and plied with questions, or asked to re-create the circumstances of the tale of the end of the Seventh Mental Structure. For the most part, Atkins does not speak of it.

The long war with the Silence is over, and the dreadful deeds he did, he does not care to revisit. Man-shaped forms, he has but few. With these, on some stylized Earth-replica planet somewhere, he tends to his apple orchard, cleans and practices with his weapons, or sleeps under the mountain, awaiting the next war.

COPYRIGHT NOTICES